Colin de Silva was born in [...] Lanka, and grew up there. He is an entrepreneur, in addition to being an author. He has also been an international trader, a member of the Ceylon Civil Service, a commissioned officer in the British Army and a diplomat. In 1962 he emigrated to Hawaii, where he now lives.

His first published novel, *The Winds of Sinhala*, was published in 1982 and quickly became an international bestseller, followed by the equally successful *The Founts of Sinhala* (1984), *The Fires of Sinhala* (1986) and *The Last Sinhala Lions* (1987).

COLIN DE SILVA

Taj

This edition published 1994 by
Diamond Books
77–85 Fulham Palace Road
Hammersmith, London W6 8JB

Published in paperback by Grafton Books 1990

First published in Great Britain by
Grafton Books 1989

Printed and bound in Great Britain

Set in Janson

Dedicated to
all those remarkable men of Richmond College, since
dead, who taught me the English language in its pristine
purity:

The Rev. Alec A. Sneath
K. Dahanayake, Esq.
E. R. de Silva, Esq.
Herbert Keuneman, Esq.
Professor Lyn Ludowyk

Let the victors when they come,
When the forts of folly fall,
Find your body by the wall.

Note

In telling this tale I have taken liberties with historical facts
    and events,
creating fictitious characters; Prince Chara, a composite of
    historical characters, and General Wahid are among the
    principals
integrating the throne room of the Fatehpur Sikri palace
    into the Agra audience hall
eliminating the suffixes 'pur' and 'nagar', meaning 'city', in
    order to shorten place names for the benefit of non-
    Indian readers
changing the actions of personages as reported in history
altering layouts of buildings, even the Agra palace, using
    my imagination in regard to their interiors the better to
    accommodate events I have created.

All of it is, however, from a careful study of the history of
the times. The Emperor Jehangir began life as Prince
Salim, Shah Jahan was Prince Khurram, Prince Husrau
was Prince Khousrau.

    Neither Asaf Khan's wife nor Nur Jehan's mother were
dead at the commencement of the story.

    Nur Jehan was the elder sister of Asaf Khan.

    Ghiyas Beg was known as Itimad-ud-daulah.

    I make no apology for these liberties, because *Taj* is a
novel, *not* a history book or a documentary. In writing
historical fiction, one should never ruin a good story by a
rigid adherence to facts!

Colin de Silva
Hawaii, 1988

Acknowledgments

My deep appreciation and thanks go to:

Grafton Books for its continuing faith in me.
My editor, Anne Charvet, who helped me decide what
should follow my Sinhala quartet, and always gave me
unfailing courtesy and professional support.
The staff of Grafton Books, with special thanks to
Pam Brogan.
My secretary, Marcia Krueger, who was almost my local
editor and whose devotion to typing and producing this
novel once again went beyond the line of duty.

SPECIAL ACKNOWLEDGMENT

Kaye Hall was always available to listen and advise when I
wrote *The Winds of Sinhala*.
Her devoted help, including typing of the earlier
manuscripts and encouragement, were an invaluable
contribution to its success and the start of my career as
a writer.

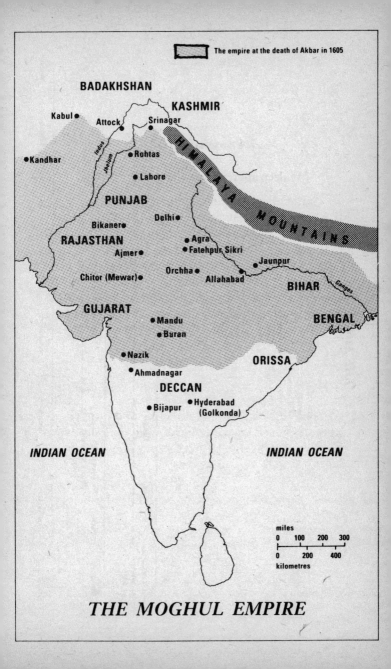

THE MOGHUL EMPIRE

THE MOGHULS

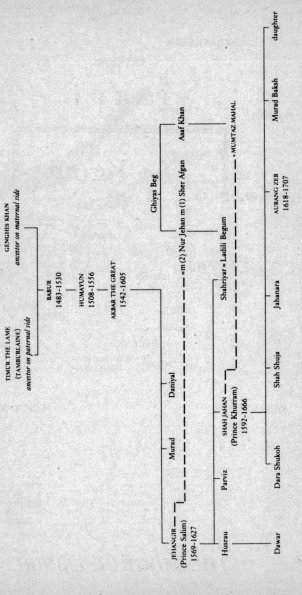

TIMUR THE LAME
(TAMBURLAINE)
ancestor on paternal side

GENGHIS KHAN
ancestor on maternal side

BABUR
1483-1530

HUMAYUN
1508-1556

AKBAR THE GREAT
1542-1605

Ghiyas Beg

Murad

Daniyal

=m (2) Nur Jehan m (1) Sher Afgan   Asaf Khan

JEHANGIR
(Prince Salim)
1569-1627

Shahriyar = Ladili Begum   .... MUMTAZ MAHAL

Husrau

Parviz

SHAH JAHAN ——
(Prince Khurram)
1592-1666

Dawar

Dara Shukoh   Shah Shuja   Jahanara   AURANG-ZEB   Murad Baksh   daughter
1618-1707

PART I

The Young Prince

Chapter 1

September 1605

Prince Jahan watched the two rival war-elephants, guided by their red-turbaned *mahouts*, hurriedly pacing in the morning sunlight, throwing great shadows on the grass of the *maidan* below. Up and down, down and up, glowering sideways at each other. Today's elephant battle was no ordinary event, but a deadly contest that would determine the Moghul succession and affect the history of an Empire embracing the entire Indian continent. His grandfather, the Great Emperor Akbar, had so decreed.

At thirteen, Prince Jahan had never been allowed friends of his own age; his grandfather had sternly instilled in him from his earliest days that he should think and act as a man. It was all in the tradition of his illustrious Moghul ancestors, from the Mongol Genghis Khan and Timur-il-Leng the Turk to Babur the Great who had commenced his rule in distant Kabul at the age of only eleven.

The Emperor Akbar had torn down the brick wall of the old Agra fort when he built the new one, which he enclosed with a seventy-foot rampart of dressed red sandstone surrounded by a thirty-foot moat. Within the fort were palaces ornamented by gardens inlaid with lawns, marble pavilions and gleaming fountains. The residences of nobles and traders, shops and a central bazaar were within the walled capital, outside which were open fields, orchards and peasant cottages diminishing to the wretched mud hovels of the poor on a sparse earth. The Emperor's palace adjoined the eastern rampart wall at a place where the River Jumna bent like a bow. A series of viewing pavilions, raised above the battlements, lined this rampart, leaving the flat *maidan* between the moat and the river open, so that the Emperor could witness the sport he loved best, elephant fighting, from his personal pavilion, high above his subjects who thronged the river bank. Tall gold-turbaned guards, magnificent in red tunics and ballooning gold pantaloons, lined the rampart wall.

Standing to the right of the Emperor's dais in the royal pavilion, beneath the high *jarokha*, the balcony pavilion that separated the royal presence from his subjects, Prince Jahan was glad that he had rigorously followed his grandfather's precepts. With the future of the world at stake, he, the Emperor's favourite grandson, had been named by the Emperor to head the team of referees that would decide which elephant won. The imperial crown would go to the prince whose elephant he declared the victor.

Today's encounter would be more fierce than ever before. The giant beasts, enemies from way back, had been so maddened to anger against each other that their small eyes flamed hatred. Though their vision was poor and their trunks dangled instead of being upraised to scent each other, their instincts told of the approaching struggle in which they had been urged by their *mahouts*, who spoke the elephant language, to batter the opponent to death. Even the two support elephants standing by, long grey trunks curling and uncurling, were imbued with the same ferocity.

As for all such sporting events or to view the Emperor when he made his daily appearance on the *jarokha*, people lined the green river banks in thousands. Since the great red ball of the slow-rising sun was behind them, Prince Jahan could not distinguish faces, but he felt an affinity with these people. Tall Pathans towered over their neighbours, bearded Sikhs mingled with Afghans wearing brown waistcoats and black fez. Men, women and children of the diverse races and religions of the Empire had gathered as part of a single nation. The mystery of nationhood suddenly touched Prince Jahan. He was too young to identify it as more than a feeling for the indeterminate masses, of common pride at being of the rich earth and air that was India. The clamour of voices died down to a curious silence. A stentorian voice across the turgid, grey water of the moat had called for order.

'Our Great Emperor Akbar, Lord of the World and the Chosen of Allah, has decreed that, since there is some doubt as to who should rule his dominions when he passes to Paradise, in accordance with our time-honoured customs, the decision should be sought from Almighty Allah through a duel between the elephants of the two contenders for the throne. To our right is Giranbar, belonging to the Great Emperor's eldest son, Prince Salim Jehangir . . .'

Loud cheering interrupted the announcement. 'Long live Prince Jehangir! . . . the Chosen of Allah!' . . . and faintly, 'Down with usurpers!'

The shouting was hushed by the upraised hand of the announcer. A sudden breeze from the river caused the flags along the rampart wall, the royal purple and gold interspersed with the bright green of the star and crescent of Islam, to flutter. Prince Jahan looked to the wind's source, the river which had been tapped at its bend to serve a broad canal that connected directly with the moat. Its waters sparkled silver as they wheeled eastward on their journey to distant Bengal and the ocean, reminding him vividly of the vastness of the Moghul Empire. All the surrounding territories, south, east and west of the river and onwards to the enfolding Indian Ocean, as far north as the distant snow-capped Himalayas and west beyond them to Afghanistan, were under the dominion of his grandfather and would pass to the prince chosen by today's battle.

He turned his attention to the voice of the announcer. 'To the Great Emperor's left is Abrupa, owned by Prince

15

Jehangir's eldest son and therefore the Great Emperor's eldest grandson, Prince Husrau . . .'

The cheering this time was not so widespread, but more vociferous, coming principally from groups of Rajputs, identifiable by the side-flaps of their turbans. The ensuing confusion, reflecting obvious conflicts of loyalties, suddenly threw up a contrast for Prince Jahan. He had a clear perception of his own destiny. He would be the Great Emperor some day. Almighty Allah had created him for it, had endowed him with the necessary brains and diligence, courage, determination and, above all, the desire to learn. Young as he was, he had fulfilled each and every task allotted to him in such an exemplary fashion that he always commanded attention and respect. When and how would he ascend the throne? Would he too encounter confusion and conflict? A savage resolve to overcome all opposition seized him before he glanced at the other three referees, standing beside him to the right of the royal pavilion.

Raja Jagat Singh was a broad-shouldered, black-bearded Rajput, the portly Prince Asad was the Emperor's Chief Minister and the aged Mullah Qasim his favourite seer. Prince Jahan turned to face the Emperor. He could recognize himself and his father, Prince Jehangir, in the man whom they both resembled so closely. Though only sixty-three, the Emperor was sick and nearing his exit to heaven. Yet the lined face beneath the jewelled purple turban, a huge glittering diamond hanging from it at the centre of his forehead, was still strikingly handsome because of its heavy bones and the sharp, dark eyes topped by unusually black brows that ran straight into each other. A droopy black moustache, which Prince Jahan's father also favoured, relict of the Mongol inheritance, a black mole on the side of the broad nose and the ruddy complexion which not even illness had caused to turn pale, all combined to give the Emperor an imperious, sardonic look, while the famed strength of a lion was still evident in his stalwart frame, the arms unusually long and the chest of extraordinary breadth. He wore a royal purple tunic today, shot with gold, with two panels of amethysts and diamonds down the middle, the sleeves sprinkled with pearls, the broad belt of shining gold studded with red rubies and green emeralds. A long double necklace of huge pearls hanging to his waist was matched by his single-pearl earrings, a family heirloom which Prince Jahan knew would be handed down to him some day. If his grandfather was given to ostentation, the precious metals and gems added to his majesty as he sat cross-legged but erect on his ornamental throne placed on the *jarokha*'s raised dais at a level high enough for no man to look down at him. To this end, the pavilion was served by six steps, leading to its open front. All its floors were covered by Persian carpets patterned in red, blue and green. The carved side windows of the pavilion were of delicately filigreed white marble, studded with gems. The whole effect made it seem that the ruler was seated alone in a lofty, sparkling heaven.

Some day, I shall sit on that throne, Prince Jahan told himself. I shall look just like my grandfather, for everyone and the palace mirrors tell me that I am the image of him. I wish with all my heart for the likeness, but even more for the dignity, the sense of justice, the dedication to honour and the awe-inspiring majesty that characterizes the Great Emperor Akbar.

What of the royal princes, his father and brother? Ornamental chairs had been placed for them on the carpeted floor of the smaller pavilions at each side of the royal pavilion. They were a study in contrasts. His father's enigmatic face bore the striking family likeness. His eighteen-year-old brother, Prince Husrau, had the long aquiline features of his Rajput mother's clan and showed signs of nervousness,

17

the long tapering fingers of his right hand beating a tattoo on his knee.

A cross-vibration directed Prince Jahan's gaze towards a tall, hawklike, dark-visaged figure sitting beside Prince Husrau. The deep-set eyes straddling a great hooked Rajput nose had been blazing hatred at the Emperor but transferred to him for a moment before being quickly averted.

Why should young Prince Chara hate the Emperor and me, Prince Jahan wondered. Six of my father's eight wives, including Prince Husrau's mother and mine, have been Rajput princesses. Is this twenty-year-old prince, entirely of Rajput birth, so concerned with a pure bloodline that he considers people of mixed birth, like me, contemptible? Could it be that as a Hindu he hates us Muslims? Or does he loathe the Moghuls because he desires a Rajput Empire? Whatever the cause, he must see me as a rival.

Prince Jahan's disquiet was removed by a change in the wind's direction, which had wafted to him the fragrance of drying grass, heavily inlaid with the Emperor's frankincense. A surge of pride filled him. The Emperor, fine-tuned to him, picked up his reaction, directed a glittering gaze at his favourite grandson. Noting his obvious admiration, the Emperor's expression softened. He beckoned Prince Jahan forward with an inviting forefinger.

'Prince Jehangir's elephant has a slight disadvantage,' the Emperor remarked, when Prince Jahan knelt before him, resting on his heels. His grandfather was given to addressing an unrelated subject when personally moved. 'Giranbar's tusks are slightly smaller than those of his opponent.' The dark eyes sobered; the curiously delicate fingers drummed on the mother-of-pearl inlay of the arms of his throne. He lowered his voice so that the gorgeous array of princes and nobles seated on either side and to his rear could not hear. 'It is your father's conduct that has placed

18

him in a humiliating position today. As our eldest son, he would normally have been assured of the succession under Muslim law and Moghul tradition. But he has been ambitious, impetuous and has allowed himself to be misled. We do not wish to speak ill of your father to you, *baba* (child), but it is a lesson you must learn. Our position would have been serious when your father invested this very capital city, Agra, in our absence, had not the governor resolutely denied his rebel forces entry. And when we had forgiven your father his grievous error the first time at the imploring of your own royal mother, he rebelled yet again. Luckily for him, this time he heeded the advice we sent him by messenger that he remain loyal, patient and obedient. We therefore decided to give him yet another opportunity for the succession, but it has to be by the will of Allah, which shall be manifested today through our time-honoured custom of letting the battle between each contestant's elephant judge the issue of succession.'

Although his loyalty to his grandfather had made him hate his father's revolts, Prince Jahan felt one of those twinges of compassion for his father which he had experienced since the Emperor announced this method of determining the succession. It was indeed a most humiliating experience for the rightful heir to be placed in competition with his own son. 'He personally attended Your Imperial Majesty's palace the second time and literally kissed the royal threshold, begging forgiveness, Sire,' he reminded the Emperor.

The fine dark eyes flashed fire. 'The act of humble submission may have atoned for the evil deeds,' the Emperor asserted flatly. 'But it could not erase the punishment. A prince must learn to serve with uncompromising loyalty before he can rule, to comply with laws and traditions if he is to benefit from them. Rights and privileges are but the product of duties and obligations.'

The Emperor was right. This was the code. But what would he do in similar circumstances? A hint of the future touched him. He would seize the opportunity to rule ahead of his time if the opportunity arose. His father was given too much to arrack and opium, contrary to the rules of the Holy Koran. Prince Jahan cast the thoughts aside. 'Are you satisfied then, Sire, that my brother, Prince Husrau, has these qualities?' he inquired boldly, careful to keep any hint of challenge from his tone.

The Emperor drew a deep breath, his wide nostrils flaring. He touched the mole on his nose with a forefinger. 'Your brother is a young man of pleasant disposition, courtliness and some governing ability,' he remarked. 'He may not make an ideal Emperor, but we are faced with a choice between two inadequately qualified princes.' He looked away into the distance, communing with himself before making up his mind. 'A pity you are not a few years older, *baba*,' he added softly, almost to himself. 'You have proven your worth, even in battle beside us. You killed your first enemy when you were eight.'

Prince Jahan's heart distended with joy, his eyes misted. 'I am your most loyal, obedient subject, Sire,' he declared. 'My only desire is that you should live forever.'

The Emperor's hand reached over, patted him on the cheek. Deeply moved, he changed the subject. 'Look, the announcer has finished and the opponents are finally ready for battle.' He nodded towards the *maidan*.

In one of those moments of sudden silence that fall on crowds, Prince Jahan heard the crump, crump, crump of the war-elephants' tread, the sound an extension of his pulse beat. A baby's wail arose from across the *maidan* and was quickly hushed.

The Emperor gestured with an outward motion of his long, heavily be-ringed fingers. The battle could begin. Prince Jahan bowed until his head touched the floor, rose to his feet and backed away. He walked to the parapet of the rampart wall, looked down at the officials standing below, raised his right hand. The chief official, dressed in white, issued a sharp order. The clamour of martial trumpets shattered the air, rousing the blood. The *mahouts*, using metal goads, prodded the two elephants towards their starting positions, about fifty yards apart. The grey beasts turned to face each other, glowering.

The trumpets' blare ended in a sound-singing silence. Prince Husrau's elephant Abrupa raised its trunk. Its own shrill trumpet of hatred and defiance splintered the morning sunlight. Giranbar raised his trunk, bellowed a defiant response. Prince Jahan's blood quickened. Unaccountably, his attention was diverted once more. Prince Chara's eyes were blazing their message of jealous hatred. Prince Jahan knew immediately that the Rajput had identified him as the real rival. The elephants below were but heralds of a future battle.

Noting the Emperor's nod, Prince Jahan waved to the chief official, who held a red flag. The flag dipped once. The *mahouts* prodded the contenders. Cheering billowed from the crowds. Trunks raised, the great grey ears of both elephants moved forward like flags. Prince Jahan never failed to thrill at this signal of the elephants' charge. The huge animals lumbered towards each other, gathered speed, two grey leviathans on a collision course.

The cheering stopped abruptly. A tense silence gripped the scene, accentuating the thud of giant feet. The lumbering became a trot. A hope flashed through Prince Jahan's mind. If his brother won, he could seize the throne more easily at some future date.

Though the distance between the contestants was too short for them to attain the speed of a charge, they connected with a sickening thud, forehead to forehead. Only such huge skulls could withstand the mighty crash.

21

The rivals screamed, blared forth their hatred. Enormous feet rooted on the green grass, they sought leverage, grey trunks entwined, long ivory tusks locked, then shoved against each other with labouring breath.

Tense minutes passed. Posed as in a sculpture, the great beasts strained every muscle and sinew. Slowly, imperceptibly, Giranbar moved Abrupa back a few inches. Hoots and whistles of joy erupted from Prince Jehangir's supporters. The clamour of the crowd mingled with the shrilling of the elephants amid the dust from their struggle.

Abrupa planted his feet four-squarely, blocked Giranbar's advantage. Prince Husrau's supporters screamed and jeered. Abrupa suddenly broke contact, drove forward with his longer tusks to keep Giranbar at bay. Would the more powerful tusks prevail? Giranbar squealed in pain. A white tusk had penetrated the hide just below his neck. He fell back. The cheers of Prince Husrau's supporters sought the heavens.

Spellbound, Prince Jahan ran a tongue over lips gone dry. His chest was tight, his heart thudding against his ribs.

The elephants locked tusks again, forehead to forehead. Giranbar swerved unexpectedly. Pushed by his own momentum, Abrupa staggered forward, presenting a grey flank. Giranbar lunged fiercely. His tusks penetrated the soft flesh behind Abrupa's foreleg like pickaxes in mud. Abrupa's shriek rent the air. Giranbar withdrew his tusks, drove fiercely again and again. Dark red blood gouted from Abrupa's wounds. The stricken elephant swung away, fled, pursued by Giranbar. The cheering of Prince Jehangir's supporters drowned out Abrupa's cries of mortal agony.

Without thought, Prince Jahan signalled the chief official who was looking up at him, expecting a verdict. Send Prince Husrau's stand-by elephant, Rathnabor, to the aid of the stricken Abrupa. Prince Jehangir rose to his feet in anger, only to subside before a stern look from the Emperor. Contenders do not enter this fray. They abide loyally by the decision of referees.

Rathnabor lumbered forward. Prince Jehangir's supporters bellowed their protests. 'Foul! Foul! Foul play!' Rocks started flying towards Rathnabor.

Prince Jahan's chest hurt, his mouth was dry. Had he overstepped the bounds? One glance at his grandfather, however, showed that, though distressed, the Emperor endorsed his decision. His grandfather always commanded fair play, as some who played polo with him had discovered to their cost. He was as insistent on sportsmanship as he was ruthless in war.

Before Rathnabor could reach the two contestants, Abrupa fled, hotly pursued by Giranbar. Officials fired rockets and succeeded in diverting Rathnabor's course. Angry crowds surged forward into the *maidan*. Soldiers and palace guards, armed with muskets and swords, advanced in long ranks to oppose them. The situation was tense, the audience silent. There was a thunderous splash. Someone pointed towards the river. Abrupa had gone over the bank to escape his tormentor, plunging into the swift-flowing water. Giranbar followed with another great splash.

Shouts of laughter broke from the crowd.

His grandfather had deliberately built the elephant arena by the river so that overheated contestants could plunge into the water and cool off. Prince Jahan glanced at his fellow referees.

'Giranbar wins,' Prince Asad declared.

'I agree,' the bearded Raja stated.

'Undoubtedly Giranbar,' Mullah Qasim intoned.

Prince Jahan faced the Great Emperor Akbar and bowed. He turned and strode up to his father, the winner, knelt beside him and kissed his hand.

Chapter 2

Her husband's brutal slap shot stars through Nur Jehan's brain, knocked her sideways. She prevented herself from falling on to the white flagstone floor only by clutching at an ornamental rosewood column. Sher Afgan was a towering hulk of a man, his name a title bestowed on him by Prince Jehangir for killing a tiger single-handed, 'Sher' being a tiger and 'Afgan', the vanquisher.

She had barely risen from kneeling to her husband in the traditional Muslim wife's greeting, when he had poured out his news: 'Prince Jehangir has been named Prince Regent and successor to the throne.'

Nur Jehan had been so pleased that she had thrown her customary caution to the winds. 'What a wonderful outcome for us and the Moghul Empire!' It was she who had engineered her husband's appointment to Prince Jehangir's staff through her father, Ghiyas Beg. Sher Afgan should have been elated. The thunderous slap alarmed her. Why was her husband so angry? Surely he could not know that she had met the handsome, gracious Prince Jehangir when she was only thirteen and had decided then that he was the man for her. She had dropped her veil, as if by accident, to attract him. And her heart told her that she had succeeded. Even after the Emperor had rejected Prince Jehangir's marriage proposal on the grounds that she was a commoner already betrothed to another man and her father had had her married to the hulking beast to whom she was already promised, she had remained determined that she would wed or bed Prince Jehangir some day.

Her father was from Persia. He had fled that country

24

with his pregnant young wife, leaving all their possessions behind, to avoid arrest for complicity in a plot to overthrow the ruling Shah. The young couple had made their way east through the north-western mountains and passes to India, where the independence of the Moghul Emperor Akbar, who was unafraid of other rulers, offered them sanctuary.

Once they entered India, however, Ghiyas Beg's wife, weary and half-starved, gave birth to a baby girl prematurely. Too weak even to carry the baby, the couple left it in a desolate area and resumed their journey. But before long, love for the baby triumphed and the mother compelled Ghiyas Beg to return to the deserted child. When they finally reached her, a cobra was coiled on her body, sheltering her from the sun. The reptile slunk away when Ghiyas Beg shouted at it and the parents picked up the baby and made for Lahore.

She had been that baby.

A curious sense of abandonment had seized her upon first learning that her parents had decided to leave her to die, in order to save themselves. It had been her father's decision to leave, her mother's to return to her. Life was that insecure for the helpless, especially for women in a man's world. There was no such thing as real love. She would put herself in a position of power over the men of her world. How?

She had first used her beauty and persuasiveness to influence her father as a child. He had been admitted to the Emperor Akbar's service shortly after he arrived in Lahore, as a man of culture and learning descended from Persian nobility, the son of a *wazir* (a provincial governor). In the year 1595, he had been appointed *Diwan* (Royal Treasurer) in Kabul. She had always made him feel loved, especially after her mother died, even during times when she resented him, and she soon had him in the palm of her hand. She learned dancing, studied voice so her golden, vibrant, sexy tones could soar flawlessly on the melody of love songs. She had the best masters teach her to play the *sirtar* (the Indian lyre). She ensured that she excelled as a student, reading widely, especially politics, government and the administrations of the great emperors. She also became a poet, a designer of fabrics and ornaments and a hunter. She worked hard, against all the obstacles of her sex and the restrictions of *purdah*, to fit herself for the historic role for which she felt destined.

She had been twelve when she first became conscious that she was always playing a part which had no association with her true identity. She cold-bloodedly accepted this fact, as a necessary adjunct to the success and power in which her future security lay. What was the point in being oneself or finding a personal identity if the result was poverty, misery or the risk of abandonment?

Prince Jehangir, as the heir apparent of the imperial crown, represented the most certain source of power and security that would extend throughout her world. But that world ended when she was given in marriage to the man who was to be called Sher Afgan. Worse, her life became a nightmare. Sher Afgan was a monster. Only indomitable courage and unwavering determination revived her hope of becoming Prince Jehangir's wife some day. After all, married women often became widows!

When Prince Jehangir revolted against his father, her husband deserted to the Emperor. Far from being dismayed, she saw this as a golden opportunity and sent her first secret messenger to Prince Jehangir: 'Tell the prince that I am so overawed by his majesty and his godly presence that I must serve him before husband, parents, family or even my king.'

Did Sher Afgan somehow know of this?

She closed her eyes, as if from the pain of the stinging

26

slap, pretending to cower while she sought answers to the questions spinning in her brain. Was Sher Afgan secretly in negotiation with Prince Husrau? Had he been promised far greater rewards if Prince Husrau became the Emperor? Did her husband hate her for not giving him a son, but only a single daughter? Was that an affront to his seed? Could he be jealous because she admired Prince Jehangir? Sher Afgan was a very secretive man. She would not learn the answers directly from him.

Through the spinning lights of these questions, a flame suddenly blazed. The knowledge of where her husband's loyalty really lay was a source of power to her. She did not quite know how, but her woman's instinct and God-given brains told her she could exploit it. Now that Prince Jehangir had been officially named the Emperor's heir, she would use that knowledge to leave this fiend and become the new Emperor's wife.

The Emperor's wife! She opened her eyes to the reality of her chamber, her husband towering above her, his black-bearded lips drawn back in a snarl. She took care to keep her eyes downcast, fold her arms across her chest, hugging the embroidered blue *kurtha*, bordered with silver at neck, sleeves and hem. Her silver bangles jingled. She hoped the sound would not irritate this monster. The heavy silver and blue turquoise neck chain felt cold at her slender neck. If she dared look directly at Sher Afgan, if she did not display complete submission, his unbridled rage would unleash itself in foul abuse which would work him up to a merciless assault. He was a powerful giant and she was helpless before him physically.

She became aware of the heady, almost pungent scent of incense curling grey smoke from the heavy brass brazier on the rosewood cabinet at the far end of the chamber. A clock struck the noon hour and the tinkle of a *sirtar* arose from the adjoining *harem* chamber. That would be young

Hamida, her husband's sister, practising. The sound and scent reminded her of the first night with her husband after the wedding ceremony, five years ago, when she was only fourteen. She had removed her veil for her husband to the scent of incense and the lilt of music. Had he sensed her revulsion that night, in spite of the brave show of lovemaking she had put on as instructed by the *harem* mothers? Was that why he had beaten her so brutally when it was over?

No one had lifted a hand to her before. Her dead mother had of course smacked her occasionally, but these slight blows were the products of love, to train her, as animals and birds did with their young. Her father and her older brother, Asaf Khan, never suspected what was happening within her marriage. Her implacable hatred of her husband was veiled by her proud indomitable spirit. She was a descendant of sultans, while Sher Afgan was merely a Persian adventurer. She would give him her body, her attention, her seeming submission, all of it illusion, while her mind and spirit remained her own, as did her loathing of him. Some day she would avenge herself, she had always told herself. Now that day had come closer to hand.

'Do you know why I slapped you?' Sher Afgan demanded, standing before her, arms akimbo. He had a curiously high voice for such a big man, with a husk to it.

'No, lord.' She kept her voice low, infusing it with a fear she did not feel.

'Look at me when I talk to you, bitch.'

She composed herself, raised her eyes slowly from his gold brocaded sandals, past the narrow green pantaloons, the long, calf-length green satin tunic, tightened at the massive waist by a cloth-of-gold sash, the ends hanging down to tree-trunk thighs, up to the black beard and moustache adorning the broad face. Her gaze came to rest on small, mean eyes, pale brown pebbles with a black dot at the centre, but she was careful not to allow it to lock into his.

'Ah, that's better. Now let's see by what beauty the heir to the Moghul crown is so enthusiastically supported.' He reached out a brawny arm, grasped the top of her *kurtha* and tore it away from her breasts. A gasp escaped her. Unaccountably, she felt as if she had been stripped completely naked, but she dared not raise her hands to cover herself.

'H'mm.' Sher Afgan started to pace around her, surveying her as if she were a slave at auction. Why did he love to humiliate her? 'Tall, full figure, voluptuous breasts – I should know! – flawless complexion, creamy against black eyes and raven hair! You have grown in beauty through the years, my dear.' He was sneering now. 'Like all useless women of the *harem*, you spend most of your time beautifying and adorning yourself. I must say that in your case, unlike most of the sows of our Muslim world, the results are excellent, even stunning. A fit woman even for an Emperor!'

Dear Allah, did he guess at the truth?

'Sit down!' Sher Afgan's changed tone puzzled her. She obediently took the ornamental stool he indicated, but only after he had sprawled, massive legs extended, on the white cushions of a divan. 'There is something I want you to do for me,' he continued. The pale pebble eyes bored into her, but his expression was more relaxed.

Nur Jehan looked demurely at her gold-sandalled white feet. They were long, slender and more shapely than many a woman's hands. 'Your slightest wish is my command, lord,' she replied, her tone submissive. 'I am your slave.' It was no more than the truth, because she had no other estate.

'Your father and your brother have much influence with Prince Jehangir, to whom they have given unquestioning loyalty and support at the risk of antagonizing the Emperor. Prince Jehangir is especially fond of your brother. They drink together,' a note of scornful disapproval had husked the high voice even more. 'It is against the tenets of Islam to take wine, arrack or other liquor. Such intemperance is even against the rules of *Din-i-Ilahi*, the new religion which our Emperor Akbar seeks to establish, as a faith consisting of the good principles of all religions, based upon reason and not the authority of any man. It is your family's influence with Prince Jehangir that got me on to his staff in the first place.' A bitter note entered his voice. 'Me, a nobody on my own, though I am endowed with more brains and physical strength than any high official in the Empire.'

'Indeed you are, my lord,' Nur Jehan murmured. She had long since ceased to be surprised by his appalling conceit, deducing that it must be a front for inherent weakness. 'It is not the intercession of my father and my brother that earned you the appointment, but your reputation and obvious magnificence. My family but opened a door. It was your endowments that made Prince Jehangir beckon you to enter through it.'

He preened himself on the divan, stroking his black beard, yellow teeth showing above it in a smug smile. 'How intelligent of you! Why is this the first time you have admitted it?' His bushy black eyebrows shot up questioningly.

'Forgive me, lord, but this is the first time you have raised the subject.'

'True. True.' He grew serious again. 'Since I have refused to support Prince Jehangir in his unfilial attempt to seize power from the Emperor, however, my career has stagnated. Your father and brother must speak to Prince Jehangir on my behalf.' He paused. 'I wonder whether the Prince suspects that it was I . . .'

He stopped abruptly, but not before a thrill of triumph shot through Nur Jehan. So it had been her husband who had betrayed Prince Jehangir's plan to the Emperor. What a choice morsel of information for someone in the seclusion of a *harem*.

'Whatever the truth of that, it is essential for Prince Jehangir's confidence in me to be restored. The Emperor's terrible diarrhoea and internal bleeding from dysentery have worsened. He will not last more than a few months longer, perhaps not even a few weeks. Though he looks well, it is only his immense willpower that keeps him going in public. Prince Jehangir will become the Emperor soon.'

Nur Jehan braved all in order to probe her husband's true intentions. Keeping her eyes respectfully lowered, her demeanour humble, she controlled her apprehension. 'Yet you seemed to feel a little while ago that Prince Husrau would be a better choice,' she ventured.

Relief flooded her when she heard her husband laugh. 'Very perceptive of you, my dear,' he remarked airily. 'Prince Husrau is a man of more dignity, restraint and sense of responsibility.'

'We who live in the *harem* know little of such things. We have to depend on the opinions of our wise lords and masters.'

'Of course. Of course. The world outside is not a woman's world.' He paused and that high-pitched giggle she hated, so incongruous in anyone but a eunuch, escaped him. 'A wife's chamber in the *harem* is one of the safest places in the world to hatch plots. No man can hear you.'

How true I shall make that, she thought sardonically. But if the world outside is not a woman's world, why do you seek my help? She felt savage at being thought so helpless. She would prove to all men that a unique woman could rule their world. 'I shall certainly speak to my father

31

and brother when they visit me this evening,' she said aloud.

'Good. The sooner the better, before the sycophants and panderers get the best figs.'

Buoyed by new confidence, she decided to ask a bold question. 'Forgive me, lord, but how will your obtaining advancement in the new Emperor's staff help Prince Husrau?'

Assured of her support, Sher Afgan was totally relaxed and expansive now. 'That's where men are more intelligent than women. The higher my position with the new Emperor, the greater will be my authority and hence my value to Prince Husrau when the time comes for him to overthrow his father.'

I thank Thee, dear Allah, for delivering this cruel beast to me at last.

Though the dinner meeting was Prince Chara's own idea, he had taken care to make Prince Husrau believe that he himself had conceived it. So it was Prince Husrau who had extended invitations to the portly Raja Man of Amber, Jaipur, and to the skeletal Aziz Koka, Prince Jehangir's foster-brother, after the elephant battle that morning.

The four had gathered in Prince Husrau's dining chamber in the palace of princes within the Agra fort shortly after dusk. This was a rectangular room with floors of pink marble covered by a great black and red Turkish carpet. Two huge elephant tusks on gleaming brass stands at one of the narrow ends of the chamber formed an arch, beneath which an exquisite sideboard of filigreed white marble held brass burners glowing with musk-scented incense. The window arches were studded with diamonds and mother-of-pearl. Gold-cushioned divans lined the walls. Above them were tapestries in pink and red depicting the two-year-old Akbar wrestling with his cousin for a painted drum and scenes from one of the Emperor's hunts, in which he cut through the neck of a lion with a single stroke of his sword. Low pink marble-topped tables served each seat, but to accommodate the visitors, one of the divans had been placed opposite the central divan on which Prince Chara, as a guest of the palace, and Prince Husrau reclined.

Prince Chara did not favour the flamboyant Moghul styles revealed by the warm golden glow of the crystal glass oil-lamps hanging from the vaulted ceiling, their intricate metal ornamentation of pure gold. He preferred the chaste half-moon hanging like a huge lemon lozenge in the bright blue sky beyond the high windows grilled in red and black lacquer.

The meal, served on gold plates, had been sumptuous, heavily spiced in the Moghul tradition. Course had followed course: flaming lamb kebabs, *alu matar* (peas and potatoes), roast pheasant, chicken *pilau*, curds and an assortment of vegetable dishes ending with choice desserts, *gulab jarman*, *kurfis*, *halva*. Finally the white-robed, red-sashed attendants, tall Afghans imposing in their turbans, had placed huge golden platters of fresh fruits, purple plums, apricots, red apples and even yellow mangoes on the table. After the golden ewers filled with scented water, the gold wash basins and white linen napkins for the washing and wiping of hands, had been used, the attendants retired on orders from Prince Husrau, closing the great double doors of the chamber, leaving behind the odours of roast meats and spices to mingle with the headier scent of camphor incense.

Most of the meal had proceeded in silence except for some sucking and slurping noises which Prince Chara found offensive. Such conversation as there was had been general. Belching, the Moghul tribute to a good meal, was successfully performed immediately after the attendants departed. Prince Chara managed only the tiniest squeak, upon which

Aziz Koka had lifted sunken eyes to him and commented drily, 'Ah, a virgin, I see!'

Prince Chara took a closer look at the two men. The portly Raja's cheeks were flushed pink, accentuating the blackness of his moustache and beard. Though possessed of a hearty appetite, he had eaten in a well-mannered fashion. Very relaxed, he was delicately wiping the side of his unusually small mouth with a white napkin. The painfully thin, white bearded Aziz Koka had eaten greedily, his shaven head and tall hunched figure making him look like an eagle-hawk. As for their host, Prince Husrau, he had seemed preoccupied tonight, pecking at his food. He half-smiled apologetically when Prince Chara's searching glance fell on him. Was this the prince who lost, or the lost prince?

'Our Emperor must be sick indeed to depend on an omen from Allah to determine the succession.' Raja Man opened serious conversation in his usual blunt manner, his voice rich and strong. 'Why would such a strong, decisive character need an elephant battle to decide who should rule his vast Empire? Faugh!'

'When one has lost contact with God's true identity and the tenets of His prophets, such conduct is inevitable, because latent liberalism has eroded strength of character.' Aziz Koka had the deep grainy voice usual in men of his build. His larynx wobbled, his sunken black eyes directed a sharp gaze at Prince Husrau. 'Understand, Prince, that we orthodox Muslims are placing our faith in you to follow middle ground between the new universal religion, *Din-i-Ilahi*, your grandfather has evolved and the ultra-conservative Shi'a beliefs to which Prince Jehangir extends lip service. I'm sure this is of concern to the Raja as well.'

Raja Man nodded vigorous assent.

'What do you mean about my father?' Prince Husrau demanded.

'Please forgive me for speaking frankly, but you well know that he is addicted to alcohol and opium, feasting and women, all of which are contrary to the orthodox Muslim beliefs he professes.' Aziz Koka sniffed his contempt.

Prince Husrau shrugged. 'I cannot fault you for what you say. As for me, all of you know that my conduct always accords with my beliefs.' He glanced at the Raja, then at Prince Chara. 'I can adhere to my own religious beliefs and still grant to my Rajput relations full rights to their ancient religion. Sincerity is the key.'

Prince Chara felt an urgent desire to tweak the pontificating Aziz Koka's intellectual nose. 'In our Rajput ideology, strength will always prevail, even over what is legitimate. The laws of nature are far more compelling than those made by man, such as rights of succession. Witness the countless times pretenders and usurpers have seized power. The people believe that this is willed by gods, but they are mistaken, for gods do not determine lay consequences. The fittest survives, the strongest succeeds, simply as a matter of cause and effect.' A smile twitched the sides of his mouth. 'Though I'm neither Buddhist nor Jain, but just a common heretic, I have observed the unfailing operation of this law.' He arched an eyebrow at Raja Man, stretched out long limbs beneath the table. He was deliberately trying to keep the conversation at a non-treasonable level, in case of eavesdroppers.

'I do not penalize anyone for his beliefs,' the Raja rejoined smoothly. A chuckle escaped him. 'Not until he tries to inflict those beliefs, whatever they may be, on the people. But if he scoffs at the religious convictions of others, or speaks disrespectfully of his own, he blasphemes, the ultimate sin.'

'I happen to believe that those who look to God or gods for support weaken themselves,' Prince Chara observed.

'That is why we Muslims submit to the will of Allah before we pray to Him for aid,' Aziz Koka interjected.

'I want you to know, Prince Husrau,' the Raja continued, 'that you have had my open support for the succession because many of us Hindus feared that your father's ultra-orthodox attitudes might pose a threat to our ancient religion. It has happened throughout history, commencing with your great ancestor, Babur, who even ordered the sacred art of the Jains to be painted over because he considered it lewd for private parts to be depicted in a public place!' The grey eyes twinkled, the chubby cheeks quivered in amusement. 'Would that the indignities suffered by other religions at the hands of any fanatic, including Babur, were as harmless.' He shrugged beefy shoulders in apology at Aziz Koka, who had begun to bridle. Muslim invasions throughout nearly eight centuries had been accompanied by fire, sword, Koran and appalling brutality.

'Harm lies in any invasion of religious rights, not in the magnitude of the deed,' Prince Husrau responded.

Prince Chara became thoughtful. He had always recognized that he could and would use the religious beliefs of others, with their attendant fears and superstitions, for his own ends. The problem with true believers such as the orthodox Muslims was that they handed over their future to tenet and Allah, losing control over their own destinies, as witnessed by the many abortive *jihads* (holy wars) throughout Muslim history. 'Real strength does not lie only in power on the battlefield, but in generalship, political acumen and tolerance where desirable,' he commented, changing the direction of the discussion. In cunning too, he thought, especially to exploit the weaknesses of others – weaknesses such as ambition and idealism, lust and trust, even apparent strength, certainly over-confidence. He himself had one goal, to be Emperor, but he would not permit it to become a compelling ambition. 'The strongest substance in all creation is air. You punch it and it gives, you withdraw your hand and it flows back, yet when whipped to cyclone force, it creates hurricanes, tidal waves, destroys tree and mountain, habitation and man, turns fire into holocaust. It is the only element with the power to whip the other elements, fire, earth and water, to destruction.'

'What can we do now?' Prince Husrau suddenly cut in.

Prince Chara felt a stab of annoyance. Why am I supporting this amiable idealist so openly, he wondered, a man who would talk treason where we might be overheard. Perhaps because this makes him the best stepping stone for me. 'We can get a breath of fresh air on your balcony if you will permit us, Prince, that's what we can do now,' he responded.

The Raja and Aziz Koka nodded their understanding approval. They rose to their feet, to the accompaniment of the Raja's grunts and, Prince Chara could swear, the creak of Aziz Koka's bones. The dining chamber was located on the upper floor of the three-storey palace, so its flat roof was on a level with the red sandstone rampart surrounding the fort, served by a flight of steps.

Rooftops are the havens of warm summer nights in the tropics. A breath of cool air from the River Jumna fanned Prince Chara's face as he emerged into the open and strolled to the parapet. The half-moon, now gold, was almost directly overhead, sailing swiftly westwards on the sky's blue ocean through tiny waves of white cloud. Dark figures and voices gentled by the velvet semi-darkness told of others enjoying the rooftops of adjoining buildings.

There were several palaces in the Agra capital. The Emperor's was the largest. It housed several hundred of the nearly five thousand women, including wives, concubines, female relations, attendants and servants, in his various palaces. Although the Shi'a Muslim sect would have allowed him only four wives, the Emperor followed the Sunni tradition that permitted extra-legal wives. He had married the daughters of powerful rulers and sub-rulers, such as those of the Rajput dominions, to strengthen his Empire.

What filled Prince Chara with bitterness was the entire concept of this capital and those at Lahore and Allahabad. Their magnificent palaces reflected the extravagances of the Moghuls. Agra alone was nearly one and a half miles in circumference. It had two gates and five hundred buildings of the polished red sandstone that the Emperor Akbar favoured, the stone beams that held up the buildings supported by intricately carved brackets. It all came from the blood of the Indian people. Rulers needed to maintain a lifestyle that would generate awe and veneration, but from time immemorial, the Moghuls had raped the native Indians, carrying away incalculable treasure and booty in the early years, and misusing it locally thereafter. While the taxes of the native Indian feudal system afforded Indian rulers luxurious living too, Moghul extravagance could only be supported by robbery.

Other sounds emerged from lighted windows, the throb of a drum, the wail of a Naga trumpet, the laughter of children.

This is my India, Prince Chara thought as he stood by the protective parapet, his eyes tracing the shiny outline of the river running east from its great bend, visible in dark moon-silver strips between treelined banks. Some day I shall have absolute power over all of it, over *my* India. I am not for race, or religion, caste, creed, or people. *India is for me*.

'Me, me, me . . .' the unexpected call of a night bird echoed his fierce thought. He fleetingly considered it an omen, but discarded the fancy as weak.

'The Emperor's decision poses a real problem,' Prince

Husrau began. He leaned against the balcony wall, his back to the river, and beckoned the others to gather around him. He pointed at the distance in order to make it seem that they were holding a normal conversation. 'What do we do now?' He was repeating his earlier question. Monotony, the privilege of the weak.

They crowded beside Prince Husrau, pretending to look in the direction he was pointing. The fatuous ploy sickened Prince Chara.

'Nothing,' the Raja replied firmly. 'We do nothing.'

'Absolutely nothing for the present,' Aziz Koka echoed. 'We wait and watch. According to his chief physician, who is a close personal friend of mine, the Emperor does not have long to live. His dysenteric bleeding cannot be stopped. He is being sedated with opium much of the time. When the loss of blood weakens him sufficiently, other complications will set in. There is no way in which we can prevent Prince Jehangir from ascending the imperial throne. He now has all the popular support of a named heir from a people, be it Muslim or Hindu, Buddhist, Sikh, Jain, Parsee or even Christian, who worship tradition. Your father will weaken his position only after he starts to rule. We can then look to an opportune moment, but it may take a couple of years.' He glanced around furtively, as if expecting spies to materialize from the night air.

'You all agree that we do nothing?' Prince Husrau inquired, looking disappointedly at each of the two older men in turn and receiving their nods of agreement. His gaze finally alighted on Prince Chara.

'I agree that there is nothing we can do about the succession,' the prince declared quietly. 'But there *is* something we can do immediately to avert a danger far graver from a source other than Prince Salim Jehangir.'

Three pairs of questioning eyes turned towards him in the moonlight. A cold hardness entered his being. It seemed suddenly as if the entire world were standing still, waiting to hear his words.

'The greatest threat to Prince Husrau's accession to the imperial throne is not his father.' Prince Chara paused for effect, directed a burning gaze at each of the others before letting it come to rest on Prince Husrau. 'It is your half-brother, Prince Jahan.'

A tense silence ensued during which Prince Chara became aware of the slow-growing conviction of the others that he spoke truly.

'What do you propose we do?' Prince Husrau finally demanded, low-voiced.

'It is not for me to propose anything, merely to point out the danger. All I will add is an old Indian saying, The baby cobra carries the same poison in his fangs and becomes the killer cobra one day.'

'Prince Jahan's fangs must be drawn.' Prince Husrau hissed out the words. He pondered a while. 'It would be more important to . . .' His unsaid words hung on the air.

Prince Chara shrugged, giving the appearance of nonchalance. He was not going to draw snake's fangs for anyone. Knowing now that he had the support of these allies, he would secretly arrange for Prince Jahan to be eliminated, a giant step towards achieving his own ambitions. When that deed was done, everyone must be made to believe that Prince Husrau was responsible. This sort of move required style!

Chapter 3

The Great Emperor Akbar limped across his private chamber in the royal tower of the Agra palace, dragging his left foot a little as usual, though he was not lame. He sat cross-legged on the rose-pink cushions of the gilt French settee, gesturing Prince Jehangir and Prince Jahan towards two of the matching chairs. Prince Jahan always delighted in the delicately hand-painted rural scenes on the backs of these chairs. They were part of the elegance of the entire drawing room, a gift from Rudolf Aquaviva, the Italian aristocrat who had come to meet the Emperor in February 1580. Its upholstery matched the burgundy and green Persian carpet and the pink marble of the floor and the fireplace perfectly. The room was entirely European, with great crystal glass chandeliers sparkling from the glow of their lighted oil-wicks, an ornate writing desk placed diagonally across the far corner, a black *boule* sideboard, Spanish paintings and Dresden china.

The Emperor frequently received visitors from abroad in this chamber to impress them with the breadth of his culture and horizons. From here, he would throw out tidbits of his knowledge of the politics of Europe and its reigning kings. He always referred with admiration to 'my twin brother', King Henry IV of Navarre, who finally brought peace to France after thirty years of bloody civil war. He was indifferent towards Philip III of Spain, who was also Philip II of Portugal, in spite of Portugal's powerful naval presence in the Indian Ocean, though recognizing King Philip's contributions to art and literature. He frequently prophesied the rise of the Netherlands as a commercial power and the problems that would face King James of England because he had not ruthlessly stamped out popular freedom movements. Whenever he was present at such discourses, Prince Jahan never failed to be amazed at his grandfather's knowledge and wisdom, tucking every bit of information away in his mind for future use.

It had been a momentous day for all of them. For the first time in years, Prince Jahan found his father relaxed and happy. He had not fully comprehended until now how much a man's unfulfilled ambitions could overpower him. It was like a dragon residing within his spirit, devouring peace of mind, burning out with the fiery breath of discontent all he did not have and all he yearned for, destroying the capacity for deep enjoyment of all that he did have. There was great wisdom in the Buddha's saying, 'Desire causes clinging, clinging causes suffering.' Prince Jahan himself was content with the verdict he had handed up to the Emperor that very morning, for the event had drawn his grandfather, his father and himself close together at last. Until now, it had been just him and his grandfather; a possessive part of Prince Jahan had to fight against antipathy towards the intrusion of his father, but he knew that no one could ever rule his grandfather's heart as he did.

They had dined with the other princes and noblemen of the Emperor's household in the great dining hall. The Emperor, once of prodigious appetite, ate sparingly these days. Then, at the Emperor's request, the three of them had adjourned to his private chamber, where Persian sweetmeats and thick black Turkish coffee, the fragrance of which filled the room, awaited them. They were very private here, within solid walls that excluded outside sounds, so the swishing of the *punkah* which cooled the room with its regular to-and-fro motion and the ticking of the gilt French clock adorning the wall behind the Emperor's settee were very clear.

Prince Jahan's one worry tonight was his grandfather's appearance. The Emperor was dressed in a green tunic glittering with emeralds and diamonds. His heavy face was unusually pale and tired beneath its tan; the right eyelid drooped. Could it be that now, having made one of the most momentous decisions of his life his grandfather would let go? Never! The fierce denial was as much a statement of Prince Jahan's need for his grandfather as of his knowledge that this valorous man, near a god, would never give in, even to death.

'You may wonder why we wanted to talk to you both alone tonight.' The Emperor's heavy voice was as listless as his countenance. 'We want you to pay the closest attention to what we have to say.' He paused, eyed each one of them in turn, his glance fierce and bright once more, commanding their attention. 'No one can live forever, but regardless of our station in life *we* are the forever of each one of our ancestors, and our descendants are our *own* forever, without end until the human race is terminated by the will of Allah.' A spasm of pain crossed his face; his nostrils dilated in a deep breath; the large heavily be-ringed hands pressed beneath the gold belt against his stomach.

'Are you all right, grandfather?' Prince Jahan inquired anxiously. 'Shall I summon your physician?'

The Emperor waved away the inquiry, the great red ruby ring on the middle finger of his right hand sparkling in the warm golden glow of the lamplight. 'It is the duty of rulers, especially Emperors and most particularly Great Emperors, to leave behind direct spiritual as well as tangible legacies. As you know, we never had formal schooling, having enrolled in those greater schools of life, the battlefield, war and politics, from an early age. Yet people consider us educated, do they not? Tell us, Prince Jehangir,

43

as our eldest son, having had the benefits of extremely wide and deep tutoring and being an acknowledged intellectual, what do you think?'

Prince Jehangir cleared his throat. He has drunk too much wine, Prince Jahan thought.

'I consider you the most educated person in the world, Sire,' Prince Jehangir responded. 'Apart from your unmatched practical grasp of everything that makes up our lives – war, politics, government, administration, culture – you have even evolved a new religion which is the harmony of each of the world's great religions combined with tolerance, the blend with which you have held all the diverse nations of your Empire together. To fulfil your concept of expanding the Empire, you have wisely adopted the Sunni interpretation of the Koran which gives implicit permission for *muta*, the lower form of marriage which our Prophet condoned among his followers, as against *nikah*, the orthodox marriage between a Muslim man with a free Muslim woman, limiting the number of such wives to four, which alone the Shi'a accept. This has enabled you and us, your sons, to consolidate territories by marrying royal women of other faiths, strengthening by union in addition to conquest, binding your Empire together with the iron hoops of family.'

The Emperor shot him a sharp glance from beneath the straight black, beetling brows, intent on seeing how much of this statement was flattery, which he loathed. Seemingly satisfied, an impish gleam crossed his dark eyes. 'When you become Emperor, we commend religious tolerance to you, for you will then no longer require the factional support of the orthodox Muslims who backed your revolt,' he observed soberly. 'But to proceed with what we were saying before we so rudely interrupted ourselves, the forever of Emperors exists in almost every facet of life. On the physical side, we can leave behind monuments to beauty, like this fort and

44

our palaces, which only violent acts of Nature, such as earthquakes or the pillaging of man may erase. Magnificence is not enough; beauty is essential. We commend beauty to you, remembering that, whatever its source, it brings delight to all human beings, like the notes of a *raga* which haunt mankind forever.'

Prince Jahan gazed at the Emperor almost in awe. He had never known his grandfather to express himself on the subject of beauty before. He had observed his grandfather's monuments with admiration, but had not realized the delicate feelings that moved their creator, feelings that were an echo of his own, like the melody of an exquisite song.

'Then there are the legacies of spiritual life,' the Emperor continued. 'If *Din-i-Ilahi* is perpetuated, it will be a new religion that will prove an eternal blessing to posterity, regardless of whether or not the human race remembers who created it. *This* is what the power of office affords. One can use that power to create and to perpetuate, or to destroy. We have just referred to your main support base, the orthodox Muslims. They regard our so-called liberalism as a menace. How can tolerance be a danger except to those who are insecure in their faith, or to those who would use that faith to dominate others or for their own emotional or material gain? When you become Emperor, Prince Jehangir, you will be the father not only of your orthodox Muslims, but of the people of all religions that exist in the vast household we call our Empire.'

'Regardless of whether or not the human race remembers who created it,' his grandfather had just said. Some people believed that the Emperor was so eager to be known as the New Prophet, one greater than Mahomet, that he even used the ancient cry '*Allahu Akbar*', God is the Greatest, to imply, Akbar is God. Prince Jahan had never believed this allegation, but he was fiercely glad that the Emperor's statement gave the lie to such charges.

'You have taught me the wisdom of tolerance already, by your generosity in forgiving my rebellions and naming me your successor, Sire,' Prince Jehangir stated earnestly. 'I shall endeavour to follow your noble example.'

The great head with its silver-grey hair grown in defiance of the Muslim requirement that heads be shaven for cleanliness, nodded. 'Finally, there are the legacies of achieving unity, peace and prosperity for all our peoples, of tempering justice with mercy, ruthlessness with compassion. Listen to your subjects; reform their lot drastically where needed and they will carry you in their hearts. Thus will you perpetuate yourself forever. All this can, however, only be achieved through strength and resolution, courage and daring in all walks of life, the physical, the material, the mental, the spiritual.' Unaccountably, the Emperor sighed. 'It is hard to accomplish . . . so very, very hard.' He emphasized the last words, raising a forefinger. 'To whom much is given, from him an equal much is demanded. That is one of the balances of life and Nature that are always in perfect equilibrium.'

In the ensuing silence, the surusuru, surusuru, surusuru, flutter of a moth's wings rose delicately above the swish of the *punkah*. Prince Jahan's head felt tight with his concentration.

'Prince Jehangir, it is our desire and command that when your life is ended and you too pass into the greater forever, you name your son, Prince Jahan, and no one else to be your successor.'

The words tore into Prince Jahan's consciousness like a peal of thunder followed by a blaring of trumpets and pounding martial drums. His eyes moistened, but, as always, the tears did not come. He met his grandfather's gaze speechlessly. The Emperor's face softened momentarily, before his eyes returned to his son. 'Do you swear this sacred oath to us, Prince Jehangir?'

'Indeed, I do,' Prince Jehangir readily responded. 'You have personally trained my son for this role. He has received the best schooling of any prince in your dominions, not only from his tutors, including such men as Raja Saliwahan who taught him swordsmanship, horseback riding and rifle-shooting, but from you, Sire. Whether it be the symbol of the tent you bestowed on him when he had killed his first enemy, the pilgrimages he shared with you, the discussions with holy men which you arranged for him to witness or the deliberations of the Great Council to which you exposed him, he has shown himself by nature, character and disposition, worthy of becoming Emperor some day.'

Pleasing words, enormously pleasing praise, a great promise for the future, except for that little phrase at the end, 'some day'. When would that day dawn? Prince Jahan wondered, suddenly impatient for it. He stole a glance at his father, still youthful, and suddenly a cross-thought from Prince Jehangir jolted him. Would his father wait for the 'some day' before he himself became the Emperor? He had tried twice to accelerate his day by armed revolt. Now he was within the palace. Had the Emperor allowed the fox into the chicken coop?

Prince Jahan cast the thought aside as unworthy, but an undercurrent of apprehension remained. He resolved to remain in close proximity to his grandfather at all times, in order to protect him from his newly named heir.

The French clock struck the hour of ten. The Emperor stifled a yawn. 'There is one more item of the realm's business we must accomplish tonight.' He half-turned in his seat, his head tilted as usual to the left. He stretched out the left leg he favoured when he walked. Was his limp affected or natural, Prince Jahan wondered irrelevantly. If natural, was it part of the forever of the Emperor's fierce ancestor, Timur, known as il-Leng – the Lame – after he acquired his limp from a battle wound, so Tamburlaine? 'News of our appointment of Prince Jehangir as our heir and successor is already on its way throughout the length and breadth of our Empire by fast horse-relays,' the Emperor continued. 'We desired word to be carried speed-ily in order to give stability to the realm. Only the requirements of protocol remain, so we are sending royal ambassadors to carry the news personally to the principal rulers, from far-flung Bengal, the Deccan and Kabul, to those nearer our capital. You, Prince Jahan, will be our ambassador to Rana Amar of Mewar at his Chitor palace.'

'Mewar, Sire?' Prince Jehangir exclaimed. 'Pardon me, but would that be safe?'

The Emperor's grin beneath the sinister Mongol mous-taches was as near wolfish as Prince Jahan had ever seen it. 'Entirely. Prince Jahan shall be accompanied by a suitable military escort. He can leave early the day after tomorrow and be back in eight days. During that period, Rana Amar's son, Prince Chara, who has been visiting your rival, Prince Husrau, will move here into our own palace, as our most . . . er . . . protected guest!'

Her elder brother, Asaf Khan, was Nur Jehan's favourite person. He was a slim, tall javelin of a man, with a flat stomach and a triangular face which revealed pearly white teeth beneath his thin, reddish brown moustache whenever he smiled. A devil-may-care disposition matched his expression, but he combined all this with an unusual sense of honour and rectitude. This last had been of concern to Nur Jehan in her manipulations, until she came to realize that people of rectitude are the most malleable of all because they are so predictable that one can use their very idealism for one's own purposes. Yet she was also genuinely fond of Asaf Khan and this showed itself in the affection of her greeting that night when he was finally able to break away from duties in the Emperor's palace and return home after dinner to the mansion which they both shared with their parents. Her husband had insisted that she speak to her brother that very night and had deliberately delayed his own return home to give her the opportunity to fulfil the mission without embarrassment to him.

Asaf Khan took his usual seat on the divan in her chamber, while she sat poised gracefully on a settle which she had placed immediately in front of him. His dark eyes gleamed with excitement as he recounted the events of the afternoon. 'This announcement opens up endless opportunities for Father and me, for the very reason that we remained neutral when Prince Jehangir rebelled,' he concluded.

'How could that be?' Nur Jehan inquired. 'Would Prince Jehangir not want to appoint his loyal supporters and favourites to the best posts?'

Asaf Khan threw back his head and laughed. 'That is not the way it works,' he declared. 'How can a ruler trust someone who rebelled, even with him, against constituted authority?'

In a trice her quick mind grasped the significance of her brother's words. 'Especially when the rebellion was not against tyranny?' She was too loyal to her idol, Prince Jehangir, to add, 'but a product of ambition.' Head to one side, she considered her brother. 'But how can you be sure?'

'Prince Jehangir has already sent a trusted messenger asking me to see him at his palace tomorrow morning. The play begins!'

Her pulse quickened. My play too, she thought. 'That is simply marvellous.' She hesitated. 'A gift from Allah, especially for me.'

'How?' His bright eyes twinkled. 'You will not be able

to accompany me and drop your veil again, this time before the legal heir to the imperial throne!'

A hot blush mantled her cheeks. It was this brother whom she had persuaded to present all his ladies, dutifully veiled, one by one, to the handsome young prince – and then dropped her *yashmak*, by seeming accident, for the prince to see her startling beauty. Soon after that fateful moment, her astrologers had confirmed her belief that she would occupy the seats of power in the Empire some day. 'You are so *bad*,' she exclaimed, flirting with him in a sisterly way.

'So are you,' he responded.

'We are twins.'

'Hardly. I can give you some years.' He grew serious on the instant, as such laughing men can. 'But tell me, how is my visit to Prince Jehangir a gift to you?'

The moment for directness had arrived. 'As you know, Sher Afgan incurred Prince Jehangir's displeasure by openly supporting the Emperor. He desires an early audience with the prince to explain his actions, in the hope that he will receive promotion and favours when the prince succeeds. Sher Afgan is very ambitious and very able, as you also know.'

'Would that his ability and discretion matched his physical strength and ambition,' her brother retorted. 'I want you to love and respect your husband, but frankly, as I have told you before, he was the wrong choice. Even our father realizes that he made a mistake.' He shrugged. 'But we all have to live with it . . .'

And I have to endure it, Nur Jehan thought angrily. You do not know even a fraction of the dreadful choice our father made when he arranged for me to marry such a monster. Aloud she meekly commented, 'It is the will of Allah that we women should be obedient . . .'

His ripple of laughter stopped her. He shook his head in

amusement, gestured towards himself with a bent palm. 'Beautiful sister, this is me, your brother and confidant, remember? I know your true feelings about the position of subordination to which our *mullahs*, damn them, have consigned Muslim women. Someone like you, with more brains and ability than most men I know, should not have to spend your time preening yourself before a looking glass, gossiping, indulging in idle pleasures. Few princes have obtained as much tutoring as you and this makes you more capable than ever. You would make a wonderful Empress!'

For once she could not keep up the dissimulation. 'It is not the Prophet but those who followed him that have interpreted his words to suit their own purposes,' she asserted fiercely. 'Men so afraid of their lack of masculinity that they had to hide the witnesses of it. I know what Allah wants of me. The fact that I am a woman may seem to make my role and my destiny more unattainable, but I tell you I am going to use it to make it easier.'

He gazed at her in such astonishment that for a moment she wondered whether she had overshot the mark. Then he laughed again, quietly this time, his brown eyes reflective. 'I am convinced that you will.' He nodded as if he were truly seeing her for the first time. 'A lot of things fall into place.' He stared into space, then fixed a serious gaze on her. 'I am confident that you will utilize whatever you are, whomever you are, for the fulfilment of your goals.' He turned unusually solemn. 'This is a moment of destiny.'

An icy calm settled over her, before joy flooded her mind in a warm rush. She had known since this noon that her time had finally arrived. 'Then you will arrange for my husband to see Prince Jehangir tomorrow.'

'More than that, I shall take him with me and ensure that Prince Jehangir and he have a few minutes alone together.'

'You will not regret it.'

'I desire no reward. I am my own man.'

'I know.'

He seemed to recall something with a start. An amused smile twitched the sides of his face. 'Tomorrow will be your husband's day with princes,' he informed her.

'Princes, did you say? How?'

'Prince Husrau sent me a message to meet him at his palace after dinner tonight and to arrange for Sher Afgan to see him in his palace first thing tomorrow.'

Clearly her brother took Prince Husrau's request for a meeting with Sher Afgan for granted because her husband had secretly supported the prince, but it puzzled her. Her brother could meet anyone freely without being suspect, but why would Prince Husrau need to see Sher Afgan at such a momentous time?

Prince Jehangir considered it more prudent to discuss secret matters, whenever possible, in open gardens rather than within palaces, where the very air seemed to have ears to hear and mouths to repeat. He had to be especially careful because he was not residing in his own palace but in that of the Emperor. Rulers had all sorts of ways by which to eavesdrop on private conversations, among them secret passages in the walls of rooms, small trap doors in panelling and hidden shafts.

As he walked out into the sunshine that morning, to meet Asaf Khan and Sher Afgan in the royal pavilion at the centre of the small lake that formed a focal part of the royal gardens, Prince Jehangir should have been pleased at the outcome of the previous day's contest, but he was not. He was consumed by humiliation, which would not end until he was on the throne. The heir to the Empire, selected by elephant battle! The thought choked him with rage. His son, Prince Husrau, was not the real culprit, though he would some day wreak vengeance on the young man for daring to compete with him. It was his own father, the Emperor.

It had begun long ago, when he was a child and his father was too involved in war and politics to pay him much attention other than providing him with the best tutors. As a boy, he often thought that he would give up all the knowledge imparted to him for the certainty of his father's love, for a display of paternal affection from the man he had venerated. Respect was shown to him, consideration for his position as the Emperor's eldest son, expressions of faith that he would develop the qualities of a good ruler, but no warmth of fatherly love. He had made excuses for his father for many years, even asking himself whether the fault was his, because the Great Emperor Akbar did seem capable of great emotions and had lavished affection on his youngest brother, Prince Daniyal. But Prince Jehangir came to see that neither he, nor Prince Murad, his next younger brother, nor even Prince Daniyal came up to the Emperor's expectations. Needing some refuge, Prince Jehangir sought it in wine and arrack. To satisfy his dreams, he turned to opium. To feel fulfilled as the man his father did not think him to be, he sought the arms of women.

When his son Prince Jahan was born in the year 1592, he noted with bitterness the special love the Emperor began to display towards the baby prince. It did not alter Prince Jehangir's own love for the boy, or deter him from the course of a father's duties, but he had frequent bouts of jealousy. For him, family was a stern reality of official life, a matter of rights and privileges, duties and obligations, but nevertheless he began to feel rejected by the growing relationship between the two. In order to absolve himself of blame, he snatched at defects in his father's character and rule. They made him drift towards dissident elements, principally the ultra-orthodox Muslim faction led by such men as Mizra Ali.

He also came to like the devil-may-care Asaf Khan, whom he found a prince among men and the soul of honour, and who became his close friend. The most memorable event in their association, however, was the night he dined at Asaf Khan's family home and saw the naked face of his sister, Nur Jehan, for the first and only time. He fell in love with Nur Jehan on the instant. The black pools of her eyes, the way they locked into his gaze, startled by the meeting, the apologetic blush that mantled her fair cheeks, were so deep-etched in his mind they haunted his dreams. He would have taken her for a second wife, but the Emperor refused his request. Further, marriage to a Muslim would have created problems with the Rajputs at a time when he needed to woo them. The thought of taking Nur Jehan as a concubine never entered his head.

He was in despair when Nur Jehan was finally married to Sher Afgan, but then Asaf Khan sought to have Sher Afgan assigned to his staff and hope sparked. Soon, however, he was torn by new jealousies and his twin ambitions became possession of the kingdom to satisfy the reality of his official life and marriage to Nur Jehan so that possessing and being possessed by her could at last give substance to the mirage of his emotions.

Though it was he who had given Nur Jehan's husband the title Sher Afgan, he loathed the man, all the more because his hatred had to be kept suppressed. This was why Sher Afgan never rose in his service. He could not bear to give the man any advancement that would bring them into closer contact, a constant reminder of the massive Sher Afgan's sexual contact with Nur Jehan whenever he pleased.

Having endured countless moments of jealous torment

through two years, Prince Jehangir found his release in hope as well as in the winecup, the arrack mug and the opium pipe. He told himself that some day, when he was Emperor and Nur Jehan his wife, he would abandon such crutches. He had tried to accelerate that day with his two rebellions, but had been forced to capitulate each time. The last occasion had been especially humiliating. He had placed his lips on his father's royal threshold with shame in his heart, the desire for vengeance bursting in his head. What did Nur Jehan think of this act? Did she despise him? His heart told him that she would cherish him regardless. If that was self-delusion, he needed to cling to it in order to retain his sanity, his manhood and his hopes.

Now the prospect of achieving both his ambitions had opened. Once he became Emperor, he would have the power to eliminate his rival and marry Nur Jehan. Like a thirsty man reaching for water, he needed urgently to shorten the waiting time, which was why he had asked Asaf Khan to bring Sher Afgan to him that morning.

He noted a new respect for him from the princes and courtiers, a special obsequiousness in the salaams of the palace attendants, as he strode alone along the marble-floored corridors and gilded hallways of the palace into the glittering sunshine, but it left him unmoved. His head ached from too much drinking last night after his father's sermon, which he recalled with contempt. His mouth tasted vile from liquor gone stale; his tongue was coated, his breath stank and he knew he was bleary-eyed.

He tried vainly to find solace in the beauty of the central pleasure garden through which he walked. Tall trees threw their shade on carefully manicured lawns, still sparkling here and there with diamonds of dew. Brilliantly coloured peacocks strutted in the sun, homely grey mates following, necks bobbing as they pecked at the soil. A cool breeze rustling through the branches brought the delicate scent of roses to tinge the more spicy aroma from the yellow marigold beds immediately bordering the red sandstone walkway. Fountains gushed and splashed on either side of him, silver in the sunlight. Brush warblers trilled, pigeons cooed and parakeets screeched around him. Overhead, an eagle-hawk soared on dark-sail wings against the pale blue sky.

Prince Jehangir's eyes fell on the two figures awaiting him across the green marble archway of the matching pavilion at the centre of the shimmering waters of the tiny lake. The man he almost loved, slim, rakish, elegant as a javelin, and the giant he hated with such passion. Had the beast made love to Nur Jehan last night? He firmly set the thought aside, composed his face into a smile and adjusted the bejewelled red turban on his shaven head as he walked across the ornate bridge. Dissimulation was sometimes a requirement for rulers and diplomats, while subjects had to pretend all the time!

He acknowledged the salaams of the two men who awaited him, noting Asaf Khan's elegance in white satin and Sher Afgan's black outfit. 'Ah, my friend, Asaf Khan, how good it is to see you,' he remarked affably, indicating that his visitor should take one of the marble garden seats, inlaid with mother of pearl, that adorned the pavilion. 'And you, Sher Afgan, how are you this morning?' He clasped his hands together across the cloth of gold tunic he was wearing. Sher Afgan, killer of tigers, dressed like an executioner. How fitting today! He restrained the impulse to laugh aloud. 'Rather cool, this breeze across the water. We can escape it when we are seated.'

Asaf Khan sat very erect. 'I am honoured to be called your friend, my prince, but even more so to become your humble subject.'

'I too am honoured to be your subject, Sire,' Sher Afgan echoed.

56

I have never liked your brown pebble eyes, Prince Jehangir thought. 'Not yet, Sher Afgan,' he stated. 'Not yet my subject.' He reflected a while, drew out his left leg, vaguely aware that he was copying one of his father's mannerisms. 'As a matter of fact, you would not have been my subject but Prince Husrau's if your misguided loyalties had worked.' Nothing like putting this giant on the defensive to give effect to his plan.

A tremor passed through Sher Afgan. 'For that I am truly sorry, my lord prince,' he declared earnestly. 'And it was to explain my actions that I had already sought an audience with you before I received your gracious summons.'

'To be in my employ, to receive your pay from me and in effect to support my rival for the succession against me, who gave you the finest opportunity of your life, is an act of the basest ingratitude.'

The giant hung his head. A splash diverted Prince Jehangir's attention to the blue kingfisher skimming away from the water with a tiny carp in its beak.

'I humbly beseech my lord prince's pardon for that base act.' Sher Afgan's high voice had become huskier than ever. 'I implore you to give me the opportunity to explain my conduct.' He raised pleading eyes to his accuser.

'Proceed.'

'I was misled.'

Aren't we all, Prince Jehangir thought cynically. The murderer, the robber, the rapist, the seditionist are always misled when confronted with the consequences of their crimes. 'I was told that you would never be appointed by the Emperor to succeed him. I reasoned, wrongly as I see now, that if I could obtain the confidences of the new Emperor, I could better serve you in due course.'

Ho, ho, ho, Prince Jehangir thought, this is certainly a new twist. What a cunning bastard you are, Sher Afgan.

Then the idle thought came from nowhere, absurd, without justification. I wonder whether you detest me because your wife loves me. 'In that event, why did you not tell me of your plan?' he demanded.

'My lord prince, I never had the opportunity. Begging your royal pardon again, my position on your staff was . . . er . . . still is, so lowly that I am hardly ever in the radiance of your person. Please remember, I am a humble commoner, while you are a prince of the most royal blood.'

Prince Jehangir turned to their companion, who had remained silent, as was proper. 'What do you think, Asaf Khan?'

Asaf Khan frowned. 'There is an old saying, my lord prince, The Devil himself knoweth not the intention of man. I would add to that, even man seldom knoweth his own intention! Since I am unable to answer your question,' his eyes twinkled, 'I doubt whether even the Devil can answer it. I would humbly ask you to remember, however, that loyalty can be expressed in many forms. For instance, though my father, Ghiyas Beg, and I love you and are more loyal to you than any other subject, we remained aloof from your rebellion and took no part in the competition as to the successor because we are devoted to principles which we believe can serve you better than words or swords.' He spoke proudly, sincerely, his head high, his gaze direct, and Prince Jehangir's heart went out to the man. 'As you know, I even met Prince Husrau in his palace last night. One should always hold out a hand to the vanquished.'

'Well put,' Prince Jehangir observed. 'And we are grateful to you, our friend, for introducing a note of levity at times to lighten the tedium of too much earnestness.' He directed a merciless gaze at Sher Afgan, deliberately allowed tension to build through a monumental silence. 'As for you, we should send you back to the obscurity from whence you came, but that is not the way of princes. We neither believe nor disbelieve what you say, but we shall give you the opportunity to prove your loyalty as well as your abilities as soon as we become Emperor.'

The sigh of relief that escaped Sher Afgan was unmistakable. He rose to his feet, knelt before Prince Jehangir and kissed his hand. 'You will never regret it,' he declared, raising his massive head.

I'm not so sure, Prince Jehangir thought, loathing the contact. Aloud he murmured, 'The opportunity may arise soon, but we all hope that the Emperor Akbar will live forever.' Allah forbid!

'May Allah so grant,' Asaf Khan repeated.

Prince Jehangir noted with interest that Sher Afgan did not echo the sentiment. Good. 'You may resume your seat, Sher Afgan. I need further converse with Asaf Khan here, but first let me talk to you in private, in order to find out more about what motivated you. I do not wish to heap humiliation on you by questioning you in your brother-in-law's presence.' He turned to Asaf Khan. 'Why do you not take a stroll through the gardens, friend, and join me when you have seen Sher Afgan depart.'

'Certainly, my lord prince.'

Prince Jehangir watched Asaf Khan's lithe figure until it was across the bridge before fixing Sher Afgan with a stern gaze. He noted with satisfaction a twitch of the giant's cheek muscle and the single wobble of his larynx. He allowed another monumental silence to soften up the man, waited until Sher Afgan dropped his eyes and shifted his feet uncomfortably.

'You were once known as Ali Quli, were you not?' he demanded softly, menace in his voice.

'Yes, my lord prince.'

'I understand you are closely related to Hakim Ali, our Emperor's personal physician?'

The great head nodded, but Sher Afgan still stared at the white marble floor. 'Hakim Ali and I are indeed closely related and we are also bound by bonds of deepest personal friendship. As a matter of fact, I once saved Hakim Ali's life.'

'Ah, so he owes you much.' Prince Jehangir leaned forward. 'Now listen carefully to me, Sher Afgan, for your whole future depends on my words.' As he continued speaking, the giant started to tremble, but soon composed himself. He slowly raised his head, the brown pebble eyes finally holding Prince Jehangir's gaze.

Hope has entered your soul, Prince Jehangir thought, but if you ever betray me, I'll have you shredded to pieces so your black soul may rot in hell.

When it was over and Sher Afgan had accepted his assignment, Prince Jehangir wondered whether he had been wise to accede to the giant's request that he should proceed straight to the palace of princes to meet Prince Husrau one last time, ostensibly in order to break off his allegiance to the prince face to face.

The homes of lost causes are quickly deserted, so Prince Husrau had no other visitors. His study was a small room on the second floor of the palace. Through its high-grilled windows lacquered red and green, Sher Afgan could see the pale blue sky, already burnt from the now fierce sunlight, though the day had not yet turned warm enough for the *punkahs* overhead to be operated. He had never been inside the palace before and he took the opportunity to look around. The room was furnished in Indian rather than Moghul style, with a white Kashmiri rug decorated with red and green leaf motifs on the inevitable pink marble floor, a low table for writing, with settees and settles of brown Indian oak, all heavily carved, the seats upholstered in red. Only the tapestries of holy scenes, again in vivid reds and greens, spoke of the Moghul influence.

A side door opened quietly and Sher Afgan turned towards it. He was amazed when Prince Chara, whom he knew only by sight, walked into the chamber. He salaamed, however, ready to extend an affable greeting when he noticed that the prince's hatchet face was grim.

'You know who I am?' Prince Chara demanded coldly, not bothering to ask the visitor to be seated.

Sher Afgan's stomach began to churn at the prince's tone. 'Yes, my lord prince.' What was happening here?

'We have but a few minutes in which to talk alone,' Prince Chara stated. 'So listen carefully, because this conversation may be the most important in your life.' He paused deliberately, his deep-set eyes glittering. 'I know you to be Sher Afgan, but I also know who you really are. You once raped, assaulted and brutalized at least three married women. I have evidence of your guilt which can be proved in a Muslim court. For a Muslim man who fornicates and commits adultery, the punishment is death by stoning.'

Sher Afgan choked with fear. Though Prince Chara's accusations were true, his first instinct was to brazen this out. Some implacable certainty in Prince Chara's eyes, however, held him back. Just when everything seemed to be going right this had to happen. As the enormous danger of his position smote him, his chest suddenly became so tight he had to reach for breath and his bowels turned soft, ready to let go. He had never dreamed that anyone knew his secrets. Prince Chara was surely the devil incarnate. He resisted an impulse to gibber. 'How . . . how do you know?' he stammered, then changed his mind. If Prince Chara were determined to betray him, he would have done so already. No, the prince must have something else in mind. Hope gleamed in Sher Afgan's fogged brain. 'I understand, my lord prince,' he declared, steadying his voice. 'I beg you to spare me.'

'I will certainly do that if you cooperate with a simple request. Time is short. I want you to have Prince Jahan kidnapped.' The words were spoken as casually as if they were a request for Prince Jahan to be taken for a walk. Prince Chara looked carelessly out of the window.

Sher Afgan stared at Prince Chara in blank amazement. The predatory head, black hair coiled under the white turban, slowly swivelled around. Hawk eyes held his gaze. Big man though he was, Sher Afgan felt like a transfixed bird. Beneath the shell of Prince Chara's closed impersonality was a tenacity of purpose such as Sher Afgan had never experienced before. 'How would I do this?' he inquired timorously.

'I understand you have close relationships with a group of *thuggee* (assassins).'

Sher Afgan nodded involuntarily. Was there anything this fiend did not know? 'How soon should this be done, my lord prince?' he inquired, sensing urgency and dreading it.

Prince Chara told him when, where and how.

'Why so soon, my lord prince?'

'Prince Jahan leaves for Mewar early tomorrow with a strong escort immediately after *zuhr* (the morning prayer) and *durbar*. The deed has to be done before then.'

'I shall do it, my lord prince.'

Prince Chara turned to leave. 'No one must know that you and I have even talked,' he threw over his shoulder. 'Especially not Prince Husrau, Prince Jehangir, Asaf Khan or your wife. If anyone learns of it, I shall say that you are spreading falsehoods because I have evidence of your past sins, which of course I shall then reveal to the authorities.'

'When I have accomplished this task for you, will you swear on your sacred Rajput honour never to use it to force me to your will?' Sher Afgan felt like blubbering, but he steadied himself with a desperate effort. He stood before the pits of eternal hell and had to save himself. 'Please, my lord prince. What assurance will I have that I will not become your bond slave for life?'

'None!' The word hung on the air like a death sentence as the side door closed softly behind Prince Chara.

Chapter 4

Prince Jahan had always enjoyed the pre-dawn horseback ride with his grandfather on the *maidan* between the moat of the Agra palace and the Jumna River. They seldom conversed, but the boy had found contentment in the feel of the cool air flowing past his face in a fast canter or a gallop, the quiet thud of hooves beating in unison on the grass beneath him, the smell of saddle cloth, leather and horse sweat in his nostrils. Most satisfying, however, was the communion from rhythm of man and mount in perfect balance and himself and his grandfather in perfect harmony.

After the exercise, his grandfather would return to his private chambers to be bathed and robed before making his public appearance, symbolically at dawn to match the risen Emperor with the rising sun, in the royal *jarokha* on the rampart wall. This daily ritual assured his subjects assembled on the *maidan* a glimpse of their ruler, evidence that all was well with his health and the state of the realm. At this time, the *muezzin*'s call to morning prayer, the first of five each day, would bring the Emperor and his Muslim subjects to their knees, facing the holy city, Mecca, bound as equals by the bond of their religion.

The Emperor had abandoned these morning rides the previous week, on the advice of his chief physician, but had directed his grandson to continue on his own until they could ride together once more. Prince Jahan had dressed each morning with the hope of youth that his grandfather would join him, but in vain. The Emperor had been available only for his public *durbar*. Today, the prince had been filled with an unaccountable despondency from the moment he awoke. His gloom had become tinged with a vague apprehension, while he changed into his riding clothes, which was not dispelled even by the feel of his long curving sword in its gold scabbard when he buckled it on to his broad black leather belt or the sharp dagger in its jade sheath at his waist.

It was still dark when he emerged onto the red sandstones of the palace courtyard, so the flares around it remained lit, their acrid odour puncturing the cold air. Across the courtyard, two sentries stood at the huge entrance gates, matchlock rifles at the order position, motionless as the dark cypress trees that bordered it. The sneeze of a horse drew his attention to the group gathered around several mounts at the right of the palace entrance doors. The glossy black, almost seventeen hands tall, unusual for an Arab, named Samt, meaning the highest, was his very own charger, a gift from his grandfather. Next to Samt, the Emperor's Scindhi, Kismet, meaning fate, stamped an impatient hoof as if disappointed that his master had not emerged. As always, the horses were surrounded by grooms dressed alike in short red tunics, white ballooning trousers and turbans, blanketed by large brown cloaks that protected face, mouth and ears against the chill. Farther away, the usual escort of ten uniformed cavalrymen was drawn up in two ranks facing the entrance gates. A hoof clopped as one of the horses restlessly pawed the ground.

'The lord prince is here!' one of the grooms announced.

The figures separated, sprang to attention and salaamed. 'My lord prince rides alone again today?' Ishtaq, the chief groom, a tall, dark Pathan, inquired, his teeth white in a smile between his black moustache and beard.

'Yes.' The reply came out politely, but Prince Jahan's tone made it clear that he was in no mood for conversation.

'Samt is in high spirits this morning, my lord, full of oats. He could do with some hard exercise.'

'He shall have it.'

The groom holding Samt's bridle led the charger forward. Prince Jahan stood to one side of the horse, fondled Samt's neck, whispered his daily formula into a cocked ear. 'You and I have been in battle together. Let us enjoy a peaceful ride today.' Knowing that he did not like to be assisted, no one came forward to help him mount, but the stirrup had been placed low enough for him to reach comfortably. He grasped the reins in his left hand. He placed his left foot on the stirrup, hands at the pommel and rear of the leather saddle. Facing the animal's rear, he levered himself up and stood for a moment on the stirrup, balancing himself. Still facing the rear, he swung his right leg over the saddle in a smooth motion, sitting without the slightest bump. He dropped his legs, drew his heels back so he could just see his toes below his knees. Ishtaq adjusted the left stirrup before stalking up to his own horse and swinging into the saddle. Prince Jahan relaxed his reins, squeezed lightly with his thighs and Samt stepped forward automatically, slow-clopping. Ishtaq followed to his left and slightly to the rear. The cavalry escort formed behind them with a clattering of hooves. The sentries came to life, saluting as Prince Jahan walked Samt through the gates.

Once on the city street, Prince Jahan turned right, broke into a posting trot, heading for the western Delhi gate. Within the city, the broad main street ran straight as an

65

arrow past the shuttered residences of princes and noble-men. The few people around were labourers cloaked in brown blankets against the cold. They skipped aside at the sound of the hooves, salaaming. An open cart, drawn by two black oxen, trundled past, milk jars clanking, wheels rattling, probably going to the Emperor's palace. Lighted barracks windows appeared. Dark figures of soldiers moved around the central parade ground.

The twin towers of the city gate loomed ahead; sentries on the battlements were blobs. Cannon poking snouts through their embrasures were barely visible. Ishtaq trotted ahead to have the gates opened. The groaning of chains and the squeak of wheels were followed by the vast creak of the great gates as they slowly swung open. The open country yawned darkling beyond.

Prince Jahan rode past the saluting sentries, his escort behind him. He signalled the men to ride ahead, while he stopped to face the fort. The hulk of Agra loomed before him. The solid rampart walls, the two sentry towers, were such a reminder of his grandfather who created them that his throat tightened. How could such a creator die? 'Can you imagine that one man alone, the Emperor Akbar, conceived and built this entire fort?' he inquired softly of Ishtaq, who had paused beside him.

'Your grandfather is the greatest builder of all time,' Ishtaq responded. 'When he tore down the old Lodi family fort to construct this one, he even built a temporary pleasure city seven miles south to use while it was being erected. He raced his dogs and flew birds there and started playing polo at night with his new invention, a ball of smouldering *palas* wood whose gleam the players could follow. After he built Agra, he created a new city at Sikri Fatehpur, to honour the holy *shaik* whose prayers made it possible for his baby sons to survive this life, besides forts and palaces at Ajmer, Lahore, Attock on the Indus, Allahabad and Srinagar. This is more than the work of a man, for to build is to create, to create is godly.'

Ishtaq was unusually talkative this morning, but what he said was true. 'To build is to create, to create is godly.' H'mmm . . . I like that, Prince Jahan reflected. These words shall be the inspiration of my ambition to create exquisite edifices, but of marble, not the sandstone of my grandfather's cities. Curiosity about Ishtaq's nervousness was extinguished before the need to press on with his ride and return to the palace in time to bathe, change and attend the Emperor. He turned Samt north-east and skirted the rampart walls until he reached the river, where he reined in at the passage leading to the eastern *maidan*. The sky before him lightened and roosters began crowing at the false dawn. The cavalry escort wheeled to form two lines behind him.

As usual, Ishtaq and the escort remained at the north end of the *maidan*. Today, Prince Jahan rode south alone, along the *maidan*. The silent rampart of the fort, the moat below it, was to his right, the broad, swift-flowing Jumna splashed and swirled at his left. His depression began to lift when he trotted Samt, broke into a light canter, enjoying the motion, moving only from his waist, his seat firmly on the saddle. He got into balance before urging Samt with the beat of his leg to a faster pace. Air, thick and tepid, glided past his face. He took in the far bank, a flat expanse of dark mustard fields until the sharp bend in the river on its journey east, between lines of tall, dark cypress trees. An open boat, poled by a single boatman standing erect, moving swiftly with the current, appeared close to the bank nearest him. The river is life and a source of living to boatmen, he thought. The dark gap of the canal that fed the moat appeared across his route, about a hundred yards ahead. The sky darkened again, but a sudden spasm of light revealed two black rocks in his path at the river's edge. He slowed his canter as he approached them.

What were two black rocks doing on the open *maidan*? From the corner of his eye, he noted that the boat had stopped at the river's bend.

Every instinct screamed that something was amiss.

The rocks erupted into life. Dark blankets flung aside, two hooded men leapt to their feet. One jumped for his horse's bridle, the other whirled something overhead. A noose hissed towards him.

For the first time that she could remember, her husband spent the entire night with her. A Muslim man is required to bless his legal wife or wives regularly with his sexual favours. Some blessing! Nur Jehan had always regarded this admonition as more than a little extreme! The colossal vanity of men made them imagine they were designed by Allah to bring bliss to women from sexual union. The act itself was comical, with its sweaty, groaning bodies and the ridiculous pumping movement that brought stimulation for the final seconds of climax. All that effort for a few moments of bliss followed by the inevitable slump of exhaustion. Why couldn't men seed women for the joy of its purpose, offspring, the sacred door to the forever? Males were merely incidental to the process, providing seeds which the wind scatters to sprout on the womb of mother earth. Whenever the male of some species tried to devour its young, the female would defend it. Females enjoyed their offspring and it was a female's natural function to nurture and help her children to prosper whatever the cost. Nur Jehan's little daughter, Ladili, though fathered by this monster snoring beside her, was growing up in the *harem*, cared for by her wet-nurse. Ladili was little more to Nur Jehan than a plaything, but when the girl grew up and the day came, she too would place Ladili's happiness before that of everyone else . . . well, excluding herself, since her well-being was essential for the child.

Why had her husband elected to spend the whole night with her? She puzzled for the answer each time she woke from her fitful sleep, unaccustomed as she was to another body on the divan that served as her bed at night. This body was so huge and immovable, it was like sleeping on a towering cliff's edge. She had to keep turning to avoid his bulk. Besides, it was disgusting to have his sexual excretion within her and to endure it on him mingled with the odour of his night sweat. Not even her favourite rose-scented incense glowing in the brazier could erase these smells. To add to it all, the night had been dreadfully hot and close and she had finally fallen into a deep sleep only to be wakened by the crowing of cocks at the false dawn. What was her husband's secret? Why had he started awake a couple of times, staring at the ceiling? Why had he humped her so cruelly this time, as if to punish her – or could it have been someone else? – on and on almost ceaselessly after her sexual ministrations, staring at her beauty as if he would devour it, before climaxing with great cries?

His massive body stirred beside her. Through the windows, the sky had paled at the approach of dawn. Barely heard, unidentifiable vibrations told of the rising household. The furniture in the room was becoming visible. Thank Allah, the night was over.

Sher Afgan sat up with a start, pig eyes staring. 'Where? What?' Even in the semi-dark, she could see the spit drool from the side of his small mouth.

'You are with me, your loving wife, Nur Jehan,' she murmured, sitting up cross-legged beside him. 'You had a disturbed sleep, my lord.'

He wiped his mouth with the back of his hand. 'How do you know?' he demanded crossly.

'You were having nightmares, lord, and you talked in your sleep.'

His massive head jerked suspiciously towards her, alert on the instant, the pebble brown eyes sharp. 'Oh! . . . what did I say?'

'Not much that was identifiable.' She tried a shot in the dark. 'You seemed to be afraid of someone or something.' She noted with triumph the hint of alarm in his expression. She recalled his visit to Prince Husrau. 'It seemed as if someone was forcing you to do something you really did not want to do.' She was watching him like a hawk but kept her expression dreamy. This must be the way fortune tellers extracted secrets before divulging them! 'Something you had to do immediately.'

A groan escaped him, but he recovered. 'Probably too much *pilau* last night,' he declared. 'It is said to give one nightmares.'

'You seemed to be in mortal fear,' she persisted. She hesitated and took the plunge, risking his anger and another brutal assault. If something had been planned against Prince Jehangir, she had to know. 'I want you to remember that I am more than your wife, lord. I am your friend, the mother of your child and your help-mate. I have also what the Parsees call *mithra* for you, the loyalties of our contract. Besides, I am nothing without you. If you have an intolerable burden to bear, why not share it with me and lessen your load?' She eyed him steadily. 'You may do so with the knowledge that it will remain *our* secret.' Then cunningly, 'Remember too that I am not entirely helpless, for my father and brother have the right connections, of which you are aware.'

He held his head in his large paws. For a moment she almost felt sorry for him, but the hatred and loathing of the years soon took over.

'There is indeed something that troubles me,' he declared

into his hands. 'Something that may be happening at this very moment, but I cannot speak of it.'

Alarm bells had begun jangling in Nur Jehan's brain. Could Prince Husrau have persuaded Sher Afgan to have Prince Jehangir assassinated? 'Is it something that is going to be done to Prince Jehangir?' she inquired.

His thunderous slap sent lightning forks through her agonized brain. She blacked out before careening over the divan bed.

For a split second Prince Jahan panicked. Then his natural coolness in danger quickly reasserted itself. The noose was already snaking over his shoulders. He reached for his sword. Too late. The rope was around his arms, tightening. He would never be able to draw the weapon.

There are two of them, he reasoned swift as lightning, and one of me . . . no . . . not one, two. He applied the aid, started leaning forward so his upper body would be at right angles to the ground at all times during the movement. Samt reared on his hind legs. Prince Jahan lightly squeezed his right rein so the horse wheeled slightly left. The assassin holding the bridle lost balance.

'Now!' Prince Jahan shouted, and the great hooves came crashing down, the left one four-squarely on the hooded face. The assassin was flung back on the turf. Samt whinnied his fierce battle cry.

Elation shot through Prince Jahan. We are both warriors, he exulted. The triumph was short-lived. The second assassin, who had been tightening the noose, ready to tear him off the horse, had paused, but only for a split second. Recovering swiftly, he jerked fiercely at the rope.

Prince Jahan tried vainly to swing Samt around. The trained battle-charger knew what he had to do. He reared and kicked, kicked and reared, keeping the assassin occupied, but the noose was slowly pulling Prince Jahan to the ground. A vicious jerk nearly toppled him over. He let go the reins, clung desperately with both hands to the martingale. If only he could draw his sword, he could cut the rope. But his upper arms were held as in a vice. His sweat was making the saddle slippery. He started teetering again, clung tighter to the strap. How to cut the rope? In a flash of inspiration he remembered the dagger at his waist. He suddenly stopped resisting against the pressure of the rope, moved both upper arms inwards. The pressure slackened. He reached down with his left hand.

His sweaty fingers touched the tip of the dagger's hilt. Slipped.

Dear Allah, help me, he silently implored. One desperate downward jab of his left hand. His fingers clasped the dagger.

Clinging to the martingale with his right hand, renewed in strength, he drew the dagger. With a last desperate effort of his thighs, he gripped Samt's flanks more firmly. He transferred the dagger to his right hand, bent his elbow, pushed the blade under the rope at his armpit.

One tremendous slash. The keen blade sliced through the rope like a scythe through mud. The assassin staggered back from the release of his own mighty pull. Blessed, blessed relief. Prince Jahan's arms were free at last. He dug fierce heels into Samt's flanks. The charger leapt forward. Recovering the reins, Prince Jahan replaced his dagger, brought Samt under control. Blood pounding, Prince Jahan circled wide into a full gallop, came racing back towards the dark figure of the assassin who had turned and was fleeing towards the river.

Rage such as he had never known, even in battle, flamed like a forest fire within Prince Jahan, drove him mad.

'Ai . . . a . . . a . . . Ai . . . ye . . . !'

The wild cry of his Mongol ancestors reached the heavens as he charged. Thundering hooves rapidly closed the gap. The assassin looked back, swerved, trying to avoid the charge.

Prince Jahan deliberately set Samt at his enemy. The assassin leapt desperately sideways, but the pounding hooves smashed into him, trampled him underfoot as if he were a giant rag doll. He sprawled on the ground, his body smashed to pulp.

The boatman had been watching the action. Panic-stricken, he began poling away.

'Ai . . . a . . . ai . . . ye . . . !' Prince Jahan headed straight to the river bank. Horse and rider forded the water with a tremendous splash. The boatman was poling desperately now, not looking back.

Prince Jahan directed Samt towards the boat. He drew his dagger, grasped it by the point, flung back his arm, sent the dagger straight and true as he had been taught, aimed for the heart.

A soggy thud. A great groan.

The boatman flung up his arms, let go the pole. His body arched. He collapsed slowly, like a nautch dancer in motion. He tried to come erect. Staggered. The boat rocked violently, throwing him sideways. The boat capsized, flung him with a great splash into the water. A thousand drops of silver arced up, fell into the hollow of the man's sinking. The wet wooden hull gleamed. The boat was caught by the current, gathered speed and headed swiftly east, between the dark cypresses, towards the glow of the unrisen sun.

Leaning forward in the saddle, Prince Jahan urged the dripping Samt up the river bank. His cavalry escort, drawn swords flashing, now lined the edge, anxious. No one dared to help him. 'Are you all right, my lord prince?' the captain called out.

'Yes, thanks to Allah,' Prince Jahan replied. He was in no mood for talk. Now that the danger was over, reaction had set in and he needed all his willpower to control the shivering of his body and the chattering of his teeth, which were not from the cold.

Samt stood firmly on all fours, shook himself violently, spraying drops of water on the grass. He blew through his nose, snorting. Prince Jahan patted him on his glossy neck, leaned forward to whisper in his ear. 'You won this battle. You are indeed Samt, the highest and the greatest.'

'So young, only thirteen, and he overcame three assassins singlehanded,' he heard a trooper say quietly to his neighbour. 'He is an Emperor already.'

He was not too numb for pride. 'I heard your words, trooper,' he responded. 'And I thank you for them, but the real Emperor is my horse, Samt, whose mighty hooves destroyed two of them.'

Prince Jahan's eyes sought the two bodies on the grass. To his surprise, Ishtaq had dismounted, long naked sword in hand, and was standing over the nearer one. Suddenly the chief groom grasped his sword with both hands, lifted it high and brought it down in a tremendous blow below the hooded head. Thwack! The neck was cleanly severed. Before anyone could stop him, bloody sword in hand, Ishtaq ran to the second man.

'No!' Prince Jahan called and spurred Samt forward.

Too late. Another great Thwack! The second head fell.

Ishtaq stood up to face his master. Eyes flaming with rage, he saluted with his sword, red blood dripping from it.

Prince Jahan reined in his horse. The cavalry escort wheeled around to form a protective circle around Ishtaq and himself. 'Why did you do that?' Prince Jahan quietly demanded.

'Because these filthy assassins attempted to kill my lord, my prince.' Ishtaq was panting lightly.

Prince Jahan thought quickly. He turned his head towards the river. Boat and man were gone. He looked

74

down at Ishtaq. 'Did you not realize that we needed at least one of these men alive to make him talk, so we could discover who is behind this obviously well-planned attempt?'

'I'm sorry . . . I'm sorry, my lord prince . . . I . . . I went mad at what they tried to do to you.' He drew himself to his full height. 'I am a Pathan, lord. It is my duty to protect those I serve. It is a matter of honour. Let no man stand in my way.' He hesitated. 'It never struck me that these dogs could tell us . . .' He shrugged.

'Didn't it?'

'What, my lord?' Was there a hint of something else lurking behind the seemingly innocent rectitude?

Pondering how exactly to tackle this man, Prince Jahan suddenly felt grown up. Why, he wondered? The answer snapped back. Because for the first time in your life, you faced danger totally alone, battled it with the resources at your disposal, including your beloved Samt. And won. His response came easily. 'Because you may have wanted to make certain that these men were dead and unable to identify their accomplices.' Though pretending careless-ness, he was watching Ishtaq's reactions like a young hawk.

Only the tiniest twitch of a black-bearded cheek betrayed the groom's apprehension. Prince Jahan remembered the lesson he had learned from the elephant battle. Swerve and lunge. He made to wheel Samt around, as if he had no suspicions and was not concerned about an answer. Ishtaq's body loosened.

'Why would I do that, lord?' Ishtaq inquired, puzzlement in his expression.

'Perhaps the answer is in your sword,' Prince Jahan flung out carelessly. He noted from the corner of his eye that the groom's eyes had dropped to his bloody sword blade as if seeking what evidence could be there. In the tense silence, one of the cavalrymen shifted in his saddle, leather creaking, and a horse pawed the ground.

'Here, give me that sword,' Prince Jahan directed. 'I will show you.' He noted Ishtaq's hesitation, then the spark of apprehension. 'The hilt towards me.'

Blood from the blade stained Ishtaq's pale palms. He walked slowly forward to Prince Jahan's right and presented the hilt. 'Ah! A heavy sword.' Prince Jahan hefted it in his right hand. 'Sharp too. See, the blood is already beginning to clot on it.' He paused, eyed Ishtaq mercilessly. 'Why would a groom need a sword such as this?'

A barely perceptible tremor went through the groom. 'It's a family sword, my lord. We are a warrior tribe.'

'What did the *thuggee* threaten you with, Ishtaq? Or what reward did your masters offer you?'

The deepset, dark eyes widened. A dribble of saliva appeared at a corner of Ishtaq's mouth, just beneath the sweeping black moustache. 'I am no betrayer, lord,' he protested.

Prince Jahan suddenly flipped the sword up, its point at Ishtaq's right eye. 'You will tell me the truth now, groom, or lose this eye . . . then the next. And if that does not work, the torture chamber of the Emperor awaits you.'

A sob escaped Ishtaq, but he kept his head erect, his eyes on the point of the sword. 'Have mercy on me, lord. I have a young wife and two small children.'

'Ah! So that was your weak point? Family.'

Disregarding the unwavering sword point, Ishtaq fell to his knees. 'Will you spare me if I tell all I know, most compassionate prince?'

Prince Jahan felt no compassion, only a ruthless purpose. From that purpose alone, he extended mercy, aware of the eyes of the cavalrymen gaping spellbound at the spectacle. 'Yes, if you satisfy me that you have told the truth.'

'I did not know the *thuggee* before, lord.' Ishtaq was

whimpering now. He wiped the snot streaming down his hawk-nose with the back of his hand. 'Two hooded men intercepted me when I was returning home from the palace last night, dragged me into an alley. They threatened to kill me if I did not agree to their demands. When I refused, they said they would kill my wife and two children instead. They wanted to know all about your movements this morning and during your ride. They promised they would not harm you, that they only wanted to detain you for a short time and have you ransomed in exchange for some of their comrades who have been imprisoned. Oh, my lord, that is all I know. I beseech you to forgive me.' He fell forward, kneeling, his white turban touching the grass, the long, lean body racked with weeping.

I believe the man is telling the truth, Prince Jahan thought. We will extract no more from him under torture. But if I am to be a ruler I cannot extend any mercy to a wrong-doer. Not out of compassion then, but merely in the interests of honour, for I have given my word, I shall extend that mercy to him. 'You may rise, Ishtaq, and return to your family. Take them and flee the city immediately, for when the Emperor hears of this incident, he will want to take you and yours, flay you all alive, pour honey over you and hang you upside down for the ants to eat your eyes out before devouring the rest of your bodies. Go now.'

Ishtaq scrambled to his feet. 'My *daevas* bless you, my lord. My family and I will be eternally in your debt. We shall have a lamp burning for you perpetually . . .'

'Go!' Prince Jahan screamed, pointing. He flung the sword to the ground. 'Take your sword with you and the horse. You may keep them both. Never let me see you again.'

Ishtaq scrambled to his feet, grabbed his sword, mounted his horse. With a single backward glance, he galloped away.

Suddenly, Prince Jahan felt only thirteen again. I should still be at school, he thought, playing with other children.

The well-trained guards, swords drawn, had, as was proper, remained watchful spectators. The guard captain rode alongside Prince Jahan.

'Please forgive me if I seem presumptuous, my lord prince, but I am amazed at your perception, restraint and wisdom. It would have been remarkable in an adult, but at your age?' He raised expressive eyes upwards. 'We are indeed fortunate to serve you. As for your mercy in letting Ishtaq go, it is beyond belief.'

'It was not mercy but good sense,' Prince Jahan replied, flattered by the praise, but strangely unmoved by it. 'He will be tracked down and followed by the Emperor's men. He will live in the hell of his terror. He may lead us to his source, but I doubt it. As for your words of praise, I'll have you know that they belong to the Emperor. Thanks to him, I am not a thirteen-year-old. I have never been a boy and never shall be.' Except for an inner part of me of which no one is aware, the vital part of being a human being, which I shall never divulge to anyone.

'I do not know what to say, my lord prince.'

'Then do not say it!' Prince Jahan smiled to rob the words of offence.

'Shall we return to the palace?'

'Yes.' He had to bathe, change, join his grandfather in the *jarokha* on the ramparts. The sun, ready to rise too, was breathing red-gold fire into the eastern sky above the dark treetops. People were beginning to file onto the *maidan*. It was almost too late for all he had to do before departing for Mewar.

He squared his shoulders, held his head high. 'I'll race you to the Delhi gate,' he called over his shoulder. Before he dug his heels in Samt's flanks, he realized that he had issued the challenge of a boy.

'Certainly, my lord prince. But first tell me, how did you know Ishtaq was guilty?'

'A groom never carries a sword. Ishtaq had it hidden beneath his cloak. He panicked when I escaped, forgot himself and drew the sword to destroy the evidence. He destroyed himself instead.' He wheeled Samt around.

'Ai . . . ai . . . yee . . .' The battle cry of his Mongol ancestors escaped him, as he dug his heels into Samt's flanks.

Chapter 5

Life had been freer for Mumtaz Mahal before she reached puberty last year. She could wander about her home more or less as she pleased, talking to the servants, climbing trees like the tomboy she was, skipping, playing with the boys of the household. Then came the bleeding. She had been warned about it by Sati who, having wet-nursed her when she was a baby, had automatically become her foster-mother and remained her governess. No warning could diminish the panic and revulsion she felt when she woke that night to find blood between her thighs and soaking her bed linen. Ugh! The cramps were bad enough, but being imprisoned within the strict rules of *purdah* forever added torture to injury. Not even the luxury of the mansion her widowed father, Asaf Khan, shared with his own father, and his sister, Nur Jehan, whose giant husband Mumtaz detested, could relieve her restlessness. Apart from her father and grandfather, the only men she ever saw now were the obese eunuchs of the household, vegetable marrows padding about silently on flat feet, spying on the ladies, milking them of their money in exchange for secret favours and emitting high-pitched giggles at their own dry jokes.

Mumtaz had woken with the cramps this morning, so the cursed event was not far away. Her bloated stomach told her it would be a fierce blood-letting this time. In addition, the night had been so warm and close that her tiny, windowless bedchamber had been like a furnace. Yet, while she envied people who had larger rooms, she loved having her own special place which only Sati shared. Here, lying on her gold-cushioned divan or seated on the brown sandalwood chest in which she kept her clothes, the only piece of furniture in the room, she could enjoy her fantasies or wallow in her miseries.

A groan escaped her.

Sati, asleep on a yellow quilt spread over the white mohair rug beside the divan, was up in an instant. Normally clean and scented, she smelled of bedclothes and sleep saliva and it made Mumtaz gag.

'What's wrong, little house-sparrow?' Sati inquired, her voice soft and mellow, concern in the large grey eyes. She mechanically started gathering up her silver hair to tie it in the usual loose knot at the back of her neck. The lighted glass oil-lamp hung from its brass chain directly above her, so her face was in shadow, but the delicacy of her pale complexion was nonetheless evident. 'Are you sick?'

'No, but I think I'm going to be.'

'Oh, it's that time of the month again, is it?'

The concern had left Sati's voice, its tone now so casual that a gust of fury shook Mumtaz. 'Oh, it's that time of the month again,' she mimicked. 'As if I were a chicken laying an egg.'

'Chickens don't lay eggs, hens do . . . and not once a month.'

Mumtaz stifled her scream of rage in case it was overheard. 'Oh, oh, oh, you are an unfeeling monster,' she cried. 'Here I am, suffering unimaginable torture, and all you can do is make jokes. What kind of mother are you?' She swung her legs over, sat up, glaring at Sati.

The grey eyes twinkled. 'A wise one, I hope.' Sati finished tying up her hair. 'I've told you time and again that if you give in to pain, and if I give you sympathy, you will suffer even more. I've also told you that when you get married and have your first baby, the cramps will cease.'

'But the bleeding . . .'

'That too while you're carrying a child!'

'You are horrid.'

'And you are spoilt.'

'That's not true. My father never sees me as he used to; my aunt has no time for me. I have no one.' She pretended to wail.

'You have me, little house-sparrow.'

Detecting that Sati was weakening a little, Mumtaz grabbed her stomach, exclaimed with pain and doubled up. 'Ooh . . . ooh!'

Sati was beside her in an instant, a plump arm around her shoulders. 'My poor baby, where does it hurt?'

Having won, Mumtaz started to giggle.

Sati drew away, releasing her arm. 'You little cheat!' She reached out, grasped Mumtaz by the shoulders. 'I ought to shake you,' her voice softened, 'but I love you instead, especially because you're so incorrigible.' She sat down on the divan and drew Mumtaz to her. Sati's plump breast was always comforting. Mumtaz snuggled up against it. 'Mm . . . m . . . that's better.' She sighed contentedly. 'Do you love me?'

'Yes. I love you.' They had agreed long ago that Mumtaz was not satisfied with a mere 'yes' answer to that question.

'Most of all?'

'Most of all.'

'That means you love others too. I do not like that.'

'There is no one else but you, little house-sparrow, and you know it.'

'That's nice.' Then, with one of her usual quick changes of mood, she drew away sharply, stood up. 'It's so hot in here.' She drew out the blue silken nightdress that clung to her body. 'See how wet I am.' She raised her right thumbnail to the light so she could see her face in the tiny circular mirror attached to it, part of the standard equipment of ladies of the *harem*. 'Ee . . . eck! I look a mess.' She straightened a curly black lock that had fallen over her white forehead. 'How terrible. The *kohl* has smudged on my eyelids. It makes my eyes look black instead of brown.' She half-sighed. 'Well, I have the whole day in which to repair the damage. What else is there to do in these accursed *harems*, but to preen ourselves like *pea*cocks all day?'

'Hardly pea*cocks*.'

'You know what I mean.' A wave of impatience swept through her. 'Why do you always pick at my words? Peck, peck, peck all the time, like a mynah.'

'Because you use words so loosely and that's no way for a sharp, intelligent lady to be. You have a remarkable future. Even the astrologers say it.'

'Like today,' Mumtaz interrupted her. 'We shall go to the toilet rooms, perform our morning exercises into the stinking buckets, then wash or bathe before breakfasting in the dining room, a whole bunch of chattering women.'

'Mynahs,' Sati commented drily.

'Whatever. Then will come the eternal powdering, rougeing, beautifying, before the business of the day with the eunuchs for the older ladies like my aunt.'

'Nothing wrong with business.'

'Then what about funny business, like my cousin Rowena yesterday. Ha! She pretended to be sick, so when the physician came and the eunuch removed the shawl which is placed around his head in case he sees any of the

82

ladies, she took his hand through the bed curtains to show him where the pain was, kissed it, bit it gently, then put it you know where.'

'That is not the kind of story a lady should listen to, still less repeat,' Sati admonished sternly.

'Then how about this? Our housekeeper Farida the Giantess sets aside the choicest chicken livers and gizzards for Mano, that sweet little Chola chambermaid of my aunt, Nur Jehan. Do you know why?'

'No.'

'Then you do not contradict it?'

'Why should I?'

'Well, Farida and Mano are lovers. They rub tits and clits whenever they have a chance.'

Noting Sati's grey eyebrows rise in shock, a peal of laughter escaped Mumtaz.

'How can you say such things, child?' Sati demanded.

'It's the truth, is it not?'

'That doesn't mean you have to repeat it.'

'The Prophet has said that we should always speak the truth.' Mumtaz rolled pious eyes heavenward.

'He did not say that we should *speak* the truth always,' Sati retorted. 'What you must always do is be a lady.'

'Do you know that Nur Jehan is fast becoming very rich?' Mumtaz shot off deliberately on one of her tangents.

'That's true, but she deserves to be rich because she has devoted all her time to studying and learning to *be* someone. She is a student of politics, administration and business. She is a great poet, a singer and a dancer. Such an accomplished lady.'

'Are you trying to make me jealous?'

'No. I am hoping to make you better than her because you have more in you.'

'That's good. But I am lazy at times.'

'It is natural at your age. Many changes have taken place

83

in both your body and your mind. You have enormous energy nonetheless, so don't be concerned about the laziness. One day you too will have a purpose in life. Then the laziness will go away.'

'I wish these stupid cramps would go away.' Mumtaz clutched her stomach again. 'But, as I was saying, I have no business interests, so I can only listen to the ladies haggling with the eunuchs for better profits from their produce or the boats they own. My aunt is actually thinking of buying a big trading ship.'

'Ladies of the *harem* grow wealthy on the presents given them by their husband, brothers, father or sons. Then they increase their wealth.'

'That is why I want a rich husband. Nur Jehan's husband is poor. Most of what she owns came from my grandfather as dowry.'

'You too will be given a dowry by your father.'

'I shall marry a prince and will not need a dowry.'

'You are worthy of a prince, but I don't know where you'll find one.'

'My father will find one for me.'

'Any ideas as to who it might be?' Sati was being sarcastic.

Mumtaz stood evenly on both feet. Arms akimbo, she stared down at Sati. Suddenly in a trance, the words came out of her in a whisper. 'Yes. It shall be Prince Jahan.'

Keyed up by the action they had just been through, Prince Jahan on Samt won the race to the entrance gates. In the miraculous fashion of forts, word of the attempt on his person awaited him. Mounted guards were assembled, ready for action. Sentries on the ramparts must have observed the entire incident through the lightening gloom of the eastern *maidan* and reported it. What did the soldiers think when, having endured such an ordeal, he casually appeared at the end of a routine race with the guard captain? It was almost worth having endured the terror to see the comical expression on the face of the fortress commander, a great bearded Sikh riding a tall bay.

'They were coming to rescue us,' he murmured drily to the guard captain who had drawn his horse alongside. 'I am sorry to disappoint them. Even so, by the time this story reaches the people, I will have been attacked by a whole band of dacoits, all of whom I slew single-handed with sword and dagger!' He would have to find another dagger, the haft of which would match the green jade sheath buckled to his belt.

'All is well,' he called out to the fortress commander. 'I must hurry now to attend the Emperor. The guard captain here will tell you the story.'

'Praised be the gods,' the fortress commander responded fervently. He saluted, then nodded. 'Make way there for the prince.'

Followed by the rest of his escort, Prince Jahan fast-cantered to the palace, the thunderous clatter of hooves on cobblestones clearing a way for them. Determined not to be late, he rushed through his ablutions and reached the eastern rampart wall minutes before the Emperor was due to appear. Prince Jehangir was already present. Prince Jahan knelt and kissed his father's hand. Before they could exchange a word, the Emperor appeared. The roar of the vast crowds assembled on the *maidan* greeted him. He acknowledged the homage with gracious waves of his right hand, palm inwards.

One look at his grandfather's face and Prince Jahan's heart sank. The Emperor looked wan and drawn, his face etched with lines of fatigue. Only the opium sedatives and his indomitable will were holding him up after a night of pain.

As the princes, nobles and attendants knelt to the

Emperor, the sentries saluting, he slowly mounted the steps, turned and faced the east. Prince Jahan dismally realized that the Emperor was no longer the symbol of the rising sun but of his own approaching night.

The Emperor bowed, sat on his throne, raised his legs up with an obvious effort to cross them beneath him. 'Pray be seated, princes, lords and gentlemen,' he commanded, but his voice lacked its usual strength.

'Prince Jahan, come forward.' The Emperor's voice showed some of its normal strength. He waited until Prince Jahan knelt before him. 'We received news, just before we left our robing room, of an attempt on your life when you rode on the *maidan* this morning.'

'Yes, Sire. I believe, however, that it was an attempt to kidnap rather than to kill me.' He noted his father's quickened interest.

'H'mm. We have heard the story at second hand. Give us the details.'

The Emperor listened attentively while Prince Jahan retailed all that had happened, sticking to the facts, avoiding the slightest embellishment or words that would smack of any heroism on his part.

Only the long tapering fingers of the right hand, drumming twice on the arm of the throne, and an occasional fingering of the black mole on his nose, hinted at the Emperor's emotion. 'You have done extraordinarily well,' he commented when Prince Jahan concluded his story. 'Some may question your judgment in letting this traitor Ishtaq escape, for the cruellest and most inhuman punishment should be meted out to such criminals. But we for our part commend and endorse the maturity and wisdom of your decision. Ishtaq will be traced and secretly followed in an attempt to track down his masters. We feel, however, that this may be an abortive search, for he and his family will be murdered if those who hired him find that he remains a threat to them. Better for him that he vanish completely from the face of the earth.' He paused, eyed Prince Jahan keenly. 'And you will depart for Mewar shortly?'

'Yes, Sire, as soon as the morning prayer and your gracious *durbar* are over.'

'Good. You shall carry out the mission and not return until it is accomplished, regardless of the state of the realm.'

Now why had his grandfather interjected those last words? The depression that had gripped Prince Jahan returned in a flood.

When Nur Jehan came to, her husband had gone and she was alone in her chamber lying across the divan. Dawn light brightening the two rosy rectangles of sky through her grilled windows, the first warblings of doves in the court-yard and the love-birds whistling merrily in their cages mocked her mood. An odour of blood behind her nose made her clear her throat. She leaned over and spat into the shiny brass spittoon beside the divan. There was no trace of blood. She sat up. Far from acceptance of her lot, the years of abuse had made her more determined than ever to end it. Not long to wait now. Excitement at the certainty that major changes were impending stirred beneath her hatred for Sher Afgan. She gently massaged the back of her neck, sore from the jolt, wiggled her head from side to side to ease it.

Her husband's reaction had confirmed what she suspected. He somehow knew of the invisible tie between Prince Jehangir and herself and was insanely jealous of it, not because he loved her but because she was his chattel that no other man could even touch. It was the knowledge she had gained from their conversation, however, that was invaluable. She had to act immediately in case there was some danger to Prince Jehangir.

87

She rose and pulled the gold-tasselled bell-rope to summon her maid. Within moments, Mano was at the door. Nur Jehan had inherited Mano from her late sister-in-law, Asaf Khan's wife. Mano was a sixteen-year-old Chola from South India, with a small-boned oval face, dark brown skin, sparkling black eyes and teeth that shone like mother-of-pearl in a perpetually bright smile beneath the red *pottu* (caste mark) at the centre of her broad forehead. Her glossy black hair, middle-parted, was tied in a tight knot at the nape of her slender neck. Her yellow *sari* and blouse showed her trim figure and pouting breasts to good effect. She made the *namaste*, palms of her hands together at forehead level.

'Prepare my bath immediately,' Nur Jehan directed. 'Scent it with roses as usual. Then have a message delivered through my eunuch, Pali, to Lord Asaf Khan before he leaves the mansion requesting him to join me at breakfast.' By custom, even for Emperors, it was generally the midday meal that the men of the household shared with their ladies in the *harem*. Asaf Khan would know from the requested change of custom that he should see her without delay. 'Have breakfast served here in my chamber. We will have only *chuppati* with *ghee*, *sarsaparilla* root crushed in goat's milk and fruit. Hurry now.' My brother and I are Muslims, she thought, but we both start our day with the food of the Brahmins.

She felt much better by the time she knelt to her brother in greeting and occupied her usual settle opposite the white-cushioned divan on which he sat.

'Mm . . . Smells good.' He inhaled the scent of hot *chuppati* and warm goat's milk on the low table between them, glanced at the hands of the clock on the far wall. 'Twenty past eight. I have not much time, I'm afraid.' She had known from the moment he strode into the room that he was troubled, though he was outwardly his usual smiling self.

'I assumed from your summons to an immediate audience that you had something serious to discuss,' he continued, after the door closed behind Mano. He reached for a *chuppati* which had already been rolled with *ghee* and took a bite. 'Ah, delicious!' His bright eyes sought hers. 'We share the same cook, but his *chuppati* tastes like sawdust when it is made for me. I suppose everything tastes so much better when I am with you!'

'Flatterer!' She loved his gallant speeches. 'I know you are busy so I shall not detain you longer than necessary. I believe that Prince Jehangir is in mortal danger.'

'Why? How? From whom?' She now connected his visible alarm with the trouble she had sensed and her heart started beating faster. 'I do not know how, but my husband is somehow involved.'

'That cannot be, for only yesterday . . .' He paused. 'Tell me all about it,' he bade her quietly.

She told him of the incident that morning, for once omitting nothing. His dark brows arched when she told of the slap, his eyes blazing with anger. 'You mean he actually struck you?' he demanded.

'Yes.'

'So hard you fainted away?'

She nodded.

'Has this happened before?' His voice was deadly soft now.

Thrilled that he was more concerned about her well-being than the important state news she had given him, she simply stared at the carpet.

'By the blood of the Prophet, I'll have him flayed alive,' Asaf Khan ground out. 'Tell me more. Tell me everything.'

She told him in measured tones, deliberately confessing to her infatuation with Prince Jehangir, her conviction that the prince loved her and her certainty that they would be married some day.

Only when she had finished did she raise her eyes. His expression held such fury as she had never seen before. 'Our father and I are responsible for this,' he confessed bitterly. 'Believing the marriage to be for your security, we never dreamed that this would happen. But that is no excuse. Now it remains to have this monster punished . . .'

He made to rise, but she leaned forward and placed a detaining hand on his arm. 'Please sit down for a few minutes longer,' she begged. 'We have not discussed the matter about which I sent for you. It is far more important than revenge for all I have endured these years.' Her tone hardened. 'Be assured that vengeance will come. But Sher Afgan is the father of my daughter, Ladili, and we should not do anything that would hurt her. When Sher Afgan's time comes, it shall not be Allah's punishment but mine that he will have to endure.'

He gazed at her, stunned by the cold menace in her voice. Long moments passed. He shook his head, a hint of sadness at the corners of his mouth. 'I never suspected such hatred in you, but I do not blame you.' He recovered his poise. 'Well, to the business at hand. It is not Prince Jehangir who was the target today, but Prince Jahan.' He told her the story of the morning's incident which he had learned at the *durbar*.

'Prince Jahan?' she demanded, incredulous, when he had finished. 'Why would anyone want to harm the boy . . . unless . . . ?'

'Unless, what?'

'Well, he is the Emperor's favourite and the Emperor would have paid anything, done anything, to ensure his safety.'

Asaf Khan raised a finger in comprehension. 'Even to changing his heir?'

'Possibly.'

'Perhaps that is where the real danger to Prince Jehangir lies, in being replaced as the heir through a trick or blackmail. Which means that Prince Husrau must be behind the kidnap attempt.' He slapped a palm on his thigh. 'By the beards of our ancestors, your husband had an audience with Prince Husrau only yesterday morning, immediately after we both saw Prince Jehangir. He may well be the connection. Incidentally, the Emperor's health took a sudden serious decline last night. Being the person he is, however, he appeared in his pavilion as usual this morning, even strolled up and down the rampart wall in full view of the people as if he were in perfect health and insisted that Prince Jahan should depart on a mission to Mewar to inform Rana Amar Singh personally of the decision regarding the succession.'

'Most interesting,' Nur Jehan observed, thinking furiously. 'Most interesting. H'mmm.' Intuition flared within her. 'Prince Jahan is the coming man. We need to get him on our side.'

'What?'

She smiled dreamily. Things were beginning to fall into place. 'Young as he is, Prince Jahan is worthy, brave and all that Prince Jehangir will require of an heir. Prince Husrau is a well-meaning idealist, while the next brother Prince Parviz is incompetent and playful. Prince Shahriyar, the youngest, is of course as yet unproven.' Her voice hardened with conviction. 'We should make Prince Jahan our ally.'

'How?' he demanded in amazement.

'By establishing a family connection.' She projected the serenity of her gaze to him. 'We must expose Prince Jahan to your charming daughter, Mumtaz Mahal.'

For once, her normally self-possessed brother's jaw dropped and he could only gape at her.

* * *

91

Prince Chara's silent fury at being held hostage in the Emperor's palace changed to impotent rage when Prince Husrau called on him that morning with news of the failed kidnapping of Prince Jahan. He nonetheless maintained his usual calm exterior, merely shrugging when Prince Husrau asked him for his opinion as to who could have been behind the attempt.

'It must be Prince Jehangir,' Prince Husrau insisted. 'He is either trying to remove all possible competition or plans to hold Prince Jahan hostage, with a ransom demand from the kidnappers that the Emperor step down immediately as the condition for his favourite grandson's release.'

Prince Chara saw no reason to disagree with this theory, but suggested, before Prince Husrau left, that the latter should arrange a meeting with Sher Afgan in the Emperor's palace. 'Sher Afgan, being on Prince Jehangir's staff, might be able to ferret out information as to who was responsible for the kidnap attempt. If we can get him to point the finger of guilt at Prince Jehangir, the Emperor will certainly rescind his decision to appoint Prince Jehangir his successor and name you instead.'

Prince Husrau had fallen for the ploy.

As he faced Sher Afgan alone in the ante-room of the chamber allotted to him in the palace, Prince Chara's fury at the botched attempt was only tempered by satisfaction at how easily he had remained behind the scenes, his manipulation unknown to anyone but this hulk of a man standing before him. His plan for meeting Sher Afgan had been simple. He had invited Prince Husrau to dinner, and it was Prince Husrau who had requested Sher Afgan to meet him in Prince Chara's suite for after-dinner coffee. Meanwhile, Prince Chara had instructed the attendants to place the Turkish coffee pot and demi-tasse cups on the low table in front of the divan, after which they were to show Sher Afgan into the ante-room, where he was to be left until Prince Husrau could emerge for a meeting with the visitor. Prince Husrau was such a trusting fool that he would make an ideal Emperor – easier toppled from the throne than his father, or used as a royal donkey-head while Prince Chara ruled from behind the scenes. As for Sher Afgan, his knowledge was so dangerous that a death sentence already hung over his head, to be executed immediately his usefulness was over.

Prince Chara had listened for Sher Afgan's arrival. When he heard the doors to the suite close behind the attendants, he excused himself from Prince Husrau on the pretext of going to the adjoining privy and slipped into the ante-room through a small connecting corridor.

Sher Afgan was so tall his shaven head nearly reached the large crystal glass oil-lamp that dominated the ante-room. His bulk, clothed in an ill-fitting brown tunic and white pantaloons, was incongruous in the elegantly furnished room. The giant was obviously ill at ease, rubbing his hands together in a washing motion, sweating in spite of the coolness of the air from the swaying *punkahs*. Prince Chara looked up to challenge the pale pebble eyes. Injecting menace into his gaze, he brought Sher Afgan under his spell; allowed moments of silence to pass in order to intimidate the man.

'You failed.' Prince Chara said the words as a pronouncement of guilt.

'I beg my lord's pardon,' Sher Afgan stuttered. 'But it is not I that failed. Your lordship asked me to hire *thuggee* for the kidnap. I obeyed your orders and hired them. It is they who failed.'

'They were *your* agents,' Prince Chara hissed, controlling his mounting anger. 'Their failure is *your* failure. You know the price of failure?'

Sher Afgan looked down at him pitifully. He shrugged beefy shoulders, gestured with his hands helplessly. 'Yes, lord.' A cunning gleam momentarily entered the pig eyes. 'But if your lordship delivers me to judgment, you will have one agent less to carry out your commands.' Obviously encouraged by Prince Chara's lack of response, he proceeded more boldly. 'Besides, if you were going to deliver me to judgment, you would have done so already.' His body relaxed; his cheeks creased in a half-smile. 'You obviously have use for me, lord. Perhaps you have another plan? Meanwhile, let me give you some secret information that will show you I am more useful alive and where I am, than shamed and imprisoned.'

Prince Chara pretended to frown. 'I am listening,' he stated grimly. 'But the information had better be worth your life.'

Sher Afgan beamed, ran a palm over his bald head. 'Part of my discussion with Prince Jehangir the day before yesterday was entirely private, just between him and me.' He stopped abruptly.

'That tells me nothing.' There was no point in attempting to intimidate this donkey. He would offer a carrot instead. 'But you are right in assuming that you would be more useful to me alive than dead,' he added agreeably. 'It is obvious that you have brains as well as physical strength.'

Sher Afgan preened himself at the compliment. His smug smile ill-fitted the small mouth. 'That is why Prince Jehangir summoned me to meet him in the first place and assured me of a higher post and greater responsibility once he became Emperor.'

Prince Chara deliberately lifted his eyebrows. 'He did?'

'Yes, lord. In such a position, I would be much more useful to you and Prince Husrau than as a hirer of assassins.'

'Why would you make common cause with us?'

'I look to you for better rewards.'

The man was obviously lying. 'You have more reason

than that,' Prince Chara retorted with an air of knowledge. He decided to try a shot in the dark. 'Remember you are talking to one who knows many of your secrets. Suppose I suggested that you have personal cause to hate Prince Jehangir?'

Sher Afgan's pig eyes flamed. 'I do indeed have cause to loathe and detest the man.' That was enough. 'But begging your pardon, Prince, I shall not discuss such personal matters. All I say is this. I hate that drunken drug-addict and whoremonger. You can have me stoned to death, but I am committed to my resolve to do all I can to destroy Prince Jehangir. I also happen to . . . er . . . believe that he is attempting to hasten the Emperor's death. I doubt it will take more than two weeks longer.'

Prince Chara was hard put not to whistle in surprise. This was big news. Keeping an unconcerned demeanour, he shrugged. 'You will tell me all at the appropriate time.'

'Yes, lord. For the present it is in your best interest and mine that Prince Jehangir becomes Emperor as soon as possible.'

Prince Chara suddenly made up his mind. With the Emperor's health rapidly declining, it would be best for him to postpone all action for the present. 'Before I leave for Mewar next week, I shall find a means for you and me to communicate without anyone else's knowledge,' he stated. 'No one, no one at all, must learn of our connection or this meeting.' He injected merciless cruelty into his gaze. 'Not even your wife or your brother-in-law. If anyone comes to know of it, you and you alone will have been responsible and will suffer the consequences. Do you understand?'

'Yes, lord.' The pale eyes were sincere, earnest, but Prince Chara knew that this man should never be trusted.

'Also, Prince Husrau must not know that you and I have spoken now. Hold yourself at my future command.'

He had barely closed the door of the corridor leading to the privy when he heard the chamber door open and Prince Husrau's voice greeting Sher Afgan.

Chapter 6

It was late evening, two weeks later, when Prince Jahan returned from Mewar. He had been received graciously at the Chitor palace, by the ruling Rana Amar, his safety assured by the presence of the Rana's eldest son and heir in the Emperor's palace at Agra, as an 'honoured guest'.

Prince Jahan was well accustomed to Rajput manners and customs, since his mother had been a Rajput princess, and it was obvious that Rana Amar had grown to like him during his short stay in Chitor. Rana Amar's gifts for his return to Agra included a long Rajput sword, its golden scabbard studded with gems, for himself, two war-elephants for the Emperor and a black Scindhi charger for Prince Jehangir.

While he would normally have made the return journey in a more leisurely fashion, Prince Jahan had hurried home, pursued by demons of depression and foreboding. Even before he dismounted in the courtyard, he sensed the gloom that had settled over the palace, seeming even to enshroud the lighted windows.

He hastened to his first-floor chamber, perfunctorily acknowledging the salutations of the guards and attendants and the occasional courtier who greeted him with a 'Welcome back, Prince.'

His chief attendant, Mansur, a lean, taciturn Punjabi, quickly helped him to take off his riding clothes and prepared his warm, scented bath. 'How is the Emperor?'

he inquired of Mansur, when the attendant began to massage him in the steam room.

'Very sick, my lord prince.'

The news, though expected, hit him in the pit of the stomach. His grandfather, his guardian, guide and friend, the immortal Emperor, was dying. For the first time, the consequences dawned on him. The Emperor had always protected him. How would his father treat him once the protector was gone? How would his two elder brothers, Prince Husrau and Prince Parviz, whom he knew to be jealous of him, react? He would be as naked before his enemies and rivals as he was on this massage table.

Then something his grandfather had once said floated into his consciousness, like a faint crescent moon on a dark night. 'The steed of fear is ignorance, its spur is lack of self-confidence.'

What am I afraid of? he asked himself. Have I not proven myself in battle and in the Councils of State? The answer came back with irresistible force. You are just a boy.

He began to sweat harder and it was not from the steam but the inner sweat of fear. Two weeks ago, he thought he had grown up, but now it seemed that the boy remained. He slowly started to reason. My grandfather was eight when he began his first campaign, not yet fourteen when he ascended the throne of a divided empire. My ancestor Babur was but eleven when he became king and faced two rivals converging on his realm from different directions. I am of their blood, a Moghul. I must stand on my own two feet right now, this very instant, if I am not to perish from my own timidity. He swung his feet to the ground and stepped out of the steam room, resolute, but totally isolated from the rest of the world.

Knowing that he intended visiting his grandfather that night, Mansur had laid out a tunic of pale blue silk with

white pantaloons for him. His toilet completed, the frankincense scent which was the Emperor's favourite heavy in his
nostrils, Prince Jahan strode along the brightly lit palace
corridors, past salaaming guards and attendants, until he
reached the Emperor's audience hall. It was as if he were
seeing the magnificent chamber, one of his grandfather's
innovations, for the first time. The Emperor's pavilion
faced sixty-four columns, one for each of his ministers. It
rose immediately above the flat marble dais on which the
prime minister normally stood. Its central supporting
column was intricately carved where the lowest cornice
would normally have been; instead, the beam spread out in
polished red sandstone like separate narrow petals of a huge
flower. These petals supported a circular platform with a
balcony rail of filigreed sandstone topped by polished
rosewood. The platform was served from two directions by
walkways linking it to the corridors of the upper floor. It
was from one of these corridors and across the walkway
that the Emperor emerged for his audiences to sit like an
imperial eagle on the glittering throne placed upon the eyrie
of the platform. Prince Jahan's eyes misted as he hurried
through the empty audience hall to the wide stairway
beyond that led to the second floor. Would his grandfather
ever be seated on that throne, isolated from the world in
regal splendour, again? Isolation! That was part of the price
one paid for dominion.

He had been told that the Emperor had elected to occupy
the European room while confined to his suite. The uniformed guards at the entrance saluted and opened the great
teakwood double doors for Prince Jahan. The ante-room
had very few people at this hour. He brushed past them,
ignored the protest of the attendants at the door of the
European and stalked inside. He paused in shocked
disbelief.

The central chandelier had not been lit, so the room was

in darkness save for the glow from two night lamps at the back of the sofa on which the Emperor reclined. He recoiled at an acrid stench of crushed herbs overlaid with frankincense. The windows of the chamber were closed, the *punkahs* were still and the air was hot and stifling. His grandfather lay on the sofa propped up by gold cushions. A small gnome of a man bent over him, as if casting a spell. A scene from a nightmare.

Even before the physician turned sharply at the intrusion, Prince Jahan recognized him as Hakim Ali. One finger to lips, the physician flapped his other hand in a rapid backwards motion, impatiently directing Prince Jahan to be gone.

'Who is it?' The Emperor's voice was weak, his breathing rough and uneven. A spasm of coughing rumbled through the chamber, the worn body shaking with the effort.

Prince Jahan waited until the paroxysm ended. 'It is I, Grandfather,' he replied boldly.

'Please rest, Sire,' Hakim Ali advised. His voice was surprisingly deep for so emaciated a man. 'Only rest will cure you. I shall have the prince leave immediately.'

The Emperor ignored him. 'We wish to speak privately to the prince. You may leave now, physician, and return after he has departed.'

Sweating profusely from the heat, Prince Jahan waited until the door had closed behind the hunchback physician before approaching the Emperor. If he had been shocked by the appearance of the chamber, he was stunned at the deterioration in his grandfather. The heavy face, tilted as usual to the left side, was drawn, the skin in dark pouches, the mole on the nose a blemish, the whole a death's head. The brilliant eyes, a film over them, had sunk into hollows, even the Mongol moustaches seemed limp, while the once magnificent body drooped on the golden cushions.

Two weeks and a virile, vital leader of men had become

a living corpse. How? Prince Jahan had read all the treatises about dysentery. While it could weaken and drain a victim rapidly, how could the effects have become so drastic? Having to conserve his strength in order to function as Emperor had even kept his grandfather away from the *harem* and his devoted wife.

'Come closer, *baba*.' The Emperor's voice, a little stronger, interrupted Prince Jahan's reflection.

A shrivelled hand was raised to him and Prince Jahan grasped it firmly, willing his youth and strength into this man whom he loved so much. 'Are the medicines helping you, Grandfather?'

'The physician took us off all medicine the day you left for Mewar. We awaited your return. You were not expected until tomorrow, but we knew you would return tonight. We are so glad to see you, *baba*. Someone who really cares at last. We wish we were in the *harem* with the Empress as well.'

Prince Jahan choked at the last words. But why had his grandfather been taken off medication? 'I pushed hard to get here tonight instead of tomorrow, Grandfather.' He knelt and placed the wrinkled hand to his lips. 'Just as you wanted me to come, I *had* to return to you as soon as humanly possible.' His voice broke as he rose to his feet.

'Remember the rules of princes, *baba*,' the Emperor admonished. 'Feelings can only be expressed in a princely manner.' He hesitated. 'But we are so pleased that you have them.'

'I love you, Grandfather.' The words were forbidden between parents, grandparents and offspring. Prince Jahan no longer cared. His grandfather and he had never declared their love for each other. It was simply there, known, acknowledged, expressed in deeds but not in speech. Now, his sorrowful heart was overflowing with love, drowning him, while horror at his grandfather's condition made him reckless.

'We . . . I . . .' He heard with amazement the Emperor drop the royal plural for the first time, but the whispered words still came out harsh. 'I . . . love . . . you, *baba*.'

The floodgates were released. Weeping bitterly, his grandfather's hot, dry palm pressed to his cheek, Prince Jahan fell to his knees beside the divan, placed his head on his grandfather's chest.

A trembling hand reached out, felt his head, began stroking it gently. It was the first physical contact between them and it touched his soul. Absorbing his grandfather's fast-fading life force, he began to shiver, his heart pounding.

'Weep now, my *baba*, my little one,' the Emperor whispered. 'We made a man of you from your earliest days.' The breath of a sigh lived in his rasping speech. 'Too soon perhaps, because it meant that you never had a boyhood. But that is your destiny.' The hand stopped stroking his head, pressed upon it firmly. 'Have you bled enough, my *baba*?'

Prince Jahan understood and nodded. Sniffing, he raised tearstained cheeks, his eyes blurred with tears, to meet his grandfather's almost stern gaze. 'Yes, Sire.'

'Then rise and fight again.' The Emperor's voice was suddenly harsh. 'You have wept for the last time in your life. You shall never weep again, save in your heart.'

From then on Prince Jahan could not bring himself to leave his grandfather's quarters. Extinguishing the flame of suspicion that had flared within him at learning that the chief physician had stopped all medication, he merely questioned Hakim Ali as to why treatments should not be resumed. After much argument, the physician agreed that this would be done.

The Emperor's condition only worsened. It seemed to Prince Jahan that, dejected by his failure to hold his family together when he had been able to contain a whole Empire, his grandfather was letting go of life. The nauseating smell of asafoetida pervaded the Emperor's suite and a strong astringent that Hakim Ali administered brought high fever and painful strangling of his urinal tract.

On Friday, 21 October in the year 1605, the Emperor Akbar sent for Prince Jehangir. Only Prince Jahan and Hakim Ali were present at the meeting. The imperial turban and sword of Humayun, the Emperor's father, had been placed on the sofa beside the dying man.

Prince Jahan watched silently as the Emperor, no longer able to speak, motioned to Prince Jehangir to wear the imperial turban and gird on the ancestral sword. The succession thus bestowed, the Emperor died.

Prince Jahan's father now occupied the magnificent throne which the Emperor Akbar had caused to be created at enormous cost. The jewels in it cost over ten million *ashreties*. The gold used in it weighed three hundred *mauns*. The legs and body were filled with fifty *mauns* of ambergris. Yet the throne was so built that it could be taken apart and transported from place to place, whenever the Emperor changed residence, even to his war camps.

The imperial crown was a glittering work of art. It was studded with two hundred flaming red rubies. Each of its twelve points contained a single large diamond, while the point in the centre of its upper part held a single huge pearl.

This was the throne, this the crown on which Prince Jahan had set his heart.

Following his accession, the new Emperor commanded the *nuggaurah*, or great imperial state drum, to be beaten

102

without ceasing. He had costly brocades and gold-embroidered carpets spread many yards around the throne, burned fragrant incense and placed nearly three thousand camphorated wax lights, three cubits in length, in branches of gold and silver perfumed with ambergris, to illuminate the scene from night till morning.

Rank upon rank of young men, dressed in costly materials, woven in silk and gold, their amulets sparkling with diamonds, emeralds, sapphires and rubies, awaited the Emperor's commands, day and night, as did the nine sub-rulers of the Empire, covered from head to foot in gold and jewels. The celebrations went on for forty days and forty nights, impressing the world with imperial magnificence.

PART II

A Woman's Ambition

Chapter 7

Barely four months had elapsed since the Emperor Jehangir ascended the throne and here was his father talking about revolt already. Had he heard aright? Prince Chara looked at Rana Amar, trying to hide his amazement. The Rana was entirely serious. 'I say the time to overthrow this upstart Emperor is now,' he repeated, this time pounding the rosewood dining table so hard that he rattled the gold salvers containing *pan*, betel leaves, areca nut, sweet sesame and spices to sweeten the breath after the meal.

Since there were only five tonight, dinner had been served in Rana Amar's personal dining room in the Chitor palace. The room was furnished to facilitate private discussion. The white mountain crystal floors were covered with a black and red Rajput carpet. Gold ornaments and bowls rested on rosewood sideboards, which matched the dining table and chairs; the walls were hung with red and green tapestries of Hindu myths. The room was intimate though its heavy colours were somewhat overpowering.

The conversation had been casual and informal while the meal was served, but after the servants, attendants and liveried footmen who stood behind each guest had departed, the Rana had immediately turned to the short-comings of the new Emperor. Prince Chara was delighted, because it was for this that he had manipulated the visit of Prince Husrau, Raja Man and Aziz Koka to Chitor to attend the Rajput New Year celebrations, but he had not expected his father to go this far. He had never seen the normally calm Rana so outraged and decisive, and all the more arresting since he was a big man, with massive shoulders, silver-black hair and dark eyes now flashing through the golden glow of the great hanging oil-lamps.

'We must fight *now*!' the Rana cried, as if to answer the ensuing silence. 'Now! Now! Now! The events following the coronation and the Emperor's new appointments are making a mockery of us rulers. They are but a prelude to the elevation of his favourites and discrimination against those he does not like.' He looked challengingly around the table, feeling out each guest in turn.

Prince Chara reflected with satisfaction that his plan was working beyond his expectations. His father did not realize that he had been manipulated into inviting the three guests. When the time for armed rebellion came, however, he, Prince Chara, would no longer be behind the scenes, but at the forefront of the rebellious troops, leading them to victory.

The burly Raja Man sat back on his heavy rosewood chair and shrugged beefy shoulders. 'I have no cause to love the new Emperor,' he declared. 'Sher Afgan, who is also your guest at these festivities, has been promoted to distant Bengal, as *faudjar* of the Burdwan province. Like him, I too have been kicked to Bengal, though elevated to its throne. I suppose I should lie on my back and allow the Emperor to tickle my tummy! Bengal is virtual exile, hardly the sort of place that makes one believe it better to rule in hell than serve in heaven. Not the most lucrative part of the Moghul realms either, nor its most entertaining. Despite my aggravation, however, your suggestion, Rana Amar, has caught me by surprise. Would it not be premature to move against the Emperor so soon?' He paused, glanced at the Emperor's foster-brother. 'What do you think, Prince?'

The gaunt Prince Aziz Koka placed lean elbows on the table, stared across it at Raja Man from the sunken sockets of his eyes. 'The personal conduct of the Emperor is

108

becoming more and more intolerable,' he grated in his dry, deep voice. 'Immediately after his accession, he abstained from liquor and drugs, worshipped religiously. I began to think, praise be to Allah, my foster-brother has reformed at last. Well, the grand reformation lasted as long as it took the God of Israel to create the world. Seven whole days! The most significant products of his sobriety were his twelve edicts, intended to show him as an enlightened monarch and to rally the support of the common man at the expense of princes, nobles and administrators throughout the realm. I knew then that we were in dire trouble, but the appointments of Ghiyas Beg as Diwan (Royal Treasurer) and Beg's son as Grand Vizier soon followed. What caused these appointments? Why was Sher Afgan promoted, like you, to Bengal, my dear Raja? Surely my revered foster-brother must have some connection with or obligation to that family. I shall find out what it is. For the present, the Emperor has returned to his dissolute ways, alcohol, opium, women, with no restraint.' He raised a long bony finger. 'I agree with Rana Amar. Let us act before it is too late.'

'His Twelve Commandments have assured the Emperor a straight passport to heaven without even the need to observe any of your holy Muslim rituals,' Prince Chara interjected. 'The old fable has been repeated. Our Emperor's new clothes but reveal his nakedness.' Secretly, he thought, you may give any specious reason for your betrayal of your Muslim brother, but I know that you are moved by the most bitter envy of him because he is legitimate and you are only of bastard birth. You are dangerous, being a religious fanatic, and motivated by jealousy, two causes that can only have disastrous effects. Prince Aziz Koka, you would be willing to fight the Emperor to the last Rajput and Muslim fanatic you can hire.

'Prince Husrau, as the Emperor's eldest son and his successor, you have the most at stake.' Raja Man Singh had directed his gaze at the lean hawk-like prince seated at the right of his host. 'What do you say?'

The young prince had been looking down thoughtfully, seemed to make up his mind. 'I knew all along that this would happen,' he declared in a low voice. 'Much to my sorrow, I have found my father to be a man devoid of principles. Even before he took office, I had received secret emissaries from powerful princes and nobles in Lahore and Kabul, urging me to strike immediately for the imperial throne and assuring me of their support. Since then, I have had many similar messages of concern from all over the Empire. The Muslim world is deeply disturbed by reports of a Muslim ruler who honours his faith only in name. Hindus are afraid for the inviolacy of their own religion. Any ruler, be he Rajput or Muslim, Jain or Buddhist, must have a religion and observe its principles rigidly in his own life, but without fanaticism. Only then will people of all religions feel secure.'

The shit of a cow, even if it is a holy cow, is just as much shit as that of a pig, Prince Chara reflected without rancour. We have had innumerable examples of holy shit from Moghul emperors for hundreds of years, and you are spewing out another lot. I do not spare a curse for any religion, but if you were an orthodox Muslim and not a liberal one, I would not trust you, however much benevolence you protested, to be fair to other religions. As for the ultra-orthodox Muslims of the west who are backing you, they would surely expect you to despoil Hindu and Buddhist shrines which are a sacrilege in their eyes.

'Since we are an Empire of varied religions, and especially since so many of our people are Hindu, tolerance of other religions is an essential quality for the Emperor,' Prince Husrau continued. His deep-set, dark eyes began to blaze. 'Can I assume that you, Rana Amar and you, Prince Aziz Koka, are giving me the assurance of your support?' He lifted his head, chin out-thrust, and Prince Chara found himself staring at the great nose. 'My lords, I am but your instrument, your servant in fact. Give me word tonight and I shall act tonight.' He stared challengingly around the table, a picture of decisiveness and resolve.

You poor, well-meaning fool, Prince Chara thought in the sudden stillness of the room, its tension hardly soothed by the swishing of the moving *punkah*. Do you think rebellions are made with mere assurances of support? And what can you achieve tonight, except relieve yourself at the privy and go to sleep with the woman we have provided you? Your mind is surely in a good man's fog, but that is just as well for me.

'Prince Chara?'

Since he was not normally invited to participate in such decisions, Prince Husrau's question caught Prince Chara unawares. 'When we last discussed this question in the Agra palace on the day your fate was decided by the toss of an elephant's tusk, you decided to wait a year or so to observe how the new Emperor fared,' Prince Chara began, feigning caution. 'Though such a delay may have been desirable, it must surely have eroded your support amongst those who were already disgusted by Prince Jehangir's rebellions against his father, his dissolute ways and obvious incompetence. The late Emperor Akbar used the time-honoured expedient of those who are uncertain, seeking an omen, thrusting the burden of a difficult decision on a deity, or so he thought, but in reality on an elephant.' He interjected a note of passion, which he did not feel, into his voice, his mind being cool as ice on the high mountains. 'A throw of the dice. At stake, in this case, succession to the largest empire in the world, embracing many proud races.' He smiled cynically. 'Our future was decided at a game of dice. Do we wait for more blunders on a Great Emperor's scale? If so, for how long?' He had been careful not to commit himself. He feigned piety to win over his father. 'Today, we have worshipped Lord Varuna, the god of rain, Lord Vayu, god of the wind and Lady Shankranti, goddess of plenty.' Why not use other people's superstitions to one's own advantage? 'What better way to celebrate our New Year than with yet another dedication, this one to the deity whose birthplace is so close to Agra, playful Lord Krishna, god of war?'

Prince Husrau's chair grated on the floor as he shoved it back. Face glowing, he rose to his feet. 'Rana Amar, you are the acknowledged leader of all the Rajput clans,' he cried. 'Mewar has ever been in the forefront of independence movements. Do you pledge me on your sacred Rajput honour that you and your kingdom will support me in an immediate bid to overthrow my father and rule in his place?'

Rana Amar stood up, towering above the prince. He raised his right hand. 'I do!' he declared fervently.

Aziz Koka rose to his feet. 'I do too!' he declared. 'On my sacred honour as a Muslim.' That is all you can offer, and it is nothing since you have no honour, Prince Chara reflected cynically. Not one soldier to bring to the cause, merely prestige and a nebulous influence.

Raja Man followed. 'I pledge you my support,' he boomed.

Prince Chara remained seated, resisting the temptation to applaud the histrionics.

The men sat down, chairs creaking in the sober silence that filled the room. Prince Chara broke it. 'Such a rebellion will require the most careful planning,' he stated. 'Our own army is always ready, but your support, Prince Husrau, will come from widely separated groups. The entire uprising should be meticulously planned and coordinated, so there is no risk of failure. We can hardly strike a blow tonight!'

'How can coordination be achieved when our rebel forces will stretch from Kabul to Bengal?' his father demanded, somewhat displeased at his son for taking the lead.

'It is for that very reason, my lord, that strategic planning is essential before we make our first overt move, with close coordination and intercommunication thereafter. These are essential ingredients for success. Our enemy will be an integrated whole, the Moghul army. While uprisings in many parts of the Empire could cause the Emperor to dissipate his force, he may well decide, as his father did on many an occasion, to ignore all else and pursue his main enemy, Prince Husrau in this case, with the entire imperial army.' His keen gaze rested on the young prince. 'The old principle of smash the head and the snake will die. Never forget the might of that imperial army.' He smiled grimly, taking care to avoid his father's accusing gaze. The autocratic Rana never liked being led.

. 'Pah! The imperial army consists mainly of mercenaries, Azbegs, Turks, Pathans.' His father waved a contemptuous hand. 'Our own troops are all patriots.' His voice rang out pompously. He half-turned towards Prince Chara. 'It is men who win battles, but if we do decide on all this planning, coordination and intercommunication of which you, my son, speak, who will be responsible for all of it?'

'With your permission, my lord, I will!'

'You?' The sarcastic note in his father's voice momentarily infuriated Prince Chara. 'And pray tell us how you, who have only led troops on the *battlefield*, will handle the responsibilities of an overall commander?'

Prince Chara calmly outlined his plan. When he had finished, he saw with fierce satisfaction the grudging admiration in his father's face. What he had not revealed was that this plan would not only smash the cobra's head, it would

113

also destroy its brood, including Prince Husrau and Prince Jahan.

She had never once had a disagreement with her brother but the time for a confrontation had arrived. Ever since he took up duties as Grand Vizier, Nur Jehan had barely seen him. The daily visits were ended and he had not even responded promptly to her messages. She was upset by it, not least because it was she who had engineered his appointment as well as that of her father as Diwan. The bait to the new Emperor, conveyed through her father since her proud, idealist brother would never have stooped to seek high office for himself, had been the suggestion that her husband should be kicked into high office as a *faudjar* in distant Bengal. When the Emperor acceded to this request, Nur Jehan's heart leapt in triumph. The bait had been taken. It would not be long before Jehangir made overtures to her. She had had her first real taste of power. The two appointments, the results of a respectful letter she had sent the Emperor, again through her father, greatly increased her importance in her father's eyes, but her brother remained his old self. He had taken four days to respond to her dinner invitation. Four whole days! It was insulting.

A new, more palatial residence, compatible with his high office, had been allotted to Asaf Khan, but he used it only for official purposes, preferring to continue living in the old mansion with his father and their entire family, so he could easily have made time to see her.

Now Nur Jehan could hardly wait for the servants to clear the meal in order to retire with her brother to her private chamber. Normally dynamic, he was radiating an intense inner energy tonight, though a hint of black beneath the dark, daredevil eyes told of sleepless nights in pursuit of his new duties. Far from sympathizing with him, his obvious dedication to his new office only infuriated her the more, because it demeaned her. His appearance was, however, impeccable as always, from the trim reddish-brown moustache to the clothes that fitted his slim, tall figure to perfection. His gold tunic ended in a long gauze skirt through which pantaloons with wide vertical stripes of gold showed; his broad sash matched the long double-stranded necklace of blue lapis-lazuli. Altogether the elegant nobleman, Nur Jehan thought with a faint stirring of pride in her family, for she knew that she reflected her brother's elegance. Her dark blue *kurtha* was bordered with gold to match the heavy dark blue sapphire necklace and bangles. Her perfume was a distillate of roses, which she had invented.

Seated on the white-cushioned divan, Asaf Khan reached gracefully for his tiny coffee cup. He sniffed its aroma.

'Be careful, it's hot,' she warned. 'You may burn your mouth.'

He smiled his thanks, took a delicate sip. 'What more can a man ask for?' he murmured. 'The most delicious coffee in the world in the company of the most beautiful woman there has ever been.'

'Flatterer,' she said, her anger somewhat diminishing. She leaned forward on her settle. 'But you are not here tonight to ask for more,' she stated with a harsh change of mood, her expression fierce. 'You are here because there are some pressing matters of State about which *I* have to ask *you*. So it is *I* who need more, but first, have you become so important, now that you are Grand Vizier, that you have no time for me?' Her eyes challenged him. 'Do you not know that *I* was responsible for your elevation?'

His eyebrows lifted in amusement. 'I presumed I was appointed Prime Minister because I am well qualified for the post,' he responded urbanely.

'There are many people in the Empire well qualified to

be Grand Vizier,' she retorted, her glance challenging him again.

He met the challenge with a deep sigh, then unexpectedly crinkled the sides of his eyes. 'How could I forget my highest qualification when I am reminded of it by the source?' he inquired, shaking his head in amusement. Then he grew serious. 'If what you say is correct, however, I owe you an even higher duty for having brought me this coveted plum than I owe my Emperor who extended it. I can only fulfil that duty if I am at my post night and day. The imperial administration had deteriorated to a shocking degree during the last months of the late Emperor's reign. Our father, as Diwan, has also unearthed widespread corruption and cheating throughout the realm, at the expense of the Royal Treasury. He and I face awesome tasks. Moreover, both of us have to prove our worth to the Emperor, the princes, the nobles and the people. If we do not, we shall betray you and you will never be able to achieve your own goals.'

She felt she had been slapped in the face with her own hand. 'Surely you can take two hours off to see me?' she demanded, more weakly. 'What if I had been sick?'

'But you were not!'

'But supposing . . .'

'Please give me your understanding,' he cut in. 'It is essential now and for the future. I cannot have anyone say that I neglected important official duties to have dinner with my sister. They might well question, why does he do it? Is she so powerful? You must never be suspect.' His dark eyes were boring into her now. 'In the final analysis, however, it is a matter of personal pride for me to do anything I undertake to perfection. You are the first priority of my heart and loyalty, but I cannot set your needs above my duties to my Emperor and the people.' His gaze intensified, hardened. She had never seen the steel before

116

and it made her pause. 'I will always serve your cause,' he declared. His voice turned tough as a sword blade. 'But I will not be your slave or your lackey.'

She glared back, her anger mounting again. This man, her own flesh and blood was abandoning her, as her parents had once done. Suddenly she recalled the story of the cobra that had protected her. She had been a baby then. Now she must be her own cobra. The tension between her and Asaf Khan became physical. 'Have a care, about rejecting me,' she warned, her voice low, intense. 'What goes up can come down.'

To her amazement, he burst out laughing, the sound rippling merrily through the golden glow of lamplight, his teeth white beneath the moustache. 'As to that, all material things that go up must certainly come down,' he declared, his wide shoulders shaking. He grew serious, raised a long, slender forefinger. 'But what of the human spirit? Ah, that can soar forever, unhindered except by Allah. My own spirit bends before no one but Him. I shall resign from the position of Grand Vizier, if you compel me. I would never retain office at the expense of my ideals or my self-respect.'

This was a new Asaf Khan. She had suspected the strength and idealism, but had never fully comprehended their intensity. She realized in a flash that she could not accept his challenge. She needed him to be Grand Vizier more than he needed the office.

He reached over to place his hand on hers. His touch was warm and comforting. 'You know that I would never abandon you, little sister,' he assured her gently.

His deep understanding of her, his knowledge of where her insecurity came from, touched her. She glanced down at the strong hand, noting the fine reddish hairs on the back of it. Red is the symbol of fire, of warmth, she thought. The warmth spread slowly along her arm, up into her body, found her heart. Handle each man according to the person he is, she reminded herself. Men are like food, some must be ground, some chewed, some merely moistened before swallowing. Being on the verge of power, do not over-reach yourself, because it is you who might come down. 'You are right,' she conceded. She could not bring herself to say she was sorry, not to her brother nor to anyone. To her husband certainly, but only when she lied to escape his brutality and felt triumph at the deception.

'Now that we understand each other, let us solemnly promise that we shall never again resort to hurling . . . er . . . platitudes at each other,' he suggested. 'They are so boring.' He released her hand, reached for his coffee cup, leaned back on the divan. 'So, to business again. I am sure you did not wish to see me merely to berate me for my failure to attend you more punctiliously!'

'Yes, I do have important things to discuss with you.' She could not resist a dig. 'Not as important as your duties, but nonetheless urgent affairs of State.'

'Well put,' he stated, acknowledging the thrust. He took a sip of the coffee. 'This coffee is almost as cold as your disposition was a few moments ago.' His eyes twinkled as he replaced the cup. 'The Grand Vizier prefers cold coffee to being in hot water as your brother. Tonight, no more coffee for the Grand Vizier, thank you, and no more recrimination for your brother!'

She felt a flash of irritation that he was treating her so lightly, but allowed the feeling to burn out. 'Have you wondered why Sher Afgan was invited to attend the Hindu New Year festival in the Chitor palace?'

'Your husband's social engagements are hardly an affair of State, my dear,' he murmured.

'Perhaps not, but when combined with invitations to Prince Husrau and his loyal supporters, Raja Man Singh and the Emperor's foster-brother, Prince Aziz Koka, what would you say?'

He grew serious on the instant, stared at her, thinking. 'I would confess that we have been so preoccupied with administering the realm that we may have forgotten the need to secure it,' he finally declared. He looked at her with admiration. 'Perhaps also that a woman's perception and intuition are often better than a man's judgment.' He nodded to himself. 'This bears looking into.' He scratched his jaw reflectively. 'I had assumed that with Raja Man Singh and your husband posted to distant Bengal they were no longer a threat. Also, more fundamentally, that once the Emperor took office he would have no challengers. But one should never grow complacent.' He squared his shoulders. 'Be assured that I shall follow this line of inquiry with diligence.'

'And what of my suggestion that Prince Jahan become betrothed to your daughter, Mumtaz Mahal?'

He grinned. 'Now *that* you will not be able to berate me about. I have already suggested it to the Emperor . . . er . . . as coming from you and he readily agreed. As a matter of fact, he will be speaking about it to Prince Jahan tonight.'

'Oh, *that* you did not forget, did you?' She could not resist the dig. 'A fine marriage for your daughter.'

His eyes flashed with an anger so steely that she quailed before it. 'That is an unworthy inference,' he stated quietly. 'If you believed it to be true, you would not entrust me with your confidences. You *need* me, little sister. Let us proceed from now on without insults or petulance.' He looked away, staring into space, his dismissal of the subject dismaying her more than any challenge.

Once again, she could not apologize. 'You are right,' she agreed. 'It shall be so in future. You are your own man and I shall respect that.' She paused. 'You will convey my fears to the Emperor?'

'Yes.'

'You will let him know that it is my abiding concern for

119

him that makes me think day and night of his security? And you will inform him that I am the source of your intelligence?'

'Of course.'

'The time is also right for you to have the Emperor to dinner again, so he can see me in the flesh.'

'You would let your veil drop once more?' His eyebrows lifted.

'Why not? Only this time it will remain dropped for much longer.'

'You cannot dare . . .' he began.

'I dare all,' she flashed, eyeing him levelly, soberly. 'Please remind the Emperor that I once betrayed my husband's proposed disloyalty to him, because my devotion to Prince Salim Jehangir, as he was then, was greater than to my husband. Assure His Imperial Majesty that my loyalty to him continues unabated and my humble submission as his subject transcends even that which I have for Allah.'

He looked at her in astonishment. 'Is that not a bit extreme?'

'Words are hollow things. They have no substance except whatever those who hear them invest them with.'

'You are cynical?'

'I am determined to fulfil my ambition.'

'May Allah have mercy on you.'

'Allah knows what is in my heart,' she retorted. 'He takes no note of my hollow words.'

'Blasphemy?'

'Is a concept of human beings who create gods in their own image and ascribe affront to deities who are above such frailty.'

Young as he was and accustomed to giving implicit obedience, Prince Jahan rebelled automatically at his father's decision. But as a prince of the royal household, his betrothals and marriages were not his to control. The Emperor alone decided when an alliance was politically necessary and such alliances sometimes proved useful to the betrothed prince as well.

Had he heard aright the command his father had just issued so abruptly? 'You shall become betrothed to Mumtaz Mahal, daughter of our Grand Vizier, Asaf Khan.'

How would this benefit the Empire or himself personally? Why was the Emperor reaching out with advancements for this particular family?

As always, however, Prince Jahan gave no evidence of his feelings. They had retired alone to the European room of the Agra palace after dinner. Prince Jahan hated being in that room with anyone else. As his grandfather's favourite place, it brought back many memories to his mind and a tear-drop to his heart. In contrast, having drunk too much wine and arrack during dinner, his father's eyes were slightly glazed and he had avoided slurring his words only with difficulty, all affronts to that near-sacred room.

'I am Your Imperial Majesty's servant,' Prince Jahan responded steadily. He decided to couch his questions in obedient terms, keeping his voice low, his eyes downcast. 'In your infinite wisdom, you know what is best for your Empire as a whole and for each one of your subjects. So that I may learn of that wisdom, pray tell me, Sire, how such a betrothal will help your gracious Majesty and the Empire.'

The Emperor spread out his legs, yawned. A drunken giggle escaped him. 'Our Empire is strengthened by men of ability regardless of their rank or station in life,' he declared ponderously. 'Loyalty to principles is the first essential of a loyal subject. Ghiyas Beg and Asaf Khan are both loyal to principles, therefore they will extend loyalty to their principal, the Emperor. We trust them and desire the union of our two families. Remember, you will have many a betrothal and many a wife before you ascend to heaven.'

I would rather ascend to the throne first, Prince Jahan thought instinctively. 'Your wisdom is infinite, Sire,' he replied.

'Besides, we understand from Asaf Khan that the girl is only twelve years old, most comely in a unique, elfin way, cultivated, bright and gifted. You may find her intriguing as a contrast to the concubines you sleep with and a bright adornment to your *harem* when it is established.' He smiled smugly. 'However, you will have the opportunity of viewing this jewel personally tomorrow, for we have decreed it to be one of the *contrary days* of the Royal *Meena* Bazaar in our *harem* here. You have studiously avoided visiting the Bazaar up to now, being more concerned with your duties and your career, but it is time you took on the duties of manhood as well.'

The Royal *Meena* Bazaar was a private market place at which ladies of the aristocracy bought, amongst other things, the dyes and oils, waxes and perfumes required for their beautification. No man dared trespass the *Meena* marketplace. If caught he would have his hands and feet chopped off at the executioner's block. On one or two *contrary days* of the month, however, the seemingly shy, docile wives and concubines of the Court reversed their roles and became shopkeepers, flirting and bargaining with young princes, nobles and courtiers, who, being allowed to attend contrary to the rules of *purdah*, competed for attention and showed off their wit by inquiring about prices in rhymed Persian verse. Prince Jahan could not imagine anything more boring or wasteful of his time than attending one of these events. Now he was being forced into it by royal command, to gaze at a girl who was not really qualified by birth to become the wife of a prince. If that was what his father wanted, however, he would accept.

What did he have to lose? But there must be some connection between the Emperor Jehangir and Asaf Khan's family. He was convinced of it now. Assured loyalty and trust alone did not justify the Emperor's actions. What could that connection be? The question intrigued him.

'You have been a good son to us,' the Emperor declared, a sentimental warmth in his voice. Prince Jahan loathed it when his father grew maudlin. It was unbecoming in an Emperor. 'There was a time when we and your brothers resented the way your grandfather removed you from the care of your mother and entrusted you to his own ageing childless wife, Salima Begum. No grandparents can substitute for loving parents. You had a lonely childhood.'

'I had great rewards in all that I was able to learn, Sire, including how to be alone and independent.' The tears of the wakeful nights of his boyhood, when he had longed for the company of his brothers, suddenly returned like monsters from some dungeon of hidden anxiety, the times when he would have liked to run to his mother for comfort, but could not. Those tears had been drained by his grandfather's stern dictates, but had left a hollow never to be filled.

'Yet we must always remember your grandfather's unique achievements.' His father's voice seemed to come from a distance. 'He was a man of genius. He invented three varieties of matchlock rifle, a device for firing fourteen rifles at the same time, a portable war tent with two bedrooms, great pontoons to transport elephants and large weapons along rivers and the cannon so huge that it needs a thousand oxen to draw it. The cannon may have been impractical for campaigning, but was nonetheless an ingenious achievement.'

'The Great Emperor also established our entire system of government, did he not, Sire?' Prince Jahan asked the question to give himself time to regain control of his emotions. 'Pray tell me of it.'

'Yes, indeed. Your grandfather divided government into thirty-three law-making divisions. He then organized local government, right down to the level of the *panchyats* (village councils) to be complementary with those thirty-three divisions, all of them subordinate, however, to the central government here in Agra. He standardized currency, minting new coins, and re-classified land, grading it according to fertility for tax purposes. He established a new system of weights and measures, and a mail system that includes our express pony service. He set up an administrative machine and by building roads, forts, inns and way stations for travellers helped reinforce our Empire. We can be proud to be his descendants.'

'I am proud to be your son, Sire.' The words that escaped Prince Jahan were more a product of protocol than an outpouring of sincerity.

The Emperor glowed. 'We have discovered each other.' His gaze was still over-sentimental. 'And we are proud to have you for a son.' He stroked his Mongol moustache, nodding. 'We still remember your words at our coronation, when the traditional Shiraz melon was brought to us, cut into five pieces, during our first family ceremonial. We asked you for the significance of the five portions. Do you remember your response?'

'Yes, Sire. "They represent union in separateness between my revered father, my mother and we three brothers."'

'You are correct and it pleased us no end when we invited you to eat your share of the melon first and you hesitated, before finally responding respectfully that it would not be fitting for you, as the youngest in the family, to take the lead.' He nodded again. 'You are a good boy, a good boy. We trust you. When we are gone and it is your turn to rule the Empire, you will have dire need of such men as yourself.' He stared into space, not at the painting of the French countryside across the room, but at a distant future. 'You will have much conflict before you get there.'

Prince Jahan decided to come out with what had been on his mind. 'Sire, I am very much afraid that there may be conflicts in your own time, for there are those that might oppose your gracious rule.'

'Like whom?' The Emperor sat up, instantly alert.

'My elder brother, Prince Husrau,' he replied boldly. 'He is not a person of ambition, but can be misled by those of ambition who lie to him.'

'You are apprehensive about the social event at Mewar?' the Emperor inquired soberly.

Prince Jahan was amazed at his father's sagacity. His face must have registered his surprise, for his father proceeded smoothly, 'It is not a coincidence that brought Prince Husrau and his supporters to the palace of our arch enemy, Rana Amar Singh. We recognize it, but cannot prevent such meetings in our open society. We can only respond to proven treason or outright rebellion.'

'Should we not warn my brother, Sire?'

'No.' The Emperor's look of fiendish cruelty reminded Prince Jahan of their common Mongol ancestry. 'Remember this for all time, Prince Jahan. If we warn those who would plot against us, we but reveal that we know of their designs, give them the information they need to bury their plots deeper. Our own technique is to be strong enough to combat any plot, however deep, overcome any revolt, however widespread. We shall permit traitors to reveal themselves and then deal with them so harshly they will never rise again and the Empire will tremble before the example we make of them.'

* * *

The Sher Afgans of this world were simply kitchen utensils to be used and rewarded with a place on the shelf or cast aside. When he included Sher Afgan in the list of guests for his father to invite, Prince Chara had expected that the giant brother-in-law of Asaf Khan might be able to shed some light on the reason why that family had suddenly been promoted to high places, but he was also moved by a deeper impulse. The one rival to the fulfilment of his aim to become Emperor of the Moghul realms was Prince Jahan. That young boy was the only prince of any ability in the entire Moghul family, therefore the only person who stood in the way of his ambition. He hated Prince Jahan with a cold passion for all his attributes, including his birth and his obvious destiny. Prince Jahan had to be eliminated.

Prince Chara recognized the dangers of such deep impulsive hatreds. They drove men to indiscriminate actions. He would never allow this to happen to him. The Great Emperor Akbar was dead and the Emperor Jehangir would never concede the throne in exchange for Prince Jahan's life and liberty, so kidnapping Prince Jahan would be futile. Prince Chara rather suspected that deep, deep down inside the Emperor Jehangir, there must also be envy of his son. It would require only the right amount of digging to unearth that envy and unleash it. For the present, however, the only way to remove Prince Jahan from the arena was to have him killed.

It was customary for princes and nobles to do things in their own time. It was the privilege of commoners to wait upon the timing of their superiors. So Prince Chara had thought nothing of directing the commoner, Sher Afgan, to retire to his suite on the ground floor of the Chitor palace after he had dined in the great hall and to keep a look out for him in the courtyard into which the bedroom of the suite opened.

With so much to discuss as to their moves and the usual

futile talk that bolsters the courage of men who have made far-reaching decisions, and with more than a dash of recrimination to justify those decisions, it was nearly midnight by the time Prince Chara was able to retire from his father's dining chamber to his own quarters. Although these were located on the first floor of the two-storey palace building, he had ready access to the courtyard, and he had allocated Sher Afgan rooms in the same wing of the palace, though it was normally reserved for royalty.

The night was cold and still. A half-moon, having struggled with heavy clouds and lost, was a disappearing glow in the west. The only movement on earth was the constant creak of crickets. Prince Chara looked towards the palace as he paced the walkway in the courtyard opposite Sher Afgan's rooms. It lay there, a solid dark mass, redeemed by a few rectangles of golden light. None of its ornamentations and embellishments were visible. Paved with white flagstones, the walkway was bordered by wide beds of shrubs and flowers, lawns with fountains beyond, silhouetted against the dark, shadowy shapes of *neem* trees. What is the reality, Prince Chara mused. What I see now, what there is by the light of day, or nothing at all, save for someone with human or animal vision? Is that squeak of a mouse I have just heard reality? The scent of crushed green bug tells me a cobra is abroad. This, I must accept as reality, for I would be foolish merely to philosophize about a cobra in my vicinity! Smiling grimly to himself, he opened his cloak and loosened his long sword, making it easier on the draw.

Sher Afgan's door opened, revealing the bulk of the man in a new rectangle of pale golden light, then closed. Prince Chara blinked his eyes against the immediate night-blindness, identified Sher Afgan's bulk again, now looming towards him. He coughed lightly to reveal his presence.

He could sense Sher Afgan's apprehension when the

giant bowed deeply, salaaming, hand to breast, mouth and head, before coming erect again.

'I'm glad you are here,' Prince Chara declared quietly, opening the conversation, as was proper. 'I hope your quarters are comfortable?'

'Magnificent, lord,' Sher Afgan replied hoarsely. 'This night air is not good for my cold, but my heart is warmed by your noble presence.'

If there's anything worse than cow shit from an infidel, it is pork shit from a true believer, Prince Chara thought savagely. Obvious flattery irritated him. It was insulting, but that was the system. He decided to come directly to the point. 'You remember all I know about you?' he coldly reminded the man. 'That is the background of our collaboration.'

'Yes, lord.' Taken aback, the giant was immediately defensive.

'Then tell me, why has the Emperor Jehangir suddenly started elevating members of your family to high office?'

'They are men of rare ability and experience, lord. My father-in-law – '

'Cut the pork shit, Sher Afgan. This is *me* you are talking to, remember?'

'Yes, lord.' The giant hesitated. 'I can only conjecture – and I would not want to mislead you with guesses.'

'Then tell me something of which you should have more direct personal knowledge.' He was keeping his voice low, but he injected a cutting edge to it. 'Why have you been elevated to the rank of *faudjar* of Burdwan?'

'I served the Emperor loy . . . faithfully when he was Prince Jehangir, so he is aware of my abilities.'

'Your words are foul wind and have the odour of a fart.'

Sher Afgan fidgeted in the dark. Prince Chara decided to go for the kill. 'Why have you been sent into exile in distant Bengal?' he demanded remorselessly. Even as he asked the question, the answer illuminated his mind in a great flash of light and everything suddenly fell into place. 'Tell me, Sher Afgan, how well does Emperor Jehangir know your father-in-law's family?'

'Very well, lord.'

'Has he ever visited the mansion of Ghiyas Beg in the Agra capital?'

'Yes, lord. Many times.'

'Had he visited it even before you were married to your wife, the daughter of Ghiyas Beg?'

The giant looked away, staring into the darkness.

Prince Chara could sense rather than see his great frame trembling. 'So the relationship has been a long and friendly one,' he observed, not wishing to reveal his hand. He nodded to himself, his mind racing. He had intended using Sher Afgan to target Prince Jahan. Now it dawned on him that he could somehow use the giant to crucify the Emperor as well. When he looked back at Sher Afgan, he thought he saw tears in the giant's eyes. He despised men who cried. 'It is likely that within a few months the Emperor will move north with his army on a mission that must remain secret even from you for the present. He will undoubtedly take Prince Jahan with him. This will give you another opportunity to take the prince, only now you shall have him killed. And remember, no more bungling.'

'But my lord, I shall be stationed in Bengal, how can I – '

'Your *thuggee* connections remain. Arrange it all immediately you get back to Agra, before departing for Bengal. You leave Chitor tomorrow, don't you?'

Sher Afgan nodded slowly.

'The *thuggee* will not be hampered by a deadline on this occasion. They can join the Emperor's army train and finish the job at leisure.' Prince Chara hesitated, then decided to give Sher Afgan the bait. 'If you do this, there will be one less competitor for Prince Husrau to contend with,' then added casually, 'and I promise you there will be no more Emperor Jehangir for you to serve but only the Emperor Husrau.'

Sher Afgan squared his great shoulders and smiled for the first time, a yellow grin that slowly spread over his little mouth. A high-pitched giggle escaped him, floated away into the dark.

Chapter 8

The Chief Eunuch of the Agra palace *harem* was a black Nubian named Tafari. Prince Jahan knew him from way back when he had been merely one of the eunuchs of Salima Begum, chief wife of the late Emperor, into whose care he himself had been entrusted from the custody of his natural mother. Salima Begum's stern rule of the *harem* had helped shape his character almost as much as the Emperor Akbar's example and precept.

Prince Jahan was aware that Tafari had worked his way up to his present position not only by fawning and loyalty to those that mattered and betrayal of those who stood in his way, but also by his cunning, deceit and that special devotion to his duties, official and moral, which had made him well nigh indispensable to those whom he directly served. The *harem* was really a city within the palace. Its outer guard, positioned around the high walls, consisted of the toughest, most ruthless infantrymen, armed with rifles and orders to shoot intruders on suspicion. The next circle of guards consisted of the eunuchs, flat-footed males, with high voices and the certainty of becoming flabbier by the year, who made up in guile for what they lacked in sexual potency.

Tafari met Prince Jahan at the outer entrance to the *harem*, to conduct him personally to the *Meena* Bazaar. As was to be expected of someone who was in a position to accept bribes, sell favours and indulge in trade and commerce of various sorts, Tafari's giant frame was richly clad. His tunic and baggy pantaloons were of cloth of gold, his broad belt encrusted with jewels. His necklaces were of emeralds and rubies with which the gold turban poised on flowing black hair was also studded. He was a huge man. The tiny wrinkles on his face were held together with paste, the whites of his eyes were eggs nestling beside the black hens of *kohl* lining their lids.

'My lord has not visited our *Meena* Bazaar since he left the household of our Imperial Highness, the Begum.' Tafari responded to Prince Jahan's greeting in a soft, high-pitched voice. 'This is indeed an honour.'

'It is an honour for me to enter the royal *harem*,' Prince Jahan stated appropriately.

'Be pleased to follow me, Your Royal Highness.' Tafari led the way down the broad corridor, which was well nigh littered with eunuchs in gorgeous outfits of blue, red, green and purple, gold attire being the sole prerogative of the chief eunuch. To make it obvious that he was conducting an honoured guest of vastly superior rank, Tafari kept turning back deferentially as he waddled, with the annoying persistence of a house fly returning to the attack.

'Your Royal Highness has been so dedicated to his studies and martial pursuits from childhood that his visits to his grandmother became more and more infrequent until his links with our little world were virtually non-existent. Alas, it has been our great loss,' Tafari sighed.

Until now Prince Jahan had avoided contact with women because his youthful belief was that they could either drag

131

a man down to the depths of hell or elevate him to the stars. For the latter, there had to be true mutual love and respect, which were difficult to find in a *harem*, where everything, even love, seemed to have a price.

His ideals were contrary to the beliefs of others, especially of princes who could have concubines by the dozen and most of whom therefore had no more respect for womankind than for any other bought chattel. Unaccountably, Prince Jahan felt that he should share a part of his beliefs with the chief eunuch, who could become a useful ally. 'If I have not visited the *harem* of late it is because I believe in the freedom of all human beings, indeed of all living things,' he declared solemnly. 'This was fostered in me by the late Great Emperor, who was a strange paradox. As a ruler, he would gleefully watch a prisoner being tortured to death, but as a human being had unshed tears for a wounded bird.'

Tafari slowed down automatically in astonishment. A kindly gleam flickered in his dark, inscrutable eyes before he resumed his pace. 'Living beings exist within the *harem*,' he stated, lowering his voice. 'Babies are born, children grow up, play and go to school within its confines, with markets and bazaars, laundries and butcher shops, schools and playgrounds to serve them. As for the ruler, he can find peace, quiet or excitement here. We are not a different part of the world, or some freakish other world, Your Royal Highness. We are of *this* world, so your views do you honour.'

Prince Jahan surveyed the broad back of the waddling eunuch, recognized that he had struck a chord of friendship, decided to develop it into a melody.

'Like any city of our world, the *harem* has its walls and its governing hierarchy,' he volunteered. 'Its sovereign is the Begum, its rulers the wives and close relations of the Emperor. Its subjects range from concubines and eunuchs to guards, ladies-in-waiting and slaves for all types of work, including cleaning, cooking and tending the baths and latrines. All of them people, though secured by your three lines of guards: the male infantrymen stationed on the *harem* walls, you eunuchs, who also ensure discipline in the *harem*, and finally the innermost line of the Tatar women, the Uzbegs, who have been compared favourably with the Amazons. All of them, people!'

They walked on in silence.

The *Meena* Bazaar was held in the inner courtyard of the *harem*, a large pleasure garden built in the Moghul tradition with lawns, dark green sculptured shrubs, flowering shade trees and mosaic stone walkways around a small central lake, its waters shimmering in the morning sunlight to serve marble-lined cascades and sparkling fountains. On the four sides of this courtyard, booths had been set up in the wide open verandahs beneath the second storeys.

The cacophony of voices reached them before they arrived at the courtyard. Customers were already strolling past and selecting their wares. Tafari sensed Prince Jahan's reaction to it with the uncanny perception of his kind. 'Human beings are the same in every bazaar,' he observed. 'Whether in a palace or a village, the bazaar is a great revealer of the human race. We have the same shrill-voiced vendors here – in this case the ladies of our palace – calling out their wares, loud-voiced customers haggling, laughter, screaming children.'

The Amazonian Uzbegs, clad in brown leather corselets, who now lined the corridor, gleaming scimitars at the ready, stared stonily to their front, but Prince Jahan could sense their alertness.

As they approached the rectangle of silver morning sunlight that heralded the courtyard, the noise from the bazaar became deafening.

'My godly prince will join this throng of human beings

alone, and he lends it distinction.' The flattering words of the chief eunuch held a sincere inflection.

'The Emperor commanded me to make this visit by myself.' Prince Jahan realized that Tafari was fishing for information. 'He will only be able to attend later due to the pressure of his duties.' This was not strictly true. His father had deemed it wiser for Prince Jahan to make a visit of this nature on his own, so as not to give the appearance that human merchandise was being inspected.

'His Imperial Majesty, like his illustrious father, sacrifices his personal pleasure for the welfare of the realm,' Tafari responded sycophantically.

This was hardly true of his father, Prince Jahan knew and so did the eunuch, but it was a nice sentiment, in keeping with the other images of palace life. He personally disliked flattery, and when he became Emperor, would discourage it. He would also maintain the rigorous austerity he had always practised, no unnecessary feasting, certainly no liquor or opium, no dallying with wives and concubines. He did not need women and yet the thought of someone who would love him for himself, whom he could truly love, had been part of unexpressed childhood longings which had become increasingly submerged until his grandfather died. Then, the feeling of being completely alone in the world had caused the desire to gush forth through the dark recesses of the nights on which he could not fall asleep.

'My instructions are to conduct Your Royal Highness to the entrance of the bazaar and to leave you free to inspect our wares at leisure.' Tafari's knowing smile made Prince Jahan wonder whether the eunuch knew or suspected the truth of his mission. They were a remarkable breed these eunuchs. They had to be, in order to survive in the world of other eunuchs and women. Tafari, for instance, had an elaborate network of spies throughout the palace and it was lewdly suggested that while he could only pass wind, not his seed, he knew when everyone else did both.

Prince Jahan had no special curiosity as to what Mumtaz Mahal looked like. Being betrothed to her would be just another incident in his princely life, but as he shouldered his way through the throng of people milling around – for everyone was equal here – he glanced at each booth, wondering about the girl for the first time. Matchmakers always extolled their wares, his father being no exception. Yet it was strange that none of the other princes had ever discussed Mumtaz Mahal when raving about this noble-woman or that, or making clever remarks about the coy, fat ones. 'The girl must have a bust like an overblown cow's udders,' or 'She looks like a public monument, not modern, but from ancient times.' Or, mooning over some unattainable beauty, 'She gleams in white beauty like the snow-capped Himalayas!' To this last Prince Jahan had responded drily, 'In other words, she is a mountain of a woman who has given you a chill response,' and received a frozen glare from the love-lorn prince in return.

Why had no one mentioned Mumtaz Mahal? She must be more than ugly, she must be plain. Well, it really did not matter. He passed the booth containing perfumes, with a mixture of scents so exotic that it was oppressive. Though the morning was cool enough, the presence of hundreds of bodies, close-packed, was beginning to make him sweat. He was thankful to have selected a white, satin tunic and pantaloons for the occasion, reflecting sardonically that the garb was appropriately virginal. As usual, he wore no jewellery.

There were no customers at the next booth, which contained precious stones displayed in velvet-lined racks. It was tended by a slim, slight figure, clad in a pale blue *kurtha* and pantaloons. Her back was turned to him, but her raven black tresses fell to her waist. He was about to pass on when the young woman stiffened.

She turned. He saw her face and his heart seemed to stop beating. Something began hammering in his head, making him dizzy. Her skin was fair, the complexion flawless. Her triangular face had incredibly small bones, above a long, slender, swanlike neck; the bust beneath was full for one so slender. It was the expression in her large brown eyes that held him spellbound. They literally sparkled, underlaid by an ever-present cheerfulness that spoke of ready smiles. She gazed back at him in a wonderment of recognition though they had never seen each other before, a startled acknowledgement that was the echo of his own. This was no voluptuous creature of the average male's desiring, no sophisticated lady of arts and wiles, no experienced siren to entice, but a slip of a girl who could bring natural brightness into life, an elf to enchant.

· They stared at each other. Her cheeks twitched, broke into a smile from deep within her, showing white teeth perfectly matched like a string of pearls and clear pink gums. That smile was so natural, it reached directly into his already smitten soul.

'You are not dressed like the other popinjays and peacocks of this court, Sir,' she said, her voice mellow, but clear as a silver bell. 'Yet you must be of royal birth. You must be Prince Jahan.'

How had she known? 'And only you can be Mumtaz Mahal,' he responded hoarsely. His heart was beating again, faster now, an inner excitement mounting within him.

'We know each other,' she declared, a strange mystery in her gaze. Her eyes lifted beyond him, not at the crowds, he knew, but at some distant past or future. 'I am delighted and honoured that you should grace my booth.' She grinned this time, looking like a mischievous child. 'I am here because my father commanded me to come. As you can see, I am not pressed by customers, or suitors.' She grew serious in a sudden change of mood. 'I prefer it this way. People can be so boring.'

'I am here for the same reason.'

'You find people boring too?' Amusement lurked beneath the dark brown eyes.

He gestured to hide his confusion. 'No, *my* father commanded me to come.'

She threw back her head and laughed, a wholesome laugh that rippled through the morning air. He laughed with her and they were one in it. Life is good when I can laugh like this with another human being about something so silly, he thought, as the bubbling within him subsided.

'Does that mean you have sold nothing as yet?' he inquired.

'Not really. A few of my relations passed by and took pity on the deserted booth and a stray traveller or two paused before this solitary cactus!'

He thought that very poetic, if untrue. He glanced at the blue velvet display racks. A large pearl caught his eye. It could only have come from the oyster beds of distant Ceylon.

> 'No cactus, but the fairest pearl of all
> So none can pay your price.
> At your white feet the earth must fall
> All gods, all men and even mice.'

The little joking verse in the Persian mode spun out of him involuntarily, while the dashing princes and cavaliers who shopped at the *Meena* Bazaar spent hours composing to impress the women who attracted them. She stared at him, astonished. She blinked once, then her eyes reddened and misted. He could see that she was moved.

'No one has ever made up a poem for me.' Though she looked at him, she seemed to be speaking to herself.

'My own life has been dedicated to war and administration,' he rejoined. 'No lady has ever inspired me to compose a poem before, nor have I ever tried my hand at poetry.' He shrugged, suddenly embarrassed. 'I was taught the mode at school, but it is not my line of work and no doubt you will soon forget it altogether.'

'Oh no, my lord prince!' She reached out long, delicate white fingers as if to touch him, then drew them back. 'It is the most beautiful poem in the world.'

He felt himself blush. This girl had the ability to reach the boy within him, a boy he barely knew to exist because he had always been expected to behave like a man. He laughed joyously, noted that it made her eyes crinkle with delight. She shook her head in wonderment, the ready smile broke forth, sunlight sparkling after rain, he thought, becoming conscious of the sunshine in the courtyard, the clamour of voices, the mingled smell of sweat and cross-bred perfumes. A world out there. The world of the *harem* which was not separate, but a part of the whole world, Tafari had said. He recognized that now, but Mumtaz Mahal and he were in a world of their own.

He gestured towards the pearl.

> 'So, I would buy that gleaming pearl
> The closest to its mistress.
> Knowing I'll never own the girl
> It may console my distress.'

Her eyes sparkling again, she responded in kind.

> 'O gentle prince, why do you waste
> Your wealth on what is but a stone?
> Its owner, humble, proud and chaste
> Would bend the knee for you alone.'

The price she had been instructed to quote for the stone was ten thousand rupees. Though the sum was far beyond his immediate means, he bought the pearl.

'I shall keep this precious pearl until I have the right to give it to the girl I love,' he stated. 'Princes never carry money, as you know, so please give me pen and manuscript and I shall write a note authorizing the Treasurer of the Royal Household to pay you.'

Her eyes were tear-filled when she handed over the writing implements. How wonderful, he thought, you laugh when you are happy and you laugh when you are sad. Deep inside him a bleak question intruded. Are there tears in every laugh?

He was too young to know the answer, still less to seek it. He knew, when he finally walked away from the booth – floated would more exactly describe it – that he had fallen in love.

Since Nur Jehan had confronted him, Asaf Khan had made it a point to dine with her at least once every week, so she was aware that the Emperor Jehangir had heeded her counsel to such an extent that he had placed Prince Husrau virtually under house arrest in the imperial palace. Now these regular dinners were not only a concession on her brother's part to his love for her, but also a clear indication that he valued her judgment and recognized her potential power. Nur Jehan also had a sneaking suspicion that the Emperor had commanded it, but Asaf Khan would never be the one to make her feel that he was merely obeying his monarch's dictates.

They were seated in her chamber, as usual, Asaf Khan on the divan and she on the settle. She had ensured a specially fine meal of fifteen different courses, because she wanted her brother in the correct frame of mind for what she had to discuss. He certainly seemed in the right mood when he replaced his tiny coffee cup on the table before him, leaned back patting his flat stomach and grinned. 'That was an incredible meal, little sister. Thanks be to Allah I partake of them only once a week, else I should have to watch my waistline. Just when I think you have run out of recipes, you come up with something new. How do you do it?'

'My culinary spies are everywhere in the world, from Cathay to France and the Netherlands, my imagination is ever-present to serve you.' She inclined her head submissively.

He laughed, then sobered on the instant. 'You will never serve anyone except to have them serve you,' he declared. 'You and I are one in that respect.'

She eyed him levelly. 'I can have no secrets from you.'

His laugh broke out again, causing her a flash of irritation this time. 'There are no secrets in a *harem*, except those in the innermost minds of its residents,' he observed. 'And those are deep and unfathomable as the ocean, because they emerge from the wellsprings of loneliness in a crowd.' He paused, his eyes crinkling with affection. 'But I believe there is one secret you can never keep from me, because my love for you gives me the awareness of concern: I always know when you have something on your mind.'

She had always found the expression of his love for her irresistible. She recognized that it could be a weakness and weakness was not a luxury she would ever permit herself, but tonight she would enjoy his brotherly feelings and of course exploit them. 'There is something of great import-ance to me that I want to share with you,' she stated, fixing a loving gaze on him. 'But first, will you concede that my analysis of the possibility of a revolt centred on Prince Husrau was correct?'

'Yes indeed, and your prior suggestion that Raja Man Singh be sent to Bengal was brilliant.'

'And what of my conclusion that if Prince Husrau was placed under house arrest, we would at least buy ourselves time to discover what was impending?'

'Remarkable. You reasoned that with the departure of Raja Man Singh and your husband for Bengal, we would only need to check closely on their long lines of communication and of course those between Prince Husrau and Chitor, which we have done to good effect.'

'My own spies tell me that Sher Afgan is secretly soliciting assistance for Prince Husrau's cause,' she lied calmly. One of her trusted spies did indeed work for her husband and was even now in Bengal with him. Though she had received no communication from the man so far, her brother was not to know that and he had already begun to attribute a bigger organization to her than she had. 'It is time . . .'

The knocking on the door was so insistent that even as she broke off in mid-sentence, she knew it must be important. 'Enter!' she called.

The eunuch who padded in was a cleanshaven, thin, older Nubian, with crinkly white hair. His lean, dark face was a comical combination of consternation at the news he was bringing and self-importance that he should be its carrier. Asaf Khan leaned forward expectantly on his divan.

'What is it, Ras?' Nur Jehan demanded, giving the eunuch his title.

'News of the gravest import, my lady.' He must have noted the flicker of impatience in her glance, for he plunged straight in, his voice quavery, knowing from experience that she wanted the news first and the details after. 'Prince Husrau has escaped from the palace and is riding north, at the head of three hundred and sixty men loyal to him. He is presumed to be making for Delhi and Lahore, where his strongest support exists.'

Nur Jehan's only reaction was one of elation.

Not so Asaf Khan. 'How did he manage to escape?' he cut in, his voice nonetheless calm. 'Or don't you know?'

'It is reported that during the second watch tonight, the *chiraghtchey* (lamp director) of Prince Husrau's household was checking on the extinguishing of lamps when he discovered that the prince was not in his quarters. He immediately reported this to the supervisor of the household, who communicated it to Amir Umra, who had just ended an audience with the Emperor. The Amir went post-haste to the prince's quarters, where he verified through the eunuchs that the prince had in fact fled. He immediately contacted the Emperor who by then had retired to his *harem* for the night.'

'So the Emperor is aware of the event?'

'Yes, lord,' the eunuch replied.

'Has any action been taken?'

'I understand that Sheik Farid has been commanded to leave at dawn tomorrow in pursuit with a large force of troops. If Prince Husrau does not surrender, or if he takes up the sword, Sheik Farid has orders to slay him.'

Nur Jehan was seeing her brother in official action for the first time and could not help admiring his concise questions. 'How do you know all this?' she inquired, though she already suspected the answer.

'A messenger brought the news for our noble Grand Vizier from the imperial palace.' He bowed towards Asaf Khan. 'This messenger had been given the fullest details.'

Nur Jehan thrilled, knowing that the Emperor, aware that his prime minister was with her, had intended the message for her ears too. She was beginning to taste power, the appetizer of a banquet, forecasting the delicacies to come.

'His Imperial Majesty commands the presence of the Grand Vizier in the palace forthwith.'

In her mind, Nur Jehan commended the astuteness of

the eunuch. He had given the details of the message so they could be absorbed before he caused anxiety to obey the summons. 'Any other points of importance in the message, Ras?' she questioned.

'No, my lady.'

It will not be long now before you address me with higher titles than that, she reflected as she dismissed Ras. She turned to Asaf Khan as the door closed behind the eunuch. He had risen to his feet, the light of action bright in his eyes. She knelt to him quickly. 'I know you must leave without delay,' she said, when she stood up. 'But I have two messages for His Imperial Majesty, which I hope you will deliver tonight.'

'What are they?' He paused in his stride towards the door.

'Will you deliver them tonight?' She was deliberately slow, noting his impatience to leave.

'Of course.'

'The first is that while he has acted with decisiveness in having Sheik Farid pursue Prince Husrau, he should not permit the Sheik to apprehend the prince and become the hero of the hour. He should gather as much of his army as is prudent with the requirements of the security of the capital and follow no later than a couple of days hence. Even if the Sheik does apprehend Prince Husrau, the Emperor will then get the credit for it, besides impressing those in the dissident factions with his decisiveness and might.'

Asaf Khan shook his head in amazement. 'You are the loveliest, fairest, most womanly lady in the world,' he declared. 'But you think and reason like a man. You have the qualities of an Emperor.'

She blushed at the compliment. Coming from Asaf Khan, she knew it was sincere and the highest praise. Conscious, though, that he wished to hasten to the palace, she quickly broached her second request. 'An Emperor has of necessity to be a male,' she stated. 'The world may be a worse place for that! But I also happen to be a woman, one whom the Emperor Jehangir desires and to whom he listens. That is the reason for my second suggestion.' Prince Husrau's departure could not have been better timed to suit this, her special, unswerving goal.

'And that is?' Asaf Khan was suddenly very quiet, as if knowing what was coming and tensing to ward off a blow.

'This precipitate action of Prince Husrau must have been inspired in part by support in Bengal.' She looked at her brother meaningfully. 'At the very least therefore it could inspire dissidents in that distant outpost of the Empire to revolt. Those responsible and those who may become supportive must be eliminated.'

'You are surely not suggesting that another imperial army should set out to the east?'

'No. There are other ways.'

'How?'

She told him, knowing that this would not only appeal to the Emperor Jehangir's head, but also to his heart.

Prince Husrau's secret message had reached Rana Amar, at the Chitor palace, three mornings earlier. On being given the news by his father, Prince Chara had shaken with silent fury. His carefully laid plans could be aborted by the over eagerness of the idiotic prince whose proposed escape was premature. Father and son agreed that Prince Chara should hurry to Agra immediately in order to advise Prince Husrau to postpone his departure, as the Rajputs of Mewar were certainly not ready yet for the proposed revolt.

Having ridden post-haste, with a minimum escort to ensure speed, Prince Chara arrived in Agra three mornings later to discover that he was too late. Prince Husrau had left the capital the previous evening, pretending to his guards that he was making a pilgrimage to the mausoleum of his grandfather five miles away in Sikandra. The prince was reportedly on his way to Delhi, at the head of some three hundred and sixty horse, consisting of loyal supporters. From Delhi he would pick up more supporters before proceeding north to Lahore and Afghanistan, perhaps Kabul, the latter being the stronghold of constant opposition to the Moghuls.

The premature revolt made Prince Chara's blood run cold. Having received the news from the guard commander at the gates of the capital when he arrived that morning, he could see that the city was agog with it. He therefore headed for the Emperor's palace, deciding quite cynically that he would mend fences and make a loyal gesture of his hurried call.

Though his visit was entirely unexpected, he was readily lodged in his former quarters in the royal palace, through the good offices of Prince Aziz Koka, whom he immediately contacted. The Emperor's foster-brother was also both furious and worried by the turn of events. Though the ruler was busy conferring with his ministers, staffs and army chiefs, Aziz Koka was able to persuade him to give Prince Chara a private audience that very afternoon.

The Emperor received Prince Chara in the European chamber which was more private than any other room in the palace.

The last time Prince Chara had seen him, the Emperor had been the heir apparent. As he raised his head from making obeisance, the change in the man astonished him. Whether it was due to the dignity of the high office or to the reserves of strength and character it could command, the Emperor Jehangir presented a picture of resolution, controlled anger and majesty, as he sat on the gilt French settee that his father had once favoured and gestured to Prince Chara to be seated opposite. His short, stocky frame, with the powerful shoulders, was so richly clad that he seemed to shine like the sun. He wore a sheer gold gauze robe over a green satin tunic and pantaloons, studded with diamonds. His necklaces and earrings were of diamonds and emeralds, with which his turban too was sprinkled. His heavy face, so like that of his father, was cleanshaven except for the Mongolian moustaches, drooping because to point them upwards to heaven would be sacrilege. His slant eyes were alert.

Prince Chara had never visited this chamber before and he could not help but be impressed by its rich elegance, as opposed to the normal vulgar Moghul magnificence. The gilded ceiling shone from bright daylight outside. The great Persian carpet, the gold and ivory ornaments on the black *boule* sideboards lining the walls and the rich tapestries hanging above them, all reflected good taste.

'You have heard the news of the day, Prince Chara?' The Emperor came directly, almost abruptly, to the point. 'Our son has fled the capital, obviously to raise the standard of revolt against us, taking advantage of our generous compassion in permitting him certain degrees of freedom from his house arrest. In our view it borders on sacrilege that he should have pretended a visit to his grandfather's mausoleum when he had really planned to flee. Those who permitted him to escape have already been suitably punished; now it remains to deal with the offender himself.' The heavy lids of the Emperor's eyes lifted as he stared at Prince Chara with a glance that would have made anyone else quail. 'Tell us, were you and your father, the Rana, privy to this plot and any part of it?' he demanded abruptly.

The blunt question was fraught with a possible accusation of treason, but Prince Chara was never one to be intimidated. He had already recovered from his first reaction and was sure of his ground. 'If my royal father and I were a part of any such plot, I would surely not have come to your imperial presence today, Sire. I would have avoided

Agra as if it suffered an epidemic of the bubonic plague.'
He lifted his head proudly. 'Besides, in such an event, I
would have been in Mewar at the head of our troops, not
in your imperial palace offering you our submission and
support.' He continued to eye the Emperor levelly and was
rewarded by the tapping of forefinger on knee, indicating
that contemplation had replaced the Emperor's suspicion.

'You are right and we are grateful for your offer of
assistance. Please convey this sentiment to your royal father
as well. It is the support of rulers like him that inspires us,
but we will not require it at the present time. Meanwhile,
pray tell us, Prince Chara, what does bring you to Agra so
unexpectedly?'

'We heard rumours of this very problem and the Rana
despatched me post-haste to bring them to your royal
notice and to assure you of our submission.'

'Good.' The royal forefinger ceased its tapping. 'You are
well quartered and looked after?'

'Yes, thank you, Sire.'

'Your friend Aziz Koka was present at Chitor early this
year, along with Prince Husrau. It was this visit that
alerted us to the possibility of subversion and caused us to
have our son placed under house arrest. Did you sense
anything amiss while he was in Chitor?'

'If we had, Sire, we would surely have brought it
immediately to your royal notice. Besides Raja Man was
also our guest in Chitor at the time and, as you know, he
had by then been deputed by you to take over the government of Bengal, for which parts he has since departed, I
understand. We were hardly a likely band of plotters to
overthrow your gracious rule, Sire, if I may be permitted
to say so!'

'True, true.' The Emperor paused. 'Why was Sher . . .
never mind.'

With a thrill, Prince Chara realized that Sher Afgan was

somehow a giant thorn in the Emperor's side. 'May I inquire what steps you propose taking against Prince Husrau, Sire?' he asked, deliberately changing the subject.

'A strong force, under General Sheik Farid, left for Delhi this morning in pursuit of the renegade prince.'

Prince Chara's mind flashed to his one personal enemy. It was essential that Prince Jahan leave with the imperial force if Sher Afgan's *thuggee* were to assassinate him as planned. 'I hope Prince Jahan accompanied General Sheik Farid,' he murmured. 'The prince is among the ablest of your retinue.'

'Prince Jahan remains in the royal palace for the very reason that he is among the ablest of our staff.'

Damn, Prince Chara thought.

'The prince, our favourite son, shall accompany us when we follow with the imperial army in about two days.' Prince Chara breathed an inward sigh of relief while the Emperor shook his head sadly. 'How could our eldest son behave thus to a father who has been so good to him, who generously forgave his attempt to usurp the throne from us?' He sighed heavily, then his face became mottled with a sudden access of fury. 'In the concerns of sovereign power, there is, however, neither child nor kin. The alien who exerts himself in the cause of loyalty is worth more than a thousand sons or kindred. The son who in the presumption of his heart forgets the duty which he owes his father, and the unnumbered marks of royal bounty so liberally bestowed, is to us, in every sense, a stranger. Prince Husrau is no different from a man who saps the foundations of his house and builds upon the upper terrace. His action brings to mind the distinguished Islamic example of the Emperor Osman, who, to ensure the stability of the realm and his royal authority, considered it expedient to preserve but one of his sons as heir, killing all the rest.'

The man obviously favoured outbursts of oratory when he wanted to impress himself!

You revolted against your own father, who forgave you not once but twice, Prince Chara reflected. How could you forget your own perfidy? Surely convenient loss of memory is the prerogative of the hypocrite in every human being. I for my part am different. I would certainly betray my own father a hundred times if it brought me the Mewar throne. As for the Moghul crown, I would betray the world and readily proclaim my perfidy to wear it.

'We will never, with our own hands, consign the power delegated to us by the Almighty Supreme to those ruinous contingencies to which the world would be exposed from the shameful effects of profligacy and ignorance resulting from Prince Husrau's accession to the throne,' the Emperor continued almost to himself.

Prince Chara marvelled at the regal pomposity, so foreign to Jehangir before his accession. Was not this the clue? While the office had changed the man, the change could only be a reflection of what was already in him, hidden or unperceived. Once Prince Jehangir became Emperor, the Chosen One of his Almighty Supreme, he developed the megalomaniac image already within him, mirroring even his past with all those virtues he required from those around him to retain his power. Now he was as addicted to high-sounding phrases as to wine and opium, all of which he needed to sustain him. Rulers were prone to such afflictions. He, Prince Chara alone, would always be too cynically aware of these human frailties to become infected.

The Emperor's next question confirmed his delusion of grandeur. 'What will history say of this event?'

History be damned, Prince Chara thought savagely, for we will not be around to witness it. Aloud he soothed the Emperor. 'That an ungrateful son betrayed his noble, blameless, sovereign father.' How easily the lies came when needed! Yet he simply could not hold back the more cynical truth. 'And yet, Sire, history today is no more than the futile effort of each human being to perpetuate himself.'

The Emperor gave him a sharp glance. 'How so?'

'What we call history is the product of our blind searchings into the past, through time and the mists of time, for some obscure origin which we will never discover because we never had it. What motivates this senseless voyage into the past is the subconscious hope that it affords us perpetuity *after* we die. None of it is important.' He suddenly deemed that a return to blatant flattery of this vain man would be timely. 'Especially to great monarchs like you, Sire, for you are already one of those divine monuments of history to which men will point back in the future forever.'

There was admiration in the Emperor's eyes. 'You have a nice wit, Prince, and a keen sense of philosophy, which we never suspected in you. We should take you with us on our pursuit of this wretched betrayer, Prince Husrau. You could enliven those campfire deliberations with our *mullahs* and holy men which help relieve the tedium of the march.'

Your Allah and my father's gods forbid, Prince Chara thought aghast, cursing himself for trying to show off his cleverness. 'That would be an overwhelming honour, Sire, and nothing would give me greater joy, not the least because my sword would then be at your royal disposal.' He sighed with calculated deceit. 'But do you not think that I can better serve you at this time by joining my royal father in Mewar?' Inspiration flamed, causing him to add, 'Besides, having my people upset in your absence from the capital, in a mistaken belief that you have taken me along as some kind of hostage, might create unnecessary outrage. You know how people are, Sire, and what opportunities troublemakers seize upon at such times.'

'You have foresight as well as wit,' the Emperor nodded approvingly. 'Well, we shall have to be content with taking our younger, less experienced model with us. Prince Jahan will hardly like to leave Agra at the present time, for very personal reasons which we will not disclose at present, it being a secret between father and loyal son, but he will, unlike his miserable elder brother, always respond readily and cheerfully to the call of duty.'

That disgusting rebel, Prince Husrau, has made the Emperor see my mortal rival as some kind of saint, Prince Chara reflected savagely. I could kill Prince Husrau with my bare hands. He calmed down, however, before the realization that the effect of this transference of the Emperor's faith had been to include Prince Jahan in the imperial train, headed for Delhi and Lahore, where death awaited him at the hands of Sher Afgan's *thuggee*. He would leave Agra for Chitor tomorrow in order to avoid any possible suspicion of involvement in that assassination. But what was this personal secret?

'When do you propose returning to Chitor, Prince?' The Emperor's question seemed to have emerged from an uncanny perception of his own thoughts.

'Since my loyal duty has been accomplished, though I arrived too late for it to be effective, I would like to leave early tomorrow, Sire.'

'You are welcome to remain here as our guest for as long as it pleases you.'

'With your departure, Sire, the light will have been extinguished from the royal palace and I shall be bereft of any desire to remain here in total darkness.'

The Emperor beamed, then seemed to lose interest. 'You add a nice turn of phrase to your other qualities, Prince,' he declared somewhat absently.

Chapter 9

The Emperor Jehangir's mind was a confusion of conflicting emotions tonight. Hatred and contempt for Prince Husrau alternated with love and compassion. Confidence that tomorrow's battle against the army of the rebel prince would result in victory clashed with the fear of defeat. He had concluded giving battle orders to his commanders earlier that afternoon. Facing the final outcome of the threat to his throne from Prince Husrau, which had commenced four months earlier, he had not even been able to enjoy his sumptuous dinner or the usual glasses of wine that accompanied it, so sunk was he into depression.

The rebel enemy had encamped at the opposite end of the Great Bharowal plain that afternoon, about one mile from the foothills which his own imperial army had occupied for four days. He had awaited the advancing forces there so he could give them battle on ground of his own choosing and preparation, after Prince Husrau's rejection of the message he had sent through a nobleman, Jamal Deen, entreating the rebel to retrace his steps in time, to beware of the awful responsibility of the blood of untold thousands, and repair to the imperial presence where he would be forgiven. 'Having proceeded thus far, I have no alternative but the sword,' Prince Husrau had responded. 'God Almighty will give the crown to that head which He knows to be most worthy of the Empire.' So the ensuing days had afforded his imperial staffs the opportunity to reconnoitre the surrounding terrain thoroughly, which, together with his superior firepower, somewhat discounted the enemy advantage of almost two to one in numbers. But the imperial nose was running, the regal throat was sore and parched, and the entire sovereign body so depleted of energy that all he wanted was to lay down his head. Hardly a condition for the Ruler of the World, he thought dismally while listening to the final report from his army commander, the burly, bearded General Bahadur Khan, confirming that the imperial forces had been positioned for the forthcoming battle.

The general and he were alone in the cosy golden lampglow from the crystal chandeliers adorning the royal tent. For once, the Emperor was finding scant comfort in his luxurious surroundings, or in the background of soothing night music from tinkling *sirtars* and gentle drumming in the adjoining tent. Camphor-perfumed smoke wisps curling through golden braziers, rich Persian carpets, gilt ornamental writing desk and chair, gold-brocaded cushions for sitting and matching bolsters for leaning were stern reminders that he might have none of it tomorrow night, that playing the role of Emperor from the security of a palace was quite different to *being* one on the eve of a battle for his throne!

'Your royal commands have been carried out, Sire,' the general reported. 'Sheik Farid's force of three thousand cavalry is in position at the entrance to the plain, and will commence its assault at dawn. Our pikemen have been placed between the foothills immediately behind the cavalry, preceding the elephant contingent. They are supported by our one thousand musketeers, infantry elements and one hundred cannon spread out in two ranks facing our front and protecting our flanks. The cavalry reserve of three thousand is in the rear, while General Husein's mounted detachments, each of two thousand men, have already departed on their mission.'

'Good!' the Emperor grunted. General Husein's mission had been his very own idea, from his extensive knowledge of past Moghul and Tatar military tactics. He resumed his contemplation, allowing the deep voice of his stalwart Sikh general to drone on around him.

He wondered what Prince Husrau's quarters were like. Would the prince be residing in this imperial encampment tomorrow night? Located at the rear of the imperial army, which was spread out over a few miles on the low foothills, the royal enclosure was two hundred yards square and protected by the imperial guard, an elite corps of one thousand men. Its outer walls were wooden screens, secured by leather straps, covered with scarlet sackcloth. The enclosure even contained a *jarokha* for the Emperor's daily public appearance. His private bedroom, sitting and dining room, bath and privy, were in the centre so that the sounds of his army, some shouting, the sudden blare of a trumpet, raucous laughter, reached him but faintly, past the halls of public and private audience, a travelling mosque and space for the *harem*. He had hardly visited the *harem* during the entire four-month chase of Prince Husrau, because his mind was full of the prospect of winning Nur Jehan for his own at long last. Nur Jehan was the only woman he desired.

Nur Jehan is my guardian angel, the only source of light in the infernal darkness of this sad night. She not only brings radiance to my soul as its mate, she also sheds sunshine on all my imperial duties.

How remarkable Nur Jehan's advice had been! It was she who suggested that he despatch Raja Man as overlord of distant Bengal. What a wonderful token of her dislike of her husband and her feelings for her Emperor, the ruler of her heart, that she should have also requested him to promote Sher Afgan to an office in that same distant eastern outpost. He had been able to sleep more easily since Sher Afgan's departure from the nuptial bed, instead of tossing on his own jealous imperial couch. How masterly were

Nur Jehan's sources of information, how penetrating her analysis of the significance of the meetings in the Chitor palace earlier that year. She had been proved one hundred per cent correct. As for tonight, was it not her wisdom in beseeching him to take to the field personally that had brought him to the verge of victory over his rebel son? Victory? Remembering the reported strength of his son's army, over thirty thousand men, momentarily deflated the Great Emperor, but he was soon reinspired by thoughts of Nur Jehan and thrust the doubts aside. With his elephants, greater fire-power, the support of his beloved and the mandate of Allah, he would win.

Another doubt intruded. Had he been wise to heed Nur Jehan's last-minute advice, on the night before he left on this campaign, to leave Prince Jahan behind in Agra as head of the Council of Regency in charge of the central government of the Empire in his absence? He dismissed the question as disloyal to the source of his inspiration. Nur Jehan had been sent to him by Allah and God's messenger could never be wrong. Proof of that was her choice of him above every other man in the world. And had she not placed her entire future in his royal hands with the plan she had evolved for dealing with her husband in Bengal once he vanquished Prince Husrau? As the first move he had already despatched Khubu Khan to take over as governor of Bengal, under the suzerainty of Raja Man.

The Emperor literally trembled – and it was not from his head cold! – at imagining what it would be like for Nur Jehan to hold him in her sinuous arms and make love to him. Perhaps she would sing to him in the golden voice that had such a caress to it. He would drink in her splendid white limbs, the softness of her flesh, the fragrance of her. Those limpid black pools of her eyes would envelop him. Yes, he needed to be enveloped by love, to be mothered, subjugated. No one suspected this need. His own mother had been an aloof though compassionate woman. Not one of the five thousand submissive women in his *harem* had ever given a thought to dominating him. Only Nur Jehan held the promise of it. And she would respect him the more for her mastery, because after all he was the Emperor and it took greater strength in a ruler, as opposed to an ordinary mortal, to be willing to accept such domination, even to need it. He would not fail her, nor she him.

General Khan had commenced by giving details of troop strengths. Facts that could not be altered or used bored him. Addicted as he was to total luxury and comfort, protocol and the familiar routine, camp life was not for him. He preferred loving to fighting. Thoughts of killing others held no terrors for him, even appealed to a part of his nature, but each time he thought of being killed, maimed or defeated himself, his guts went weak, his chest tightened, throwing bitter bile at the back of his throat.

Another question intruded. Notwithstanding Prince Chara's philosophical speculations, which he had taken to heart, would history hold him responsible, either as a parent or a ruler, for Prince Husrau's revolt? Tonight was definitely not the best time of his life!

He leaned forward from his reclining position against the cloth of gold bolster, took a sip of his wine. It was tasteless in his mouth. He wondered whether to reach towards the low table nearby for the silver opium pipe, but decided against it. All sounds of the encampment had died down to a silence in which the unexpected hoot of an owl sounded ominous. He shivered. He must awaken early tomorrow and be fit and ready for the battle. Involuntarily coughing, he spat into the golden spittoon beside him, blew his nose into it. A golden spittoon does not give royalty help in mental affliction, he reflected dismally, then turned his attention to the general.

'So finally the future of the Empire is in our own hands, Sire,' General Khan concluded resolutely.

'We are but the instruments of Allah!' the Emperor interjected with his customary concession to superstition. 'But God Almighty has already sent us favourable omens of His Will.'

'And what may those be, Sire?'

'We visited our father's resting place at the commencement of this march and had not even proceeded a mile thence when a man came to us, who could not possibly have known we were the Emperor. On our demanding to know his name, he stated it was Murad Kaujah. Note the Kaujah, meaning "good fortune", General, and also that Murad is the name of our deceased younger brother. Farther on, near the tomb of our ancestor the Emperor Babur, we met another man, carrying a burden of thorns and driving before him an ass laden with firewood. Upon inquiry, his name turned out to be Dowlet Kaujah, which means "Sir Fortune".'

'Miraculous,' the general murmured, without conviction, stroking his black beard.

'We thereupon expressed to our immediate retinue what a clear sign from God Almighty it would be if we met yet a third person bearing the name Saadet Kaujah, "omen of victory". Proceeding a little farther, we observed a little boy grazing a cow on the bank of a rivulet to our right. Upon venturing to ask his name, with some hopeful concern we might add, he replied that his name was Saadet Kaujah.' He looked at the general triumphantly, his hopes buoyed by recollection of the omens.

'It would appear that we are indeed assured of victory,' the general responded, summoning a little more enthusiasm this time.

The Emperor decided it was time to give the general some words of appreciation to strengthen his morale before

157

dismissing him for the night. 'Prince Husrau left Agra with only three hundred and sixty supporters,' he declared. 'His first encouragement along the way was from Beg Badakh with three hundred horse, which enabled him soon to swell his ranks to twelve thousand and thereafter to intercept an imperial convoy and seize several hundred thousand rupees with which to pay more troops. Between Delhi and Lahore, the traitorous prince was joined by Abdul Rahman, the *diwan* of that province, whom the prince appointed his *wazir*. We shall remember those two traitorous vipers, Badakh and Rahman. At Taran, the prince received the benediction of Arjun, the fifth *guru* of the Sikhs. One of your own people.' He eyed the general fiercely, forgetting his intended concessions towards the latter's morale.

'Every race has its traitors and renegades,' the general assured him urbanely. 'My own presence here tonight is a symbol of the loyalty of my people to Your Imperial Majesty.'

'True, true!' The Emperor remembered what he had intended moments earlier, to strengthen the morale of his commander-in-chief. He knew that his attention wandered at times, and occasionally asked himself why, but was not concerned enough to seek out a reply. 'It is the loyalty and devotion of subjects such as you that inspire us in the daily labours we dedicate to our rule.' Perhaps a warning hint coupled with the offer of a plum might be timely. 'If any entire race were to oppose us, it would feel our might. Where the Sikhs are concerned, however, they are assured of our constant endeavours on their behalf and our generosity towards them because of the exemplary conduct of brave men such as you, General. Be assured too that at the end of this campaign your own rewards shall be great.'

'I do not serve you for rewards, my revered Emperor,' the general responded proudly, 'but for honour.'

'For that very reason, your rewards shall be the greater.'

The Emperor paused, trying to recall the trend of his original statements. 'Ah yes, Beg Badakh, Abdul Rahman and Guru Arjun, on the other hand, shall be suitably punished.' Having already decided what those punishments would be, he savoured them for a moment.

The general's eyes flashed fire. 'Surely not the *guru*, Sire,' he protested. 'You would not punish one of our priests.'

'A *guru* ceases to be a *guru* and a symbol of sanctity and holiness when he blesses a traitor.' He decided it would be prudent to abandon that subject. 'We shall, however, give the matter further deliberation. On a more cheerful note, the governor of Lahore, Dilawar Khan, who refused Prince Husrau entry, closed his gates and resolutely defended the city when our son besieged it, is yet another cast in the mould of honourable men such as yourself. He too shall be amply rewarded after our victory in tomorrow's battle.'

All of which reminded the Emperor that if he was to put himself in a position to bestow rewards on loyal subjects, he had best turn in for the night. He dismissed the general and lay back on the gold cushions, reflecting on the enormous sacrifices he made for the Empire and his subjects.

He reined in Samt by the water's edge, close to where the *thuggee* had once lain in wait for him, and Asaf Khan slowed his bay alongside. Prince Jahan had recommended his daily pre-dawn horseback ride on the *maidan* a few days after his grandfather's death, but he had ridden alone with his sad memories until shortly after he met and fell in love with Mumtaz Mahal. He had then invited her father to join him on the morning rides, but had been careful to avoid personal topics in their conversations, since it would not have been proper for him to discuss Mumtaz Mahal, still less his feelings for her. Any overtures as to betrothal or marriage had to come from his own father, the Emperor, especially since it was the latter who had first suggested that he take a look at the young lady.

It had, however, given Prince Jahan an undefinable sense of being close to Mumtaz Mahal to ride each morning with Asaf Khan, and of course it was a learning experience for him, of which he took full advantage, to spend time alone with the man who was Prime Minister. While sorry not to be in the middle of action against the rebel forces, he was elated that the Emperor had commanded him to remain in Agra as head of the Governing Council, a signal honour.

The mornings had become warmer as summer progressed, but there was a cool eastern breeze blowing the scent of eucalyptus across the river. To their right the dark moat linked the river's course with the rampart wall. The sky ahead was lightening with the first rosy glow from a sun still below the horizon, throwing grey and black clouds into travail, seeming to thrust the dark silver waters of the Jumna rippling and splashing towards them when the river was really flowing in the opposite direction. The black sentinels of cypress trees lining the far banks were taller companions of the mounted guards, motionless at regular intervals on the near bank and along the edge of the moat, the product of the late Emperor's command after the attempt on his grandson that the cavalry should guard the *maidan* every morning, whether Prince Jahan rode or not. The sight of those guards never failed to remind Prince Jahan of his grandfather's love and protection, which he sorely missed.

'It is strange that Ishtaq was never found after the kidnap attempt,' Asaf Khan remarked, his thoughts obviously an echo of Prince Jahan's. 'He is probably in hiding somewhere in the mountains of Afghanistan by now, protected by his family.'

Prince Jahan often wondered about Ishtaq during these

rides and even whether Samt missed the former chief groom, but Asaf Khan's words had brought concern that he had known for months to the forefront of his mind. He had hesitated to voice it before, but now felt close enough to Asaf Khan to express it. He placed his hands on the pommel of the saddle, eased himself forward on it. 'Which raises an interesting speculation.' He lowered his voice. 'As you know, just before he departed on this campaign against my brother, my father appointed your cousin, Khubu Khan, to be governor of Bengal under Raja Man. This was the culmination of a series of appointments the Emperor made, including your own and those of your father and brother-in-law. While these are most deserved tributes to the loyalty and capabilities of the various members of your family, it places you as a family unit in a position of great power, which I personally welcome. Is there any special significance in Khubu Khan's appointment?' Voicing the question released bad feelings that had lain unrecognized in the depths of his mind and were allied with his suspicion that his beloved grandfather had been poisoned or otherwise done to death by Prince Jehangir. 'I know that the Emperor acts on his own initiative from his infinite wisdom,' he added. 'But I could not help wondering whether this appointment neglected other considerations that my poor young intellect cannot perceive.'

Asaf Khan smiled, stroked his moustache with his right hand. His bay pawed the ground in reflexive response at the movement. 'You are wise beyond your years, Prince, to credit the Emperor with more than his readily perceived wisdom. It enhances my admiration for all you have achieved as head of the Council of Regency during these past months. You have improved security in the city, especially of the royal vaults and throughout the palace, strengthened the defences of the fort and proved yourself a superb administrator. Indeed, some of our older noblemen are likening your capabilities to those of your illustrious grandfather and your formidable ancestor the Emperor Babur at the same age. I have even observed your resoluteness and confidence in the way you sign the *firmans* (royal edicts).' His teeth shone briefly white in an apology at the flattering words, so unusual from him that they had made Prince Jahan glow. 'You are right to assume that there is a special undisclosed significance in Khubu Khan's appointment.' Asaf Khan had lowered his own voice. He glanced swiftly around. 'You may not be aware that Raja Man was appointed overlord of Bengal because his own loyalty to the Emperor was suspect.' Asaf Khan gazed unseeing along the river, then turned his head sharply towards the prince and lowered his voice still further. 'Do you give me your sacred oath that you will hold what I am about to tell you secret?'

'I do indeed.'

'You spoke just now of the growing power of my family. While I have any say in affairs of state, that power shall be exercised fully and with uncompromising loyalty and obedience to the Emperor, unless the dictates of honour compel otherwise.' He paused, his expression grim. 'We have reason to believe that a member of this same family, Sher Afgan, is a traitor.' He took in Prince Jahan's shocked silence, nodding slowly. 'Worse, that Sher Afgan may even have been behind the attempt on you last year, here on this very *maidan*. Please do not ask me for details.'

'Is the Lady Nur Jehan aware of all this?'

'More. She is one of our sources of information. I would have you know, Prince, that my sister is a lady of exemplary virtue, as dedicated to the service of our Emperor as you and I.' His eyes narrowed; he stared at the distant horizon. 'Allow me to let you in on a great confidence. My sister has little cause to love her husband.' He paused, then ground out, 'Sher Afgan is a brute, a monster, a wife abuser who shall be destroyed.'

Prince Jahan's mind had been spinning with his companion's revelations. Now he was appalled. Like the first glimmers of dawn in that distant horizon, he was beginning to see how the future was shaping. Reasoning had always told him that there was more to his father's confidence in Asaf Khan's family than appeared on the surface. Could there be some connection between his father's interest in having him meet Mumtaz Mahal and a widowed Nur Jehan? It was only a flash of suspicion, dying instantly, but it left him wondering about his own future. His father was addicted to the pleasures of life, had never been emotionally involved with any woman or willing to accept any responsibility of a personal nature. He was also a poet, a writer and a great romantic, given to supporting or rejecting people by emotion instead of logic and reason. How could he, Prince Jahan, use this situation to fulfil his destiny of becoming Emperor? Playing a loyal, subordinate role to the Asaf Khan family would help, but he could not remain a loyal subordinate all his life. Young as he was, as a student of history, he saw this now in moments of startling clarity. Loyal, faithful Prince Jahan, forever the faithful adviser of Emperors, a sterile role he had no desire to play.

Your family is becoming the power behind the throne, he thought dismally. Where will that leave me? He was gripped by the sense of aloneness and insecurity he had felt the day his grandfather died. He breathed deeply, the air cold in his nostrils, fighting the feeling resolutely.

'We believe you are the coming star of the Empire, Prince, and you may be sure that our family regards you as one of us and will support you to succeed your father, who will assuredly return in triumph over Prince Husrau.'

Bells sounded in Prince Jahan's head before it started to

163

spin with delight. Had there been a promise of more than the imperial crown in Asaf Khan's words?

He had not felt like getting out of bed when he was awoken, as usual, by the sound of gentle music which had grown more insistent to ensure that he did arise; but once on his feet, his blood circulating again, the Emperor felt better. He was almost his normal self after his bath, robing, breakfast and prayers were over. It was not yet light when he stepped outside his tent, followed by his valet and attendants. The air was cold after the warmth inside, but fresh and invigorating. Trumpets and drums in the near distance began quickening his blood. Clad in black leather armour, his hand on the glittering hilt of his long sword in its golden scabbard, the thought of the battle ahead suddenly exhilarated him. Good, for it was essential that he display a regal carelessness to his troops. And after all, was he not a Moghul?

How much easier it is for an Emperor or any commander to be brave than for the common soldier, he reflected, as he strode past the dim figures of prostrate attendants, eunuchs and staff towards the entrance of the royal enclosure. The appearance of being brave, even bravado, regenerates courage within a commander in a kind of mutually supportive cycle, until fear becomes non-existent, or at least unrecognized. Not having to set an example, the common soldier had the more difficult role of generating his own courage. Men of whatever station, however, who do not know the meaning of fear must be stupid, ignorant or unimaginative. Fear makes one take care, produces real courage, though it can be the worst enemy on the battlefield, far worse, far more insidious than opponents with their swords and horses, guns and elephants. The truly brave are those who know fear but overcome it for whatever reason.

His war charger, a tall black Scindhi held by uniformed

grooms, awaited him at the head of his entourage, just outside the entrance to the enclosure. Since there were no elaborate formalities on the battlefield, his staff was already mounted. General Khan walked his great bay forward, saluted. 'The gods be with you today, most revered Emperor,' he called out in deep tones, so everyone present could hear. 'We await your royal command.'

'We are in the hands of Allah, but total victory is our order of the day,' the Emperor declared, trying to make his voice ring out through its muffler. 'Victory or death in the cause of righteousness.' He mounted the gold-plated steps, grasped the reins, placed one foot on the stirrup and swung onto his charger.

Saddles creaking, they clattered through the nearly deserted encampment. The squeak and rattle of cannon-wheels, the distant blare of trumpets and shouted commands became louder. They rode past great barrows of cannon balls that served the thrusting snouts of the great guns, evil-looking in the red-gold glow of flares that would be extinguished with daylight. The gun crews were dark, silent shapes huddled in cloaks. Then the grey masses of elephants appeared, their *howdahs* merely shadows containing blurred outlines of fighting men. The clicking of metal announced the musketeers, checking their weapons. They veered right and made for the crest of a high hill which had been selected as the royal command post. Here, the Emperor reined in his charger and surveyed the scene. With the east behind them, the lightening sky revealed the grey-green world of the great plain. 'The sun will be in their eyes,' he threw over his shoulder to the general.

'Your Majesty's choice of battleground was astute. As for the dispositions of our army, they are magnificent and assure us of victory.'

The general had not lied. Immediately to their left were the masses of elephants and musketeers, preceded by the pikemen in the re-entrants of the low foothills, their weapons bristling like a series of great hedgehogs spreading on both sides of the command post to merge into the near darkness. Ahead of the pikemen, Sheik Farid's cavalry was massed, pennants in rows, banners here and there fluttering in a light breeze that swept across the vast plain. The whinny of a horse floated up, echoed by another. Several of the mounts snorted violently to clear their nostrils, while others pawed the ground restlessly, the cavalrymen sitting erect, motionless in their saddles. One of the riders towered over the rest, the shoulders of his leather corselet almost at the level of the turbaned heads of his comrades. The Emperor nodded in his direction. 'There's Colonel Nasrin, Sheik Farid's deputy, the tallest man in the Empire,' he remarked. 'The cavalry certainly make a brave display.'

'They are ready to obey your royal command, Sire, victory or death,' the general responded. He rose in his saddle, peered across the plain at the blare of enemy trumpets rolling across it, followed by the roar of distant voices.

At that very moment, the sun cleared the trees behind them, throwing the shadows of the hills over Sheik Farid's cavalry, while the plain ahead lightened. Was it an omen? The Emperor shivered involuntarily.

'The issue approaches!' The general relaxed onto his saddle again. 'The enemy cavalry is charging.'

'Prepare to advance!' Sheik Farid's command was echoed down the ranks. The cavalrymen stiffened almost imperceptibly in their saddles, then relaxed.

'Advance!' . . . 'Advance!' . . . 'Advance!'

A moment's hesitation and the massed horses moved forward as one, saddles creaking, hooves thudding. The Emperor's inheritance, breeding, training and sense of majesty broke through the confines of self-interest. The blood began to race in his veins. He longed with all his heart to be at the head of those men, leading them to victory or death. His eyes misted with tears of frustration. 'We are confined to this command post, like a cripple to his crutches,' he cried.

The drumming of enemy hooves arose before the entire mass of Sheik Farid's cavalry had trotted into position on the plain. When the last rank of the Sheik's men were well clear of the foothills, fresh commands cracked out. 'Form Line!' . . . 'Form Line!'

Masses of riders in the rear veered right and left, to string across the plain. The Emperor could identify their individual figures now, the broad backs of hundreds of horses and riders all covered in leather armour.

'Prepare to charge!' The command went rolling across the ranks. 'Prepare to charge!' . . .

'Chaa . . . aa . . . arge!' Trumpets blared.

The two lead ranks of cavalrymen took off, thundering across the plain, pennants on lances a-fluttering. The approaching enemy became visible, a sweep of cavalry shaped like an arrowhead growing larger by the second. 'They are trying a different formation,' the Emperor observed excitedly to the general. 'Sheik Farid's men have levelled their lances, but how will they make contact with the enemy?'

The general clapped a hand to his thigh. 'What the arrowhead formation heralds, Sire, is the attack we expected on one or both of our flanks.' He turned to his aide, a hawk-faced Rajput with a black moustache. 'Send messengers to alert the flanks,' he commanded.

The aide barked an order. Two mounted men took off in either direction.

The opposing forces met at the centre of the plain. A brief pause and the arrowhead of enemy cavalry sheared through Sheik Farid's line like a gigantic scythe through mud. Horses reared, men fell. Hand-to-hand combat commenced. Shouts of rage reached the Emperor, screams of agony. The whinny and neighing of horses mingled with the clash of weapons. Almighty Allah give us victory, he prayed.

Though initially taken aback by the enemy tactic, Sheik Farid's flanks now started folding inwards, closing in on the arrowhead, but their charge had lost momentum. Soon the imperial cavalry was being rolled back remorselessly across the plain. Sheik Farid's trumpets sounded the order to retire, then blared forth again for the next ranks of cavalry to charge through their returning comrades.

'They should charge in inverse V formation, so . . .' the general began, then exclaimed aloud with satisfaction. 'Ah! They have done it. That will expose the enemy's lead elements to encirclement.'

Enemy trumpets sounding the retreat for its first ranks of cavalry rose above the din and clamour of battle. Men disengaged, wheeled their horses and thundered away, leaving bloody friend and foe, the scattered dead and wounded with here and there a fallen steed, a horse struggling to rise, a riderless mount galloping away.

The cavalry battle swayed back and forth across the plain for over an hour, every charge ending with groups of men in face-to-face combat. Neither side effected a penetration. Fallen men and horses could be seen on the plain each time it cleared. The Emperor could almost smell the stench of blood.

Postriders from the imperial army flanks rode in almost simultaneously. 'We are being heavily attacked!'

'The classic move!' General Khan observed coolly. 'Frontal assault followed by heavy attacks on both flanks. It is time for us to withdraw to the second command post, Sire.'

'Certainly.' The Emperor smiled as he turned his black war charger around.

The general signalled the six mounted aides who had been awaiting his command. They galloped away to deliver his orders.

With a final backward glance at the battle raging on the plain, the Emperor relaxed in his saddle, gently squeezed with his thighs. As he rode down the hill, Sheik Farid's trumpets began blaring out the general retreat for the imperial cavalry.

Her father had returned from his pre-dawn ride with Prince Jahan but, once again, he had not seen her. Each morning since she had learned of these rides, Mumtaz Mahal had hoped that her father would bring her back some message from the prince, some token of his love, but in vain. The new clock that adorned the wall of her tiny bedroom showed 7.30, so her father would already have left for his duties in the palace.

She flung herself on her divan bed and buried her face in a white silken cushion.

'He hates me,' she moaned. 'He probably does not even remember that I exist.'

Sati smiled placidly, without interrupting her knitting. 'Whom are you talking about?' she inquired, as if she did not know from having gone through this ritual every morning for over four months.

Mumtaz sat up with a start, faced Sati accusingly. 'You play this game with me every morning,' she complained.

'Who?'

She jabbed her forefinger repeatedly at Sati. 'You . . . you . . . you!'

'It is indecorous for anyone, most of all a lady, to point a finger.'

She glared at Sati, unbelievingly, but dropped her hand. 'Why is it indecorous to point?'

'Because it implies that the person you are talking to is not taking notice.'

'You certainly do not notice my misery!'

'Then you should point at your misery.'

She grabbed a cushion in exasperation, flung it at Sati. 'You are hateful, as always, and I point the finger of hate at you.'

'Better to hate than to feel you are hated.' Sati's voice took on a stern note. 'Now pick up this cushion and put it back on the divan. The attendants have tidied your room for the day and I shall not ask them to return.'

'Let the cushion remain there then, until they return tomorrow.'

'Nur Jehan will soon come to check on your room and will blame me because it is untidy.'

'And you will be to blame because you will not summon an attendant to pick up the cushion.'

'You threw it, so you shall pick it up.'

Mumtaz stamped her foot. 'No!'

'Now you are being disobedient and your aunt will fine me a day's wages for it.'

'Oh, oh, oh . . . you . . . you.' She knew she had lost the battle because she would never want her 'mother' to be punished. She loved Sati too much. 'You are a cunning old vixen beneath your sedate grey hair and placid smile.' She leapt off the divan, picked up the white cushion and threw it back. Knowing that this could bring about another battle that she would lose, she daintily arranged the cushion in its proper place, ran her palms down the waistline of her pale blue *kurtha* to smooth it and sat sedately on the edge of the divan with hands folded across her lap. 'There now! Am I in a fit state to receive your understanding?' she demanded. 'After all, you give it only if I am proper and decorous. If I were bleeding to death and dishevelled you would ask me to tidy up before you tended me.'

'I have given you understanding already.'

'How?'

Again that placid smile, which she should hate but loved. 'The cutting edge of your misery has already been blunted.'

Sati looked at her, her large, grey eyes moist with love.

'What would I have done without you?' The question escaped Mumtaz involuntarily.

'What would I have done without you, little house-sparrow?'

'Why do you always call me by the names of birds?'

'Not by the name of any bird. Never the eagle or the hawk, the owl or the bat. Just the little ones, like the sparrow and the bee-eater, with their nervous flights and those tiny beating hearts which a harsh breath could destroy.' Sati looked down at her knitting again to hide her emotion.

'Oh!' Deeply moved, Mumtaz leapt towards Sati. She sat on the white mohair rug and laid her head on Sati's comfortable lap. 'Your voice is as fair and soft as your skin, little mother.'

Sati set down her knitting with a sigh, began stroking her hair.

'I'm so happy,' Mumtaz declared spontaneously, then instantly conjectured what Sati must be thinking. 'But I'm still miserable that Prince Jahan ignores me, though I swept him off his feet the day he met me at the *Meena* Bazaar.'

'There is no way in which Prince Jahan could send you a message, least of all through your father. It would be . . .'

'Indecorous.' Mumtaz finished the sentence with a short laugh. 'I dream of a man who would set aside all rules, including those of decorum, for love of me and this is what I get.'

'You dream of Prince Jahan all the time, even though he has not set aside the rules of decorum for you. But he is just a boy, not yet a man, though I hear he is now fulfilling a man's responsibilities as head of the Council of Regents in a most manly way.'

'I love him *so* much. If he does not send me a message tomorrow, I shall kill myself.'

'So when a message comes thereafter it will be to a beautiful corpse?'

She raised her head with a jerk to gaze up at Sati. 'Do you really think it will come?'

Sati nodded, picked up her knitting. 'Yes, but not as soon as you desire. And when it does come, it will be from the Emperor through your father, a royal command, not the plea of a girl-struck young lover. Nothing will happen, however, until the Emperor returns from his campaign.'

'All very proper, decorous and unromantic.' Mumtaz grinned at Sati. 'When I become the Begum, I shall issue many decrees, one of which will be that lovers may freely converse with each other, become betrothed and get married.'

'Then your decree would have established what is decorous, so you would not have abolished decorum, merely changed its rules!'

'You are so wise, you have an answer for everything. When I become the Begum, you shall be my chief adviser.'

'And my first advice to you would be to retain all existing rules of decorum.'

Mumtaz burst out laughing.

'As with all children who pretend to be wilful, you have Allah's saving grace of being able to laugh at yourself,' Sati observed. 'May you always retain your sense of humour.'

Embarrassed though pleased, Mumtaz shot off in a different direction. 'I heard at breakfast this morning that the eunuchs believe Nur Jehan to be the power behind the imperial throne, because the Emperor is smitten by her. If he is, my aunt must have had a charm placed on him.'

'She has enough charm of her own without needing to place one.'

'Then it means that the Emperor has met her, seen her.' A thrill of triumph at her own astuteness shot through Mumtaz. 'That's right! He must have met her when he visited our house. Perhaps they slept together!' She pondered a while. 'In any case, I believe that Khubu Khan has been sent as governor of Bengal at her instigation, to kill her husband Sher Afgan.'

'Shh . . . child! You must not say such things. Your aunt might hear.'

'If she does, and she is not guilty, she will merely be pleased to think that I ascribe so much power and influence to her. If she is guilty, she will not dare punish me, because she will be afraid that her guilt would be exposed.'

Sati stopped her knitting, looked down in wonder at her ward. It gave Mumtaz a warm feeling. 'You are wiser than I ever believed,' Sati declared.

You do not know the half of it, beloved 'mother', Mumtaz thought. Nor do you know of my dreams for the future, how I shall love, cherish and look after my beloved Prince Jahan, especially after he becomes Emperor, dreams which I can only share with Allah. Aloud she said, 'I believe that Nur Jehan is indeed the power behind the throne today. I do not know when or how, but some day she and I will clash for this position. Until then, I shall be obedient to her, because she alone can get me to where that conflict will surface, but far down in the depths of my mind it has already commenced.'

The risen sun was bathing the foothills and valleys. Silver light and dark shadows glanced off cannon snouts and burnished *howdah* roofs, gleamed on matchlock rifles, swords and spears, by the time Emperor Jehangir reached his second command post on the crest of a taller hill. The

173

smell of blood mingled with odours of gun oil and the scent of drying grass to penetrate the sandalwood paste scent he was wearing. The clash and clamour of battle, the screams of men, the shrill neighing of horses reached for the pale blue heavens from the entrance to the plain, through which the enemy cavalry was pouring in hot pursuit of Sheik Farid's retreating horsemen.

As planned, the Sheik's riders wheeled in both directions and sped between the spreading foothills to support the imperial flanks. Suddenly, the path of the enemy was cleared as if by magic, but its irregular line of riders in brown leather armour, lances couched and levelled, came to a screeching halt before the barrier of the imperial elephants. Flashes along the line of *howdahs* followed by ear-splitting rattles announced musket fire from the royal troops. Shouts of agony arose, enemy riders fell, horses reared, others were swivelled around. The unearthly shrilling of angered elephants trumpeting rent the air.

'We have trapped them as planned, Sire!' General Bahadur Khan exclaimed gleefully, as the great grey elephant mass surged forward, from walk to trot, trot to canter. With the second shattering musket volley from the *howdahs* the enemy cavalry line broke. The men had realized that they had crashed through the imperial pikemen only to walk into a trap. They wheeled around to flee, but dozens were laid low by the hail of musket fire from the *howdahs*.

The enemy horses finally galloped away. The royal elephants thundered in pursuit, the earth shaking beneath their massive tread.

'Look, Sire!' General Khan shouted in alarm, pointing across the battle scene. Hundreds of fire-balls, trailing smoke, were arcing towards the elephants.

'They knew we would use elephants,' the Emperor ground out. 'That accursed son of ours has studied history too. This is what our ancestors did against the Rajputs. We can only hope.'

The fire-balls containing fuel to spread on the *howdahs* and the leather armour of the elephants, dropped on the charging herd. Shrill trumpets told of giant beasts in agony; some of them were soon enveloped in flames.

Miraculously, the *mahouts* managed to hold the elephants on course. Their charge was resumed. The acrid smell of burning leather smote the Emperor's nostrils, but he began breathing more easily.

'O gods of my fathers, they are well prepared,' the general smacked an impotent thigh.

The Emperor suddenly knew an immense calm. This is my legacy from my ancestors, he thought, to be steady in a crisis. 'The battle is not lost, General,' he began. 'Remember . . .' He broke off, staring at the scene beneath him.

A second round of fire-balls had splattered the elephant throng. Fresh screams arose from the beasts, red fire streaking across grey backs, down leather and over bronze *howdah* tops. *Mahouts* leapt from elephant backs, musketeers from the *howdahs*. Beast crashed against stampeding beast, trumpeting in fear, trying to escape the deadly fire.

Enemy infantry appeared in solid lines, increased their pace, roaring defiance. The elephants broke and fled.

O Allah, lead the elephants' flight in the right direction, the Emperor silently prayed. And Allah answered his prayer. The elephants careered madly through to the rear of the imperial dispositions. The shrieks of the wounded combined with pathetic gibbering left the Emperor unmoved, so intent was he on the unfolding of his battle plan. Clearing the first valleys, the enemy infantry advanced in solid lines, spears raised. They soon spread into the folds and hollows between the hills.

'Now! Now!' the Emperor muttered under his breath.

'Ah!' General Khan exclaimed in satisfaction.

Tiny sparks of tinder, great flashes along the lines, bursts of smoke, were followed by the deafening roar of the great guns, jerking backwards in recoil, drowning the whistling of cannon balls overhead. The stench of burnt cordite swiftly penetrated the air.

The enemy lines of infantry seemed to fold inwards. Now it was from their ranks that the cacophony of groans, screams and shrieks arose. Cannoneers poured water on hot barrels, started reloading immediately.

More blinding flashes, smoke and a second thunderous roar announced the firing of the second line of cannon. The enemy ranks wilted and broke. Screaming and roaring, the imperial infantry surged forward into the folds and hollows in the planned counterattack.

'It is time we joined the action!' the Emperor shouted above the din. He dug his heels into his black charger's flanks.

'Pray the gods that General Husein has arrived,' the general grated and set his bay down the slope.

And General Husein had indeed arrived. The Emperor had flung two contingents of cavalry far beyond the flanks of the enemy to take them in the rear. Their flank attacks repulsed, their own cavalry caught in the act of regrouping on the plain, their infantry hemmed in between the charging imperial infantry and newly arrived cavalry in the rear, Prince Husrau's forces, totally disorganized, with no command control, fought in groups, bolted away or surrendered.

Shortly before noon, Prince Husrau fled the field, accompanied by a small group of followers. The battle was over. The Emperor Jehangir's battle plan had worked and he was the victor.

Chapter 10

Having proceeded to Lahore after his victory on the Bharowal plain, the Emperor Jehangir was holding full *durbar* this August morning from the royal pavilion which had been built by the Emperor Akbar on the rampart wall of the principal tower of the palace. This was the occasion for rewarding all those who had been loyal and for punishing transgressors. Since his birthday was only two days away, the *durbar* celebrated both events and the Emperor was in an excellent mood.

He loved pomp and pageantry, provided he was its centrepiece, especially on a clear, bright morning such as this, with pale blue skies and a gentle breeze to fan his brow. The stimulation of victory had banished his head cold and his mind was sharp because he had deliberately modulated his drinking the previous night the more to be able to enjoy this *durbar*. Most importantly, he had been in a constant state of euphoria since despatching the imperial relay conveying his royal mandate to Governor Khubu Khan in Bengal on the very afternoon of his victory over Prince Husrau. Dressed in a long cloth-of-gold tunic, littered with jewels – red rubies and green emeralds from Burma, purple amethysts and blue sapphires from Ceylon, sparkling diamonds from the Empire, his triple necklaces of great lustrous pearls also from Ceylon – he glittered in more splendour than the sun as he sat cross-legged, wearing the imperial crown, on the golden throne of the Moghuls. The perfume of the ambergris in the legs and body of the throne reached out to all who stood nearby or approached the balcony window within the royal pavilion.

Since he had issued orders that the *durbar* was to be conducted with the utmost panoply, in order to impress all his people, especially in the dissident areas near Lahore but even in distant Kabul when news of the celebrations was received there by imperial relay, the rampart walls were a riot of colour and sound. The princes and nobles standing on either side of the raised royal enclosure were all dressed in their most resplendent attire. In high turbans crowned with flashing gems, tunics of gold, green, blue, scarlet and white satin blazing with jewelled necklaces, they were all his subjects, gathered to offer him homage: tall bearded hawk-visaged Pathans and Punjabis, broad-chested Baluchis, squat Gurkhas with their Mongol features, even a sprinkling of great-nosed Rajputs. The soft music and drumming that always accompanied the imperial presence was occasionally rent by a blare of trumpets announcing each munificent award and the strident cheers that sprouted from the incessant murmur of the vast crowds gathered below. The Emperor took in the spreading mass below him. Men, women and children, all gaily dressed, stood in orderly ranks, dark, fair, brown, even yellow, cleanshaven, bearded, brightly clothed, save for the priests in white robes; Muslims in red fez, Hindus in white caps and various Indian tribes wearing their distinctive turbans. Vendors selling sweetmeats and drinks in trays slung from their necks walked in front of the crowd, shouting their wares. The imperial cavalry, swords drawn, motionless on their tall steeds, were evenly spaced in front. These too were his subjects, each one of them an individual, capable of joy and sorrow, pain and laughter, loyalty or betrayal.

Ah, betrayal! He had already punished dozens of leaders of the revolt the two previous mornings by having them trampled to death by the elephants who would normally have been fighting each other on that *maidan*. He loved the sport of elephant fighting, but had enjoyed the gruesome executions even more. He had imposed a fine of two hundred thousand rupees on the renegade Hindu guru Arjun who had dared to bless the rebel enterprise. He half-hoped the son-of-a-whore would not pay.

The slow blare of trumpets announcing the arrival of the grand betrayers interrupted his reflection. A hush fell on the ramparts, extended downwards to the teeming crowds below. The last notes of the trumpets echoed sadly, vanished into thin, silver-gold air. In the deep silence, the harsh croak of a raven was like a warning. A cold, implacable purpose gripped the Emperor as he heard the first clank of chains approaching along the rampart.

Prince Husrau came up, manacled hands in front of him, dragging chained feet over the sandstone of the rampart walls. Beg Badakh was on his right side, Abdul Rahman at his left, both similarly chained. They were flanked by six guards with drawn swords. The Emperor searched his own heart for an ounce of pity for his first-born child.

Found none.

This was no son of his, but an accursed traitor to lineage, tradition and person who had dared to contest his claim to the crown. He recalled the humiliating experience of the elephant battle to determine a succession that was rightly his, the prince's escape from the palace, the gathering together of his enemies, the bold seizure of the royal treasure train and the final insulting messsage six days earlier rejecting a truce. He glanced incuriously at the prince's dark, Rajput features, now so drawn that they were haggard, the hooked nose jutting outwards like a great beak. This was a predator bird that had to be destroyed.

But first the spirit. That was most important. He must break the supposedly tender, sensitive spirit of this upstart prince.

His feelings must have shown even in the impassive countenance he was presenting to the world and the wretched prisoners, who now stood before him. Trembling before the imperial presence, Prince Husrau began to weep. He placed his palms together and started to raise his hands in worship, bending at the knees.

'No!' the Emperor roared. 'We will not accept prostration from those we shall never forgive.'

Two of the guards standing behind Prince Husrau grabbed him by the arms, jerked him erect again. He stood there dumb, not daring to speak until he had royal permission, save through the tears that were rolling down his sallow cheeks, trickling on to his black moustache and dribbling on to his long chin.

The Emperor deliberately allowed moments of grim silence to pass. 'You, Husrau, are a prince by birth and rank, not by breed or showing,' he finally declared in deep, solemn tones. 'You not only betrayed your father, you betrayed your Emperor, our Moghul tradition and an entire people. If you had not finally betrayed your traitorous followers, we might have found some spasm of regard for you in our royal heart, and would at least have accepted your prostration. Can your constant weeping of the past four days atone for the deaths of thousands, the wounds of thousands more, the agony of the maimed, the anguish of women and children, families and friends, all bereft? No! We now owe a duty to our subjects to cause them to beware of the great betrayers such as you who walk only in the traditions of Shaitan, whose every prostration may herald betrayal. We would have sentenced you to death this day, for treason against the Empire and your Emperor, but that would be too easy a punishment for you and not lesson enough for those who might be tempted to follow in your despicable footsteps.'

The Emperor paused dramatically. While Prince Husrau stood transfixed, Badakh eased his position, the clank of his manacles disturbing the hush on the rampart walls.

'We sentence you to imprisonment in chains within the palace tower for the rest of your natural life, or until pardoned by us.' He drank in the general reaction that followed his words, revelling in the pitiful reaction of his son, then slowly announced the further punishments he had formulated from his bitter, vengeful contemplation of the past few days. He was rewarded by the stunned silence that followed, broken only by an involuntary sob from the prince.

This he would watch, if only to derive the greatest satisfaction from the punishments he had decreed. His one regret was that he could not be close enough to Prince Husrau to observe his reactions in detail. The holes for the posts, three hundred and fifty on either side, had been dug the previous day along the length of the *maidan* below, creating an avenue about eight hundred yards long. Attendants dressed in red and white imperial uniforms had brought in the large stakes immediately after he dismissed Prince Husrau from his royal presence, placed them in the sockets, the sharp pointed ends upwards, and tamped them firmly down with small rocks, pebbles and soil. The seven hundred chained and manacled prisoners had been forced to shuffle into the avenue and now stood in line each before one of the stakes. The fourteen hundred chosen executioners, black hoods over their faces, devils' eyes peering through hollow slits, had taken their places on either side of each prisoner. The throng of princes and nobles on the ramparts, the guards and attendants lining them, the packed crowd and the impassive cavalrymen watched in awed silence, broken now by an occasional sob or cry for mercy from one or other of the prisoners. The Emperor felt utterly ruthless, completely devoid of the pity he would normally extend to a wounded bird or an injured child. 'Execution by impalement is one of the most torturous forms of punishment,' he declared in solemn tones to those

181

around him. 'It is being meted out to the rank and file of Prince Husrau's supporters. They flocked to make his rebellion come *quickly* alive, so we have made them congregate for a *slow* death. You all know that the most excruciating agony, lingering over many hours, awaits these despicable sons of Shaitan before the hand of death finally relieves them. But how can this match the unending torture of those they betrayed?' His entire being quivered with the ferocity of his purpose. 'Let what is about to take place be a warning to those of like mind forever. Let the scribes who have taken down our words inscribe and reinscribe them a thousand times so they can be despatched to the outermost regions of our vast Empire as our covenant against treason.'

The Emperor signalled with upraised hand. Trumpets crashed into the stillness, conveying the order of execution. The hooded men stepped forward, grasped each of the prisoners by head and heels, reversed them so they faced downwards, swung them from side to side, lifted them high, moved on either side of each stake. A moment's pause for timing, then down came the bodies viciously, almost as one, with a great thwack! Shrieks of agony rent the air as seven hundred stomachs were pierced by the pointed stakes. Scream upon scream followed, slobbering cries, deathly groans and gibbering anguish. A slow wail rippled through the assembled crowd.

'We are giving our people a spectacle, a circus they shall never forget!' the Emperor declared to no one in particular. 'Bread and circuses, as the old Roman Emperors gave their people.'

The thousands of spectators, as if needing to find some release from the shock of the impalements, erupted into roars of rage against the wretched men screeching from the stakes. Someone threw a small rock. Others followed. The cavalrymen came to life, turned mounts around to subdue the crowd. The stone-throwing subsided, the shouts and imprecations babbled on. A hundred trumpets slashed at the ugly cacophony of human sound, blaring forth the call of the victor. The tumult slowly subsided, save for the mortal cries of the dying.

At the far end of the *maidan* two strange objects appeared, led by royal muleteers in the imperial livery of purple and gold, brilliant against the mere red and white uniforms of the guards.

'The man with the fresh skin of an ox sewn tightly around him is Beg Badakh,' the Emperor explained to those immediately around him, as if they did not already know. 'The skin of the ass was reserved for Abdul Rahman. They are both seated on asses, where they belong, each facing the tail, the right direction for the accursed. They are the advance guard.'

As the gruesome little group entered the avenue of screeching, whimpering, groaning men, trumpets rent the air again, this time sounding the fanfare for the imperial approach. A gaily caparisoned elephant followed the group, walking with slow majestic tread. The *mahout* on its back, trident in hand, was also dressed in the imperial purple and gold livery. The *howdah* slow-teetering from side to side was golden. Even at that distance, the figure seated on the golden throne within the *howdah* could be seen to wear a crown.

'Prince Husrau desired the royal elephant, our throne and the imperial crown,' the Emperor announced blandly. 'He now has them all, as he rides in state behind his advance guard, reviewing his impaled troops. But the throne is made of thin board, the crown of paper, both painted with gold. As he parades down the avenue of the damned, listening to the groans and supplications of his followers, he will witness the benefits he has conferred on his loyal, misbegotten subjects, for it is he and he alone who caused them to be impaled on those stakes.'

* * *

Since he was acting as head of the Council of Regency, Prince Jahan had been given leave by the Emperor to use the European room of the imperial palace for official purposes as freely as he desired. His father probably knew how much he loved this room, so he appreciated the gesture even more for its thoughtfulness and used the privilege to the full. He felt his grandfather's presence in the room.

A vast structure such as a palace, with all its guards, attendants, courtiers and bustling people, can never be a home any more than an entire city can, he reflected now as he listened to Asaf Khan in this familiar room. So the rulers, the princes and other inhabitants of the palace must look to a single chamber, or even a bed, as the private possession that is home.

'Since you spent this entire weekend on the royal barge checking on tax gatherers along the Jumna River, you would only have received news of the Emperor's victory over Prince Husrau's army on your return to the palace this morning,' Asaf Khan stated. 'I requested this audience so that I can brief you thoroughly with all the facts available to me before the meeting of the Council of Regency at 10 A.M.' He smiled. 'Before I proceed, may I be permitted to say that I have missed our morning horseback rides on the *maidan*?'

A wave of affection for the dashing Prime Minister swept through Prince Jahan. 'And I too, with all my heart.' Afraid that he had demonstrated too much, he added, somewhat lamely, 'But we must all put duty before pleasure, must we not? And our hearts are first for the Empire.'

'Well said, Prince.' Asaf Khan's white smile flashed beneath the trim reddish-brown moustache.

This is a sensitive man, Prince Jahan thought and that quality gives him quick perception and understanding. 'Please proceed with your information, Prime Minister.'

Prince Jahan listened with total concentration as Asaf

Khan recounted all he knew about the battle. 'So my brother is the prisoner of my father,' he murmured, when Asaf Khan had ended. 'It's a sad day for our family, but the really sad day was when Prince Husrau commenced his revolt.' He stared into space, considering his brother's actions a moment, remembering the elephant battle and his momentary temptation to help his brother, the weaker candidate, so he could fulfil his own ambitions. 'Perhaps the saddest day of all was when Prince Husrau first decided that he should compete for the imperial throne.'

'You are so wise, not just for your years, Prince. I hope I shall be able to serve you some day in your capacity as Emperor.'

The words, from the man with whose daughter he had fallen completely in love, escaping without seeming thought, were obviously sincere and they moved Prince Jahan. 'That would be my privilege and my honour,' he asserted. I shall make it happen, he decided.

As always, Asaf Khan returned swiftly to the point. 'Apparently interrogation of prisoners revealed to the Emperor that there were other conspirators. In consequence of this intelligence, the Emperor issued a *firman* immediately to Governor Khubu Khan, removing Raja Man from the overlordship of Bengal and appointing Khubu Khan as Raja in his place. This *firman* is already on its way to Bengal by the post-haste relay established by your royal grandfather. The sentences imposed by your father on the ringleaders of the revolt, trampling to death by elephants, will have been executed during the last two mornings. Today,' he glanced at the gilt French clock ticking on the wall, 'at this very moment, the punishments decreed for the rank and file rebels and for Beg Badakh and Abdul Rahman are being carried out, with Prince Husrau to witness them.'

Was there a sadness within Asaf Khan at revealing these

dire sentences? Well, a Prime Minister could afford such a luxury. Prince Jahan himself felt neither pity nor compassion. His grandfather had not bred any such within him for rebels, malefactors and traitors. The responsibility for maintaining law and order for the benefit of millions of people had to transcend all personal feelings. Otherwise, one was not fit to rule. He decided to change the subject. 'What of the guru Arjun?' he inquired. 'Will he be punished for blessing this unholy rebellion?'

A shadow crossed Asaf Khan's face. 'I am afraid so, my lord prince. The Emperor has decreed that he pay a fine of two hundred thousand rupees.'

'But Arjun is a holy ascetic, he does not have any money of his own.' Prince Jahan could not see this as a wise move. In times of rebellion, one should not create more enemies than needed, was the policy his grandfather had instilled into him.

'Nor he does. Perhaps the faithful will raise the funds for him.'

'He is a proud man. He will refuse the money.'

'Then the Emperor, having taken the first step to punish the guru, will have no alternative but to have him executed.'

The finality in Asaf Khan's tone sent a chill through Prince Jahan. Here was a man who could combine sagacity with decisiveness, compassion with a ruthless adherence to the dictates of the system. 'Do you have any other news of significance, Prime Minister?' he inquired, deliberately changing the subject, because he recognized that neither of them would or should criticize the Emperor's decisions.

'Only as an adjunct to what I have already told you, Prince. The *firman* issued to Khubu Khan – I suppose we should title him Raja from now on – also commands him to summon my brother-in-law, Sher Afgan, to the Bengal palace for questioning as to any complicity he may have had in Prince Husrau's plot.'

186

Intuition told Prince Jahan that Sher Afgan's days were numbered. Why? Because he had refused to side with the Emperor, when he was but a prince and the heir apparent, in his rebellion against his own father, the Emperor Akbar? No, Sher Afgan had subsequently remained in the then rebel's employment. Why that clemency? Why his virtual exile to Bengal, though admittedly assuring him of much higher income? Why the appointments of Ghiyas Beg and this handsome, dashing capable genius seated opposite?

At that moment, Prince Jahan finally came to the conclusion that there was some connection between the Emperor and Sher Afgan's wife, Nur Jehan. His mind reached back to recall something his grandfather had mentioned when he was a child . . . something . . . something . . . he could not track it down.

Then the cold, stark nature of the punishment inflicted by his father on Prince Husrau struck Prince Jahan with blinding force. It was obvious that his father was fearful of Prince Husrau. Why? A voice whispered in his brain: *because he is afraid that what he did to his own father will befall him.* The Moghul legacy?

At that moment, Prince Jahan knew with certainty that his father had been responsible for the premature death of his grandfather, the man he had loved beyond measure. At that moment, he hated his father with an infinite, implacable passion. At that moment, his Moghul blood demanded vengeance for the deed. He suddenly saw his grandfather, the handsome features drawn, walking into the room. There was pleading in the slanty eyes. *Will you not avenge me,* baba? Some day, Grandfather, but not yet. I must first get to where I can extract that vengeance. Grant me help from heaven.

The vision passed. He found himself staring through the morning light at Asaf Khan, who seemed puzzled by his unusual preoccupation. This was the father of Mumtaz

Mahal. When the Emperor returned, he would beg permission to become betrothed. Betrothed! That was it. He remembered now what his grandfather had mentioned in passing all those years ago, and he knew the course he would follow.

Chapter 11

The last time Raja Man had dined with Prince Chara and his father in the small private dining room of the Chitor palace, Prince Husrau and Prince Aziz Koka had been present and hopes had run high. Now, eight months later, a political gestation period had produced a crippled baby. Prince Chara had revised his initial conviction that his plan for a timed revolt had been demolished by Prince Husrau's impetuosity and had become convinced, when he received news of the strength of the rebel forces, that Prince Husrau had deliberately proceeded on his own in the hope of seizing the throne with the support of the Muslim races and the northern Hindus alone, excluding the Rajputs who might have become too powerful in consequence. In the realms of empire and diplomacy, anything was possible, especially deceit.

The attendants and liveried footmen had just departed and the three of them were partaking of *pan*, green betel leaves, brown areca nuts, sweet anise and other spices intended to freshen the breath. Raja Man had arrived unexpectedly from Bengal late that evening. As the gracious host, Rana Amar had refrained from asking their visitor's news.

'That was, as usual, a sumptuous meal, in the best Rajput tradition,' Raja Man stated, pushing back his chair and stretching out his legs. The delightful odours of roast lamb, garlic and cardamom, of spiced vegetables and baked breads clinging to the cool air attested to the truth of his words.

'Ah Raja, your journey from Bengal has obviously been hurried, following what must have been a somewhat precipitate departure,' Rana Amar responded. 'It is perhaps the poor boards offered by inns along the route that make our fare acceptable to your refined palate.'

What unctuous humility, Prince Chara thought. We have just had a wonderful meal and you know it. When I become Rana of Mewar and then the Emperor, I shall not indulge in such hypocrisy.

'On the contrary, many of the inns along the way offer dishes of the countryside which are delicious,' Raja Man countered. He cast penetrating glances at his host and Prince Chara. 'You have hospitably received me and my retinue as your guests. I thank you. Now that we are finally alone, let me give you my news.' He paused. 'Where to begin?'

'At the very beginning,' Rana Amar prompted with what Prince Chara considered remarkable originality.

Raja Man cleared his throat. 'As you know, when I was last here, I had been kicked upstairs by the Emperor as the overlord of distant Bengal. Though this is a vaster territory than my native Jaipur, of which I was ruler by birth, it was hardly a promotion. That man, Sher Afgan, was despatched along with me as *faudjar* of Burdwan, yet another questionable promotion. I wondered about my appointment and came to the conclusion that the Emperor must have been aware that I was making common cause with Prince Husrau against him.' He grew silent, stared into space.

'A not illogical deduction,' Prince Chara threw into the

189

pause. 'It must have been the imperial astrologers that warned him!'

His father snorted disapproval at the frivolous interruption. The Rana still had not quite abandoned the idea that his children should be seen, if their appearance could be a credit to him, but not heard.

Raja Man smiled, a little sadly Prince Chara thought without sympathy. 'The Ghiyas Beg family now heads the team of imperial astrologers,' he declared. 'Anyhow, I had just begun to settle down in my new palace when I received news of Prince Husrau's confinement to his residence in Agra and then of his escape, obviously to commence the revolt, contrary to our plan. On the heels of this news, Khubu Khan arrived with an imperial mandate, appointing him governor under my overlordship. It seemed an imperial insult, which I was not disposed to stomach, but I felt it would be prudent to await further developments before responding, particularly since I had no news as to how Prince Husrau's plans fitted in with those we had formulated while I was here. The wisdom of my restraint was demonstrated when I received news of the Emperor's victory over Prince Husrau in battle on the Bharowal plain, included in another imperial *firman* sent by the post-haste messenger service stripping me of my position and power and appointing Khubu Khan as Raja of Bengal.'

'What?' Never one to hold back an explosive reaction, Prince Chara's father pushed back his chair, thumped a fist so hard on the table it rattled the salvers, spilling some of the areca nut. 'How dare he treat us hereditary Rajas and Ranas as if we were imperial lackeys!' he ground out.

'He dares anything, because his power and resources make us his lackeys,' Raja Man retorted bitterly. 'The man is a megalomaniac.'

'That is amply demonstrated by the punishments he meted out to his son and the chief rebels.' His father's voice was calm, but Prince Chara rather suspected that there was more fury to come.

'I have only heard gossip along the last stage of my journey,' Raja Man said. 'What did our maniac Emperor do?'

Listening to his father give details of what had taken place in Lahore, Prince Chara could not help a sneaking admiration for the Emperor's punishments. It was the sort of thing he would have liked to administer in similar circumstances. Any ruler had to be ruthless. A supreme ruler, answerable to no overlord, had to be supremely ruthless. The Emperor's victory and subsequent actions had demonstrated that he was not just a large bag of cotton, soaking up alcohol and opium, but a ruler with regal qualities, not only inherited but in him by disposition. He would have to be tested by other means than direct confrontation in a single battle. This made it doubly unfortunate that his own original plan for the revolt had not seen the light of day. Prince Chara thrust this last thought aside; he had trained himself not to succumb to the 'if only' syndrome. That was the prerogative of lesser, weaker men. His policy was to face existing facts and turn them to his advantage.

'Even more shocking was what then happened in my palace, which Khubu Khan immediately took over,' Raja Man quietly resumed. 'His first act was to send an escort to invite Sher Afgan to the palace to explain his connection with Prince Husrau's revolt.'

'Escort . . . invitation?' Rana Amar lifted an eyebrow at the paradox. 'Sher Afgan was to participate in our overall plan, but the Emperor had no knowledge of that and Sher Afgan certainly played no part in Prince Husrau's idiotic revolt.'

Their guest smiled grimly, with his mouth, not with his eyes. 'That's exactly what I feel. To cut a long story short,

Sher Afgan arrived in the palace that morning. Khubu Khan met and questioned him in the courtyard, as if he were some dog unworthy of entry.' He nodded slowly at the sudden alertness of his hosts. 'In fact, Khubu Khan treated him so insultingly that, as was to be expected, the giant flew into a rage. He drew his sword and ran the new Raja through.'

'Wonderful!' Prince Chara's father exclaimed excitedly. Stupid, Prince Chara reflected, for the giant fell into the trap. 'What happened then?'

'The escort fell on Sher Afgan. I wish I had been there to witness the fight. I was told that Sher Afgan went berserk. You know his reputation as a fighting man. He killed nineteen of the guards before he was felled.' He grew silent for a moment, to steady his voice. 'They then butchered him. They were not content to despatch him with a single blow, which they could quite easily have done. On orders from the wounded Khubu Khan, the gods rot his *atman*, who lay on the courtyard floor refusing help and watching the scene, the guards hacked Sher Afgan to death in slow degrees. But they did not get one sound out of him in the long minutes of his torture other than an occasional involuntary gasp at a blow. I do not know how he lived, any more than I comprehend the why or wherefore of his execution, but he challenged death in order to establish his dignity and died honourably, a hero.'

He certainly did, Prince Chara reflected. And yet it would have been better if he had lived to establish his dignity. Now I have no one to use for any personal attempts against Prince Jahan's charmed life. Should I not therefore abandon that part of my programme for the present? Prince Jahan's turn will come, but I had best deal with the Emperor first, a man who has demonstrated a formidable capability, acting with speed, decisiveness, great military skill and remarkable astuteness. Why did he want Sher

Afgan killed? And why in such a brutal manner? It was almost an act of vengeance. In a flash, the motive became obvious. The Emperor was sending a message to someone and from what Sher Afgan had hinted at during their last meeting, it must be to Nur Jehan.

'What happened to Khubu Khan?' Rana Amar bridged the shocked silence that had filled the room.

'He died shortly afterwards.'

'Good. At least the giant Sher . . .' He was interrupted by an urgent knocking on the door. He cocked an impatient eyebrow in its direction. 'Enter!' he called.

The chief attendant, a tall grey-haired Rajput dressed in the palace uniform, made obeisance. 'I pray thee forgive the interruption, my lord Rana, but a visitor from the Agra palace requests immediate audience with you.'

'At this hour? Who is it?'

'Prince Aziz Koka, my lord.'

Prince Chara could not but admire his father's calm, though all three of them were stunned. The hell's broth was brewing.

'Bid the prince enter,' Rana Amar commanded.

It was a somewhat dusty Aziz Koka who entered the room and bowed. All three stood up to greet the prince. Now it only required Prince Husrau to appear for the cast of characters from their previous meeting to be complete. What dire event could have brought this skeletal figure, neatly dressed in spite of his long journey, so precipitately into the palace?

'You have obviously travelled in considerable haste,' Rana Amar said when they were all seated around the table. His voice took on a grim note. 'If it means that you have escaped the Emperor's wrath, please be assured that you and your retinue are safe in our palace, as our honoured guests.' He paused. 'Would you like some refreshment before you retire to your usual rooms?'

'I thank you for your welcome and your assurances.' Prince Aziz Koka's voice seemed more thin and dry than ever from his ride and his obvious agitation. 'I am in honour bound, however, to tell you my situation first.' He glanced at Raja Man. 'I am not surprised to find you here, Raja. I suppose you made our hosts aware of the news from Bengal?'

'In the fullest detail.'

'Good. Let me then tell you my side of the story. Immediately he heard of the death of Sher Afgan in the imperial palace, the Emperor called at the residence of the widow, Nur Jehan, in Diwan Ghiyas Beg's mansion, and conveyed news of it to her.'

'Rather odd, don't you think?' Rana Amar interjected with a characteristic lift of one eyebrow.

'What followed was even more odd. The Emperor Jehangir commanded that the widow be henceforth under his protection.'

'More to be feared than a wicked husband,' Prince Chara interjected.

'Then hear this. The Lord Protector of Widows also appointed Nur Jehan chief lady-in-waiting to the late Emperor Akbar's widow, Salima Begum, and arranged for her to move to the *harem* of his palace.'

'I do not believe it!' Rana Amar exclaimed.

'On the contrary, this incident puts everything into proper perspective,' Prince Chara intervened smoothly. 'The Emperor is obviously infatuated with Nur Jehan, has been for some time. He desires her so he had her husband killed, ostensibly on the grounds that the man was guilty of plotting with Prince Husrau. Now we await the next thrilling episode, an announcement, after a respectable period, that the Emperor has taken the widow for a wife or concubine. I doubt that it would be the latter, because the woman happens to be the daughter of the Emperor's Diwan and sister of his Prime Minister. It is now clear that even those two appointments were caused by the Emperor's infatuation. The despatch of Sher Afgan to Bengal, the appointment of Khubu Khan as governor and subsequently as Raja were also aimed towards this one rather . . . ah! . . . interesting goal. Interesting because any mad infatuation is a weakness that can be exploited. If nothing else, get a man into a bedchamber with a new wife for whom he thirsts and he will in turn be drained so dry that his enemies can conquer him.' He paused, chin lifted confidently at the others.

'Remarkable!' Aziz Koka exclaimed.

Noting his audience's appreciation of his quick perception, Prince Chara decided to show off. 'Which is the true story of what happened to Samson in the Christian Bible. It was not in his hair that his strength lay, but in his mind and body, especially his scrotum. When he drained away that strength in the bedchamber with Delilah, he became so weak through sexual and alcoholic excess that his enemies were able to overpower him. Cutting off his hair was merely a symbol of shame which the enemies inflicted on him. When he was blinded, he must have cursed the real blindness that preceded it! By the time his hair grew back, he had long recovered his famous physical strength and was able to destroy the palace building by pulling down its central column.' He stretched long legs comfortably under the table. 'We can certainly anticipate a stage at which the Emperor Jehangir will succumb to his demonstrated weaknesses.' He glanced at Aziz Koka, grinned agreeably. 'Pray forgive my interruption, Prince, and proceed with your story.'

'There is not much else to say except for the outcome. When I advised the Emperor of the unwisdom and the immorality of these actions, which are contrary to the tenets of Islam, he flew into a rage, accused me of plotting against him and summarily dismissed me from his presence. Warned by Asaf Khan, an honourable man unconnected with all this deviousness, that the Emperor was planning to have me arrested as soon as possible, I left behind the excuse of a visit to ancestral lands and came to the one place where I knew I would be safe from the imperial madman's actions.'

'And indeed you are safe here,' Rana Amar assured him. 'The Rajput regions of Mewar and the Deccan do not fear Moghul Emperors, though we acknowledge their suzerainty.' He drummed on the table with his fingers. 'How about some refreshment now?'

'Some fruit and sarsaparilla juice if I may?'

'Certainly.' Rana Amar reached out and pulled a long sash attached to a pulley on the ceiling.

The chief attendant appeared, made obeisance.

'Fruit and *nannar* juice for Prince Aziz Koka,' the Rana directed. 'Also have his usual rooms aired and prepared for an indefinite stay. His retinue has been suitably fed and lodged?'

'Yes, lord.'

Prince Chara waited until the door had closed behind the uniformed figure. 'I venture to suggest that the time has come for us to commence planning our own rebellion against the Emperor,' he stated pleasantly. 'Only this time, we must do it alone, as our people once did when they went to war against the Emperor Akbar almost forty years ago, in the year 1567.'

'Your timing will be perfect,' Aziz Koka declared emphatically. 'You may recall that the Emperor imposed a fine of two hundred thousand rupees on the holy priest of the Hindus, guru Arjun, for blessing Prince Husrau's cause. I heard just before I fled the palace that the venerable guru has refused to pay the fine and the Emperor has ordered his execution.'

A chill swept the room. Prince Chara recognized that he alone was not appalled by the news, but elated.

'The first Arjun is mentioned in our great epic the *Maha Bharata*.' Rana Amar's voice was sad and reflective for once. 'He was a prince, the younger brother of King Yudhi. In that epic work, our sacred Testament, the *Bhagavad Gita*, a sermon is given by god Krishna to Prince Arjun, who has quailed at killing his relatives in a war to support his older brother. Prince Arjun says:

> ". . . Alas, what victory
> Can bring delight, O Krishna, what rich spoils
> Could profit, what rule recompense, what span
> Of life itself seem sweet, bought with such blood?"

'The reply of god Krishna is:

> "Let them perish, Prince, but you must fight."

'God Krishna then explains that the soul is eternal and cannot be slain. By killing his cousins, Arjun will do them the favour of moving them forward to the next life; being a member of the warrior class, the dictates of *dharma*, the duty of his station, demand that he fight. And if Arjun does not fight, his enemies will call him a coward.'

Rana Amar gazed into space for a few moments, then seemed to come suddenly alive. '*Dharma* demands that we avenge this impious act,' he stated with such quiet simplicity that it impressed even Prince Chara.

'You will not be alone,' Raja Man cut in quietly. 'The Hindus of Sind, Baluchistan and the Punjab will be with you. Nor do I intend remaining here, a refugee under your hospitable roof, for the rest of my life. I shall return to Jaipur as soon as possible, to raise the standard of revolt there.'

'By making war on our own, Raja Man, we will ensure a

return to our old suzerainties, free of Moghul and Muslim domination,' Rana Amar responded.

Prince Chara cast a swift glance at Prince Aziz Koka, just in time to catch the ugly shadow that for a fraction of a second had crossed the gaunt Muslim's face.

Extracts from the Emperor Jehangir's Diary:

At the period when I took my departure from Lahore it happily occurred to me that the different *zamindars* (land-holders) on that route should plant at every town and village and every stage and halting place, all the way from Lahore to Agra, mulberry and other large and lofty trees affording shade, but particularly those with broad leaves and wide-spreading branches, in order that for all time to come the way-worn and weary traveller might find under their shadow repose and shelter from the scorching rays of the sun during summer heats. I also ordered places of rest and refreshment, substantially built of brick or stone, to be erected at the termination of every eight *kosse* (twelve miles) for the whole distance, all provided with baths and a tank of fresh water, with a certain number of servants for each *serai* (resting place) and convenient bridges where needed along the route.

The news of Khubu Khan's death fills me with rage. My one source of joy is that Sher Afgan has been sent to hell, and I hope that the place of this black-faced scoundrel will always be there.

Chapter 12

This meeting would decide her entire future. As befitted a woman just widowed, Nur Jehan had selected a white *kurtha* and pantaloons with no jewellery apart from a single pearl necklace for her audience with Salima Begum, who ruled the royal *harem* of the Emperor Jehangir.

The low hum of conversation died down as she entered

the vast private chamber, emphasizing the soft tinkling of *sirtars* underlaid by an occasional light drum tap.

The Begum was seated at the far end of the chamber on a long divan upholstered in cloth of gold, very erect, hands folded on her lap, disdaining the purple and pink satin cushions on which she could have leant. Nur Jehan could not but be impressed by her majesty, which had nothing to do with the regal splendour of her surroundings.

Nur Jehan was led past a private pool inlaid with blue turquoise. The fountain gushing silver at its centre wafted heady sandalwood perfumes into the chamber. Ladies-in-waiting, all of them young, clad in rich outfits of shiny white satin, stood gracefully along the rear walls of the chamber. Female attendants dressed in white linen lined its sides. The Begum was reported to favour white for her immediate entourage, as a background to her own brilliance, while continual presence of young women rejuvenated her.

The floor was of pink marble, the squares so perfectly matched they looked like a single sheet. An enormous Persian carpet covered the area immediately in front of the long, central divan, from either side of which two great ivory elephant tusks, their massive black ebony stands embellished by broad bands of gold encrusted with emeralds, sapphires and rubies, rose to form an arch over the Begum's seated figure. Two supple Nubian girls, in diaphanous skirts and blouses of pale blue, the only touch of coloured clothing, black midriffs bare, slowly waved great peacock feather fans just enough to circulate the cool morning air. Salima Begum's personal majesty was innate, the product of birth, breeding and circumstance, and since the Emperor Jehangir did not have a favourite wife, she had remained head of the royal *harem*, over which she exercised an iron rule.

Totally unexpected, her recent appointment as chief

lady-in-waiting to the Begum had revealed to Nur Jehan that the Emperor's decisiveness as a ruler could extend to his personal life as well. She was frustrated and angry, however, because the Emperor had unwittingly thwarted her plan to continue wielding power from her father's mansion until the Emperor married her. Having breached the fortress gates of her marriage through her husband's demise, he intended to sweep into her citadel. While she had some feelings of love, admiration and protectiveness for the ruler, every instinct warned her to resist the pressure he was applying. If the Emperor were to accept her suggestion that Prince Jahan should be betrothed to her niece, Mumtaz Mahal, it would signal his belief that royalty could wed commoners. But still she must play hard to get. Most men, though giving the appearance of strength, were so basically insecure that they needed challenges to prove themselves; whereas truly strong, secure men would walk away from mere challenges to do whatever they desired.

Her own task now was to win over Salima Begum, this tough, old autocrat, whom she knew only slightly and to use her both as a channel of communication with the Emperor and a shield against those of his immediate intentions that might conflict with her own ambitions. However, her hope of playing a powerful role as lady-in-waiting or even a *harem* attendant to the Begum had been shattered when she was kept waiting three days before the old lady summoned her to an audience.

Salima Begum's appearance was not unfamiliar to Nur Jehan. Today, the white hair beneath a golden crown, cheeks that would have resembled dried grapes if they had not been so pink and overlaid with make-up paste, exquisite facial bones framing emerald green eyes, all held a new hauteur which Nur Jehan recognized as directed towards her. Those large, piercing eyes, their clear whites accentuated by black *kohl* lining the edges and delicate green shading on the lids, were especially cold. Not hostile, for this great lady would never descend to hostility, or allow anyone, even a husband, the intimacy of high emotion such as anger or resentment.

When Nur Jehan stood in front of the Begum, her head bowed in submission, the two female attendants who had ushered her in began to back away. A gnarled hand, ridges of blue veins rising above brown freckles, long, bony fingers glittering with diamond, pearl, cat's-eye and lapis lazuli rings in heavy gold settings, was slowly extended. She placed her own hand just beneath the extended fingers, without touching them, and sank on both knees before the Begum. The tiniest hint of relenting in the green eyes, as she rose to her feet again, was her reward. She had planned this move to attract the Begum's attention. By not presuming to touch the royal hand she would convey her total humility. A thrill of triumph shot through Nur Jehan. Not only had her plan worked, her reasoning had been correct.

The hand she had bowed over was waved upwards in a gesture of dismissal. 'Leave us alone,' the Begum commanded her entourage. Her voice was youthful, clear as a silver stream.

With a rustle of clothing, everyone present, most of them obviously puzzled by the unexpected directive, backed out slowly. The music faded into silence.

The Begum and she were alone. Even with her eyes downcast, Nur Jehan was aware that the Begum was entirely self-possessed, probing her for signs of weakness or defiance. Head bowed, Nur Jehan deliberately relaxed the knot in the centre of her stomach, firmed up the churning beneath it while the long moments of the Begum's deliberate silence passed.

'Our stepson, the Emperor, has, in his infinite wisdom, decided that our entourage should be supplemented by one of the most beautiful young women in his realm.' Had there been a note of irony in the clear voice? 'We have accepted his imperial command, as always ... er ... joyously. But first, should we not extend our sympathy to you in the sad loss of your husband, especially under such tragic circumstances?'

The words of sympathy couched in the form of a question meant that the Begum probably suspected the true circumstances leading to Sher Afgan's death. It sent an invisible shiver through Nur Jehan. She remained silent.

'We trust that you and your orphaned daughter – what is her name? ... Laidli? ... are suitably lodged and looked after.' The words came out slowly, each a crystal dew drop.

It was now or never. Nur Jehan recognized with unerring instinct that she needed the Begum as a patron, but without patronage. She raised her eyes to meet the old woman's piercing gaze four-square. She had no intention of staging a battle of glances or wills. That would be impudence, bringing disaster. 'My daughter's name is Ladili, Your Majesty. I only dare to give you her correct name because she, like me, has been placed under your royal protection – for that is what the position to which our Emperor has deigned to appoint me, with your gracious approval, now affords a widow and her orphaned child. I must state with the deepest humility and the utmost submission, however, that the protection my daughter and I need and desire more is the radiance of your smile and your gracious acceptance of us as loyal, obedient subjects of this, your domain, the royal *harem*. Protection against the world, we could somehow have found. What we need more vitally is the security of peace and dignity that only being in your personal favour can ensure.' She lowered her eyes, staring at nothing, seeing only the dark red and green of the carpet at her feet.

She could sense the Begum's perplexity, without any softening of the attitude. 'We had been informed that you are a unique human being.' The clear silver of the voice had become slightly sharper. 'While we are always submissive to His Majesty's dictates, what makes you imagine that we would automatically extend our favour to you on a personal level, which only Almighty Allah can command?'

'Your Majesty, I am assured of your royal favour officially because you have always followed to the letter and the entirety of the spirit, the dictates of the Emperors who have been fortunate enough to extend their confidence to you. Such is your nobility which has earned their trust. But my daughter and I desperately need more than your *royal* favour. We require it from you as . . .' She deliberately paused, glanced briefly up at the Begum and smiled with her eyes, '. . . as a unique human being.'

A silence, broken only by the splash of water in the fountain, told Nur Jehan that the Begum was taken aback. 'You have either a great intellect or a great heart,' the Begum finally stated. The haughty note re-entered her voice. 'Why do you presume that you could ever enjoy our favour as a human being when we do not even know you?'

It was the question Nur Jehan had been hoping for. She raised her eyes again, this time holding the Begum's glance levelly, again with no hint of either presumption or submission. 'Because you were in the same position nearly forty years ago, Your Majesty, when almost the same age as I am today. You were the daughter of the Emperor Humayun's sister and therefore the Emperor's first cousin. Although he loved you, I believe the Emperor Akbar did not wed you because your family relationship forbade it under certain of the laws he administered and he was too unsure of his position at the time to test these laws. He therefore gave you in marriage to a man he could trust implicitly, his guardian and chief supporter, Bairam Khan.'

The Begum's chin had lifted at her words. The green eyes surveying her from above the pasty pink cheeks had become opaque, staring, Nur Jehan knew, into a distant past. 'Go on,' the Begum murmured, her red-painted lips merely forming the words.

'Your husband, being the young Emperor Akbar's Regent, wielded great power, excited much jealousy. Those who wield power, especially on behalf of others, are extremely vulnerable, frequently to their own failings, like vanity and overweening self-confidence. Regardless of the causes, the Emperor Akbar removed your husband from his exalted position with the time-honoured excuse that he should fulfil his lifelong ambition to visit Mecca, a holy pilgrimage the offer of which no true Muslim can refuse. The events of your husband's subsequent rebellion, defeat, pardon and final journey are a part of history. On the way to Mecca in the year 1560, your husband's party was attacked by a band of Afghans and he was repeatedly stabbed until he was dead, leaving you a widow and your infant son an orphan. My husband Sher Afgan too was sent into virtual exile and was repeatedly stabbed until he died. Your Majesty, I say to you in the strictest confidence that my husband was brutal to me. From the very day we were married, he assaulted me unmercifully. Yet I grieve at the manner of his dying.'

A swift lifting of green eyes revealed that she had struck home. The Begum must have suffered the same treatment from her first husband and also endured remorse at the way he had been killed.

'When the Emperor Akbar then took you and your son under his protection, you must have had doubts as to his intentions,' Nur Jehan resumed quietly. 'Since my plight today is the same as that which you faced so many years ago, what other human being could understand it more than you, Your Majesty? That is why I dare to hope that I can depend on your gracious favour as a human being.'

The Begum's chin was slowly lowered; her eyes regained

their piercing quality, faceted emeralds. Have I over-reached myself, Nur Jehan wondered. Well, I have nothing to lose.

The Begum's gaze now seemed to penetrate her very soul, but she held it steadfastly. 'As you imply, dear Nur Jehan, we must confess for the first time ever that the Emperor Akbar did love us all along. You are most wise or cunning to have perceived a truth that no one else has suspected.'

'Even if I do possess one or both of these attributes, Your Majesty, neither wisdom nor cunning are required for me to perceive the truth of the Emperor Akbar's love for you. After all, once his position had been more firmly established, did he not marry you and depend on you the rest of his life?' She smiled with sincerity. 'How could he have resisted you?' Then grew solemn. 'The fact is that when Almighty Allah decrees that a man and a woman be joined together in holy marriage, the vows are inherent in their souls, their inner beings. The spoken words, the *kadi*'s blessing, are but human benedictions, the presumptuousness of a licence granted to consummate the eternal.'

'What immortal words.' The Begum slowly shook her head from side to side in wonder. 'How do you know all this?'

'By observing from my humble life to your own noble one, Your Majesty; for in essence we are both human beings, though you were born to rule and I to serve.'

The Begum had completely recovered her poise, but she was no longer distant. 'It has taken us forty years and more to discover a kindred spirit,' she declared softly. She gazed dreamily into the distance. A prophetic note entered her voice. 'It is obvious that your own future will match our past, Nur Jehan. You may have been born serving, but you will not serve forever.'

'Your Majesty, it is to continue serving that I humbly

beseech your protection,' Nur Jehan stated firmly, playing her loaded dice. 'I have no desire to become the Emperor's consort in any form whatsoever,' she lied. 'I am a woman, just widowed, with a small orphan daughter. I need no pity. Indeed, I would resent it. But under no circumstances would I want to become a concubine, even of an Emperor.' She felt fierce satisfaction at having stated her position so openly. 'I would kill myself and my daughter sooner than suffer such humiliation.'

Wife and queen, yes . . . concubine, never. She had injected deadly earnestness into her quietly spoken words and she now raised her eyes to the Begum to convey chill determination. 'All that apart, however, whatever the intentions of the Emperor towards me, should we not both protect him from the evil tongues of men and the calumny of history?'

'What do you mean?' The words were a challenge.

'While I will, as a loyal subject, obey the Emperor's slightest command, it would be intrinsically disloyal of me to do so if it would hurt the Emperor in any way.' She deliberately injected a note of passion into her voice. 'I would rather die than have it said that the Emperor deliberately engineered the cruel murder of my husband in order to possess me.'

The moment she uttered the words, a split-second widening of the Begum's eyes told Nur Jehan the one truth that even her great imagination and intellect had not laid bare. Just as she and the Emperor Jehangir had engineered Sher Afgan's death, so had Salima Begum and the Emperor Akbar arranged for the death of Salima Begum's husband, Bairam Khan.

Once again, the truth of that trite saying, history repeats itself, had been demonstrated, this time in a most devastating manner. What did the future hold? Nur Jehan's triumph at having won over the Begum was clouded by a bleak question. Would history repeat itself with the Emperor Jehangir's sons?

When Prince Jahan received the Emperor's summons to attend him immediately at the regular morning public audience in the Agra palace, he was surprised. His father knew that he had fallen off his horse the previous morning and was resting. True, the worst he had suffered was a badly bruised thigh – having taken the fall correctly, he had avoided any damage to his spine – and injured pride, but the physician had recommended complete bed rest and the Emperor was usually considerate of sickness when he knew there was no malingering. Something of urgency must have inspired the summons.

The large ante-room was crowded with suitors, the subdued hum of conversation and the inevitable music that for Emperors formed a background almost continuously. The chief usher, a huge Pathan dressed in the imperial purple and gold livery, towering above those present, shouted: 'Make way there for Prince Jahan to answer the Emperor's summons.' The scents of sandalwood, camphor and wild rose smote Prince Jahan's nostrils as a passage was respectfully cleared for him.

Preceded by the chief usher, trying hard not to limp, Prince Jahan threaded his way past the brightly dressed throng, sprinkled with the white robes of priests. He climbed the pink marble steps of the broad circular stairway leading to the high platform, encircled by its red sandstone railing, in the centre of which was the royal enclosure built by the Emperor Akbar to look like the eyrie of a royal eagle. The Emperor Jehangir was seated cross-legged on the golden throne, a god dispensing justice from on high. Asaf Khan stood on the dais to the right and slightly to the rear of the throne, while the Imperial Treasurer, a silver-haired and moustached version of his son, the dashing

Prime Minister, save that his tall figure was leaner and slightly stooped, was on his left. Father and son were dressed alike in calf-length tunics of dark blue satin, gold pantaloons and belts, neck-chains glittering with diamonds and sapphires, matching the turban jewels. Prince Jahan's arrival seemed to stir an unusual interest and he wondered why. A royal court, especially an imperial court, was an arena in which anything could happen, a victor one moment being vanquished the next.

The Emperor waved away the two suppliants kneeling before him, then beckoned to Prince Jahan, who sank on both knees, head bowed, before the imperial throne.

'Ah, Prince Jahan, we learned with regret that you fell off your high horse yesterday morning.' The Emperor guffawed at his own weak joke, looked around to acknowledge the sycophantic titters of those nearest him. 'We summoned you because we have decided to elevate you in a totally different sphere.' He paused, placed his right elbow on his knee, held his chin lightly with his hand, thumb beneath. 'Being nearly fifteen years of age now, it is time you took on the responsibilities of manhood.' He removed his hand, looked around again, nodding his head rapidly, reproducing the acknowledgments he expected from those present. He stroked his moustache reflectively. 'While you will assuredly contract marriages to strengthen our ties with the ruling princes of our Empire, we deem it essential to your personal well-being that you, who have steered a lonely course all your life, should share your life with a lady who can be your helpmate.' He sighed. 'We know only too well how our own life would be enriched if we had such a person in it.'

What is going to happen to me, Prince Jahan wondered dismally. I have done better than anyone else so far. I need no woman in my life to complicate it, unless it is the girl I love, the elf who bewitches my dreams, Mumtaz Mahal.

'Having given this matter due deliberation and aware of your extreme usefulness to our rule, our appreciation of which we have demonstrated in the rich rewards and distinctions liberally bestowed on you, recognizing that you are now the fittest of our sons to be our heir, we have chosen for your betrothed a well-born young lady of noble birth, of surpassing beauty, charm and accomplishment.' The Emperor paused, obviously expecting some response.

'Sire, I am deeply touched by your infinite thoughtfulness,' Shah Jahan lied. How could he tell the Emperor that he felt like a trapped animal? As a royal pack mule, he would gladly accept any burden of work and responsibility, but he preferred not to become an imperial stud! 'Your slightest wish is my command.'

'Well then, that is settled. You are now betrothed. You may . . . er . . . what?' The question had been directed with an impatient frown at Asaf Khan, who had moved forward a step, bowed and spoken to the Emperor in a low voice. 'Ah!' The royal brow cleared. 'The young lady to whom you are now betrothed is the daughter of the highest official in our Court, Prime Minister Asaf Khan. She is named Mumtaz Mahal.'

Shah Jahan was dazed. 'Sire . . . S . . . Sire,' he stammered. 'You are too kind. This is granting me more than a wish, it is the fulfilment of a dream.' He was tempted to declare his love in public, so word of it could spread throughout the Empire, but the years of training in reticence, combined with an innate caution against revealing what might be exploited as a personal weakness, held him back. And beneath the joybells that were clanging in his head, he heard a more ominous tolling: You are being used by your father to get closer to the object of his own unfulfilled dreams, so be careful.

'Before you leave, Prince Jahan, we desire to discuss the situation in Kandhar.' The Emperor's voice, reaching him through the clangour, cleared Prince Jahan's head. 'You may sit beside us.' He gestured gracefully to a low stool on the step below his dais. 'Prime Minister, present your preamble before we announce our decisions.'

Asaf Khan remained silent until Prince Jahan took his seat. Neither of them looked at each other in spite of the personal tie that had just been created. 'Owing to its strategic and commercial importance, Kandhar, located in south central Afghanistan, is vital to the Empire.' Asaf Khan had raised his deep, mellow voice so all those present could hear.

'It is a gateway to India from the west and a natural base of operations for any invader. Possession of its fortress by an adventurer could pose a threat to Kabul. The Emperor Babur captured Kandhar in the year 1522, but it passed into Persian hands in 1558 upon the death of the Emperor Humayun. Recognizing its value, the Great Emperor Akbar recaptured it in the year 1594. Recently, Afghan chieftains in the area, whether under instigation or not, attempted to seize Kandhar, but the governor of the fortress held out resolutely. Subsequently, as you are all aware, our Emperor Jehangir despatched a strong relief column to Kandhar, at the approach of which the attackers fled in disarray. Thereupon, Shah Abbas, the ruler of Persia, disclaimed knowledge of the incursion, rebuked his chieftains and offered his apologies to our Emperor, indicating that he submitted to our sovereign rights.'

'We are certain that all of you here present believe that the matter of Kandhar thus ends satisfactorily.' The Emperor lifted his chin, surveyed those he could see beneath the balcony rail. He nodded sagely, a smile hovering beneath the droopy moustaches. 'The wisdom that Almighty Allah has seen fit to bestow on us warns otherwise. The strongest support for our errant son, Prince Husrau, came from the north-western regions. Had he not decided to launch a precipitate attack upon our army, he could have outnumbered us not just by two to one but by many times more. We have therefore decided to visit these parts.' His single nod was decisive and grim this time, the massive jaw clenched. 'We shall leave for Lahore with the bulk of the imperial army within a few weeks. We shall then proceed to Kabul. When we have displayed our might there, we shall winter in Lahore and return to Agra. A show of our immense military strength, combined with some generous concessions to the nobles and people of the region, will be timely. Both our sons, Prince Jahan and Prince Husrau, shall accompany us on this mission. In our absence, the defence of the capital will be in the hands of our Prime Minister, Asaf Khan.'

The bells that now tolled in Shah Jahan's head were doleful. He did not want to be betrothed to Mumtaz Mahal merely as a token. When he could have met her again, had communion with her, enjoyed her charm, he had to leave the capital. And why was the Emperor taking himself away at this time? It must be a ploy.

For the first time in his life, Prince Jahan faced a stark fact that he had taken for granted up to now. People are merely the pawns of their rulers. With that knowledge, the warm love he had begun to feel for his father at the announcement of his betrothal, which he had thought to have been inspired by parental concern, turned cold as frost, flowed into the compartments of hatred created by his belief that his father had organized the murder of his beloved grandfather. This was no thoughtful father, no enlightened Emperor, but a selfish, conniving man to whom people were merely the means to attain his personal desires, all of it a game, a play he was directing not through passion or conviction, but solely on the impulse of each moment.

A sense of hopelessness seized Prince Jahan. Dominated by drink and opium, a libertine life and an all-consuming desire to possess another man's wife, now a widow, the Emperor's rashness could only become progressively worse. Some day, the Empire, religion, morality, good conduct, would need a saviour, and he, Prince Jahan, was the only one capable of filling that role.

Mumtaz felt a tremor of apprehension when she received the formal summons from her father that morning, through Ras, the Ethiopian who was Chief Eunuch of the Ghiyas Beg *harem*. What had she done wrong now, or what had she not done that she ought to have done?

Since her earliest years she had always been in trouble. More recently, her life had fallen into a more sedate pattern, yet the tomboy in her had not yet grown into the disciplines of the life of a young lady, so trouble always lurked within reach of her independent spirit and outspoken tongue.

She swiftly searched her mind for the cause of the summons. 'What have I done wrong, Sati?' she questioned her lady-in-waiting, while tidying her make-up, the eunuch waiting outside to escort her.

'You tell me,' Sati bade her quietly. Mumtaz knew that her 'other' mother hated any reprimands for her charge even more than she did herself.

'It could be one or more of many things. I pulled the hair of Rowena's little daughter this morning for being cruel to a puppy. She is a little tattler but would never reveal *why* I did it.' She pondered a while, debating whether to divulge her secret even to Sati, then broke down. 'I sneaked the poor shivering little puppy into the kennels, so it could be fed and protected.' No more pets had been her father's edict. 'Oh, and I wandered around the garden yesterday, listening to the birds, when I should have been reading the Koran.'

'Well, listen to what you are accused of first,' Sati advised, deftly plaiting Mumtaz' hair. 'Then admit to it if

212

you are guilty. Otherwise deny it. The truth always pays, but you don't have to go blurting out your wrongdoings unasked.'

'You are *so* good to me.' Mumtaz noted her eyes glowing in her tiny thumbnail mirror. She reached up and patted Sati's plump hand affectionately. Deep inside, she knew that she was growing up into disciplines of her own. Her meeting with Prince Jahan had inspired her to identify some of them. 'I know I am *bad* at times. I wish Prince Jahan would help me to become better. I am so hopelessly in love with him I would even accept any outside disciplines.'

'We all need inspiration at times,' Sati responded.

'Who inspires *you*?'

'My little house-sparrow.'

'Oh Sati, you are such a darling.' She reflected a moment. 'You know, Sati, we are living in an age that is more romantic than practical. Princes and noblemen who are interested in single ladies of the *harem* wait outside the *harem* gates and call in their respects to the lady of their choice through one of the eunuchs. If the lady is pleased with the man, she responds by sending him a present of some sort, such as a jewel or an ornament, the mark of her favour. Regardless of how the man fulfils his physical needs, love links his spirit with that of the lady, an exquisite love that causes him to tremble and emote in verse. I have a poem and a silken handkerchief for my Prince Jahan, as tokens of my favour, but since I first met him at the *Meena* Bazaar, I have endured a ponderous, even overwhelming silence from him. He has not even come to the bazaar again. Why? Is he so busy, or so high and mighty? I cannot believe that he is ignoring me out of cruelty. After all, he paid ten thousand rupees to buy my Ceylon pearl, when he could not even afford it.'

'Princes of high rank, such as Prince Jahan, have to

follow certain standards of decorum, especially those dictated by the ruler. Have faith that your prince loves you. It is only a question of time.'

Impatience welled up within Mumtaz. 'Decorum! Decorum! Decorum!' she exploded. 'Always decorum. When am I going to live? I am getting older by the day, the hour, the minute. I might die tomorrow.' She stopped abruptly as a chill dread entered her being.

'If you die tomorrow, it will not be of old age.' Sati's rejoinder was made in the no-nonsense tone she usually adopted for her ward's emotional outbursts.

For once, that dread prevented Mumtaz from retorting. Sati's deft fingers stopped their work on her nearly completed hair-do. 'What is it?' the older woman inquired. 'Why are you silent? Are you sick?' Then more light-heartedly, referring to her ward's stock source for sympathy. 'The cramps, perhaps?'

'N . . . no . . . Sati.' In an access of terror, Mumtaz reached with both hands, grasped Sati's poised fingers, stood up and faced her. 'Suddenly, I'm afraid that the time is short. Hold me, please hold me.'

Sati was waiting for her when Mumtaz returned an hour later. Holding the little box hidden in hands clasped behind her back, she had planned to tease Sati, but one look at her 'other' mother's anxious expression caused all mischievous thoughts to flee.

'Oh Sati, give me your mother's blessing,' she cried. 'I am the happiest girl in the world. I am betrothed to Prince Jahan, by the Emperor's order. And guess what my prince has sent me as a token of his love and delight?' She held out what she had been hiding. It was a little gold box, glittering in the morning sunlight from the sapphires, rubies and emeralds that studded it. She lifted the lid. Reposing on a

214

dark blue velvet lining was a single pearl the size of a small bird's egg.

'Look! It is the pearl he bought from me!' Mumtaz squeaked with delight. 'He has written me another poem too, in the Persian mode, which I have hidden in my *kurtha* pocket. I shall not share this poem even with you, but it says that he kept this flawless stone until he could give it to the pure heart from which he first obtained it. And if he had not been able to give it to me, he would have smashed it to powder rather than have it adorn anyone else.'

She saw the tears of joy in Sati's eyes. 'Oh Sati. He loves me, he loves me. I am so happy, I do not know whether to laugh or cry.' She proffered the jewelled box to Sati, who took it gingerly. 'I shall dance instead.'

She whirled around the room, singing a song of love that needed no melody. She stopped abruptly, giggled. 'Do you know one of the things I thought my father had discovered?'

Sati shook her head in amazement at the change of subject. 'No.'

'That horrid girl, Fatima, had managed to smuggle a whole radish and a cucumber into her room. You know that vegetables which look like a man's thing are forbidden in the *harem* unless they are chopped so they cannot be inserted in the you-know-where.' Her eyes twinkled with mischief. 'Well, I sneaked into Fatima's room, cut up the vegetables and spoilt her fun, because it is a sin to do such things and Fatima is horrid anyway.'

Her merry laugh rang through the little room.

Chapter 13

Despite his disappointment at having to leave Agra so soon
after he became officially betrothed to Mumtaz Mahal,
Prince Jahan had looked forward to the journey north with
the Emperor's army for one major reason. He would see
Kabul.

Kabul! Magic word from his boyhood.

The first time he had seen the beautiful gardens Babur
had created outside the capital city of Agra, to remind him
of his beloved Kabul, Prince Jahan had been captivated.
Ever since, he had felt a kinship with Kabul.

In the secret recesses of his mind, Kabul, the ancient,
had always been his spiritual home. He could not account
for the feeling. He sometimes thought that a profound love
for it had become implanted in the very seed of the Emperor
Babur, founder of the Indian part of the Moghul Empire, a
love that had passed through the seed of four generations of
descendants to surface in him, Prince Jahan.

The journey had drawn him closer to his father. They
had hunted, made pilgrimages together and had many
philosophical discussions.

The barrier of his conviction that this man had caused
his beloved grandfather to be killed could never quite be
removed, but he had got to know his father as a human
being for the first time and this had generated a new respect
and some affection for him.

When they finally reached Kabul he knew he had been
in the city before, though he could not understand how.

It had taken the imperial army four months to get there,
with stops in Lahore and Kandhar. The vast force was now

encamped in the city and its environs, spreading many miles south along the valley. The only peace to be found was not in the palace, but in the royal gardens created by Babur, now reserved for the exclusive use of the Emperor and his immediate family.

Standing in the great cave dug into the hillside that was part of the pleasure garden in the Pratap Bagh, he watched the westering sun casting purple shadows on the dark red crags of the northern mountain.

The city was perched on a plateau at the junction of the ancient caravan trails. On the west was the mountain range known as the Koh-i-Baba, its peaks rising nearly seventeen thousand feet, behind which the blazing red fireball of the sun was fast seeking its bed. To the north was the enormous massif of the Hindu Kush mountains, glinting black-red and silver with its granite and the ice of winter.

Kabul was shaped like a horseshoe lying on its side, the closed end to the east fronting the river. The silver spear of a canal plunging into the waters now streaked them crimson, the dark shapes of boats seeming to float on blood. The walled citadel was built on the high hills of the curve of the horseshoe. Shining minarets of mosques sprinkled the landscape. He could imagine the people on the streets, dark-skinned Afghans with flashing eyes and great hooked noses striding along with lithe step. They would be clad in loose white trousers, long white overshirts reaching below the knees, dark brown waistcoats, turbans with one end hanging down. The women following them were shapeless masses in the brown *chador* of traditional Islam. Some men would have feminine-looking male companions. His ancestor Babur had favoured such company.

Alone for the first time, in the peace and solitude of the gardens, he was able to identify some of his unexpressed desires. He needed above all else to be an Emperor in the adventurous mould of his ancestor, Babur, who had commenced his career right here with but two hundred followers. Descent from Timur-il-Leng, Timur-the-Lame, had been his only heritage. Shah Jahan too yearned to create beauty. Not just the forts, palaces, monuments and their inevitable gardens laid out in traditional mode of which his grandfather had been the greatest builder, but a creator of a unique style that would bear his seal and give delight to endless future generations. He would build of marble instead of sandstone. His gardens would be laid out in designs of his own invention. Beauty vibrated within him, transcending all else.

While the discovery of these fundamental needs elated him, he also felt a calm determination to fulfil them. He looked west, south and east at the walls which enclosed the high plain on which the city had been built. Northwards, stark ridges rose like the scaly backs of legendary monsters that were said to have once inhabited the earth. The citadel within which he stood was set apart, on the ridge nearest the city. Pleasant gardens, watered by silver springs and the canal, spread green below him, with splashes of colour from immaculate flower beds laid out in precise squares and rectangles. The air was cold and crisp, scented with jasmine. The vibrant calls of birds wending their way across a pale blue sky mingled with the faint roar of the voices of people dotting the bazaar, vendors calling out their wares, women at the water troughs, men price-haggling amid the booths. Twelve languages were spoken here and a large population of Muslim Sunni lived in harmony with their Shi'a brethren and with Buddhists, who once formed over one-half of the population, Hindus, Jews, Parsees and a sprinkling of Christians. The rich were very rich, the poor almost destitute.

A caravan approached along the southern highway, hastening to enter before the city gates were closed for the night. Where was it coming from? The caravan routes linked India with Persia, Iraq and the Fertile Crescent of the Middle East. He could almost distinguish the long necks of the laden camels bobbing back and forth, the horse-guards slow cantering alongside. He thought he detected the faint creak of wagons above the city noise.

Magnificent buildings and countless pleasure gardens dominated Kabul, contrasting starkly with mud hovels in the distance. The destroying Moghuls had created beautiful edifices. Was it to demonstrate to history that they were not barbarians? Moghul was the Persian word for Mongol, the destroyers who came from the east, typified by his own ancestor, Genghis Khan. It was unusual for a Moghul to wonder in such a way, but then he was an unusual Moghul!

It was a vibrance rather than sound that first made him aware of the man approaching the cave. It was not safe to be alone here at this time of the evening. His eyes darted around to see whether the man had companions. Finding none, his hand went to his sword regardless and he pulled back into the darkness of the cave.

The intruder was dressed in the white hooded robe of the Parsee. He was short of stature, his face youthful beneath the hood, the pointed features as trim as his dark moustache and beard. He walked with a slow pensive step, passed the cave entrance, looking sideways at the city below, paused facing west.

Prince Jahan drew his sword. The long, naked blade gleamed in the darkness. He cat-footed towards the man, sword outstretched. He stopped when he was close enough to place the point at the nape of the neck.

'Do not move!' he quietly commanded.

A tremor went through the intruder. He became perfectly still, continued gazing into the distance.

'Who are you?' Prince Jahan demanded.

219

'I am called Ustad Isa.' The voice was cultured, its tone unruffled.

'You are unafraid. Why?'

'If you were going to harm me, you would not have asked who I am.'

A highly clever individual this. Prince Jahan knew an urge to prick the drum-skin of his composure. 'And if I harmed you?'

'It would not have mattered.'

'Why not?'

'Life has no meaning for me. Death at least might have some significance.'

The man slowly turned round. Beneath his hood, his long hair was completely white. Yet his fair skin was tight-drawn, youthful. The dark eyes were wet with tears. In the instant that their gazes locked, some strange connection was established in Prince Jahan's mind, of a like nature, yet not the same, as that now existing between him and Kabul. Was it the sadness of the man's expression, a hint of tragedy that was not evident except in the tears and some liquid sorrow within the haunted eyes, that had established the connection? Common suffering, fusing them?

'I did not give you permission to turn round,' Prince Jahan said lamely, wanting to hide his thoughts.

'I did not ask your permission,' Ustad Isa responded gently.

'You are obviously a Parsee. What are you doing in the Emperor's private garden?'

A gentle smile this time. 'Walking around, breathing its air, enjoying its beauty.'

Prince Jahan remembered the aura that had emerged from the man, linked it with the tearstained eyes. He sheathed his sword. 'Why are you sad?' The question escaped him involuntarily.

'Is it my tears that make you think I'm sad? People cry when they are happy too, you know.'

'I would not know,' Prince Jahan declared proudly. 'We Moghuls never cry.'

'But as you can see, I am not a Moghul, just a human being and I cry sometimes.'

He accepted the quiet chiding without anger. He had never met anyone like this Ustad Isa before, so gentle he was unbelievably strong. Instinct told Prince Jahan that he could learn much from this man. 'Why do you come to our private pleasure garden to cry?' he demanded. 'Outsiders have no right in here. You could be imprisoned or even killed for trespassing.'

Again that gentle smile. 'As I told you, I have no fear of death. I have a right to be here, however, as a guest of the Emperor. I take it from your questions and your . . . er . . . boast that you are a Moghul, that you are of the royal family. By your age, I would guess that you are Prince Jahan.' He made no move to genuflect or salute his superior by birth.

For the first time in his life, Prince Jahan did not mind, even acknowledged mentally that it was not necessary. He liked this man immediately. 'That was a good guess. Why are you in the palace?'

'I am the architect whose presence the Emperor commanded. I arrived yesterday and am lodged here.'

'Ah! The renowned architect from Shiraz. I had expected you to be much older.'

'I am not sure about being renowned, yet at twenty-seven I have lived too long already!'

The words had been lightly spoken, but the truth of them smote Prince Jahan. He covered up. 'I am very interested in architecture.'

'I know.'

'Who told you?'

221

'You did.'

'What I said just now?' Prince Jahan was puzzled.

'No, *all* of you.'

'Oh!'

'You have the essence of a creative genius. Not only a builder, like your illustrious grandfather, but a true artist.' A prophetic note had entered the gentle voice. 'You will not merely build, you will *create*.'

'How do you know?'

The thin shoulders shrugged, the pale hands gestured briefly with long, delicate fingers. 'I don't know how I know.'

They laughed together as if they were old friends. 'Let us sit down on that bench, so you can tell me about Shiraz.' Prince Jahan changed the subject to avoid embarrassment and to return into his shell. 'Also about your religion and architecture.'

They sat side-by-side on one of the pink marble benches overlooking the city.

'First tell me about the Parsee religion,' Prince Jahan requested. He felt comfortable with Ustad Isa.

'As you know, one can only be born a Parsee; it is not a religion to be adopted. It was conceived nearly twelve hundred years ago by the prophet Zarathustra, Zoroaster as some call him, who discovered Ahura Mazda, the one God, the Creator, for mankind. Parsees believe in Spenta Mainyo, the holy spirit of the one God, the truth and the light, represented by the sun and by fire. It opposes Angra Mainyo, the destructive spirit of darkness. As with the Universe and the Earth, the conflict is also in men's hearts.'

'Do you practise your religion?' Prince Jahan did not know why he asked the question, unless it was that he sensed that a man such as Ustad Isa would not succumb to primitive beliefs, as he considered them, such as the powers of light and darkness.

'No.' The architect hesitated for the first time, stared into space a while. 'I have recently inclined to the philosophy of Gautama Buddha.'

'The Buddhist religion?'

'Buddhism is neither a religion nor a philosophy, nor even a way of life. It is a manner of living for each individual.'

'Based on *kharma*, with no God?'

Ustad Isa smiled. 'The Buddha did not say there was no god, merely that we make our own destinies without divine intervention.'

'Faith in Allah, acknowledgement of His will and acceptance of the Prophet Mahomet's Holy Koran are the fundamentals of *my* existence.'

'Each of us has different needs. A bee seeks honey, a vegetarian milk and vegetables, a Muslim lamb, a Christian pork. Regardless of one's beliefs, the laws of *kharma*, which is cause, not retribution, and *vipaka*, effect, remain. It is by seeking to prevent causes having adverse effects that Buddhists attempt to make their way towards Enlightenment, the escape from the cycles of causation which are suffering.'

'I listened to many philosophical discussions between holy men, mainly between our Muslim *imams* and my grandfather, the Emperor Akbar. He had the time and leisure for that sort of thing during the long months of his campaigns. Through these discussions he was able to evolve his own religion, *Din-i-Ilahi*, which embodies the best of all religions. But this is the first time I have heard Buddhism so simply and clearly expressed.'

'It is easier to be simple and clear when one is not learned.' A gleam of mischief had flickered across the architect's face. 'Now, on to architecture, where I think your interest primarily resides. I studied at the great University in Shiraz where they deem architecture to be one of the five cultural arts, the others being literature, music, painting and drama. As with all art forms, the sole function of architecture is to give delight. Unlike a song, however, or even a book or painting, good architecture has an ever-present drama. Whether it be a pleasure garden, a building or a monument, it is always there, the vibrance of its spirit enriching us each time we observe it.'

Prince Jahan was amazed. The man was putting into words all that he himself had been about to identify that very evening, just a few minutes ago. Surely he was a messenger from Allah, pointing from that secret part of his own nature to this aspect of his destiny. He knew that Ustad Isa would say no more about architecture. When one had produced a perfect gem of speech one should not embellish it and the architect was sensitive enough not to try. In case he did, however, the desire to prevent him was suddenly urgent in Prince Jahan's mind. He abruptly changed the subject. 'Shiraz, Herat and my ancestral Samarkand have always fascinated me,' he confessed. 'I asked my father only yesterday for leave to visit them, but he denied my request.'

'Shiraz is the capital of the Persian province known as Fars,' Ustad Isa began, nodding to acknowledge both the change of subject and its reason. 'It is located within the Zargos mountains on the vast agricultural lands of South Central Persia.'

'You were looking towards Shiraz just now, were you not?'

A flicker of pain, barely perceptible, crossed the dark, haunted eyes. 'Yes,' Ustad Isa whispered. He pulled himself together with an effort, shrugged again. 'It is natural to look towards home whenever the blinds of night are slowly drawn over the sky.'

'Especially when you are haunted by the tragedy you left behind.' Once again, the words emerged from Prince Jahan without thought.

Ustad Isa stared into space. His larynx wobbled once.

'I am sorry,' Prince Jahan said softly. 'Would you like to tell me about it?'

Long moments passed while the architect struggled for composure, wanting to speak, but obviously afraid that his voice might break. 'You are very perceptive, Prince, and compassionate.' He was approaching the subject obliquely to allow the truth to emerge unfettered by his emotions. 'I was married to the most beautiful woman in the world. I loved her so deeply that no one else will ever exist for me.' His voice broke. He cleared his throat. 'Why do I tell you of this thing when it has been a secret locked in my heart for over a year now?'

'Because you were meant to share it with me alone.' An intense dread gripped Prince Jahan, chilled his entire being. Was this a premonition? 'Because you and I were meant to share the bitter fruit of your tragedy,' he ended, speaking to himself.

'My wife Laila died with our baby in childbirth.' The words emerged as a painracked cry that suddenly shattered the evening air. Its echoes were flung back from the sky, from the city below, seemed to fill the world. The man did not have to say more, nor the boy to ask.

Prince Jahan knew then that the grief had turned the architect's hair white overnight. He heard the sound of a great rushing wind. It caused waves of air to sweep over the city below, over the palaces and mansions, minarets and pleasure gardens. An agonizing grief started in his heart, spread throughout his entire being. The world grew dark before the mystery of anguish. He was alone. The wind, now chill, turned his body, mind and spirit to ice. He reached out a despairing hand, clutched only the empty, clouded air. The loneliness became unbearable, turned to an intense longing. *Dear Allah, help me.* Out of the opaque waves below him, a golden spire emerged, then a marble and gold cupola.

A grey dove was suddenly perched on the spire, baring its pale pink breast to the setting sun. He cupped his hands towards it and in a trice it had nestled in them, its heart palpitating against his palms.

'Babur!' he cried, recognizing the dove.

By some magic of a moment, he became the dove, cupped in the hands of his ancestor of the heavy face, black moustache and beard beneath the jewelled imperial turban.

'I inherited nothing but my birth and two hundred loyal men,' Babur murmured. 'With these I carved out an Empire. You are seed of my seed. Go forth and be worthy of me.' He flung the dove that was Prince Jahan back into the clouded air.

With a fluttering of wings, Prince Jahan came back to earth. The dove had vanished.

'My life no longer has any direction other than the creation of beauty as homage to my Laila.'

Ustad Isa's words hung before Prince Jahan, etched against the cupola as if he could see them. The chill began to leave him, the waves of air dissipated, carrying the cupola and its spire with them; the sound of the wind died down.

In an instant, Kabul lay beneath him, somehow barren.

The message of the dove glowed brightly in his heart.

Prince Jahan's father was very pleased to observe the friendship that had sprung up between his son and Ustad Isa. Impressed with the architect, the Emperor had suggested that he should accompany the royal party back to Lahore, to design a new summer palace and pleasure garden. He also allocated a mansion in the Pratap Bagh gardens in Kabul to Prince Jahan, giving him an unlimited budget for embellishing the building and grounds.

Plunging wholeheartedly into this project, under Ustad Isa's guidance, Prince Jahan found it a fascinating outlet for his own creative endeavours. It was a new experience to conceive, plan and create a work of art, one that appealed to his very soul.

Another of the highlights of Prince Jahan's stay in Kabul occurred when he celebrated his fifteenth birthday. His father had him weighed in gold, silver, nine other precious metals and silks respectively, all of which went into his private treasury, along with costly gifts from the Afghan chieftains. The most politically significant event of the day was the *dastarkhwan*, the royal levée his father held in the Kabul palace that night. He was given pride of place at the right of the Emperor, who personally fed him the royal Shiraz melon.

While all this was heady stuff for Prince Jahan, he could not help feeling sorry for Prince Husrau, confined in his quarters at the Kabul palace. But his brother had gambled for high stakes and lost. He alone was responsible for his sad fate. Though the outcome of it had been beneficial to himself, Prince Jahan's happiness was, however, tinged with compassion for his brother.

All the while, his love for Mumtaz Mahal remained constant, a single, shining star on a dark night. While he longed intensely to be with her, the knowledge of their love exhilarated his every conscious moment.

On the journey back to Lahore Prince Jahan was able to spend many an evening with his new friend, his soul-mate in the creation of beauty, the architect, Ustad Isa. The prince could not escape the feeling that they were destined to create a monument of great beauty together.

Chapter 14

May 1607

Preparations for the revolt had gone forward steadily from the Chitor palace. Since Rana Amar had placed him in charge, Prince Chara regarded this as a token that his father finally recognized his talents. Either way, he did not give a flea's fart for his father's opinion. He could make his own life.

Two things about his father concerned him. First, the Rana was too impatient to get the revolt started. Success depended on timing and he, Prince Chara, had other plans than merely raising the flag of rebellion by refusing to pay taxes and tribute. Second, the Rana trusted Aziz Koka too much. The skeletal figure was everywhere, participating in every discussion, listening avidly to every detail of the planning. It was the last which had caused Prince Chara to accompany the Rana on the wild boar hunt this morning.

'Prince Aziz is a Muslim, joined in blood to the Emperor,' Prince Chara had warned his father. 'His ties with Agra are deeper than any he may have with us in a common cause. Once we overthrow the Emperor, Aziz may even join another of the Moghuls to ensure our continuing subjection.'

'Prince Aziz is an orthodox Muslim,' Rana Amar had retorted. 'He hates the Emperor's dissolute ways and infidel behaviour. He is bound to us in heart and spirit. We can trust him implicitly. Look how much he has done these past months to assure us of the support of Muslim leaders. Besides, he is Prince Husrau's father-in-law.'

Prince Chara could not contradict these last statements.

Unlike their overlord, the Emperor, the ranas and shahs who ruled the imperial regions did not have large standing armies. They and those nobles who were so endowed by any Emperor had the right to so much income (*zats*) and to raise and retain so many men (*sawar*) for the Emperor's use. In consequence, it was impossible to assemble a rebel force of thousands of armed men at a given place and expect it to grow. News of the movement would soon reach Agra and the Emperor's troops would march to crush the rebels before they became too powerful. What had happened with Prince Husrau, who had quickly attracted enormous numbers to his banner, could not be repeated in the south. The trick, as Prince Chara saw it, was to enlist the support of powerful rulers, princes and nobles and have them join forces at an appointed place and time. None of those who had acted otherwise, flinging down the gauntlet from the head of a few thousand men, scoring minor victories and expecting dissidents to join them along the way, had ever succeeded. If the Rajputs were to spearhead a revolt, they had first to unite, create divisions in the predominantly Moghul areas at the same time and then strike north at the imperial capital.

'It is what happens after we overthrow the Emperor that concerns me,' Prince Chara had protested.

'Let us worry about that once we get there,' the Rana had insisted. 'Remember our old Rajput saying, Bake your *chuppati* before you try to share it, otherwise all you have is a large lump of dough.'

Prince Chara hated his father's homespun sayings. Did people actually believe that this was wisdom?

'Surely we should be able to bake our *chuppati* in peace without having our hungry neighbours alerted to the fact that we have prepared the dough.'

'Enough is enough,' Rana Amar had finally declared. 'You keep preparing the dough. I alone shall decide who shall know of it. Your repeated attempts to discredit Prince Aziz, a trusted ally who has suffered so much at the hands of the Emperor and is an honoured guest in our royal palace, are becoming monotonous. If I may commend one of your own fancy intellectual flights to you, monotony is the ultimate sin because it creates boredom and to be boring is grossly bad manners.' The Rana's white grin beneath the black moustache and beard had been one of malicious enjoyment.

Chagrined, Prince Chara had to be content with keeping as much information as possible from Aziz Koka. This was, however, difficult because Prince Aziz was indeed everywhere, snooping for news, poking his beak nose into every council whether invited or not and the Rana shared every bit of information with the prince during dinner, almost as if he had a death wish to be betrayed.

Prince Chara had therefore organized the three-day hunt at short notice, to be able to get his father completely alone for once. He had set aside the first morning for a wild boar hunt on horseback, knowing that the Rana would gallop ahead once the beaters flushed out a boar, eager to claim the kill for his own.

The base of the hunt was a great encampment in an open meadow by a clear stream. It consisted of tents, men and animals, including horses and elephants for the hunt and pack mules. Trackers would go out into the forest each evening to locate the animals – tiger, wild boar, deer and antelope – at the water-holes. Tiger were hunted by leaving a kill to entice them, then cornering them and driving them towards the hunters who were generally mounted on elephants. Deer and antelope were chased on horseback after a herd was located. Boar were flushed out by beaters spread across the forest, then pursued on horseback or on foot.

In recent years, Rana Amar had preferred to hunt boar

on horseback, pig-sticking as Prince Chara contemptuously thought of it. His father was growing old, needed to be replaced! He himself preferred to hunt this most ferocious, unpredictable, dangerous of beasts on foot in the classic way, an infinitely more exciting operation. He would await the boar in an open glade into which the beaters would drive it. There he would confront the maddened beast with only spear in hand, awaiting its sudden charge. He would plunge his spear at the exact point below the left ear, arresting the charge, pinning the boar and using the stuck spear to vault over its body. Once it was laid thus low, he would hold down the struggling animal until it died. Now *that* was a real fight, he reflected as he followed his father's tall chestnut, crashing through the undergrowth beneath the vast canopy of *neem* trees that obscured the morning sun.

The boar finally turned to face its tormentors on the far side of a small grassy glade. Prince Chara reined in his bay to watch his father. The clanking of the beater's iron cans and the rattle of drums had died down, leaving an eerie stillness, broken only by the snorting of the horses and the harsh breathing of the wild boar at bay. It was a gigantic creature, the top of the brush of black hair above the ridge of its neck almost four feet from the ground. Surely this king merited the classic kill rather than being stuck from the back of a horse.

All those years to grow to such great size, then this end, Prince Chara thought, steadying his own breathing. That is life. My father too has grown to great size. Should I have him die in this glade? He sighed. The timing was not right. His father had stature as well as size. He himself had to acquire a certain status in the eyes of the Rajputs first. Let his father pull the chestnuts – an appropriate phrase, he thought, cynically observing the colour of the Rana's mount – out of the fire.

The sun was halfway up to its noon point. Prince Chara briefly observed its shimmering silver disc to his right, glaring down from a pale blue sky above the treetops. The harsh cries of parakeets intruded upon the near-stillness. The reek of decayed leaves was overlaid by the strong stale animal smell of their prey.

Man and beast erupted as if they had chosen the moment by common accord. The boar charged straight across the glade and the Rana's mount shot forward. The Rana anticipated the boar's swerve to the fraction of an instant. Split-second timing, Prince Chara noted with grudging admiration, as the spear flashed to smash into the mark at the nape of the neck. Still grasping the spear, the Rana jerked his chestnut to a shuddering stop, almost on its haunches. The thrust was so effective that the boar, its power of motion shattered, was immediately halted in its stride. A squeal of rage and agony suddenly ended in an anguished scream as it collapsed on its side. Blood gushed from the lacerated wound, white ligaments and pink flesh showed beneath the grey hide and spindly black hairs. The Rana let go his spear. The boar gave a shuddering sigh and died. The stench of its faeces smote the clear air.

Prince Chara sought his opportunity after they had dismounted, inspected the dead animal, remounted and were awaiting the arrival of the beaters, who would follow the horses' tracks.

'He's a huge bastard!' the Rana exclaimed proudly.

'As big as an Emperor,' Prince Chara observed.

The Rana's great bulk turned towards him. 'Now what the devil do you mean by that?'

'Timing is as important in a revolt, Sire, as it is in the hunt, over which you have just displayed a superb command.' He eased his long, lithe body on the stirrups. His bay jerked its head upwards. 'The Emperor will leave Kabul for Lahore before long. When he is there, we must arrange an antelope hunt, to which he is addicted almost as much as to wine. Shortly before we declare our revolt, we shall make a dead imperial pig of our Muslim Emperor while he is out hunting.'

The Rana clicked an impatient tongue. He was more interested in his kill of the moment. 'Why talk about the improbable?' He paused, scratched a reflective chin, eyed Prince Chara. 'You must have a scheme in mind. Spit it out, Prince.'

'Only on condition that you assure me on your sacred honour that you will not breathe it to a soul,' Prince Chara demanded boldly. He hastened to add, 'An attempted assassination is not like a rebellion. The fewer people who know of it the better.'

'All right, you have my word,' the Rana stated reluctantly. 'But your whole attitude is presumptuous.'

To hell with you too, Prince Chara thought. 'Pray forgive me, Sire, but my sole purpose is the restoration at all costs of our sacred Rajput honour. Having instituted a search since the beginning of this year, I have had a secret visit from a nobleman of Lahore named Noor Deen. He has been closely in touch with Prince Husrau and others of rebellious mind, including Itibar, a powerful eunuch of the imperial *harem* in Lahore. He told me that whenever the Emperor goes out hunting antelopes, he races ahead of his entourage for the kill.' He smiled faintly. 'Such impetuosity appears to be a prerogative of rulers! Since the Emperor is alone at such times, he opens himself up as the prey of anyone who wishes to hunt him!'

A rustle of undergrowth and the hum of voices heralded the approach of the Rana's men. Prince Chara quickly outlined details of his plan to his father. By the time he finished, the Rana's turban was slow-nodding in approval. Crashing sounds announced men forcing their way towards the glade. The hum of voices became a babble. The reek of the great boar's corpse was a grim reminder of what lay ahead for the Emperor, the imperial pork flesh of a Muslim, Prince Chara thought.

September 1607

When General Wahid limped into his suite overlooking the ornate western garden of the Lahore palace that morning, Prince Jahan had no inkling from his urbane exterior that anything important required attention. It was only when the general suggested that he might like to take a walk in the gardens that the prince realized something serious had occurred. The craggy-faced general, with the bristling iron-grey moustache and shaven head, was not only a distinguished cavalryman, whose limp was the result of wounds sustained in the Emperor Akbar's last campaign, but also currently the security chief of the Emperor Jehangir.

As he rose and strode decisively towards the door, Prince Jahan realized that he was no longer reacting like a boy prince who had never had a boyhood, but as a man. The visit to Kabul had changed him.

With General Wahid beside him, he strode past the saluting guards along the wide palace corridors and emerged into the morning sunlight. They exchanged pleasantries until they reached the red sandstone walkways which lined both sides of the long pools, coloured turquoise by their tiles. Pruned shrubs of pentax separated wide beds of marigolds, whose spicy scent tinctured the air. Only the flow-sounds of cascades, the splashing of fountains, the screeching of mynahs in the *ashok* and eucalyptus trees and the hum of an occasional bee disturbed the stillness.

When he was certain that they were alone, the general broached the subject on his mind. 'Your Royal Highness, I may have uncovered a plot to assassinate your father.' He spoke soberly, but his deep voice bore the sharp edge of outrage.

Prince Jahan paused, the general with him. They pretended to look at the silver-gold fish in the waters of a pool, through the reflection of a pluming white cloud from the blue sky. 'Give me the details,' he requested casually, as if he were seeking information about the fish, realizing that his calmness had registered favourably with his companion.

'I have yet to discover the exact details,' General Wahid responded. 'All my sources have unearthed is that a dancing girl from Egypt, named Nadia, revealed it to her friend, another dancing girl. This girl mentioned it to her merchant lover, whom she did not know was one of my trusted spies.'

Prince Jahan was tempted to ask who the merchant was, but refrained because such sources were best kept secret. 'Seems a little far-fetched at third hand,' he commented. 'And yet the timing would be right. Our presence in Kabul, demonstrating the might of the imperial army, so intimidated Shah Abbas of Persia and the rebellious Afghan nobles and chiefs that they almost grovelled in their submission to our Emperor. The only way to dislocate the unity and strength of the Empire today would be to assassinate him. I suppose the Persians, the Afghans or the Pathans are behind the plot.'

'That is my perception too,' the general rejoined, glancing sideways at a plop which revealed a kingfisher skimming away from the water with a small fish in its beak. 'Throughout history, rulers who could not be beaten in battle have often been foully murdered.'

If the attempt succeeds, I shall ascend the throne, Prince Jahan thought. Or would I? Would it not be my brother, Prince Husrau, whom the powers that be in this part of the world would support? 'I presume you will investigate this rumour thoroughly?'

'Of course, but I came to you directly I heard it so you could take precautions to prevent the Emperor from exposing himself to any risk. For instance, he would be well advised not to go out hunting tomorrow.'

'Certainly. But, as you know, if the Emperor thought we were trying to protect him, he would deem it his duty to expose himself to danger, with confidence in himself and faith in Almighty Allah's protection.' Prince Jahan did not wish to add that, in his view, his father was addicted as much to such acts of bravado as to wine. He pondered a while. 'He will never permit cancellation of tomorrow's antelope hunt! How do you propose proceeding?'

'I shall first cause inquiries to be made of this dancing girl, Nadia, bring her in if necessary.'

Prince Jahan thought swiftly, became filled with a sense of urgency. Any hunt, but especially an antelope hunt, would expose the Emperor to enormous danger. 'When and where does she dance?'

'Every night at the Seven Veils Tavern.'

'Do you know where she lives?'

'No.'

'She would ply her other trade between dances at the tavern?'

'Almost certainly, though like all those of her profession, she will be well guarded there.'

'If there is a plot, we must uncover it before tomorrow's hunt. You and I shall visit the Seven Veils Tavern tonight.'

The more he thought about the rumour during the rest of that day, the more Prince Jahan became convinced of its truth. A great hunt was the perfect place for such a deed. Following a tradition established by the Emperor Akbar, the forest area selected for the hunt, the *qamargah*, was sixty miles long by four miles wide. For the past four weeks, ten thousand specially selected soldiers of the

236

imperial army had surrounded a vaster area, acting as beaters to drive the jungle animals into the *qamargah*, where the Emperor, accompanied by selected courtiers and armed variously with bow and arrow, sword, lance, musket or even a lasso, would hunt for five days. He would on occasion ride alone, a practice which he unfailingly followed when hunting antelope. At the end of the five days, the nobles, the lords and ladies-in-waiting, the troopers and soldiers respectively would take their turns in the *qamargah*. At this stage, traditionally, holy men would appear to beg that the lives of the remaining animals be spared.

General Wahid had timed their departure from the palace that night. They slunk out unobserved at 10 P.M., disguised as attendants, a man and a boy in dark cloaks, going off-duty to visit the city taverns. They walked side by side in silence until they reached the tradesmen's quarter. There were few pedestrians abroad at this hour. The shops lining the streets were shuttered for the night. The occasional palanquin, revealing gay colours in the red-gold light of the street flares, was accompanied by the pad, pad, pad of the bearers' feet. Every clippety-clop-clop of the hooves of horses drawing closed carriages, intertwined with rattling wheels, left behind odours of horse sweat and dried dung. A drunk staggered past, mumbling to himself.

The first herald of the Street of Taverns was a constant hum of voices, underlaid by tinkling strings and the deep thud-beat of drums, dislocated by an occasional burst of raucous laughter. Never having visited this street before, Prince Jahan felt a throbbing anticipation unconnected with the purpose of the visit. Kings and princes are largely denizens of palaces. They never visit the beating heartlands of their cities and forts, merely ride through them when necessary. They do not enjoy these sectors of sin, least of all at night, but have its pleasures brought to their residences. Tonight would be a new experience for him, merely as an onlooker though, not a participant, because his heart was given to Mumtaz Mahal. 'I appreciate your acceptance of my decision to visit the tavern with you,' he remarked to General Wahid.

'I try not to oppose or object to the inevitable. In this case, I considered you sufficiently mature and responsible to make up your own mind. I also appreciated your decisiveness.'

Prince Jahan experienced a rush of gratitude and respect for this strong man. 'That's wonderful, especially as you are exposing yourself to the risk of harm befalling the Emperor's son.'

The general shrugged broad shoulders. 'All life is a risk. Your royal father and you are under my protection. I'm confident that you can look after yourself tonight.' His smile became mischievous. 'Besides, you *want* to do this yourself. And it should be a lot of fun!'

The noise increased, coming from beneath the glow cast upwards from the multi-flares of the Street of Taverns towards a pale night sky scattered with stars. The hum of voices became loud and discordant, the music and drumming a clash of harmonies and rhythms, the raucous laughter hoarse and drunken. Chanting and singing in fractured cacophony disturbed Prince Jahan's senses. This was no way to appreciate culture, but then people were not here for culture but for enjoyment from the desert of life in the oases of the taverns.

When they turned into the street, Prince Jahan discovered another world. No vehicles, only palanquins, were permitted along its length, which ran straight between two-storeyed attached buildings, with never a tree or a shrub, to end abruptly in darkness far beyond. People in all types of clothing jostled one another, their races as always distinguishable by their headgear, the red Muslim fez dominating. Huge Pathans, tall Rajputs and Sikhs, mingled with white-capped Egyptians, black-capped Afghans and many a soldier's leather helmet. A dwarf in a gold cloak waddled beside a giant blue-clad Gujarati. Groups of men stood in front of the taverns, just gawking, their eyes inquisitive, faces gleaming in the flarelight. Odours of sandalwood, spicy camphor, frankincense, myrrh, stale sweat and sharp urine punctured the cool night air.

'Many of these men are waiting in the hope of seeing their favourite entertainers,' General Wahid remarked, as they threaded their way through the crowds. As if to prove him right, a palanquin was deposited in front of a tavern across the street. They paused, noting the lighted sign of the tavern which announced Paradise Seraglio in Arabic letters. The bare-chested Nubian bearers came erect, arms folded, black torsos gleaming with sweat. The pale blue curtains parted, a hooded, cloaked female figure emerged, paused to acknowledge the splattering cheers of the onlookers and hurried to the barred entrance door. A small latch was opened to her knock, an eye must have surveyed her for she was quickly admitted and the door slammed shut again.

'The woman is obviously a famous nautch dancer,' General Wahid volunteered.

'Do all these places exercise such a rigorous security system?' Prince Jahan inquired, surprised.

'The more exclusive places need it, otherwise the most beautiful singers and dancers in the Empire would be kidnapped! Remember Lahore is infested with some of the wildest men in the world. There are, of course, taverns and brothels for the general public farther down the street. Entry to the exclusive places is, however, restricted to regular patrons or by invitation.'

'How are we going to get into the Seven Veils Tavern?'

'I have arranged for it. Hence our disguises, beneath our attendants' cloaks, as a visiting merchant from Kandhar and, forgive me the liberty, Your Royal Highness, his son, with plenty of money, out on the town for a night.'

The Seven Veils Tavern was located on their side of the street, about halfway down. The crowd congregated before the tavern was even greater than that in front of the others. Nadia must be among the more famous of the dancers. At the shuttered door, they went through a ritual to gain entrance. The general produced a scroll, unrolled it and held it up for the eye peering through the peep-hole to scrutinize. The eye roved quickly up, down and across the street before the door was opened and hastily closed behind them.

They stood in a marble-floored ante-room, in the glow of shaded lamp-light. Prince Jahan's first impression was of a delicately perfumed incense that not merely clung to the air but *was* the air. The soft strumming of an Egyptian lyre set the mood of the place. There was no other sound. As uniformed attendants silently took their cloaks, a large man, almost as round as he was tall, glided forward with the grace that many fat men display. His face was broad, pudgy and shiny, his black moustaches seemed to spread across his face, reaching for circular golden earrings. His eyelids and lashes had been darkened with *kohl*, leaving the thin black slits of the eyes almost hidden by their folds. His forehead was broad beneath a high gold-coloured Egyptian Pharaoh cap.

'I am Anwar, the humble owner of this poor tavern,' he announced in a sing-song voice, a child reciting an oft repeated lesson. 'You honour me with your presence, Lord Latif and his son, Lord Ahlip. Please follow me.'

He led the way through another ante-room, much larger this time. 'We like our patrons to be assured of privacy,' he stated, explaining the absence of guests in the rooms. He opened a door and they suddenly faced an Arabian Nights dream of a garden. Lit by the glow of pink, red and green lanterns, with a large pool as its centrepiece, it was open to the stars. In the middle of the pool was a stage, served from the rear by an arched bridge. The garden consisted of sculpted shrubs, pruned low enough for the patrons who occupied private rooms lining the open verandahs that ran along three sides of the garden, to watch the performances in state.

As they followed Anwar to their private room, dead centre with the stage, pleasant odours of cooking titillated Prince Jahan's appetite. Their room was narrow but deep.

'Our world-famous belly dancer Nadia appears at midnight,' Anwar informed them when they were seated. 'The dance of the seven veils. When it is over, she will visit you personally, should you desire . . . er . . . more private entertainment.' He rubbed his pudgy hands together, his white-toothed smile as delicate as the suggestion. This was no common brothel! General Wahid must have paid a pretty price for the event.

A long low brass table in the centre of the room contained a small golden wine ewer and three gold wine goblets with beautifully chased handles, two matching opium pipes and a tiny golden bell. Anwar, having been paid in advance, had obviously prepared the room for his two guests and Nadia. He bowed, mostly an inclination of the head, the best a man can do whose huge stodgy torso gets in the way, and gestured them to be seated.

Placing their staffs beside them, Prince Jahan and the general sat facing each other. Anwar raised his hands and clapped three times. A tall servant appeared as if in answer to an Al-il-deen rubbing his magic lamp.

'Pour wine for the noble lords,' Anwar commanded.

Since he never drank wine or other liquor, as the servant moved forward, Prince Jahan glanced questioningly at the general, who raised a restraining palm. 'We are both true

241

believers, forbidden to take wine,' he stated. 'Some pome-granate juice perhaps?'

Anwar gave his oily smile. 'Certainly, my lord.' He glanced at the servant. 'See to it,' he commanded. He watched the man depart. 'The scriptures do not forbid you other forms of delectation, my lords. As arranged through your generous patronage, you shall have the personal attendance of our famed Egyptian belly dancer, Nadia, who is honoured at the privilege you are extending to her.' His smile was roguish, but Prince Jahan sensed the tough cunning beneath it. 'You may make such arrangements with her as you desire. She has a comfortable suite upstairs . . .' He left the purpose of the suite deliciously vague. 'Please ring that bell should you need service. And now, if you will pardon me, my noble lords . . .' He was gone, moving as smoothly as a huge well-oiled wagon wheel, before Prince Jahan could grasp the fact of his departure.

'A remarkable character!' Prince Jahan observed, shaking his head in wonder. 'Straight from the Arabian Nights.'

General Wahid smiled. 'He is the most successful, wealthy taverner in Lahore.' He nodded towards the plat-form across the water. 'Notice how cleverly he has stage-managed the principal act. The performance can be clearly witnessed from every one of the rooms, the red velvet hangings of which can be released and drawn for complete privacy. Dancers act only as guests in these rooms, provid-ing the main course . . . er . . .' He grinned. 'Any needed dessert is served upstairs!'

The meal that followed, served from gold-plated con-tainers on gold platters, was a feast worthy of the imperial palace. Each dish – marsalas, fish kebabs with onion and green capsicum slices, *tandori* pheasant, roast lamb with curds and pickles, chicken biriyani and every type of bread – was accompanied by the odour of the more delicate spices, basil, fenugreek, lemon-grass, sweet anise. Fruit, desserts, Persian sweetmeats and Turkish delight followed, the containers being left on the table against the guests' continued desires.

Finally, when Prince Jahan's stomach was tight as a drum, the single clang of a bell broke through the subdued hum of conversation around him. Total silence followed its echoes. They both glanced towards the stage. Two rows of huge Nubian torchbearers, their bare black chests gleaming above silver loin cloths, muscular thighs powerful in the golden light, marched slowly on to the stage and took their places at its rear. A single drum started a slow *tap . . . thari kitha . . . thari kitha . . . thari kitha*. A reedy pipe took up the beat, dissolved into the haunting traditional belly dance melody. Stringed instruments joined in. Slow tinkling finger cymbals announced Nadia's arrival. In the breathless hush that followed, the jangling of her brass ornaments was a sudden gasp of sound. But sound alone, not sight.

Caught up in the atmosphere, all thoughts of his mission, even of Mumtaz Mahal, forgotten, Prince Jahan waited expectantly for Nadia's entrance.

Still she did not appear. Instead, the rhythmic jangling rose to a swiftness and an unbelievable crescendo that dazzled the senses.

When he finally thought he could not bear the suspense any longer, she appeared. Gliding, bare feet softly thudding a slow rhythm on the boarded floor to the forward motion of each alternate hip. Unusually tall for a belly dancer, the skin of her arms and the face above the pink gauze veil was ivory, contrasting sharply with long hair gleaming jet black, tight drawn from a noble forehead and held in place by a glittering tiara of diamonds. She was dressed in a long garment of pink, so diaphanous that her curves were revealed, full breasts, tiny waist curving to beautifully contoured hips and generous thighs, without revealing any part of her body.

'A divine gift from Allah!' the general muttered to himself.

And indeed she was, Prince Jahan silently agreed. He watched enthralled as she came to the centre of the stage, paused, made the *namaskaram*.

She began to dance. Eyes glued to her, the music merely a forgotten dream in the background, Prince Jahan watched with rapt attention as she revealed the seven veils, changing the rhythm and the pattern of her dance as she removed each veil, from the hip thrust to the wiggle of shapely buttocks, the side sway, sinuous arms waving, neck moving as if it had a side-to-side life of its own and, finally, a hip swing that kept them both shaking their heads in amazement.

'Dear Allah, she must have a hundred-inch circular hip swing!' General Wahid exclaimed. 'No wonder she has never dared perform in the palace. She would have been retained permanently as a slave!'

Nadia removed her seventh veil to a mighty clash of cymbals, tambourines, strings and drums. She was breathing deeply, nostrils dilating, huge breasts rising as if they would burst through the pink gauze. Revealed but not seen, Prince Jahan thought again. He had an erection so stiff that it hurt. From the earliest days of his sex-consciousness, he had determined that he would not respond to any demands of sex or the desire for wine and opium. He had seen how dissolute ways, over-indulgence of the body's pleasures, had destroyed people. His grandfather had encouraged him in these disciplines. Notwithstanding all the offerings and the compulsions of the palace, his only experience of sex had been in his wet dreams, often without the actual dreaming, a pleasant passing out of his fluid, with the awakening to sticky stuff on his night robe and the raw odour, both of which he loathed.

His erection remained while Nadia stood there, seeming

244

lost in a trance. Shouts, cheers, the banging of spoons on golden platters rose around her. A continuous clinking on the marble floors announced the flinging of gold coins which would be collected for Nadia by the servants, but only later, to satisfy decorum.

General Wahid reached into his tunic pocket, fished out a few gold coins and flung them outside. 'A rare experience, my lord prince, well worth the price, don't you think?'

'Absolutely,' Prince Jahan breathed. He could neither take his eyes off Nadia nor loosen his erection. She remained standing motionless on the stage. The torchbearers slowly trooped away. The applause died down to a hush again. Servants in long golden robes arrived with dippers and slowly, deliberately extinguished the torches, one by one. The stage grew dimmer and dimmer, turning Nadia's pale figure into a shadow. The goddess of light gleamed faintly, ethereal in a faint glow. Then total darkness. The end of reality or illusion.

She entered their narrow room preceded by the low jingle of anklets and the high scent of myrrh. She bowed to them in salutation. The servant who had escorted her drew the curtain closed and departed. The moment her dark, magnetic eyes above the veil fixed themselves on Prince Jahan a contact was established that sent a thrill through his entire being. She bowed in salutation, those eyes remaining intently on his, as if locked into his gaze and imprisoned there.

He had seen many women dancers, poets and musicians before, but all of them had been presented to him in Court, respectful, submissive, generally available for the taking. He had never had interest in any of them. The ladies of the imperial *harem* could only be seen at the *Meena* Bazaar. He had had no interest in them either. When he met Mumtaz Mahal, he knew why he had remained a virgin man. It was to hold his body for Mumtaz alone. His behaviour was unique in a prince, especially a Moghul, who was expected to prove himself sexually by bedding as many women as possible, as frequently as possible. He was certain that his father and others in the imperial court regarded him as freakish or impotent. They knew he was no homosexual, as his ancestor Babur had been. Tonight, he was seeing a woman on personal terms for the first time. This one was of such startling beauty and exuded such incredible magnetism that he was in her thrall. He had sunk into a morass of desiring, the focal point of which was his rock-hard penis. He wanted to grasp this woman to him, to feel the fragrance of her breath on his face, to plunge his virgin penis into her and ease its pain.

Incredibly, she knew all this.

'Pray be seated, Madam.' General Wahid's voice cut into Prince Jahan's desires. He shivered, trembled and tried to relax, but his thoughts were confused.

She did not kneel in greeting, but sank gracefully on to a cushion and removed her veil. Her face was small, exquisite, the nostrils thin and fine, the skin like alabaster, the eyes black as onyx. She exuded a tantalizing odour of fresh sweat now, combining with the heady scent of myrrh to further arouse Prince Jahan's desiring.

'You are not a Muslim?' Prince Jahan inquired, feeling his callow youth before this woman of the world.

'No, I am a worshipper of *Ra*, the sun god.' Her voice was mellow gold with the hint of a caress to it.

She declined the wine which the general offered, sipped some pomegranate juice instead, ate a purple plum, split open a pistachio with long delicate fingers and popped the nut into her mouth. Prince Jahan watched her every movement with fascination, she was so naturally graceful. They talked about her early days in Cairo, the school of dancing at which she studied, the ageing belly dancer who

246

finally taught her how to use her talents to the fullest, the journey through the Middle East. Her language was refined, her manners perfect, but Prince Jahan somehow sensed that all of it was to create an image, to fill a gap in time. He knew he was right when she shot a question at them out of the blue. 'Do you both want to lay me, or is it just one of you?' The unexpected, blunt words combined with a hungry gaze she directed at him made Prince Jahan quiver like a soft curd.

'We would both like to go upstairs with you,' General Wahid volunteered, causing Prince Jahan to wonder whether the general was interested in bedding the woman too.

'Follow me then.' She had suddenly, subtly taken command.

Prince Jahan and the general picked up their staffs. No one even spared them a glance as they followed Nadia down the verandah, up a broad staircase at the rear of the building. They proceeded along the balcony verandah, lit by flares, overlooking the central courtyard, to great double doors of brown teakwood directly above the dance platform. The ante-room they entered was lit by subdued lamps with red shades that created a rosy glow. Wine-coloured carpets were scattered on pink marble floors, rose-tinted cushions against walls adorned with tapestries depicting sex scenes. The heady scent of frankincense from glowing braziers on marble stands joined with the furnishings and the total silence to create an exotic trap.

'The young one first,' Nadia stated and led Prince Jahan into the bedroom. It was furnished in similar style save that it had only a huge rosy cushion in the centre. Nadia closed the door behind her, turned to face him.

'How old are you?' she demanded.

'Fifteen,' he replied, tremulously.

'Good. I can only reach my orgasm through teenage

cocks. I love them, but you're the first to come here. Have you ever had a woman before?'

'No.'

'You lie.'

Anger flamed within him, but he was powerless to express it, so filled was he with the atmosphere of the room and the magnetic presence of the exotic woman. He could feel the caress of her being as if she were enveloping his whole body with hers. 'I never lie,' he shot back. 'I have avoided . . .' The memory of Mumtaz Mahal for whom he had desired to hold himself pure came flooding back. Oh my beloved, save me, he implored, but the beseeching was less than half-hearted. Mumtaz was hundreds of miles away. Nadia was here and now, with wild desire for her setting him afire.

Her gaze on him intensified, grew deeper, and he knew that she was not pretending. Courtesan she may be, but she desired him too. The knowledge stimulated him so much that his erection pushed against his pantaloons. She approached him slowly, one hip before another, a tigress stalking its prey. He, the prey. Despairing and yet in an ecstasy of anticipation.

She paused directly before him. Her breathing fanned him, smelled fragrant with liquorice root. The fresh odour of her sweat transfixed him, semen stirring in his scrotum. He had to hold back. Dear Allah, he simply had to hold back.

The recollection of Mumtaz Mahal returned. Almighty God, save me from impurity.

But he did not really want to be saved. Nadia's hands reached out, touched his thighs, just above the knees, moved slowly upwards, fingertips caressing ever so lightly, white fingers, nails painted purple, stirring him.

Her nostrils distended. Desire overpowered him. He reached blindly for her.

Chapter 15

She woke with a start and had to stifle the scream welling up in her throat. She sat up staring wildly about her, trying to focus on her surroundings. This was her small room in the family mansion. Through the dim, turned-down light of the hanging lamp, she could make out Sati's figure lying on the carpet beside her divan bed, huddled beneath a white bed-sheet, smelling of night-clothes.

Mumtaz Mahal did not want to disturb the sleeping woman, but even as her wild heartbeats started to steady, Sati flung aside her sheet and sat up. 'What is it? Are you all right?'

'Yes . . . I think so . . . yes . . . but I had a terrible nightmare and it is still with me.'

'You and your dreams . . .' The older woman was about to turn over and go to sleep again, but something about her ward arrested her. 'My poor baby, you are shivering.' She rose to her feet, sat beside Mumtaz, held her close.

The warmth and softness of her 'other' mother's body was comforting, but the terror remained in Mumtaz' mind, seeming to flood her whole being. 'I dreamt that my betrothed was about to be enveloped by a horrible cloud . . . He was standing in an open meadow and I was running towards him. He kept looking towards me, seeing only me and suddenly there was this horrible thing . . . it was like a black cloud . . . uh . . . but it wasn't either, because it was sticky, steamy and oily . . . slowly approaching him across the meadow. I tried to shout a warning to him, but no sound would emerge. I ran towards him but my legs were so heavy I could not lift them because the meadow had become a bog and my leaden feet were sticking in the mud. And all the while . . . all the while he kept looking at me . . . and I suddenly knew with horror that he was aware of the danger, was begging me to save him. But I could not. I was helpless to move. Oh Sati, I *know* my prince is in mortal danger. I'm terrified. What can I do?' She was sobbing now, unable to restrain the tears that were pouring down her cheeks.

'Hush, little paddy-bird. Hush the beating of your heart. I do not want to say that you are being fanciful. If you feel it so strongly, your prince may need your help. We women are destined to endure the torments of the damned for our loved ones, from a distance. The one thing we can do at such times is to pray to Almighty Allah to extend His divine protection to the one in danger.' She released Mumtaz, gripped her by the shoulders, stared into her eyes.

Mumtaz looked at the woman with wonder. She had never seen Sati's gaze so hypnotic and compelling.

'We are both going to *will* the danger away from your prince,' Sati continued. 'We shall call on Allah to give us *strength* of *will* to do it, even if we have to concentrate on it all night.'

It was one of those rare occasions when Prince Chara dined alone with the Rana. He had of course engineered it and they had just finished a pleasantly dull dinner in his father's small dining room. The attendants had cleared the table and left the room leaving only coffee and the inevitable breath-freshening spices in golden salvers on the Indian mahogany table.

As Prince Chara had expected, an unnamed visitor was announced, the odd hour making it obvious that the matter was urgent. His first impression of the man who was ushered in by the chief attendant was that he was dusty, obviously from a long, hard ride on horseback. When he came erect from bowing to the Rana, he was revealed as a lean, tough-looking Sikh of about forty with a trim black moustache and beard, dressed in dark blue *jodhpurs* and white tunic. The bow rather than obeisance indicated that he was not of greatly inferior rank. He waited until the door had clicked shut behind the attendant before announcing himself. 'I am Lord Jared Singh. I have just arrived from Lahore.' His thin, high voice sounded almost as dusty as his long ride must have been.

'You are more than welcome, Lord Jared,' the Rana stated. 'This is my son, Prince Chara.' He motioned towards the prince who nodded. 'Please sit down. Some refreshments after your ride?'

Lord Jared straightened his shoulders, placed his elbows on the dining table. 'Later, if you don't mind. My news is more important. The beating of animals in the Lahore forest into the *qamargah* has been completed. The Emperor leaves on his hunt tomorrow morning. His first chase will be after antelope.' His smile was as thin as his voice. 'The stage is set for the hunt of the imperial tiger.'

'Pig!' Prince Chara interjected.

'We shall raise the standard of revolt here tomorrow,' the Rana stated.

'How will you do that?' Lord Jared inquired, as casually as the Rana had declared his intention.

The Rana's eyes flickered towards Prince Chara.

'By a very simple gesture,' Prince Chara replied pleasantly. 'Tomorrow happens to be the day the imperial tax-gatherers collect their blood from the peasants who farm the Crown lands claimed by the Emperor. We shall send out messengers tonight directing our own tax collectors not to deliver their collections to the imperial bloodsuckers.'

'Tell Lord Jared how we propose dealing with the blood-sucking imperial auditors who have arrived in Chitor. They

251

will assess our own contributions from what is now the *jagir* of Mewar, our own former kingdom, no longer hereditary, which has so generously been granted to us by the Moghuls who conquered it.' The Rana's tone was harsh. He was referring to kingdoms and lands possessed through conquest, over which *jagirs* were given to rulers and nobles who were responsible for revenue collection in their areas. This revenue represented their agreed salaries, any excess being poured into the imperial treasury. It was *zat*, representing rank, that regulated the salary of the holder. A *sawar* was the number of soldiers he had to provide for the Emperor; the larger the *sawar*, the greater the *zat* to support its numbers. The Emperor Akbar had gradually converted the system of tax gathering from goods and services to cash, precious metals and jewels.

'By another simple gesture,' Prince Chara could not keep a diabolical note from underlying the affected charm of his voice, 'we shall return them to Agra . . . er . . . minus any tribute and minus their greedy, grasping right hands. Is that not the punishment for robbery under Muslim law?'

The mixed scents of Nadia enveloped Prince Jahan, over-powering him. He reached for the suppleness of her lithe body, held it with eager hands. Her skin was smooth as a snake's, yet underlaid by a hint of soft give which drove him wild. Eyes closed, dimly aware that he was no longer in control of himself for the first time in his life, he did not care, not even when a fork of lightning flashed Mumtaz in his fevered brain. It was just as quickly extinguished. Nadia's breathing, tinctured from deep down inside her with desire, was a caress on his face. She pressed a soft pubis against his bursting penis. The downy feel of it nearly caused him to explode. Some Moghul legacy of having to prove manhood gave him desperate control.

She clasped his penis with one hand. He shivered. 'Mm

252

. . . m . . . h.' The sound was a growl from deep within her. She reached out the cool fingers of her other hand, began unbuttoning his silk *kurtha*.

'Let him go!'

The low, sharp command penetrated the fog of Prince Jahan's brain. It had come from some other world.

Nadia released him, turned around in a flash. 'Get out!' she hissed.

What was happening? Prince Jahan opened his eyes. A tall figure was framed in the open doorway. Who was this? Merciful Allah, it was General Wahid. The mission. It all came flooding back into Prince Jahan's fevered brain. The general's gaze at him was magnetic, stern, commanding, as if Nadia did not exist.

'Leave us alone. Get out!' Nadia's voice was low, intense with fury. She raised a hand, finger pointing imperiously. 'I said, get out.'

Yes, yes, get out, General Wahid, how dare you interfere, Prince Jahan echoed in his lust-driven mind.

The general continued to ignore her. 'We don't have much time,' he quietly advised Prince Jahan. 'Remember all we have to do before morning.'

The harsh reminder of duty brought shame flooding through Prince Jahan.

A low cry of rage escaped Nadia. In one swift movement, she reached into her tunic with her right hand, raised the hand high. A long-bladed knife gleamed between her clenched fingers. She advanced slowly, cat-like, on the man who had thwarted her craving. In a trice, Prince Jahan's young mind comprehended how this woman had fought for everything she desired, clawing her way to the top of her world. Every instinct told him to leap to the general's rescue, but he hesitated. He had never laid hands on a woman before, never fought two to one, never interfered with another's pride, so he merely followed Nadia like a shadow.

To his surprise, General Wahid continued standing at the doorway, relaxed now, an amused smile on his face. He remained motionless as Nadia plunged the knife downwards, with a wild shriek, then whirled her arm around to thrust forward and upward with the speed of a striking cobra. Only then did the general move. He slashed swiftly down and sideways with his left hand, deflecting the blow, grabbed her arm at the elbow with his right hand. He must have pressed the nerve inside with his thumb. A grunt of pain escaped Nadia. The knife clattered on the marble floor.

Powerless in the general's steely grasp, she tried vainly to claw at his face with her left hand, then slowly gave at the knees, bending to ease the pain from his grip. He held her there. 'Now, lady, if you resist or scream, I'll destroy your hand and you'll never dance again.' He spoke with a deadly quiet certainty. 'We don't make war on women. We are here with a purpose, though one of us nearly forgot it.

'Will you listen quietly?' the general continued, staring at Nadia. 'You can become one of the dregs of humanity, or earn riches beyond your dreaming.' He must have sensed her fury evaporating. 'Riches that will place you above men who take their pleasure of you for a price, men whom you loathe and despise. Riches that can give you all the teenage boys of your desiring, the unspoilt, frenetic young with the crystal clear mountain springs, the fountainheads of sex. What do you choose?'

Moments of total silence passed. The suspense was unbearable. Prince Jahan no longer saw Nadia as a beautiful, desirable, exotic woman, but a pathetic creature, stripped of her mystery. With wonder, the recall of Mumtaz Mahal enveloped him. The maiden of sparkling magic, real magic. In a flash, he comprehended the true mystery of a man and a woman, love. Love that gives meaning to physical union with each act.

Wide-eyed, he saw the tall figure of General Wahid and the half-bent, sideways-twisted body of Nadia, the belly dancer, motionless, as if sculpted.

'You are hurting me. Please release me, I shall listen without calling for help.' The whispered words held a note of pleading.

Prince Jahan knew then that the skirmish had been won, but it was General Wahid, not he, who had been the hero of the hour. Savage determination seized him. He, not any general, was the man of destiny in the Moghul Empire. Never again would a woman deflect him from his purpose or another man best him.

As he stood in the large ante-room of his *harem* at the Lahore palace, facing Prince Jahan and General Wahid, the Emperor Jehangir was angry, frustrated and irritable. To be woken at 3.30 A.M. on any day was outrageous, but he was in neither mood nor fit condition this particular morning. The trusted messenger from Salima Begum at the Agra palace who had arrived last night had brought him the most miserable personal news he had ever received. He had been at dinner in his *harem* at the time and it had driven him to drinking so much that he had passed out on the cushions before the meal was over. Since the imperial custom was that when the ruler 'left' the guests departed, all the concubines who had been attending him had fled away, probably on tiptoe so as not to disturb the sleeping monarch, while the eunuchs had quietly extinguished the tapers.

When he had been abruptly woken up by the hammering at the door, he had thought at first that the banging was in his head. Not all the attentions of a warm perfumed bath, a brief massage, scents and unguents and robing from his hastily summoned female attendants had eased his headache, grainy throat, or the weight of his eyelids. He had continued to feel awful while he strode down the dimly lit *harem* corridors. Thanks be to Allah, at least it was not daylight, for he could not have borne the sun's glare.

Nur Jehan had turned down his invitation to join his *harem* as a concubine and that damned Salima Begum was backing her refusal. How could he hit back? He had promoted Asaf Khan and Ghiyas Beg to the highest rank. They had proved themselves so loyal, dedicated and capable that the imperial treasury and the administration of the Empire, both of which had suffered during the final years of the Emperor Akbar's reign, had been vastly improved. So he could not even dismiss the two men without hurting himself. He had cleverly organized the murder of Sher Afgan. He had attempted to use the betrothal of Prince Jahan as a bait.

All of it had failed. Nur Jehan would not become his chief concubine. He would never lie on that luscious body, gazing at those lustrous eyes. Damn! damn! damn!

When he faced his son in the ante-room, he suddenly identified Prince Jahan with his intense disappointment. Here was someone he could wound so he would have a bed-fellow in his misery. The boy was in love with Mumtaz Mahal. He would put into effect the alternative plan he had evolved, against the very event he now faced, Nur Jehan's refusal of his request. Life was no different from a military battle. One should always have contingency plans. It satisfied a sadistic streak in him, scratched the itch that was cruelty, to think of how miserable Prince Jahan and this Mumtaz Mahal creature as well as Ghiyas Beg and Asaf Khan, the whole stinking lot of them and mostly Nur Jehan, would be when he put this plan into effect. He would teach Nur Jehan not to resist a Moghul Emperor.

* * *

Prince Jahan noted with contempt that his father's eyes were bloodshot and his breath stank from excessive wine-drinking the previous night. His appearance took Prince Jahan back, by contrast, to the dignity of his grandfather. The Emperor Akbar did like his wine but generally partook of it in moderation, an example which his three sons had not followed. The second boy, Prince Murad, and the youngest, Prince Daniyal, had both been addicted to alcohol. Their princely duties had been seriously affected by excessive drinking and both of them had in consequence died young. It was these sad examples, which he had despised and pitied since his earliest days, that had encouraged Prince Jahan to abstain from drink and sex.

Now he kept his eyes lowered. 'I beseech your royal pardon, Sire, but we have uncovered a plot to assassinate you while you are out hunting antelope tom . . . er . . . today.'

'What? A plot to assassinate us, you say?' It finally registered. 'A plot?' Incredulity turned to rage. 'Who dares to plot against us?'

'My brother, Prince Husrau, Sire.' Prince Jahan felt numb as he uttered the words, from conflicting emotions of rage at the impudence of such an attempt, incredulity at the gamble, the stern need to take action, a dash of pity for his brother and recognition of the benefit to himself.

'That is impossible. Prince Husrau is a virtual prisoner in the palace.' The dark, slanting eyes grew contemplative. 'We did of course permit him to roam the gardens of Kabul and, now, Lahore without fetters, but he has seemed to prefer solitude and even begged to be excused on the two occasions we invited him to attend Court functions. It has been apparent to us that he loathes us for the effects of his own sinning. Give us the details.' The news had sobered the Emperor like a splash of icy water on a fuddled head. He was alert now, no longer irritated.

Prince Jahan told of the rumour reaching General Wahid and their encounter with Nadia, omitting details of his personal involvement with the woman. 'The dancing girl learned of the plot from Prince Uzbeg and a wealthy merchant friend of his, both of whom are her ardent admirers. Two nights ago, the prince, while drunk, promised her the world,' his smile was deprecating, 'or, more accurately perhaps, a part of the Empire in exchange for the additional favour of giving up her profession to belong exclusively to him. When she inquired how this was possible, he boasted that he would soon be one of a triumvirate governing the Empire under Prince Husrau, who would be the Emperor in your place, Sire.'

'Prince Uzbeg dared say that. The low, conniving product of pig's offal. We shall have him flayed alive and fed to the ants. As for your brother . . . but go on, Prince. You have more to report and we have interrupted you.'

'General Wahid and I sped to the palace immediately and arrested Prince Uzbeg. On a promise of pardon,' he waited to the count of three for the Emperor's explosion, was relieved when it did not occur, 'Prince Uzbeg revealed the details of the plot to us. Besides himself and Prince Husrau, the leaders are Lord Noor Deen and Lord Ullah. Also involved is the Chief Eunuch, Itibar, as the financier of the conspiracy, and the Sikh, Lord Jared Singh. You were to be killed by Lord Ullah when you went out hunting antelope this morning and raced ahead of the rest of us in the chase, as is your wont, being such an expert rider and hunter. The triumvirate would then have seized the palace with four hundred loyal followers who were privy to the plot and ready for the task. It would have declared Prince Husrau your successor and ruled in his name without hindrance.'

A tense silence fell on the ante-room while the Emperor slowly assimilated the reality of what had been proposed.

He took a step forward, turned, hands clasped behind his back and began pacing the room, his gold sandals clacking on the marble floor. Once up, once down and he stopped, turned his head in Prince Jahan's direction. 'What action have you taken?' His voice was calm.

'With Prince Uzbeg already under confinement, the general and I arrested Lord Noor Deen, Lord Ullah and the eunuch Itibar. We found written evidence of the conspiracy and the involvement of all concerned in Itibar's residence. We have thrown cordons of trusted soldiers around Prince Husrau's quarters and the residences of every single one of the four hundred conspirators. The entire plot has been aborted.'

The Emperor turned to face them. 'You accomplished all this in three hours?'

Prince Jahan glanced sideways at General Wahid, then looked down in embarrassment.

'Your life was at stake, Sire,' the general stated.

'We not only wanted to nip the plot in the bud but also to ensure that every single person who was involved in such a cowardly, damnable conspiracy was punished.' Prince Jahan looked at his father fiercely, challenging him to punish all concerned, including Prince Husrau.

'We get your message, Prince. You are personally satisfied as to the guilt of all concerned?'

'Without a doubt, Sire.'

'And you, General Wahid?'

'I have no doubt whatsoever, Your Majesty. Every single one of them is guilty. Some have already confessed and implicated the others.'

'Good. You, Prince Jahan and General Wahid, are to be commended for your uncompromising loyalty, your wisdom, your zeal, your swift and relentless actions.' A pleased grin touched the corners of the imperial mouth. The Emperor brushed back a moustache with a broad finger. 'Praise be to Almighty Allah, we can now go on the antelope hunt without worry!'

Was that the only important result of this stunning event? Prince Jahan could not believe his ears.

A dreamy look entered the Emperor's face. 'Our punishment shall be as swift and terrible as your investigation. Prince Uzbeg shall be spared since you promised him clemency. We must honour such promises if we are to obtain the cooperation of guilty informants in future. Noor Deen, Ullah and Itibar shall be flayed alive and have honey poured on their bodies. They shall then be tied to stakes and left in the broiling sun for the ants to devour.' He licked thick lips, savouring the tortures his enemies would endure. 'All the other conspirators shall be trampled to death by elephants in our presence next Monday morning. As for Prince Husrau, ah, that is another matter entirely. He is our eldest son and legally our heir. We cannot have him executed.'

Why not, Father? Prince Jahan questioned hotly in his mind. He is my brother, but if he attacked you in my presence, would I not kill him instantly? Is there a special law, different justice, for the Emperor's heir? Should not such a one be vested with a greater duty than anyone else in the land to protect you, rather than cause your death? My grandfather would . . . Prince Jahan paused, remembering how the Emperor Akbar had twice forgiven Jehangir. But surely a rebellion could not be compared to a dastardly assassination attempt? The thoughts, the questions were whirling around in Prince Jahan's head like dervishes. From their core, a question emerged: Do you not want your brother executed to give you a clear line of succession to the throne? His spirit went bleak, because he did not know the answer. Or was it that his dedication to nobility and honour prevented him from facing up to the truth, was making a hypocrite of him?

Suddenly he felt weary. In a daze, he heard his father mutter. 'How to render Prince Husrau totally ineffective without executing him? Emasculation? H'mm. Not a bad idea. Who would want a eunuch for an Emperor?' He seemed to roll the prospect around his brain with relish. 'No, on second thoughts that would not do. We cannot have a Moghul eunuch. It would degrade us all.' His clicked his fingers, straightened up, eyed his son levelly.

'The perfect punishment.' The Emperor chuckled throatily. 'It shall be carried out while we are out hunting this morning. Prince Husrau shall be blinded.'

The Emperor obviously enjoyed the shocked silence that greeted his words. A harsh, merciless, almost bitter expression entered the slanty eyes. 'There is another matter that requires our immediate attention.' He fell to musing. 'We had a message from the Agra palace last night that indicates to us that the family of our Prime Minister, Asaf Khan, is not as . . . er . . . loyal to us as the Prime Minister. It has therefore become expedient for us to separate ourselves from his distaff side. Asaf Khan and his father, Ghiyas Beg, are all we could want in their respective appointments and their dedication to us, yet at times . . .' Unusually for the Emperor, who was seldom at a loss for ideas or words, he hesitated, before plunging on. 'Prince Jahan, although you are betrothed to Asaf Khan's daughter, Mumtaz Mahal, we are now of the view that our Moghul Empire is more in need of an alliance with Persia.'

What on earth was his father talking about? Prince Jahan's brain went numb before the awful realization of the truth, then began a rhythmic pounding.

'We shall have emissaries depart for Persia this morning to arrange for your betrothal to the Princess Amira, daughter of Prince Safawi, who is descended from the Shahs of Persia. A notable family and a lovely girl, we understand.'

The cruel twist of the Emperor's mouth more than the

miserable words caused the roaring in Prince Jahan's ears. Why was the Emperor doing this? Dimly he perceived that the man's pursuit of Nur Jehan had been thwarted. He and his beautiful Mumtaz Mahal were being made the victims of imperial revenge.

Was this his reward for having saved the Emperor's life?

At that moment, Prince Jahan hated his father with such a passion that he trembled before it.

Then the training of years took over. If a prince has any worth, he remains calm in bitter situations. Resolutely Prince Jahan steadied himself. The Emperor could marry him off to the corpse of the late Queen of Sheba, but could not assail his celibacy. He would never, never, never, bed any woman but Mumtaz Mahal. This one thing no ruler could compel him to do. When the time was right, he would marry Mumtaz Mahal, but a *brachmachariya* he would remain until then.

Meanwhile, obedience had to be the order of the day. A cold, fierce determination took over. The correct words emerged. 'Your slightest wish, Sire, is my most imperative command.'

As the days had gone slowly by, Nur Jehan had adapted to life in the imperial *harem* of the Agra palace. She had come to like and respect Salima Begum. Here was someone who could teach her how to wield power from behind the throne. After their first meeting, the old Begum had treated her as a daughter. So when the Emperor sent his missive from Lahore, through a trusted messenger, declaring his love for Nur Jehan and inviting her to become his chief concubine, Salima Begum shared her outrage. Unlike Nur Jehan, however, the Begum's reaction had quickly returned to her customary serenity and self-assurance. 'Leave this in our hands, daughter Nur,' she had insisted. 'We shall reply to the Emperor on your behalf.'

And so it had transpired. The Begum's response had been a masterpiece of specious nothing. Nur Jehan's period of official mourning for her dead husband was not over; she had to consult the *imams* as to the disgrace of a widow becoming a concubine, even of an Emperor, and of the reaction of the entire Muslim world to such an act which was contrary to the teachings – unspecified – of the Holy Koran.

This morning, news of the Emperor's retaliation had reached them while they were in the Begum's chamber. The Begum had immediately cleared the room. Sitting erect as ever, a precious toy clad in gold gauze, her glance at Nur Jehan was sharp and bright. 'The Emperor is showing his teeth,' she advised. 'Do not worry, daughter Nur.'

'I am mainly concerned about the impact of this on poor Mumtaz Mahal, who is, I understand, deeply in love with Prince Jahan.'

'The Christians would say that this is a cross your niece has to bear. Pray Almighty Allah that bearing it this early in her life – she is only fifteen, is she not? – means that better times lie ahead for her. Let us face the facts. The high appointments bestowed on your father and brother were imperial bribes offered to you, the betrothal of your niece to Prince Jahan was a message of family connections to be established. You have rejected the reason for the bribes, so the Emperor is flashing a warning to you.'

'Will he now remove my father and brother from their appointments?' This was the only area in which Nur Jehan felt vulnerable.

'We doubt it. They have both acquitted themselves so well since taking office that they are indispensable to the Emperor, especially at the present time, with the revolt in Mewar, of which he was obviously unaware when he received your rejection of him. If he removes your father and brother from office now, the truth would leak out and impair the image of manhood, fairness and invulnerability the Emperor seeks. He cannot behave like a petulant boy who throws stones at the neighbour's garden when he has been denied its fruit.'

'You are so wise.'

'We are so *old*, daughter Nur. One cannot remain in this gilded prison we call a *harem* without developing the ability to survive against the onslaughts from the world outside.'

'What can we do now?'

'Nothing. This is *our* war. Let the Emperor reveal his strategy. However long it takes, we shall remain non-committal, because the real initiative is with us.' She smiled her alert, white bird smile. 'We do nothing . . . until the enemy is ready to do as *we* desire. There are advantages to being hidden behind *harem* walls!'

'You are right, Your Majesty. It is the lot of women to suffer in silence, to use their brains to bring happiness to their hearts. After all, we women are the earth, men are but planters of seed within us. They plant and move on. The travail of bringing forth life and sustaining it is ours. It is all the will of Almighty Allah.'

A smile hovered around the Begum's paste cheeks. 'Regardless of what the *imams* say, to ascribe will to Allah, the Almighty, the Eternal, the Infinite, is to reduce Him to the level of man. Allah simply *is*. He has no will, no desire, no justice, no love as man conceives it. Allah does not create or destroy, which are merely effects we, dwelling within his body, observe churning around us. Do we humans willingly create or destroy the substances within us, of which we are made? No. Then why would Allah? The Emperor Akbar had the right knowledge when he evolved his new religion, *Din-i-Ilahi*.'

Nur Jehan was amazed. A true believer up to now, she

had accepted the tenets of Islam without question. 'If we women are not the earth, what are we?' she inquired.

'Anything we want to be, so long as we do not try to achieve our desires as men would do.' The Begum paused. 'What is the strongest substance in the world?'

'Rock, iron?'

The neat head shook from side to side. 'The strongest substance in the world is air. You punch it, note how it gives, only to return the moment you withdraw your hand. It is invisible, life-giving, seemingly compliant and weak. Yet when it gathers itself in fury, its storms can lash the great oceans, create tidal waves, remove mountains, acquire the heat of raging fires to whip them back to more dreadful intensity. Fire, earth, water, air, the greatest of these is air. Women can be the air of life, to sustain it or to destroy. If we women are the earth, then we must also act like the other three elements, fire to inflame, water to douse the flames, air to control everything.'

Mumtaz Mahal gazed at her father in horror. 'You mean I am no longer betrothed to Prince Jahan?' she demanded. Suddenly she felt as if the walls of her small room were closing in on her. For once, Asaf Khan, who had ridden back from his visit to Lahore to convey the news personally, was visibly in torment. 'No, you are still betrothed, but Prince Jahan is also betrothed to another, a Persian princess.'

'How may that be?'

'It is the way of princes.'

Mumtaz Mahal knew that her father would never openly criticize his ruler. 'Is that the way of *my* prince?' The tears were not far away, but a great, sad calm settled over her. It had all been too good to be true.

'Never. I believe he loves you truly and this is not what he wants. It is the Emperor's decision.'

'Did my prince not protest against it, rebel?'

'Such is not the way of princes.'

'Surely it is the way of lovers, Father.'

'Sit down, Mumtaz.' He patted the small divan bed and she perched herself beside him on its edge. He took her hand in his. It was the first time he had touched her since she was a child.

His steely strength flowed through her, but it could not ease the pain. The reality of the news her father had just given her was beginning to seep through the initial numbness of shock. 'We all face major adversities in life,' he began earnestly. 'It is how we react to them that matters, for it is that reaction which reveals who we really are and conditions what we are going to be. Do you have faith in your love for Prince Jahan and his love for you?'

'Yes.' The word came out in a whisper. Her chest was now tight, her throat dry.

Is this how a heart breaks?

'Then have faith.'

'And meanwhile?' She fought back a sob. The hours that lay ahead, the days, weeks, perhaps months and years, filled her with dread. A sudden thought reeled through her. 'Will Prince Jahan have to . . . have to marry this Persian princess?'

His grip on her hand tightened. 'It is likely. You will need to be as strong as a rock.'

'Oh Father, a rock does not have to *feel*. If Prince Jahan marries her, I shall kill myself.'

'*You will not.*' His gaze became stern, compelling. 'Even if you wish to – and *I hope you do*, because that would be the measure of your love, *you will not* take your life. You will bleed, but you will live.'

'I have no refuge, Father.' She almost moaned.

'I would like to say that *I* am your refuge, but that would not be true. The test of nobility lies in how we respond to calamity. If you want to be worthy of your prince, you must be as noble as a princess. You must show the world how well-bred people take their grief.' He gripped her so fiercely by the shoulders that she nearly gasped with pain. 'Let no one – not even your foster-mother, Sati, witness your grief, for this sorrow is like none you have ever shared with her before. I know this from my own life and the death of your mother.' His voice broke slightly but he steadied himself. 'Your refuge shall be our Holy Koran. Remember always that giving way to grief is a form of idleness. Spend all your days learning the Koran by heart and your grief will slowly be absorbed by your reverence. Endure pain with faith in yourself, your future and Almighty God, for then you will be blessed by the crown of life . . . perhaps the crown of the Moghul Empire. That is your only refuge. If it does not prove to be so, you are indeed a lost soul, lost only because your love and your faith failed you.'

Prince Jahan had reached the depths of despair by the time the army returned to Agra. His whole world seemed to be disintegrating. Even his new-found friendship with the architect Ustad Isa had ended, because the Emperor had paid the architect a large sum of money and sent him back to Shiraz, since he had decided not to proceed with the building of a new palace in Lahore.

Why then had Prince Jahan felt that Ustad Isa and he had a common destiny? Had that perception been a myth like the entirety of his life? Only his princely training combined with his ambition inspired him to perform his normal duties and to display filial affection as if his spirit was serene. His only source of comfort was that if he could demonstrate such fortitude in the face of disappointment when so young, it would stand him in good stead later in life. 'Your emotions are like the muscles of your body,' his grandfather Akbar had once advised him. 'Disappointments must exercise your emotional muscles, give them strength, not weaken or destroy them. Thus controlled, the muscles become strong and supple, to be used by you, not to drive you.'

In his moments of despair, Prince Jahan clung to this advice and found it to be so true that he could reach for his other source of comfort, that all trials and tribulations overcome would lead him to the imperial throne. When no one was able to dictate to him he would take Mumtaz Mahal for his wife.

News of what the Rajputs had done to the imperial tax-collectors and other atrocities had reached them while they were still on their way to Agra. The timing of the revolt had convinced the Emperor that it was part of the assassination plot. He had decided to send an army, not only to subdue the Rajputs, but to achieve what his father had never been able to accomplish, the conquest of all of Mewar. With Prince Husrau blinded, though only partially as a last-minute reprieve, and completely out of the way as the Emperor's successor, Prince Jahan was certain that he would be selected to command the expedition. Not only would it give him great experience, it would also bring him enormous glory and ease the pain in his heart.

The imperial party had raced ahead of the main column, reached the Agra palace late the previous night. A message that Prince Aziz Koka had returned to the fold and awaited the Emperor's pleasure was conveyed to them immediately on arrival.

Strangely, the Emperor's reaction had been positive. 'So the stinking, skeletal fart has returned to us as if we were his rectum. Tell him to wait on us in the European room at 9 A.M. tomorrow. He can give us first-hand news of what is going on at Mewar. Prince Jahan, you and Asaf Khan will attend.'

The amiable reception that morning of a man who had virtually deserted to the enemy camp had surprised Prince Jahan until he realized that what had triggered Prince Aziz Koka's decision to leave Agra had been the Emperor's action in taking the newly widowed Nur Jehan into the protection of the palace *harem*. Now that the ruler was upset with Nur Jehan, he was ready to welcome his foster-brother again. So much for the intransigence of rulers.

'We told you so,' the Emperor observed, beaming at his own cleverness from his seat on the gilt French settee, when Prince Aziz Koka had bent his knee in supplication for forgiveness, been magnanimously granted it and had furnished his report. His excuse for his conduct, that he had gone to Mewar because he suspected the plot and wanted to act as a spy by pretending to identify with it, was such a palpable lie that it had caused Prince Jahan to exchange a sceptical glance openly with Asaf Khan.

If the Emperor shared such doubts, however, he hid them behind his normal impassive exterior, merely stroking his moustaches, the slanty eyes enigmatic. 'All this was part of a single plot. They kill us in Lahore, revolt in Mewar and the north-west and regain their ancestral auton-omies. Faugh! It was their internal dissensions and dis-cords, their incompetence as rulers in the first place that made them an easy prey for invaders. Without us, they are nothing, merely echoes of the farts of their ancestors.'

'Precisely, Sire,' the gaunt Prince Aziz Koka observed. He shifted his skeletal frame uneasily on his chair, the sunken eyes sycophantic in the morning sunlight streaming through the open windows. The harsh croak of a mynah intruded from the palace gardens below. 'Now it remains to deal with the revolt. I humbly crave Your Imperial Majesty's approval to lead your army against our foes.'

No, no, Prince Jahan protested silently. *I* shall be the one to command the army. At that moment he hated Prince

269

Aziz Koka in addition to despising him as a coward and a traitor.

'We appreciate your offer, Prince, but this revolt must be dealt with by a member of our immediate family – one of our own sons, in fact.'

Prince Jahan's heart began beating faster with joyous anticipation. His wish would be granted. At least he had *something* to cling to.

'Prince Parviz, our second son, shall proceed to Mewar at the head of twenty thousand horse and bring the Rajput dogs to heel.'

PART III

Angel
of Honour

Chapter 16

The Emperor seldom enjoyed his meetings with Salima
Begum, so he kept them to the minimum. He had called on
her in her reception chamber at the Agra palace this
morning only because he needed her advice. It was now
four years since he had named Prince Parviz to head the
imperial forces sent to Mewar to put down the revolt, and
stalemate stared him in the face.

As for the Begum, he might be the Emperor, with the
power of life and death, the power to move huge armies
and build new cities; his merest wish had the force of an
imperial dictum, yet dealing with her even on a purely
polite, social level, was like trying to command a gentle
breeze.

Seated erect, as she was this morning, on her favourite
divan in her luxurious reception room, perfectly painted
and ever respectful and agreeable, exuding total dignity and
an innate majesty, she made him feel that it was she who
held court, granting him audience, instead of the other way
round. From the moment she rose to her feet, from kneeling
to kiss his hand in the traditional Muslim greeting, she
turned him from an Emperor into an awkward schoolboy.
And yet, while she made him furious at himself, he could
not be angry with her or resist seeking her wise counsel,
not only in affairs of the *harem* she ruled and its subject
people, but also in crises within the imperial family and the
calamities of the entire realm.

In view of the real purpose of his visit to the Begum
today, he had decided to even the scales somewhat by
adopting the physical stance of authority. He had paced up

and down the chamber while she remained seated, an unusual privilege which he accorded few people and then only when it seemed advantageous to himself.

Since they were alone, he had hoped to distract her, to affect her perfect poise, putting himself in command of the discussion by towering over her while he spoke, and forcing her to follow his movements. He had even worn a cloth of gold tunic studded with rubies, and necklaces and rings also of rubies for the occasion.

It was a dismal day outside, reflecting his own mood from a hangover caused by last night's dissipation and the state of the realm. Heavy rain splattered the palace roof in great flurries, driving in the smell of wet sandstone through the large open courtyard beyond, to mingle with the exotic perfumes of musk and myrrh from the fountain and the gold incense burners surrounding the chamber. Thunder rolling ominously in the distance sounded its warning as to the Empire's future, caused his sick stomach to clench.

'The war in Mewar is not going well, is it?' the Begum inquired, after the initial interchange of pleasantries. She might as well have been talking about the health of his favourite horse as of an important matter of State.

He waved an airy hand. 'It is going as well as can be expected.'

'Of course. After all, it's only been going on for nearly four years.' Her tone was dry.

'Guerilla stuff. Nothing to worry about.'

'The late Emperor Akbar, your father I think,' the sharp green eyes twinkled, 'once said of his own Mewar campaign, that the guerilla wins until he is killed and the imperial army loses until it wins.' She paused. 'But what do we women know of such things? We have wars in the *harem*, but we never permit guerillas!'

He stopped his pacing. Arms akimbo, he looked down at her. 'You are trying to tell us something?'

'We would never presume to tell an Emperor anything he does not know already.'

The need for guidance, which he was too proud to seek from his official advisers, most of whom he suspected of bias, surged within him. He clasped his hands behind his back. 'It is possible that we took the Mewar revolt too lightly,' he conceded. 'Remorseful at the punishment we had meted out to our eldest son, we appointed Prince Parviz to lead our army against the Rajputs. We also thought that since we had subjugated the north-west during our own expedition there in 1607, and this had brought tranquillity to all other parts of the Empire, Prince Parviz could concentrate on his task and put down the revolt with ease. As you know, we were mistaken. Rana Amar stopped our army in battle at the Dawar mountain pass. Although both sides claim victory, the Rajputs certainly did not lose.' Remembering the dictum of his father which the Begum had just quoted, he fell silent, stared at the pink marble floor in gloomy contemplation.

'Since then, you wisely recalled the army, after it had ravaged the plains in the vicinity of Dawar,' the Begum intervened. 'Even if he got through the mountain pass, Prince Parviz would have to take Chitor before he could claim victory and that is a task which proved well-nigh impossible for the entire Moghul army when your father invaded Mewar. Your appointment of Sagar as a puppet Rana, to create dissension among the Rajputs, has not succeeded. Who would support a Rana without a realm?'

'Chitor, Chitor . . . why is it necessary to take Chitor?' he demanded, suddenly feeling stubborn before the inferior position to which Salima Begum had once again relegated him. Damn the woman, he thought, but then the secret voice within him questioned whether this was not the position to which he had really relegated himself.

'We can only quote another of the Emperor Akbar's

dictums,' she responded sweetly. 'A war is not won until the victorious infantryman stands within the enemy citadel.'

His head had begun to throb again. 'You are full of wise platitudes this morning,' he burst out unpleasantly.

She arched a thin eyebrow. 'We of the *harem* have to depend on the sayings of our lords and masters,' she rejoined, still sweet. 'We have no wisdom of our own.'

Pork shit, he thought savagely, then calmed down. He was here for advice, not confrontation. 'Since then we have sent two more expeditions against the Rajputs, the first under General Mahabat, the next commanded by General Abdullah. Both were met by guerilla tactics. General Abdullah won the only open engagement against Prince Chara, but to no purpose. Laying waste Rajput territories has had no effect. Meanwhile, the Deccan is simmering, like a volcano about to erupt and we have news of disaffection in Bengal. A very serious situation, all in all.' He glanced at her questioningly. 'Especially if the north-west revolts too.'

'We can only offer you the wisdom of our late husband . . .' A heavy splatter of rain on the roof drowned out her voice. Vivid flashes of lightning caused him to look at the blinding sheets of rain outside. Sudden rolls of thunder reverberated through his entrails. 'Whenever such military problems arose, he chose the right man . . . the imperial armies . . . himself as a last resort.' Neither thunder, lightning, nor rain could affect her composure.

'Whom do you consider to be the right man?'

'Prince Jahan.'

'Never . . . er . . . not yet. He is only nineteen and inexperienced for such an important task.' In his mind, he knew that Prince Jahan was his whipping boy for the frustration of Nur Jehan's rejection of him. His signal to her, the marriage of Prince Jahan to the Persian princess, had failed miserably, because his son had not even fathered a child of the marriage which had taken place over a year ago. What was wrong with the young man? Was he impotent?

'Then you must lead the imperial army yourself,' the Begum said.

He knew this to be best, but he did not have the energy any longer. In recent years, he had been more given to words than deeds. This was quite unlike him, for he had always been a decisive man of action, as he had proved to his father and the world. He told himself that this condition existed because he needed Nur Jehan as his concubine to inspire him. Rejected love was eating into him, driving him to seek solace . . . he stopped short of admitting that it was in drink and opium, preferred to say dispiritedness. 'We shall do so when the time is right,' he declared, airily now. The possibility filled him with elation, the deed imminent from his mere admission that it would be done. 'Meanwhile, it would help if we had the necessary inspiration.'

'What more inspiration should an Emperor need but the welfare of his subjects?'

He held back the expletive that had replaced his euphoria. Bugger the subjects, he thought angrily. Aloud, he said, 'We need Nur Jehan to be our concubine, to inspire us to valorous deeds.'

'In the bedchamber?' The sharp green eyes feigned innocence.

He controlled himself. 'In our day-to-day duties.'

'Why do you need her or any woman to inspire you in your day-to-day duties, Your Imperial Majesty?'

The ironic tone of the Begum's last words were not lost on him. The truth escaped in words. 'Because she is so *strong*.' Having admitted it, he examined that truth with wonder, then went on speaking more to himself than to the Begum. 'She would be a source of strength to us in the performance of our office. She would be strong in the bedchamber too.'

'You mean dominant, Sire?'

He recognized the shrewdness of her question. How did she know? 'Perhaps.' He was not prepared to admit his innermost yearnings, some of which he had not even clearly identified for himself and could not divulge to anyone, least of all this old witch.

'She will never be your concubine.'

In a flash he returned to reality. 'Who dares say that?'

'We do.' The cotton-pad tone, meant to seduce him to confession, had given way to steel in a silken sheath. The emerald eyes held a warning glint. 'Nur Jehan does not wish to be your concubine and while she is under our protection, she never shall be.'

Suddenly the conflict in the air was not from the elements alone, from which a smell as of gunpowder had intruded into the chamber. 'We are the Emperor,' he declared wrathfully. 'No one . . . but no one . . . shall thwart our desires.'

'We, Salima Begum, head of our own empire, your imperial *harem*, shall thwart the ignoble desires of any living person towards the subjects we are sworn to protect.'

'What authority . . . d . . . do . . . you have against us? How would you d . . . dare oppose our imperial will?' He was spluttering with rage.

She reached a slender, gnarled hand beneath the cushion beside her, drew out a scroll bearing the red imperial seals. She raised the scroll aloft. 'We have the imperial *firman*, a decree of the Emperor Jehangir here, entrusting Nur Jehan, the widow of Sher Afgan, to our absolute protection. Not even the Emperor himself may rescind the decree for his personal whims without bringing dishonour on himself and his ancestors.' She eyed him levelly, without fear or rancour. Even her tone had been gentle as that of a mother

278

advising a son. 'Nor may the Emperor Jehangir violate Islamic law by facing a charge of complicity in the death of her husband, which could turn an alleged execution into a planned murder. Else the Emperor would go down in history as a monster and a tyrant, to be reviled by succeeding generations.' The silken sheath was removed, baring only the steel in her voice, sharp as a blade. 'Nur Jehan is under *our* protection. Not even the Emperor shall violate her without first engaging Salima Begum, no mere guerilla, but a formidable foe, in open battle. Least of all can you afford that in this time of emergency.'

He knew when he was beaten. Suddenly overwhelmed by anguish, he dropped the royal plural. 'I love Nur Jehan *so* much. I think of her night and day. I cannot get her out of my mind. What should I do?'

'Do? Abandon all thoughts of concubinage. Bestow upon yourself the highest imperial honour of seeking her hand in marriage.'

The war seemed far away that afternoon, when Prince Chara rode with his father and their mounted escort to the village near the Chitor citadel, though it had taken its toll on all the people of Mewar. They had been about to return to the fort from visiting a neighbouring village, when the Rana decided to accept the invitation of the head of the *panchyat* (village council), a man named Hari, to have their afternoon meal at the small local inn. Hari was a village elder, a tall, thin Rajput in white tunic and pantaloons, built rather like Prince Aziz Koka, except that he was naturally bald beneath his black turban. His grey moustache and beard were luxuriant, his brown skin wrinkled like a dried apricot. He had a deep voice, emerging from a prominent voice-box in an unusually long neck.

The village was typically Indian, a dusty street flanked by tall tamarind trees, their small leaves scattered brown and green on the ground, but this village was more prosperous than most. Its homes, sprinkled irregularly on either side of the street, were of whitewashed mud on wattle frames, with thatched roofs, occasionally surmounted by green creepers, especially watermelon, all behind wooden fences. This was where tenant farmers lived, the men who tilled and sowed their overlord's fields beyond, black and fallow at this time of the year in readiness for the spring sowing. Black, brown and brindled cattle were tethered in the fields to provide manure for the crops, its odour high in the torpid noon air. Prince Chara restrained a shudder at the thought of the stink of human excreta of those who, having no privies, simply littered the open ground. Pi-dogs snoozed in the noontide heat. One of them squatted on its haunches, scratching its ear for fleas. A double bullock cart trundled lazily by, wheels creaking above the clip-clop of hooves, avoiding the sacred white cows that drooped in the street. The birds nesting in the tamarind branches were having their noon-day siesta. The only flying creatures were bees seeking honey and whining gnats, searching for blood.

The inn was a small, single-storey red sandstone building with a flat roof, set in a wooded garden beside the wide stream that served the moat of the Chitor fort. They tethered their horses to the inn's hitching posts. Since they were now in safe territory, the Rana despatched the cavalry escort back to the fort for their own meal.

The innkeeper was a nondescript, cross-eyed Rajput, both unusual characteristics in an upstanding race. Prince Chara, the Rana and Hari sat on brown teakwood settles around a trestle table placed on the courtyard paving in the shade of a tall Indian teak tree. The sun was fairly blazing down, a spinning ball directly overhead, glaring from a burnt blue sky. On one side of them the stream chattered and splashed above black and orange stones, alternating silver and grey in the light and shadow shreds of overhanging branches. Above the flat roof of the inn, the tall rugged cliffside of the fort arose, its roadway wall slashing steeply upwards to the massive battlements and sentry towers towering towards the heavens.

'Our fort' is impregnable,' the Rana declared. He eased out his massive frame, stretching long, thick legs, the white *jodhpurs* cased in brown leather riding boots.

'Its impregnability is in the valour of the Rajputs,' Prince Chara responded. 'And unlike in the past, its main defences lie on the borders of our kingdom.'

'Would that our valour were as impregnable as your words.' For all his perspicacity, Prince Chara never knew whether these remarks of his father were meant as personal thrusts at him. Certainly nearly four years of war, with no progress, had made him more cynical, even bitter. The support he had expected from Raja Man had petered out, extinguished when the Raja died suddenly. Help from the Deccan had never materialized. The Rajputs had stood alone against the Emperor. Their last battle against the imperial forces led by General Abdullah could have been even except that the troops Prince Chara led had become disheartened while on the verge of victory, because he had to be escorted from the battlefield by his bodyguards when he lost consciousness from the chance sword-cut of a Moghul captain. It seemed as if life itself – he did not believe in gods – were conspiring against him. The wound had healed, but it left a scar running down the right side of his face from the dark eye to the black-bearded chin, still livid at the edges. He knew that the shadow of that event and its scar would never be erased from his spirit.

The aroma of baked *chuppati* heralded the approach of the innkeeper bearing the bread, three bowls of *ghee* and large slices of pink melon on a huge wooden tray. He set it down carefully on the table with hardly a clatter, his cross-eyes making it seem like a conjurer's trick. He placed goblets and platters before each of them, poured red pomegranate juice. 'I shall bring you the roast chicken as soon as it is done, my lord Rana,' he stated and withdrew.

'I trust this humble offering of our village will satisfy your lordship,' Hari, the elder, volunteered in his deep voice. He was obviously awed by the unusual honour of sitting at the same table as his ruler. 'If we had had the time we would have prepared a more fitting feast.'

'We are hungry,' the Rana responded. As if it were reply enough, he reached eagerly for a *chuppati*. He placed it on his platter, broke a piece gingerly because the bread was still piping hot. He dipped the bread in the *ghee* and tasted it. 'Wonderful! Why is it that our palace kitchens can never duplicate a home-cooked meal?' He paused, munching. 'M'mmm . . . this is a double treat for us, Elder Hari, because we rarely get the opportunity to mingle with our people in such a domestic way.'

'It has the sanction of unfamiliarity,' Prince Chara observed, reaching for a *chuppati*.

His father took him seriously. 'You mean we would not enjoy this if we had it regularly?'

'One can grow as tired of plain food as rich fare. Human beings generally take for granted what is readily available.' He grinned maliciously. 'Like a wife, or peace, or freedom.'

'But never servitude,' the Rana interjected. 'Especially if one is a Rajput.'

'Another lofty sentiment,' Prince Chara sneered, openly this time. 'By the way, Sire, talking of freedom and servitude, I omitted to mention to you that . . .' He stopped abruptly, glanced in the direction of the highway, at the thunder of a horse's hooves in furious gallop. 'Something tells me that we have a messenger from our advance forces.'

In a few seconds, the rider appeared between the cottages, heading in their direction. As he drew closer to the inn, he slowed his mount to a canter, then a trot. The building hid him, the sound of hooves ceased. A few seconds later, the visitor hastened on foot round the side of the inn. A grizzled cavalry veteran, his solid frame was clad in a dusty red tunic and white *jodhpurs*, the armpits of the tunic damp. Beads of sweat covered his face from his ride in the sun. He made obeisance to the Rana.

'I am Captain Das, with the cavalry regiments near Dawar,' he reported. 'While on patrol, my company intercepted an imperial messenger from the Emperor to Prince Parviz. My commander and I thought it sufficiently important to bring the news directly to the palace. The guards at the gates informed me as to your whereabouts. I beg your royal permission to deliver my report.'

'You have it,' the Rana jerked out.

'On the twenty-fifth day of May, the Emperor Jehangir will take the widow of Sher Afgan, named Nur Jehan, under Muslim law, for his lawful, wedded wife.'

Chapter 17

She awaited the Emperor in her quarters at the Agra palace with fierce anticipation underlaid by apprehension. Tonight would determine her future. Nur Jehan had planned and plotted for this day for over seven years, almost four of which she had spent in the Agra palace *harem* preparing herself for the role in every way, making use of her new position as chief lady-in-waiting to Salima Begum to improve her talents. She had been hailed as a poetess, a singer and a creator of fabrics, dresses, ornaments and carpets. Her designs had a unique style that had begun to dominate Moghul fashion. She read avidly to acquire knowledge of politics and government. She had even gone hunting, taking care to observe the rules of *purdah* strictly, and on one occasion had used only six shots from the closed *howdah* on an elephant's back to kill four tigers.

Nur Jehan's secret drive had, however, been to discover discreetly all she could, from the numerous ladies he had bedded through the years, of the Emperor's needs and desires in the bedchamber. Believing that the way a man with access to almost any woman performed sexually would provide vital clues to his character and his most basic needs, she had concluded that the Emperor had deep needs, probably even unidentified by him, which had never been satisfied.

The light that had emerged at the end of the long, dark tunnel of her inquiry had revealed a theory which coincided with her own woman's assessment of him from the very beginning, and which had made her resist all the Emperor's efforts to get her to bed with him, so inflaming him with longing that he took refuge in the concept of a hopeless love in order to satisfy his egoism. The fact that he had finally succumbed to the pressure of his own desiring to accept marriage to her proved several things. Deep, deep down inside, the Emperor was a romantic, but also weak. Having had no maternal protection against the pressures of that incredibly strong man, the Emperor Akbar, he had always been compelled to play a role, finally challenging his father in open revolt on two occasions, to prove himself a man. Simultaneously, he played the role of the Moghul stud in the bedchambers of the *harem*, like most emperors and rulers of the time, in order to prove his manhood. Proving something, Nur Jehan knew, may be satisfying, but it is not necessarily fulfilling. Fulfilment depends upon the satisfaction of subjective longings, while proving is an objective impulse. One man might ride a fiery steed to prove to the world and to himself that he could do so, without deriving any joy from the ride or the contest with the animal. Another might bed six women in one night without being fulfilled. Within these roles of the Emperor Jehangir was a man, essentially a hollow man, who vainly used alcohol to fill the void and opium to satisfy his dreams. *She* would now fill that void.

She had also decided that the Emperor was very lonely. He desperately required someone with whom he could be at peace, the peace of being himself with neither pretensions nor fear that his true self and weaknesses would be betrayed to the rest of the world.

The wedding ceremony that night had been a quiet one, attended only by Ghiyas Beg, Asaf Khan, her daughter, Ladili, Prince Parviz, Prince Jahan, the Emperor's youngest son, Shahriyar, and Salima Begum. Nur Jehan had nodded her assent to the Chief Mullah's traditional query and was now the Emperor's official wife. Although maintaining an outward air of perfect composure, her mind was in a daze. She could not believe that all she had planned for, hoped for, agonized for, had at long last been realized. Yet she was alert enough to tell herself that this was not the end, but only the beginning of her progress towards supreme power. By becoming the Empress she had merely proved herself. Fulfilment lay only in wielding power. She needed that for her security too. The baby daughter of Ghiyas Beg had once been abandoned. Her position as offspring had given her no security whatever. Security was something she desperately needed. She could only obtain it by being the mistress of her own destiny and the destinies of those around her, *including* the Emperor.

As she waited in her bedchamber for the nuptial visit of her new husband, she had to steady her breathing in order to control the beating of her heart, beating not with the excitement of a bride, but with apprehension at the daring of her plan. If it worked, the future would be hers. If not . . . with iron determination, she resolutely cast the negative thought aside. *She* would *not* fail.

Much to the surprise of her ladies-in-waiting, she had declined the traditional bath in perfumed water, the applying of scented oils and exotic perfumes, the special seductive robing. She did not tell them that she wanted none of these illusions that always beset the bedchambers of the *harem*, nor soft pink cushions and lights, erotic tapestries, wine and haunting music. Unknown to her staff, she had personally cleared the bedchamber of all these aids, depositing them in an adjoining room. Her bedchamber now consisted of the bare floor of pink marble, glowing cold in the bright lights, and a white mattress. She herself smelled clean, of fresh sweat. She was dressed in her riding clothes, baggy white trousers tucked into black riding boots, a short black *kurtha*. She had requested that there should be no wine-drinking or revelry that night and the Emperor, eager to bed her, had so decreed.

She stood at the far end of the room, feet apart, hands behind her back, the symbol held in her left hand. She heard the front door of her suite open and close.

'Nur Jehan, my white beloved, where are you?' It was her husband's voice from her reception chamber, loud, clear, demanding.

She did not move while his confident footsteps clattered on the marble floors, then stopped. 'Where are you?' he called again, answered himself. 'Ah, how wise, how submissive, you await your husband-lover in your bedchamber. Are your pink limbs spread naked to receive him?'

The door to the chamber opened with a click. The Emperor, clad in a gorgeous cloth of gold robe, studded with diamonds, stood framed in the doorway. 'There you . . .' His slanty eyes blinked once. Puzzled, they took in her clothes, roved around the room, fell on the bare mattress. 'What in the name of the Hindu hell is this?' he demanded, furious. He took a step forward. 'Tell us,' he demanded, his chin lifting imperiously.

She spoke for the first time, her mellow voice cool and clear as a mountain stream. 'You are a naughty boy, Jehangir, a cheeky brat. From now on, it is never *us*, in *my* bedchamber. There is no Emperor *here*.' She could not stop the pounding of her heart, but remained outwardly calm.

His jaw dropped. Rage entered his eyes. 'Wha . . .' he began.

She kept her left hand behind her back, used the other to unbutton her black *kurtha*, partly exposing a pink-white breast for a quick moment before swiftly buttoning it again. 'You want this?' she inquired. 'You can take it by force, but that would only be the Emperor snatching whatever he desires, never *holding* it.' She paused, allowing her words to sink in. 'Do you understand that, Jehangir? You have always reached for things, but have you ever *held* anything? Tonight, because I love you,' noting his eyes widen and soften the tiniest bit, she repeated the words, 'because I love you, because I love you as Jehangir, a prince who is a princely man, not as an Emperor except that you rule my heart, you have the unique opportunity of your lifetime. You can be loved for yourself, you can possess as a human being,' she gestured inward with long white fingers, 'the most desirable woman in the world, by being possessed.'

She held his gaze, thrilling at the dawn of comprehension in his expression, witnessing the struggle of Jehangir, the man, against the Emperor born and bred to his role. 'You dare . . . this?' He grated, but his voice lacked resoluteness.

'I dare all for the man I love. The part of my life when I gave my body to a man merely because I had to, as his wife, is over. No man has ever had *me*, the real me. Will you be the first?' She decided that the time for testing had

287

come. 'Are you submissive enough as only a man who is truly strong can be? I have nothing for the Emperor or any man in authority over me, but I am ready to give all of me to my lover, who will also be my friend, my protector,' she raised her voice, 'and my *son*.'

Tears sprang to his eyes. She knew she had won. This was a totally new experience for him. He tried to hold the tears back, but two large drops rolled down his ruddy cheeks to remain poised on each of the russet Mongolian moustaches. 'All these years . . .' He paused. 'Are you saying that it requires true strength to display dependency?' he whispered, his eyes focused on her.

'Yes, but only with someone you can trust not to exploit that weakness, or to betray you.' She deliberately delayed her next words. 'As you would be submissive before a truly loving mother, who cherishes you for yourself alone.'

He blinked again as the words struck home. 'A *truly loving mother*,' he mused. 'Something one had hoped for but never experienced.'

'You have had to prove your manhood in the bedchambers of the *harem*,' she proceeded, sure of herself, ruthlessly in command now. 'It is the tradition of Moghul emperors and princes. While you had something to strive for, the crown, the throne, you found the willpower to have your erections. Once you became the Emperor, you had to prove nothing, for you were already there. Your organ grew flaccid. It required wine, coaxing, ministrations to bring you to erection. Since you had no more to rise to in life, there was no inspiration for your manhood to rise, any more than for any derelict human being to waken in the morning. Fear entered your being and the more you drank to overcome it, the worse it became.' She allowed her words to sink in, watched apprehension blanch his face. 'With me, you are already a man. You do not have to prove yourself. You shall in future bed me alone and I shall brag of your prowess. The world will hold you in the highest esteem as an emperor capable of instant erections, elevated to a human being and the Emperor of Love.'

He nodded slowly. 'You have touched me as no one ever before has dared, Nur Jehan,' he said humbly. 'It has been impossible to find true love in the *harem*, where only artifice exists.'

'You and I are going back a long way to your boyhood, when you first needed love, discipline from and submissiveness to a loving woman.' She withdrew her left hand from behind her, revealed the riding crop it held. She watched his eyes focus on it, widen and seek hers again. She made her loving glance even more melting. 'This is going to hurt me more than it hurts you,' she declared simply. 'Pull your pantaloons down, Jehangir. You have been a naughty boy and must be punished.'

He stared at her, seemed ready to erupt in outrage and her heart sank. Had she over-reached herself? She held his look steadily, without displaying even a tremor of anxiety. He exhaled loudly, it was almost a sigh. Eyes fixed on her, he slowly removed his gem-studded gold belt, let it go with a clatter on to the floor. He took off his glittering robe, dropped his baggy pants to his ankles, stepped out of them.

'Come here!'

He advanced step by step until he was two paces away from her, then stopped. She noticed without looking that his penis was flaccid. He waited, head bowed, a child awaiting punishment.

'Kneel down.'

As in a trance, he obeyed her, his head now just below her crotch. He looked up at her pleadingly. She brought the crop cracking sharply down on the bare pink imperial bottom. The thwack resounded through the room. 'Uungh!' the Emperor cried.

'Remain on your knees, but straighten up.'

Again he obeyed her in silence, his gaze now adoring. She dropped her eyes to his penis. It was large and rock hard, thrusting forward like the beak of a predatory bird.

So I was right in assuming that you wanted to fuck your mother, Nur Jehan thought triumphantly.

Holding his eyes like a cobra its prey, slowly, deliberately, she undid the buttons of her pantaloons with her right hand, pulled open the fly sideways with both hands to reveal the soft copper down of her pubis, surrounded by pink flesh. He gazed fascinated.

'Down again!' she directed him.

He went down on all fours. She tapped him lightly on the buttocks with the end of the crop. She spread her legs, held open her fly with her left hand. 'Come forward and eat me,' she commanded. 'Notice that I do not smell of scents but of a fresh, clean, raw female organ.'

He hesitated. The crop came down so hard on his bottom that he gasped. 'I said, eat me!' she growled.

Still kneeling submissively, the Emperor raised his head, sniffed like a dog, buried his face in her crotch. She could tell that his penis was so inflamed it must hurt him.

Only when he had given her an orgasm with his mouth did she allow him to couple with her, from behind, like a dog mounting a bitch, one of the infinite variations she had planned on the theme she had created for him. He went at it long, hard, punishing her.

Whenever Prince Jahan met Asaf Khan, he was sharply reminded of the Prime Minister's daughter, whom he loved. As they sat in his study sipping coffee, he could not help but think how wonderful it would have been if Mumtaz Mahal had been there.

Since he had wed the Persian princess, Prince Jahan had been allotted a separate palace, adjoining the imperial palace in the Agra fort. This had previously been occupied by

Prince Husrau, now a prisoner in the main palace. Was his father giving him the message that he, and not either of his two elder brothers, was now the heir to the throne? His father's attitude to him since that night in Lahore had been nothing short of ambivalent, a sort of love-hate combination that resulted in mixed messages. He had on occasion even wondered, without conceit, whether his father was jealous of him, a throwback to earlier emotions when he had been the Emperor Akbar's favourite. Or could it be that the resoluteness with which he abstained from wine, opium and women, in spite of his father's requests and even admonitions, had affronted the Emperor?

Being very much alone, with neither friend nor relation to talk to, Prince Jahan had decided to await events, accepting honours and accolades with the graciousness of one accustomed to them and setbacks as if they had not occurred. As his grandfather would have pointed out, all this was good for his character. But how many setbacks did Allah have for him before he became the Emperor and could marry Mumtaz Mahal on a decision of his own making, as his father had just wed Nur Jehan. That marriage had given him hope again that he would be permitted to marry Mumtaz Mahal and brought the realization that he would only be the master of his own destiny when he ascended the imperial throne.

He had been curious as to why Asaf Khan had requested that they meet in private after the wedding ceremony. The Prime Minister looked dashing as always. He was dressed in pantaloons of white satin, his long tunic of cloth of gold, but he was one of those rare men who did not need ostentation to be striking. In the golden lamplight, the triangular face with its fair skin tight-drawn over high cheekbones, script-thin moustache and devil-may-care eyes did that. Seated on a European-style chair opposite Prince

Jahan, sipping his coffee from a gold cup, he had a natural grace which most princes had to cultivate.

The usual courteous prologue ended, Asaf Khan placed his cup on its saucer. 'You and I, being bound by loyalty and obedience to our Emperor, have never been able to converse freely with each other on many matters springing from his policies. Since he has just done my family the honour of taking my sister to be his wife, however, I feel that a bond of family has now been created which permits us a little more latitude with each other, while still following the dictates of honourable conduct.'

Prince Jahan's pulse quickened. 'I welcome that,' he responded steadily.

Asaf Khan's eyes crinkled in the familiar smile, the lamplight seeming to dance off them. 'Then I would like to tell you frankly that, while I would unquestioningly accept whomever the Emperor names as his heir, my personal choice would be you, Prince. Let there be that knowledge between us.'

Prince Jahan's cheeks went warm with pleasure. 'I am as honoured by your opinion as if the Emperor had conferred that right on me,' he declared sincerely. 'The Moghul tradition of succession by the eldest son is, however, no respecter of persons. I remember how my grandfather agonized over this same question nearly seven years ago.'

'Was he at peace with his decision?'

The direct question took Prince Jahan aback. Peace from following tradition, yes, but peace from the knowledge that the realm was in safe hands? 'I do not know,' he replied, truthfully.

'The reason I asked a question which might otherwise seem disloyal is that I see a similar situation arising at the moment.' Asaf Khan bent his head as if contemplating the carpet, then raised it. 'Did you know that, at Prince Parviz' request, the Emperor has granted Prince Parviz and Prince

Husrau a private audience after tomorrow morning's *durbar*?'

'Both of them?' What devilry was afoot?

'I believe this to be an attempt on the part of Prince Parviz to restore Prince Husrau to his traditional position of heir apparent.'

'Very worthy of Prince Parviz.' Prince Jahan tried to hold back his mounting fury.

'Not so, Prince. Prince Parviz is, in my view, attempting to establish the traditional line of succession to cut you out and turn it to his own advantage. A partially blind Emperor can be easily removed, overthrown or turned into a puppet.'

'Should we speak to the Emperor?' Even as he uttered the words Prince Jahan knew that such an action would be fruitless, even dangerous.

'No.' Asaf Khan's smile was white and confident. 'That would not be prudent, nor, I think, will it be necessary. My sister has the same views about the succession as myself. Knowing her, I am certain that she will soon become her husband's confidante. I merely mentioned tomorrow's audience to you as proof of where my own loyalties lie. We shall, if the need arises, make common cause in this matter for the Emperor's well-being and the welfare of the realm.'

Prince Jahan's heart had begun thudding against his ribs. Was his future opening out at last?

'It was my sister who suggested and arranged for your betrothal to my daughter, Prince. I suffered much disappointment from the subsequent reversal. My daughter too.' He paused to steady himself, cleared his throat. 'The chain of my sister's influence was broken because of . . . er . . . certain disagreements between the Emperor and her, but that influence will soon be restored.' He smiled faintly. 'I know Nur Jehan.'

Would it mean that he could then marry Mumtaz Mahal?

Prince Jahan longed to ask the question, but years of princely training held him back. Suddenly the answer became even more important than becoming the named heir to the Moghul throne. Simultaneously, deep within him, like the distant rumbling of an earthquake, another question stirred. Would he be exchanging one servitude for another? He would far rather become Emperor because he deserved it than by being the nominee of another person, especially a strong woman such as Nur Jehan.

At that moment, he knew beyond doubt that some day he would seize the throne by force.

Chapter 18

When Prince Chara carried the news of the Emperor's marriage to his father, the Rana was taking an evening stroll in the Chitor palace gardens. His huge, black-bearded father, clad in purple silk *jodhpurs* and white satin short *sherwani* tunic, had paused before a fountain, its waters leaden with the approach of dusk.

The Rana turned at his approach. 'Ah, it is you.' His grin, white above the full black beard, was slightly malicious. 'We trust you have joined us for our evening stroll.' He knew that Prince Chara disliked such pastimes.

'It would have been my privilege, Sire.' He gave a mock sigh, glanced about him. 'What more can a man ask for? Silver-grey skies shading to old rose in the west before the final glare of a dying sun. Crows winging their way home or cawing from their nests in the dark branches of *ashoka* trees. A light easterly breeze wafting the scent of jasmine to please the chattering fountain.'

The Rana clapped his hands. 'Good, very good, Prince. You may turn out to be the Court poet after all.'

'Words may not a poet make,' Prince Chara retorted, uncertain as to whether his father was mocking his retort. 'But braying can only announce a donkey!' He paused briefly, noted the flash of anger in his father's eyes and proceeded smoothly. 'I regret interrupting your communion with nature, but I thought you would like to hear the news which has just arrived by special messenger from the Agra palace.'

The Rana turned towards him, bushy black brows raised in interrogation.

'The Emperor's marriage to Nur Jehan took place at a small, private ceremony last Wednesday night.'

'Why a private ceremony?'

'Probably because the Emperor undertook the marriage solely to satisfy the cravings of his privates,' Prince Chara responded drily. 'Which reminds me to ask you, very respectfully, why should Nur Jehan now keep a private school and the Emperor sit on ice?'

Rana Amar stared at him blankly. 'We are discussing matters of State and you come up with such an absurd question?' He was obviously intrigued by it, however, for he stared at the white flagstone floor, puzzling for a few moments. 'Why?' He looked up. 'Oh, all right. Tell us why.'

'To keep their privates cool!' Prince Chara answered urbanely.

A great guffaw escaped the Rana. 'Good, very good.' He glanced evenly at his son. 'See, you are not only the Court poet, you are also the Court jester. Such talent!'

I shall make a jest of your life through your death some day, Prince Chara thought cold-bloodedly. Aloud he said. 'Both must be my inheritance, Sire!' His glance was smooth. 'Let me then add, as Court jester, Sire, that our

295

war against the Moghuls is no longer a joke.' His tone was sober. 'All we have done for four years is to rebel against Moghul rule and defend our territory.'

'We have paid no taxes to the Emperor since the war began,' Rana Amar declared.

'We have lost far more through the attrition of our economy, through the sacrifices of our people and the tithes we ourselves have levied on them than we would have paid the Emperor.'

'Pride and independence cannot be measured in terms of wealth,' the Rana looked ponderous, 'any more than artistic talent.'

Hating his father's pomposity, Prince Chara felt the scar on his face itch. 'Freedom can drown in the deeps of platitudes,' he retorted, then added quickly to rob the words of the offence he intended, 'I agree with you, Sire, that we Rajputs, alone, can only defend our independence, because the Emperor can field vast armies and drive us to the walls of the Chitor fort. We do not have the resources to invade the imperial dominions. But, as I suggested before our first revolt began, there are others with whom we can join to achieve what has been impossible up to now.'

'Not again!' The Rana waved an impatient hand. 'Your brilliant plan to link up with Prince Husrau and the dissidents in the Punjab, Afghanistan and Bengal came to naught because we depended on others. So too your plan to make common cause with Raja Man and the Deccanese. None of your political plans have worked, Prince. We Rajputs have always fought a lone battle and will always have to fight alone. You are a brave soldier and a proven general. Be content to fight alone.'

'This time I suggest we should open negotiations with Malik Ambar of the Deccan. The situation there has changed in the last four years.'

'That Abyssinian!' There was contempt in the Rana's voice.

Prince Chara held back from declaring that he himself would make common cause with the Devil if it served his purpose. 'That Abyssinian, as you so scornfully call him, Sire, is one of the most brilliant generals of our times. In 1608 he successfully resisted the Emperor's attempt to conquer Ahmadnagar. He then consolidated that State so firmly that when Prince Parviz was appointed governor of Khandesh and Berar in 1610, it proved to be an exercise in futility. Since then, Ambar and his Marathas have confounded every brilliant Moghul general who was sent against him.'

'By avoiding pitched battles, yapping at the Moghul army's tail like wolves, ambushing components . . .'

'And driving the main body of the Moghul army away from Gujarat, which is not even in the Deccan proper, just three days ago.' Prince Chara dared to interrupt his father because this news too had just come in and he knew it would catch the Rana's attention.

'What? General Abdullah's imperial army defeated?'

'Routed, with severe losses.'

'H'mm.'

It was time to press home his point. 'Since the Emperor is married at last to the lady of his dreams, he will not be disposed to take the field himself with the main Moghul army. Nor will he despatch it on a major invasion while he is not at its head, giving credit for victory to someone else who might well turn with the army against him. The time is ripe for us to join forces with that Abyssinian,' he could not resist the thrust, 'and strike a major blow at the Moghul Empire.' He grew excited at the prospect. 'Why, if this could be achieved, we can be absolutely sure of uprisings in the north-west and perhaps in Bengal too. The Deccan, as you know, Sire, consists of several sultanates spreading east and west from ocean to ocean and south to the Dravidian regions. If we could rouse them all to join our struggle for independence, not even the might of the Moghuls could withstand us.'

'The Indian people will never unite against a common foe. We will always be split by dissension, since some of the differences between us are greater than those we have with the invader. Our problem has always been and will remain until the end of time, that our differences are heightened and more bitter because we are a family like any family. Rajputs, Sikhs, Punjabis, Gujarats, Bengalis, Dravids can never retain unity. We will always be more curious and suspicious of, more cruel to, each other than to our common enemies.' His deep voice sounded sad, was echoed by the concerted cawing of crows gathered in dissonant harmony for the night. 'Tomorrow morning those united crows will be fighting each other over scraps of food. The sadness of their cawing is from spirit hunger for a unity they will never possess.' He pulled himself abruptly away from the well of depression, sighed heavily. 'What do you propose, Prince?'

'That you send an emissary to General Malik Ambar.'

'Whom do you recommend?'

'Me.'

The Rana showed no surprise. 'When will you leave?'

'I have already planned to leave at dawn tomorrow.'

'You have already . . .' The Rana's laugh rang out above the splatter of the fountain. 'You will never change! Go with our blessing. Take gifts with you.'

'No gifts, Sire, only our offer of an alliance!'

Having left Chitor at dawn the next day as he had planned, Prince Chara and his six-man cavalry escort, riding hard south and west along the Moghul highway, reached Ahmedabad, on the eastern outskirts of which General

Malik Ambar was reported to be encamped, late on the Tuesday evening. Since their arrival was unexpected, they were received with mistrust at the first of the general's outposts, manned by the fierce Maratha warriors who had repeatedly proved themselves against the formidable Moghul troops. Prince Chara's escort was detained to be fed and accommodated in a bivouac, while he was conducted to the general's headquarters in a valley about three miles away, where he was held up at the sentry post while word of his arrival was carried to General Malik Ambar.

Tired from his long, hard ride, Prince Chara's limbs began to stiffen. Unused to being kept waiting, insulted by the stares of every passing soldier, officer and camp follower, the prince controlled his rising anger with difficulty. One hour went by, lengthened into two. Darkness began falling and the smells of camp-roasts cooking on open pits reminded him that he had not eaten since dawn.

He was nearing the end of his restraint when word finally came back that the general would see him. Remounting his black Scindhi, he was escorted by six Maratha cavalrymen to the general's tent. On dismounting, he had to endure the further ignominy of a search for hidden weapons by a staff officer, who permitted him to retain the long sword at his side. Only then was he shown into the general's large field tent.

Unlike the Moghuls and most Indian rulers, the general obviously did not believe in luxury on the campaign trail. In spite of his irritation at the indignities he had suffered, Prince Chara had not failed to observe the alertness and efficiency of the rebel army. He was further impressed to discover that General Ambar maintained the kind of lifestyle for which only the Spartan warriors of old were reputed. In the uncertain light of lanterns hanging from its overhead poles, the tent was bare of furniture, except for a long trestle table of some white wood in its centre, on which maps had been spread out. A dozen settles of matching wood, with rope seats, scattered around it indicated that a conference had just ended. He noted a yellow sleeping mat rolled up on the bare grass, with clothes hanging from hooks above it at the far left end of the tent, before giving his attention to his host who stood behind the table.

General Malik Ambar was in his early fifties at this time. He had the medium height and stocky build of a Gurkha warrior with the same broad facial bones and quiet aura of power. The resemblance ended there, because the general was very black and had crinkly hair, the like of which Prince Chara had never seen before. His uniform, white *jodhpurs* tucked into black riding boots and short white tunic, was as Spartan as his tent. When he advanced to meet the general, Prince Chara noted the flat nose with splayed nostrils bridging deep-set, inscrutable dark eyes.

Neither of them was willing to concede rank, so they greeted each other without formal salutations, the general with a smile that was surprisingly white in a dark face hairless as that of a baby.

'Thank you for seeing me without formality, General Malik Ambar,' Prince Chara responded to the smile. He stopped at the opposite end of the table.

'It was no more than I could do, because of your reputation as a soldier,' the smile became a little crooked, 'not by virtue of your rank as a prince which would have required weeks of protocol before you and I could meet.' The general had a strangely husky voice, yet it was forceful.

Well put, Prince Chara thought, warming to the man. You acknowledge that I am here as a fellow-soldier, while putting the prince in his rightful place.

'I apologize for keeping you waiting as long as I did, but I was in conference with my general staff and had instructed my aides that I was not to be disturbed. I understand that you have had a long, hard ride. Would you care to join me at dinner? It will be served here as soon as I have made rounds to ensure that my staff has been fed. I'm afraid our fare is more plain than that to which you are accustomed, for all of us, men, officers and generals, eat the same food, but I hope your welcome will make up for it.'

'Not to mention the honour you do me by inviting me to your board.' Though he normally hated flattery, Prince Chara could turn a nice phrase when he was so disposed.

The general's eyebrows, if he had any, lifted. 'I had been given to understand that you are not one for the idle speeches of courtier-fops,' he remarked. 'H'mm.' He gestured towards a settle. 'Please be seated. I assume that you would like to talk before being shown to your tent.' Noting Prince Chara's nod, he sat down on the opposite side of the table. 'Would you like some water to drink? I'm afraid it is all we can offer you.'

'No, thank you.' Prince Chara took one of the settles directly across from the general.

'Now, what is the purpose of your visit, Prince?'

This was a man after Prince Chara's own heart, direct, honest, with no time to waste on status. Would he be a source of competition when the Moghuls were driven out of power and the rulership of the Empire became open? Prince Chara decided not. Firstly, no foreigner, least of all a Chinese, European or Abyssinian, would be given fealty by the ruling princes, the nobles, or the Indian people. Secondly, the general was a fighting man and a superb administrator. He would make a great Prime Minister and Army Commander, not a king.

Feeling easier in his mind, Prince Chara explained all that the Rajputs had achieved since the latest revolt and propounded his observations and deductions as to the political situation of the Empire, which he had done so frequently with his father. 'Since we have a common foe, the Moghul Emperor, and a common purpose, the termination of that Empire, I thought it timely for the Rajputs to join forces with you and evolve a common strategy,' he ended.

General Ambar had listened with the total attention of the born commander. He now stared thoughtfully into space for a while. The dark eyes gleamed, causing Prince Chara to wonder for the first time whether there was some flaw in his plan. He hated being dependent on others. It was a relief when the general broke the silence. 'It strikes me that while we have a common desire to rid ourselves of the Moghul yoke we may not have a common conclusion as to how far we should go to achieve it. We of the Deccan would be satisfied with not having to pay imperial tributes and taxes. Your own goal is more far-reaching. You wish to drive the Moghul completely away, a very laudable aim but one that, if achieved, could leave a vacuum of power and stability. I, for one, see nothing wrong with peaceful co-existence with the Moghul dynasty so long as it does not extend its tentacles in our direction.'

Spoken like a guerilla, Prince Chara reflected, disappointed in the man as well as at his response. 'In politics, as in war, it is necessary to understand one's adversary,' he countered. 'Since the days of Genghis Khan and Timur the Lame, the Moghuls have been adventurers. There is no such thing as a Moghul with a limited suzerainty any more than there is a stud with limited sexual power.'

The general smiled. 'Well put, Prince.' He pondered the remark. 'I like that . . . and you may be right.' He stared into space again as was obviously his wont when he was thinking hard. He finally raised his eyes to meet Prince Chara's four-squarely. 'What strategy do you propose?'

'An alliance that would immediately place the Emperor

on the defensive, with our combined armies advancing on Agra.'

'Turning ourselves to cannon fodder at the first major engagement? Surely not.' The general's tone implied that such a move would be foolhardy.

'We will not engage the imperial army in open battle. Having previously selected the site, once the two forces are massed and poised for battle, we will pretend to withdraw, in different directions, causing the enemy to split up, then destroy him piecemeal, as you have so successfully been doing these past five years, but on a scale large enough from our combined strength to do real damage to the imperial army, which is after all the true thorn in our side.'

The dark eyes sparkled momentarily in the lamplight. What he had shrewdly suggested was a strategy that placed General Ambar on familiar ground.

'It might work,' the general declared. 'And I am willing to try it, but I can't agree that we should give effect to it immediately merely because the Emperor is preoccupied with his woman. If driven, he will leave his bombardments on his wife's warm bed and emerge with his real cannon firing.' He smiled faintly at his jest. 'That is a risk we can't afford to take. I suggest as an alternative that we draw the main imperial army out in slow degrees. My victory in driving it out of Gujarat will undoubtedly evoke a strong military response. Let us combine forces to meet that response and turn it to our advantage.' He looked directly, compellingly at Prince Chara. 'Agreed?'

'Agreed,' Prince Chara replied. It was not what he had wanted, but he had no alternative. He extended his hand across the trestle table, palm down.

The general placed his own hand firmly on it.

Chapter 19

In the glow from the hanging lamps that were never extinguished, the wall clock that Nur Jehan had installed in her bedchamber to serve the Emperor showed the hour of midnight. Nur Jehan was too clever – she preferred to think of herself as too wise – to attempt to influence her husband in any major way immediately after she had established sexual dominance over him on their wedding night. It was one thing to have influenced him in decisions through her brother while she was still married to another man, but as the Emperor's wife, dealing directly with him, she knew she should proceed with caution.

As she had expected, following that first sexual encounter, her husband had been watchful and suspicious when he had risen the next morning from sleeping in her arms like a baby, as if he had betrayed too much of himself. He had kept away from her bedchamber the next two nights and it was whispered around the *harem* that she had failed him sexually. Secure in her power, however, she had gone about her tasks serenely, letting it be known to Salima Begum alone, who would of course ensure that word got back to the Emperor, that her husband had proved to be a magnificent but considerate lover, whom the late Sher Afgan, slayer of tigers with his bare hands, could never have hoped to match. 'In the jungle of the bed,' she had declared, 'it requires more than physical strength . . .'.

Whether the wise old Begum believed her or not, she must have passed word to the Emperor for he had visited her again on the third night, more relaxed this time. Nur Jehan had treated him to a splendid variation of the theme she had conceived. Since then, his confidence in her discretion growing, he had begun to spend every night with her. During this period, she gradually began to discuss affairs of State with him, never proffering advice, but showing herself interested and as knowledgeable as any of his advisers. When she did start to influence him she always made it seem that the decisions he took were his alone. Never once did she ask for any favours and he never gave her any gifts such as he bestowed, as was customary, on the other women of his harem. Delighted by this, she on the other hand gave him costly presents, which he loved. The jewelled portrait miniature of himself and a gold-plated matchlock gun were paid for from her own coffers. The more tender presents, such as love poems and songs she had composed for him, a design for a new gold coin bearing his image stamped on it, came from her intellect, not quite from her heart.

They had acquired the habit of going to sleep on the bare mattress in her bedchamber after their nightly love-making. With the Emperor's approval, she had kept this room exactly as she had prepared it for him on their wedding night, letting it be known that the Emperor was a lover who had no need for soft lights, silky cushions, sweet music and exotic scents to stimulate his manhood, now that he had discovered the one true love of his life. The adjacent room had therefore become her own bedchamber. With the approach of winter she had a stove installed to heat the bedroom they shared and a supply of warm woollen rugs for additional warmth.

He had come to her chambers earlier than usual tonight. Their love-making done, they had donned their normal nightclothes and slept the sleep of complete satisfaction for three hours. He awoke gradually and she with him, as if she were a part of his being, this close had she drawn him to her.

'This is the first day of the European New Year 1613,' the Emperor murmured, his voice slumber-coated. 'You have proved yourself to be an exemplary wife, Nur Jehan, empress of my heart, giving all and asking nothing. I would be an insensitive wretch if I did not comprehend your saintliness and appreciate it. One of the things I am most touched by is your insistence that I drop the royal "We" when we are alone. It has given me an identity again, apart from the miraculous discovery of my true self which you have helped me achieve. I mean, who is "We" when I am really "Me"?' He chuckled at his sally and she laughed low with him, reached out and took him in her arms. 'You are my refuge from the anonymous and impersonal . . . you know?'

'Of course I do.' She drew him closer to her. 'I was born to serve you as wife. If you are the master, I am the mistress, a unique combination which can only derive from your strength and your confidence that you are the liege-lord of my soul.' Her words were nonetheless sincere from her thrill of pride at the wisdom, imagination and self-restraint which had brought his tribute to pass.

'Despite the setbacks we have suffered in the Deccan and the Rajput regions, the entire Empire is secure. With your wise counsel, I have refused to send an army to oust General Malik Ambar from the Gujarat. I believe he is trying to provoke me to this end, and I have not taken the bait, especially because my spies in the Chitor palace reported Prince Chara's sudden trip to Ahmedabad to visit the general last May. This could only have meant an alliance. It is often better to wait for the enemy to show his hand rather than to take the initiative. When I do move into the Deccan, I think I shall send my foster-brother, Prince Aziz Koka, with an army to augment Prince Parviz' forces there. Aziz betrayed me twice. Once when he supported Prince Husrau's claim to the throne in preference to mine and the other when he fled the palace upon my assigning you to the protection of Salima Begum upon Sher Afgan's . . . er . . . demise.'

'You are so noble to forgive and forget the wrongs done you by your foster-brother, who should have been family to you.' This was her method of denigrating Prince Aziz Koka, a man she loathed.

'You are my only family, Nur Jehan. I wish to reward you. What can I do to show you how grateful I am?'

'Be as you have been to me. Visit my chambers every night, for since I have known you, I have been introduced to loneliness for the first time in my life. Be true to me in body, mind and spirit.'

'All that you already have, my beloved.' He paused, reached out for her fingers, raised them to his lips. 'You are Great Allah's most precious gift to me, for with you I can be myself. You have made me feel a human being at last, just an ordinary decent person, each night, like millions in my realms. You and I are so much one family that, knowing you would not ask me for anything, I have decided to strengthen the bonds that bind you and me.'

'How could our eternal bonds ever be strengthened?'

'The invisible bonds of our spirits may be eternal and infinite, but we also have certain visible ties and I can think of no better way of celebrating the European New Year than by making a public announcement at my *durbar*.'

'And what would that announcement be?'

'Something I have known to be dear to your heart. Let it be my secret until the morning, when I shall bring you the news myself immediately after the *durbar*.'

To Prince Jahan it was just another levée at the Emperor's Agra palace. With no special tasks allotted to him, the struggle to keep bitterness from entering his soul, especially after the reconciliation between the Emperor and Prince

307

Husrau, who was once more publicly acclaimed heir to the throne, had been intense. He was not sure that he wanted to overcome his resentment, because he had increasingly veered to the view that a little bitterness was good for a man. So long as it did not consume or control him, it protected him from exploitation. So he carried on with the duties the Emperor entrusted to him as perfectly as ever, not expecting anything but with confidence that all of it trained him to grasp his reward some day.

This morning, following *subh* (the morning prayer), the Emperor's rooftop balcony was as usual crowded with courtiers, nobles and supplicants, all richly clad in bright-coloured velvets, silks and satins, turban-jewels, necklaces and belts glittering in the pale sunlight. Dressed in the long cloth-of-gold tunic and baggy trousers which he favoured, he stood beside Asaf Khan to the right of the Emperor's *jarokha*, with Ghiyas Beg beside him. As was normal at this cold time of the year, the public on the *maidan* across the moat below was thin.

Prince Jahan was feeling low this morning. Chills skimmed through his body, caused him to shiver. Not even his pre-dawn ride with Asaf Khan had helped bring the sparkle back to his sluggish bloodstream. He hoped he was not coming down with the winter sickness. These morning *durbars* had become so routine, even boring, that he barely heard the Emperor's unusual words.

'We are breaking with our normal procedure this morning to make a most important announcement.' As the Emperor paused, looked around for silence, it seemed to Prince Jahan that the world had stopped still. What new disaster was coming his way?

'Having conferred with Prime Minister Asaf Khan, and with his knowledge and consent, we hereby decree that our third son, Prince Jahan, shall be wed for a second time this spring for the good of his life and that of the realm.'

How Prince Jahan kept a straight face above the misery that welled up from his heart, he never knew. What did the Emperor have in store for him this time? A princess of Cathay to unite two ancient kingdoms? An African queen? It must be someone important enough politically to compensate for the resulting slap in the face of the Persian royal family, which had provided his first wife. He caught his father's triumphant glance and hoped that his forced smile did not betray his hatred. Even the humblest peasant was more free to marry a young woman of his choice than he, Prince Jahan, now twenty years old and going nowhere, while his grandfather had ascended the throne at the age of fourteen.

'The young lady we have chosen for Prince Jahan's new wife is of noble birth, unblemished character and unwavering religious disposition. This marriage will strengthen the bonds of our family. Princes, lords and all of you here present, we command you to greet the proposed bride with acclaim. Her name is Mumtaz Mahal.'

The name of his chosen new wife did not register until after the burst of cheering. 'What a noble choice . . . Such imperial wisdom . . . Long live Mumtaz Mahal . . . Long live Prince Jahan . . . Long live our Emperor Jehangir . . .'

Then the knowledge crashed into Prince Jahan's consciousness. Tears of gratitude sprang to his eyes, but he fought them back. The sickness suddenly left his body, the blood began sparkling in his veins again, overflowing in his heart. As he advanced, turned and knelt before the Emperor, the sun cleared the distant treetops, shedding a great white light on the balcony. He thought, my night has finally ended.

Mumtaz Mahal knew that the five long years of hopelessness, every morning spent, like today, in the same little room in the *harem* of the mansion of her grandfather,

Ghiyas Beg, had changed her into a more thoughtful, responsible person, yet what good was it doing, except to her immortal soul?

'Today is the first day of the year 1613 after the birth of Yasoos Christus, and where will this year take me except towards a lonely old age, for I will not marry anyone other than my prince.'

The grey-haired Sati smiled sympathetically, but went on with her sewing. 'You have asked yourself that question more times than you have asked me each morning, little paddy bird, and I must give you the same answer: no one goes anywhere.'

'Then what is the purpose of life?'

'Only the Great Allah knows. Only humans have purpose, not God.'

'His truth is supposed to be in the Holy Koran. As my father advised me on that dismal day a century ago when my spirit broke and the light went out of the sun, I have learnt the Holy Koran by heart, but I am no nearer discovering the purpose of life, Sati.'

'Perhaps you are confusing God's will with your purpose and therefore find no joy in your station. You have remained in love with your prince, you have led a chaste life in the *harem*, dedicated only to your studies. Deep in your heart, you have been preparing yourself for the day when you will become Prince Jahan's wife.'

'Do you know the unbearable agony of having him be another woman's lawful husband, the shame of being his betrothed while he beds a Persian princess? I have endured four years of this since the actual marriage.'

'You well know that I have shared it all with you, as if the anguish were mine. As for bedding the Persian princess, the fact that they have had no children makes me suspect that Prince Jahan avoids her bedchamber.'

'Oh, you are so romantic, Sati. Men are not like that.

310

Word in the *harem* is that Prince Jahan has had no children because he has no seed, or cannot get it up.'

'Do you believe that?'

'There are times, such as this morning, when I do.' She paused, smiled through the tears of the years. 'However, my heart always tells me that he is holding himself for me.' She sighed. 'But then, my heart usually tells me only what I want to hear. Oh, Sati . . .'

She glanced up at the knock on the door. 'See who it is, Sati. Say I am studying the Holy Koran and should not be disturbed.' She reached for the book, placed it on her lap, while Sati opened the door.

'Is my daughter dressed to receive me?' It was her father's deep voice.

'Oh yes, my lord. Be pleased to enter.' Sati stood aside.

Her father stood framed in the doorway for a moment, a smile making his face more dashing than ever. 'Ah! There you are my dear,' he exclaimed. She kissed the holy book and placed it on the bed, rose swiftly and crossed the room. She knelt and kissed his hand in greeting.

When she had risen again, her father moved inside the room. Sati made to leave. 'No, you may remain, Sati, because you have shared my daughter's grief during these long years. Please close the door.'

He waited until he heard it click, then reached out and took his daughter's hand. It was the first time in five years that he had touched her. The warm grasp somehow conveyed his love for her, brought a lump to her throat.

'I have some wonderful news for you,' her father said, his eyes sparkling now. 'The Emperor, having first done me the honour of consulting me in private, announced at *durbar* but an hour ago that his son, Prince Jahan, will wed you in the spring.'

At first what he had said could not reach through the wall of hopelessness which the years had built. Then it connected with her thin reservoir of faith and came crashing through that wall. Tears sprang to her eyes, the world started to spin around her and she fainted in her father's arms.

Apart from the routine afternoon calls on the women required by custom, Prince Jahan had never visited the *harem* of his palace. Nor had he increased the dozens of women whom he had inherited, the former entourage of his brother, Prince Husrau, who had in turn inherited the women but had added to their number. His new wife, the Persian princess, was the only woman that Prince Jahan had brought to his *harem* and that was because he had no choice.

He had married Mumtaz Mahal before the Mullah-i-Azam that evening in the same sort of small, informal private ceremony at which his father had married Nur Jehan. Now it seemed to him that he had waited all his life for this moment. Clad in his silver nightrobe, as he was ushered by Sati into the bedchamber allotted to Mumtaz Mahal, conflicting thoughts swirled in his mind.

He was scared. He was not concerned about being declared a stud or a cocksman, virile and potent. He loved Mumtaz Mahal so much that all he wanted was to please her, to find favour with her in the sacred ritual, as he regarded it, of love-making. He knew enough about sex to want to satisfy her. Would he be able to do so when he was totally inexperienced?

His encounter with Nadia had proved to him that he could get an erection, but since his only sexual outlets had been wet dreams and, in his early years, masturbation, he did not know whether he would last long enough to satisfy Mumtaz Mahal. He knew that she was a virgin and that he had to cause her pain to pierce her veil. The very thought of hurting her terrified him. Would it make him flaccid at the entry way, or during the process? He was well accustomed to inflicting pain, to watching people suffer torture unmoved, as was required of rulers, princes and nobles, but never where family was concerned, or innocent people, or even animals, birds or insects. In this, he was like his father and grandfather, extraordinarily sensitive to such suffering, as if nature were compensating for his seeming ruthlessness and cruelty to humans by making him extraordinarily sensitive to its other creatures.

Dear Allah, would his sensitivity cause him to ejaculate prematurely as a reflex against causing Mumtaz Mahal pain? Sex surely complicated romance! The way he felt about Mumtaz Mahal, he would have been content to be alone with her, watch her, talk to her, at most perhaps hold her in his arms. How much he had enjoyed getting to know her these past months on the weekly visits he had been permitted, under the watchful eyes of her governess, as a special dispensation from the rigid rules of the *harem* of Ghiyas Beg's mansion. There had been an inner sadness to her at first, but this had begun to dissipate after his second visit, revealing once again the sparkling girl of his dreams; but now above a depth of character born of her self-confessed years of suffering she was somehow different having found refuge in the Holy Koran and the Islamic faith.

The door clicked shut behind him and he was alone in the bedchamber of Mumtaz Mahal for the first time. The room was large, lit by shaded lights that gave it a pink glow. Recalling Nadia's bedchamber, he shuddered, partly with guilt. A large white Kashmiri carpet dominated the pale pink marble floor. The walls were framed with pink and white tapestries depicting *harem* scenes, beneath which were cushions of darker pink and low tables of filigreed ivory carrying golden braziers glowing with incense sticks that gave forth the scent of some Arabian perfume. Refreshments, the inevitable golden coffee pot, goblets of juices and bowls of fresh fruit, were laid out on a low centre table with an ivory top. The divan bed, also in pink, was set beneath the high windows of the far wall.

Definitely not Mumtaz Mahal's room, Prince Jahan thought. She will surely want to change it all. Then he saw her standing beside the door to his right that must lead to the privy. His breath caught. She was dressed in a sheer white silken robe that fell to her ankles, held tight at the tiny waist by a broad gold belt that caused the robe to flare beneath her and to reveal the full breasts above. It was the first time he had seen her body unmuffled by the loose sheath garments of *purdah*. His eyes went to her face. It glowed in beauty, the skin like alabaster beneath the long, raven black hair. But it was her eyes that transfixed his gaze. They were translucent brown pools, with a depth and a mystery that made him catch his breath. He had read somewhere about the luminosity of the virgin bride on her wedding night and now he was witnessing that marvel of life.

Eyes to eyes.

His being began to merge with hers, the air between them shimmered, diffusing his identity, so that he and Mumtaz Mahal became one.

How long they stood thus, he did not know. Then suddenly her eyes misted and a crystal teardrop welled in each, startling him. He took three steps towards her, uncertain. 'M . . . Mumtaz Mahal, beloved bride . . . tears? . . . why tears?'

She shook her head, smiled wistfully. 'Who knows?' she responded quietly. 'It is enough that they flow from the depths of my soul which is now in your possession.' Her eyes twinkled with the mischief he was getting to know so

314

well and to adore. 'So perhaps it is you who can answer
. . . Why tears?'

He laughed low. The spell of silent communion had been
broken, to be replaced by the new magic of a man and a
woman speaking freely. He moved forward, but slowly, as
if a hasty movement might end that magic. 'Perhaps you
weep because you are afraid,' he teased.

She grew serious on the instant. 'I am weeping because I
am not afraid. I am weeping because the long night is over
and in the emerging daylight I can see through my tears,
see the beloved prince of my dreams.'

'Oh, Mumtaz.'

Then she was in his arms, soft breasts against his chest,
close to his pounding heart, her face upraised. He stared
down at the beautiful elfin face. Was this one of his own
dreams? He took in every feature, the pink-white skin
tight-drawn over delicate bones, the wide mouth with
quivering red lips, the fine nostrils of the small, straight
nose, the thin-arching eyebrows and finally her doe-brown
eyes again, adoring now, the perfect whites lightly tinged
with the pink mist of desiring. This was his love, this was
reality at last. As his own love gushed forth in a torrent to
enfold her, his penis stirred, grew large, hard, pressed
against her pubis.

'Oh!' The exclamation escaped her at the contact.

Her nostrils distended, drove him to fierce ecstasy.
Blindly he released her, moved her slightly away, half-
turned her, bent and raised her up in his arms. She buried
her face in his neck while he carried her to the divan bed.
He placed her gently on it. Gazing at her, hypnotized, he
straightened up and began unfastening his robe. Her eyes
on his, she slowly undid her belt, allowed her own robe to
open, revealing her naked body. Slowly she spread her
limbs. He gazed upon her body, drinking in its beauty,
until he came to the soft triangle of dark brown down.

Driven wild, he flung his robe aside. All thoughts of foreplay ended. His penis, near bursting with its swell, pointing almost to the ceiling, he lay between her legs.

Her eyes still on his, she slowly reached down with her right hand, grasped his penis, held it gently in her soft palm. She shook her head gently at its size and hardness, rubbed it against her vagina. 'See how wet you have made me, Prince, for the first time in my life. I'm just as ready as you are.' She directed the point of his penis inside her.

Trembling, he placed his palms on the divan so as not to put any weight on her. Then he thrust gently inwards. She closed her eyes, pressing forward to take in his pressure. He felt resistance, pushed harder. Her smoothness around his penis created exquisite sensations, but the thrusting point was a wellspring of anxiety.

'Harder, Prince. Don't be afraid.'

He knew that she was trying to help him, giving freely of her pain to end years of carefully preserved virginity, her most priceless possession, more precious than all the pearls of the world. Fleetingly, in a haze, he recalled the pearl he had bought. Then she winced, exclaimed with pain and he burst through, pushing deep inside her. His ecstasy was instantly replaced by the knowledge that he had caused her pain.

His love greater than his lust, he began to withdraw from her.

'Don't pull away now, Prince,' she begged. 'It doesn't hurt anymore.'

Too late. He was flaccid again.

Seeing the disappointment on her face, he pounded the divan bed in frustration. Then she laughed low, and shame made his face burn crimson. He closed his eyes, his whole world shattered.

'My pain did that to you?' Her question trickled into his consciousness. Dear Allah, she understood. 'Oh my prince, how you must love me. How lucky I am. I thank Almighty Allah again for you. Next time there will be no pain. And every night of our lives shall be our next time.'

When they awoke in each other's arms and made love to each other that night, Mumtaz Mahal was so moved by his love, tenderness and caresses that she came quickly, easily. He knew then that their love would always be consummated in a way which removed all anxiety, that he could really satisfy her and, in so doing, experience his own deepest fulfilment.

Chapter 20

It was inevitable that he should have been given command of the imperial forces in Mewar. More than four years of ineptitude, and it had still taken the influence of Nur Jehan to achieve this.

The hour was almost midnight. Prince Jahan had spent three hours in his tent vainly trying to convince the two commanders that he was following the right policy. Finally, in order to end the endless argument, he had summoned his military secretary and dictated the order to be issued to all his troops the following day.

'Our mission is a historic one. The honour and prestige of the Moghul army depend upon our subjugating a brave and reckless enemy. We must achieve victory regardless of the cost, even if it means reducing all Rajasthan to dust and ashes. The Rajput is a ferocious being, splendid in life, magnificent in death. We shall match his disdain for living with our relentless will to conquer him. We shall never resort to diplomacy or negotiation in this campaign. The

317

good fortune of our Emperor, the Chosen One of our friend and guide, Almighty Allah, will give us the wings on which we shall soar to total victory.'

The manuscript contained his first order of the day. Prince Jahan placed his palm impression on it. It set the seal upon the iron determination that had entered his exultant spirit the moment he was named by his father to lead a larger army than any that had ever taken the field during the long campaign against the rebellious Rajputs, in order to bring them finally to heel. Although he was saddened to leave his new bride, the one real cloud dimming the sparkle of his elation was that, concerned at his total lack of field command experience, the Emperor had named as his principal adviser Prince Aziz Koka, whom Prince Jahan held to be a traitor and a secret Rajput sympathizer.

Remembering the policy of his military hero, the Emperor Ky-roos of Persia, to attack only from strength, Prince Jahan had moved from Agra only when he was satisfied that he had been given a sufficiently large force, well enough equipped with cannon and muskets, ammunition and weapons, elephants and the all-important supply train, to carry out the plan he had in mind, a repetition of the military strategy of his ancestral heroes, Genghis Khan, Timur the Lame, Babur and Akbar.

Having placed his signature on the document, he now glanced coldly at the two men seated at the trestle table in his private tent, which he also used as command headquarters. Prince Aziz Koka continued shaking his head in disapproval and he obviously had the support of the Rana Surjan seated next to him. The Rana was the brother of Prince Jahan's Rajput maternal uncle, the late Rana Udai Singh, but an avowed friend of the Moghuls in this struggle. The Rana's ambition must be rulership of Mewar, as a vassal of the Emperor, in place of the present ruler,

Rana Amar. The Emperor had appointed him Prince Jahan's chief aide, another reminder of the prince's lack of field experience.

Even after Prince Jahan had signed the document, Prince Aziz Koka refused to give up. 'You should reconsider your order, Prince,' Aziz Koka insisted. He looked more skeletal than ever, his deep-set eyes in shadow from the uncertain lamplight of the tent.

'I have signed it.'

'But you have not issued it.'

'The moment I place my signature on any document, it is issued though no man may set eyes on it.'

'It is the privilege of the young to be headstrong at times, especially if they are men of unique worth,' Rana Surjan intervened smoothly. He stroked his long white beard, which would have made him look like a Muslim *mullah* were it not for the typically haughty Rajput features, hawk eyes, prominent nose and noble forehead beneath a tight black turban. 'I can say with the utmost certainty that my cousin, Rana Amar, is finally disposed to discuss terms now that *you* have arrived at the head of such a large army.'

Prince Jahan was always revolted by flattery. He was about to make a sharp rejoinder when he remembered his new position. The commander of a Moghul army should not take personal issue with his subordinates. Yet he was tired, drowsy from having ridden most of the day to reach the camp, immediate inspections, discussions with his field commanders and most of all the frustrating argument with these two advisers. 'Let me tell you both for the umpteenth time, as simply as possible, the strategy I shall follow.' Recognizing that his voice was an unseemly growl, he softened it. 'The words of my order contain a clear statement of our object. We are here to subjugate this territory, *not* to negotiate for it. I requested the Emperor, and he graciously extended to me, all the resources necessary to

319

achieve this object. Even the late Emperor Akbar never conquered the whole of Mewar. He merely besieged Chitor and briefly occupied it. I intend that our Emperor Jehangir shall be the first Moghul Emperor in history to bring all Mewar under his suzerainty.'

'We will only be wasting more men and material,' Prince Aziz responded. 'We are not here to create history, but to end this revolt, amicably if possible. You intend a scorched earth policy. What would then be left to the conquerors? A desert containing a starving people with only the thousands of Rajput and Moghul corpses to feed the vultures?'

'The Moghuls will not starve,' Prince Jahan insisted, still holding on to his temper. 'I have already ensured that through the system of supply trains I have organized. As for the Rajputs, they will fight to the death if they are not starved into submission.'

'Where do you expect to have the final battle that will give you victory over the Rajputs?' Prince Aziz Koka demanded, pounding the table with a bony fist.

'I will not give battle to the Rajputs.'

'Will you then besiege Chitor and Udaipur for months, possibly years?' Rana Surjan inquired smoothly.

The time had come to reveal his true plan, which only the Emperor knew of and had approved. 'I shall besiege nothing. I shall march across Mewar taking possession of all sources of food and water needed for our own sustenance, destroying the rest. I shall blockade the frontiers of the kingdom so that nothing gets through. I shall avoid any and all major contact with Rajput forces, especially open battle. I shall not allow myself to be trapped in river beds, ravines and mountain passes. The entire Moghul army shall play the terrorist guerilla.'

In the shocked silence that followed, a trumpet sounding the midnight hour seemed to blare forth a message of doom.

'No . . . no . . . No!' Prince Aziz Koka banged the table

320

once more, stood up. 'You dare not, Prince,' he croaked. He looked wildly at Rana Surjan who was shaking his head slowly from side to side in disbelief.

Prince Jahan rose to his feet. Not quite as tall as his foster-uncle, he had to raise his eyes to meet the man's blazing gaze. 'Sit down, Prince Aziz Koka,' he commanded.

'I shall never sit down in the face of such . . . such monstrosity. I shall always rise up for the poor oppressed against barbarism.'

'Have I not told you that the Emperor has approved this plan?'

'I still oppose it . . . rise up against it.' The sunken eyes were so demented now that Rana Surjan placed a restraining hand on the sleeve covering the bony arm.

'As you once took up sides against the Emperor?' Prince Jahan snapped viciously. 'As you opposed him not so long ago and fled to Mewar? Let me warn you, Prince Aziz Koka, that I am beginning to mistrust your motives. It is the generosity and compassion, especially to members of his family, that has always characterized our Emperor which saved you from imprisonment, even execution. Are you finally a loyal subject of the Emperor, or is your sympathy for that rebellious entity you call the poor oppressed greater than your dedication to your ruler?' His anger finally broke loose. 'Answer me!' he roared. 'Where is your loyalty?'

'My first loyalty is to my religion, which means to Almighty Allah and his Prophet Mahomet.'

'And what of your temporal loyalty?'

'It is to wisdom and restraint.'

'Are you saying then that the Emperor's proposed policy towards Mewar is lacking in wisdom and restraint?' Prince Jahan calmed down. Should he concede to Prince Aziz Koka's principles? Was this man a traitor or a saint? No, a fanatic Muslim perhaps, but never a saint! Remembering

321

Prince Aziz Koka's past actions, Prince Jahan decided to treat him as dangerous, a man who might even betray the planned strategy to the enemy.

'Do not put words in my mouth, Prince Jahan.'

Instantly, Prince Jahan recalled another of his grandfather's warnings: There is no room in the field for half-heartedness or prevarication; those who are not whole-heartedly, uncompromisingly, with you are against you and must be treated as traitors.

He suddenly became cold and sober as a judge. 'Prince Aziz Koka, as your commanding general, representing the Emperor in this campaign, I now order you to accept his policy for conducting it.'

'As your chief adviser, duly appointed by the Emperor, I shall resist the policy you propose. Pending appeal to my sovereign, I shall open diplomatic negotiations with Rana Amar tomorrow and prove your plan to be the product of a wild, headstrong, ambitious youth.'

This was it. Too much was now involved, including the effectiveness of his command of the Moghul army. If he did not act quickly and decisively, he might as well return to Agra. 'Prince Aziz Koka, as of this moment you are under arrest for insubordination and traitorous intentions.'

The moment he entered her suite of rooms for the night, Nur Jehan knew that the Emperor was worried and in a bad mood. It was the custom of kings, princes and nobles to have the noon meal in the *harem* and visit it at night only when they desired fleshy desserts after dinner. But as he became more and more dependent on her, the Emperor had started to have dinner too with her, whenever possible, after which they would adjourn to her bedchamber. While encouraging this practice because it helped him to reduce his intake of wine and opium, she took pains to ensure that he continued his feasts with the princes and nobles, who were one of the principal sources of the support he needed in order to govern the Empire.

Tonight, for instance, at her suggestion, he had dined with a visiting embassy from Persia, which included a group of philosophers and learned priests. Now he had come to her. One look at his face, the slanty eyes focused inwards in sombre reflection, the Mongol moustaches drooping, its whole expression set in harshness, warned her that she must use the utmost wisdom to restore him to his normal self.

As soon as she had knelt and kissed his hand, she took his arm and led him directly to the mattress in her bedchamber. She unrobed him in silence, her every touch a caress, pouring out all her love-energy to soothe him. With the pressure of her hand on his bare shoulder, she gently urged him to lie on the mattress and relax.

'Rest flat on your back, my lord, with your legs stretched, your hands beside your body, the palms up. Roll your eyes backward in the calm manner of death. Concentrate only on what you are doing. There must be *no* other thoughts in your mind.' She adjusted his legs and hands. 'Now concentrate on your toes and start relaxing them as if there is no life in them . . . now your feet . . . your ankles . . . your calves. Now your thighs . . . They must be completely lifeless.' She lifted his right leg a few inches, dropped it. It flopped down without life. 'Wonderful. Now your hands, starting with your fingers.' She repeated the process, checked his arm to ensure that it too flopped without weight on the mattress. 'Now your waist . . . your stomach . . . your neck . . . your face.'

When he lay completely still, she disrobed herself, while he stared, sightless, at the painted mosaics on the ceiling. She knelt beside him and started to stroke his head, moving soft fingers very gently over his hair at first, then gradually running her fingers through it until she was scratching his head lightly with her nails. She kept her eyes on his head all the while, never uttering a word, projecting towards his whole being a love of infinite tenderness.

Presently, she felt his mind relax. The head settled down completely on the mattress. He had closed his eyes, his breathing was slow and even. She placed light middle fingertips on his temples, felt the pulse beats. Pressing lightly, she moved the fingers in a slow, circular motion. Rotating her hands back, leaving her middle fingers pressing more lightly now on each temple, she touched him below each eye, just beside the bridge of his nose, with the tips of her thumbs. She located the tiny pulse beats and drew the thumbs ever so slowly along the frontal bones until they reached the middle fingers. He sighed when she repeated the movement. She drew down her middle fingers until they were pressing just at the entrances to his ears. 'Open your mouth by dropping your jaw,' she bade him gently. 'Let the jaw too hang lifeless.' She pressed with her middle fingers, repeated the stroking of his frontal bones with her thumbs.

He opened his eyes, smiled at her. 'You are my wonderful, caring mother,' he murmured.

'You are my most wonderful, obedient son,' she breathed, responding with one of their magical formulas.

'Come and lie down beside me. I need to feel your body against mine, to talk to you, to get your advice.'

Here it was, at long last. All that she had worked towards with wisdom and restraint. For the first time ever, he was openly seeking her advice. The event was delicate as fine porcelain, had to be handled as such, using the utmost care, lest it shatter.

Taking pains not to make a single jerky movement, she lay on her side facing him, felt the cool silk of his skin above his body warmth. He clasped his hands behind his head, stared at the ceiling again, collecting his thoughts.

'Our young general in Mewar has created a situation of extreme difficulty for me, possibly a crisis,' he began. 'I am not sure that Prince Jahan was the right choice to lead the expedition.'

In her wisdom, she still did not utter a word.

'Prince Aziz Koka, whom I appointed Prince Jahan's principal adviser, representing *me*,' he gestured towards his chest with his fingers, 'dared to disagree with him openly on the strategy he intends to pursue against the Rajputs. The prince has placed Aziz Koka under arrest for traitorous conduct.' He turned his head towards her, eyebrows lifted inquiringly. 'Imagine that! A young prince, just turned twenty, places the most senior prince in my household, three times his age and my foster-brother, under arrest. What do I do now? I can deal with any contingency of peace or war in the Empire as I have amply demonstrated all my life, but this conflict within my family is quite another matter. I mean, Prince Aziz Koka is also a respected general, an elder statesman and my representative with our Mewar army. I cannot permit a hot-headed young field commander to take such drastic action.'

Thoughts were whirling like dervishes through Nur Jehan's head, but she gave no sign of them. How best could she use this occasion to earn the Emperor's trust and confidence, make it so that he would come to her again and again for advice until she would be the one wielding the power, through him at first, later on, directly? Now that the possibilities were unfolding at last, they awed her, but also generated an icy determination to make them materialize. She had already started influencing policy once again through her father and brother, but it was not enough. The three of them were proving an effective team, but it galled her to be an adviser at second-hand, merely because she was a *harem* woman. Also, the only way in which she could displace Salima Begum's suzerainty over that *harem* was to have the old lady poisoned or to wield supreme power over the entire Empire, leaving the Begum her vassal with the right to rule the *harem* kingdom. The latter thought intrigued and excited her. Having someone murdered, as the Emperor had done with Sher Afgan, was such an *ordinary* thing to do! Using one's brains was superior.

At that moment, as she stared at the Emperor's profile, the noble forehead, bushy eyebrows, straight nose curving upward at the tip, the resolute chin, the rugged strength of the whole, she saw Prince Jahan's likeness to his father. She had always considered Prince Jahan the most worthy successor to the throne, which was why she had cleverly organized his betrothal and marriage to her niece, Mumtaz Mahal. The similarity of appearance established a connection, divulged to her the course she should follow. Prince Jahan was the brightest star in the Moghul firmament. She had to support him and make him too a vassal of the kingdom within the Empire, the kingdom of power and responsibility, rather than territory, which she was building, *her* kingdom. Her father, her brother and Prince Jahan would then form the Nur Jehan Cabinet. That was it, the Nur Jehan Cabinet. She liked the phrase. It carried the ring of history.

'Who was it who uncovered your eldest son's plot to assassinate you, beloved of my soul?' she inquired gently.

'Why, Prince Jahan of course.' He frowned. 'But I cannot extend my gratitude to him so far as to permit him to usurp my own . . .' He stopped short, snapped a finger, turned his head sharply to gaze at her in admiration. 'By the Almighty, you are so wise. Your questions always stir my own wisdom. Prince Husrau was my own son, but I allowed Prince Jahan a free hand in arresting him . . .' He stopped short, the frown still creasing his brow.

'As the traitor whom Prince Jahan exposed him to be,' she completed the sentence.

'And I dealt with Prince Husrau myself for his crime.' His brow cleared. 'I *then* meted out the punishment of *my* choice to him.'

'You have such infinite wisdom. You have seen that Prince Jahan uses his God-given initiative to protect you, but leaves you your rights as a ruler. As I understand it, Prince Jahan has only arrested Prince Aziz Koka for traitorous conduct. What exactly transpired?'

She listened quietly while her husband poured out the story based upon the reports he had received from both antagonists in the dispute.

'While Prince Aziz Koka's report contains opinions, Prince Jahan has stuck to the facts, it would seem,' she observed when he had finished. 'The truths of truth lie in the statements of both men. Prince Aziz Koka does not deny that he would act on his own initiative to open negotiations with the Rajputs even after Prince Jahan assured him that such was not your policy.' Noting that his expression had relaxed, she pressed home. 'I see that you have come to a conclusion without any assistance from me,' she lied. 'All you needed was to speak your thoughts aloud. Will you share your decision with me, liege lord of my heart?'

'Of course.' He looked so serene now, that she knew something positive, even cruel, was in the offing. 'The only way in which I can save face in the light of Prince Aziz Koka's actions and retain my authority is by supporting Prince Jahan's decision to the hilt. I shall have Prince Aziz Koka brought back to Agra in chains and sentence him to the dungeons for one year. That will teach him not to pass wind in *my* commander's tent!'

An atmosphere of gloom had slowly begun to invest Chitor during the winter. Tonight Prince Chara recognized, for the first time, that it had infected his father. The Rana was outwardly his confident, cheerful self as they sat down to dinner together, but there was something indefinable, confirmed by the rather cheerless way in which he said, 'Give us your report, Prince,' as if he already knew that he would not learn anything favourable.

Prince Chara had just returned from three months in the field at the head of the Rajput army, much of that time spent in camps, bivouacs and village inns. His preference for tonight would have been to be leading a combined force of Mewar's Rajputs and the Deccan's Marathas against the Moghul army led by his arch-enemy, Prince Jahan. Since that was not possible, he was ready for some of the luxuries of the Chitor palace life, typified by the soft glow of light from the hanging lamps of the small dining chamber on the polished Indian mahogany dining table and the ornaments on the matching sideboards and by the blessed sounds of silence which were never available in the field. The dinner had, however, hinted of austerity; the roast lamb was rationed, with hardly any spices to flavour it, the fruit consisted only of some red plums, the dessert his father's shrug.

'Our forces are being rendered ineffective by the sheer weight of numbers of the Moghul army with its own watertight supply and service plan,' he reported. 'We knew when the Emperor sent such a huge, well-equipped force that open battle was out of the question, unless General Malik Ambar joined us from the Deccan with his entire army. The very size of the Moghul invasion force, however, discouraged General Ambar from following through with that plan. Having achieved such remarkable progress in the Deccan and Gujarat, he was reluctant to gamble on a single throw of the dice.'

'Understandably so.'

A flicker of impatience streaked through Prince Chara. The scar on his face began to itch. 'I believe it to be a grave mistake,' he countered. 'If the success of our own endeavours is delayed – ' he for one would never admit that they might fail – 'General Ambar will face a formidable foe on his own. Prince Jahan's own strategy is obvious. If he defeats us, it will be the turn of the Deccan next.'

'What do you consider to be Prince Jahan's final plan?' Rana Amar demanded heavily.

'As you know, he has avoided open battle and any form of investment or siege, either of Chitor or Udaipur. He has also kept clear of mountain terrain where he might be ambushed. Meanwhile, his army, as a single entity, has pushed steadily into the heartland of Mewar, razing villages to the ground, setting fire to standing crops, seizing those that have been gathered. He has poisoned wells and reservoirs, blockaded towns, wrecked bridges, blown up major highways. He has inflicted the barbaric punishments of the Moghuls on collaborators, as he calls those who support us. And all the while he maintains a relentless pressure on our main body, stabbing wherever possible to inflict heavy casualties. It has been like having a huge forest fire following us, with great tongues of flame frequently licking out to destroy. There has been no way in which we could retaliate, except with sporadic raids on his outposts, wiping out the occasional patrol, like putting out the forest fire with water buckets.' His shrug was helpless, but bitter frustration engulfed him with a more deadly hatred than ever of Prince Jahan.

'Our people are suffering the tortures of the damned.' The Rana shifted his huge bulk on his chair, placed an elbow on the table, cupped his chin in his hand. 'Reports are pouring in daily from all parts of the country of starvation, disease, epidemics, thirst, death and destruction. The will of the people is being sapped. We are a race of fighters, not penitents mortifying the flesh. Prince Jahan is the absolute reincarnation of his ancestors – not the

Emperor Akbar, but Babur, Timur the Lame and Genghis Khan.' He stared into space a while, in open gloom now. 'What do you propose?'

'Rajput honour and freedom are involved,' Prince Chara responded fiercely, near demented in his determination. 'We shall never submit or yield to cruelty and oppression.'

'The young prince is relentless. Is it honourable to offer our people from the security of this palace the freedom to suffer so dreadfully with only death as their release?'

Prince Chara was appalled. Weary, frustrated, bitter, angry from the past three months of constant retreats, he had never expected this from his father. 'I have not suggested anything from the security of the palace,' he exploded, banging a fist on the table. The unusual display, disrespectful as it was, acted as an outlet, restored his balance. 'I am sorry for the outburst, Sire,' he apologized. 'But this has been a most trying time for me. I have witnessed all I have reported to you at first hand and it has filled me with such loathing for the Moghuls and, yes, Prince Jahan, that I would rather die than yield to them.' He paused. 'As to your request for suggestions, I would recommend that we keep on retreating before the enemy, inflicting even pin-pricks of damage, wearing him out. An army can never destroy an entire nation. We must outlast the barbarian horde, attempt to rally all freedom forces in its Empire to our cause. When the time is right, we shall unite against him.'

'When will the time be right?'

Prince Chara's smile was crooked. 'When the snake's head is removed from its body.'

'Forest fires, snakes. You sound confused. What do you mean?'

'I have already organized a death squad of patriotic Rajputs, who believe that dying for *dharma* (the duty of station) will give them the eternal reward of good *kharma/*

vipaka. They will remove Prince Jahan permanently from the scene. Meanwhile, your cousin Rana Surjan is standing by, ready to commence peace negotiations with us on honourable terms which the Emperor will surely approve when his brilliant,' he spat out the word, 'favourite son is dead. All our talk of gods of justice is pork shit. There is no such thing as justice in the universe. Justice is a human concept. Witness drought and flood, fire and famine endured by helpless people. So we must inflict, I repeat inflict, our own justice on these barbarians.' His ferocity caused him to bare his teeth like an animal at bay.

The Rana brightened. 'You are remarkable,' he declared appreciatively. 'Never without an alternative. Is our cousin . . . ?'

Prince Chara cut in before his father could complete the question he would not answer. 'I prefer to be regarded as relentless, Sire.'

He would not even mention his Agra plan.

As he lay with Mumtaz Mahal, the slow beat of rain began on the palace roof. It was dark in the bedchamber so he could not identify the furniture in it, but his wife's body was soft and warm beside him. How cosy it was, home at last. Mumtaz was his home.

'Mumtaz, my pearl,' he murmured into her soft hair.

'Mmm . . . mh,' she responded drowsily.

The beat of the rain increased in stops and starts of drumming. Attendants shouted, so the rain must have leaked through the windows. He wanted to get out of bed and summon Sati, but he was somehow chained to the divan by the bedclothes and the weight of his wife's leg across his thighs.

The drumming became a pounding. The shouts turned to screams of pain.

Prince Jahan awoke with a start. It was pitch dark in his

tent. He was not in Mumtaz Mahal's bedchamber. He must have been dreaming, but the clatter, thuds and screams persisted. His mind cleared away its sleep-mist on the instant. In a flash, he comprehended that his dream had been linked with reality. The sound of hooves was interspersed by the angry neighing of horses, shrill whinnying, the clash of arms and agonized shrieks. A battle was raging near his tent. Alarm forked through him.

What in Allah's name was happening? How had the enemy broken inside his lines?

He grasped the long sword which was ever present beside him while he slept, flung aside his field blanket and leapt out of bed.

Where were his bodyguards?

The blood pounding in his veins, he rushed to the entrance of the tent, thought better of it, sped to the rear, ducked under the tent flap.

The ghost-riders came swooping down on the tent like a pride of lions on a herd of antelope.

Near panic, his right foot caught on a tent rope and he went sprawling on the damp grass.

Tonight was the night. Wrapped in his cloak against the chill air outside the barn where he headquartered, Prince Chara could not hold back a shiver. He knew it was not from the cold, but from suspense. His mind was white, bright as the starlit sky above him. If he had been unable to sleep, it had not been because of the dark stench of straw long stored within the barn that still remained in his nostrils, or the odours of manure and horse-sweat from the nearby stables. The three-day-old crescent of a moon had set, so it was nearly midnight, and if his plan worked, the rising star above the Muslim crescent would have been extinguished even at this moment.

He listened to the sounds of the darkness about him, the

constant creak of crickets, the croaking of bull-frogs from the nearby marsh. The barking of a dog in the distant village leap-frogged through the other sounds, petered out into loneliness. The certainty that Prince Jahan was dead gripped him, filled him with elation. He raised clenched fists to the heavens, restrained a cry of joy.

Soon the long weeks of misery and privation would be over. With the death of their champion, the Moghul army would become dispirited, the Emperor dismayed. The next death would totally crush him so that he would be ready to accept Rana Surjan's offer to negotiate a favourable peace.

He sensed the presence before he detected the dark shadow. He whipped around, flinging open his cloak, drawing his sword in the same movement.

Nur Jehan was restless for once. Unable to sleep, she tossed and turned on her divan bed, trying vainly to identify the cause of inner disquiet that had brought her wide awake barely two hours after she first fell asleep. Her body felt chill, yet she found the pink silken cushions and covers uncomfortably warm as she tossed and turned. She wondered whether she was getting an attack of the ague, from which her husband was suffering tonight, but immediately realized that if she did have the ague it was in her mind, the source of it unaccountable dread. Since the Emperor made it a point never to visit her when he was really sick, she was alone in her new upstairs two-bedroom suite, adjoining his own bedroom, that overlooked the gardens of the royal *harem* of the Agra palace.

The suite consisted of a foyer, a large reception chamber where she spent most of her time during the day, working beside the indoor pool or entertaining her friends. Her hunting trophies lined its walls and the matchlock rifle with which she had killed her tigers, always fully loaded, hung above the fireplace, with tinder and wicks on the mantel-piece. All the rooms were side-by-side, opening out to the balcony which ran the length of the suite. She had redecorated it herself. Knowing that her husband had a partiality for the small European chamber which the Emperor Akbar had created to impress his foreign guests, she had the reception chamber and the first bedroom done in formal French style to provide him with a change from the splendour of the heavy Moghul and Persian mix of the rest of the palace. The second and last bedroom was sparsely furnished with settles of polished ebony along the walls, a white marble floor and two crystal chandeliers. She never divulged to a soul that this was the room for ritual sex, merely let it be known that the Emperor liked a bare room at times, to contrast with all the extravagance and opulence around him.

Restless, Nur Jehan finally rose, slid her bare feet into her warm silk bed-slippers. In the uncertain light from the lamp at the far end of the room, the only one lit for the night, the arms of the ornate wall-clock pointed to midnight. She shivered, reached for the pink satin robe hanging on a golden peg beside the bed. She donned the robe, padded silently to the balcony. The darkness here was comforting. The palace gardens, lit by flares along the paved walkways, stretched into blackness beyond. She could almost hear the splash of the fountains and the rush of the cascades that ornamented the elaborate water features which, together with the dark sculpted shrubs and tall cypress, were a feature of every Moghul garden. Imagining that she heard the chink of a cobra, she shivered again, for the very reason that the cobra was her protector. Did the cobra's presence mean that she needed protection? She shivered again, this time with a dire premonition of evil. She found the scent of rose incense, which she favoured for her bedroom, overpowering. Caught between the dread within her and the suffocation of the incense, she decided that she would try to sleep in the bare bedroom at the end of the suite. She turned to walk towards it.

The tiniest creak drew her attention to the bedroom door. Slowly, ever so slowly, it had begun to open. Startled, she paused in her stride. Could it be Mano, now her chief lady-in-waiting? Cold reason instantly told her that neither Mano nor any other attendant would enter without knocking and being granted leave. And absolutely no one would ever open her bedroom door, least of all in the middle of the night. It must be an intruder.

She stifled a scream.

Her heart began to pound. Reason connected with her earlier dread. Should she shout for help? No, that would be futile. She was alone here with someone, a rapist or an assassin. How could anyone have got past the guards, eunuchs and other attendants? An idle question. What she needed was to protect herself. Panic-stricken, she shrank back into the shadows, watched in horror as a huge, hooded figure dressed in black, with slits for eyes, slipped quietly through the half-open doorway, paused to stare fixedly at the divan bed, trying to penetrate the semi-gloom. He wanted to identify her sleeping figure!

The assassin cautiously slid a black-gloved hand inside his robe, withdrew it, revealed a curved scimitar, dully gleaming in the dim lamp-glow. He raised the scimitar aloft. Nur Jehan's terror mounted, reached for her throat. Petrified, she watched the assassin move slowly forward.

He leapt high in the air, landed six paces away, his sword grasped in both hands at waist level pointing at the intruder. For the flicker of a second, Prince Chara recalled with thankfulness that he had been taught this trick by a military visitor from Cathay.

A gasp escaped the dark figure emerging from the gloom

of the barn doorway. 'It is me, Prince.' The man was terrified.

Prince Chara remained poised for a moment, the blood still tingling in his veins. 'Never, never come upon me without warning,' he gritted, staring across the darkness to impress his deadly seriousness on his aide. 'Not if you wish to remain alive.' He relaxed the sword, so it pointed down at the dark grass.

'I'm so very sorry, lord. I humbly beg your pardon.'

The quaver in Selvam's voice reached Prince Chara's tension, caused it to demand an outlet. He sheathed his sword, dropped his voice. 'Since you startled me, you will have to ease me,' he breathed. He moved forward, brushed past Selvam, caught a glimpse of the young man's tanned face, the skin tight drawn over delicate bones, the dark eyes lustrous in girlish features, before plunging into the gloom of the barn. The odour of damp straw smote him, mingled with his aide's night sweat. He turned, heard the squeak of a field mouse before the barn door creaked shut. He moved slowly forward until he sensed Selvam's body vibrate near his and heard the young man's quickened breathing.

He reached for Selvam's crotch, felt the rock hard erection and grunted with satisfaction. All other thoughts fled as he fondled his aide's magnificent member, out-thrust like the prow of a ship.

Chapter 21

Thwack! Thwack! The great scimitar came down twice on the cushions. Frozen, Nur Jehan watched in horror, heard the sounds she was never meant to hear except when they blended into a single moment of excruciating agony that would have been her awareness before death.

'For Itibar, foul bitch!' The words muffled by the hood reached her, jolted her numbed senses back to the need for action. As the scimitar was raised aloft again, she recognized, coolly now, that she had but a few seconds before the assassin realized that he was hacking away at empty cushions and began searching the bedroom. If she was lucky, he would make for the second bedroom before searching the balcony where she stood.

But what could she do? Pray that he went first to the other bedroom? Prayer would not help here, only action. Already the upraised weapon had been poised too long. Doubt had sprung in the assassin's mind. He released the scimitar from his left hand. Still holding it upraised in his right, he bent, began fumbling with the cushions in jerks with his free hand. She heard the hiss of his escaping breath. He had failed to find a body on the bed. He searched more frantically, finally rose to his full height. The deadly weapon still held aloft like a brand in his right hand, his head swivelled sideways, this way and that, searching the room. A fiend in a horror play.

She shrank back into the shadows. Her heart had stopped pounding, but it was still beating rapidly. Thanks be to Almighty Allah, all the rooms opened out on to the balcony. If the hunter came to the balcony, she would make a run for it to the reception chamber. If he did not, she would race to the second bedroom, slip inside, play hide and seek with him until . . . She steadied her breathing as the seed of an idea sprouted in her mind. A cold purpose gripped her stomach. She gritted her teeth. She was Nur Jehan, the Empress. She would remain cool . . . and resolute . . . and survive!

The huge figure silently knelt to look under the bed. She was tempted to run, but held back. She needed to wait. He

337

rose to his feet. Knowing that he would first glance in the direction of the balcony entrance, she deliberately looked away from him, closed her eyes, held her breath, removed all consciousness of him from her mind. There is no better way to attract someone's attention than to focus oneself on that person. It required every ounce of her willpower, especially when her brain screamed out that those death's-head eyes were boring straight into her through the slits in the hood and she simply *had* to check. With indomitable resolution, she defied her brain, concentrated totally on her heartbeat, excluded all else from her consciousness.

She had her reward. A rustle and a muttered, 'Damn you, bitch, where are you?' told her she was undiscovered. Totally calm, she opened her eyes, quietly drew a breath. Her resolve had entered her mind as well.

The assassin had turned around, was probing the far corners of the room, his head moving in sharp jerks this way and that, his gaze fumbling in the semi-darkness as his hand had fumbled on the bed-cushions. She waited until he stopped moving. His eyes on the entrance to the second bedroom, he stalked silently towards it. He paused at the door, a huge figure of doom, trying to penetrate the darkness beyond.

It would not take him long to search the semi-bare bedroom. She had but a few seconds. With a super-human effort, she took her eyes away from him again. She slipped slowly forward, careful not to make a jerky movement. Slowly, ever so slowly, walking erect, she made for the glow of light that was the opening from the reception chamber to the balcony. It spelt safety.

Would she ever make it? Now at least she could run. Take a chance on reaching the entrance to the suite ahead of him. Shout from there for the guards. What guards? Suppose they had been bribed? Suppose this was part of a major palace plot? No, if that were the case, the assassin would have needed neither hood nor stealth. Encouraged, she made steadily for the rectangle of light.

She paused to look inside. The glow from the single hanging lamp showed that the chamber was empty. She looked to her left. The balcony lay dead in the gloom. She was damp with sweat in spite of the chill of the night air. Again the chink of that cobra. The cobra was her friend. She was the Empress. She would never scream for help.

She stepped into the chamber, sped to her objective.

Thwack! Thwack! He heard the soggy thud of the flung spears against the tent flap. His fall had saved him. Allah be praised. The thump of footsteps told him that the night-rider assassins had seen him. And flung their spears. Two thwacks meant two spears. At least two opponents. Deliberately, he cooled his fevered mind.

His first instinct was to run, but honour forbade it. He would turn and fight his foes. Die facing them, never with his back turned.

Out of that indomitable resolve, inspiration flashed. In a trice, sword upraised, he sprang towards the taut tent guy rope nearest him. One fierce downward slash and the rope severed neatly. The tent sagged . . . just enough to halt the assassins who were almost at the flap. He sped to the second guy rope. Another mighty slash. The tent collapsed. Savage curses arose beneath it. He saw the lumpy outlines of the heaving figures.

Wild exhilaration mingled with overpowering rage. Regardless of danger, he leapt forward. Hacking, thrusting, smashing at each of the figures in turn. Their muffled screams of agony maddened him the more. 'Bastards!' he screamed. 'I'll teach you!'

The screams faded into groans, gasps. He only paused in his merciless onslaught when the great lumps fell silent, lay still in the gloom.

* * *

She stood by the fireplace, facing the door to the bedroom, commanding the balcony entrance as well.

He emerged from the main bedroom, a huge, menacing figure. His gaze fell on her immediately. With a shout of triumph, he raised his scimitar aloft, shot forward, then paused as he noted what she held in her hands.

Calmly, coolly, as when she had been hunting tiger, she aimed the matchlock rifle at his chest. Not his head. She wanted to be able to identify him.

He leapt towards her, brandishing his fearsome weapon. She gave him two steps. Pulled the trigger that sent the already lit match to the touch hole. The weapon erupted, flashing flame. She gave with its thunderous blast. The shot hit the assassin four-squarely in the chest, halted him for a fraction of a second. He keeled over. Unearthly screams ripped through the hood. His sword clattered to the marble floor. One hand reached for his chest before he sprawled backwards.

Fierce as a mountain lion, Nur Jehan bounded forward. Smoking rifle in hand, the reek of gunpowder in her nostrils. In seconds she reached the jerking figure lying on its back. She raised her rifle aloft, brought down the barrel on his head.

Thwack! Thwack! Poetic justice, she exulted. The giant figure gasped once. Lay still. Blood oozed from the gaping chest wound. Lacerated pink flesh showed beneath the scorched hole in the black robe.

When the Uzbeg female guards and eunuchs raced in through the entrance door of the suite, they found Nur Jehan facing them. She stood beside the body, her right foot on its stomach, her right hand grasping the rifle semi-upright, its butt held against her haunch.

Nur Jehan, the hunter. A figure of triumph.

They paused, shocked into silence.

'You may remove this assassin,' she directed calmly, in

340

even golden tones. 'Those of you who were a party to the plot will wish you had never been born.' Her every instinct told her that, apart from lax guards, there were no other conspirators in the palace, otherwise Tafari would not have attempted to murder her himself.

She glanced down at the body. 'This was our Chief Eunuch, Tafari.' Who had sent him? She would never know.

He became conscious of his surroundings in an instant. Whirled round to face possible foes.

'Prince Jahan, thank Almighty Allah you are safe.' The voice was that of General Wahid, now his chief aide. The general limped forward, naked sword in hand. He stopped in front of the prince and saluted. Even in the darkness, Prince Jahan could discern the anxiety on the rugged, hatchet face. Guards carrying flares and officers with drawn swords crowded behind.

'What happened?' Prince Jahan inquired of the general.

'As far as we can tell, a death squad of Rajputs broke into the encampment. Their aim was obviously to murder you.'

'How did they get past the guards? Our outposts are a mile away.'

'They knew when we change guards. It is always at midnight. They had inside information as to their dispositions.'

'So one or more of our own betrayed us?'

'Yes, Prince. But who?'

'We shall soon find out. Bring the prisoners to me.'

'There are no prisoners.'

'What?'

'Every single one of the assassins has been killed.'

Prince Jahan was about to explode against such stupidity when the recollection of his own savage fury of a minute

341

earlier flashed through his brain. 'I understand how it happened,' he responded quietly. 'I understand only too well. We shall never find out who sent them.'

The memory of his chief groom, Ishtaq, who had killed the two *thuggee* who had attempted to kidnap him on the *maidan* of the Agra palace years ago to prevent them from betraying their sponsors, intruded. History had repeated itself. He would never discover the traitor.

As if to open the door to his suspicions, however, the silver-haired Rana Surjan appeared, half-clothed, full of alarm. 'What in the name of the gods is all this?'

Prince Jahan shrugged and turned away. 'Merely an attempt on my life.'

'By whom?'

'A Rajput death squad,' General Wahid snapped.

'Any prisoners?'

Ah, my dear Rana, why are you so concerned about prisoners? I shall never discover the truth of who conspired with the Rajputs to attempt this murderous deed, but you are not to be trusted.

'Remove the bodies,' Prince Jahan coolly commanded. 'Send them back to the nearest Rajput village with a message, "Jahan is invincible." Reinforce the guard posts. General Wahid, alter the guard schedules to changes at irregular intervals without notice or warning to anyone at all. Have the camp-followers re-erect my tent. We can all do with some sleep.'

My beloved Mumtaz, Allah saved me for you. I hope I will continue my dream of you tonight.

One year after Prince Jahan took over command of the Mewar expedition, Rana Amar offered unconditional surrender. During that year, the Moghul invasion force had turned the entire kingdom of Mewar into a land of starvation, disease and death. The worst blow that had struck the

Rajputs, however, came from whichever of the Rajput's pantheon of gods wielded such power. The winter of 1613 brought torrential rains that resulted in great floods that destroyed crops. A drought in the following spring played havoc with the sowing. The result was famine and the inevitable pestilence. Cholera, typhus and smallpox epidemics ravaged the kingdom as heavenly deities allied themselves with the young Moghul army commander to destroy it.

Prince Chara's hatred for Prince Jahan became all-consuming.

Friendly nobles inevitably began deserting Rana Amar Singh. With Prince Chara always in the field, the Rana had no one sufficiently close to him to share his anguish at seeing his land laid waste, his people sinking to unequalled depths of misery, his allies deserting him. When he sent an embassy led by Prince Shub and Prince Das offering total surrender to Prince Jahan, it was in the teeth of Prince Chara's opposition. Inexplicably, it had taken Prince Jahan several weeks to accept the offer of surrender. When acceptance finally came, Prince Chara and the Rana were puzzled by the procedure requested by Prince Jahan. Normally, under such circumstances, a victorious commander caused the enemy ruler to attend his headquarters, frequently under the most humiliating circumstances, and acknowledge abject defeat. Prince Jahan's message stated that he would attend the Rana in the audience hall of the Chitor palace shortly after dawn two days later. The fortress gates were, however, to be opened to his troops, with the battlements unmanned, the previous day, so that advance units of the Moghul army could take over the fort to secure it for Prince Jahan's arrival. The Rana was to be present in his audience hall, accompanied only by his personal advisers, at 7 A.M., to receive the victorious prince.

'I told you that this upstart Moghul would heap humiliation upon us,' Prince Chara had been unable to keep from
snarling at dinner the previous night. 'What greater insult
can there be than to have him, as the victorious invader,
dictating terms to us here in our own citadel? Chitor, which
held back the Emperor Akbar outside its gates for months
on end, belongs to him without the firing of a shot.'

'Perhaps he is coming here instead of having us go out to
him like miserable captives in order to do us honour.' The
Rana's voice had, however, held no conviction.

'Honour, Sire?' Prince Chara had demanded incredulously. 'What do the Moghuls know about treating enemies
with honour? Throughout history they have trampled
shamefully on those they have defeated. They have
wreaked vengeance, exacted their toll on the conquered
territory and its people, humiliated its rulers.' A bitter
laugh had escaped him. 'Tonight, we are prisoners in our
own citadel, with Moghul soldiers manning our battlements. Our cannon have been turned inwards to wreak
destruction on the palace, if necessary, a clever move,
worthy of the diabolical cunning of that young Moghul
arch-fiend. Make no mistake about it, Sire. The victor
comes to claim our very hearth. We are doomed to dishonour. Death on the battlefield would have been
preferable.'

'Death is an alternative that is always available to anyone
who desires it,' the Rana had rejoined. A great calm had
suddenly settled on him.

Bitterness consumed Prince Chara as he watched the victorious Prince Jahan emerge like a god of Hindu mythology
through the wispy trails of dawn-mist, the thunder of a
thousand hooves clattering behind him on the damp grey
cobblestones.

The year was 1614 AD of the Christian calendar and he

would surely remember this day of shame forever. Nor would he forgive his father for having delivered Chitor the impregnable to the enemy. Chitor was a true fortress on a steep, rocky eminence surrounded by a moat and located within a vast cactus-laden plain. An enemy who got past the murderous fire from across the moat would have had to scale the near-cliff slope of the eminence, only to face high rampart walls of granite, with embrasures for cannon and muskets that denied entrance to the lofty plateau on which the city was located, the palace at its centre. A narrow road, winding up the cliff-face, led to the city's main gate. The surrounding countryside offered neither food, shelter nor sustenance to the invader, while the city itself was still provisioned to withstand many months of siege.

Weakened by famine, crushed by pestilence, Chitor had finally become the stronghold of ghosts and wraiths, the home of the walking dead amid the lonely smoke and foetid stench of burning flesh from corpses on *ghats* in the plain below. Yet it should never have been surrendered. Better to have had the Moghul destroy it stone by stone.

When Prince Jahan, on his black charger, headed for the palace to accept the Rana's submission, Prince Chara knew that the victor and his cavalry escort would have ridden through the silence of empty streets. No proud Rajput would show his face to a conqueror. The thousands of eyes that gazed unseen from behind shuttered doors and half-closed windows must have been filled with the same shame and hatred that consumed him.

Standing on the first-floor balcony of the Chitor palace, he watched Prince Jahan's approach through the entrance gates, up the long avenue lined by the silent *ashok* trees, standing like tall, mournful sentinels clad in dark green. Prince Chara turned and walked slowly downstairs to receive the conqueror at the entrance doors of the palace, as he had been commanded by his father. The edges of the scar on his face itched and burned.

He was barely at the great teakwood doors when Prince Jahan, his mounted men in a solid phalanx behind him, reined in his horse at the empty front courtyard of the palace. Two tall red-uniformed grooms, white moustached and bearded, their top-knots held up by white turbans, rushed up, one to hold the charger's head, the other respectfully to help Prince Jahan dismount. Graciously declining the offer, the young man swung lithely off his horse, tossed the reins to the waiting groom and turned to face the palace. Proud, tall, erect, clad in black leather armour and helmet, arms akimbo, long curving sword at his side, he looked every inch the conqueror. Prince Chara ached with hatred for him.

The first ray of the day's light slanted from the east as if it were a messenger of the sun god, and lit up Prince Jahan's face, revealing heavy saturnine features, their sombre aspect belied by large, dark eyes, the slanting almonds of his ancestry, glittering with power and purpose. His figure was solid, yet tight-knit and dynamic. The bones of his wrists and ankles were curiously delicate.

Gazing at this interloper, Prince Chara recognized, in a moment of eternal consciousness, that the Moghul campaign had not been one of ambition or a lust for territorial expansion. Nor had it been between the Moghul and Rajput races, the Arabic and Sanskrit languages, the Hindu and Muslim religions. It went far, far deeper to the roots of the human race, the ancient struggle of people who had grown from a soil against those who had adopted it.

He saluted Prince Jahan as an equal, escorted him to the audience hall with no consciousness of his surroundings. Rana Amar Singh sat on his great ebony throne upholstered in red silk brocade, embellished with emeralds and rubies studding the great bands of gold on its arms and legs. Clad in a royal purple silk tunic with silver *jodhpur* pantaloons for the occasion, the great figure of the Rana somehow portrayed his defeat. It made Prince Chara, clad in the white satin pantaloons and sombre black silk tunic he had selected as appropriate for the mournful occasion, hold himself more proudly.

Perhaps to avoid witnesses to his shame, the Rana had decreed that only Prince Chara should be present at the meeting. Why had Prince Jahan come alone? To display his courage, assert his personal triumph and authority?

Prince Chara suppressed a wild, desperate desire to run the man through with his sword. 'Your Majesty, I have the honour to present to you the Moghul Prince Jahan, commander of the Emperor's army in Mewar.' He had selected his words with care, giving his father full rank and title, *presenting* a man of lesser rank, a prince, to him as commander of an army in Mewar, while the Rana was commander-in-chief of all his armed forces, small as they were.

The Rana did not rise from his throne, merely raised his right arm in greeting.

If Prince Jahan felt any discomfiture or anger, he did not show it. Instead, he advanced to the dais, mounted the steps leading directly to the throne, extended both his hands seeking the Rana's outstretched hand. Prince Jahan grasped the hand, knelt and kissed it.

Prince Chara could not believe his eyes. Prince Jahan was the victor. He could have treated the vanquished with contempt. Instead, he was honouring the conquered king as a monarch and, undoubtedly, an elder. This must be a trick of some kind.

The Rana's broad back shook. Had a sob escaped him? 'You may speak, Prince,' he declared, exercising his sovereign right to speak first.

Prince Jahan released the hand and stood up, his countenance grave. 'Your Majesty, you have done me great honour by receiving me cordially in your palace. In doing so, you have honoured my master, the Emperor but, more profoundly, you have honoured yourself and your race. This audience is a fitting finale to the valiant struggle of the Rajputs against overwhelming odds. Yours has been a bitter fight. By permitting my presence here, you have signalled the end of the war. That decision, even if dictated by circumstances, is still yours and yours alone, an honourable end to your honourable campaign. My personal presence here, when other arrangements might have been dictated, signifies my recognition and that of the Emperor that you have honourably won the peace.'

Prince Chara had become more and more amazed as he listened to Prince Jahan's words, delivered in a deep, melodious voice, its tones grave. He was seized by an almost demonic fury. If he had hated this victorious prince before, for his skill in war and politics, he absolutely loathed him now for his nobility. The Rana rose to the occasion. 'Your presence here, your conduct and your words do you more honour, Prince, than the long months of war you have waged. If we Rajputs had to fall, we could not have chosen a more triumphant end than at your hands.' He paused deliberately. 'Tell us now, what are your terms?'

Now the blow, padded in velvet speech, would fall, Prince Chara thought.

Prince Jahan bowed. 'My lord, the Emperor has commanded me to inform Your Majesty that, since there has been no defeat, there are no terms,' he stated slowly and clearly.

The Rana raised his head, shrugged his great shoulders in disbelief. 'What . . . uh . . . what then is the position?' he inquired hoarsely.

'All Rajput territories seized by the Moghul Emperors since the time of the Emperor Akbar are hereby restored to Your Majesty. The Emperor will hold the traditional imperial *durbar* to celebrate this event, but Your Majesty will not be required to attend it. Prince Chara would be most welcome as your representative. Unlike the other Rajput rulers, your house will not be required to enter into a matrimonial alliance with the Emperor's family. Your Majesty is only requested to acknowledge the suzerainty of the Emperor and to refrain from fortifying your capital, Chitor, on the understanding that imperial troops will come to your aid if any other ruler seeks to invest the city.'

'Is that all? No tribute to be paid?'

'That is all, Your Majesty. No tribute to be paid.'

'A trap,' Prince Chara grated.

'Silence!' Rana Amar Singh roared. 'You would bring the stench of disbelief to such a noble event?'

Prince Chara controlled his fury, leaving no doubt, however, as to the malevolence seething within him.

'We apologize for our son's lack of . . . er . . . decorum,' the Rana stated, the words bitter gall for Prince Chara. 'Tell us, Prince Jahan, did the Emperor come by these decisions on his own, or did he heed the advice of his field commander?'

Prince Jahan hesitated. 'The Emperor's decisions are always his own although . . . er . . . they are sometimes made on the advice given him.'

'You have told us what we need to know without saying it,' the Rana declared. He impulsively raised his right hand, drew out the great ruby ring that flamed on his middle finger. 'This ring has belonged to our family for centuries. It is not only of priceless worth, it represents the heart's blood of Rajput honour and that of our family.' He held up the ring in his right hand. 'See how it glitters even in this uncertain light.' He extended the ring to Prince Jahan. 'This birthright ring has always been a symbol of our nobility and honour. You have earned it today, Prince

349

Jahan, victor not only of territories but of your own *atman* (soul). Wear it always with pride.'

Prince Jahan's eyes glistened with emotion, the strong nostrils quivered. He took the ring in his right hand, examined it with obvious admiration. 'What a priceless treasure,' he murmured. He raised smiling eyes to the Rana. 'It is your desire to give me this valuable token, the gesture, that matters. For when you and I are gone from this life, the ring will remain without an owner who may have earned it.' He extended the ring to the Rana. 'In token of my own esteem, admiration and love, I beg you to accept this ring from me, Your Majesty. It is too precious to grace other fingers than those of honourable Rajputs.'

Prince Chara had listened to the interchange with silent fury. These two play-acting fools. Did they not know what war and politics was really about? He would have to teach them.

Chapter 22

The fourteen months that had gone by since her nominee, Prince Jahan, had compelled the surrender of Mewar, had seen Nur Jehan firmly entrenched as the power behind the throne, wielded through her three-man cabinet.

As a prince of the royal blood and virtually heir to the throne, Prince Jahan led the way into her chamber for their regular Friday morning meeting, followed by Asaf Khan, as befitted his rank of Prime Minister and Ghiyas Beg, the *Diwan*.

Nur Jehan felt some gratitude towards Prince Jahan. It was his victory over Mewar, confirmed by a formal treaty that had been executed in Agra nine months earlier at a

Great Durbar in which Rana Amar Singh had been represented by his son, Prince Chara, that had enabled her to start acting openly as the leading figure in the Empire. Yet she would never concede that anyone other than she herself had been responsible for the eminence of her position. She alone knew the grief and frustration, the bitter disappointments, the years of nonentity, the laborious study, the clever planning, the sacrifices, that had propelled her to the position of power she now occupied, with the Emperor a willing tool in her hand. And she always searched the faces and expressions of these three men for signs of contradiction, rebellion or any covert attempt to usurp her authority.

Today their expressions were respectful and sincere when they took their usual seats at her command. Both the handsome prince, dressed in cloth of gold, and her brother, wearing silver *jodhpurs* and purple satin tunic, did, however, bear watching. The young prince had hidden ambition, her clever brother an unfortunate addiction to moral principles and idealism. For this reason she sat facing them, with her stout, bald-headed father at her side. Ghiyas Beg had started wearing white homespun garments not long after he was appointed *Diwan*, in order to play down his role and emphasize his integrity. Men were given to playing games; it made them easier to manipulate once you comprehended what and how they played.

Her own manipulations had culminated in her having the three most brilliant men in the Empire to help her rule it. Her father was an astute, experienced, conservative financier. Her brother was sharp and enterprising, with a memory like that of an elephant and a complete grasp of every department within the Empire and its far-flung outposts. He was now acknowledged to be the finest administrator the Moghuls had ever known. Prince Jahan was the doer, a general more capable, daring and ruthless than his illustrious grandfather, Akbar the Great. She was indeed blessed by Allah, not because of these three but because of the brains and ability He had bestowed on her to find such men and make them dance to the tunes she piped from her gilded cage, the *harem*.

'We thank you for your presence, gentlemen,' she declared formally, leaning forward on her divan. She nodded towards the silver sunshine pouring on to the white marble courtyard outside. 'A beautiful spring morning. The green of the tangerine bushes with their round, golden fruit, the whistling of love-birds merging with our man-made scent of roses from the incense braziers are a perfect combination of the work of the Almighty with the divine gifts He has given humans.'

'Not just any human, Your Imperial Majesty,' Ghiyas Beg stated. 'Only such as you, who are gifted to create. After all, was it not you who invented the attar-of-rose perfume?'

'You do us honour, *Diwan*, as always,' Nur Jehan responded. She loved praise, but never let it influence her.

'Yet the most divine gift of Allah, which does the greatest honour to God's creations and those of men, is that of human perception, the ability to witness, experience and admire,' Asaf Khan interposed. He flashed her his bright smile, crinkly eyed, teeth white beneath the thin auburn moustache. 'It is that perception which brings us to *you* on such a beautiful morning, Your Majesty. When we could be enjoying God's creations elsewhere, we are here, ready to serve you.'

Her brother had the rare ability to disarm the expression of any philosophy that differed from her own with a personal compliment and she was never sure whether it was all sincerely meant or part of his quality of laughing at the world in general and himself in particular. Of course, he was too well-bred to hold even an ounce of malice and too decent a human being to laugh *at* other people, only *with* them.

'Although Almighty Allah has given us bright sunshine outside the Agra palace today, dark clouds still hover over the Deccan,' she responded, adroitly bringing the meeting to the matter she wished to discuss. 'The Deccan considers itself an independent entity, a buffer between our own southern territories and those of the Chola kingdoms of the south, which have traditionally repudiated Moghul suzerainty. The Emperor Akbar subjugated Kandesh and a part of Ahmednagar in the Deccan. Upon his accession to the throne, our present Emperor decided to extend his dominion to the rest of Ahmednagar and the two remaining independent States of Bija and Golkonda, so he despatched General Khan at the head of 12,000 hand-picked cavalry in 1608 to conquer the Deccan. You are well aware of the disastrous results of that expedition and what has taken place in that territory during the last eight years.'

'General Khan was opposed by a military genius, Malik Ambar, Abyssinian by birth,' Asaf Khan stated gravely. 'Since General Khan could not maintain the morale of our troops, the Emperor gave command of the campaign to Prince Parviz, appointing him governor of the region. Malik Ambar refused open battle, adopted guerilla tactics and ambushed our forces more than once. In 1611 our two-pronged drive into the Deccan failed because General Abdul, who commanded one of the pincers, advanced too impetuously and caused the decimation of his troops. We then pulled back to Gujarat. All our subsequent campaigns against the Deccan have resulted in failure.'

'Precisely.' Nur Jehan's eyes flashed. 'It is a situation which our Emperor will no longer tolerate.' She raised her hand and slashed it down. 'The Deccan *shall* be conquered.'

'It can, if the Emperor in his infinite wisdom will entrust us with the responsibility for planning an all-out campaign, giving us the fullest power to achieve his goals,' Asaf Khan volunteered quietly.

'He has delegated the responsibility to us alone,' Nur Jehan gestured towards herself, 'with the fullest powers.' She glanced at her father. 'The first essential for the task is funds. What do you say, *Diwan*?'

'All funds needed for whatever men and material you demand will be readily available, Your Majesty, without the need for further taxes. It would be impolitic to conserve the Empire's resources at the expense of imperial might.'

'Will any such funds have to come from the Emperor's private treasury?'

'Not unless an expensive campaign drags on and on.'

'Good. What we plan is a single campaign, more powerful than any before. We expect to put 50,000 men in the field, including infantry, cavalry, musketeers, artillery and elephants.' She glanced at Prince Jahan. 'You have been silent, Prince. What are your views on our object?'

He smiled deprecatingly. 'The timing would certainly be right if the army moves early this spring. With Mewar rendered virtually helpless, our army's rear would be safe and General Ambar deprived of an ally that might have been dangerous.'

'You seem to have some doubts though.'

Prince Jahan shrugged his broad shoulders, looked down at his feet. 'I do not quite know how to put this, Your Majesty.' He glanced sideways at Asaf Khan, as if for support, then his slanty eyes fixed on her with fierce intensity and the words came out in a rush. 'An army is only as good as its general. Throughout history, even before the time when the two-hundred-thousand-man army of the Emperor Xerxes was held up on the Grecian plains by two hundred Spartans, under Leonidas, who manned the mountain pass at Thermopylae, numbers have never counted. With all due apologies, Your Majesty, Prince

Parviz could not take the Deccan if he had two hundred thousand men!'

'You are right, Prince,' Nur Jehan replied quietly. 'We have given personal thought to this question and selected another brilliant general for this campaign.'

Prince Jahan's eyes flashed in anger. 'And who might that be, Your Majesty?'

'You.'

Salima Begum had changed during the past years, especially the last few months. What had begun as a loving, almost maternal attitude when Nur Jehan needed her strength and support had deteriorated to one of studied courtesy clothing the invisible steel of a rigid insistence on the Begum's rightful position as head of the imperial *harem*, even though Nur Jehan had become Empress of the realm. With the perspicacity of the truly clever person, without which neither a climb to power nor retaining it once reached was possible, Nur Jehan recognized that the change was in her own self and that the Begum was merely responding to that change. Yet it irked her that, like the Emperor, she had to bow to the customs of the *harem* while shaping the destinies of the Empire. But she had not challenged the Begum's rights except by subtle hints of superiority and authority during their weekly meetings. She had come to regret having made it a practice to visit the Begum formally for the luncheon meal immediately after the Friday morning session of her Cabinet. It made her feel rather like a girl reporting the events of the school day to her mother. What was more painful, however, was having to endure the cloak of cynical humour that the Begum now unfailingly donned. Containing an intellectual and regal superiority more subtle than anything she herself could conceive, it was an irksome reminder to Nur Jehan that she was not of royal birth.

This morning, when she rose from kissing the gnarled old hand, a custom she now loathed but had not dared to break, the amused twinkle in the old lady's green eyes, emerging through the heavy make-up on wrinkled cheeks, grated on her. The gnarled hand gracefully continued its motion, indicating Nur Jehan's usual settle opposite the divan on which the Begum sat, her slender figure erect as ever, then waved away the young waiting women and attendants, clad in their usual white. This has become like a mosque ritual, Nur Jehan thought, in which I find myself alone in the presence of a female Allah! I wish I could stop it, but the only way, unless the old tyrant dies naturally, is to hasten her demise, which is too low a stake for gambling away the power I now wield.

Seeming to concentrate on the splashing of the silver fountain in the blue pool at the far end of the chamber, the Begum listened in silence while Nur Jehan gave her a brief run down on the affairs of the realm, ending with the appointment of Prince Jahan to head the campaign against Malik Ambar in the Deccan.

'Such ponderous affairs of State,' the Begum finally commented. 'We ourselves are so fortunate to have been but a *harem* woman all our life, leaving it to the Emperors to make imperial decisions. You are terribly brave to shoulder such responsibilities.' The bright eyes twinkled maliciously. 'But then, unlike us, you have no choice, with the hangover of circumstances requiring your superior wisdom and strength.'

The cleverly veiled reference to her husband's drinking problem was not lost on Nur Jehan. The battle had begun. 'Effective decentralization is a key to the good government of an Empire as vast as ours,' she countered. 'We would like to think that it is the Emperor's own infinite wisdom and strength that causes him to bestow imperial responsibilities on those of proven wisdom and strength.' She had deliberately emphasized the word 'imperial'.

'Emperors sometimes bestow power with the recklessness of persons scattering bad breath. Thanks be to Almighty Allah, we have not found our step-son, the Emperor Jehangir, to be one of these.' The Begum paused, twinkling again. 'He has neither bestowed bad breath nor the intoxicating fumes of imperial power upon us!'

Damn you, old bitch, Nur Jehan thought savagely. But she rejoined sweetly, 'The Emperor knows exactly where to delegate power. That is why he has vested you with the responsibility of ruling the *harem*, an empire of souls over which there can never be darkness.'

A tiny nod at this reminder of the Begum's limited domain acknowledged the thrust. 'Ah, souls! Now you are committing fifty thousand souls to the risks of a military campaign to conquer hundreds of thousands of other souls. How brave.'

'It requires bravery to maintain an empire,' Nur Jehan flashed.

'To extend an empire demands the heedless courage of the non-combatant.' The words were a murmur. 'Subduing the Deccan might prove to be an experience of dubious value.' She sighed, genuinely this time, looked down at the Persian carpet. 'But who are we to ponder on trifles like the death and maiming of countless bodies, when we have the souls of our own little empire to mind?' She lifted her gaze to meet Nur Jehan's. 'You have certainly selected the right general to head the campaign.'

'Prince Jahan?'

The white head nodded slowly. 'Yes. His grandfather had enormous faith in him, even told us once that Prince Jahan would challenge Allah to rule the Empire at an early age.' The sharp eyes had become challenging.

The words hit Nur Jehan in the pit of the stomach. Never before had the Begum spoken so directly about Prince Jahan's ultimate destiny. She herself had been taking pains to get the young prince into her power and to manipulate him, so he would succeed her husband but remain her puppet.

'He is too strong to remain anyone's puppet.'

The Begum, with her uncanny gift of perception, had slammed into that first blow with the power of a sledge-hammer. This was something which Nur Jehan had always feared. The harsh croak of a raven intruded on the whistling of love-birds. Though always compliant with her slightest command, Prince Jahan had been showing an unexpected strength of late, especially in leading the life of an orthodox Muslim, for which Nur Jehan suspected Mumtaz Mahal was mainly responsible. After all, the girl was of almost fanatic faith and, being her father's daughter, must have inherited some of Asaf Khan's independence. Well, she would watch for the slightest sign of rebellion in Prince Jahan. If she detected it, she would put into effect the plan she had already devised, sooner rather than later. As for this old bitch, cunning as she was, the Begum would never dream of what Nur Jehan had in mind.

'Have you met the Princess Mariam again?' The Begum's reference to the ageing wife of a Persian prince who had been visiting the Agra court indicated a studied change of subject to shallower waters.

'No. It is not our most burning ambition. The princess is a bore and we keep our meetings with her to the minimum required by courtesy.'

'Her problem is that her ancient lineage implores her to look down on everyone, even her superiors, with the consistency with which most dowagers have neuralgia. I presume you have been presented to her husband, Prince Badiyi . . . er . . . doubtless under the strictest rules of *purdah*.'

Nur Jehan ignored the reference to her stretching of the rules of *purdah* in recent months, extending even to sitting beside her husband during his early morning *durbars*. 'Indeed. And I seemed to have met him before somewhere,' she responded flippantly.

The thin eyebrows arched. 'But he has never visited our courts before and you certainly have no acquaintance with the Persian court.'

Got you, this time, Nur Jehan thought. 'He has a perfectly recognizable moustache, which I have undoubtedly seen before.'

The wrinkled hands clapped lightly with delight. 'Ah, dear Empress, you are adding a nice wit to your repertoire of superhuman powers.'

'Why is wit superhuman?' She could not help asking the question.

'Firstly, because it is not the privilege of ordinary mortals, else it would be as commonplace and as unworthy of recognition as the middle classes. Secondly, because there is no wit without malice, a quality which when carefully controlled is a delightful adjunct of upper-class behaviour.'

'Don't the middle classes have wit?'

'The lower classes love buffoonery because it makes them feel superior. The middle classes, being clowns themselves, adore clowning. The upper classes alone, being neither buffoons nor clowns, appreciate wit . . . er . . . because they do not understand it.'

There must be either some truth or fallacy there, but Nur Jehan was not disposed to probe. 'Don't the middle classes *have* wit?' she persisted.

'If they do, being a new tribe, they display it with the pride of a single ripening plum pretending to fill the entire fruit bowl, its own beauty and pungency lost at the source, pretension.'

'We must get accustomed to the emerging middle classes,' Nur Jehan retorted primly. 'They are becoming increasingly wealthy and a source of power.'

'Never of wit. Anything midway, like a half-way house for recovering alcoholics, lies between black and white, uncertain. The middle classes are grey. They will eventually destroy civilization.'

'Then we must educate them to our standards by accepting them, letting them grow on us.'

'Like some sort of fungus? My dear Empress, can you imagine a man wearing a crown merely because he is middle aged? Do you see a successful merchant, an actor or a mummer, wielding supreme power?' She sighed, heavily this time. 'It will happen in this world some day, because it is the much-bred not the well-bred that survive. But praise be to Almighty Allah, we shall not be around to see that day, that empire, or the decline of the world from it.'

While she reacted to the innate snobbery of these sentiments, Nur Jehan could not escape the conclusion that they emerged from the deepest most eternal wisdom of the times, which had kept the Begum in power, influencing even imperial policies, since the days when she had charmed the Emperor Akbar. 'We wish we had your wisdom,' she declared impulsively.

How really deep the Begum's response was, Nur Jehan realized only later. 'You would be better advised, Empress, to be infected with our wit!'

His appointment as army commander of the Deccan operation meant that the young Prince Jahan was acknowledged the most brilliant general of the Moghul forces. While participating to the fullest in the discussion that had followed Nur Jehan's announcement, aware of all that had to be done if he was to get his army on the move in the spring, Prince Jahan's one urge had been to rush to give the news to Mumtaz Mahal. She alone, not his ambition, was now his true inspiration. Her constant admiration, her loving warm welcome whenever she saw him, had made her his whole world.

Owing to the breakdown of a ferry boat, he had returned only this morning, after being away from Agra inspecting some of his lands, just in time to rush to his weekly meeting with Nur Jehan. So he had not seen Mumtaz for six whole days. It was almost noon when he arrived at her suite. As he awaited her in the reception chamber, he strode up and down in anticipation, like a schoolboy with his first love. She still was and always would be his child-bride.

He was shocked when she slowly entered the chamber, her gait uncertain, the proud lift of her head gone. As she knelt to kiss his hand, he noticed the drawn cheeks, their fine bones protruding. The sockets around her large doe-like eyes were dark and her gaze was listless.

Panic-stricken, he reached for her. 'Mumtaz, beloved, light of my life, what has happened?'

She let him hold her, but without melting into him as usual. He placed a forefinger beneath her chin, tilted the pert face upwards. 'What is wrong, Mumtaz? Are you angry with me? Why don't you let me hold you?'

'Because I do not wish to be sick all over you, my lord.' The words came out hesitantly.

'You are sick?'

'Very.'

'Why? How? Do you have the stomach disease? Vomiting? Are you sick both ways? Any blood?'

'No, it's nothing like that, my lord.' Her smile was less wan. The impish look he loved so well shot briefly through her eyes. 'I do not have any such disease, but you have given me something that has laid me low for the first time in my life.'

Alarm flared through him. Could he have given her a disease he had contracted on one of his campaigns which had lain dormant in him? 'L-like what?'

'Your baby, my lord.'

'My what?' His jaw dropped and he gaped at her.

'Your baby. But you do not seem pleased.' She managed one of her adorable pouts.

'Pleased? Oh, my beloved, you can be sick all over me as often as you want.' His joyous laugh echoed through the chamber as he gripped her tightly.

She clung to him with near desperation, shivered once. 'Are you scared, my beloved?' He murmured the question into her dark hair that smelled of musk and sweat.

She nodded. 'I have felt awful, but now that you are back, all will be well.'

The wondrous news he had just brought would be bad news for her personally. Should he postpone telling her of his appointment? 'They say that morning sickness lasts only for three or four months at the most,' he ventured.

'I do not have morning sickness,' she wailed. 'I have day and night sickness.' She lifted her face to his, revealing a bared-teeth smile. 'I need you with me twenty-four hours a day, every day.'

'You are truly one of Allah's angels,' he breathed. 'That is what I too would want more than anything else, but you know I have my work to do. Almighty Allah's will for me must be fulfilled.'

'You are so cunning,' she said. 'You always use my faith to have your own way. You obviously have something on your mind.'

'Never *my* way, always *our* way. Do you not want me to fulfil my destiny?'

'Of course, you cunning fox.'

'I have great news connected with it.'

She drew her head back, her eyes searching his face. 'You are to be appointed the Emperor's heir.'

He laughed aloud. 'Not yet, my honey bird, not yet. But something that will get me there.'

Her face clouded as she pulled back from him. 'You are going away again.' It was a statement not a question.

Dear Allah, she was so much a part of him that she always knew. 'Not yet, my honey bird.'

'You said that before, including the honey bird. Everything is not yet and when it does happen, you always have to leave me.'

A gush of tenderness swept through him at the strange illogical logic so characteristic of her. 'I have been appointed to command the greatest expeditionary force to be sent to the Deccan since my grandfather's time,' he blurted out.

Her face fell for an instant; she gulped and ran out of the room, her hands to her mouth, mumbling something. He stood there nonplussed, not knowing what to do. He thought to follow her to the bedchamber, but heard her retching inside the privy and decided to wait. He stared blindly through the open windows at the glaring noontime sunlight, vaguely aware of children's voices singing in the courtyard below. Children. One day his child would be singing there too.

The minutes ticked by. He grew impatient. When she emerged through the door, she looked shame-faced. 'I am sorry, my revered husband,' she said. 'Your finest hour and I had to be sick.' Her breath smelled of vomit, but he did not care, only ached with his love for her, his eyes brimming with tears he would never shed. 'Know, however, that my mind and spirit share your joy, with pride at your accomplishments. This is no honour conferred on you by the Emperor, my lord prince, but an honour you bestow on him by accepting such a gigantic task. You will succeed.' Her voice was prophetic. Gone was the child-bride. In her place was an ancient soul. 'When do you leave? Come sit with me and tell me all.'

He sat on the divan, she on the Persian carpet beside him. He marvelled at the strength of her. Her face lifted to his, he told her all that had transpired that morning. 'It will take at least three months to prepare for the march,' he concluded. 'Especially as I have requested eighty thousand men instead of the fifty thousand proposed. So I shall be here through your sick period.'

'Can you not make it eighty thousand and one?' she inquired.

'Who would be . . . Oh, *you*?' He roared with laughter. 'That would make it perfect for me personally but it might be a trifle inconvenient for the army commander.'

'Why?'

'You will be at an advanced state of pregnancy then.'

'You could use me as a battering ram!'

'I have other uses for you when you have recovered from your day and night sickness.'

'Oh, you propose being *my* battering ram?' she inquired archly.

'Something like that.'

'That would make you an old goat.'

'Why?'

'Because a ram is a male goat.'

He spluttered with delight. 'I ought to take you as the Court jester.'

'You shall never go to bed with the Court jester,' she asserted with mock primness.

'You know, there's one thing I love about you.'

'Only one thing? Let me guess. It must be the smell of my vomit.' She clapped a delicate hand to her mouth as if to shut out the smell.

'Seriously. You always make light-hearted remarks even when you are sick. That is true gallantry. And you always get the better of me. That is unfailing victory!'

She dimpled, suddenly grew serious. 'There is one thing that causes me concern.'

'Like one thing I love about you?' he teased.

'Seriously. As I have frequently warned you, I fear that Nur Jehan is manipulating you for her own ends. When you return from this campaign, successful once again, she will not only be jealous of your popularity, but will fear your increasing influence with the Emperor. Having sucked you like an orange pip, she will spit you out. I know this in my head, my heart and my spirit.'

'I am well aware of it too, my love.' He smiled. 'How could I fail to be, with your constant reminders!'

'Both of us are also constant reminders to Nur Jehan and the Emperor of the error of their ways. That does not bode well for you.'

'What do you mean?'

'We are strictly orthodox Muslims who follow the Sunni dogma, while both your father and the Empress are more liberal. You live the life of the true faith, which upbraids those who allow calls of the flesh, drink, opium, unbridled sex, to dominate their existence. They are going to find you such a constant reminder of their own shortcomings that they will resent you bitterly, now that you are on the ruling scene.'

'Surely not. Why should they care about my lifestyle?'

'It is an affront to their shabby conduct as lesser mortals. Don't you remember the number of times your father – your own father – tried to persuade you to drink wine – "just one little glass", he would say?' Her eyes flashed with anger. 'What kind of a father would teach his own son evil habits? As for Nur Jehan, beware of her always, especially now that the moment of truth is drawing near.'

Though it was nearly midnight, the heat of summer had laid an almost imperceptible veil on the air in Prince Jahan's tent, where he was seated with General Wahid.

It had been a long day while the imperial army settled into its miles of encampment on the plains just across the wide river south of the city of Burhan, which Prince Jahan had decided to use as the base for his Deccan operation. He was still elated at having received news the previous night by fast messenger, that he was now the father of a lusty boy and that mother and son were in excellent health. They had commenced the final stage of the march at dawn and even the delays of the river crossing had not diminished his elation. When the city surrendered in fear at the sheer size of the Moghul army, he regarded his new-born son as a bringer of good luck.

'Your demand that our army be increased from fifty to eighty thousand men has already yielded dividends, Prince,' General Wahid remarked. His hatchet face looked strangely youthful in the pale amber light from the hanging lanterns. He certainly showed no signs of the tiring day.

Prince Jahan, seated across the table, smiled grimly. He looked forward to these last moments of each day, when his other officers and staff had departed, leaving him and the general alone to talk freely. At such times, the tent felt secluded from the sounds of the sleeping encampment, the subdued murmur of voices, the shouted challenge of a sentry, the distant barking of a dog. A trumpet blared the midnight call for the change of sentries. Other trumpets took it up in the distance. The smell of the roast meats and boiled beans that had been served for dinner still clung to the air inside the tent.

'The Emperor acceded to my request when I explained my strategy,' Prince Jahan stated. 'I'm glad it has worked.' He did not wish to add that it was Nur Jehan who had given the imperial approval. He placed his elbows on the table, leaned forward, dropping his voice. 'I have kept my plans very much to myself as you know, but I now want your help in achieving them. Warn General Khan to attend my tent by himself at dawn. I shall have orders for him.'

'Certainly, Prince.' If General Wahid ever had any

curiosity, he never showed it. Prince Jahan warmed even more to the man, a soldier's soldier in every sense of the word.

'Since you will not be present, let me tell you what I have in mind.'

'I am at your service, Prince.'

'General Khan, with thirty thousand men, including cavalry, musketeers and two regiments of artillery, no infantry or elephants, will force-march south, cross the Godavari River and occupy Pathri as his base. Leaving ten thousand men there, he will send another contingent of ten thousand west to Surat, while he himself, with the remaining ten thousand men, will speed on to invest Bija. He will ride fast and avoid open battle with General Malik Ambar's troops. I have carefully mapped out all the routes to prevent our forces from being trapped in ravines or otherwise ambushed, while my system of flying patrols will save them from guerilla attacks.'

Realization had slowly been dawning on General Wahid's face. 'Brilliant!' he asserted. 'You will effectively cut off General Ambar's rear and also prevent any allies from farther south linking up with him.'

'Precisely. I have taken the added precaution of bribing the Portuguese Viceroy in Goa, without divulging the source of the bribe, to send a powerful punitive expedition east as far as Dawar to keep Rana Adil on the run.'

'Knowing the Portuguese, they might take the bribe and not perform.'

'Knowing the Portuguese, they will only receive one-half of the bribe, with the balance, which represents their profit, later, after we have brought the Deccan to heel!'

'Splendid! And what do you propose doing here, Prince?'

'Nothing, but I shall send a contingent of ten thousand infantry and elephants south-east to Bihar. Within a few weeks, General Ambar will realize that he is encircled by our armies to the south-east and north of him with the ocean to his west. He will receive exaggerated reports of the strength of our armed forces and the reinforcements we are expecting. Tension will confuse his men and make uncertainties arise within his ranks. Meanwhile, the presence of our forces in these territories will cause the people immense hardship, for which we shall blame General Ambar. His people will fear that the fate of Mewar may be in store for them and we shall do nothing to discourage this view. During this time, we shall also make secret offers of rich rewards to Ambar's junior commanders for the transfer of their loyalties.'

'How do you conceive these things?' General Wahid shook his bald head in wonderment.

'From history, from the ruthless triumphs of my ancestors and the wisdom of the Emperor Ky-roos,' Prince Jahan laughed deprecatingly, 'combined with the will of Allah, who has bestowed flashes of insight upon me, his humble servant, and the inspiration provided by my beloved wife. Also it is better to lose money, rather than men, to win.'

In Malik Ambar's tent outside the city of Ahmad, Prince Chara eyed the Abyssinian-born general with good-natured tolerance. He had sent notice of his intended visit well enough in advance this time so had been received with the honours due his rank. The journey from Chitor had taken three weeks because he and his small cavalry escort had followed a circuitous route, heading south-west towards Cambay on the Indian Ocean, proceeding south along the coastal highway, then cutting east to Ahmad. Having arrived the previous evening, he had deliberately pleaded a fatigue which he did not feel and retired early to his tent, stating that he would await the general's pleasure in the morning. He would teach the black son of a whore a lesson for the treatment he had received during his last visit!

If General Ambar felt any discomfort from the ring of Moghul armies encircling him, it was not evident. His shiny black face with its wide nostrils, dark expressionless eyes, their whites very white, lying flat on the wide cheekbones, was expressionless.

'I trust you are as comfortably housed as can be expected in an encampment, Prince?' the general inquired when they were alone. A smile touched his mouth, revealing his pearl-like teeth. The silence of the tent was broken by sharp commands from outside, the pounding of hooves on the parade ground and the squeak and rattle of wagon wheels.

Was the black bastard trying to patronize him? The scar on Prince Chara's face started to itch. 'I am well accustomed to the noise and discomfort of army camps,' he retorted. 'We Rajputs have been warriors since time immemorial.'

'Pity you had to surrender.'

Prince Chara restrained a flaming urge to slap the general across his face. 'As matters turned out, we surrendered to circumstances,' he stated, smiling with his teeth. 'The peace vindicated Rajput honour. Unlike Moghuls and other foreigners, we owe a responsibility to our people.'

The general nodded affably. 'Well put,' he declared. 'I deserved that. You must forgive me if I am testy today. The tactics adopted by the Moghuls have left me nonplussed. I am a guerilla, used to open battle only when I have the strength or the tactical advantage. Prince Jahan's tactics have left me powerless. That is why I welcomed your offer of a visit. You have great experience of this prince who wins victories without fighting.'

The fierce hatred he felt for Prince Jahan spewed forth within Prince Chara. 'If you had joined me when I requested your alliance, we could have driven him out of Mewar and you would not be at a loss today!'

Two tiny sparks of red seemed to glow for a split second in the general's dark eyes. 'On the other hand, if I had

369

joined you, I might have shared your fate and we would not be here discussing history today,' he declared brusquely.

Prince Chara kept his patience. The years of frustration had taught him to pretend urbanity, but the scar on his face now burned. 'Let us then discuss the future,' he stated shortly.

'By all means. You obviously came here with a purpose.'

'You have recently suffered defections of junior commanders from your ranks, have you not?'

'Yes.'

'The Moghul armies encircle you and the Portuguese have a dagger pointed at your rear.'

'Yes.'

'Then there is only one course open to you.'

'And that?'

'Surrender while you can make an acceptable peace.'

'Never!' The word was barked out.

'Listen, general. Everyone imagines that peace means the end of war. That need not be the case. Peace can be the continuation of war by other means.'

'Like . . . ?'

'Spending the peaceful years in making strong alliances, in creating dissension amongst the enemy's top ranks.'

'Top ranks?'

'Consider the situation in Agra. A drunken Emperor, a power-hungry Empress pretending to rule through a Cabinet while she gradually accumulates supreme authority. A young general with command of over a hundred thousand men who is, however, not the direct heir to the imperial throne. It is a simmering pot that, given time, will boil over to our advantage.'

'Supposing it does not?'

Prince Chara told him.

When he had finished, General Ambar nodded his

crinkly head slowly, the dark eyes showing open admiration. 'You are right,' he finally declared in a low voice. 'We must bring time on *our* side. I shall send Prince Jahan my offer for an honourable peace today.'

Chapter 23

Having just received news of the capitulation of General Malik Ambar, the Emperor Jehangir was in a jovial mood while holding the regular evening *durbar* in the Agra palace. He had dressed with special care because he had agreed to receive the ambassador appointed to his court by James, King of England. His rich turban was plumed with herntops, an inset ruby as big as a walnut dangling on one side, a diamond of the same size on the other. He wore a huge heart-shaped emerald on his forehead. His tunic and trousers were cloth of gold, the tunic studded with pearls, emeralds and rubies. His sash was wreathed with a gold chain on to which great pearls, rubies and diamonds had been drilled. He wore a triple chain of large pearls around his neck and at his wrists, his armlets were set with diamonds and every finger had a blazing ring on it. His shoes, the tips sharp-curling, were embroidered with pearls. He glittered like the sun for this representative of the distant island kingdom which had become increasingly powerful in the Indian Ocean.

In addition to the good news from the Deccan and the consciousness of his splendour, the Emperor also felt physically fit. He had refrained from taking any liquor for a whole week and was emotionally uplifted by the presence of his veiled wife, the most beautiful woman in the Empire, on her chair to the left of him.

No man's head was above his on the balcony. As always, his Prime Minister, Asaf Khan, stood below him to the right and his *Diwan*, Ghiyas Beg, to his left. The display of family unity gave him a great sense of security; the affairs of the realm were in safe hands. Two richly clad attendants, in striped robes and turbans, stood on two great wooden elephants at the foot of the balcony, waving fans, so he was cool in spite of the heat of the summer afternoon. A glittering array of princes, nobles, courtiers and suppliants crowded the hall beneath him. Each of the sixty ministers was in front of his tall column below and all officials and courtiers stood at precisely measured distances from his throne, the most senior within inner railings, the next within a second row. Persons of lesser importance stood on the three sides of the railings.

'An impressive scene, eh?' the Emperor inquired of Nur Jehan. 'Even a country like this powerful England, which we understand has many fair women and a foul climate, can never hope to match it.'

'No being in the Universe can even begin to match your splendour, Your Majesty,' Nur Jehan responded, dropping her voice to add, 'shining light of my life.'

What a woman. He was indeed blest of Allah. Last night had been particularly satisfying. She had actually managed to make him get it up, when so often in recent years even she had not been able to penetrate the fog of liquor that invariably left him limp and flaccid, the spirit avidly desiring, the flesh totally weak. 'This ambassador, what did you say his name is, Prime Minister?'

'Sir Thomas Roe,' Asaf Khan replied, leaning forward. 'You may recall, Sire, that he landed at Surat a year ago, with credentials from His Majesty King James. Sir Thomas is a man of about thirty-five and his principal mission is to establish trade relations with us, displacing the monopolies of the Portuguese and the Hollanders, especially in spices, calico and indigo.'

'H'mm. Did he not have some trouble with you and our young Prince Jahan when he arrived?'

'Indeed, Sire. Your recall is extraordinary. He demanded over-imperiously that all his baggage should be permitted into the country without let, hindrance or customs dues, but Prince Jahan had several crates impounded to remind Sir Thomas of his mortality. Being a clever man, Sir Thomas countered that these crates contained presents for Your Imperial Majesty, so Prince Jahan equally cleverly had them held in bond for delivery to you at the time the ambassador presented his credentials. May I remind you, Sire, that the ambassador has obtained your gracious approval to use the salutation of his own country in greeting Your Imperial Majesty, rather than our *kornish*, bowing with the palm of the right hand pressed against the forehead, signifying the head as being in the hand of humility and presented to you, which is something an ambassador cannot offer since he represents his king.'

'Pity we did away with the full prostration decreed by our own father for the disciples of his religion. That indicates a fitting reverence without any such delivery.'

Suddenly remembering the presents brought by the ambassador, the Emperor brightened visibly. He adored receiving presents, insisted upon it whenever he could, demanding them from his subjects even when he was out in the countryside. Presents from abroad were of course the most exciting. 'Do you know what the presents are?'

'The latest edition of Mercator maps of the world, some English paintings, an ornamental box with a glass side, portrait miniatures . . .'

'Tchk! Does he not have anything of value? Velvets, precious stones, gold, weapons,' he could not keep an eager note from entering his voice, 'a new matchlock rifle perhaps, gold plated, studded with gems? We would also like an English horse.'

'No, I regret to say, Sire.'

'Do the maps show our Empire as the largest in the world?'

Asaf Khan hesitated. 'Er . . . I have not seen them, Sire.'

The Emperor noted his Prime Minister's hesitancy. 'Bah! These Europeans! What do they know of our dominions? They are forever showing their own as the largest.' He sniffed, fingered his jaw, reflecting. 'Most English people are mad,' he finally asserted. 'Was it not this ambassador's priest, a man called Edward Terry, who referred to our holy prophet Mahomet, as the *ringleader* of the Muslim religion?'

'Not all people on this earth have our sense of decorum, Sire.'

'And that other Englishman, Cory . . . Cory . . . something?'

'Thomas Coryate, Sire.'

'That's right, Thomas Coryate. Thomas Roe, Thomas Coryate! Are they as short on names in England as they are on sanity?' He guffawed at his own wit, pleased at the trill of laughter, muffled by her *yashmak*, that escaped Nur Jehan.

Asaf Khan smiled his own appreciation, then grew serious. 'Thomas Coryate is the Englishman who said he was tired of hearing our *mullahs* proclaim from the high tops of our mosque turrets five times a day *La Allah illa Allah*, *Mahomet Resul – allah*, there is no God but one God and Mahomet, the Messenger of God. So he himself ascended one day to the highest turret in Surat opposite the great mosque and roared back, *La Allah illa Allah*, *Hasaret Eesu Resul – allah*, there is no God but one God and the Lord Christ the Son of God! He added that our Prophet

Mahomet was an impostor. The assembled crowd would have torn him limb from limb for these unspeakable blasphemies, but someone reasoned that the Englishman was mad, a punishment inflicted on him by Allah which should be left to take its fullest course.'

'All of which reveals to us that Europeans have no manners,' Nur Jehan murmured. 'They were barbarians until two centuries ago and have developed wealth without true culture, which is not painting, music, literature, drama and architecture, but living in a civilized, mannerly fashion.'

'Well put as always, star of our soul,' the Emperor interposed. He was so proud of his wife's intellect. He shoved his forefinger beneath his collar to reach an itch. 'Many say that European civilization goes back several centuries, but look how barbaric they were during their Crusades, which were missions of pillage in the guise of *jihad* (holy war).' He paused, gazed towards a commotion at the far entrance doorway. 'Ah! Here comes the ambassador.'

'Make way there for His Excellency Sir Thomas Roe, Ambassador of His Majesty King James of England,' an usher announced in stentorian tones.

'Such a common little name to accompany the high-sounding titles!' the Emperor muttered to his wife.

'I understand the word "Roe" means fish-eggs in their language, Sire,' she murmured back. 'He certainly has the eyes of a fish.'

'His parents were probably fish and he the roe,' the Emperor tittered behind his hand.

The man who strode purposefully through the crowd which parted before him was certainly no ordinary fish. Of commanding height and presence, he had a long saturnine face, a long saturnine nose, a high saturnine forehead and a short French beard of reddish hue supporting bristling

moustaches that, spreading importantly sideways, contra-
dicted the otherwise elongated features of the man. His
hair was beginning to thin at the high forehead. He was
dressed in European fashion, in a doublet of dark blue
velvet with slashed gold breeches and netherhosen. He
carried a feathered hat in his right hand. He advanced
towards the balcony with the self-assurance of a man
confident of his master's authority and came to a halt
several paces away.

A curious hush fell on the great hall. The ambassador
could not speak until the sovereign bade him, but why did
he not make the promised reverence? Instead, he just stood
there, proudly, imperiously, his gaze challenging. The
Emperor's gut tightened and from it anger began to mount.
By Allah, he would teach this dog, fish, whatever he was,
not to fart in his court. That head would not look so proud
impaled on a stake, with the moustaches quivering in the
wind.

A sigh rippled through the hall, as if all those present
had been holding their collective breath. The ambassador
had slowly grasped his hat in his right hand, extended it,
drawing his right leg back and his left hand to his heart,
and bowed, the right hand circling in a flourish. He came
upright, advanced a few paces, then repeated the bow. The
third bow brought him almost beneath the balcony.

The Emperor acknowledged the salutation with a graceful upward wave of his hand. 'You are welcome to our
Court, Sir Thomas Roe,' he declared, speaking in Arabic
with Asaf Khan as interpreter. 'Your credentials have
already been presented to our State Department and we
have found them to be perfectly in order and therefore
acceptable to us.'

To his delighted surprise, Sir Thomas responded in
Turkan. 'You honour yourself and my sovereign lord, King
James, by your courtesy, O Emperor.' His voice was deep

and resonant. 'This ensures a valuable ally for you in the Indian Ocean.'

'How so? You are a new power to these waters.'

'We are the greatest naval power on earth, Sire. I have the great pleasure to inform you that we have just trounced the Portuguese navy in two major engagements in Indian waters.'

'What?'

'Indeed, Your Majesty.' To the Emperor's added surprise, the words were spoken low-key, as if the man had announced victory at a game of draughts. There was no hint of boastfulness or triumph in the ambassador's expression, merely a certain grim strength which sent a chill down the Emperor's spine. This was a new breed of supreme power, he reflected, more deadly than the vainglorious Portuguese. The thought brought inspiration flaring within the Emperor. Perhaps he could turn the Portuguese reversal to his advantage. Abandoning the rules of protocol, he broached a subject dear to his heart. 'You are undoubtedly aware, Sir Ambassador, that we are supreme in all our territorial waters because no power dare oppose us.'

The graceful nod of Sir Thomas's head may have been a concession to good manners rather than to the good sense of this statement, so the Emperor hurried on. 'The Portuguese command the Arabian Sea, however, and have insisted that our Muslim pilgrims on their holy journey to Mecca should carry Portuguese passports, bought from the Portuguese – bought, mark you! More despicably, these passports are stamped with pictures of the Christian Mary and Jesus. Sir Ambassador, we of the Muslim religion abhor idolatry at any time, but on a sacred pilgrimage to Mecca? It is a preposterous, diabolical requirement, a fiendish insult to our religion.' He rather thought that this tirade should cull him added popularity from all segments of his Muslim subjects, especially the *mullahs*, then suddenly realized that he would acquire enormous prestige in the Muslim world if he could get the system of passports abolished. 'What say you to protecting our pilgrims from this harassment and our religion from such sacrilege?'

'My sovereign lord is dedicated to establishing freedom of the seas, Your Imperial Majesty. I shall certainly bring your gracious request to his notice. Meanwhile, I shall also send despatches to the admiral of our East Indies fleet advising him to take all necessary measures to protect your pilgrims.'

The Emperor grasped at the words without understanding their full diplomatic intent, for they contained no promises. 'Splendid! Magnificent! Your sovereign lord will not regret such intervention.' He paused, desiring to show this man a special mark of his favour. 'But why remain standing there? Come up to our *jarokha* and sit here.' He indicated a settle at his feet.

The ambassador strode up the stairs, but paused before him. 'Sit down! Sit down!' The Emperor gestured towards the settle.

'Your Imperial Majesty, I cannot sit with my head below yours,' Sir Thomas countered gravely, in a low voice. 'Being here now as the accredited representative of my sovereign lord, I am His Majesty King James in person on all official occasions and must be treated as such.'

The Emperor heard the hiss of Nur Jehan's indrawn breath and became aware that Asaf Khan had taken a step forward. He remembered the story of this Englishman's courage. When he had attended the court of Prince Parviz in Surat, refusing all commands to bow down to the ground, he had marched steadily through a row of mounted troops and courtiers and had insisted that he be allowed to climb the three steps up to the prince, or be provided with a chair immediately below. Though this was denied him, he had been permitted to lean gracefully against the pillar supporting Prince Parviz' canopy. The Emperor also recalled that Prince Parviz had invited him to the palace that night for a more intimate discussion, which had not taken place because Sir Thomas had presented the prince with a case of wine that had laid the prince low during dinner. His second son was a drunkard, who could not hold his liquor. His eldest son . . .

Tension in the hall had begun to mount again though few would have guessed at what was taking place. Anger conflicting with admiration of the Englishman's courage combined with an unwilling recognition of the justice of his stand. These ambassadors! They always created problems in the names of their sovereign lords. He did not want confrontation to mar his sense of well-being today after the news of the Deccan's surrender. Besides, this newcomer, England, would be a better friend than a foe. Peace with honour was what he should achieve. 'We are of the same view, Sir Ambassador, and had already decided that you may stand at the rear right-hand pillar of our *jarokha* during this audience and all your future attendances at our *durbars*.' He waved his right hand in a circular motion three times, beamed. 'You even have our permission to lean against the pillar if you so desire.'

Prince Chara had timed his visit to the Agra palace to make it seem that he was felicitating the Emperor on the Deccan victory. He had decided upon Sunday to pay his formal call on the new English ambassador, because Sunday was the Christian day of rest and he was certain to be given more private time for the discussion he intended. He had given a sudden, urgent need to return to Mewar as his excuse for disturbing Sir Thomas on his holy day.

The Emperor had made a large house within a compound of the Agra fort available to the ambassador as a residence.

Prince Chara rather suspected that this was motivated as much by a desire to keep an eye on Sir Thomas as to be hospitable.

Summer had not yet fled, so the late morning heat and the scent of dried grass were beginning to creep in through the open windows from the flagstone courtyard which served the reception chamber in which Sir Thomas had received him. A large painting of a king, in a heavy gilt frame, dominated the room from above the ornamented fireplace, beneath which burnished copperware had been placed. Except for the large Persian carpet, all the other furniture was European. Straight-backed chairs of dark mahogany, upholstered in a cream-and-red-striped satin, stood along the walls. A gilt sofa, on which Prince Chara sat with his host, and two chairs, which Prince Chara knew to be French from the room in the Emperor's palace, occupied the centre of the room.

It was strange how Europe could be forced into a Moghul setting, accentuated now by the ambassador's presence. Sir Thomas had a ruddy skin which was beginning to show the effects of the climate. He was formally dressed in blue velvet doublet and slashed white silken breeches, so it was no wonder that he had to keep mopping his brow with a large cream silken handkerchief. The polite pleasantries over, Prince Chara decided to show his understanding. 'Our climate is not exactly suitable for Europeans,' he ventured. 'I am also sorry that your experience down south in Surat after you landed there over a year ago was not of the best.'

Sir Thomas shrugged. 'It is over now, but you are right. I could only find lodgings in a private *serai* (rest-house) where I occupied four chambers like ovens, no bigger either, round at the top, with brick exteriors. I caught a fever there which nearly killed me.' He bared his yellowing teeth in a feral smile. 'But nearly is never good enough, especially when Death visits the English!'

Prince Chara seized the opportune moment. 'It is a pity too that the Emperor's agents failed to show you that respect due your rank and position, where your belongings were concerned, which the Emperor himself would assuredly have extended.'

The ambassador's sharp blue eyes flashed. A man with a temper, Prince Chara noted. 'M . . . mm. Pity is that it was the Emperor's own son who was responsible,' Sir Thomas snapped.

Prince Chara pretended a sigh. 'Prince Jahan treats me like a brother after his victory in Mewar,' he stated with mock appreciation. He paused, as if finding it difficult to be frank. 'The truth is that men whom the stars favour forget to keep their feet on the earth.' He smiled apologetically. 'Please accept my sincere apologies for the shortcomings of my brother, Prince Jahan.'

The thin, long eyebrows shot up. 'You are his brother? Surely not, Prince.'

Prince Chara smiled deprecatingly. 'No, no, we are brothers by circumstance. Our family relationship is through Prince Jahan's mother, who was a Rajput connected with our family.'

Sir Thomas eyed him levelly. 'Now, Prince Chara, I do not for a moment believe that you came to visit me in order to commiserate with me on my misfortunes and to wish me good health,' he stated abruptly. 'You obviously have something on your mind. Why not do me the honour of ceasing to insult my intelligence and come to the real purpose of your visit?'

Prince Chara was taken aback, but he maintained an urbane exterior. 'You are right, Sir Thomas . . . and a very clever man. I appreciate your frankness. It is how I myself like to deal, with total honesty.' The pantheon of gods forbid that I should ever be frank unless it is to my advantage! He injected a sad earnestness into his voice. 'My concern is the independence of my homeland. You, coming from a small island nation that has fanned out to become a world leader, can appreciate the patriotism of our ancient Rajput race.'

Sir Thomas nodded slowly. 'We have heard of you Rajputs even in distant England. Your outstanding valour throughout the centuries, your dedication to the warrior tradition and your fierce independence have won our admiration.'

'Thank you, Sir Ambassador. It is good to know that there are people in the world who appreciate and would support such principles.'

'Do not put words in my mouth, Prince. I did not say we would support them, merely that we admire them.' His tone was blunt.

'Admiration is the strongest form of support,' Prince Chara responded calmly. 'We Rajputs have always fought our own battles.'

'How can I help you fight your own battles, when whether as the representative of my sovereign lord, or in my personal capacity, I would neither say nor do anything that would conflict with my appointment here, my position as a guest, or my conscience?'

'By putting yourself in a position of power and influence in this court.' Prince Chara raised a hand. 'The Rajputs are not looking for dominion, merely freedom from interference under the benign suzerainty of the Emperor. What you *can* do for us is to ensure that the Emperor is not influenced by selfish power-seekers.'

'Such as?' There was a challenge in the deep voice.

'Prince Jahan.'

'M'mm . . . You think he is a powerful influence in the Court?'

'Not yet, but he will be, now that he has scored his second major victory over yet another proud, independent people.'

'How does one stop a charging elephant?'

'By swerving and lunging. That is what another elephant would do.'

'Explain yourself.'

'Prince Jahan is charging along. We must swerve from his path and lunge from another direction.'

'You speak in riddles, Prince.'

'You started the metaphors, Ambassador,' Prince Chara snapped back and was rewarded by a glint of amusement in the blue eyes. He realized then that there was only one way to deal with the Englishman. You had to demonstrate strength and fearlessness to him, earn his respect.

'*Touché!*' the ambassador responded.

'Whatever that means, I shall accept it as your apology.' He went on smoothly to avoid any debate on that issue. 'The real power behind the throne is the Empress, Nur Jehan. She must be made to feel that Prince Jahan's successes are a direct threat to her position.'

'Why do you not bring this to her notice yourself?'

'Firstly, she would imagine that I am a sore loser who is trying to extract vengeance from the victor. Secondly, she would suspect my motives.' He shrugged, spread out his palms. 'Finally, I am not her favourite person.' He grinned. 'You, on the other hand, are a victim of Prince Jahan's arrogance. Though he hides it well, Prince Jahan left humility behind with the maladies of childhood. You obviously have nothing to gain from taking sides, and are a man of enormous authority, wise in the ways of Courts. You could be a great attraction to the Empress.'

'Her brother, the Prime Minister, is Prince Jahan's father-in-law. He joined Prince Jahan in the outrageous act of confiscating my baggage.'

'Asaf Khan is unswervingly dedicated to his principles. Such a man is a source of danger to himself and to others.'

'How may that be? Surely men of principle can never be dangerous.'

'Principles are marvellous so long as they are right. What happens when they are wrong, Ambassador? Those who advocate them become dangerous addicts.' Tired of play-acting, he could not help a return to his normal, cynical self. 'Ah, principles! The refuge of the poor. Whenever addiction to principles occurs in politics, it does so with sickening thoroughness.'

The straight eyebrows lifted, a glint of appreciation filtered through the piercing blue eyes. It encouraged Prince Chara to proceed. 'Any man addicted to principle, like Asaf Khan, has the soul of a bread without yeast – it will not rise above its doughy self! As for Prince Jahan, he will some day undoubtedly follow the main occupation of Moghul sons, rebelling against his father. The only member of the Nur Jehan Cabinet – an entity of which you are doubtless aware – who will give her unquestioning loyalty, is her father, Ghiyas Beg; he, being a financier, has the dedication of a moneylender to the well-being of his debtor's collateral, in this case the power of his daughter.'

'You suggest that I get to know the Empress and bring these matters to her notice?'

'No, I suggest that you contact the Empress and win her confidence. We have been talking frankly.' He smiled faintly. 'This conversation has never taken place, so let me tell you that the Empress is at base a vain, insecure woman. She can fairly easily be encouraged to take measures to protect her position.'

'What are those measures?'

'Probably some she has considered already,' Prince Chara began, then went on to explain.

Sir Thomas listened attentively, nodded thoughtfully

when he had finished. 'You seem to be covering all possible ground in your assault on Prince Jahan,' he finally declared. A shrewd look entered the blue eyes. 'It's strange how far some people will carry a personal vendetta.'

'I am not pursuing a personal vendetta,' Prince Chara flashed.

'What other motive could you possibly have? In the distant past, you may have had some hope of ruling a unified India, but that was shattered when Prince Husrau mistimed his revolt.' The ambassador's smile was wintry. 'Oh yes, I know a great deal about the recent history of the Moghul Empire. A necessary ingredient of my work here. You will become Rana of Mewar on your father's death. With new leaderships in the Deccan, such as that of General Malik Ambar, you have nowhere else to go. So let us understand each other, Prince. We may make common cause because we share a common . . . er . . . detestation.'

Prince Chara grinned. He liked this man. Sir Thomas was tough as steel, with a mind like a trap. 'I accept you as an ally,' he stated. 'But I want you to know that I do have somewhere to go. When I succeed my father, I shall move to take over all Rajasthan. Merely being Rana of Mewar will not satisfy me. Then, it would be logical to dip down into the Deccan.' He shrugged elegant shoulders. 'Who knows what will lie ahead thereafter? A weak Moghul Emperor is essential for my plan. Prince Jahan would be far too strong an individual for my comfort or ambition.'

'M'm . . . m. All that is wishful thinking, Prince,' Sir Thomas retorted. 'For the present, let us be satisfied with being allies to overthrow a common foe.'

'Accepted.'

'In that event, I strongly urge you to speak to Nur Jehan and give her counsel. The more she is bombarded by doubts the surer we can be that her dream castle Cabinet will fall.'

Prince Chara laughed heartily, enjoying the ambassador's lifted eyebrows. 'Now that we are allies, I can divulge to you what I could not if I merely wanted to entrap you into the alliance.'

'You have already spoken to the Empress?'

'Of course.'

'And her reaction was positive?'

'Let us say it was watchful.'

'M'm . . . m. You really are a sod, aren't you?'

The word appealed to Prince Chara's sense of dramatic irony. For all your cleverness, he thought, one thing you don't even suspect, Sir Thomas, is what a sod I really am, in every sense of the word!

Before he left, Prince Chara decided that he should offer to help Sir Thomas in the mission for which he had been appointed by the young East India Company, with letters of credence from King James, to obtain a trading agreement for the company with the Emperor. The Portuguese had exercised a monopoly of the trade in calicoes, indigo and spices for over a hundred years, since their Admiral Vasco da Gama discovered the sea route to India which pre-empted those in the caravan trade. The Dutch, following those sea routes, had begun making inroads into that trade. The English were newcomers, but their recent mastery of the seas would soon put them ahead of all others.

'I would like very much to commence trading relations with your Company, Sir Thomas,' Prince Chara stated. 'We produce many of the goods you require in Rajasthan. I can arrange for a trade cartel to make these goods available to you, but it would be up to you to obtain the necessary export permits from the Emperor. You would ship the goods from Surat, which is a more sheltered port than the Portuguese stronghold of Diu.'

Sir Thomas showed immediate interest. 'I would be most

grateful,' he declared. 'That would save me several steps in the business. Your association would also give my attempts the credibility they lacked until the Emperor accepted me in the imperial court.'

'You might consider chartering one or more of the Empress's ships though you have your own merchant fleet.' He grinned slyly. 'It always helps to give those in power a stake in your business. If I may advise you, however, make the overtures through her Chief Eunuch who handles all such affairs of the Empress. It would never do to have it seem as if you were both common traders, but then I hardly need remind you of such niceties.'

The cold fish-eyes gleamed. 'What a splendid idea!' Sir Thomas declared. His expression said, I may even get to like you one of these days!

The ambassador did not know that the Empress's previous Chief Eunuch, Tafari, had been his, Prince Chara's, agent when the Empress blasted his chest with her matchlock rifle.

From the Diary of Sir Thomas Roe

This evening I had the privilege of attending the Emperor while he held *durbar* in the *diwan-i-an* where the public part of the Empire's affairs are conducted, primarily appointments and presentations. Oddly enough, wrestlers, jugglers and tumblers were on hand to fill in the gaps. This *durbar* over, we withdrew to a private council (*ghusl-khana*) in a separate chamber to which only the highest officials were admitted. Here, the real decisions of State were debated and made. I am of the view that I was invited to be present in order that I might be impressed with the diligence and attention to detail the Emperor brings to bear on his rule and I have a shrewd suspicion that the debates between officials had been planned in advance in order to display their brilliance and the decisiveness of their master!

Ironically, since it was now evening, those attending had their breath sniffed at the door by a guard for signs of alcohol, but as the event progressed business was prevented by *drowsiness which possesseth His Majestie from the fumes of Backus*! I have been told of occasions on which the Emperor suddenly lay down during these councils and fell asleep, when the tapers were immediately snuffed by attendants and those present had to fumble out through the darkness. Boredom is an affliction that rides with Backus.

My influence with the Emperor increased greatly when I was able to give him news of an English ship that had arrived in Surat the manifest of which included some '*toyes*' for him. He was quite shameless in demanding what there was. Did I have an English horse?

In a land where the nature of the gift determines the extent of the favour, imagine my mortification at receiving leather cases gone mouldy, faded velvet, looking glasses with the mercury peeling, the glue of the frames unstuck. The Emperor was astonished at the offerings his royal brother in England had sent him. Fortunately, the parts of a magnificent coach had also arrived, which I was able to piece together and thus placate him, though he has ordered that the upholstery be replaced with richer brocade and the brass rails with silver. I have been constrained, however, to give the Emperor my personal possessions as gifts, to maintain the reputation of my king.

The Emperor has given me a small portrait of himself set in gold with a huge pendant pearl, which is a mark of great favour, since even the greatest nobles of his court receive only gold medallions of his head.

He was much taken by my paintings and has hung some in the alcove behind his throne, somewhat indiscriminately I might add, for the portraits of the royal family are mingled with those of a citizen's wife of London and of the Countess of Somerset, who at this very moment is awaiting trial in London for the murder of Sir Thomas Overbury. But I shall not be the one to tell the Emperor, since no other is likely to and what pleaseth the eye need not be jaundiced by knowledge, as a serpent is beautiful if one is unaware of its sting. Suffice it to say that the Emperor is almost as addicted to painting, literature, music, drama and architecture as he is to alcohol and opium!

* * *

I have this day concluded the first agreement containing the Emperor's approval and seal, obtained through the Chief Eunuch of the Empress, for a cargo of spices to be shipped to London on one of the Empress's ships. This is certainly the first breakthrough and I am grateful to Prince Chara for his advice. The Emperor is reluctant to enter into a permanent trade treaty until we have demonstrated our ascendancy over the Portuguese in the Indian Ocean and the Persian Gulf by forcing them to abandon the system of Portuguese passports for travellers to the Holy City, Mecca.

The Emperor left on a tour today. I give here a verbatim account of his departure: *He descended the stairs with such an acclamation of 'health to the King' as would have outcried cannon. At the stairs' foot, where I met him, and shuffled to be next, one brought a mighty carp; another a dish of white stuff like starch, into which he put his finger, and touched the fish and so rubbed it on his forehead, a ceremony used presaging good fortune. Then another came and buckled on his sword and buckler, set all over with great diamonds and rubies, the belts of gold suteable. Another hung his quiver with thirty arrows and his bow in a case, the same that was presented by the Persian ambassador.*

To my delight, his gloves, which were English, were stuck in his girdle and he drove away, attended by an English servant, whom I have procured for him, in a replica of the coach I had gifted him, while his wife followed in the original coach, complete with new upholstery and silver nails!

My compatriot and chaplain, Edward Terry, has described the Emperor's entourage when on the move as 'ambulans republica', a walking republic. Indeed, the Emperor himself has estimated that to supply the imperial army on the move, in barren areas, grain sellers with at least one hundred thousand fully laden bullocks must accompany it. When the entourage is encamped for the night, it covers an area well nigh twenty miles in circumference equal to almost any town in Europe for greatness, with regular streets in which each noble or tradesman has an allotted area in which to pitch his tent. The king himself and the nobles have two sets of tents each, so one could always be sent ahead to be ready for the owner's arrival.

* * *

I saw the Emperor being weighed on his birthday today, against a great variety of precious metals and stones. He sat on one side of a huge pair of golden scales, while bags of gold were placed on the other to balance him, followed by silver, jewels, precious cloth and foodstuffs. I was not impressed by the precious metals. As one commentator said, '*It being in bags might be Bibles!*' Moreover the sacks were intended for distribution to charity, but since they were transported inside his palace, I assume in this case charity began at home. A fat Emperor would otherwise bestow much money on other charities than his own.

In contrast, I passed today a camel laden with three hundred men's heads, sent all the way from Kandhar by the Governor in present to the King.

Chapter 24

Suddenly, for no accountable reason, the Emperor had sunk to his knees and vomited without warning. Nur Jehan gazed in horror at the blood spewing out of his mouth. He stared wide-eyed at the mess of blood, mixed with yellowy remnants of half-digested food, staining his bare chest.

As she sank to her knees in alarm, one hand on her husband's shoulder, Nur Jehan noted his expression of puzzlement beneath downcast eyelids. 'That's funny,' he said, as if to himself. 'How did that happen? I had a fine dinner with the Persian ambassador and looked forward to being with you.' Dropping the royal plural in this bedchamber had become a habit with him. 'I felt perfectly all right when I came in just now, having had only three glasses of wine at dinner so I could make love to you. Why should I be sick?' He lifted questioning eyes to her. She realized with added alarm that his sickly sweet breath had a slightly faecal odour to it.

She had an instant's premonition of disaster before responding, 'It is probably something you ate, light of my life.' But her instinct told her that this was no trifling symptom. It was somehow connected with his excessive drinking over the past twenty-five years. She had never actively discouraged him from drinking, at times had even taken advantage of it to accumulate and maintain power. Now, for the first time, she was staring at the consequences of her policy, nature's first warning.

'There, I feel better already,' he declared, forcing a smile. 'See how my soul bleeds for you, its star!'

She tried to match his attempt at light-heartedness, but it was from a heavy heart. 'You can hardly bleed from your soul, Sire. And never for a star.' Concern for him had begun to seep into her fears for herself. She did love him in her own way.

'Ah, the unattainable star,' he responded seriously, then placed a swift hand to his mouth and bent his head to gulp out another small trickle of blood. 'Tchah! Not again!' he exclaimed in disgust. His slanty eyes glazed with tears from the involuntary effort, he gestured helplessly.

'Let me summon the physician,' she volunteered, rising hastily to her feet.

He reached out a hand to her wrist. His touch was clammy. Sweat beads were forming on his face. 'No! Not yet. There is no cause for concern. I feel fine. As if some poison has been ejected from my stomach. Calling the physician will only create alarm in the court for what is surely a passing ailment. I would prefer not to summon the attendants either. Let us keep this to ourselves. Just bring me a bowl of water from the privy please and wipe away this mess.' He shrugged broad shoulders. 'Even an Emperor is sometimes brought down to his knees. Better to bleed from a poisoned stomach than a demented heart!'

'You shall not be brought down by anyone or anything,' she cried vehemently, her gaze hypnotic.

She walked towards the privy to get the water and a linen cloth.

'You can explain away the blood by saying it was from your period,' he called after her. She laughed at his jest, but in her heart was the sickening knowledge that it was time's cruel jesting that she faced. She recalled her superficial talks with Prince Chara and separately with the English ambassador, a man she was beginning to like for his courage, forthrightness and dignity. That had been fifteen months ago, shortly after Prince Jahan and Mumtaz Mahal had their first son and heir, Prince Dara. Since then, they had yet another boy, Prince Shuja, and Mumtaz Mahal was very likely to become pregnant again and again. Such a prolific couple, while she herself had only the one girl. Her own husband, the Emperor, obviously had no seed.

She needed to reorganize her present to meet her future.

Prince Jahan caught the angry flash of Nur Jehan's eyes. The Friday morning meetings of the Cabinet in her reception room, once so harmonious, had in recent months taken the complexion of an audience at which her will alone had to prevail. It seemed to Prince Jahan that the more power he himself acquired in the Empire, the less influence Nur Jehan was willing to allow him. He was accustomed to Moghul heads exercising imperial authority but dictation from a female surrogate disturbed him. He also regarded impatience and irritation as signs of inherent disrespect which had serious cumulative effects on both the person expressing them and those towards whom they were directed. Although loyalty had prevented them from ever discussing it, Prince Jahan could tell from his father-in-law's reaction of aloof amusement that the Prime Minister shared his perception and concern.

Prince Jahan himself had been driven to the belief that the honours showered on him by the Emperor after his return from the successful Deccan campaign, much of them on Nur Jehan's enthusiastic recommendation, including the grant of the title Shah and the unprecedented elevation of his *mansab* to thirty thousand *zat* and twenty thousand *sawar*, giving him virtually a private standing army, had finally begun to bother the Empress. His successful treaty with the Deccan ruler probably caused her to fear competition from him. Mumtaz Mahal frequently warned him of this, and since the birth of their first child and the arrival of their second baby, had repeatedly emphasized, in her usual uncompromising manner, that Nur Jehan was jealous of him and increasingly apprehensive of her position now that he had male heirs who could create a new line of succession when the Emperor died.

Shah Jahan himself recognized that he had been growing up and was no longer the blindly obedient princeling, but a man of twenty-five who had established his ability. He needed to think and make his own decisions. He attributed some part of Nur Jehan's changed attitude to the English ambassador, whose influence in the Moghul Court had increased greatly in the past year. Nur Jehan obviously liked and trusted Sir Thomas Roe for she had taken to granting him regular private audiences, while he had hated both Shah Jahan and Asaf Khan from the time of the Customs incident.

The astrologers had warned Shah Jahan only the previous week that he was entering a dangerous period in his life, with the malign planet Saturn ascending in his *lagna*. Any children he might sire over the next three years would be unlucky for him. It was his belief that people, especially family, could bring a man either great good luck or misfortune. Had not Mumtaz Mahal's entry into his life coincided with the start of his remarkable career? Had not the birth of his grandfather, the Emperor Akbar, completely changed the fortunes of that Emperor's own father Himayun after they had reached their lowest depths?

Apart from her anger and annoyance, Nur Jehan also seemed preoccupied today. What trouble lay behind the eyes now flashing fire above the black *yashmak*?

'The treaty with King Adil does *not* preclude us from imposing new taxes on the people of the Deccan,' Nur Jehan reasserted, anger in her mellow voice. She turned to her father, who was as usual seated on the sofa beside her. 'We need to raise the money to increase our standing army against the possible threat from Persia, do we not, *Diwan*?' Her tone was imperious.

'We certainly do, Empress.'

Nur Jehan directed her gaze to Asaf Khan. 'And you are certain that the intelligence reports you have received of a slow gathering of the Persian Shah's forces are accurate, Prime Minister?'

Asaf Khan's white teeth showed beneath his red moustache in a lazy smile, obviously intended to calm Nur Jehan. 'Intelligence reports of this sort could be inaccurate, but I have had these particular ones verified.'

'We need the increase in our imperial army. We need funds for the purpose.' Her eyes lifted to Shah Jahan. 'Therefore, we should tax the Deccan, which has caused us the unnecessary expenses of repeated campaigns to quell its rebellions over the last ten years.'

'It was arbitrary taxation for imperial purposes that was one of the principal causes of the Deccan revolt in the first place,' Shah Jahan insisted. 'As a matter of general policy, under the feudal system of mutual rights and privileges, duties and obligations, any taxes raised in a territory should be used mainly for the direct benefit of that territory. The late Emperor Akbar, one of the finest administrators in our

Moghul history, repeatedly emphasized this. Besides, freedom from arbitrary taxation was one of the conditions of our treaty with the Deccan.'

'Our Emperor Jehangir is a finer administrator than any other in Moghul history,' Nur Jehan flashed back. 'As for the Deccan treaty, show us where it says there will be no arbitrary, as you call it, taxation.'

Shah Jahan was hard-put to restrain his own annoyance. He resented the inference that anyone, least of all his drunken father and this power-crazy woman, could be superior to his grandfather. Restraining himself, he replied in a level voice. 'There is no specific reference in the treaty, but it was implied in the spirit, Your Majesty. After all, having negotiated it, I know more about the spirit of the treaty than anyone else,' he had been tempted to say 'in this room', but held back before the needs of harmony, 'also what the desires and intentions of the accord were, since I was personally in touch with both King Adil and General Malik Ambar.'

'You are always over-generous with our rebellious subjects,' Nur Jehan countered impatiently. 'It is not the person who negotiates but whoever signs a treaty that interprets it.' She turned to Ghiyas Beg. 'Our final decision is that these taxes will be imposed.'

Asaf Khan's swift hand placed on his wrist prevented Shah Jahan from erupting. 'We will abide by Your Majesty's decision,' the Prime Minister said smoothly. 'Your wish is our command.'

'Good. We are glad there is some regard for authority in this room.' Nur Jehan directed a cold stare at Shah Jahan.

'I have always respected properly constituted authority, Your Majesty,' Shah Jahan responded. 'This too was instilled in me by the Emperor Akbar.' He paused, his gaze solemn. 'It is my duty to advise you, however, that this taxation will cause the standard of revolt to be raised once more in the Deccan. I know those people as only a field commander can know his enemies. They will not rebel immediately, but in a year or two, after they have quietly gathered their forces, a revolt will be inevitable. This decision will return to haunt us.'

She had ensured the same absolute privacy for the encounter that Friday afternoon with Sir Thomas Roe and Prince Chara as she had for the morning gathering of her Cabinet. This was Nur Jehan's first meeting with the two men together, but the time had come to form an alliance of those opposed to Shah Jahan. Perhaps for the very reason that he had guessed the cause for the summons she had sent to Mewar by secret messenger, Prince Chara had audaciously sought and received the hospitality of Shah Jahan's palace in the Agra capital for his visit. She thought this a nice, amoral touch, calculated to throw off suspicion.

Shortly after moving to her new suite of rooms adjoining those of the Emperor on the first floor of the Agra palace, Nur Jehan had caused full-length curtains of green velvet to be installed in the middle of her reception chamber; these were drawn on the infrequent occasions when she gave non-family males audience for the transaction of the business of the Empire.

She now sat on her usual divan facing the curtains, which were closed to leave the merest slit through which she could observe her two visitors, though they could not see her. Even she had to observe the rules of *purdah* very strictly if she were not to incur the malicious digs of Salima Begum.

Without wasting too much time on trivial formalities, Nur Jehan briefed the two men on the situation created by Shah Jahan's increasingly independent attitude, especially his continued and determined opposition to taxation in the Deccan.

'We summoned you both here because you have had

your own experiences of the arrogance of this young prince,' she ended. 'At the meeting of our Cabinet this morning, he actually threatened to raise the taxation issue directly with the Emperor. If there is one thing we cannot stand, it is ingratitude. We were responsible for giving Shah Jahan every opportunity that has brought him to his present level and he now turns on us.' Deep inside, she knew that this was not entirely true. Shah Jahan had risen to his present heights through merit, but these two men knew nothing about the facts and she needed to manipulate them. 'The walls of our chamber do not have ears, so we may talk freely,' she added. 'Sir Ambassador, will you commence?'

She suspected that the English ambassador would have more to offer than Prince Chara and she did not want the prince to feel small by leading with too little and having Sir Thomas supplement his advice. About thirty-six years old at this time, Sir Thomas looked worldly wise. The codpiece he wore, she considered ridiculous; according ill with his elegance, it was a typical symbol of male European bravado, to pretend that something of significance was there when it was not. But Sir Thomas's experience with the East India Company had been useful to her in expanding the vast trade she now carried on through her eunuchs. He had also influenced some of the changes she had effected in Moghul Court protocol to bring it into line with European styles and of course she appreciated his honesty and caustic wit.

'Hr . . . r . . . mph . . .' Sir Thomas cleared his throat, stroked his ginger beard slowly. The long sardonic face with the fish gaze assumed a reflective expression. 'Ah, taxation!' he exclaimed. A humorous glint appeared briefly in the cold eyes. 'It is the method God has provided for rulers to live beyond other people's means, Madam. All decent aristocratic people live beyond their means. Some do it better than others. A creditor or tax payer should have no right to dictate where the funds he extends should be spent. Would you not agree, Prince Chara?' The man was playing before plunging.

Nur Jehan could not avoid a quiet ripple of laughter. The ambassador's remarks had real wit because they carried the germ of truth in them. But they had also lightened the proceedings. She directed her gaze at Prince Chara.

Sombrely dressed in white *jodhpurs* and short black tunic, Prince Chara rose readily to the occasion. His deep-set eyes twinkling, he rubbed the side of his long Rajput nose with a forefinger. 'Shah Jahan is a very serious-minded young man,' he volunteered. 'He reminds me of the Jainist flagellants who mortify the flesh for the good of their immortal souls, as if beset by some special divine grace denied ordinary mortals.' He shrugged slim shoulders. 'No one who is not addicted to good wine and bad morals could possibly have an immortal soul.'

A smile twitched the sides of Sir Thomas's face. His whiskery moustache seemed to quiver in acceptance of the invitation to levity. 'M-m-m . . . Shah Jahan reminds *me* of our crusaders who invaded the Middle East to establish Christianity and their divine right to the fabled treasures of Middle Eastern rulers,' he contended. 'He has no redeeming vices but the earnestness of a food reformer gives him that subtle air of spiritual superiority extended by those who drink only water and fruit juice towards us poor wine-bibbers.'

'Which brings us to a very important aspect of the problem,' Prince Chara broke in seriously. 'Shah Jahan is an ultra-orthodox Muslim, powered by his over-pious wife,' he bowed slightly in Nur Jehan's direction, 'your niece. We Indians of non-Muslim religions fear such fanatics. It is the liberal views that you, Madam, and the Emperor, hold that

398

have given non-Muslims the confidence to place our destinies in your royal hands.' He smiled carelessly. 'I for one do not give a fig for religion, which I believe to be the opium of the masses, but the millions under your suzerainty do. And I repeat, they do not want a Muslim fanatic on the imperial throne. Shah Jahan neither smokes, drinks nor indulges in sexual pleasures outside his marriage. An altogether admirable young man, but what kind of a ruler would he make? I venture to suggest that the grant of the title of Shah to him and the elevation of his *mansab* and *sawar* were wholly unjustified.' He leaned forward in his chair, eyes flashing. 'Prince Jahan has not won one single battle! I realize that you, Madam, were probably responsible for obtaining these honours for him, but the truth must be placed on record.' He leaned back in his chair, very relaxed.

'You are right, Prince,' she agreed, seeing the truth of Shah Jahan's military roles with sudden clarity. 'We recommended his rewards to the Emperor for conquests that we now realize he did not achieve as a general but as', she glanced at Sir Thomas hoping he would imagine her smile, 'a diplomat.'

'Success came too easily to this young man,' Sir Thomas stated flatly. 'This is specially dangerous for those of ambition. Our celebrated dramatist, William Shakespeare, who died last year, put it rather well when he spoke of "vaulting ambition that o'erleaps itself and falls on the other". You have besides, in Shah Jahan, a most dedicated man. Dedicated to what? To his religion alone? No. To his family? Probably. To what he believes is his destiny? Certainly. It is a form of dedication that rather inhibits self-denial!'

'The late Emperor Akbar undoubtedly helped convince him of his destiny,' Prince Chara intervened smoothly. 'Which brings up a most important factor, family. Shah

Jahan now has two children, both male, and his wife will undoubtedly draw only a breath or two between periods of gestation. Few things make a man's mental glands secrete faster than the product of his physical glands. Male off-spring represent to insecure men the illusory promise of immortality. Shah Jahan would want the imperial throne not only for himself, but for his male progeny as well.'

'And his wife would see in her children the source of the continuance of her power.' Mumtaz Mahal was the Empress's competitor, desiring what she too needed most, total power to determine her future. Power today and especially after the Emperor died. She did not need to carve out a place in history; she was concerned only with wresting total security in this life.

'In my view, the Princess Mumtaz Mahal has considered you a rival from her earliest years.' Sir Thomas echoed her thought. 'You are everything that she is not. More, you have always had the love and admiration of her father, your brother, whose loyalty you now command. It would be logical for the princess to set her husband, over whom she undoubtedly has considerable influence, against you. As for Shah Jahan, the rivalry between father and son is primordial. The young bull will some day challenge the old bull for mastery over the herd!'

She knew this to be true, but the ambassador's statement nonetheless caused her stomach to flutter. 'What do you suggest, Sir Thomas?' She already had her own solution, so needed the support of these two men, not their advice. But men were so self-important; to feel their own non-existent influence, they must think that theirs was the advice.

'Your Majesty, at the heart of the problem is the succes-sion.' Remembering the Emperor's vomiting fit, Nur Jehan's interest quickened at the words. Even this sagacious

400

ambassador could not possibly guess how true his deduction was. For the first time in her life, she wished she had been a man. 'With his eldest brother, Prince Husrau, physically incapacitated and the next in line for the succession, Prince Parviz, virtually disqualified by his . . . er . . . excesses, Shah Jahan is the logical successor to the imperial throne. He will succeed your husband or, I'm sorry to say, seize power, if the succession is . . . um . . . too long deferred. Should he succeed, your position would be . . . um . . . extremely precarious to say the least. I venture to suggest that you should take some positive action immediately to safeguard yourself.'

'Timing is, however, important,' Prince Chara interjected. 'Much as I would like to see the departure of the man who won a war against our kingdom without fighting a single battle, there can be no denying Shah Jahan's present power and influence, especially with the imperial army. It is vitally important not to create an immediate crisis.'

'We rather think that both you gentlemen have a solution upon which you have agreed,' Nur Jehan countered.

Sir Thomas glanced at Prince Chara, whose nod encouraged him to be the spokesman. You are crafty, Prince Chara, Nur Jehan thought. You want the ambassador to be the one to make the suggestion and bear the responsibility should it fail. You and I have much in common.

'You might consider marrying your daughter, the Princess Ladili, to Shah Jahan's younger brother, Prince Shahriyar,' the ambassador advised. 'You could then groom Prince Shahriyar, over whom you would have . . . um . . . the absolute control which would ensure the well-being of the Empire, for the succession. As to timing, which is essential, you might merely announce for the time being that a betrothal is contemplated. European custom is replete with such events.'

Nur Jehan clapped her hands. 'Wonderful!' she exclaimed. 'What a brilliant idea!' She had already decided on this solution, but seeing Sir Thomas beam at her praise she knew it had been well bestowed. 'We like the idea of timing.'

Sir Thomas smiled complacently. 'It is what our English admirals, who now command all the seas of the world, would describe as firing a warning shot across the bows of a hostile ship.'

Having deliberately left Nur Jehan's audience chamber at the same time as Sir Thomas, Prince Chara paused with him at the entrance doors of the palace while footmen raced outside to have the grooms bring up their horses. The sun beat fiercely down on the flagstone courtyard.

'Beastly hot day,' Sir Thomas observed, mopping his brow. 'That was quite an eventful meeting. The Empress has a distinct flair for dramatizing even the commonplace.'

Prince Chara grinned. 'Only the three of us can make the meeting eventful,' he observed. 'In which case it will be hotter for the Empress's opponents.'

A sardonic smile revealed the ambassador's yellow teeth. 'And cool for a conniving bastard,' he replied pleasantly.

Prince Chara warmed towards the man. 'Now who would that be?' he inquired innocently. 'Prince Aziz Koka is one of the few bastards in this court who might have qualified, but he died in prison last month after a heart attack. Probably hastened by his imprisonment. The only other bastard is of course Prince Shahriyar, who is the son of a palace slave!' He was all wide-eyed innocence which he knew the ambassador would appreciate.

Sir Thomas turned to face him squarely. 'Mm . . . m . . . When General Malik Ambar revolts again, it will weaken both the Deccan and the Empire. After the Emperor dies, with Prince . . . er . . . Shah Jahan and

Prince Parviz away from Agra but still contenders for the imperial throne and a weak Prince Shahriyar the named heir, the Empire will be further weakened by internal dissension. Your suggestion that Princess Ladili be betrothed to Prince Shahriyar will weaken the Empress too, rather than strengthen her position.'

'As I recall, it was *your* suggestion!' Prince Chara countered urbanely.

'Whatever the case, someone is going to foment revolts in Bengal and the north-west as well. The contender who has the strongest power base will have a very good opportunity to extend it. Mewar has been recovering from its crucifixion by Shah Jahan.' His grin was positively feral. 'I suppose it will be a united Rajput front that comes to the fore.' He paused. 'What a splendid opportunity for . . . er . . . the ruling Rana of Mewar.'

The clippety-clop of horses' hooves came from the courtyard.

Mind-reading like this was the result of observation and deduction from experience. 'I hope the English king will then decide to make common cause with . . . er . . .' Prince Chara paused, his expression mock-serious, 'the ruling Rana of Mewar!'

Lying naked beside the Emperor on the solitary mattress in the inner chamber of her suite in the Agra palace that night, Nur Jehan decided that the time was opportune to brief him. 'You were magnificent tonight, lord of my soul,' she murmured, feigning tiredness in her voice. 'You wore me out.'

'I did, didn't I?' Though lying on his back, obviously spent, he brightened, placed his palms behind the back of his head, slanted his eyes towards her.

She had cultivated what few, if any, *harem* women could do. The clutching of the vaginal muscles, the ready orgasms, pretended or otherwise, the cries and moans were regular assets of all who plied the sex trade, wives, concubines, prostitutes. She alone knew the secret of the Emperor's need to be dominated before mastering the object of his worship. She had therefore practised until she could come like a man, from deep within her, the deflowered clitoris, rendered insensitive as with all Muslim girls immediately they reach puberty to deter arousal, throbbing and spurting juices like a male's ejaculation. It was a gift Allah meant her to cultivate and exploit. She reached out to fondle his flaccid penis, beneath the now bulging stomach, half-revolted as always at his breath which contained that sweet, slightly faecal odour and by the smell of raw emission. 'How could I help it with a great stud like you?' she inquired seductively. 'I do not know what I would do without your divine protection.'

'You certainly have that,' he assured her grandly. 'You need not fear anyone or anything.'

'I need it more than ever now.' She glanced down at the smooth motions of her hand. 'My, my, the little boy is starting to grow again.' It was not strictly true, but her reward was an induced jerking as he tried to enlarge his penis. He was so like a child, for a moment she felt protective towards him before her cultivated instincts took over from the natural. 'I fear Shah Jahan,' she whispered.

'What?' He raised himself on one elbow, his almond-shaped eyes sharp. 'Why should you fear him? He is our near-heir and our most loyal son, is he not?' He blinked once, his forehead creasing in a frown as he reached for the concentration which he found increasingly difficult to achieve in recent times. 'Or is he?'

'Shah Jahan's first loyalty is to himself, my lord.'

'Not even to his wife and children?' There was a note of incredulity.

'I fear we have been mistaken in Shah Jahan. His

404

ambition is so great that he has come to regard his wife and children, his father and brothers, as but chattels for his use. Even Sir Thomas Roe has warned me of this.'

The Emperor sat up, absently scratched the reddish brown hairs on his bare chest. 'You have discussed this family matter with an outsider, a foreigner at that?' His disapproval was unmistakable.

'I would never discuss such matters with anyone but you, lord.' She sat up, placed a palm on the mattress, eyed him levelly. 'You know me well enough. Sir Thomas requested a special audience with me to warn me of possible enemies. You know how wise he is from his experience of foreign courts.'

'Shah Jahan would never betray us,' the Emperor muttered, automatically reverting to the royal plural which he had seldom used in that room since their first sexual domination scene. 'Or would he?'

With growing concern, Nur Jehan realized that her husband was having difficulty focusing on a single line of thought. 'But it is not Shah Jahan's political ambition alone that I fear,' she ventured. 'I believe we can easily take care of that by ordering him to lead an expeditionary force to the Deccan, where trouble is brewing again. That would remove him from the centre of things. When that happens, I suggest that we send Prince Husrau with him, to eliminate any moves against you by Prince Husrau's supporters.' This would clear the way for her to advance Prince Shahriyar as the heir to the throne. 'Prince Parviz too should be removed farther from the scene.'

'Prince Parviz loves wine and women more than he does power.'

'Power can give him all the wine and women he needs. He is timid, egoistic, lazy and superstitious. His only way to power is to be near it, to court the princes and nobles, especially whenever you and I are away from the capital.'

'You have a point there.' Eyes downcast, the Emperor reflected a few moments. 'Where would we send him?'

'To govern Bihar. In the distant north-east, he will be far enough removed to eliminate any threat.' She noticed that the Emperor had begun to sweat though the room was cool. In case it was caused by alarm, she hastened to add, 'We can explain to him that in view of your frequent absences from Agra, you want trusted men in charge of the farthest outposts of the Empire. These moves, combined with the announcement of the impending betrothal of Prince Shahriyar to our daughter, Ladili, should ensure against any rebellious actions from your sons.'

'You are a very astute lady. You have our approval.'

You have never suspected how astute I am, she thought, plunging in with her final thrust. 'There is only one other source against which I desperately need your divine protection, lord of my life.'

'And what is that, star of my soul?'

She pretended to hesitate, forced tears to her eyes. 'I pray daily to Allah that He will take me away before you, so I can await you in Paradise.'

While she was certain of the existence of Almighty Allah, she did not believe in heaven or hell, considering them the manacles which prophets, priests and *imams*, who needed to dominate people, especially rulers and the rich, used to bind the credulous and enslave them to codes of conduct. 'But I do know this. If I have the rank misfortune to remain when you are gone, I shall have to take my life and forever forfeit any chance of meeting you in Paradise.'

'Why?' He tilted his head, slanty eyes round in wonderment. 'You are not a Hindu woman to submit to *suttee*, immolation on your husband's funeral pyre?'

She listened to the ticking of the wall clock. It spelled the passage of time, an extension of her heart-beat. 'Do you recall what your father, the Emperor, did with Salima

Begum years ago and how Shah Jahan has carved himself in the image of his grandfather?'

'My father was married to his Prime Minister's . . .' The Emperor paused, an incredulous expression on his face. 'You are not suggesting that . . .' He shook his head like a dog its wet body. 'No, that is impossible.'

'Everything is possible, lord, because, unlike you, all other men are disgusting creatures. They are greedy and ambitious, vain and lustful. You must not worry about what I say, because I have already taken steps to thwart any such aims, but Shah Jahan respectfully requested permission to remain behind when the meeting of our advisers ended today and tried to embrace me when we were alone.' She held up a restraining hand. 'Now remember, he will be gone soon, so you need do nothing about it.'

'The dirty, filthy pig.' The imperial eyes, reddened by excessive drinking, were bulging with rage, the veins on his forehead had knotted. 'We'll have his penis and balls cut off. We'll flay him alive . . . We'll . . . we'll . . .' He paused, reaching for breath.

'No, no, lord,' she implored. 'We beg you to calm down. Remember, we must not create a crisis for the present. Let us act with wisdom. We must do everything to retain the stability of the Empire at this time of danger.' She deliberately dropped the royal plural. 'I would have a dagger ready for Shah Jahan and for myself if he ever attempted to violate my womanhood.' She injected magnetism into her gaze to steady him. 'You may be assured of that. Our best form of revenge is to reduce him to nothing in the Empire.'

She had placed a hand on his arm to steady him, but it was in vain. He heaved upwards with his chest, eyes wide, nostrils distending, trying desperately to breathe. His clawing only produced dry rasping sounds until his breath finally broke through. He leaned forward, deep sounds of phlegm rumbling in his chest.

It was the worst attack of asthma he had ever had and she wondered whether she had induced it with her deliberate lie about Shah Jahan. If so, she might use it at some future date when her own plans for the succession were secure. Nothing would alter her implacable resolve to retain power.

PART IV

Brothers in Arms

Chapter 25

It had taken almost two years, longer than Shah Jahan had estimated, long enough for Mumtaz Mahal and him to have a daughter, whom they had named Jahanara, and for Mumtaz Mahal to become pregnant once again, before the Deccan did erupt. Shah Jahan had always known that the treaty of 1617 was only temporary, an armistice. Unlike Mewar, which he had brought to its knees before achieving its surrender, the Deccan had been strong when it capitulated to a much stronger force. When Asaf Khan gave the Nur Jehan Cabinet the news that Friday morning, Shah Jahan's only surprise was that General Malik Ambar had taken so long to revolt.

Shah Jahan was well aware that the announcement, made so many months ago, that the Princess Ladili was to be betrothed to his younger half-brother, Prince Shahriyar, the weak-kneed son of a palace slave, was a weapon that Nur Jehan intended to hold over his head and that the official betrothal and subsequent marriage would take place only when Nur Jehan considered the time right. He had therefore decided to play a waiting game himself. Meanwhile, he had accepted the bitter lesson that imperial patronage is illusory, the price for it, bondage. The only way a man could be completely independent was to put himself in a position from which he could exercise independence. In 1617, he was already impatient for his hour. Now it had become clear that the Emperor Jehangir was declining in health. Having diagnosed the problem as a combination of a damaged liver and asthma, the Court physicians leeched and bled the Emperor, gave him laxatives and even sent him to the more salubrious climate of Kashmir for a few months, during which time Nur Jehan was the virtual ruler of the Empire, but to no avail. He was in such poor health that Nur Jehan remained in power even after he returned to Agra.

They were seated in their normal places in Nur Jehan's reception chamber this morning, Ghiyas Beg on the divan beside her, Asaf Khan and Shah Jehan on chairs facing her. As the background to Asaf Khan's ill news, a summer storm raged outside, casting its grey pall on the open courtyard. Dark, lowering clouds sent gusts of rain drumming on the roof. Lightning flashed vividly, followed by the distant roll of thunder. They had to raise their voices to hear one another speak.

'In short, General Malik Ambar has formed an alliance with the sub-kingdoms of Bija and Golkonda,' Asaf Khan concluded. 'They jointly launched an attack on our governor, General Khan, who retreated to the fortress of Ahmad, where he is now besieged. The Deccanese forces are, however, carrying on their guerilla tactics elsewhere, with several successful raids as far north as Mandu.'

'Why should these people revolt?' Nur Jehan demanded. 'We have been so good to them.'

'We have also taxed them for purposes other than the needs of their own territory,' Asaf Khan reminded her drily. 'They are the products of a militantly feudal order, deriving from the time, eight hundred years ago, when Emperor Chandragupta Moriya established a very explicit set of mutual duties and obligations between ruler and subject.' He shot a knowing glance at Shah Jehan.

Since this was precisely what he had warned against when the taxation issue was first raised two years before, Shah Jehan could not avoid a throb of triumph but, having acquired the virtue of restraint, he kept his expression impassive and his eyes downcast.

'What are we going to do now?' Ghiyas Beg inquired. His face and frame had become gaunt. His voice was quavery and his stomach protuberant from a growth which was increasingly diminishing his energies.

'Fight,' Nur Jehan hissed. 'We shall send an imperial army to destroy these rebels and make an example of them. General Malik Ambar shall be brought to Agra in chains.'

Wonderful, Shah Jahan thought. You create the grounds for people to revolt and are then prepared to fight them to the last imperial mercenary. It is so easy when you do not know what war means: death, maiming, hunger, thirst, the utter weariness of body, mind and spirit of men driven beyond their capacity to endure, the anger, the bitter hatred, the abject fear.

'Is the Emperor aware of the situation?' Asaf Khan began.

'The Emperor, knowing the moves which General Malik Ambar was making, alerted our General Khan to resist with all the resources at his disposal,' Nur Jehan replied. 'He also decided that, if General Khan could not put down the revolt, an imperial army would be sent to deal with it.'

Asaf Khan shot another glance at Shah Jahan. 'Who would lead the expeditionary force?' he inquired blandly.

Nur Jehan looked at Shah Jahan with a twisted smile. 'Why, the general who produced such a transitory peace in the first instance, our most brilliant Shah Jahan.'

A spasm of rage convulsed Shah Jahan as his conjectures were confirmed. The crafty Empress planned to have him out of the way in distant Deccan when his father died, so that she could nominate Prince Shahriyar as the successor. He resolutely held back any eruption, presented a seemingly grateful face. 'I am honoured by your confidence in me, Madam, and that of the Emperor. I shall set out on the mission without delay.' He must be back before the Emperor died.

'There is one condition which the Emperor insists on,' Nur Jehan intervened.

Something in the tone of her voice made Shah Jahan tense. 'The Emperor's every desire is my command,' he replied without enthusiasm.

'You are acknowledged throughout the Empire as our most brilliant general. Meanwhile, the legal heir to the throne, Prince Husrau, languishes in ignominy. Desiring to bring some joy to the life of his eldest son, the Emperor commands you to take Prince Husrau with you on this campaign, so he can observe your superb strategy, perhaps participate in the fighting and share some of the glory.'

Shah Jahan was taken aback. This was Nur Jehan's move to get the legal heir out of the way. With Prince Parviz in Bihar, the way would indeed be clear for her nominee to the throne. What he did not know was the added dimension to Nur Jehan's plot that had been hatched for her privately by Prince Chara.

Though Mumtaz Mahal was advanced with child again, the charm of her face had not diminished, but was accentuated by the bulge of her stomach. Even in pregnancy her body was tight-knit, elegant. After the Friday morning meeting of the Cabinet, Shah Jahan had as usual hastened to his wife's reception chamber. His heart went out to her at her response to the news.

Mumtaz Mahal's eyes flashed in anger. She held her stomach so she could lean forward on the divan. 'The betrothal of my aunt's daughter to Prince Shahriyar was announced this morning, the event timed to take place in your absence, as a slap in your face and a blow to your rights.'

'She clearly wants to warn me against showing my independence.' He felt curiously objective now that he was sharing his outrage with Mumtaz.

'It is all too fundamental to be merely a warning,' Mumtaz Mahal countered. 'My aunt will buy time while you are away, to discredit you and gather support for what she intends.'

'You think so?'

'Is it not obvious? Face up to reality, husband of mine.'

'No one shall stand in my path.'

'It is time you grew up from the noble ways of childhood,' Mumtaz Mahal advised in a low voice. 'Imperial power is not a game of polo to be played according to rules of sportsmanship. Because you follow the code instilled in you by your grandfather, you are always too predictably honourable. But your grandfather did not play politics by those rules either, so why should you? You *must* start playing the deadly game by its own rules, which are *no* rules, which you *can* do without abandoning your cherished ideals as a human being.'

'I must think on that.' He was not contesting the principle, merely considering how he could follow it while remaining true to himself.

'While you are doing so, also remember this, my beloved. Your grandfather's major problems arose when he deviated from our time-honoured Muslim tradition of delivering succession to the eldest son. You and I both know that your father was unworthy of receiving the imperial crown, but the principle of succession should have been more important to your grandfather than the individuals concerned. Yet today, you and you alone are the only *eligible* heir, so go for the crown, lest Prince Shahriyar inherits it. This is an extension of the law of succession.' She tapped her stomach fiercely. 'I bear here your fourth child. I know it will be a boy. We shall name him Aurang Zeb. I would strangle him at birth if I thought he would ever contend with any *eligible* elder brother to succeed you. The only true test of succession is eligibility.'

He seemed to be emerging from a fog. 'You are right,' he stated. 'I have been blessed by Almighty Allah with the capacity to be the greatest Emperor in our history. With Prince Husrau ineligible to succeed and Prince Parviz totally incompetent, only I can save the Empire from the machinations of this ambitious woman. I still revere my grandfather, as I revere obedience, filial loyalty and honour. But I now face a situation similar to that when my father postponed my marriage to you after having us betrothed, taking away what was even dearer to my heart than becoming his heir.' He looked at her deeply, his eyes moist. 'You know that you are my whole life, Mumtaz, that I would gladly give up the throne for you.'

'Indeed, I do, my beloved.' The tears sprang to her eyes. 'And I would give up my life, which is all I have, for you.'

She looks most beautiful when her eyes glisten thus, he thought, for her soul is then mirrored in her tears.

'Those were dreadful years,' she whispered, looking back. 'I could easily have killed myself, I wanted so much to be with you.' She brushed her cheeks with the back of her hand, sniffed. 'See, I still do not have all the graces of the Court. Sati would chastise me for not behaving like a lady and using my silken kerchief.' She sniffed again, smiled suddenly, the dazzling smile of a sun breaking through clouds that always brought sunshine to his heart. 'At least that part of it is over and we are together whatever happens.'

'You are my only source of joy,' he responded. 'And the inspiration for my destiny.' He paused. 'You are right. I have tried to be the angel of honour, while others, especially our cunning, ruthless Empress, play the devil. That has now ended.' He found himself speaking with cold finality. 'I shall act honourably towards all individuals, but I shall fight by every means, fair or foul, against my enemies and those who would thwart my honourable designs. I love this country and our people. I know that of all those who might become the Emperor, I alone care about the people who make our nation. I shall work for rich and poor alike and bring glory to the Empire.'

While pushing day and night to get his expeditionary force ready for the move to the Deccan, Shah Jahan had sought earnestly for some device, some gesture, some stirring call that would reach the hearts of the people and inspire his predominantly Muslim expeditionary force to victory. It was Mumtaz Mahal who reminded him of what Babur had once done. He had called for *Jihad*, holy war! Shah Jahan's was a more difficult task in an Empire that now included millions of people of other religions. He had to instil in his men the belief that they were fighting a holy war without raising a cry that would alarm those of other faiths, causing them to unite with the rebellious Deccanese against Moghul might.

How could this be achieved? When he finally hit upon the solution, it was so simple that he laughed aloud. He would kill more than the proverbial peacock with a single arrow. It pleased him to be thinking like a Moghul conqueror.

Adapting the Emperor Babur's example to suit his own needs, he took a solemn vow and caused it to be announced by beat of drum throughout the city and countryside:

> I shall never again pollute any part of my body by taking alcohol or opium to my lips. I shall forever follow the path of righteousness laid down in the Holy Koran.

With this one move, he incidentally flung down a gauntlet at his besotted father and the drunkard Prince Parviz. As he had anticipated, the powerful Syets and other orthodox sections of the Islamic nobility responded to his vow with tremendous acclaim.

In order to dramatize the announcement, Shah Jahan once again followed Babur's example. On the morning before his army set out to the Deccan, he summoned all his commanders, right down to the junior ranks, to assemble on the *maidan* bordering the palace and the Jumna River. Here he had piled all the wine-drinking accessories from his palace. Gold and silver cups, bowls, flasks and flagons, worth a fortune, gleamed in the bright morning sunlight. His entire stock of priceless Persian and Moghul wines and other liquor was stacked in heaps alongside. Crows sailed slowly across the sky, cawing sadly as they eyed the glittering treasure. The assembled men watched in hushed silence as giant bare-chested Nubian slaves, wielding great sledgehammers, methodically broke up all the treasure, then cast the battered remains into the river.

When it was done, Shah Jahan strode forward and proclaimed his order of the day in stentorian tones:

'Most social evils spring from alcohol, which converts man into a devil. We of the imperial Moghul army are in duty bound to observe the moral codes of the Holy Koran, which demand total abstention from alcohol and other intoxicants. We are about to leave on a mission that may lead us to death. Each one of us therefore pledges that we will be true followers of the Prophet Mahomet in all our actions. Thus alone will we be assured of the success of our mission and of a place in Paradise if we die.'

The cheers that rent the air scared away the crows, soared to the heavens. With one voice, every single commander took the oath. 'Allah-u-Akbar! . . . Allah-u-Akbar! . . . God is great,' they bellowed.

Glittering swords were raised to the Creator; Moghul muskets rattled and artillery thundered their own royal salute. Shah Jahan was consumed with fierce elation. He had flung down the gauntlet. His message would be heard all the way to the imperial palace.

* * *

418

Preparing an army to take the field is no mean task. It not only involves assembling men, weapons, animals and materials from various supporting princes and nobles, some far removed from the assembly point, but also the logistics of supply and service, ammunition, transport, food, clothing, medical services and camp followers. Yet the situation was urgent, for Malik Ambar was reportedly planning to move towards Mandu, which was well north of Ahmad, the farthest he had been before the peace treaty. If Mandu were lost, a dagger would be pointing at the Empire's heartland.

Shah Jahan had worked round the clock with such astonishing speed that he had achieved the miracle of having his expeditionary force ready to move from Agra within twenty-nine days of receiving his orders. The army moved out at dawn the next day, through a light mist, led by a vanguard of five thousand cavalry ten abreast, pennants fluttering on gleaming lances, under General Prince Baz. Instead of being at the rear of the column, complete with all the paraphernalia of a luxurious camp life, as most rulers did when they went to war, Shah Jahan rode his black charger, unusually tall for an Arab, immediately behind the vanguard. He was accompanied only by his chief aide, the grizzled General Wahid. The milling crowds which had already packed the streets to witness the spectacle began shouting his name, 'Shah Jahan! . . . Shah Jahan!' He was undoubtedly their idol. Their thunderous acclaim would reach the palace as had the roar of artillery the day before and deliver its own message to the Emperor and Nur Jehan, confirming the start of a different war, undeclared, silent, grim.

He thought of Mumtaz Mahal and how the cheering would please her. He missed her already. Last night . . . He put the fond memories resolutely away from his conscious mind, locked his spirit with hers, resumed total awareness of his immediate surroundings and circumstances. His vision for whatever he had to do became clear again. It was the only way to retain sanity.

His remaining troops followed, thirty thousand trotting cavalry, fast-stepping infantry, mounted musketeers, bowmen and great plodding grey elephants. The artillery trundled in the rear just ahead of the rattling supply corps and camp follower wagons.

As he rode out of the city gates and headed south, the sky to his left turned rose-gold with the dawn. The sun, still beneath the dark-red horizon, shot three great rays of light upward. 'An omen! An omen!' the men shouted. An omen indeed, he silently rejoiced. The silver ribbon of the Jumna River heading towards the east, between its dark guard-of-honour of tall cypress trees, reminded him of his escape from kidnapping and death more than thirteen years before. Had that been in another lifetime? Had it happened to him? Surely a silver ribbon leading towards a rosy sky was yet another good omen.

Shah Jahan wanted to take General Ambar and the Deccanese by surprise. Moving faster than any Moghul army had done in recent history, they covered over three hundred miles in twenty days and encamped for the night on a great plain near Ujjain, a hundred miles north of Mandu. As usual after dinner with his senior commanders, Shah Jahan was alone in his tent with General Wahid when General Prince Baz was announced.

The man who strode in and saluted was a tall and slim aristocrat by birth and bearing. His shaven head beneath the plumed black leather helmet was held proudly erect. His ruddy face was cleanshaven. Haughty black slanty Mongolian eyes straddled a small nose that rose very little above the wide cheekbones and tight-lipped mouth. He was dressed in the black tunic, riding boots and baggy white trousers of the imperial cavalry.

Only an emergency could have brought the vanguard commander to him at this hour of the night. Shah Jahan could not avoid a spark of concern. 'Ah, sit down, general!' He indicated one of the settles opposite the plain white deal table at which he and General Wahid were seated. 'Have you dined yet?'

'Yes, thank you, Prince.' General Baz sank his lithe form on to the settle.

'Do remove your helmet,' Shah Jahan bade him. 'We can be informal at this hour.'

The general eased his helmet off and laid it on the ground beside him. In the light of the hanging lanterns, his bald head shone with sweat.

Shah Jahan leaned forward, elbows on the table. 'Now, your news.'

'We gave shelter to a group of pilgrims of our Muslim brotherhood returning home from Surat this evening.' The general had a soft, husky voice. 'They warned us that about ten thousand Deccanese troops, under a black general with crinkly hair, were making for Mandu.'

'Malik Ambar himself!' General Wahid exclaimed. 'At least he has not reached Mandu yet.'

Shah Jahan coolly appraised the situation, but his heart had begun to beat a shade faster. 'How far was he from Mandu at the time?' he inquired.

'The pilgrims assessed that he would reach Mandu about four days from now.' General Baz took a deep breath, eased slim shoulders beneath the black tunic. 'The black general need not be General Malik Ambar himself,' he ventured. 'Why would Ambar, who reportedly commands nearly fifty thousand men, lead an expedition of only ten thousand?'

'Warned of our approach, he plans a pre-emptive strike, so important that he will personally lead it,' Shah Jahan responded. 'Never dreaming that we would leave Agra so

421

soon and maintain such a tremendous speed, he was probably grouping normally until he had news of our advance. He will now hasten to the attack.' He paused, reflecting. 'H'mmm . . . His move is to strike a vital blow, essential to his strategy. Why not? Mandu is the southern gateway to our territories. If Ambar takes Mandu, it would not only be a tremendous set-back to our prestige, with grave effects on the morale of our people and soldiers, but would also help his efforts to capture Buran and Ahmad, both of which he has already besieged in order to drive us from the Deccan and our other southern territories.' He raised a cautionary finger. 'Such a situation would also bring all dissident neighbouring kingdoms to Ambar's cause, including Mewar again, and who knows what effects it will have on our eastern and northern territories.' He banged the table with his fist. 'That's it. We must relieve Mandu without delay at all costs.'

'Pray Allah, General Taqi has taken steps to hold Mandu,' General Baz growled. 'He must surely be aware of the enemy's approach by now.'

'You arrived with your aides?' Shah Jahan demanded.

'Yes, Prince.'

'Good. Send out a fast patrol to General Taqi,' Shah Jahan commanded. 'Give the patrol three days in which to reach him. He is to hold Mandu against Ambar's forces to the last man, if necessary. We shall be there with our entire cavalry vanguard to relieve him in four days.' He returned to General Wahid. 'Summon all the commanders immediately. That includes you, General Baz. The entire army moves at dawn tomorrow. The cavalry vanguard leaves two hours earlier, led by me.'

The problem of keeping a large force of five thousand cavalry moving at its highest speed is that the supply wagons cannot keep pace with cantering horses. Having estimated that, by using field rations, he could afford to have the rest of the army and supply train one day behind, Shah Jahan reached the outskirts of Mandu at the head of the cavalry vanguard on the fourth evening. Messengers from General Taqi confirmed that General Ambar had crossed the river that very morning and surrounded Mandu, but the three thousand Moghul defenders under the general had resolutely beaten back Ambar's first attempt to take the city.

The hill city of Mandu was located on the northern bank of the river, which formed its southern defence. Its main gates facing north, it was surrounded by red sandstone rampart walls, including turrets for defence and embrasures for cannon. General Ambar's main force, having crossed the river, would be encamped in an arc on the plain around the city, the bulk of his troops at the main gates to try to force them.

They were a little over ten miles from Mandu that evening, when Shah Jahan halted the column, established a field encampment and sent out reconnaissance patrols to try to establish enemy strength and dispositions. The reports he received by midnight confirmed his analysis of those dispositions. He thereupon issued orders for the attack on the Deccanese at dawn.

The plan he had evolved was a novel one. Two thousand of his cavalry would attack the main body of the enemy in arrowhead formation, the point slicing through the enemy lines to make for the main gate in order to link up with the besieged garrison. The base of the arrow would then circle pockets of the enemy on either flank and destroy them. Meanwhile repeated attacks by his remaining three thousand cavalrymen would keep the enemy flanks from turning.

Shah Jahan was excited by his plan. He would show his

detractors, especially Nur Jehan, that he could win military as well as political and diplomatic battles.

The pre-dawn air flowed smoothly past Shah Jahan's face as he rode his black charger, Samt II, at the head of his cavalry column towards the plain fronting Mandu. Through the clatter of hooves on the cobbled highway behind him, he heard the crowing of roosters in a little village they passed at an easy canter. Dim lights in the rear of the cottages beneath the ghostly outlines of tall trees he could not identify, told of wives preparing the morning meal of *chuppati* for husbands getting ready for a day's toil in the fields. Such peaceful occupations, through which he and five thousand men rode into battle, to danger and agony, terror and death. He abruptly closed that avenue of thought, deliberately evoked enjoyment of the creak of leather, the clinking of an occasional weapon, the familiar smell of horse-sweat, the sneeze of a mount and his oneness with those who rode with him in the common cause. *Jihad*, holy war, had been his order of the day.

The sky to the east was lightening, slow-turning the dark world of night into grey, when they hit the plain. The walls of the city loomed in the distance, pricked by an occasional light behind them. He could distinguish the black shapes of enemy wagons stretching on either side of the broad, straight highway. He noted with satisfaction the gap in between, more than sufficient for his cavalry arrow-point to pierce the enemy ranks and head for the city. He detected the movements of the great body of the enemy stretched across the plain.

Without pausing, he removed his lance from its socket, raised it high to signal his men. He couched the lance and dug his heels into his charger's flanks. The noble war-steed must have smelt the battle ahead. With a shrill whinny of rage, it took off like a bolt from a catapult. The cavalrymen were well trained for the attack. He sensed them surge behind him. The rapid drumming of hooves soon pounded into his body. His pre-battle fears vanished, his whole being sparkled with delirious excitement and he cried aloud, he knew not what, in mad exultation. *Battle is in my blood, war is my heritage*. The words were one with the thudding of his own charger's hooves.

They crashed into the gap before the enemy comprehended what was taking place. A group of foot soldiers tried to block their passage. Shah Jahan's wild shout of 'Allah-u-Akbar!' was echoed by the men behind him. Stooping low in the saddle, he shivered his lance on a giant Maratha. The man gawked, leaned forward, grasping the lance with both hands even as Shah Jahan let it go. Screaming aloud, Shah Jahan drew his sword and hurled his mount into the enemy mass. His horse began pounding with deadly forehooves at anyone who stood in his way. Men cowered sideways, only to be smashed by General Baz's and General Wahid's mounts. Tumultuous cries and screeches arose as the ruthless Moghul cavalrymen behind the tip of the attacking arrow, wheeled, cutting, chopping, to encircle the enemy flanks. The clash of metal, the thud of hooves, the screams and curses of men, the squealing of horses, rent the air. Thrust, withdraw, hack, cut, chop. Shah Jahan kept forcing his way through the enemy, but the barrier of men in front of him was becoming thicker. Through the clamour of battle and his own blood lust, a thought flashed. He had to find General Malik Ambar and kill him.

The entrance arch of the city gates appeared in a brief gap in the human wall. Screaming with triumph, Shah Jahan spurred his mount, striving to force a way through. Out of the corner of his eye, he saw that the battle had broken into little groups of men fighting to the death. Not so good, when he was heavily outnumbered. A wild thought of withdrawing, regrouping and attacking again was suddenly replaced by the red mist of determination. He would never yield ground. His sword arm had begun to ache from an hour of fighting, but he did not care. His two generals were still on either side of him. He began to distinguish enemy faces. Great bearded men, cleanshaven youths, bestial expressions, teeth bared with hatred, the enemy.

The shrill sound of trumpets streaked through the cacophony of battle. Artillery boomed. Cannon balls whistled and ploughed directly ahead of him. Piercing shrieks arose from wounded enemy.

Surely his main body could not have arrived? The human wall in front of him shuddered and gave. In a flash, he knew what had happened. The valiant General Taqi, barricaded in the city, had fired his cannon at the enemy and launched his cavalry through the city gates. Taken in front and rear, the enemy was fleeing towards the flanks, fodder for his own flanking cavalry movements.

Laughing madly with the certainty of victory, Shah Jahan plunged into the battle with the ferocity of his Mongol ancestors.

Immediately after the victory, Shah Jahan sent despatches by fast messenger to the Emperor in Agra, commending General Taqi for his resolute defence of Mandu and his 'singularly daring action to safeguard the frontiers of the Empire. The victory is due to the intercession of Allah on our side, but steps should be taken immediately to station at Mandu a force sufficiently strong to prevent future challenges by rebellious elements.'

Despite urgings of his senior commanders for consolidation, Shah Jahan spent only two days at Mandu, to give his army rest and to re-victual, then rode out of the city at the head of twenty thousand men. Heading south, he crossed the river and set a hot pace south-east for Buran, his double object being to prevent General Ambar's defeated forces from regrouping and to protect Buran from falling into enemy hands.

As he rode through the dawn, he recalled the warning General Khan, governor of the region, who had just ridden in from Buran, had given him the previous night. 'General Malik Ambar is reported to have seventy thousand dare-devils under his command. We should await reinforcements from Agra before advancing to take him on.'

'I have studied General Ambar's strategy through the years,' he had retorted. 'Never once has he massed his forces and risked them in a single battle. He is not a military gambler. He knows that if he loses one great battle, he is finished forever. If he does win, it would be at great cost, but the might of the imperial army would still be available to the Emperor. General Ambar understands that even if he wins such a battle, the war would not be ended.'

'You may be right,' General Baz had intervened thoughtfully. 'We have just received reports that roving bands of Deccanese have been heading for Buran and Ahmad. There does not appear to be any plan to consolidate their forces.'

'Meanwhile, we must ensure that those key cities are not taken,' Shah Jahan had responded. 'They will become our own strongpoints, from which we can hold territories, as we have traditionally done for over a century.'

Had he been right? If he had misjudged General Ambar, his entire army group might be annihilated and his own future would end. He remembered his ancestors. Moghuls had been victorious against overwhelming odds. He was a Moghul. He would prevail regardless.

Shah Jahan's advance elements reached Buran, about one hundred miles from Mandu, in ten days, just in time to prevent enemy encirclement of the city. He was elated that his judgment had been proved correct, especially as the relief of the city was accomplished without the firing of a single shot.

Rather than enjoy the luxury of the city's accommodation, Shah Jahan elected as always to remain in his simple tent in the encampment of the main body of his men on the outskirts. This had been established just north of the river that flowed beneath the city's southern rampart walls.

The night was hot, underlaid by tremendous humidity in the air. Shah Jahan had a thin film of sweat on his body as he sat with his generals around the table beneath the hanging lanterns. The acrid odour of burnt oil from a smoking lantern mingled with the scents of roast lamb and baked breads remaining from their meal.

All the men were in field uniforms, black tunics, baggy white trousers tucked into black riding boots, swords at the side. The governor, General Khan, sitting at Shah Jahan's right, was a stocky Pathan of about fifty-five, with enormously broad shoulders and a wide face streaked by a black moustache, his chubby cheeks glowing in the lamplight.

Seated on Shah Jahan's left, General Vickram was a lean, tall Rajput, well over six feet in height. Cleanshaven, he wore his gleaming black hair in a top-knot beneath a white turban. His piercing eyes and high-bridged nose gave him the appearance of an eagle.

'You were right to push on to Buran, despite our own best advice,' General Hassan stated. He was a diminutive Muslim, with pointed features, sharp black eyes and a trim moustache, seated directly across the table from Shah Jahan. 'We should continue with that strategy and proceed to Ahmad at our best speed.'

'I'll endorse that, Prince,' General Khan conceded. 'You were right to push on in spite of my protests.'

'Mm . . . I'm not so sure that it is a worthwhile risk,' Raja Bhim, seated on General Hassan's right, demurred. He was a burly Rajput of about forty, his heavy body and round face already running to fat. 'Mandu and Buran were different propositions. They are a part of the Empire's heartlands. From here on we are virtually in enemy territory. Our lines of supply and communication are lengthening, our home base is getting farther and farther away and we are slowly dissipating our forces.'

'I agree with all you have said, Raja, but I think your last point is the only vital one,' Shah Jahan responded slowly. He pushed back his settle, eased legs stiff from the day's hard riding. 'Remember, gentlemen, we are an army of twenty thousand now, having left ten thousand men at Mandu. We are opposed by seventy thousand seasoned fighters. The logic of numbers cannot be ignored, but we cannot wait for reinforcements from Agra either. I propose that we pause here to institute a massive drive to increase our strength locally. The *jagirdars* (wealthy landowners) in this region have had their lands confiscated by General Malik Ambar and his sultans. An immediate recruitment drive, with money, promises, bribes, should rapidly increase our strength by another thirty thousand men. Meanwhile, we shall also make overtures to Sultan Rahim to hold at bay the Shi-ite sultans who have given their support to General Malik Ambar, until we are ready to take on the general.'

'Wonderful!' General Khan exclaimed, an approving smile beneath his black moustache. 'We can scout the region, send fighting patrols out to keep the enemy off balance and also call for reinforcements from Agra.'

Shah Jahan felt a flash of anger. 'Never from Agra.' He pounded the table with his fist, then remembered. Caution before pride. 'We have been sent here by the Emperor with a mandate: Seek out and destroy the enemy. He gave us some of his best regiments for the task. Meanwhile, he has to keep his forces in Agra on the alert in case of trouble from the Persians, the Afghans and Pathans or from the east.' He calmed down. 'No, this is something we have to do on our own, with whatever resources we have and can make available from the region.'

'Sounds good to me,' Raja Bhim stated. 'You have always combined absolute daring with good sense. I commend your caution on this issue. I imagine you will take at least six months to achieve these objectives?' He raised inquiring black eyebrows.

Shah Jahan smiled. 'I thank you for your praise and take you up on it. This time I expect to combine both virtues.' He surveyed the men gathered around him grimly. 'Gentlemen, whatever time we take is lost to us and gained by the enemy.' He nodded firmly. 'I shall certainly give you enough time in which to achieve my objectives. We shall march against the enemy, neither in six months, nor in three, but two months from now. Otherwise, the monsoon will be on us too, bogging down our operations.'

The Rana Amar reined in his Scindhi bay on the bund of the small reservoir, turned to face the muddy pools of water, the skeletal black legs of a dead cow sticking up from one of them, accusingly pointing to heaven. Prince Chara drew his Arab alongside. The pre-noon sunlight beat relentlessly down on cracked earth, scorched almost black by the drought, and on the little fields beyond, parched yellow. Except for two vultures slow-sailing beneath a burnt blue sky, the only movement was the restless pawing of the Rana's horse, the only sound the murmur of their escort's quiet voices.

'The whole of India is dead and we are visitors from another planet,' the Rana remarked quietly. 'Look at those two walking corpses.' He gestured towards the side of the reservoir.

The two men had emerged from a hovel to stare incuriously at the visitors. They were emaciated, ribs showing on bare chests, skins wrinkled and burnt dark by the sun.

'India died when the Mongols invaded us centuries ago,' Prince Chara observed, wanting to make a point. His own belief was that there would always be the rich and the poor. It was not a question of someone's fate or *kharma*, but the law of cause and effect that governed all creation. Rich soil produced; desert soil was barren. It was as simple as that. Breast-beating and compassion were for the weak.

The scene before them proved his belief. The hovels around the reservoir had been put together, not built. Their walls were of brown mud, the roofs of dried straw. Tattered mats served as entrance doors. There were no windows. The people lived in such dire poverty and filth that they were too apathetic to improve their lot. They were like those emaciated cows, drooping listless in the shadows of the hovels.

'These people have lost all hope,' the Rana burst out. 'They have been abandoned by their gods.'

But first by their rulers, Prince Chara thought. When the sun goes down, they will sit in front of their homes without even the energy to drive away the flies that settle on their sores. 'They are now in the hands of moneylenders and tax-gatherers,' he said aloud. 'Mortgaged for genera-tions to come. That is why they have lost hope.'

The Rana snorted. 'Our tax-levies have always been fair and reasonable.'

'We never know what the tax-collectors impose on these people,' Prince Chara retorted. 'On the other hand, every-one in the kingdom contributed to the war of liberation which we lost and most of the privation has been caused by the Moghul barbarians who systematically destroyed our land.' He thought the moment opportune to speak up, risking his father's wrath.

To his surprise, the Rana remained silent, staring at the two men who had squatted at their entrance. 'These are *our* people, *our* family,' he muttered.

Cow shit, Prince Chara thought savagely. They are the aliens, the creatures from another planet. 'The only way we can improve their lot is by shaking off the shackles of Moghul taxes which together with our taxes create a double burden on them,' he remarked.

'A hopeless task.'

'We can keep trying.'

The Rana swivelled sideways in the saddle, stared piercingly at him. 'You are planning something,' he asserted. 'What is it?'

'You know me so well, Sire,' Prince Chara stated. Not really, but I want you to think that! 'I have sent a secret messenger to Shah Abbas, ruler of the Persian kingdoms.'

'You what?'

'You heard me, Sire. Hear me out, please. With Shah Jahan in the Deccan and Prince Parviz in distant Bihar, the only sons of the Emperor capable of defending the Moghul Empire are far removed from the capital, at its southern and eastern outposts. I have suggested to Shah Abbas that, with a dying Emperor at the centre of things, he will never have a more splendid opportunity to expand his dominions. If he takes Kandhar and Kabul, we in Mewar will be ready to rise again, and when we do, this time all the Rajputs of Rajasthan will unite with us.'

'You believe that?'

'Not necessarily, but it seemed a nice sentiment to express to Shah Abbas.'

'We have only now recovered from the effects of the Moghuls' savagery. We shall never again permit war in this kingdom as long as we live.'

Urine from Prince Chara's horse began splattering on the bare brown earth. Piss on you too, my father, Prince Chara thought. Nur Jehan believes she is making use of me, but she is really my tool now. If the Emperor is besieged on three sides, by his two sons and Shah Abbas, and if the two sons are preoccupied with revolts in the Deccan and Bengal, I shall be where I wanted to be years ago, when that fool Prince Husrau bungled my spectacular planning. This time, no one is going to stop me. Since you intend trying, you have not long to live.

Chapter 26

By the time Shah Jahan relieved the City of Buran, Prince Chara had learned of the victory at Mandu and decided to visit Agra. He sent a message to Nur Jehan, now at the zenith of her power, requesting an audience. His confidence that she would welcome him was substantiated when she invited him and his escort to stay in the Emperor's palace. However, when he entered Nur Jehan's audience chamber that Friday afternoon, he was surprised to find Sir Thomas Roe already seated beside the blue waters of the pool.

The entire scene, in front of the green velvet curtains, drawn except for Nur Jehan's peephole slit between them, was so familiar, it was like the re-run of a play, except that today the stage set was different. Spring sunshine beat fiercely on the marble courtyard outside and querulous murmurs emerged from the cages of the love-birds, complaining against the heat. Slow-moving *punkahs* overhead cooled the chamber, but the sallow-faced English ambassador occasionally mopped his forehead with a large cream silk handkerchief. Sir Thomas's grand clothes were hardly suited to the Indian climate, when even his own cotton garments, the black tunic and white *jodhpurs* he always wore, did not keep Prince Chara cool.

As was proper by virtue of her position, though it conflicted with her female estate, Nur Jehan opened the

433

discussion. 'Gentlemen, we would first like to assure you once again of the total privacy of this chamber and the completely confidential nature of our discussions.' The mellow-gold voice floating through the slit in the curtains had a new authority, and once again Prince Chara wished that he could see the woman who had captivated an Emperor with her beauty. His interest in her was purely objective, not as a sex symbol but as an ally who might one day become an antagonist. 'You have undoubtedly heard of the quick success of Shah Jahan at Mandu and his rising popularity in consequence.' Had a slightly strident note entered her voice? 'This time, he seems to have proved himself as a soldier and a general, to add to his past successes as a politician and diplomat. We are convinced that he personally led his men and joined the fray deliberately, in order to capture the popular imagination.' She paused. 'We have informed the Emperor of the success of our army at Mandu, but have given full credit for the victory to General Taqi. The Emperor is seriously ill and should be spared news that might cause him the apprehension of suspecting that we may have in the wings one who might attempt to usurp the throne.'

'You have so much wisdom, Madam,' Prince Chara commented appreciatively. Or is it cunning? I'm glad I'm on your side, though you would make such a formidable opponent that it would be sheer intellectual pleasure to challenge you and win. 'I can confirm that Shah Jahan is the hero of the hour in all the Rajput kingdoms and those sultanates which border it.' This was not strictly true, but he saw no harm in inflaming Nur Jehan's fear of his life's adversary whose successes he readily but privately conceded were bitter gall to him.

'Apart from the danger he poses to the succession, the young man will be personally more insufferable than ever, if he returns victorious,' Sir Thomas interposed smoothly.

He tucked his handkerchief back into the white lace at the wrist of his doublet. Trim-bearded chin out-thrust, he stroked it reflectively, the fish-eyes cold and chill. 'You should consider taking immediate measures to stop his popularity.'

'What measures can one take to stop a runaway horse?' the voice behind the curtain inquired. 'Shah Jahan commenced his campaign with a shrewd move that immediately belittled us and made him a Muslim hero. We refer to his stirring performance on the banks of the Jumna, which harnessed religious energy, especially Muslim, to his purpose.'

'Mm . . . m . . . He certainly made a Mahomet's mountain out of the molehill of an oath, complete with cannon firing, muskets rattling and thousands of voices swearing renunciation. All that the event lacked were celestial trumpets and angel choirs. Shah Jahan's appeal especially touched women, who have an unfortunate tendency to worship anything assuring them of sobriety and restraint in men.' The saturnine cheeks creased with good-humoured malice. 'Such extravagances of adoration come as naturally to women as sexual and alcoholic excesses do to men.'

'As I have observed it, women fear the *depths* of frailty in men, *not* their excesses.' If Prince Chara's experience of women was more objective than subjective, he remained convinced that this made him a better observer than if he had any involvement with them. As for his sexual experiences with men, ah, that was another matter, for he took his pleasure of them without risk of emotional involvement. 'A woman will more readily forgive her man nights of drinking with friends and carousing with loose women, none of which pose any serious threat to her, than even a mild love affair. Don't you think so, Sir Thomas?'

'You are right. A woman's belief in fidelity is confined to what she does not know. She assumes that if her lover is being unfaithful, she will discover it through gossip, or through the diminution of his sexual ardour, while if it is her husband, his performance on the marital bed would have become a trifle . . . er . . . absent-minded.'

'All of which is very entertaining, gentlemen,' Nur Jehan's normally mellow voice had a definite edge to it, 'but does not solve the problem at hand. We are well aware that Shah Jahan has acquired tremendous popularity with women of all races, because he is a faithful husband perched on the pillar of morality. The question is, how do we counter this?'

Prince Chara felt a flash of irritation at Nur Jehan's tone. 'Topple him off his perch, Madam, by having him fornicate with a sacred white cow in the public square of Agra palace,' he drawled. 'That would offend people of every religion and persuasion. Hindus, to whom the white cow is sacred, would be outraged. Women, who would rather Shah Jahan seduced them if he *had* to stray from the marital bed, would scream for his head since they could not have his body. Muslims would be disappointed that he failed to degrade himself truly by selecting a white sow instead. And everyone who publicly berates perversion because of secret suspicions that perversions link the human race far more than righteousness, would want him crucified for exposing the truth.'

The exclamation of impatience from behind the green velvet curtains was barely stifled. You are so scared about the entire situation that you have lost your customary sense of humour, Prince Chara reflected. And why not? Your husband is dying. It is reported that your father too is mortally ill. Your Cabinet is crumbling and your entire future is threatened by the powerful Shah Jahan, while all you have on your side is the imbecile Prince Shahriyar, now officially betrothed to your daughter. Since the ideal-ism of your brother the Prime Minister makes him a doubtful ally in any power-grab, you need Sir Thomas and me.

The ambassador revealed yellow teeth in a smile of appreciation at the reminder to Nur Jehan that neither of them were pupils in her schoolroom. 'What about the Buddhists?' Sir Thomas urged Prince Chara, deliberately ignoring the Empress's impatience.

'Buddhism is neither a religion nor a philosophy, Sir Thomas. It is a manner of living, so self-centred that it does not even require the existence of a god or gods. It advocates compassion merely to add to the credit side of a personal ledger of good and bad deeds in the accounts of a moral *baniar* (moneylender) they call the *kharmic* cycle. A Buddhist's response to the seduction of a sacred white cow in the public square of the Agra palace might well be to preach Right Conduct to the cow!'

'Gentlemen, we beg you to give this matter your serious consideration.' The chastened tone of Nur Jehan's voice indicated that she had got their message. 'How can we remove Shah Jahan from his pedestal?'

'Firstly, create a situation which will make him abhorrent to the public,' Prince Chara responded.

'How? He is so far away.'

'You can reach him, Madam, in consequence of the very shrewd move you made by insisting that he take Prince Husrau with him on this expedition.' He went on to explain what she might do and was rewarded by the hiss of her indrawn breath and Sir Thomas's yellow-toothed smile of approval.

'Who will have it accomplished?' Nur Jehan's quick acceptance made Prince Chara realize that his was not an alternative she had already considered.

'*I* can arrange it,' Prince Chara replied airily. He examined his fingernails as if what he had just proposed was commonplace.

'What is your price for this favour, Prince Chara?' she inquired bluntly.

Such poor taste for a woman of supreme cunning and intelligence! Why? It dawned on Prince Chara that Nur Jehan wanted him to commit himself in the presence of Sir Thomas Roe, so that she could hold him to their bargain and no more. 'Madam, we are not trading housewares,' he declared, without conviction. 'My sole motive is the public interest, my reward the improved welfare of the Empire.' He paused, stared through the slit in the curtains, knew with a thrill that he had invisibly connected with her glance. 'Of course, it is just possible that once you achieve supreme power, you may wish to extend the basic rule of all diplomacy . . . um . . . reciprocity, to Mewar, by ignoring certain events that might be in its . . . um . . . public interest!'

Catching Sir Thomas's quiet chuckle, he directed a quick glance towards the ambassador and saw the thin lips frame the word 'bastard'. He chuckled in agreement.

Shah Jahan had spent a sleepless night with the decision to consolidate for the next two months before pursuing General Ambar. There must be a flaw in the plan. By the time he awoke the next morning he had discovered the loophole. He had General Wahid summon his commanders for a 2 P.M. conference, to include Prince Husrau, who had spent most of his time thus far reading the Koran and other holy books in his own tent. This had suited Shah Jahan, for while extending all the rights and privileges of rank to his older brother, he had no intention of giving Prince Husrau undue exposure to the armed forces of the people, still less credit for successes. Yet he broke bread alone with Prince Husrau at least once a day and had timed the staff conference for the end of the noon meal.

The years had sat heavily on Prince Husrau mainly

because of the sedentary life he had elected to pursue. Watching him, as he wiped his lips with a white napkin, Shah Jahan could not help but think back on the elephant battle that morning years ago. He realized with wonder that it was perhaps the closest his brother had come to wearing the imperial crown, and the outcome had not been in his hands but dependent on the fighting ability of his elephant! How sad. He, Shah Jahan, would never let this happen to him.

Now, Prince Husrau's once lean, tall figure was girded by a paunch; the tight Rajput features had grown so flaccid that the high nose no longer looked imperious but had become merely an adjunct to the face. The left eye, blinded by their father for the second revolt attempt, had healed, but it had turned pale blue and fixed, giving the good brown eye the effect of a squint. Here was no contender for an imperial crown, but a man reduced by circumstances of his own creation and the mistakes of his youth. Why then had Nur Jehan insisted that Prince Husrau participate in this campaign? The question had hammered at Shah Jahan's brain a hundred times without any answer other than a warning of danger.

Another question had also intruded. Why had Nur Jehan not adopted Prince Husrau as the heir? One look at the inherent dignity of the man, which neither time nor circumstance had been able to diminish, gave Shah Jahan the answer. If Prince Husrau ever succeeded, he would never be anyone's puppet.

While the attendant busily cleared away the dishes, goblets and linen, Shah Jahan allowed his mind to drift to Mumtaz Mahal. Despite the recent birth of a third son, Prince Aurang Zeb, she had never failed to send him her daily letters, his favourite Persian sweetmeats, presents, by every military post from Agra. He in turn had responded with the Persian love poems he wrote every morning, so that she would know that his first waking thought was of her. She was his inspiration to virtue, the pursuit of his career and to manhood. In contrast, his brother, who had not even the comfort of a good woman in his life, was beginning to look like a eunuch.

'Thank you for briefing me yesterday as to your proposed strategy,' Prince Husrau said when the attendants had left and they were alone together again. 'You have been more than kind to me on this expedition.' He mopped his brow with a handkerchief, glanced through the open tent flap at the glaring sunlight, then directed his squinty gaze at Shah Jahan. 'I presume you have an important change of plan in mind?'

'Why do you think so?'

Prince Husrau smiled faintly. 'Listen to the sounds outside,' he suggested.

What kind of a reply was that? 'Silence?' Shah Jahan inquired.

'Precisely. The entire camp is silent, except for the vibrations of men and animals. It is the siesta hour. You would not have summoned your generals to a meeting at this time if it were not to announce an urgent change of plan.'

Shah Jahan gave his brother an admiring glance. Behind the slovenly figure, the brain inherited from Moghul ancestors was still sharp. What a pity he and Prince Husrau were not close, like brothers in normal families. Together, they could have conquered the world. But with whom as the leader? The question that always tore apart brothers of the ruling classes, especially in imperial families! Rulers bestowed the seeds of strength and ambition, ruthlessness and the lust for power on their offspring, regardless of seniority of birth. Rivalry between brothers was therefore inevitable and where it did not exist inherently, it was fomented by others of ambition who wished to make tools of potential heirs. He and his brother had never discussed the events of the night in the Lahore palace when Shah Jahan had placed him under house arrest, but he knew that Prince Husrau held him responsible in part for his blinding and downfall and the horrible punishments inflicted by the Emperor Jehangir on the ringleaders of that plot. How else could it be when, at times, Shah Jahan himself felt the weight of that responsibility on his conscience? 'A very astute conclusion,' he responded.

'Will you share your plan with me before the others arrive? I would like that.'

'Certainly.' Shah Jahan paused, scratched his moustache reflectively. 'I knew that there was something wrong with our strategy before I went to bed last night.' He shifted his gaze briefly to his rolled pallet on the grass at the side of the tent. 'The flaw hit me just before I got up this morning. By merely defending our forts and carrying on a diplomatic offensive to build up our forces, we would be surrendering the initiative to General Ambar, the greatest master of guerilla warfare. The answer to a guerilla is to keep him off balance all the time, whatever the cost. The object of this afternoon's staff conference is to work out strikes for that purpose.'

'I rather saw the flaw myself when you explained your strategic plan to me yesterday.'

'You did?'

'Is it not obvious?'

'Why did you not tell me then?'

Prince Husrau's smile was apologetic. 'I suppose I have grown more accustomed to listening than to speaking these past years. Also, I believe I am exclusively a thinker, not a doer like you. I want you to succeed on your own.'

Was his brother trying to give him a message? Most doers tend to be so accelerated by the momentum of their own achievements that they go over the cliff's edge of disaster before they can pull back.

'The Empire is in grave danger.' Prince Husrau's quiet voice broke in on his musing. 'Although I am the legal heir to the throne, I could never rule effectively. You and you alone can save all that our ancestors built and bring peace and harmony to our people. I shall do everything in my power to help you.'

Shah Jahan stared at his brother in amazement. 'You see the danger?'

Prince Husrau's smile was sad. 'How could even a blind man be blind to it? Our father is dying. The Empress is an evil, conniving woman. Why else would she send Prince Parviz to the distant east, you down south, with me to accompany you, than to remove all the possible heirs as far away from Agra as possible so she can name the successor when the Emperor dies?'

'You have thought all this out?'

'I told you I am a thinker, not a doer. And I have all the time in the world to think.'

On the instant, Shah Jahan knew that Prince Husrau spoke truly. He had abandoned all thought of becoming Emperor. The two of them could now go forward together.

Kindliness broke through the veils of his eyes for the first time ever with his brother, was met by a look of surprise in the single brown eye, then shock, quickly replaced by a curious vulnerability. Impulsively he reached out a hand across the table. Staring at him hypnotized, Prince Husrau made no move.

Do not deny me this moment of grace, my brother, flesh of my flesh, Shah Jahan silently implored.

But how could the years of bitterness be flung aside in the flash of an impulsive moment? Shah Jahan looked down at his hand lying cold on the table. It seemed so lonely there, detached from his person. No, not detached, merely the extension of the aloneness, the chill loneliness he had known all his life until he married Mumtaz Mahal.

Shah Jahan sighed heavily, nostrils dilating, closed his eyes. His chest felt as if it would burst. 'I'm sorry,' he muttered. He did not know for what. He began slowly withdrawing his hand.

He heard a stifled sob. His hand was gripped in two warm hands, so fiercely it hurt. He opened downcast eyes, noted with wonder the strong black hairs on the back of his brother's hands. He slowly lifted his gaze. Tears had formed in both Prince Husrau's eyes.

I helped blind that eye and now it weeps for me. He gulped, fighting back his own tears.

'Together at last,' Prince Husrau said huskily. 'There is no competition, therefore no cause for dissension. The curse of Moghul sons, our legacy, is that we can never be brothers. I am glad you made the first move. I have been ready for it, but could not take the initiative, because you always seemed so distant.' His smile was sad. 'And after all, having everything, why would you need a half-blind brother?'

For once, Shah Jahan was at a loss for words. And if he had them, would not have been able to speak without breaking down.

A sharp command from outside announced the arrival of the generals. Shah Jahan and Prince Husrau nodded at each other, drew their hands apart.

But the bond remained.

'Just so that you are the first to know this time,' Shah Jahan stated quietly, controlling his voice with a great effort, 'I plan a series of guerilla assaults, feints, withdrawals and counter-attacks on General Ambar's forces to divide them and compel him to keep on the run. This will include major cities. The command decision has been taken by me. This afternoon's conference will give teeth to that decision.'

'Having kept General Ambar on the run, do you intend drawing him out into open battle when we are up to strength?'

'I would if I could, but that would be an exercise in futility.' Shah Jahan could not keep a note of savagery from his voice. 'The only way to win is to wear him down. This must be done speedily.' He was suddenly filled with an indefinable sense of urgency. 'The time is short, both here, with the mission at hand, and in Agra.'

Prince Husrau nodded slowly. 'I agree,' he replied softly. 'And I shall do anything you ask to help you return to Agra in time.'

Two months later, Shah Jahan's ranks had swelled to sixty thousand, from regional recruitment alone. Meanwhile, his growing strength had caused support for the Moghul Empire to spread even in the Deccan, with a corresponding drop in the rebel's alliances. After ten days of intensive planning, Shah Jahan launched a two-pronged offensive of twenty thousand men, commanded by General Khan and Raja Bhim, against Daul and Ahmad, while he remained with the main body of his forces at Buran.

One night, thirty days later, he received word that both offensives were being beaten back by great concentrations of Deccanese daredevils, especially the deadly Marathas, through a combination of direct attacks and guerilla tactics. He immediately sent for General Wahid, Prince Husrau and General Taqi to join him in his tent.

Flying ants were sizzling against lanterns when the conference began. The camp was hushed, except for the sentries' call, 'Ten o'clock and all's well!' ringing through the warm night. The men looked tense.

'You have heard the news?' Shah Jahan inquired when they were seated.

'Yes, Prince,' said General Taqi. The others nodded

tersely. 'The situation is serious. Both our columns have begun withdrawing.'

Shah Jahan laughed. He was rewarded by the looks of surprise on the faces of all three men. 'It is what I intended,' he replied easily. 'Both our columns were sufficiently strong to produce strong responses from General Ambar's forces. Needing to restore his credibility, he has taken the bait.'

'You planned all this?' The incredulity in General Taqi's voice pleased Shah Jahan. 'Brilliant! So having drawn his best troops out, his teeth as it were . . .'

'You and I shall proceed to demolish the body,' Shah Jahan concluded.

Prince Husrau rapped the table in applause. 'Well conceived indeed,' he declared.

General Wahid shook his head, amazed. 'What will we do now, Prince?'

'General Taqi and I, each with fifteen thousand men, shall force-march for Berar and Kandesh tomorrow. Having conquered these two rebel sub-kingdoms, we shall not hold our men back. We shall give these rebels a taste of our performance in Mewar, but this time our loot-hungry men will be able to satisfy their needs to the full.' His eyes went hard with determination, his jaw set. 'We shall bring General Ambar to his knees before the year's end.'

It was past midnight before they worked out the plan of advance and intercommunication between the two forces. General Taqi retired to brief his commanders and formulate their own plans, General Wahid to do the same with Shah Jahan's contingent.

Prince Husrau lingered in the tent. 'I would like to accompany you,' he stated when they were alone, glanced earnestly with his single eye at Shah Jahan. 'But I would only be in the way of a fast-moving column. So may I remain behind in Buran?'

'I had hoped that you would accompany me, brother.'

Shah Jahan could not keep the disappointment from his voice. Since the barriers between them had been removed he had spent every possible moment with Prince Husrau. 'But I shall honour your wishes.'

'I want to go with you more than anything else I desire at this moment,' Prince Husrau countered quietly. The single brown eye roved around Shah Jahan's face, taking in every detail. 'How is it that we both have the same Moghul father and two mothers, both Rajput, but you look a Moghul and I a Rajput?' His tone grew pensive. 'Were these things determined at birth, at conception, or earlier, so that you could become the Moghul Emperor of destiny and I . . . and I . . .' he faltered, the words came out in a whisper, 'the Rajput victim of fate?'

Shah Jahan's throat began to ache; his chest felt the weight of the years of his brother's desperation and desolateness. He could not bring himself to speak.

'No matter the cause,' Prince Husrau concluded gently. 'The effect is that each of us marches to the beat of a different drum. So you must lead your cavalry tomorrow and I shall remain in Buran.'

'You can live in the Buran palace, safe within the city walls.' Shah Jahan managed to bring the words out with an effort.

'Will you do me a favour?'

'Anything.' Shah Jahan's voice was hoarse.

'Leave this tent here and let me occupy it until you return.'

Shah Jahan choked. He did not need to ask the reason for his brother's request. Battle he challenged, love always overcame him. He nodded. 'We do not intend dismantling the camp, so you will be safe here with the skeleton force.'

'Good.' Prince Husrau rose to his feet. 'Now I am satisfied.' He held out his arms.

Sending his settle tumbling to the ground with one

backward movement of his legs, Shah Jahan rushed past the deal table and was clasped in the first embrace he had ever known from a member of his father's family.

Chapter 27

In his tent near Kandesh, Shah Jahan was jubilant that night. 'Our two-pronged drive to Berar and Kandesh has had a triple effect,' he declared, as General Wahid entered. 'First, it has compelled General Ambar to withdraw troops from Daul and Ahmad, relieving the pressure on General Khan and Raja Bhim, who have now regained the initiative. Second, it pulled General Ambar into direct conflict with us and we have won every skirmish along the way. Third, our policy of devastating Berar and Kandesh, which General Ambar has always claimed to be Deccanese and not Moghul, has turned the people against the saviour who could not protect them. General Malik Ambar must by now be off balance and unnerved.'

'So unnerved, Prince, that he has sent emissaries to us seeking peace,' General Wahid responded, a slow smile stretching the scar on his rugged features. 'They have just arrived.'

Shah Jahan's heart leapt, but he kept his voice cool. 'Sooner than I thought. Where are the emissaries? How many are they?'

'Three sultans and their escort, Prince. I had a tent placed at the disposal of the sultans and arranged food and accommodation for their escort. I took the liberty of advising them that you will see them sometime tomorrow, when you can spare a few minutes from your busy schedule!'

'Good man.' He paused, grinning. 'A longer period of looting enemy territory will not harm the pockets of our troops either!'

'And further destroy General Ambar's reputation as the lord protector.'

'Did the sultans mention any of the terms of surrender?'

'They are anxious to talk. They say they will cede all Moghul territory they have seized since the Emperor Akbar's death.'

'That is all?'

'That is all, Prince.'

A snort escaped Shah Jahan. He thought rapidly. 'Then I shall not even see the delegation,' he asserted. 'Send them packing back to their master first thing in the morning with a message from Raja Vickram saying that he dare not even present such presumptuous proposals to me. We are poised for total victory. We shall require General Ambar also to cede Ahmad, repay all costs of our campaigns against him and furnish an annual tribute, the amount of this tribute to be the only point of negotiation.'

General Wahid's eyes gleamed. 'Your command is my wish,' he stated with an ironic smile.

'Oh, by the way, please also send word of this development to Prince Husrau in the Buran camp.' Shah Jahan's eyes softened. 'And have a messenger ready to take a letter from me to Agra, to my wife.'

Prince Husrau sat on one of the settles in Shah Jahan's tent outside Buran. It gave him pleasure to reread the despatch, which he had received late that evening, from Shah Jahan in Kandesh. Now it was midnight. The camp was still as the grave. Manned by a skeleton force, the usual stirrings of the field were absent. The scent of the vegetable gruel he had eaten still clung to the warm air. He glanced sideways at the pallet bed laid out for him. Though he had been used all his life to the comforts of silken cushions and sheets, he had found more peace on this pallet than in any palace bedchamber. It is all in the head and the heart, he reflected.

Filled with quiet joy at the success of Shah Jahan's mission, he made an entry in the diary he had been keeping since his brother's departure. When the feelings of jealousy, envy, competitiveness, which had been his companions through the years, vanished, he had found peace. The night he embraced his brother had brought him a great calm, and being in this tent somehow gave him comfort and a feeling of Shah Jahan's solid strength. He had elected to stay in it on an impulse, believing it would give him the sense of family he had never experienced in his life. And he had found it. The loneliness had vanished. The blindness of the soul searching vainly for some gift of sight, had been replaced by certainty. He was part of the earth, part of life again. He found quiet joy in writing of it.

He sensed rather than saw or heard the movement. Before he could turn round a large wrist pressed against his larynx, the fingers grasping the forearm of the other arm, the palm of which clamped against the back of his head. His head was in a vice. He could not move or shout. Then his larynx shattered. He rose reflexively, was brought back on to the seat, choking. His eyes began to bulge. The wrist pulled back harder. The pressure on his throat was fearful. His senses reeled. Black spots danced in circles around his blinded eyes. His sphincter released. The smell of his faeces assailed him as if from a distance.

Suddenly, he was lifted like a child. Two sledge-hammer blows thudded against each kidney. Blood and urine spurted through his penis.

'Be careful,' a hoarse voice warned. 'This must look like murder by someone trying to make it seem from natural causes.'

Prince Husrau's last thoughts came from a miraculously clear brain. My poor brother, Shah Jahan. They will blame him for my murder, and I am the only witness of his innocence and his love for me. The thoughts merged into his death rattle.

The body was laid out in a gold-plated casket which had been placed on the white dealwood table in his tent outside Buran. The magnificent casket was incongruous, almost obscene, in that setting, the white satin lining trying tiredly to glisten beneath the rusted glow of two hanging lanterns. The encampment was still as the grave, everyone in it hushed by his tragedy.

His tragedy? What about his brother, Prince Husrau, lying stiff beneath his gaze, the closed eyelids hiding the one blind eye and the squint of the other? He would never see those eyes again. Was Prince Husrau's death tragic? Any more than his life? Or had he finally triumphed in death?

Why had Prince Husrau's chief aide laid the body out here instead of in the Buran palace, where it belonged? Shah Jahan immediately knew the answer. Prince Husrau had shared with the man his intention of greeting his younger brother, when he returned victorious, in this very tent where they had discovered their love for each other. Had that been a discovery or had the love been newly born that night? . . .

I am here to greet you, in the very place where I first embraced you and the cells of our bodies recognized each other as family, clung to each other and were reborn.

He had returned victorious, but there would be no embrace. Dimly he perceived that this was life. Oddly enough, this perception had started with his grandfather's death and some knowledge of it had haunted him ever since.

Fast messengers had brought news of Prince Husrau's death to him on the field, on the very day that the emissaries of General Ambar and Prince Adil had accepted his terms for the surrender. He had rushed back to Buran, accompanied by General Wahid and a small escort.

He was thankful that he had been left alone with the corpse. The corpse! What a word to use for what had once been a living, breathing human being!

While recognizing that the questions and the philosophizing were Nature's defence against the stark tragedy of seeing this . . . corpse . . . all laid out in cloth-of-gold tunic and baggy pantaloons, he indulged in them with sad hopelessness. He had seen corpses strewn on the field, men who served under him, his friends and the no longer to be feared enemy. Why would this one corpse torment him, its full impact still to come?

His brother had not died on the field, but on his pallet bed, splattered with his own urine, blood and faeces. Dear Allah, what a stinking death! To end a stinking life? All those years, every year with its months, weeks, days, hours, minutes, seconds of anguish and despair. Why did some lives have to be so tragic?

Whatever the answers, Almighty Allah take my brother's soul to Thee in Paradise.

His mouth was dry, his throat ached, his chest was fit to burst. Still without tears, he bent and kissed the cold, hard forehead.

Did the eyelids open and the blind eye give him a mocking glance? Could it see, through dead lids, into his own soul, see the times when he had known he would even destroy his brother to reach the throne? Stifling a sob, he backed away.

As he strode from the tent into the darkness, General Wahid fell into step beside him. 'We shall need to send a despatch giving news of Prince Husrau's death to the Emperor,' he stated.

'Have my secretary prepare a scroll despatch which I shall sign and seal,' he directed. Then added bitterly, 'Receiving it on the heels of my report of total victory in the Deccan ought to please both him and the Empress. They might even regard it as one of their luckiest days!'

'What shall we state as the cause of Prince Husrau's death?'

Shah Jahan paused in his stride, then replied, unthinking, 'A severe colic, I suppose.'

Chapter 28

Salima Begum's summons was delivered to Mumtaz Mahal in person by the Begum's Chief Eunuch. As she had received Shah Jahan's letter from Buran, Mumtaz Mahal was aware of General Ambar's surrender and Prince Husrau's death and connected the summons with the news. But why would the Begum, who had a reputation for haughty aloofness, wish to see her? The best way to find out was to answer the summons! She was to be escorted by palanquin to the imperial *harem* on Friday morning. With her husband away in the Deccan and Ghiyas Beg seriously ill in his mansion, the Nur Jehan Cabinet no longer met.

Mumtaz Mahal selected a white satin *kurtha* and pantaloons, with pearls as her only ornament. Having never visited the imperial palace before, she was overwhelmed by its splendour, but not awed. None of it was to her taste. Heavy guards crowded the *harem* walls, richly clad eunuchs in shiny jewelled robes and gleaming turbans of different coloured silks and satin minced around with obvious self-importance. Silent Uzbegs, the giant female sentries, lined the wide pink marble corridors, standing still as the huge interspersed ebony and ivory stands on which fabulous gold ornaments of intricate design glittered. It was a gigantic gilded cage, ostentatious and therefore vulgar in Mumtaz Mahal's eyes. She wished she was at home with her four children.

Salima Begum's reception chamber was elegant by contrast. To her surprise, the Begum was alone, seated on a gold-upholstered divan at the far end of the room. Slim and still as she was, the splashing of the fountain in the blue-tiled pool was, to Mumtaz Mahal's perception, an affront to her dignity. The camphor scent from the gold incense braziers created the appropriate background for this perfectly painted statue, which belonged in the silence of a temple.

The doors clicked shut behind her and she moved close enough to the divan to make obeisance and kiss the gnarled hand, heavily bejewelled with rings. Only then did Mumtaz Mahal realize how old the Begum was. Not even the heavy make-up paste could hold up the wrinkles of the perfectly oval face; but the green eyes, sharp as pointed emeralds, warned of vitality and an active brain.

'Sit down, Princess.' The gnarled hand was gracefully waved in the direction of a gold-cushioned settle beyond the filigreed ivory and gold table fronting the divan.

Mumtaz Mahal sat primly down, knees together, hands on her lap, the right lightly across the left palm, as she had been taught. For all her occasional rebellion against constituted authority, she always had an instinctive respect for dignified conduct. Her heart began beating a little faster.

'Four children have left no mark on you.' The Begum's voice was grainy with age. Her white-haired head, beautifully coiffed, trembled slightly on the scrawny neck, circled with diamond throatlets which seemed to be supporting that head. Mumtaz Mahal could tell that the Begum was holding together her life as she did her body, simply by indomitable will. When she let go that will, she would fall apart one day, soon, but the remains would still be imperial. 'It won't be long now.' Uncannily, the Begum had picked up her thoughts. No wonder she had been a power in the land for over seventy years. 'But we were like you once.' A smile creased the painted lips. 'In another lifetime. One final duty in this life.'

'Beauty such as yours comes not from physical attributes, Your Majesty.' The words tumbled out of Mumtaz Mahal involuntarily. 'Emerging from the soul, which is timeless, it is eternal as the sun giving light to the earth, brightening the dust of the body for a brief while.'

'Ah, you are a poetess.' The Begum seemed pleased. 'We were seventy-four on our last three birthdays, the last thirteen to be mathematically exact. Mathematics is important in life, but we have forgotten why, except that our brethren the Arabs invented it . . . and then forgot why too!'

A trill of laughter escaped Mumtaz Mahal. This lady was a sparkling jewel.

'We like the way you laugh. One can always tell the nature of others from the way they laugh. If they do not laugh freely, they either have no sense of humour or are too constrained. The titterers are shallow, the bellowers vulgar. But a good laugh,' the green eyes twinkled, 'emerges from the soul.'

Mumtaz laughed out loud again. What a delightful person, quite contrary to her reputation as an austere autocrat, and yet obviously not someone to be defied or crossed.

'You must wonder why we sent for you and why we desired to converse with you alone.' The Begum came to the point abruptly. 'Word of this meeting will have already reached the right quarters, meaning of course the wrong people. We have let it be known that, being in the hope of imminent death, we wished to speak to the beloved spouse of the prince whom our late beloved Emperor Akbar,' the grainy, faltering voice would have broken in someone of less strength and breeding, 'loved best of all, since it is likely that we shall never see that prince again.' She chuckled. 'A gesture to sentiment, which is the truth. It will leave people who do not comprehend such sentiments puzzled, even worried, which is Nature's way of punishing them for their lack of emotional breeding!'

'I am honoured, Your Majesty.' Mumtaz Mahal fought to hold back the tears that prickled her eyes. 'Not because the Begum has conferred such a gift on me, but because of what my husband and I have in common with a beautiful human being. Yes, my husband loved his grandfather best of all. Whatever is good and noble in him, he owes to the Emperor Akbar. This is something he has divulged only to me.'

'Splendid. Children invent unseen worlds when they find their own singularly unattractive, but have the saving grace of being content to persuade themselves of the reality of the world of their creation without descending to the vulgarity of inflicting it on others of no consequence. In the case of your husband, his world with his grandfather was his only real one. Even we, who were responsible for his upbringing during his early years, could not reach him. Since others would have regarded his experience with polite scepticism, he quite rightly refrained from referring to it until he found his soul-mate. We therefore have a message for your husband from our own late husband.'

'A message?' Mumtaz Mahal was puzzled. 'Does the Emperor Akbar commune with you then, Your Majesty, from Paradise?'

The Begum knew that she spoke sincerely. 'When one has lived with someone as long and closely as we did with our husband, one speaks to the other even after death. Some of it is called comfort, some of it is wisdom, the rest we forget, if we ever knew.'

Mumtaz nodded. 'I understand.'

'Nur Jehan would never understand. Unfortunately, her perception is limited by her preoccupation with herself. An archangel proclaiming the arrival of paradise on earth only to find that it has to be postponed because everyone is watching an elephant battle, could not be more crestfallen than your aunt must have been upon hearing the news of your husband's lightning successes in the Deccan. In fact, if she could harness one of those lightning bolts, she would return it to the source!'

This was no more than Mumtaz Mahal had already deduced, but it gratified her to know that such an astute woman, possessed of the wisdom of the ages, had reached the same conclusion. 'Word of Prince Husrau's death could, however, harm my husband,' she ventured. 'There are those who would say that he murdered his brother.'

'More than that, my dear princess, it is those very people who undoubtedly had Prince Husrau murdered.'

'What?' A hand flew to her mouth. 'I am sorry, Your Majesty. Please forgive me the unseemly exclamation.'

'We might have been suspicious if it had not escaped you! The principal reason we summoned you is to inform you that, under the present circumstances, you are your husband's greatest source of danger.'

'Me? How could *I* be, Your Majesty? I love him. I would never harm him.'

The white-haired head quivered involuntarily on the scrawny neck, the jewelled circlets flashed. 'Listen carefully. The murder of Prince Husrau is, as you say, an attempt to discredit Shah Jahan. Your aunt's next move will be to send him to the far north-west where trouble is already brewing from Shah Abbas. When the Emperor Jehangir dies, Prince Shahriyar will be named the heir, but not before Prince Parviz and your husband are summoned to Agra, without their armies, to attend their dying father. All this is not new. It has happened before, the sorry plots of the Moghul legacy. Your husband is the one heir who can command public support and wrest the vacant throne for himself. Whether he answers the summons to visit Agra alone, refuses it, or arrives at the head of his army, *you*, being in Agra, will be the hostage. And he would rather surrender than have one hair of your head harmed.'

Mumtaz Mahal saw the truth in a blinding flash of light. 'How does Your Majesty know that my husband would give up all right to the throne to save me?' She almost whispered the words.

'Because his grandfather would have done as much for *me*.' There was pride in the quavery voice, in the dropping of the royal plural. 'When there is no one left who will act for you, remembering those who *would have* acted becomes a priceless heritage. Your husband and the Emperor Akbar are two of the same unique breed, loving men.'

'What can I do?' She suddenly felt helpless. What indeed *could* she do? Flee to Buran? She would be detained before she reached the Agra city gates.

'Now you are talking sense. We have arranged for you and your children to accompany a group of the faithful who are going on a pilgrimage to Ajmer. Once there, you can join your husband, wherever he may be, but do not ever return to Agra except when he ascends the imperial throne. You leave *immediately*.' She sighed, but happily. 'Now I have fulfilled my last responsibility to my husband, I too can leave.'

* * *

457

When news of Prince Husrau's death reached Prince Chara in Chitor, he knew that it would not be long before he received Nur Jehan's summons. It arrived the following week with an invitation to stay in her Agra palace.

Two weeks later he presented himself at the *harem* on Friday afternoon, as arranged, and was conducted to Nur Jehan's reception chamber by her Chief Eunuch. He was not surprised to find Sir Thomas Roe seated on his usual chair in front of the fountain.

'Gentlemen, as you know, the news is not good,' Nur Jehan stated from behind the curtains once the formal pleasantries were over. 'Shah Jahan's successes in the Deccan have been stunning. His unlikely story that his brother died of a colic has been received with polite disbelief and great grief by the Emperor, who blames himself for having placed his eldest son in a murderer's hands. It will inevitably hasten the Emperor's death. And we have just received word that the perfidious Shah Abbas, who but recently professed "eternal friendship for our brother Jehangir", is ready to march on Kandhar. Meanwhile, contrary to our expectations, Shah Jahan's popularity with the people continues unabated.'

'The people always create heroes who can do no wrong until those very people rise to destroy them,' Sir Thomas asserted. 'Shah Jahan's day will come, but it is up to you to ensure it.' His short laugh was as sardonic as the glance he shot at Prince Chara.

'The people love sensation rather better than they love the truth,' Prince Chara rejoined.

'Shah Jahan is a wild beast!' The Empress almost hissed the words, reminding him of a snake.

A snake and a wild beast. What a combination! 'The wild beasts I am accustomed to have come with proper credentials, or have been bred in captivity,' Prince Chara murmured. 'Shah Jahan is, however, a singular wild beast and must be brought into captivity, but without his herd.'

'How can that be achieved?'

'Mm . . . mm . . . There are ways, Madam,' Sir Thomas interposed, scratching the side of his long nose. 'The most obvious is to provide the bait, eh?' He winked at Prince Chara.

'Of course.' Prince Chara understood immediately, grew excited. 'Of course.' Now, why hadn't he thought of that himself? This cunning Englishman . . .

'What do you mean?' Nur Jehan demanded.

'His wife, Madam,' Sir Thomas replied. 'The perfect bait. Command him to return to Agra alone, hinting that otherwise harm might befall his wife.'

The sound of Nur Jehan's escaping breath was audible. 'Too late!' she exclaimed.

'Why?' Prince Chara knew a throb of anxiety.

'The Princess Mumtaz Mahal left this very morning for Ajmer with a group of pilgrims.' She paused. 'It was all arranged by Salima Begum.' Her fury was mounting. 'Planned, planned, planned.'

'Send an escort to have her brought back,' Sir Thomas suggested.

'Impossible. One never interferes with a pilgrimage, least of all by the use of armed force.'

'Can you exert some pressure on the Begum?' Sir Thomas began.

'Impossible!' Nur Jehan reasserted bitterly. 'The Begum died in her sleep at noon today. Her ladies-in-waiting found her lying peacefully on her divan bed. She clung to life long enough to deliver me this death blow!'

'Please accept my sincere condolences,' Sir Thomas said insincerely.

Very funny, but damn, damn, damn, Prince Chara thought savagely. His mind began to race. 'Then you have only one alternative, Madam. Summon him in the name of the Emperor to lead the imperial army against Shah Abbas.'

'Mm . . . m . . . And tell him to come alone,' Sir Thomas added. 'Send your messenger to reach him before he learns of his wife's escape.'

'No!' Prince Chara interrupted. 'Let him bring his crack troops here. Since they will be those most loyal to him personally, once he arrives here and is directly under your control, command him to leave them in Agra and proceed to Kandhar with regiments less known to him, on the grounds that the best troops are needed for the Emperor's protection.'

'That is what we had planned to do.'

Prince Chara knew a thrill, this time of triumph.

They discussed details for an hour.

'Then it is all satisfactorily settled,' Sir Thomas finally stated.

'Yes, thank you, Sir Ambassador,' Nur Jehan said. 'The only remaining question is how long Shah Jahan can be kept in the north-west. What is to prevent him from lightning success, returning to Agra an even greater hero?'

Prince Chara laughed aloud. 'Your Majesty, the craggy mountains and ravines of those regions are immune from lightning. It is the hunting ground of weapon-happy Afghans, Tatars and Uzbegs. Shah Jahan will be embroiled in an indecisive campaign that will last for years.' He grinned at the slit in the green velvet curtains. 'Especially if you do not give him sufficient men and material to demonstrate an overwhelming show of force that would demoralize the enemy.'

Her visitors had barely left when her personal attendant came rushing in, tears streaming down her fair cheeks, and prostrated herself in front of the divan. Nur Jehan looked down in amazement at Mano, the petite, big-breasted young South Indian woman whom she had brought with her from her father's mansion.

'Speak,' Nur Jehan commanded. She hated such displays of emotion.

'Oh Majesty, Majesty, the most terrible news. Your revered father is dead.'

So it had happened at last. It must have been a relief to the ailing man, but it left her completely alone. The Emperor, still addicted to alcohol, was slowly dying of asthma and a failing liver. Shah Jahan, once her protégé, was a rebel addicted to his ambition, her brother, Asaf Khan, addicted as usual to principles. The young Prince Shahriyar, whom she had selected to be her son-in-law and heir to the imperial throne, was addicted to incompetence, which was why she had selected him in the first place. Now her father, on whom alone she could have depended, was dead.

Meanwhile, she had an Empire to rule.

She had never had any deep love for her father. It was he who had abandoned her, though briefly, when she was a baby, a rejection she could never forget. Even her present husband had rejected her before deciding to marry her. Rejection, rejection! She had, however, depended on her father's always being biased in her favour. And he had been incomparable as the Imperial Treasurer.

Now, Shah Jahan, whom she finally saw as her rival for power, had gone from success to success and her plan to discredit him had failed. Shah Abbas was ready to attack Kandhar. There were rumours of possible uprisings in the east. And she had to cope with the affairs of the Empire single-handed.

For the first time in her life, Nur Jehan felt completely out of her depth.

But she would never reveal her state of mind.

'Have the eunuchs prepare our palanquin,' she calmly

commanded Mano. 'We shall go to our family mansion immediately.'

The very calmness of her own voice steadied her, brought back her resolve. Her aloneness was not new. She had known it all her life, its cause the need for security. She had fought, suffered, made sacrifices, to put herself in a position where she depended on no one but herself. Now she was at the very top of the world's ladder, though alone.

She had worked her way up alone . . . by herself . . . with her own God-given abilities. No one would topple her. From now on, she would depend on no one, not even Allah.

Her savage resolve reasserted itself. Before the doors to her reception chamber had closed behind Mano, the Empress Nur Jehan was her strong, indomitable self again, sure of her position, certain where her path lay.

He saw Sir Thomas to the entrance doors of the Agra palace. Grooms hurried away to fetch the ambassador's horse. Once again, the scene was like the re-run of a play from years ago, except that he, Prince Chara, was residing in the palace today. A glaring sun beat down on the flagstone floors of the great courtyard. Indian cypress trees drooped around its borders, but the sentries in their red and white uniforms stood alert at the gates.

'So Salima Begum has died,' Sir Thomas said, making conversation.

'Very considerate of her,' Prince Chara retorted. 'It leaves Nur Jehan undisputed head of the *harem*.' He paused. 'Tell me, Sir Thomas, why do you give such uncompromising loyalty to the Empress?' He felt close enough to the ambassador, at least in cunning, to ask the question.

The ambassador bared his yellow teeth in a cynical smile beneath his bristling moustaches. 'Uncompromising is a good word, Prince,' he stated. 'I give the Empress loyalty

462

so long as *I* remain uncompromised! It is my duty. Representing my sovereign lord, King James, in this Empire, I must act exactly as I deem *he* would. I have no personality of my own in that capacity.'

'Have you no *compromising* loyalty then?' Prince Chara asked, grinning.

The ambassador grew serious. 'That is a fundamental question. It deserves a perfectly honest answer, so you may understand me, Prince. An Englishman's first loyalty is to his king and country. We call it patriotism, from the Latin word *patria* which means the fatherland. If the call of king and country demands it, I shall betray the Empress without a thought. Her present designs, however, accord with the policies of my king, so I give her what you have chosen to call uncompromising loyalty.'

Prince Chara lifted an eyebrow. 'You are not motivated by antagonism towards Shah Jahan?'

'Mm . . . m . . . Let us say that my dislike of Shah Jahan makes me delighted to support the Empress's present plans, but should it be Shah Jahan that England needs, I would give him my support even while regretting that I cannot give him my boot instead!'

'Have you no other loyalties?' Prince Chara was becoming more and more curious about this strange man.

'Oh, there is God, naturally, and my religion, Christianity.'

'What about family?'

'As you know, I have neither wife nor children. For that sort of loyalty, there is a favourite horse or dog, or both.'

'If you did have a wife and children?'

'I suppose I would include them somewhere within the list of other loyalties.' He was beginning to sound vague. 'Family honour too, that sort of thing.'

'So an Englishman's loyalties are first to his king and country, then to his God and religion, next, to his horse or dog, then to family honour and finally to his wife and children. In that order.' Prince Chara could not hide his amazement.

Sir Thomas turned red. 'Look here, Prince, all this is damned embarrassing. Hrrumph! We English never discuss personal things the way you foreigners do.'

'Sir Thomas, I shall not apologize for any embarrassment I have caused you,' Prince Chara rejoined amiably. 'On the contrary, I am glad I did, because it has enabled me to understand you a little more. You have shown me that the English race is unique. With such patriots, your country will have a worldwide Empire some day, ruled by a handful of your countrymen. I am not given to prescience, being a very pragmatic person, as you know, but the Rajputs are divided into three groups, Lunar, Fire and Solar. I belong to the last of these, so I am certain that the sun will never set on the Empire you establish. And on a personal note, I would respectfully add that an Englishman is a gentleman after my own heart.'

Sir Thomas roared with laughter. The clippety-clop of his horse's hooves caused him to direct his fish-gaze in its direction, before turning his eyes four-squarely back on Prince Chara. '*Before* your heart, Prince, I trust, not after. For what comes *after* your black heart does not even bear contemplation!'

Clippety-clop went the hooves of the ambassador's horse, echoing the truth of his words. Prince Chara was not offended. He recalled all the privation, disease and misery this Englishman had endured during his first year in India, all for his country. He thought, your God must look *up* to you, not *down* on you.

464

Chapter 29

While extending to Prince Zain the honours due to a senior Amir and the Emperor's ambassador, housing him in the Buran palace, Shah Jahan elected to receive the Amir in his tent outside the capital. His purpose was to impress on Prince Zain the fact that here in the Deccan, he, Shah Jahan, was a field commander, not a palace puppet.

Prince Zain, whom he had never met before, proved to be a middle-aged man of considerable girth and self-importance. Although it was only 9 A.M., he was already sweating from his rich attire, a calf-length tunic of heavy brocade, the broad white satin sash at his waist and the matching silk turban studded with rubies. His face was florid, the luxuriant black moustaches spreading beneath wide cheekbones. The bulgy, pale brown eyes were cunning. In contrast, Shah Jahan had deliberately worn his field uniform.

General Wahid retired after presenting Prince Zain, whose entourage had remained outside the tent.

'Since His Imperial Majesty has deemed the matter which he desires to communicate to me of sufficient importance to have selected a senior Amir to be his royal representative, I thought that you and I should discourse alone, without any further protocol,' Shah Jahan began. 'But first, I trust that you are well accommodated and looked after, my lord prince.' He smiled. 'What we have to offer cannot compare with the style to which you are accustomed, but I hope it is to your satisfaction, for it is the best available.'

'No complaints, my lord prince. No complaints at all.' Prince Zain had a high, feminine voice. He looked around the tent, at its plain dealwood table, wooden settles, hanging lanterns, with Shah Jahan's rolled-up pallet on the side. The bulgy eyes bulged even more. 'Rather a Spartan existence for *you*, though,' he observed.

'By choice. Now, if I could only match the Spartans of old in courage, daring and fortitude as well, I should be satisfied.'

'I had heard reports of your rather odd habits on the field, but . . . hrrmph . . . we all make our own choices.'

'And live with their successes and failures.' Shah Jahan thought it about time to remind this Court popinjay of his victories.

'Undoubtedly, undoubtedly.' Like all self-important people, Prince Zain had a habit of repeating words. 'Which brings me to an effect of your recent successes.' He reached into his deep tunic pocket and produced a small scroll which he handed to Shah Jahan with a flourish. 'A missive from the Emperor himself.'

Shah Jahan accepted the scroll with both hands, bowed respectfully over it and then unrolled it. To his surprise, it was signed by Nur Jehan, under the Emperor's seal. Ignoring the platitudinous superscriptions, he read the basic text:

. . . The situation is grim. Shah Abbas, aided by tribesmen disloyal to us, is ready to march on Kandhar. Our Governor in Kandhar will resolutely oppose him, but begs for reinforcements. To make matters worse, the Emperor, may Almighty Allah give him life eternal, is much too sick to take the field. Only a lightning strike by our armies will drive the invader back and restore peace and tranquillity to the region. Almighty Allah has granted us, in you, dear Prince, the only leader in our Empire, other than the Emperor himself, to whom He has given this power.

The Empire needs you today, as never before. Hasten back to Agra immediately therefore and save the Empire.

Our ambassador, Amir Zain, is fully acquainted with our

plans. He will answer all your questions and brief you fully as to how they shall be accomplished.

He read the message twice before he decided what lay between the lines. In short, Nur Jehan wanted him back in Agra immediately, before shooting him into virtual exile in the north-west for what might be years. The last words of the text were highly significant. He was to save the Empire in accordance with Nur Jehan's plans. It did not require a closer inspection of Prince Zain to tell him that Nur Jehan had selected the shrewdest possible messenger for the task.

What did these people imagine? That he was still the teenager of his grandfather's shaping, who would immediately jump to his feet, raise his sword aloft, and shout: 'Here I come! Long live the Empire!' then summon his charger and gallop to the rescue of Kandhar?

Prince Zain's voice cut into his reflection. 'The Empress commanded me to tell you that your beloved wife, the Princess Mumtaz Mahal, and your four lovely children, are safe and well in Agra.'

One look into the pale brown pebbles of the ambassador's eyes and Shah Jahan understood the threat behind the words. His wife and children would be safe as long as he obeyed the royal commands. They were being held hostage. Fury surged within him, but he held it back.

His mind began working coolly. He should at all costs avoid going to Kandhar, getting bogged down there and losing his reputation. He now commanded eighty thousand men. He should remain with his troops and never be too far from the centre of events.

'Her Majesty also commanded me to convey her condolences to you on the death of your brother, Prince Husrau.' The high voice held a note of menace. 'She stated that it must be particularly trying for you to endure such a tragedy when a colic is such a trivial complaint. The Emperor is terribly disturbed and blames himself for having delivered Prince Husrau to . . . er . . . a situation that led to his untimely death.'

Again the implication was obvious. He was blamed for his brother's death.

His resolve took wings. If he did not meet Nur Jehan's fire with cunning, he would be destroyed. His grandfather had frequently warned him never to fight from weakness, always from strength. 'The slightest wish of the Emperor and the Empress is my command,' he asserted. 'I expect to be able to thank the Empress in person for her condolences. All that remains is for you and me to settle the method and manner of my move to Agra and thence to Kandhar.'

'I am a minister plenipotentiary on this mission,' Amir Zain responded suavely. 'I am authorized to discuss any problems you may have, and to make such concessions as may be reasonable.' He paused, the brown eyes glinting. 'Incidentally, the Empress also commanded me to convey her regrets that you could not attend the betrothal of her daughter, Princess Ladili, to Prince Shahriyar. She commends you for being in the field performing a higher duty for the Empire.'

So it had finally happened. Nur Jehan had shown her hand. The Empress was the real enemy. His own strength lay in the fact that he was needed. With this bargaining position, he would lay down conditions that would give him added strength. He needed time to work them out. Amir Zain would remain in Buran discussing problems for a long time!

As he stood in the private courtyard gardens outside the Chitor palace, watching his father's bedroom window, Prince Chara recalled how he had waited in that very place at the same hour of the night for Sher Afgan to join him. The giant husband of Nur Jehan, on his way to a new post

468

in Bengal, had however, occupied a ground-floor room. Meanwhile, what changes had transpired! Tonight, as the suite of the Rana was upstairs, his father would not be coming out to join him. On the contrary!

But something could go wrong. Prince Chara's heart started beating faster. He steadied his breathing and, with iron determination, sent the fear rising from his guts upward through his chest, reaching for his throat, back where it belonged. Nothing could go wrong.

Keeping an eye on the lighted windows of his father's bedroom, he deliberately studied his surroundings. They were all too familiar, especially as he had walked the gardens by himself on many a night, before retiring to bed. He could have been anywhere in India. The deep blue sky was a glitter-litter of stars. He could see his red planet, Mars, the great constellation of Orion and, in the distance, just above the cypresses bordering the courtyard, the Southern Cross, guide of travellers. He was travelling a new road himself tonight, but he had no star to guide him, only his ambition, drive and the goal he had set for himself. He shivered, but it was only from the coolness of the air.

Impatient for the outcome of his actions, he focused his full attention on his father's window. No shadow announced the Rana's presence. He hoped that this would not be the one night on which his father broke an unfailing routine before going to bed: the beaker of fresh pomegranate juice, the walk across to the window, opening it, placing his hands on the sill and breathing deeply of the fresh air outside before closing the window again.

Still no shadow. Once again, he calmed himself, renewed his contemplation.

After an eternity of waiting, it seemed as if the way was opening for him at last. Not defeat nor the past years when Mewar, devastated by the Moghul arch-fiend, Shah Jahan, was slowly recovering from the ravages of that war, nor tragedy, had daunted him or deflected him from his purpose. He was a Rajput, the very word meant 'descendant of kings'. Even when everything seemed hopeless he had never succumbed to despair.

Mostly, he was Prince Chara, not an instrument of destiny, but a man of such brains, abilities and indomitable will that the final achievement had to be supreme power. First Mewar, and all of Rajasthan, then the south and finally Agra, as head of a coalition of independent States that would cast aside the Moghul yoke of a hundred years. Once he proved himself to the other Rajputs, to the Marathas and the Deccanese, all races of his own region, the Sikhs and the Pathans of the north would unite with him to recreate the India that existed before the earliest army of Mongols arrived on the west bank of the River Indus in 1398 to pose the first threat to the Indian rulers in Delhi. The autonomy of the kingdoms and the powers of the rajas and ranas who ruled them would be restored. As Rana of Mewar, he, Prince Chara would also be the Maha Raja, the Great King, supreme overlord of all India.

It was all very logical in his mind.

Since today's Moghul capital Agra was already in turmoil, with internal dissension inevitable between Nur Jehan and the Emperor on the one hand and the sons of the Emperor on the other, the time had finally come for Prince Chara to position himself so that he would be able to exercise the initiative to move at will, without impediment. Tonight would see his first gigantic step. He glanced instinctively at the upstairs window. It was still bare of any shadow.

It was he who had hired the two assassins to kill Prince Husrau. Although his plan to have Shah Jahan immediately discredited as the murderer had not worked, he had no regrets over the demise of the blind fool. Prince Husrau had lost him almost fifteen years by ignoring his carefully laid plan and acting on his own when he first rebelled against the Emperor. His death was poetic justice, once again the operation of inevitable cause and effect.

The Husrau murder had not been as simple as the one he had set in motion years ago for the elimination of Prince Jahan, through Sher Afgan who had direct connections with *thuggee* assassins. This time, Prince Chara had decided to depend only on himself. His aide, Selvam, had once mentioned in passing that there were *dacoits* for hire in a certain village not far from Chitor. Disguised as a Muslim, Prince Chara contacted two of them, a father and son, who readily accepted the mission but named a high price since it involved a prince and the enormous risk of accomplishing the deed in an army encampment. One-half the price was to be paid down, the balance upon completion of the mission. If the second half was not paid, the assassins would of course reveal all to the authorities, who would undoubtedly manage to track down those behind the deed. Unfortunately, or fortunately – depending on how one looked at it – Prince Chara realized that the older of the two *dacoits* had recognized him. Without revealing that he knew of the identification, Prince Chara went ahead with his plan. It required considerable coordination with his spies among the Moghul troops at Buran, but the deed had been done.

Prince Chara smiled grimly to himself as he went over the sequel. A dark night, two *dacoits* confident of their invulnerability coming to collect their balance payment, undoubtedly with the added expectation of a big pension for life by blackmailing him. He had set the meeting for a lonely place by a swamp. His sword had proved more than a match for the *dacoits*. The first, the older man, never realized what had happened. The sharp blade severed his head from his body. The second drew his knife, only to have the reverse swing of the sword flatten him, the blade going through his heart before he could roll away. He had dumped the two bodies and, of course, the severed head in the swamp, where no one would ever find the remains.

It required cunning, coolness and skill to deal with such situations. Tonight, he was dependent on no one but himself . . .

He detected the movement upstairs before he saw it, his father's shadowy bulk against the window. He let out a long breath of relief and watched fascinated, but with his mind objective. The click of the window latch reached him clearly across the night. The window opened silently. His father stood framed within the lamplight from the bedroom. Prince Chara could not see his face. He neutralized a tiny twinge of regret with the recall of past insults.

He only thought he saw the cobra slither up his father's hand, but he did see his father's upraised palms, the step backwards in horror. He imagined the contorted face. The cry that shattered the night was as great as the body from which it emerged.

It has worked. Rather clever of me, Prince Chara thought. The poisoned drink, the angry cobra confined to its wickerwork basket poised on the flat ornamental moulding just below the windowsill, which opened with the window pane. The cobra's movement dislodging the basket, which I shall retrieve. The knowledge that my father's reflexes have slowed. Having done its duty, the snake would be coiled on my father's chest, hood extended, hissing at the attendants who would deal with it.

He had best pick up the basket now – it had just dropped lightly to the ground – hasten to his own suite of rooms and pretend shock when the attendants summoned him. It would be a nuisance, making appropriate noises of horror and grief, but his father had given him plenty of experience in play-acting. It would not be difficult in the confusion, once it was firmly established that the cobra must have stung his father, to retrieve the lid of the basket, which he had attached to the window latch with a dark, strong thread. He would do so by requesting a few minutes of mourning alone with his father's dead body. Rather a nice epilogue!

A son grieving for a parent he loved. Just the right image with which to commence his rule over Mewar. Rana Chara Singh of Mewar! The words had a ring to them.

What no one but he would know was that, regardless of whether the cobra did its lethal work or not, his father would have died of the poison in his pomegranate juice.

She had never been to the city of Ajmer before. When she had once broached the subject of a pilgrimage to her husband, Shah Jahan had replied jokingly, 'You can hardly find the time to do it between pregnancies, Mumtaz beloved.'

The pilgrim caravan had reached the outskirts of the city that same evening and was encamped outside its walls. The pilgrims would be permitted in when the gates opened the next morning. As was proper and customary for women in *purdah*, Mumtaz Mahal and Sati slept in their wagon. It was not the most comfortable mode of travel. The jogging ride from Agra had seemed interminable. In spite of the cushions, the hard wood floor made Mumtaz's back hurt. Being confined for hours within curtains in that narrow space, with two small children and a baby, was frustrating and the heat inside almost unbearable. How did people who travelled regularly in caravans endure it? Her little girl was lucky to be in the Agra palace; she had brought only the boys with her.

'None of it matters, though,' she had told Sati between the bouts of pretended complaining that brought baby-ing from her other mother. 'I am free and my beloved husband can now act as he pleases to fulfil his destiny.'

'Not to mention ensuring the well-being of the Empire,' Sati had rejoined drily, quoting what she knew to be one of Shah Jahan's favourite phrases.

'Oh, you are horrid!' Mumtaz had stormed, still pretending.

'And you are beautiful, even if sweat is smudging the *kohl* on your eyelids.'

'Do you still love me, *amma*?'

'Of course I do, little paddy-bird.'

'Then hold me to you.'

'It's too hot.' Sati had taken up a wicker fan and started fanning herself vigorously before moving it outwards to fan Mumtaz.

'You are a cool weather friend,' Mumtaz had pouted.

Now it was long after supper. The three boys were asleep in the wagon and Sati and she were both seated on the grass outside, enjoying the cool air before turning in for the night. Most of the campfires had died down. Their embers glowed in the centre of the picket line comprising the dark masses of the wagons which had been drawn up in a small circle on the open *maidan* outside the city walls looming beyond. Only the occasional murmur of the sentries patrolling the outer perimeter broke through the stillness of steady cricket-creaking.

'How odd it is that the only ugliness in this beautiful night of God's creation is that created by man,' Mumtaz said softly.

'And what may that be?' Sati inquired.

Mumtaz crinkled her nose. 'The stench of night-soil brought by a sudden breeze. Otherwise everything is perfect. It is so wonderful to be outside at night. Not on a palace roof or a courtyard, but on the free earth, with bright stars literally splattering the deep blue sky, the ghostly shapes of dark cypresses over there reaching vainly to touch their silver splendour.'

'Ah, my poet.'

'Never a poet, Sati. Remember, I am a woman, so I can only be a poetess.'

'Then it is Almighty Allah's gift you have.'

'Undoubtedly.'

'Pity he gave you the gift of being able to smell the night-soil.'

'Sati, I am serious and you are horrid. You are spoiling the beauty of the night by arguing.'

'It is you who started arguing, little paddy-bird.'

'Don't you come little paddy-birding me.'

'All right, I won't then.'

She loved these interchanges with Sati, which had never stopped even after she got married. Some women, mothers, governesses, were possessive and created trouble once their wards gave their lives to another, but not Sati. 'Don't you dare stop. Only don't do so when you are horrid to me.'

'How am I to know when you think I'm being horrid to you? Especially when it's you who started the argument?'

'What did I say?'

The lowing of an ox rent the sounds of silence. A caravan dog growled. Quarrelling people had to be like that, but Mumtaz knew that she never really quarrelled with anyone and was glad she had that gift of Almighty Allah.

'You said you were not a poet but a poetess,' Sati reminded her.

'Well, isn't that true?'

'Not necessarily.'

'How can you say that?'

'You are trying to quibble about a word, when night-soil by any other name would smell just as . . . er . . . horrid.'

'Oh, you are incorrigible.' Mumtaz picked up a cushion and flung it at Sati.

The governess caught it with the deftness of years of practice. 'You can sleep in comfort tomorrow in the palace

475

which the Emperor Akbar built in the city.' She nodded towards the dark walls. 'I'm told it's a place of wonder.'

Mumtaz Mahal grew serious. 'My husband has described it to me, but you know, Sati, I do not think it proper to seek or have comfort on a pilgrimage. And on one such as this, I should not have any more than my fellow pilgrims.'

'You are right. I knew it was what you would say. You're a good girl. Your husband is like that too, on the field.'

'Yes, he declines the luxury and comfort of the Moghul army train for the bare tent and plain food of his troops.'

'Tell me about Ajmer. I know so little about anything.'

'You know the beginning and end of love and how to bestow it with kindness, gentleness and devotion, and all that lies in between, mother of mine. Nothing else matters. Nothing else is true knowledge. There is no other fulfilment.'

Sati reached out an impulsive hand and touched her cheek briefly. Mumtaz held it closer before letting it go.

'I still want to know about Ajmer,' Sati insisted.

'The city was founded four hundred years ago with two Jain temples as its centrepiece. It has always been a place of trade and is still one of our largest local sources of linen. Located between the two Rajput kingdoms, it is predominantly Muslim, so the Emperor Babur created a strong Moghul military base here and converted one of the Jain temples into a mosque. Not a very nice thing to do, *I* think. One should be tolerant of other religions, as the Prophet required. But who am I to canvass the dictates of Emperors? I am only a woman.'

'Yes, of course. A poetess at that!'

Sati knew her so well, was fully aware that she often fretted at the lot created for women by those who had misinterpreted, as she always insisted, the teachings of the Prophet to suit their own personal insecurities and the desire to possess.

476

Mumtaz smiled through the semi-gloom at the thrust. 'The tomb of our Muslim saint Muin-ud-din Chisti was built in Ajmer and it is to venerate him that we are here.'

'And to escape Nur Jehan,' Sati reminded her.

'Of course, but I am happy just to be able to make the pilgrimage. Only one thing bothers me.'

'Other than the discomfort you pretend to complain about!'

'Seriously Sati, how in the world am I to get word to my lord? Salima Begum assured me that she would despatch a secret messenger to him advising him of my departure to Ajmer, but I have no way of sending my regular letters.'

'He will send messengers to you as soon as he learns of your whereabouts and you can then have them carry the accumulation of letters you have been writing back to him.'

'Better still, he may ask me to join him in the field.'

'And share his tent, complete with three squalling children?'

'I am committed to sharing his entire lot, the good, the bad, the ugly, whether he is rich or poor, sick or in health, until death parts us and we will have deserved, through our single-minded love for each other, to meet again in Paradise.' She shivered.

'What is it, little paddy-bird?' Sati, always attuned to her moods, inquired.

'Suddenly I am afraid.'

'Of what, my precious darling?'

'I don't know. Supposing Salima Begum does not send the message or falls ill? Supposing the messenger is killed or something happens to him on the way? My husband will be so worried.'

'Something, something! You are holding something back.'

'Yes, Sati. Indeed I am.'

'Tell me.'

'I fear death. From the Begum's death to my husband's, or my own.' She got a grip on herself. 'But please don't worry. These feelings come and go . . . like life and death.'

She realized that she had not clung to Sati as she did in the past, whenever she had such fears. She had grown up.

In the silence that followed, Mumtaz Mahal knew that Sati somehow comprehended her fears. The familiar Agra seemed so far away, yet this comprehension comforted her more than her other mother's loving arms and warm breasts. Tonight she had realized with stunning force that her fears must distress Sati. Pulling herself together, she changed the subject. 'Look all round you, Sati, listen to the hushed sounds, smell the air, yes, even the night-soil and ox-dung, and you will know how insignificant we are in the order of things. Yet to Almighty Allah, Lord and Sovereign of the Universe, each of us is important, although for that importance to be demonstrated we must cease to regard ourselves as important and submit to His will. Allah created man and appointed a fixed period of life on earth for each human being. He prescribed a code of life for us, but gave us the choice to follow it or not. Those who follow it are Muslims, those who do not are *kafirs*. Unfortunately, not all those who profess to be Muslims are true believers. They are really *kafirs* in their hearts.' She dropped her voice. 'The Emperor is a *kafir*, so is my wicked aunt, Nur Jehan.'

'Yet in accepting *tawhid*, we Muslims acknowledge that all men are the creatures of the one God and are all equal.'

'Some more than others in Almighty Allah's eyes, I'm sure.' Mumtaz Mahal smiled, but this was her true belief. Then she had one of her abrupt changes of mood. 'Oh, oh, oh, how am I ever going to get my letters through to my lord?' she wailed.

Sati brightened. 'I have an idea,' she suggested. 'Visit the military commander of the garrison here tomorrow morning and ask him to send a messenger to my lord prince immediately.'

Mumtaz Mahal reached out and touched Sati's hand. 'Oh you are so wonderful,' she declared. 'That solves everything and I can sleep in peace tonight.'

The *muezzin*'s call to *subh* (morning prayer) rang out from the towers of the mosque in Ajmer, but Mumtaz Mahal and Sati had already risen to set about their morning tasks before the children awoke. Mumtaz could imagine the white-robed Muslims wending their way to the mosque.

Subh, *zuhr* (afternoon prayer), *asr* (late afternoon prayer), *maghrib* (the prayer immediately after sunset) and *isha* (the night prayer) make up a Muslim's day. It helps establish Islam as the only religion that is practised almost continuously.

All prayer is performed facing Mecca, the sacred city, and has to be preceded by ablution, the symbolic purification of body, mind and spirit, so fountains or pumps are placed outside each mosque and when one enters, one faces Mecca. But the Prophet Mahomet had said, 'The whole world has been made a mosque for me,' so one may pray anywhere. Through the rear curtains of her wagon, Mumtaz Mahal could see the other pilgrims emerging from their wagons to the centre of the encampment, where wooden pails of water had been placed for their ablutions.

The subdued hum of conversation and an occasional shout from a wagoner were broken by the sudden drumming of hooves. Horsemen were approaching from the direction of Agra. Why in such a hurry? Why had they ridden through the night? Had a crisis brewed in the capital? Mumtaz's heart began thumping and her stomach churned with fear. Any crisis in Agra would involve Shah Jahan. She hastened down the improvised steps and helped her stout other mother down. Being women, they could not go beyond the bounds of the wagons' circle which was in effect a *harem*.

The hooves drummed down as the horsemen approached the wagons, then died. Shouted greetings followed by questions and answers split the expectant silence of those in the camps and its environs.

Minutes passed, seeming like hours to Mumtaz. 'Go as near as you can to the men and find out what is happening,' she commanded Sati.

Her eldest son, Prince Dara, awoke, crying as usual and she hushed him through the curtains. Prince Shuja smiled at her through the dark, made no move to rise from his cushions; the little devil loved his bed. The baby Prince Aurang slept through the noise and bustle outside; he was already showing signs of a quiet, determined character.

How she hated her position as a woman, not being able to go out and discover what was afoot immediately. How she loathed the rules of decorum that demanded she remain there, being a princess, until Sati brought her the information. Royalty must not betray vulgar curiosity! Her beloved Shah Jahan not only practised the doctrine, he believed in it. She wanted to please him.

Sati hastened back to her. In the pale light, Mumtaz could see that the woman's eyes were wet with tears. Alarm sent terror thrills through Mumtaz. She restrained the urge to display too much curiosity because her lord would not have wanted her to.

'Oh my lady, my lady, such sad news,' Sati cried. 'Those are imperial messengers from the Emperor in Agra to the military commander in Ajmer. Salima Begum is dead.'

For a moment Mumtaz could not comprehend what was said. She only knew relief that the news did not affect her husband. Then it dawned on her that the old Empress had died. A remarkable woman. But the cloth of her body had been held together only by the thin seam of her willpower.

Death must have been a merciful release for her. Surely she would be with the Emperor Akbar in Paradise at this very moment. So why grieve for her? But why would messengers ride through the night to bring this news to Ajmer? And to whom were they conveying it?

'Is that the only news?' She wanted to be sure.

'Yes, my lady. It is so tragic.'

'When did the Begum die? Did they say?'

'Yes, just before noon on Friday.'

'Then it was before she could convey the news of our departure to my lord.'

'Is that all you can think about at such a time of grief?' Sati's grey eyes were wide with disbelief. 'I am surprised at you.'

'Listen, Sati, to be honest, I cannot pretend grief when I know that this sudden death was a merciful relief from loneliness and the aches of ancient bones about which the Begum could never even complain – no, not even to Allah. When I saw her on Friday morning, it was obvious that she was only holding her body together with an indomitable effort of will. Now I will share something with you that I had only intended for my lord prince. The Begum told me, in effect, that she was rescuing me from the position of hostage to my aunt and the Emperor to ensure Shah Jahan's good conduct. Having done this last act for her late husband who loved my own husband as a son, she could die in peace. What remains is our sacred duty to ensure that her act is not rendered futile.'

'I understand, little paddy-bird. Please forgive me my doubt. I know you to be a human being of great compassion.'

'Thank you, Sati. Your good opinion is important to me. Now let me ask you, why would imperial messengers dash through the night to convey news of the death of the ruler of the imperial *harem*, even the Empress, to the military commander of Ajmer? Is that an event of such Empire-shaking significance?'

The sad cawing of crows rose above the babble of voices in the encampment.

Sati's eyes widened. She raised a hand to her chest. 'You mean . . . ?'

Mumtaz Mahal nodded. 'Those were not the Emperor's messengers, Sati. They were Nur Jehan's. Why did they stop here if their mission was so urgent? They were checking to see whether we had arrived. What they could not reveal were their secret instructions to the military commander.'

'To apprehend you.' Sati shook her head in wonder. 'You have grown up, my little paddy-bird. You always had the sharpest intelligence, but this?' Her face became filled with alarm, she pounded her forehead. 'What do we do now?' She paused. 'Surely they cannot take you while you are on a pilgrimage?'

Mumtaz Mahal knew a great calm. 'No, but they can escort me back to represent my husband's household. At this time of mourning, I would have to abandon the pilgrimage and accompany them to Agra without question.'

'Do we have a choice?'

'Yes.' Mumtaz Mahal responded coolly. 'We shall attend *subh* as if nothing has happened. As soon as it is over, we shall slip out of the camp, go into the city on foot and make our way to the palace.'

'Would that not be walking into the enemy camp?'

'Salima Begum's closest friend was one of the Emperor Akbar's political wives. She is the Princess Jemaliya, who now rules the Ajmer palace *harem*. Salima Begum advised me to contact her if I was ever in trouble, told me that she would help me if I simply said, "Your sister Salima sent me." She will give us protection.'

'But not against the Emperor's commands.'

'Certainly not, but she will have the right to postpone the fulfilment of those commands if they violate the Emperor's laws.'

'What on earth are you talking about?' Sati knitted grey eyebrows, clearly puzzled.

She probably imagines my mind has become unhinged, Mumtaz Mahal thought. 'The Emperor's public health laws.' She giggled. 'You see, Sati, I have just developed smallpox. As a princess by marriage, I will be segregated only in the palace *harem*. The Princess Jemaliya alone will know the truth and she will of course send messengers to my husband immediately. He had the smallpox too as a boy, you know.'

Comprehension dawned on Sati. Her face cleared. 'You will pretend to have the disease. Only the appointed physician can enter the *harem* and he cannot cast his eyes on you. Oh dear Allah, what a clever plan. You are a little devil. The *harem* does have its advantages.'

'So does the veil.' Mumtaz Mahal laughed gleefully. 'No one but you and my husband can discover whether I have scars on my face or not, since I am in *purdah*!'

Chapter 30

The imperial relay-post which the Emperor Akbar had established between Agra and all the principal cities of the Empire had arrived twice a week in Buran, with unfailing regularity. Mumtaz Mahal's daily letters to Shah Jahan had been delivered with equal regularity, except that when he was in the field, they were brought to him by his own messengers, promptly as he had commanded. It was the Great Shah of Persia, Dhar-oos, centuries earlier, who had first recognized the need for speedy communication between himself and the far-flung outposts of his Empire. He had created an efficient system of highways and relay-posts, equipped with fast horses and manned by skilled riders; news of planned plots or uprisings reached him so quickly that he was able to despatch his troops to quell them before they ever became a threat.

Today was the second occasion on which the Agra post had proved empty for him. The first time, he had merely turned away with a sick heart. This time, he became alarmed. Why were there no letters from his beloved Mumtaz? Was she sick? Had she stopped loving him? Had some harm befallen her? Amir Zain had implied on the day of their first meeting that Mumtaz Mahal was well, but now the final deadly question hammered at Shah Jahan's brain. Was his wife being held hostage by the Emperor and Nur Jehan to ensure his, Shah Jahan's, compliance with their dictates?

Until now, Shah Jahan had been motivated only by his ambitions. Suddenly, the safety of his loved one was involved and it convinced him that his family would only know real security when he wielded supreme power. Rage had burned fiercely into his brain during the day, and so he summoned Amir Zain to his tent in Buran for dinner that night.

The table had now been cleared by his attendants and the senior commanders had departed, leaving him alone with the Emperor's ambassador. As always with florid-faced men after a meal, Amir Zain looked replete, his cheeks shiny in the golden glow of the hanging lamps, the luxuriant black moustaches bristling with satisfaction. He burped loudly, proclaiming his appreciation of the food. 'Ah! The taste of that roast lamb returns with every belch,' he declared. 'It remains in the palate and its odours still hang in the air.' He sniffed appreciatively. 'Camp roasts must be the best in the world, otherwise we would have mutiny on our hands from men who have little else to compensate for the rigours of camp life.'

Amir Zain certainly did not look as if he had ever endured such rigours. 'I'm glad you enjoyed our somewhat rough fare,' Shah Jahan responded. 'Everything is relative. One can have a three-hundred-course all-night banquet without enjoying a single morsel.'

Amir Zain lifted a supercilious eyebrow. 'It is because you are of such a mind that you make a good soldier,' he stated. 'It is er . . . the enjoyment of sumptuous banquets that fits me for the lesser role of ambassador!' He paused. 'Tonight's meal, however, was fit for a king.'

'You talk like an ambassador,' Shah Jahan concluded. 'Which brings me to the principal cause of our meeting tonight. For two weeks now, you and I have discussed plans for my departure to Kandhar without reaching finality. I have now decided to move to Kandhar, through Mandu and Agra, without delay. We must thwart Shah Abbas's plans as quickly as possible. While in Agra, I shall have substantive discussions with the Emperor and Empress as to the strength and composition of the army I am finally to lead to Kandhar.'

'Excellent.' Amir Zain sucked at a tooth, causing Shah Jahan to shudder, removed a gold toothpick from one of the pockets of his gold silk tunic and ran it around his gumline. 'When do you leave?'

'Immediately my wife and children leave Agra to join me. I want them to be moved first to the fort at Ranthanbor. It is not much more than a hundred miles from Agra, but they can easily move south from there to join me on my way to the capital. The army will of necessity be proceeding very slowly, so I can leap-frog ahead of it without placing myself too far away.'

The ambassador's jaw dropped. He stared in puzzlement

at Shah Jahan. 'What possible connection . . . ?' he began, then comprehension dawned in the pale brown eyes. 'Ah, I see. Very clever!'

'I do not think you see, ambassador,' Shah Jahan retorted quietly. 'My reason is very simple. Although I have two wives and many concubines, I am a monogamous man. I miss my wife and children. Having been in the field for three major campaigns now, I have not done my duty by my family. I need to spend as much time with them as possible, before departing on the Kandhar campaign which could last for months, even years.'

'But are you not making it a condition of your departure that your family join you?'

Shah Jahan looked Amir Zain squarely in the eye. 'It becomes a condition only if the Emperor finds some impediment to granting my legitimate, reasonable and easily fulfilled plea. You are the Emperor's minister plenipotentiary, with full power to negotiate as if he were doing so himself. I would never dare haggle directly with my sovereign lord, so let me just say that if you agree on his behalf tonight and give me his *firman* by proxy tomorrow, it would serve as an inspiration and incentive for me to move almost immediately.'

A cunning gleam briefly crossed the ambassador's pebble eyes. 'I agree immediately in the name of the Emperor.'

'I shall expect your document tomorrow and shall give you in exchange a despatch for the Emperor and Empress.' But he knew that this was not a man to be trusted.

When Amir Zain had departed with his escort for the city, Shah Jahan composed his despatch in his own hand, which began:

> In obedience to Your Imperial Majesties' command, your humble servant plans to move out of Buran without delay in order to be able to kiss the royal threshold of your *jarokha* before winter sets in . . .

The winter rains were only two months away. Time had become a vital element in this drama.

Finally, he had flung down the gauntlet. His request for the move of his family was in reality a dare and both Amir Zain and he knew it. What would the Emperor's reaction be? How would Nur Jehan respond? He did not care. He was in a position of great strength with an army of over eighty thousand men, most of them devoted to him. As his grandfather had always advised, he was dictating terms from strength. The days of blind obedience were over at last. Strangely, what had triggered the change was the implied threat to Mumtaz.

The tent suddenly seemed confining. In an effort to still his misgivings, Shah Jahan walked outside, absorbing the peace of the night. The roof of the sky, brilliant with late summer stars, stretched so endlessly upward that the sense of physical confinement soon left him. None of it could ease the intolerable summer heat.

A nearby trumpet blared forth the midnight call. Other trumpets echoed it in the distance. Inevitably, dogs started to yelp. Yet the men in the tents spreading along the flat *maidan* slept through it all, no different to the campfires that were merely embers. His misgivings charged to the fore. Had Amir Zain really lied when he agreed to have Mumtaz Mahal and the children moved to Ranthanbor? Was his family still in Agra? Why had he received no letters from Mumtaz Mahal? The questions began pounding into his brain. While the uncertainties of the battle-grounds of war and politics had never overcome him, now, love for his family threatened to overwhelm him.

He reached with his spirit for Mumtaz. 'Oh, my beloved, tell me you are alive and well,' he whispered.

Suddenly, through the cold night air, Mumtaz Mahal's

spirit responded, reached out and touched his own, miraculously communing with him at that very moment. He knew with the utmost certainty that she was alive and well, loving him.

His hands dropped to his sides. 'I love you, Mumtaz, star of my soul, light of my life,' he said softly. He went inside his tent to write her his daily love poem.

> When my mind and body hungered for you
> My spirit burned to death.
> Your love reaching from afar
> Breathed life into my dead ashes
> As the love of God once did to create man.

* * *

He had been very pleased to receive Sir Thomas Roe's request for an audience soon after his father's death. Bowing to the rules of protocol, Sir Thomas had already cleared the visit with the Emperor in Agra. Rana Chara, as he had become, not only liked the English ambassador but also knew that England could become a powerful ally. His official coronation, with all the pomp and pageantry associated with such events, all of which he loathed, would only take place after the one year he had prescribed as the period of mourning for Rana Amar was over, but meanwhile he had already become firmly entrenched in the administration of Mewar.

'We are delighted that you desire to honour our little kingdom with a visit,' he stated in his reply to the ambassador. 'We invite you to honour our Chitor palace as well by being our guest for as long as your duties permit you to remain in Mewar.' He meant it too.

Four weeks after Rana Amar's death, Sir Thomas arrived at the Chitor palace and was assigned the suite reserved for visiting rulers. Rana Chara received the ambassador the following morning at a formal audience, during which he suggested that Sir Thomas might like to rest that afternoon and walk with him in the palace gardens in the evening before the official dinner which had been organized, though on a subdued basis because of the family bereavement.

Having paced the flagstone walkway, they paused by the splattering fountain. 'We are alone together for the first time since your Sunday visit to me some time ago.' Sir Thomas's fish-eyes softened. 'I remember that day so well.' Embarrassed at displaying even a hint of emotion, he quickly changed the subject. 'This is the real India,' he stated, surveying the scene. 'Your gardens are very natural, a product of the heartbeat of your soil. They are not sculpted like the Moghul gardens; even the crows winging their way across the sky seem to fly free instead of in some vast ornamental cage. You native Indians would appreciate our English gardens, with their green lawns, bright flower beds and dark shrubbery. It would be one of the loveliest times of the day back home, a summer evening, warm air, the dry scent of grass and the moist perfume of lilacs.'

Rana Chara warmed towards the man. Within the cold fish, the patriotic heart pumped blood, not ice. 'You miss England?'

'Um . . . m. Very much, I suppose.' He stared at the fountain for a few reflective moments, as if other scenes from his far-off land were reflected in its silver waters, then cocked an ear at the resounding ko . . . haa . . . ko . . . haa of an oriole from the branches of a teakwood tree. 'A call to arms,' he said and came back to his surroundings.

'We invited you to walk with us in the gardens because there are no ears in the open air,' Rana Chara stated frankly.

'I have come to understand that one does indeed walk in a palace garden in your part of the world for the good of one's health!' Sir Thomas bared his yellow teeth in that feral smile which Prince Chara had come to find characteristic.

'Have you met the Empress recently?' Prince Chara inquired.

'The day before I left Agra.'

'We trust she was in good health and spirits.'

'Apart from an unusual degree of preoccupation, yes.'

'And she still functions for the Emperor?'

'She has no choice, has she? I mean, as we say of the Christian marriage vow, she has promised to love, honour and endure him.'

Prince Chara could not resist the laugh that rang out of him. He loved the Englishman's caustic wit, which also afforded him relief from the past weeks of gruelling solemnity and earnestness. 'Has the Empress taken her father's death very much to heart?'

'The Empress has never given evidence of possessing that frail organ. Probably as a gesture towards reassuring the people, however, she has sent a private mission to Shiraz in Persia for an architect named Ustad Isa to come over and design a mausoleum in honour of her dead father.'

'Is that not a bit extreme?' He was quoting one of Sir Thomas's favourite phrases.

'People resort to the extremities when they want to impress others with the depth of their emotions. We English have a phrase "from the bottom of my heart". If the heart had a bottom, it would exercise alimentary functions. Apart from this . . . um . . . slight aberration, the Empress appeared sane in all other respects when I last met her. Oh, before I forget, she has developed one other trait, a merciless faculty for perpetually referring to her father's intellect and achievements, which she seems to enjoy even more at the nineteenth repetition than at the eighteenth. Her problem probably is that, needing to establish a family name and identity, she has to declare her father an ancestor. It is an exercise in futility in her case, because one can alter the history of one's family background, but geography will always reveal the truth.'

'Well put, Sir Ambassador.' Rana Chara was enjoying himself in the hearing even more than Sir Thomas in the telling. 'But what is this I hear about the Princess Mumtaz Mahal contracting smallpox and being confined to the Ajmer palace?'

Sir Thomas grinned again. 'Mm . . . The story is true. The Empress is torn with anxiety, not to mention chagrin, at her niece's ailment, which coincidentally made it impossible for the young lady and her children to be present at the funeral obsequies of the late Salima Begum. The Empress had actually sent a military escort to Ajmer to bring the Princess Mumtaz Mahal and her children back for the event. Such touching family devotion! Pity it was wasted because the princess was in quarantine.'

Rana Chara stared at the ambassador. 'You think then that Mumtaz Mahal lied to avoid returning to captivity in the palace?'

Sir Thomas shrugged broad shoulders. 'Who but the princess would know when her face is hidden behind the veil?'

'Very clever.'

'She is a highly intelligent, remarkable young woman of great strength of character. She has certainly earned the single-minded devotion which her husband bestows on her . . . his only redeeming . . . er . . . gesture because he has no virtues!'

'Shah Jahan's single-mindedness has its rewards,' Rana Chara countered. 'It is rendered easier because he avoids temptations by living in his tent, leading the austere life, when he is on the field. More than a side benefit of this is that, since he does not cart a *harem* with him while on military campaigns, he is a fit, alert commander and a tireless soldier in consequence.'

'Mmm . . . I am well aware that many a battle has been lost because a commander had so many erections the previous night that he could not sit erect on his horse the next day! Seeking release in sexual exploits at such a time generally betrays weakness of character, the desire to forget or set aside the promptings of timidity. But enough of that.' He paused. 'Since I have answered all your questions, Sire, may I ask a few of my own?'

'Certainly.'

'We have always been blunt with each other, have we not?'

'Yes.'

'Did you murder your father?'

'Did you murder yours?'

The long jaw dropped. Then Sir Thomas caught the cunning of the words, slapped his thigh and guffawed. '*Touché*,' he conceded. 'Now my next question. What are your immediate plans?'

'To unite the two kingdoms of Rajasthan that are separated by Ajmer.'

'How will you do that?'

'By capturing Ajmer once Shah Jahan moves on to Kandhar.'

'So Shah Jahan's move to Kandhar is vital to your plan?'

'Yes.'

'And then?'

'We shall bring Ahmad, the Deccan and the Sikhs up north into a coalition.'

'When you have achieved that?'

'We shall need the help of your country to throw aside the Moghul yoke.'

'Supposing that help is not forthcoming?'

'It will come. After all, the Emperor has only thrown the crumbs of trade at you, though you have worked for years to obtain the entire loaf. Your East India Company would pay any price for the trade *we* shall offer you. If you do refuse, we shall turn to the Portuguese, who, as you know, have been well established on our east and west coasts for over a hundred years, since the days of Viceroy Admiral Vasco da Gama, or to the newly emerging Dutch East India Company.'

'Mm . . . m. Heavy stuff.'

'Vast Empire!'

It was dusk by the time he returned to his tent from visiting the troops who were preparing for the move to Mandu, orders for which he had issued that morning immediately upon receiving the *firman* from Amir Zain agreeing to move Mumtaz Mahal and the children forthwith from Agra to Ranthanbor. Although he went about his duties cheerfully, as if he did not have a care in the world, Shah Jahan was experiencing mixed emotions. He was certain, after his silent communion with her last night, that Mumtaz Mahal was safe but, being extremely practical, it was difficult for him to depend exclusively on intuition. Doubts would occasionally creep in. Further, even if Mumtaz Mahal was safe, Nur Jehan could refuse to accept Amir Zain's *firman*, or she could deliberately misconstrue its meaning, or something could happen to his family on the journey. The possibilities for missed connections were great, but once he got to Mandu, there would at least be no more major river crossings between him and Agra.

They had endured another blistering hot day. Men within the encampment, stripped down to their loin cloths, were bathing in the cool waters of the river. He could hear the shouting and splashing and the clap-boom of those who kept ducking into the water. Lambs were roasting on spits above glowing fires and the aroma of cooking was wafted towards him by a fiery breeze.

Seated on a settle, he was about to have his personal

attendant remove his riding boots when he heard the commotion. He waved the man aside and walked to the open tent entrance. General Wahid was escorting a dust-covered cavalry captain, obviously Moghul, walking stiffly towards him. He was young and of medium build. Beneath a shaven head, his features were regular and adorned by a thin, black moustache.

Seeing Shah Jahan, he hastened his steps. This must be a messenger from Mumtaz Mahal. Shah Jahan's heart started beating faster, but he remained outwardly cool, resisted the urge to dash forward.

The captain knelt to him. 'I am Captain Raschid of the Fifth Imperial Cavalry Regiment station in Ajmer, Prince,' he announced, rising to his feet. 'I have ridden night and day to bring you important letters.'

Disappointment reached into Shah Jahan's stomach. The man was from Ajmer, so these must be military despatches. But he had said 'letters', not 'despatches'. Who could be writing to him from Ajmer?

Captain Raschid proffered a package to him, which he accepted.

'Any emergency in Ajmer, Captain?' he inquired.

'None that I know of, Prince.'

'Have Captain Raschid suitably quartered near my tent,' Shah Jahan commanded the chief of the guards. 'Meanwhile, he may like a bath and some refreshment. See to it. General Wahid, would you please attend me?'

He turned, acknowledging the salutes of the men. He called to his attendants that he wished to be alone until he summoned them, before entering his tent, followed by General Wahid. They sat on their usual settles. Shah Jahan placed the package on the table and broke open the seals. His breath caught when he saw the familiar handwriting. He fumbled with the scroll in his excitement, glancing once at General Wahid who was well aware of his concern over

494

his family. 'I am writing this from Ajmer, where our children and I are safe and well.' He nodded to General Wahid, smiling to acknowledge that all was well. Relief flooded him. How like his thoughtful beloved to start with the most important item of news when anyone else would have given the whole long story from beginning to end. His intuition had been right. Joyously he read on, learning all that had happened to Mumtaz Mahal, from the Friday morning when Salima Begum had summoned her to the time of writing. She and the children were staying with Princess Jemaliya in the Ajmer palace *harem*. The princess had proved to be as steadfast as Salima Begum. Shah Jahan smiled tenderly when he read of the bogus attack of smallpox. 'So now we can say that we have both lived through the disease!' Mumtaz had written. What a remarkable human being! Such ingenuity, tenacity of purpose and high ideals, inherited from her father. Captain Raschid was the closest friend of the Chief Eunuch of the *harem* and could be trusted not to divulge who sent him on his mission to anyone or to pry into the contents of the package.

He read of Salima Begum's death with mixed feelings, all of them detached. He remembered her from his childhood as a distant woman who saw to it that he had the proper upbringing his grandfather desired. He had been grateful to her, had respected her, but could never generate warmth or affection for her, neither of which she had ever shown to him in any physical way. Now this! How little one knew of people's true feelings.

He gave General Wahid details of Mumtaz Mahal's letter, knowing he could trust his aide implicitly. When he finished, the craggy face cracked in a smile beneath the iron-grey moustache. 'Time we had some good personal news, my lord prince,' he commented.

Shah Jahan noted the 'we' with pleasure. Beneath the stern, composed exterior, this man was another loyal human being; in fact, like his grandmother, one of a vanishing breed. 'I wish I felt more of a personal sense of loss at Salima Begum's death,' he confessed. 'Beneath her old autocratic mask, Salima Begum had genuine love for my grandfather which has carried through to concern for me. It touches me. What is remarkable is that her sense of responsibility towards both of us lasted through the years until her last loving duty to both of us was fulfilled, when she removed the will to live which had kept her body together, and the body fell apart.'

'Her reputation for being a power behind the imperial throne while her husband was alive reached beyond the *harem*,' General Wahid commented. 'She will now be in Paradise. It is astonishing how a human body can fail when the will to live ends.'

Shah Jahan grew thoughtful. 'It reminds me of the philosophy of the Buddha which Ustad Isa once referred to in one of our discussions. Lives are an accumulation of *kharmic* substances. They can end with timely or untimely death. Timely death is the exhaustion of those *kharmic* substances in due process, not necessarily old age, but because of limits or inadequacies inherent in one or more of those substances. Untimely death is when the substances are removed. Ustad Isa quoted the example of a lamp. The flame of life is supported by the size of the container, the wick, the oil. Timely death depends on the nature and quantity of the wick and the oil. When the oil is fully used, the flame splutters out. In untimely death the flame could be extinguished by a gust of wind, or someone spilling the oil or jerking the wick, all accidents, or by someone stealing the oil, thus causing premature death, or by blowing out the flame, removing the wick or deliberately spilling the oil, murder.'

'Interesting,' General Wahid asserted. 'As good Muslims, we should not be discussing other religions, but that philosophy does not, in my view, clash with the teachings of the Prophet. It could complement them. Salima Begum therefore died a timely death?'

'Yes. And since she was a model of purity and uprightness, dedication and devotion, her soul will be sharing Paradise now with the Emperor Akbar. I wish I could shed even a single tear for her in my heart, but I have no tears. What would Salima Begum want from me? Respect was more important to her than love. I have just realized with wonder that love can end or change in our lifetimes or when death takes over, but respect remains forever.'

General Wahid watched him in silence. Shah Jahan re-read all the letters, then pushed back his settle. His mind working furiously, he stared unseeing at the darkness outside, oblivious to the sounds of the encampment. 'Amir Zain is a liar,' he finally declared. 'He knew all along that Mumtaz Mahal and the children were not in Agra. When he agreed to have them brought to Ranthanbor, he was granting a concession it was not in his power to extend. Where does that leave the situation? No one in Buran but you and I know of the escape of my family. Shall I send a fast patrol to catch up with our messengers who are carrying the despatches to Agra and bring them back? Should I refuse to move until my family is actually delivered to me? Should I advance on Ajmer, seize the city and rescue my family? Should I send one of our guerilla units to do that instead? So much is at stake.' He pounded the table, unable to express even to General Wahid what he would really like to do, which was to march on Agra and seize the imperial throne.

'I have always found that when an opponent is practising a deception and we are aware of it, we have the tactical advantage if the opponent continues to believe that we have been deceived,' the general advised.

'You mean I should do nothing to let Amir Zain or the

497

Emperor and Empress know that their deceit has been uncovered?' He stared at the general.

'Yes, my lord prince.'

Head to one side, in a pose that he half-consciously knew to be similar to his grandfather's, Shah Jahan considered that. 'You are right,' he finally conceded. 'Another lesson learned from you, general.'

General Wahid beamed.

'With that, everything falls into place. I can achieve all else I need by following the present plan. While those in Agra believe that they have me dancing on a string, I shall accelerate our departure and arrive at Mandu in great strength. This will make me even more needed for Kandhar.' He pondered a while, clicked his fingers. 'That's it. My wife's quarantine period expires in four weeks. We shall time the arrival of our main body in Mandu so that I can set out for Ajmer with a strong escort to move my wife and family personally to the Ranthanbor fort, where they will be safe. I shall do this *before* I receive any response from Agra to Amir Zain's *firman*. Do you think there will be any opposition to me from the Ajmer military command?'

'You are going there for the legitimate purpose of looking after your family. Besides,' General Wahid smiled grimly, 'no one within the imperial troops would dare cross you!'

Having received Amir Zain's final despatch, Nur Jehan could not wait for Sir Thomas Roe to return to Agra from Mewar. Since her father's death, her only competent adviser was her brother, the Prime Minister, but how could she trust Asaf Khan's loyalty where his own daughter Mumtaz Mahal and her husband were concerned?

Once again it was Friday afternoon. This time, Sir Thomas sat alone, his back to the blue-tiled pool and its splashing silver fountain. Summer was drawing to a close so there was a silver coolness to the pitiless sunshine beating on the outer courtyard, which she could see through the slit of the green curtains. Sir Thomas was richly dressed as always in thick dark blue doublet, a gold medal at his chest, hanging from a heavy chain, white satin breeches and netherhosen, with gold buckles at the knee and the inevitable cod-piece. He looked more tanned, his long nose peeling from the long rides to and from Mewar.

She made the usual pleasant inquiries about his visit, refrained from asking political questions to which she knew she would only receive courteously evasive replies. She then told him about the despatch she had received from Amir Zain.

The palm of one hand on his knee, Sir Thomas listened most attentively. A broad finger tapping briefly, indicated a thought. 'Puts you rather in a quandary, does it not?' he finally inquired. 'Shah Jahan will not leave Buran until you deliver what you cannot!'

'You have acquired a flair for stating the obvious,' she responded tartly. They had grown accustomed of late to speaking freely.

He flushed. 'Then let me help you with the obvious! There's an old saying, if the mountain will not come to Mahomet, Mahomet must go to the mountain.'

'Such irreverence, Sir Ambassador.'

'Such veracity, Madam. The period of diet and rest for smallpox is, I understand, seven to eight weeks. Four weeks have already gone by, but you cannot afford to wait much longer before you pull Shah Jahan away from what is now virtually his territory. Send word to him of his wife's reported ailment and give him the *firman* he requested, signed and sealed by the Emperor. Since he has agreed to proceed immediately to Mandu with his army, leaving behind whatever forces are necessary for the defence of the Deccan and Ahmad, you will have his family waiting for him in Ranthanbor on his arrival. With the Princess Mumtaz Mahal in Ajmer, this is an easy promise to make.'

'We then lose our most lethal weapon.'

'A weapon you do not possess, Madam, is never lethal.'

She saw the wisdom of his words, but could not give in as yet. 'If we wait out the period for diet and rest, we can bring Shah Jahan's family back to Agra, by force if necessary.'

'And risk the odium of the people, cause civil war at a time when you need to defend your frontier against a foreign invader? Come, Madam, please realize that if you damage a man's heart, he will not use his head in resisting you.'

She bridled at his tone, but held her temper. 'You are right, Sir Ambassador. We are indebted to you for your good advice, which we shall follow. If we have read the new Shah Jahan aright, he will be taking steps independently to have his family join him. We might as well get the credit for it.'

He was always so desperately tired nowadays and the frequent attacks of asthma at night left him exhausted. Yet he was the Emperor and had to keep up the appearance of well-being for the benefit of his subjects. It was part of the price of his position.

Nur Jehan was his one source of comfort and joy. Beautiful undoubtedly, but also a rock, she alone knew of his every ache and discomfort. She was wife, friend, companion and mother to him. He never needed to hold anything back from her. If the day had been specially trying, he could always look forward to the peace of sharing it with her at night, as they lay side by side on the mattress in the bedchamber of her suite of rooms at the Agra palace.

'Have you been unhappy today, star of my soul?' she inquired, gently caressing his face. However tired he was, her naked body never failed to excite him, though he did not try to prove his manhood to her. In fact, it was frequently brought to his notice that she had spread word throughout the *harem* that he had been so magnificent in bed, the virile stud, that she was exhausted, when he had merely lain with her, limp and flaccid. He was specially grateful to her for these lies of love.

'No, light of my life. Mm . . . m. That is wonderful. I like that.' He was responding to the gossamer touch of her slender fingers on his skin. 'As a matter of fact, today was one of my better days . . . and now it is the best of all.'

'Flatterer!' Her fingers moved from his face to his neck. She rose and straddled him to massage his shoulders. He loved the moist warmth of her naked womanhood on his bare stomach.

Believing that the Empire was in the safe hands of his beloved wife, who nonetheless kept him informed of all important events and consulted him whenever major decisions were required, he was content with the trappings of office, like his daily *durbar*, which he loved. Frankly, he did not want to be bothered by affairs of State when he felt so wretched. He needed time to write, especially in his diary, and to investigate flora about which he had great curiosity. Since the day he first vomited blood, his health had begun to deteriorate. The Court physicians had given him a choice of abstaining from alcohol and opium to live longer or a much shorter lifespan. He simply could not give up drinking and the joys of the pipe. When the attacks of asthma commenced, it seemed as if nothing but pain and misery lay ahead for him. He could also see his stomach getting increasingly bloated and his legs becoming spindly. He recalled with sadness the days of his youth, when he was a magnificent fighting man who exercised regularly, fought hard and lived hard. Now he could not even get hard! He was caught in the vicious circle of poor health that drained him of all desire and ability to exert himself physically, and the consequent absence of exercise which further ruined his health.

'Mm . . . mm,' he went again, closing his eyes, as her kneading hands eased the tension in his shoulders. 'However dark my days, the one bright light is you, Nur Jehan. Always tender and loving, you make no demands on me, least of all in the bedchamber, where you are content to hold me in your arms all night and share the warmth of companionship instead of demanding the heat of sexual passion. You have relieved me of all my burdens, whether in governing the Empire or in my personal life. You are a tower of strength to me, while being the foundation of my existence. I am *so* grateful. To me, Nur Jehan can do no wrong.' He opened his eyes, smiled at her and closed them again, very much at peace from the magic of her touch and the feel of her love.

Her silence told him that there were problems. His deep love for her prompted him to open his eyes with the desire to share. 'Something is wrong, is it not?' he inquired gently.

'There are always crises in our Empire, my lord.' Her hands worked towards his upper arms. 'Nothing that I cannot take care of.'

He grasped her wrists, held them. 'Tell us what has happened.' His concern made him slip into the royal plural, and he saw that deep down she was still in awe of his majesty.

'I have taken appropriate steps, my lord, but the man who swore eternal friendship to you has proved himself a lying hypocrite.'

A twinge of alarm went through him. 'Shah Abbas?'
She nodded.

'What has he done? Finally attacked Kandhar?' Her eyes told him the truth. 'The despicable son of a whoring pig!'

'Yes, lord. But I have taken all necessary action. The

governor of Kandhar is holding out resolutely and I have ordered Shah Jahan to move with the bulk of his army to drive the Persian rabble away.'

'Shah Jahan? We will not permit that fornicator to come to Agra. We shall kill the bastard when the time is right.' He hated the son of a bitch who had dared to approach Nur Jehan. Traitors, traitors and hypocrites, every one of them. Only his beloved Nur Jehan was pure, true and loyal. He was getting breathless. 'We do not even want his lascivious eyes gazing at you.'

'Relax now, my lord. Breathe slowly and easily. There now.'

Nur Jehan had even taught him how to prevent his asthmatic attacks by controlling his breathing.

'I am perfectly capable of dealing with Shah Jahan now that you have given me the power,' she assured him. 'As a matter of fact, I have insisted that his family move from Ajmer, where his wife, who as you know has the smallpox, is residing. They will proceed to the Ranthanbor fort and be with him thereafter. As for Shah Jahan gazing at me,' she smiled tenderly, 'he will remain in Agra only to receive orders from me. I shall be behind my curtains. He need not even see me so long as I do not attend your *durbar* on those days.'

'Do *I* have to see him?' He was back to his role in her bedchamber now.

'It would be important as a concession to a victorious general.'

'Damn the victorious general. Why should I see such a son of a bitch?'

'Because you copulated with the bitch.' She smiled tenderly. 'Also, the world must not only know that you are giving the orders, it must see and hear you give them to him.'

'Ah, Nur Jehan, always so wise. Very well then. Go

ahead and do as you deem fit. Tell me well enough in advance when I have to give this upstart audience, so I can steel myself for the event.' He sighed at the thought, then brightened.

Whatever the drawbacks of being an Emperor, with Nur Jehan in charge, the Empire was in safe hands. But the curses of Allah on the two Shahs, Abbas and Jahan. Maybe the title Shah was unlucky for him. Perhaps he should not have conferred the title on Prince Jahan. He tried to ponder on this, but his mind started meandering as it did so frequently nowadays.

Chapter 31

They were halted by sentries with levelled muskets at the gates of Ajmer, a most unusual occurrence in an open city. The guard commander who had been summoned was striding purposefully towards them through the warm evening-gold air. He was a huge swarthy Pathan infantry captain, with the familiar turban, fierce moustaches and hot eyes.

'This is a bad sign, my lord prince,' General Wahid, who was riding beside Shah Jahan, muttered under his breath. 'They can only act this way on instructions from Agra.'

When they had reached Mandu two weeks after Shah Jahan had received Mumtaz Mahal's letters, news of Prince Shahriyar's marriage to Princess Ladili awaited them. Shah Jahan had been incensed. Nur Jehan was proceeding with the implementation of her plan.

He had left thirty thousand men behind under the overall command of General Khan for the protection of Buran, Ahmad and Bija as well as the Deccan, so he had fifty thousand, including all his crack troops, under his direct command. The Rajputs, Raja Bhim and General Vickram, his most loyal senior commanders, had accompanied him to Mandu. His highest priority now being to rescue his family, he had decided to select one of two options when he arrived at Mandu. He could either proceed onwards, with his entire army, as Agra expected, or he could remain there until Mumtaz Mahal and his three children were reported to have arrived safely in Ranthanbor. The wedding of his youngest brother to Nur Jehan's daughter had, however, thrown a different complexion on his movements. It brought Nur Jehan's cunning and ruthlessness most forcibly to his attention. She clearly intended to control the succession and was therefore quite capable of harming his family.

He decided on a third alternative. Ignoring Amir Zain's protests, pleas and warnings, he ordered his army to make camp at Mandu and proceeded to Ajmer, accompanied only by General Wahid and a small escort. His despatch to the Emperor included his reasons for his change of plan:

My men have been on the field for many months now and are battle-weary. I have pushed them to the limits in order to obey Your Imperial Majesty's commands. Now, pre-monsoon rains have commenced and we face high winds and floods along the way. Horses, elephants, cannon and wagons will get bogged down. All this my men and I would gladly endure in the interest of the Empire, but if Your Imperial Majesty's ultimate object, which is the defeat of Shah Abbas and our Persian enemies, is to be achieved, it is vital that the troops under my command be rested and fresh before they leave for Kandhar.

Under those circumstances, I humbly beseech your gracious approval to have the army under my command remain in Mandu until the worst of the monsoon is over.

Meanwhile, it would greatly strengthen my ability to provide Your Imperial Majesty with the finest fighting men if I receive the authority to demote or dismiss officers under my command who are unworthy and promote those of merit.

It would also be a boost to my effectiveness to fulfil your Imperial Majesty's goals in the north-west and an inspiration to the devoted service of which Your Imperial Majesty is assured at all times, if the *suba* (fief) of Punjab were added to my personal estate.

Finally, I most respectfully and humbly request the assurance that adequate funds have been set aside at source for the conduct of the Kandhar operation and its successful conclusion . . .

He had just told General Wahid the specific requests in his despatch. The general's response had been a lift of the shaggy eyebrows, a sombre expression and confirmation of what Shah Jahan already knew. 'Demotion, dismissal and promotion of officers have hitherto been the Emperor's sole prerogative. Setting aside adequate funds at source from the imperial treasury for a campaign is not even a practice of the Emperors themselves.' He shrugged broad shoulders. 'Well, you have created so many precedents, my lord prince, why not two more?' He grinned. 'At least the fiefdom of Punjab is negotiable!'

'I shall make all concessions necessary for security,' Shah Jahan snarled, eyeing the approaching Pathan captain. 'But I shall *not* be thwarted in my plan.' His anger began to mount. He had been to Ajmer so many times before, with his grandfather, his father and, occasionally, alone, but had never been stopped at the entrance gates, least of all by a guard captain. Besides, his heart had been literally pounding at the prospect of being with Mumtaz Mahal again. He had thought of a dozen things to tell her, teasing things, tender words and of many acts of overwhelming love. 'No one shall stop me. If need be, we shall fight our way to the palace.'

'A thousand to one? Why not?' General Wahid said quietly. 'I would ride through the gates of death with you.

But remember, it is not a gallant death we came seeking, but the life and well-being of your family. Would it not be better to return with a strong enough force to take Ajmer?'

'In my last letter to my wife, I gave her my oath that I would join her on the day she ends her quarantine. Today is that day.'

'Your life is worth more to her than the oath you gave her, my lord prince. Let me force a way through with our escort, while you . . .' he stopped, smiling ruefully at the realization that Shah Jahan would never have agreed to what he had been about to suggest.

The Pathan was nearing them. Shah Jahan felt the need to explain himself to this man who might die with him. 'An oath is absolute and inflexible,' he stated softly. 'Otherwise, life, government, even man's relationships with his God, cannot be maintained with any degree of reliance. An oath publicly taken is therefore unshakeable if we are to be held in public esteem. One privately taken is, however, even more binding if we are to retain self-esteem. I shall not do you the dishonour of suggesting that you should not offer your life for my personal oath, because I know you will ride with me to victory or Paradise.'

He stopped speaking as the guard commander halted by the head of Samt II and, to his amazement, grasped its bridle.

Having spent the entire morning in an access of fury, following the receipt of Shah Jahan's despatch, Nur Jehan had regarded it as an omen that Rana Chara had requested the Emperor's permission to call on him informally as a token of humble submission and was already in the Agra palace as a guest. She guessed that the new Rana would never be humble or submissive in his heart, but had welcomed the opportunity his visit afforded for a discussion with him and Sir Thomas Roe.

Rana Chara was to be in Agra over a long weekend. She arranged for him to attend the Thursday evening *durbar* so her own meeting with him could take place once again on Friday afternoon. She had received Shah Jahan's despatch only that morning and had opened it though it was addressed to the Emperor. It was her practice to read all correspondence addressed to the Emperor first, so she could tell him only what she wished him to know.

It was another bright summer afternoon in Agra, not as warm as the last time the three of them had met in her reception chamber. Through the slit in the green velvet curtains, she could see Sir Thomas mopping his brow. She also noted that Rana Chara's new estate had not caused him to change his plain style of dress.

'Gentlemen, let us open this discussion with our felicitations to our new Rana on his accession and our condolences to him on the death of his father, especially under such tragic circumstances.' Her voice carried the sincerity she felt. 'If the Empire had to know such a loss, it has gained by the addition of a new ruler of such remarkable character and abilities.'

'We thank you, Madam,' Rana Chara responded. She could not help wondering whether the melancholy note in his voice was not faked. 'The cobra is a sacred creature in our mythology. It guards treasures. Was it not a cobra that shielded the most sacred treasure of this Empire as a baby? Now, a cobra has killed our father.'

A hand flew to her mouth. She was glad she could not be observed. 'You are too kind, my lord Rana,' she responded, steadying herself. Then inspiration flared. 'Since we both owe our present high offices to the sacred creature, it is all the more reason for us to make common cause.' She plunged into the text of Shah Jahan's communication to her, controlling spasms of fury.

When she finished, silence reigned in the chamber,

broken only by the whistling of love-birds from their cages in the courtyard.

The two men looked at each other. 'The young Shah's demands are so preposterous, they almost amount to treason,' Sir Thomas finally declared. 'What do you think, Rana?'

'Shorn of the euphemisms of Court language, they are nothing short of blackmail.' He smiled faintly, stroked his black moustache with a long forefinger. 'The problem is, who will rope this crazed tiger at the present moment? We remember when Prince Jahan, as he was then, was a pillar of obedience. If we may be permitted to mix the metaphor, since it is Princess Mumtaz Mahal who has turned a vegetable marrow, as you once called him, into a raging tiger, perhaps that is where you should direct your attention, now that her period of quarantine is almost over. After all, if our assessment of the princess's malady is correct, her attack of smallpox is hardly likely to cause an epidemic! But Your Imperial Majesty has undoubtedly considered this course already.' He cocked an inquiring eyebrow at the slit in the curtains.

'Mm . . . m . . .' Sir Thomas communicated his approval by the tone of his voice. 'The lady obviously likes security rather better than she does the truth.'

'We have already taken steps to bring the Princess Mumtaz Mahal back to Agra, where she belongs.' Her temper flamed. 'It is not dignified for female members of the imperial family to follow their husbands throughout the country like common whores . . .'

Even as she uttered the words 'imperial family', she knew they were a mistake. She saw the flash in Rana Chara's dark, deep-set eyes. He flicked a speck off his white *jodhpurs*. 'Madam, dignity is not the sole prerogative of imperial families.' His nonchalant tone belied his inner reaction. 'It belongs to the entire human race. Unfortunately, we have kings who are peasants and peasants who are kings. It is not a matter of birth, but of cause and effect, because at base, society has ensured the evolution of the entire human race into a bunch of whores! Those of us who are Emperors and Ranas are *common* whores, Madam, because we provide our services to the *common* people for a price. A body for a night, a life for a lifetime, what's the difference? As for women, give me the whore that lies with a man for a few rupees rather than the wife who, loathing her husband, cohabits with him for a marriage licence and a permanent place in society.'

The ambassador made no comment, merely gave a grunt of approval.

You are a known homosexual who takes his pleasure from his men on the battlefield, so how would you know about wives? Nur Jehan thought, but she dared not voice the sentiment. 'If philosophy could solve such enormous affairs of State, all we would need is a few platitudes,' she commented tartly.

'Let the Princess Mumtaz Mahals of the world accompany their husbands into battle if it keeps them monogamous.' Sir Thomas adroitly steered the conversation into safer waters, quoting Shah Jahan's thesis with a straight face. He rubbed his long nose thoughtfully. 'Which brings us to the point of our discussion. In my view, you should reject Shah Jahan's demands outright and order him to return to Agra with all troops under his command in Mandu immediately. The Emperor is the commander-in-chief of the armed forces so this must include all army and corps commanders.'

'You can always issue the command,' Rana Chara intervened. 'But how do you ensure compliance? We are agreed that Shah Jahan and his men should return, but there must be a more effective way of ensuring it.' He clicked his fingers. 'We have it.' Nur Jehan could not help noting how easily he had slipped into the use of the royal plural. 'We are overlooking the nature of our opponent.'

'What do you mean?' Nur Jehan demanded.

'Don't you see? Shah Jahan's demand that his wife be moved to Ranthanbor is a ploy to get her away from cities directly under your control, but he will not remain content to have her live so close to Ajmer and Agra. It is meaningless. He will try to get her to Mandu, a well-nigh impregnable city, and his stronghold in the region he now controls. Being Shah Jahan of the lightning strikes, he will do so by an immediate personal visit to Ajmer, which he will only undertake with a small escort. He will have played right into our hands if you take steps to have him escorted, not arrested or apprehended, by royal command, back to Agra, with his beloved wife and children accompanying him.'

Sir Thomas clapped his hands lightly. 'Well reasoned, my lord,' he declared, then focused his attention at the slit in the curtains. 'Marriage can be such a fatal addiction!' he commented.

A thrill of triumph went through Nur Jehan. Ignoring the ambassador's barb, she also cast aside a vague concern about possible problems from the two Rajasthan kingdoms once the imperial presence in the region was depleted. There was no situation she could not handle. 'We are both obviously guarded and inspired by the sacred cobra, Rana. So we reason alike and are blessed with its sting. Having anticipated such a move on Shah Jahan's part ourself, we have already taken adequate steps to turn it to our advantage.'

They discussed the steps she had taken in Ajmer. To her delight, both men praised her wisdom and tenacity of purpose.

'Shah Jahan may have a reputation throughout the Empire as a wonder-worker,' Sir Thomas concluded, 'but it is the Emperor's prerogative to have his subjects perform their wonders only wherever and whenever he deems expedient. If Shah Jahan demurs, you have the power to convert the wonder-worker into a charlatan.' He paused. 'And now, Your Imperial Majesty, having had the privilege of participating with you in discussing what could be one of the most stirring events of our times, I regret that I have some personal news which saddens me exceedingly.'

Apprehension scrambled Nur Jehan's stomach. For months on end, she had had nothing but bad news. 'What is your news, Sir Ambassador?' she inquired, steadying her voice. 'Anything that saddens you would grieve us.'

'I have received orders from my own king and the Company I serve to leave India and proceed to Turkey without delay, where I shall take up similar duties.'

'But . . . why?' She already knew the answer.

'I have failed in my mission here.' The words came out succinctly, but with a careless smile. Sir Thomas would face even death with that smile.

'You mean you have been unable to obtain a monopolistic trade agreement with the Empire?' Rana Chara carefully avoided referring to the Emperor.

'Yes. It is nobody's fault. Mine perhaps. I have done my best.' His smile was wistful. 'But as a wise Sinhala prince of Lanka is reported to have said fifteen hundred years ago: Doing one's best is never enough, it is the lame excuse of those who fail.' He squared broad shoulders, lifted the bearded chin. 'I am being elevated to a higher post, so I neither need nor deserve sympathy. It is I alone who stand in judgment over my achievements or lack of them.'

Nur Jehan could not bring herself to speak. In the silence that reigned, the splattering fountain seemed to be laughing at mere mortals. See, I am water. I go on forever. You may change my form, into steam, but I always return as rain. Filling her with a strange sense of loss, it gave her an idea.

Rana Chara glanced sharply through the slit in the curtain as if he would bore through it and reach her regardless. She knew then that he too was filled with a sense of loss and that his feeling for the Englishman was the closest he had ever come to caring for someone.

'Madam,' Rana Chara asserted earnestly, 'the Empire cannot, must not, permit the loss of such a fine English statesman and . . . er . . . er . . . loyal friend. Besides, with the European sea-dogs baying at our ocean frontiers, we need the naval might of England as our ally. Give Sir Thomas the trade agreement he seeks and he can remain in India for the rest of his days, our honoured guest as always.'

Unaccustomed to praising anyone in public or private, Rana Chara had avoided looking at Sir Thomas. 'Yes, yes,' Nur Jehan hastened to agree. 'We have been remiss in not interceding with the Emperor in this matter. Be assured, Sir Ambassador, that we shall do so this very night and you shall have your treaty, executed and sealed, tomorrow morning, on only one essential condition, that it will last while you are the English Ambassador in our Court.'

'Hrm . . . ph . . . Hrm . . . ph!' Sir Thomas was visibly moved. He fished out his cream linen handkerchief and blew his nose. He replaced it and shook his head. 'I'm afraid it is too late for that, Your Imperial Majesty,' he stated with a faint smile. 'I have received my orders and the ship that conveys me to Turkey already awaits me in Surat. But I do thank you for your generosity.'

'Surely you can send a despatch back to our brother, your king, stating what has happened and our desires in this matter.'

The chin lifted. 'I am afraid I could never do that,' Sir Thomas declared. 'Once orders are received, they must never be questioned, right or wrong. Otherwise, the might of my country would be weakened.'

'But this would be carrying out the objects of your king,' she remonstrated. 'You can at least ask for more time.'

This time the English Ambassador's smile was sardonic. 'Madam, I am not a Shah Jahan.'

A hand on the left bridle of his horse! For a split second, Shah Jahan's mind raced back fifteen years. He had been a boy then, riding Samt I on the *maidan* of the Agra palace on a dark-grey dawn. Surely Samt II was no less mighty. Instinctively, he drew down and inwards on his reins, moved his knees up, giving Samt II the aid. Whinnying fiercely, in a flash, the mighty charger reared on his hind legs, almost lifting the huge Pathan captain off the ground. A tremendous lash with the forelegs caught the man four squarely in the chest. A stifled scream escaped him. He sprawled in the dust, his ribs shattered, jerked twice, then lay still.

Shah Jahan brought his mount under control again, patted his neck soothingly. The twelve-man guard detail, muskets levelled, was drawn in two ranks across the highway, the first rank kneeling, blocking his path. He noticed for the first time that a crowd had gathered at the gates, spellbound by the drama. They were all gazing horror-stricken at the fallen captain. His glance at the guard detail was deliberately casual. 'I am Shah Jahan, second surviving son of the Emperor Jehangir,' he said in clear, quiet tones. 'I command an army of eighty thousand men, all completely loyal to the Emperor and me. I have the right of free passage anywhere in this Empire and I intend exercising it without hindrance. I hereby rescind whatever orders you and your commanders may have received. My escort and I will now ride to the royal palace. If you try to stop us, you will rue this day for the rest of your lives.' He smiled with his teeth, his eyes cold and deadly. 'If you live that long!' He paused. 'Remember, you will be answerable to the Emperor if you lay your hands on a prince of the royal blood without his special warrant. And should any harm befall me or my comrades, the imperial army will march from Mandu and tear down your city, brick by brick.'

He lifted his chest, lightly relaxed the reins and squeezed with his thighs. Head up, neck curved, Samt II mince-gaited forward as if he were on display.

For a tense moment, it seemed as if the twelve men would not move from his path. Their sergeant cleared his throat, preparatory to giving the order to fire.

His brain ice-cool, his pulse beat normal, Shah Jahan eyed the man. 'Bury your dead!' he commanded.

The sergeant quailed, moved slightly aside. Shah Jahan rode through the guard detail, followed by General Wahid and his escort. The cheers of the crowd rose to the blue heavens, turned it into a triumphal march.

He rode directly to the palace courtyard. The sentries at the entrance made no move to stop him, merely saluted. He tossed the reins to the ever-vigilant grooms, commanded the chief attendant making obeisance at the doors to provide suitable accommodation for General Wahid and his escort. He nodded his thanks to the general, acknowledged his salute and strode through the wide marble corridors, attendants hurrying behind him, directly to the *harem*.

The Princess Jemaliya, an almost exact white-haired replica of Salima Begum, received him without delay in her reception chamber. She was even seated on a similar gold-upholstered divan and had dismissed her attendants. She waved him to a pink-cushioned ebony settle opposite her.

'You have come to rescue your wife,' the Princess said, her eyes smiling above her *yashmak*, 'from the ravages of smallpox. Very timely. We shall not obstruct you with unnecessary chatter. After all, you are a prince of the royal blood, commander of eighty thousand men and Almighty Allah alone knows how many cannon, horses, elephants and other impedimenta of battle.' Word of his statement at the palace gates had already reached her, he realized with wonder. Good, she was obviously a power in Ajmer, and had already proved herself a useful and loyal ally.

'My army and I would pause at your gracious feet, Princess,' he declared with sincerity. 'After all, armies are meant to oppose enemies, and to be at the disposal of friends.'

She pointed her fan at him. 'You were always the gallant one,' she stated. 'Aloof but gallant. Now go to your wife without delay. You may share her suite, since it is in our quarantine area and therefore separate from the rest of the *harem*.' She grew serious. 'Your wife awaits you impatiently, an elf with the strength and determination of a committed virgin. We would rather oppose your armies than her! You will not want to remain in Ajmer long, however, though we would welcome your stay.'

Chapter 32

She stood awaiting him at the far end of the small reception room of her private suite, opening out into a courtyard. He was barely aware of the golden glow from the hanging lamp overhead, the scent of camphor incense from the glowing braziers or the voices of little *harem* children singing in the distance. He paused at the entrance, drinking in her beauty. When Sati left, gently closing the door, he hardly heard it click.

Oh my beloved, you are more than passing fair. You are possessed of the deepest, most lustrous doe-like eyes.

516

The expression in those eyes drove all thought from his mind, the flood of love and longing pouring from them began to engulf him. All the tortured fears, the dreadful anxieties, the unfulfilled passions of the past months were released.

A cry of longing escaped him. He crossed the room in six strides. Then she was in his arms.

Her soft body, pliant as a willow wand, the large yielding breasts, the pert face uplifted to his, but mostly that gaze, that infinite, eternal gaze which only true love can produce. Heart pounding, he looked down at her, aware that he was holding her roughly and she was glorying in it.

He bent his head. His lips lightly touched her soft cheek. She gasped, closed her eyes, opened her mouth slightly. His lips melted into hers. He smelled and tasted her deep desire on her breath. She moved her pubis against his crotch.

He released her, reached down and lifted her in his arms. He carried her into the bedroom. He laid her on the divan, unbuttoned her pantaloons, pulled them off. He drew a breath at the white flesh of her thighs, released from their confines, the patch of her pubis dark brown in contrast. He reached through the slit of his baggy trousers. His penis literally shot out, proud, erect, angled upwards. Her eyes slowly drifted down to it. She smiled that mysterious half-smile, looked up at him and lifted her legs.

He entered her without foreplay. She was already moist.

She came twice before he did. The third time, they came together in glorious, long-drawn surging of united ecstasy. He did not seem to be able to stop the fluid that kept spurting from him, long stored for her alone. The clutch-ings of her vagina matched him, spasm for spasm.

He lay above her, on his elbows, sweating, exhausted. Loving her gratefully, as never before, he rained soft kisses

517

on her eyes, her cheeks, her mouth. Finally, he relaxed on her. She adjusted her body to hold him close, his cheek on her shoulder.

They slept in each other's arms, oblivious of time and space. Before he dozed off, he vaguely thought, I must see the three children, but he was powerless to attend to his fatherly duties. He could have dozens of children, but there was only one Mumtaz Mahal.

The chiming of a clock woke him. He was lying on her left side, his knee over her body. She was up on the instant. Her head turned, the large eyes, deep and slumbrous, gazed lazily at him.

'It's ten o'clock,' he said.

The elfin look flitted into her eyes. 'You see me after months that seemed like years and the first words you utter are: it's ten o'clock. Isn't that romantic?'

'I said other things,' he began, defensively.

'Uh-uh. Moans and groans don't count.'

How he adored her. 'Then let me say belatedly and at your urging, I love you,' he meant the words, 'with all my heart.'

'Too late,' she teased. 'You have to be punished for the omission.'

'I will forgive you your sins if you forgive me mine.'

'What have *I* done?'

'Your first words to me after months that seemed like years were: You see me after months that seemed like years and the first words you utter are . . . and so on and so on!'

She pouted. 'You're horrid!'

'And you're more beautiful than the night, hushed and deep, but sparkling with stars.'

She released her hands, touched his cheek. 'Oh my beloved husband, I love you. I've missed you *so* much.' Her eyes were wet with tears.

His penis came erect again, this time for being out of the

518

depths of misery, fear and uncertainty they had shared. 'You have been so gallant,' he whispered. He leaned over to kiss her.

She held his face with both hands, looked deep into his eyes. 'My darling heart, I want you to promise me that you will take me wherever you go, even to the battlefield.'

He was deeply moved. Yet the practical intruded. 'I can't do that. You know I live in a tent.' He paused. 'And I do take you with me wherever I go, in my heart and my spirit. Why, only the other night . . .' He told her of his experience in Buran, outside his tent, when his lonely, anxious heart had known despair only to be linked with her spirit so he knew she was safe and well.

'Words cannot replace deeds,' she replied gently, her eyes pleading. 'Nor can the mind and spirit compensate for the absence of the body.' Her eyes widened. 'I do not know how long we have with each other on this earth,' she whispered. The look of a seeress in her eyes frightened him. His organ went limp again. 'But I want to spend every possible moment of it with you. I am a miser, counting each second of our being together, hoarding it all to span the time between death and our meeting again in Paradise.'

'Don't talk like that,' he begged, heartsick, fearful.

'Well, my beloved, isn't it true?' she demanded, low, fierce.

'Ye . . . es. We all have to die sometime.' A platitude he thought, hopelessly.

'You may die on the battlefield.'

'Of course.' Her words made him feel a little better. She was not prophesying her death, merely afraid of his. Deep inside the thought nagged, you are trying to fool yourself.

'Do you know how many deaths I die when you are on your campaigns?'

'I can guess, but how could I ever really know?' he

519

responded truthfully. 'I can only equate it to my feelings when I think some harm has befallen you.'

He heard the fluttering of a moth's wings, gazed at the lamp, noted its vain efforts . . . sputter . . . sputter . . . sputter . . . to get to the flame that would scorch it to death.

'Multiply that a thousandfold before you can imagine what it feels like when I am safe in some palace *harem* and you are facing danger every moment.'

'You safe? Like you were in the Agra palace *harem*?' He was teasing, wanting to break the tension.

'Your presence here tonight is proof that you have known fear for my safety. Unlike me, you have the right, the freedom to come to me whenever you are worried. What do I have? Only the freedom to reach out to you with my spirit. Oh my beloved husband, it is simply not enough. Please promise that you will take me wherever you go.'

'The children . . .'

'Can come with us, or be looked after in the palaces. Didn't you in reality grow up without a father or mother?'

'Yes. But the tent, the discomfort – '

'I married you to be with you, to share your life. Where you go, I go, where you are, there I shall be, be it a tent or a palace, sharing the good and the bad, undergoing your hardships.' He could see her mind working swiftly. 'There is also something else of which Salima Begum warned me before she died.' She paused. 'Listen carefully. I am the most vulnerable part of your future. If your enemies have me in their power, they will hold a weapon against which you will have no defence. Your security and mine demand that I always remain in your protection until you become the Emperor.'

'You are cunning.' But he saw the wisdom of her words.

'No. The truth is cunning. And Salima Begum remained

alive just long enough to remove me, the weapon, from the grasp of your enemies. You are in her debt.'

'True, but I still think you are cunning.' Deeply moved nonetheless, he smiled gently at her. The tension eased as he felt her deep, deep love for him, from the fundament, the core, the source. Such love came to a man just once in a lifetime and only if he were blessed by Almighty Allah. His erection returned from a holy passion that came from beyond time.

She released his face, reached out and firmly grasped his penis, her soft fingers encircling it. That mischievous smile crossed her face. 'He is ready again, isn't he?'

'Yes.' The hoarseness of his voice came from the strength of his emotion.

'He is quite a big fellow, quite a man!'

'I hope so.'

'You want me?'

'Oh my beautiful beloved, I want you with every fibre of my being.'

'You shall have me, but only if you swear to take me wherever you go.'

'What?' He drew back, saw the elf in her and fell into her mood. 'Only whores go into battle with men.'

'I am your whore.'

'Only common whores demand a price for their bodies.' Such play had always been part of their love-making.

'I am *your* common whore.' She paused, grew serious. 'It is a high estate you bestowed on me by being true to me, faithful in every thought, word and deed. In a man's world, where men take their pleasure from every source of their desiring, where women are available by the hundred, you have given me purity. But it is not for your purity that I love you. I am Eve made from your fifth rib, destined to be your mate even if you had been the greatest womanizer in the world. I cannot help being for you in every way. So I am all that you have made me, your wife, your lover, your friend, your parent, your child and, always, your common whore.'

She had said it all. It seemed to him that they had lived this scene before. Tears prickled his eyes, but they would never fall. 'Wherever I go, you shall go with me,' he said quietly. 'My oath on it.'

They reached for each other in a delirium of oneness.

Nur Jehan had been despondent all evening. Sir Thomas Roe's announcement of his impending departure had shown her how much she had depended on this strong, haughty man, on his wisdom, knowledge and integrity, in her major battles, especially against Shah Jahan.

Shortly after dinner that night, she had obtained the Emperor's signature and seal on the *firman* she had prepared, ordering Shah Jahan to return forthwith to the imperial presence with his troops, wherever they might be.

> The siege of Kandhar will not be lifted by your monsoon. Should you be reluctant to risk rain and flood, you shall send your army to us immediately, under command of the Moghul and Rajput generals.
>
> Unquestioning obedience is the product of loyalty. Do not put your loyalty to question. The price you pay would be high . . .

The *firman* would leave by fast messenger for Mandu early the following morning. Meanwhile, she could see that her husband's condition was worse. Seated on the divan in her reception chamber, with her reclining at his feet on the Persian carpet, he seemed specially preoccupied tonight.

'We have been advised by our physicians that a change of climate would benefit us,' he finally stated, staring into space as if repeating a lesson he had learned. 'We too have

522

a yearning to leave for Srinagar, to the vale of Kashmir, where we always knew our best health.'

Her heart sank. If he went to Srinagar, she would have to travel with him. Being away from the centre of things at this juncture would be fatal, especially if he died while they were away. A disputed succession would be decided in the capital, Agra.

'We shall leave immediately,' he went on. 'The cool hills, the quiet lake with its floating gardens, lying beneath the mists of Karakoram, the waters enfolding a tracery of tree-silhouettes at their silver breast. The peace, the tranquill-ity.' He was almost mumbling now and she remembered with a shock that the desire to return to a place of youth and vitality frequently sprang in the minds of those who would never recover. Her husband was doomed. He might die in Srinagar, or on the journey up, before she had liquidated Shah Jahan's claims to the imperial throne. Prince Shahriyar was her only hope of wielding supreme power in the Empire. She had to remain in Agra.

'Ustad Isa, the architect who is to design my father's mausoleum, is due to arrive within a few months. Can we not wait until then to leave for Srinagar?'

'Bah!' The exclamation sent the ever-present faecal odour of his breath nauseatingly down on her. 'Let the dead bury the dead.' It was the Emperor speaking. The stern look in his eyes told that his fogged brain was clear again. 'Is your father's mausoleum more important to you than your Emperor's health?'

She knew she had over-reached herself and pulled back. 'You know better than that, star of my soul,' she responded. 'Only when the star shines brightly is there any light for me. Your health is more important than my life. My real concern was lest the long journey tire you. I thought it might be best for you to give yourself a period of rest in Agra, then leave for Srinagar in the spring to convalesce.'

523

She pretended to brighten, but her mind worked furiously. How could she ensure that the claims of Prince Parviz and Shah Jahan to the imperial throne were aborted while she and the Emperor were away in distant Srinagar?

'Everybody keeps telling us what to do.' He was near-mumbling again. '*We* are the Emperor. *We* make all the decisions.'

'Of course, Your Imperial Majesty.' Her use of this title always brought lucidity back to him.

Absurdly, an expression once used by Sir Thomas Roe was propelled into her consciousness: If the mountain does not come to Mahomet, Mahomet must go to the mountain. There was the solution! So simple she could have laughed aloud. Thankful for the Englishman's wisdom, she assumed the role of dutiful wife and parent, gazed at the Emperor with eyes full of love and concern. 'And do you know what we shall do to increase your well-being?'

'What? What?' His interest was only perfunctory.

'We shall command your sons, Prince Parviz and Shah Jahan to attend you in Srinagar.'

'But what about the Empire?' He paused, thinking, his mind suddenly lucid again. 'Bihar and the east could manage for a few months without Prince Parviz. He is a dru . . .' he changed the word, 'wastrel, in any case. But what about Shah Jahan? Do we not need him for Kandhar?'

'Indeed, but once he arrives in Agra, Prince Shahriyar can take over his army and leave for Kandhar while Shah Jahan joins us in Srinagar for a while. All Kandhar needs immediately is a show of force.' She hastened to add, 'Prince Shahriyar can handle that until Shah Jahan arrives to take over for his lightning strikes.' Then she thrust in, shrewdly, 'Besides, what is a couple of months' delay in comparison with our beloved Emperor's well-being.' Her gaze became adoring.

'You are a treasure,' he declared. 'Always full of the most

stunning ideas. And such a loving wife. We shall have the *firmans* prepared tomorrow.'

'On the contrary, star of my soul, the union of our family in the beautiful vale of Kashmir is so important that I shall have the *firmans* prepared immediately, so they can leave by messenger at dawn.'

'Do as you will, light of our life. Have we not handed you the Empire in return for a cup of wine and a few morsels of food!' He was quoting one of his favourite sayings, sometimes even uttered publicly.

'No, star of my soul,' she retorted. 'You have handed me the empire of your heart in exchange for mine.'

He surfaced from the sleep that followed their second love-making that night with a start, sat up on the divan. Ever since his earliest days, when danger approached, Shah Jahan would awaken thus, warnings forking through his brain. Lost in the bliss of being with his wife again, there was something he had missed. What was it? Seeing the children? No, that was responsibility, not danger unanticipated. The warning continued to nag.

'What is it, my beloved?' Mumtaz Mahal's voice was grainy with sleep, the words slurred. She was tired. You have worn me out, she had said before falling asleep in his arms.

He smiled tenderly at the recollection. Without ever trying, she made him feel a man, capable of looking after her in every way. In every way? Then it hit him. He clapped a hand to his forehead. 'Wake up, my darling heart.' He shook her gently.

She sat up, rubbed her eyes. 'Do you want it again?' she inquired, still half-asleep.

'No, I mean yes. I want it, but we cannot have it tonight. Get up now, ask Sati to pack your things and those of the children.' He glanced at the clock. It was twenty minutes past midnight. 'We leave immediately.'

'Leave?' She was wide awake now. 'My beloved husband, have you taken leave of your senses?'

'No,' he replied grimly. 'You befuddled my senses, but they are clear again. We cannot remain in Ajmer.'

'Why not?'

'Don't you see? I was allowed into the city without any further fuss after Samt II killed the guard captain. Why did they not come after me, at the very least to question me or offer apologies?'

Comprehension dawned in the doe-like eyes. 'You and I are virtual prisoners while we remain here.' She nodded slowly.

'That is why we must leave Ajmer tonight. We must do so before the military commander receives a warrant in the form of a mandatory summons to me from Nur Jehan. We shall use the fastest wagon available in the palace for you, the children and Sati.'

'Supposing the sentries at the gates refuse to open them?'

'I doubt that the garrison commander will have anticipated our leaving in the middle of the night. He will imagine that we are happily sleeping together, as indeed we were, so the men at the gates will have received no specific instructions. Just as I forced my entry, I can force my departure, with my escort if necessary. Hurry now. Have Sati pack some food too. We can eat along the way.'

'What if we are followed?'

'They will divert to Ranthanbor, while we shall keep going to Mandu.'

With General Wahid immediately behind him, followed by the wagon and his cavalry escort, Shah Jahan clip-clopped through the deserted main street of Ajmer, which ran straight as an arrow towards the south gate. The night flares were still lit. Their hissing red-gold flames cast shadows that danced before steady breezes from the north.

He thought of his reunion with the three boys. The elder two had been sleepy, but the baby Prince Aurang was wide awake. A real soldier that one. Strange though, the Moghuls had more sons than daughters, but were never really close to any of them. That was part of the price of kingship. You instilled only traits of stern duty, loyalty, respect in your children. Not love, which was something a ruler could ill afford, because it weakened him, made him vulnerable. Recognizing this truth made him involuntarily draw his cloak tighter, but the chill was from within him. He remembered his daughter, Princess Jahanara, safe in the Agra haven. He should see more of her.

It seemed as if the whole world were asleep beneath the high canopy of a sky glittering with stars. The dusky odour of empty, dry streets filtered into his nostrils. A beggar huddled in rags, sleeping beneath a narrow porch, sat up, curled back when he saw that it was not a night patrol. Two pi-dogs frisking across the street paused, gazed incuriously at the horses and the trundling wagon. They were accustomed to traffic.

The city gates, well lit by flares, loomed ahead, their two guard towers thrusting skyward. Shah Jahan steadied his breathing. He must remain cool. 'Wait here,' he commanded General Wahid. 'I shall go forward alone and see us through.'

'If they . . .' General Wahid began, then stopped. There was no need for words.

Shah Jahan rode up to the gates. The two sentries had already come alert and levelled their muskets. 'Halt!' one of them cried. Above him, a man's bulky figure appeared outlined against a pale glow of light from the open door of the right sentry tower. Obviously the guard commander.

Should he obey the halt order or not? He had better not

risk being shot by a nervous sentry. He reined his horse in. 'I am Shah Jahan,' he announced. 'Ask your sergeant to come down and identify me, so you can open the gates and let me through.'

'What brings you out at this hour of night, Prince?' The sergeant shouted the question from the tower.

'The Emperor's business does not wait on day or night,' Shah Jahan shouted back. 'Come down and identify me immediately. I insist you perform that duty. Once you are satisfied, I shall not tolerate further questions.' He had injected menace into the last words.

The sergeant hesitated. 'We have orders not to let anyone through. Of course you are different . . . ' He was surely aware of the incident outside those very gates the previous evening.

Shah Jahan decided to be bold. 'You have orders not to let anyone into the city without express authorization after the gates are closed for the night. You have no orders to prevent any responsible person from leaving at any time unless they are pimps, panderers or escaping criminals.' He laughed, knowing it would ease the tension. 'Your commanders would consider you an imbecile if you woke them up at this hour to question whether a prince of the royal blood, who is also a commander of the southern armies, can be permitted to leave!'

He waited tensely while the sergeant scratched his head. Samt II caught the tension, tossed his head nervously, stamped a hoof.

'The killer horse!' one of the sentries called nervously to the sergeant.

The man came down the stairs, sword drawn. He seized a flare from its socket with his left hand, walked up to Shah Jahan. He held up the flare. 'I recognize you, Prince,' he said, saluting. 'Please forgive me for holding you up.'

Shah Jahan returned the salute. 'I appreciate a man who

does his duty,' he asserted. 'I have use for such men. What is your name?'

'I am Sergeant Hamdoon, Prince.' He turned towards the sentry. 'Open the gates and let the prince and his party out.'

Other guards appeared at the entrances to both towers. The clip-clippety-clop of hooves and the clatter of wagon wheels announced that General Wahid had already begun moving.

The two sentries drew the huge bolts with a great squeaking and clanking. The two gates were swung open, screeching on their wheel runners. The courtyard, strewn with wagons, carts and sleeping figures, appeared outside. The open countryside beckoned beyond.

Shah Jahan eased his mount forward, controlling the urge to dash through the entrance. General Wahid, the wagon and his escort followed. Acknowledging the salutes of the sergeant and the two sentries, Shah Jahan rode into the free air.

Soon he began cantering along the pale strip of the highway, the wagon trundling behind. With a six-hour start, he estimated his family and he were safe at last.

He was stunned when he received Nur Jehan's despatch. Prince Shahriyar had been given command of the Kandhar operation and was moving north at this very moment. He, Shah Jahan, was stripped of his command and all his possessions in the north. He was to remain in Mandu and the southern states, in exile from Agra and the north. He was to send forty thousand of his crack troops to Agra, where a general named Mahabat would take command of them and proceed to Kandhar to reinforce Prince Shahriyar's army. Meanwhile, the Emperor and Empress with their entire entourage would have left for Srinagar by the time he received this *firman*.

It had to be a tactic of Nur Jehan's, but there was no way in which he could check whether any or all of it had the Emperor's approval.

Coincidentally, his astrologers had been present in his tent when he received the despatch. Mumtaz Mahal and his children were quartered in the Mandu palace, but he still used his tent, visiting the palace daily and sleeping there occasionally. All the astrologers had urged him to proceed with whatever plans he had in mind, since his planets were favourably conjoined. Only the ancient Baga had warned him. 'Do not proceed north of Mandu for any cause till the planets Jupiter and Saturn come to occupy positions of vantage in the east.'

Baga's advice accorded with his own immediate analysis of the position. Situated just south of the high plains of Rajasthan, which the Rajputs had developed from the seventh century onwards, the Deccan was a high, massive area ranging from forests and vast cultivated fields to scrubland and mountains. The monsoon governed all life here. Every spring, its soil was baked by the blistering sun and hot, dry winds. Late summer, when it seemed as if life itself must end in most areas, clouds piled over the blue oven of the sky and burst forth in torrential rain. The stifling heat ended. The earth blossomed with green, but was baked too hard to absorb the vast downpours. Flash floods struck with fearsome swiftness, sweeping away homes, men and cattle in swirling seas of mud.

It was not a time of the year when he should risk his men even to obey a command from Agra. But now, danger such as he had never experienced before also loomed like the monsoon clouds.

Mandu was cooler than Buran, but General Vickram, Raja Bhim and General Wahid were sweating profusely with the afternoon heat when they entered the tent and took their customary places on the settles around the table. They were curious at his urgent summons.

Shah Jahan quickly read the contents of Nur Jehan's despatch to them, holding back none of its contents, including news he had privately received that Prince Parviz would be visiting Srinagar. What he did hold back was the contents of a personal letter he had received from his father-in-law, Prime Minister Asaf Khan, urging him to follow the path of rectitude and obedience in response to the Emperor's commands. Asaf Khan could not possibly know the whole truth.

He looked up from reading the despatch to find the expressions on the faces of all three men stark as the sunlight beating fiercely down through the silence of the siesta hour outside. His men would be lying in their tents, inert with the heat, while vibrant drama was at hand.

'I do not believe that those are the Emperor's orders,' General Vickram finally stated. He glanced inquiringly at the others.

'Nor do I,' Raja Bhim grated. 'Some devil's work is afoot and I believe the devil is a female! Neither the decisions nor the writing style are those of the Emperor.'

'I agree,' Shah Jahan said. Suddenly, his whole future was at stake. Depending on these two men, it would be decided this very afternoon. 'Any decision as to what we do is not mine alone to make. What do you gentlemen advise?'

'Ignore the conniving bitch,' General Vickram asserted without hesitation. 'With clouds piled up in the sky every evening, the monsoon may strike even today. The highway back to Agra will soon be dangerous, not only for our army, but for any punitive expedition from the capital. In any event, once the bulk of the imperial army has moved to Kandhar under Prince Shahriyar and with the Emperor's personal regiments going with him to Srinagar, the administration can hardly spare the necessary men to take you back to Agra in irons.' His smile was grim. 'And if they did try to take you, we would hardly allow them, eh Raja?'

'Certainly not!' Raja Bhim banged the table assertively. 'The move to keep you in the south combined with the removal of your command and the seizure of your lands is a Nur Jehan plot to destroy you. I say, give up nothing. Hold fast with us here. Each day takes the might of Agra farther and farther away. I'm surprised that Nur Jehan did not realize this. Being unused to major political power play she probably assumed, quite naïvely, that a commanding general can be stripped of his power by mere written word. Let no one else learn the contents of this despatch. By the time the rains have ended, the largest part of the imperial army will be enmeshed in Kandhar; Prince Parviz will be under virtual house arrest in Srinagar and the way will be open for our move to take Agra.'

'You really mean that?' Shah Jahan's heart began to pound.

'Certainly,' General Vickram assured him. 'What other course of action can we take to defeat the evil aims of this bitch who holds her husband in thrall? We owe *her* no fealty. The Emperor cannot transfer our boundless loyalty to him to a . . . a mere proxy holder!' He spun out the last words contemptuously.

'I have only one area of concern,' Raja Bhim intervened. 'General Vickram and I are both Rajputs, in command of our army corps because of our Rajput regiments. You would be well advised in the months ahead to woo the Islamic elements of the army, probably even appoint a Muslim general to assist Raja Bhim and me in the overall command.'

Shah Jahan was deeply moved. These were such generous, sincere men. How sad that the Emperor had forfeited their trust and loyalty by handing over his powers to his woman. And what a woeful day for the Empire.

Chapter 33

He awoke to the blare of trumpets sounding the 2 A.M. watch. His heart was racing, cool beads of sweat covered his warm skin. I am Shah Jahan. I can overcome fear, he told himself, groping for his covering linen. He ducked under it, only to become uncomfortably hot, stifled. He had experienced fear of battle many a time but this was different. He was not in a death or glory situation. He faced the possibility of having to endure the agony and anguish, the humiliation and disgrace that his dead brother had known before he was murdered. Dear Allah, what a way to go, in your own faeces and blood-streaked urine.

He flung aside the linen. The coolness was better, but his body was still warm. He shivered and sweated. His breath became short. He turned on his side. His heartbeat thumped, duck . . . duck . . . duck in his ear through the head cushion. For the first time in his life, he was really scared – not dark scared, or battle scared, or death scared, but scared scared.

When he awoke again, the fear had vanished, but its aftermath remained, pins and needles throughout his whole body, vibrant in his guts.

By the time he rode out to the hillock observation fort with his generals, he was entirely calm again, but by a tremendous effort of will. He would take Agra today.

General Itbar had steadfastly refused all the offers of reward Shah Jahan had sent to him by intermediaries, for defection. With only ten thousand men to hold the capital, how would he react when he realized that it was surrounded by fifty thousand of the best fighting men in the Empire, complete with artillery, elephants and all the resources of a modern army? The question would be answered any minute now.

The rains had ended early in December, leaving the land clean. Having remained in Mandu during the monsoon, Shah Jahan was elated that there had been no defections among the troops under his command. Most of the officers and men were so loyal to him that he believed some of them would follow him to the ends of the earth. There was, however, one element of his policy that he knew the men to be restive about: his ban on looting and plunder, on pain of death. But he needed to keep his reputation clear in the region.

The entire Moghul army consisted of mercenaries, whose wages were merely the boiled rice of their existence. It was only looting whenever they were on a campaign in 'foreign' territory, as in Mewar and the Deccan, that put chicken in the cooking pot. Looting not only provided luxuries to his men, but also the means to buy a house and a plot of land in the ancestral village, for retirement.

His spies from Agra had confirmed the arrival of the Emperor and his entourage in Srinagar, where Prince Parviz had joined him, and the departure of a huge imperial army under Prince Shahriyar, on whom honours reserved for the heir had been heaped, to Kandhar. The way to Agra was clear, once the curtains of the monsoon rain were raised. The forces guarding the capital were under the fifty-one-year-old General Itbar, a sworn loyalist. The man emerging as a power in the land was, however, General Mahabat upon whom Nur Jehan had begun increasingly to lean.

Seated on Samt II, with General Vickram, Raja Bhim

and General Wahid beside him, Shah Jahan awaited General Itbar's response to his direct demand for the delivery of the capital. They were on a hillock beyond the range of the fort's artillery. The city below was bathed in morning sunlight, its minarets glittering. The *muezzins'* pre-dawn call to prayer still echoed in his head. A temple bell clanking furiously in the distance clashed with it. He thought fleetingly of Mumtaz Mahal. She had come with him only as far as Ajmer, which he had by-passed, and gone on to the safety of Ranthanbor, knowing it would worry him less.

Since they faced the west gate, he could see the broad silver ribbon of the river heading eastward between its avenue of cypress. He remembered other days.

It was strange, looking on the scene from the outside, as an invader, when he had belonged inside all his life, had been a part of the capital's heart. Within those red sandstone ramparts with their turrets and the embrasures for cannon, the snouts of which gleamed dully, was the Empire. His troops were massed behind him, his own cannon stretched endlessly along the green plain, encircling the city, out of artillery and bow shot, ready to seize that Empire.

Wings outstretched, two vultures soared towards him. There must be a rotting corpse somewhere. Suddenly, he was the vulture, the entire capital a corpse. He shivered and cast the morbid thought aside, but it made him pause.

This was the city that his beloved grandfather had so lovingly re-created, the product of a unique man's need for strength, expressing his love of beauty. Could he give the order for his cannon to blast those walls?

He had to. That was the price of the imperial crown. That was what he owed the men who had pledged him their loyalty. The price of rebellion, too gruesome to contemplate. He recalled again the obscene fate that had befallen his brother, Prince Husrau, and those who had joined him against the Emperor. He had thought of that many times these past months but had always been certain that he was not fated to endure such horror. Was that wishful thinking? In his moments of doubt, he would recall what the famous *sufi* Jilain had told him:

'Master, faith is everything, all else is nothing. Birth, life, death, the changing forms of men and all other living things are a cosmic process. But there is something higher, faith. It is by faith that mountains are climbed, deserts crossed, empires built. You have faith in yourself, faith in your destiny and above all, faith in God. Never deviate from your course, press on with your mission. If you have faith, you can never be destroyed, not even by God, because God is faith . . .'

A wrinkled old man, staff in hand, long white hair fluttering in the wind, cheeks almost parchment yellow with age. An ageless seer.

Why then was Shah Jahan, the man with faith, unconvinced that Agra would be delivered to him this morning?

The vast entrance gates creaked in the distance. 'Ah, here they come now,' General Vickram observed.

Three men on horseback emerged from a crack between the gates. One carried a white flag.

'See, the white flag, they are going to surrender!' Raja Bhim slapped his thigh, grinning.

'But they are closing the gates again,' General Vickram stated.

'We'll know soon enough,' General Wahid commented.

Shah Jahan made no comment, simply watched the three riders trot across the moat, the man with the white flag on their right. They broke into a canter, heading across the green sward towards the hillock.

A hoof flung back a sod of soft turf, a quiet drumming reached his ears.

The future approached. Once again, his entire life hung in the balance.

The passing months under his rule had seen Mewar become even stronger than it had been at the time it revolted against the Emperor. Rana Chara had not only built up the nucleus of a standing army, by calling on the princes and nobles of his kingdom to pledge their permitted quotas of fighting men to him whenever he decided to call on them, but had also been assured of the support of Bikaner, Jodhpur and Jaipur, north of Ajmer, and of Baroda, south of Mewar, as well as Kutch to its east. The Rajputs had for centuries been ever ready for a fight. As the sick and dying Emperor was headed for Srinagar with a small army, and a large imperial army moved towards Kandhar, only Shah Jahan with a total of eighty thousand men under his command remained a formidable opponent. When Rana Chara received news of the events in Ajmer, he recognized trouble between Shah Jahan and Nur Jehan, which meant a further loosening of the Emperor's grip. He therefore issued an invitation to General Malik Ambar to visit him in Chitor.

Rana Chara was elated when Shah Jahan passed through Mewar with his force of forty thousand men. Word was that he was on his way to Kandhar on the Emperor's orders, but Rana Chara guessed that Shah Jahan's real objective must be Agra. If he had been in Shah Jahan's shoes, he would have seized the capital.

Eyeing General Ambar across the dining table at a late breakfast that morning, Prince Chara was experiencing grim satisfaction that he had finally brought the general to his door. Their two previous meetings had been in the general's tent on the field. The very fact that General Ambar had accepted the invitation indicated that he too regarded the timing as opportune. He would make a useful ally, provided he was allotted a specific role and not overall command.

It gave Rana Chara some satisfaction that he had extended to this kinky-haired son of a whore the hospitality of a Rajput palace, far removed from the peasant fare of an army tent.

General Ambar too must have recognized this, for he pushed his chair back from the mahogany dining table, when they were alone with the *pan*, betel leaves and condiments, the scent of baked *chuppati* and roast lamb in the air stirred by the soft swish-swish of the overhead *punkah*. Unusually for this time of the year, bright sunlight promised a hot day. 'A delicious meal, Rana, for which I thank you,' he said. His black skin shone in the silver daylight and his wide flaring nostrils were distended with satisfaction. 'Far removed from the plain fare we were compelled to offer you.'

The man had matured socially, or was he reacting to the different environment? 'We have even richer fare for you, general.' Rana Chara stared at him challengingly. 'Are you man enough to taste it?'

General Ambar grinned, his teeth very white. 'I taste anything that is not likely to give me indigestion! As for being man enough, I have never believed in proving my manhood.' He became serious in an instant. 'I know that you did not invite me here to taste the food on your table, Rana,' he added quietly. 'You and I are both soldiers. We have always been blunt with each other. Tell me, what's on your mind?'

Rana Chara proceeded to give the general his own analysis of the political situation. He secretly watched for even the slightest reaction, but received none. The general listened intently, very relaxed, his eyes inscrutable.

'What do you think will happen in Agra?' he finally inquired.

'General Itbar is a stern, uncompromising loyalist. He will refuse to open the palace gates. It will be history repeating itself, for this is exactly what happened twenty years ago, when Prince Jehangir marched to Agra to seize the capital in his father's absence. Commanders of the major Moghul cities, especially Agra, are specially selected for their courage and loyalty.'

'Prince Jehangir retired before the refusal to open the gates. What do you think Shah Jahan will do?'

'He will blast his way in.'

'And then?'

'Civil war will break loose. The forces that Shah Jahan left behind in Bija, Ahmad, Buran and Mandu will be divided with conflicting demands made of their commanders, the entire fabric of the Moghul presence in the Deccan will be weakened.'

The general's eyes gleamed, his nostrils dilated. Ah, I have you reacting for the first time, Rana Chara thought. You look like a gorilla on the scent. Now for a final glimpse at the state of your quarry. 'As you know, our one formidable opponent is Shah Jahan,' he asserted. 'But his strength is only as good as the unity of his command.' It was his turn to grin. 'We have taken steps to bring to the notice of his Muslim commanders that they are being supplanted by two Rajputs, General Vickram and Raja Bhim, that Shah Jahan favours Rajputs because he intends revolting against his Muslim father and the Islamic establishment. That he is assured of the support of *us*,' he emphasized the word, 'Rajputs because his mother was a Rajput.' He drew a thumbnail underneath his black moustache. 'We have of course refrained from adding that the Emperor's own mother was also Rajput!'

'You're a cunning devil,' the general declared involuntarily, shaking his head.

'One has to be, to survive in a cunning world, don't you

think? You are cunning on the battlefield, because you have to be. We, being a small kingdom, are cunning in politics.'

'What roles to you expect each of us to play?'

'We would want you to tie down Shah Jahan's men in Bija, Ahmad, Buran and Mandu by a continual series of guerilla attacks, so they are unable to throw their support on to either side in the civil war. We shall then raise the flag of revolt again in Rajasthan.'

'What do you hope to achieve?'

'Independent kingdoms in Rajasthan and the Deccan, such as we had before Babur.'

'And what role would you hope to play yourself?' The general paused, eyed him bleakly. 'You are not doing all this for the sake of your health, Rana. And don't do me the dishonour of saying it is for Rajput honour.' He was that black gorilla on the prowl now.

'Our independent kingdoms have always had a titular *maha raja*.'

'You aspire to that?' the general demanded incredulously.

'Of course.'

'Well of all the damned impertinence!' General Ambar was about to explode, when he suddenly, inexplicably, fell silent. He stared unseeingly at the mahogany table, shooting an occasional glance at Rana Chara from the almost devilish dark eyes.

Rana Chara never flinched, nor did he once take his eyes off the general. His stomach had clenched, but he remained outwardly cool, though his future hung in the balance.

This was a man to be looked at . . . and watched.

She had invited General Mahabat to attend her in the Shalimar Gardens that morning, because she did not trust the security of the Srinagar palace. Seated on a bench in one of the marble-pillared pavilions, with the general standing respectfully on the steps below her, she found the setting romantic. The air was crisp and cool, as if the snow-capped Himalayan peaks gleaming white in the distance, across the silver waters of the lake, were wafting reminders of their presence. Birds whistled and trilled in the tall *chenar* trees, whose green tops were sharp-etched against an ice-blue sky. The scent of the roses she had caused to be planted was dewy.

And General Mahabat was very much a man. A single man too, being a widower with no children. His wife must have been barren.

He was only forty-three, a dashing ex-cavalry colonel. His red tunic fitted the barrel-chest and massive shoulders to perfection; baggy white trousers tucked into shiny black riding boots revealed the slightly bowed legs of the horse-man. His face was square, exuding the same power as his body. The lips beneath a cavalry moustache were red and sensuous, the skin beneath cleanshaven as his head. It was the eyes that were remarkable. Large and dark green, flecked with brown spots, they could melt like snow on those mountains or grow sharp as ice crystals.

If she had been a man, Nur Jehan would have depended on no one. Being a *harem* woman, governed by the rules of *purdah*, however much she might stretch those rules, she still needed someone in the outside world to give effect to her purposes. There were times when she positively hated being female and the frustrations made her want to scream, but she had schooled herself over the years to wield power through others. For that very reason, Shah Jahan's defection in pursuit of his own interests had created a gap. It had been partially filled by her brother but she had begun to doubt whether the father-in-law of Shah Jahan would give her unswerving loyalty. Unfortunately, her son-in-law, Prince Shahriyar, was a dolt, but then that was the operation of what Rana Chara kept referring to as the law of cause and effect, because she had selected Prince Shahriyar for the very reason that he would be her pawn and a pawn could not have brains.

She was reminded of another of Rana Chara's statements – a clever one, that Rana! – that most married women were whores. She was certainly one, because she ministered every night to a sick, drink-besotted, opium-befuddled man with stinking breath for her position as his wife and Empress. Though she loved Jehangir in her own way, it was all so boring, but the price was well worth the whoring. How exciting it had been though, a long time ago. She vividly recalled the night she had brought the Emperor under her sexual domination.

What would it be like to have General Mahabat make love to her? He would be ruthless, demanding. He would whip her with his loins. She cast aside the fantasy. Later perhaps. She could never risk her present position for anyone or anything. And unlike many of the women leaders throughout history, she had no great desire for sex.

'You may wonder how it is that we can receive you, a male person, here in the open, instead of in the palace *harem*,' she ventured after their initial greetings were over. General Mahabat was always respectful to his superiors, she had noticed, but there was an inner independence to him which told her that he accepted no one as his master. This both excited and gave her cause for concern.

General Mahabat revealed large, even white teeth in a smile. 'I never wonder at such things, Madam,' he rejoined. His voice was deep, quiet, the accent refined. 'I accept them for what they are.' The smile widened. 'Just as I accept your obvious desire to tell me, which makes me glad to listen.'

Another clever man, this one, with logic as well as words. He could be dangerous. Yet she had no option but to trust him, especially today. 'We believe you should know because you will be working very closely with us in future, General Mahabat.' She picked up his quickened interest though it was barely perceptible. 'As all men know, the Emperor has graciously commanded us to attend all his daily *durbars*, seated on a throne beneath his, properly clad in *chador* and *yashmak* of course. On the other hand, within the royal *harem* we had the curious anomaly of rule by another empress, Salima Begum. Out of respect for her, we followed the strict rules she imposed within the *harem* and confined our conduct of the Empire's affairs to interviews and discussions in our reception chamber, where we received our male guests from behind curtains. It was a rather silly concession to the principle of total seclusion of women, which our Prophet never advocated in the first place. With our dear husband ailing, he has entrusted more and more responsibility to us. This monumental task can only be fulfilled if we have greater freedom of movement, while taking care to observe the *spirit* of *purdah*.' She paused, glanced down at him. 'You are probably wondering why we are giving you this explanation?'

He glanced about him. 'On such an idyllic morning, I need no explanation as to why Your Imperial Majesty should choose to be out in the world that Almighty Allah created for man,' he said, his voice low. 'And if I may add, very respectfully, your gracious presence here transcends the beauty of nature.'

He had deliberately kept his eyes on the paved walkway so as not to seem impertinent. She appreciated it. 'You have given us the answer we had hoped to obtain from you, general. Since you are an orthodox Muslim and will be working directly under our command, it is important to us that you fully understand and sympathize with our personal manner of conducting the affairs of the Empire.'

'Your Imperial Majesty is more than gracious, but I would serve you regardless.'

543

'Thank you.' She deliberately changed the subject in order to temporize while she softened him up before making her request. 'The Srinagar fort and palace were built by the Emperor Akbar. These were later embellished by the addition of two beautiful gardens. Shalimar was the creation of the Emperor Jehangir. As you can see, it is characterized by a series of summer pavilions like this one.' She drew her *chador* closer around her against the chill air. 'Not winter pavilions!'

'Pleasant even in winter,' he remarked.

His eyes had told her that it was she who made them pleasant. 'It was our husband's idea to build the pavilions supported by these graceful black marble columns, elegantly carved, and to surround them with pools so they can be reached only on stepping stones,' she said.

'Our Great Emperor is also the Great Artist,' he murmured.

'True, but he is more besides, a visionary. He harnessed the spring at Vernag some forty miles south of here for use in his Moghul gardens. You have never been there?'

'No, Madam.'

'He caused an octagonal series of small, domed pavilions to be built there, around a turquoise blue pool. We remember so well that he had peaches brought all the way from Kabul by runners for the opening party and both of us placed gold rings on the noses of the great fish with which he stocked the pool.' She sighed. She had deliberately led into this subject. 'Those were happy, carefree days. Our beloved Emperor was fit and well. He ruled with no other help from us than that of a good wife.' She sighed again, more heavily this time. 'Things have changed so dramatically. It is the will of Allah.' She did not really believe such nonsense, but she wanted to sound convincing to this man.

'Indeed.' General Mahabat looked up at her squarely,

those green eyes opaque. Sunlight caught them, caused the brown flecks to sparkle. He knew she was finally coming to the point.

'We carry a heavy burden of responsibility towards all in the Empire.' She gave him an appraisal of the entire situation from Kandhar through Agra, Ajmer and Mewar to the Deccan and a frank evaluation of the personalities involved. When she had finished, she glanced down at him for a response, hoping, almost praying, that it would be favourable.

'Madam,' he stated firmly, 'I am a soldier, not a politician. You obviously have a role that you desire me to play. Please be frank with me, so I can give you equally frank answers. I assume the situation is urgent because of the latest news from the south?'

A thrill of alarm shot through her. 'What news?'

'That Shah Jahan was marching to Agra with fifty thousand men.'

'So he is finally obeying the Emperor's commands.'

The general's grin was cynical. 'It depends on what those commands were, Your Imperial Majesty.'

She blanched. 'What more could it be?'

'Madam, my own intelligence warns me otherwise. My officers left Mandu the day Shah Jahan issued his marching orders, raced to General Itbar in Agra with the news. He had already received overtures from Shah Jahan for the surrender of the capital, which he had resolutely rejected. Regardless of the reason publicly given by Shah Jahan for his march, General Itbar fears – and I concur – that Shah Jahan intends taking the capital. Based on my evaluation of timing, he may be poised around Agra at this very moment.'

'But Shah Jahan is a disgraced heir,' she began. 'He has been stripped of his command and his northern possessions.'

'By whom, Madam?'

For a moment she was tempted to lie. She needed this man now, more desperately than ever. Then she remembered his reference to his intelligence service. If he ever discovered her in a lie, he would never trust her again. 'By our own command,' she asserted.

'The Emperor is unaware of this?' His tone was sharp.

How would General Mahabat respond to her request now? Suddenly she was frightened, glad of the *yashmak* that hid her reactions. One look at his eyes, no longer sentimental but hard, told her that doubts were flashing through his mind.

Chapter 34

The three riders halted in front of Shah Jahan. Two of them, cavalry colonels, dismounted, threw their reins across the saddles of their chestnut mounts. The man carrying the white flag, a sergeant, remained on his horse. A light, cool breeze caused the flag to flutter and flap, but the sergeant remained motionless. Samt II jittered his skin, whisked flies off with his tail.

The colonels saluted. One stood to attention, while the other, a lithe, cleanshaven Muslim of indeterminate race, strode up to Shah Jahan. Head bowed, holding a scroll respectfully in the palms of both hands, he proffered it silently to Shah Jahan. The lean, tough face gave no indication of what message the scroll contained.

Shah Jahan's heart had stopped pounding. Now that the moment of truth had arrived, he was calm and composed. He accepted the scroll with a nod. He glanced quickly at the lean, tall, black-haired General Vickram, then at the portly Raja Bhim, before opening the scroll.

The writing was so brief in delicately formed Arabic script that he knew the capital was not being surrendered.

Long live the Emperor Jehangir.

That was General Itbar's response. The words swam before his eyes. He had lost this battle. He was about to read out the message to his generals when caution intruded. It was so loyal and historic a reply that word of it should not be conveyed to anyone. 'General Itbar refuses to open the city gates,' he announced. 'We shall take the capital by force.'

'Damn him!' General Vickram muttered.

Raja Bhim merely sighed.

General Wahid remained his noncommittal self.

'Go back to General Itbar,' Shah Jahan commanded the colonel. 'Tell him that he had better be prepared to die with all of you, his men, in the rubble of Agra.'

The colonel merely saluted, turned smartly.

'Summon my artillery commanders,' Shah Jahan directed General Wahid.

The general wheeled his horse around. The clump, clump of its hooves on the turf clashed with the thud of the horses of the three-man truce delegation as they cantered back to the city.

Shah Jahan waited in silence, lost in his thoughts. The clatter of hooves on the causeway leading across the moat was followed by the creak of the great gates. He raised his eyes to the city. Beyond the red sandstone ramparts, a minaret glittered in the bright sunlight. This city was originally created by his ancestor Babur. It was Moghul from the core outwards, brick and mortar put together by Moghul flesh and blood, transformed into a heritage.

The two vultures overhead swooped down on their invisible prey.

What was he, a Moghul, doing here? That curious sense of disorientation returned. He was a renegade Moghul, about to give orders to have the heartland of his ancestors' creation, the walls, the palaces, the bazaar, reduced to rubble. Across twenty years of time, he sensed the thoughts of his father, Prince Jehangir, the Moghul rebel, as he stood, probably on that very spot, in the silver sunlight of a winter morning.

A groan escaped Shah Jahan. His companions glanced sharply at him.

'I cannot do it,' he ground out.

'Do what?' General Vickram demanded fiercely, but comprehension had already dawned in the dark, deep-set, fierce eyes.

'His Highness cannot give the order to destroy the city of his ancestors.' Raja Bhim already knew the answer.

The deathly silence that followed enshrouded Shah Jahan's very spirit. The moments dragged on, pounding death nails into the coffin of his hopes.

'Your feelings are understandable,' General Vickram finally stated. 'But we face a serious contingency with our men if we are to continue our campaign. As you know, most of the Raja's troops and mine are Rajputs who do not care a melon for the Moghul heritage. In fact, they have been dying to rape it!' He paused, ever respectful. 'They have eagerly looked forward to great rewards from the imperial treasury within that city,' he nodded in its direction, 'ever since we decided to take Agra. It was only their deep loyalty to the Raja and me and undoubtedly to you, Prince, that kept their ranks together these past months, especially during the last few weeks when your order that looting was forbidden on pain of death created hardship and some dissatisfaction. I'm sorry to advise you that there

548

is only one way in which we can retain their support in your cause.'

His cause. Had he forgotten his cause, his destiny, his Mumtaz Mahal, before the call of Moghul tradition? His mind came sharply back to reality. It was the will of Allah that he become the Emperor. It was his own burning desire to become the Emperor. His whole life, the sacrifices, the dedication, the hours of hope and despair had been directed to that end. If he did not pulverize Agra and take it, what were his alternatives? To besiege the city, to withdraw, or to surrender.

Hideous choices.

He owed it to himself, his family, his commanders, his men, to history, to take Agra by any means. He smiled with relief. He would take this city if he had to turn it to dust and ashes. He half turned towards General Vickram. His eyes fell on the scroll he still held open in his hand: Long live the Emperor Jehangir.

Trumpets sounded in his ears, the trumpets of history.

A fanfare: Long live the Emperor Akbar.

Another fanfare: Long live the Emperor Humayun.

A double fanfare: Long live the founder Emperor Babur.

The trumpets rolled back getting fainter: Timur-il-Leng, the Lame. Genghis Khan.

The Mongols, who destroyed everything in their path, also created beauty. Never destroyed their own beautiful works. The Moghul tradition: Demonstrate to history that we are not barbarians.

His soul ached, his heart was dry, his lips parched. We shall not destroy the holiness of our own creation.

A shadow passed over the sun.

From the chill depths of his tortured being, he heard the words emerge. 'We shall not touch this city. We shall besiege it and try to draw its troops into open battle.

Meanwhile, let the men loot and pillage the entire countryside.'

Was it he, Shah Jahan, lover of his people, who had spoken the words?

A temple bell tolled in the distance. It sounded like a death knell. The death knell of his hopes? Of the morality, restraint and honour that had always characterized his career and made him loved by the people? Or of the lives of one or more of those on this hillock?

Three men on a hillock. Absurdly, it brought to the mind of the Muslim a Christian event. Calvary. Three men crucified on a stark hillock.

An icy hand gripped him. He knew the answers to his questions.

Long moments of suspense while he awaited General Ambar's response caused Rana Chara to despise the parts that life had forced him to play. Always the suppliant. Except when he took his destiny into his own hands and eliminated his father.

Those moments determined his whole future. Suddenly, for the first time, he saw the role to which he was committing his future life very clearly. Shorn of the trappings of power for which he had blindly reached, he would remain a suppliant. A suppliant of the Rajas, the Ranas and sultans in order to throw aside the imperial yoke. A suppliant for their loyalty once he became the Maha Raja. A Great King could never compare with the Moghul conquerors. The Moghul Emperors were really rulers. They were not figureheads but mighty kings. He would be a puppet up at the top!

In the bleak dark eyes of General Ambar, Rana Chara saw the truth for the first time in his life. Cause and effect. Since boyhood he had sought the highest office. For this, he had suffered insults, borne privation, faced death.

The scar on his face itched and burned.

For this? To be a puppeteer manipulated by his own puppets? It was laughable. Here he was, a grown man, also manipulated since childhood by those puppeteers of life . . . causes. And the whole grim farce was played out against the mural of a child's desire: I want to be king! A grown man moving inexorably to a destiny created by a child!

General Ambar must have sensed the doubts going through his mind, though he had given no outward sign of them. 'Your plan is brilliant,' he declared. 'Let us work out the details.'

Rana Chara knew that this man would function only to his own advantage. We are both *thieves* of fortune, he thought, masquerading as *soldiers* of fortune. We would slit each other's throats for a bauble of fate.

Too late to withdraw, but he did not wish to withdraw. If his ambitions had been those of childhood, the dislikes of his later years remained. Dislikes were more amusing than likes. They gave zest to life.

Nur Jehan with her pretentious ways. He loathed pretentiousness.

Shah Jahan, his arch-rival, symbol of the Moghul spoiler on Rajput soil.

These things still remained to give purpose to his life, but from now on he could act and react at will, unimpeded by insensate ambition, driving his future without being driven by it. To hell with earnestness and ambition.

Cold, objective, that was what he could now be. He liked that.

Life would become amusing.

She was not going to let anyone or anything intimidate her, least of all her future. And yet the old, old insecurity clawed at her stomach. Not so long ago, a young woman given in marriage to a monster who raped and brutalized her. Nur Jehan, abandoned to that fate by those who should have loved and cherished her. An Emperor who merely wanted her for his concubine and caused her to endure years of loneliness, doubt and heartache. Nur Jehan, abandoned by the romantic prince of her dreams. An Empress condemned to minister day and night to a dying husband, unable to make decisions without deception and apprehension. Yes, star of my soul. Of course, Your Imperial Majesty. Nur Jehan, abandoned by herself.

A faint slapping sound from the distance interrupted her thoughts. Below her, on the opposite bank of the lake, women, tiny figures, were pounding clothes on flat stones. Those already washed hung on lines in long rows on the green sward. Washerwomen, a bird that whistled qu . . . qu . . . qu . . . from a plane tree, a cobra and yes, a baby. Over there, to the west, a baby in the desert. Nur Jehan abandoned by her parents, shielded from the sun by a cobra.

A cobra. She knew what General Mahabat's eyes were like. A cobra's hood.

He was a cobra. He could shield her, until her parents returned.

She took command of the situation. She would never be subservient to anyone, not even Almighty Allah. 'We have for you a very interesting and challenging assignment, General Mahabat.' Her voice was warm gold, but its tones were clear as the temple bell she heard in the distance. 'You shall take the entire force of twenty thousand men who accompanied us to Srinagar and proceed south without delay to the relief of Agra.'

The green-brown eyes widened. 'Madam, I am honoured at the assignment, but what will the Emperor use for his personal protection?'

'The imperial bodyguard will remain here. They should

suffice.' She smiled faintly. 'Remember the Ten Thousand Immortals of the Great Emperor Dar-hoos? Besides, we shall send swift messengers to Prince Shahriyar to detach ten of his regiments and send them here. The defence of a border outpost may be important, but it must give precedence to saving the Empire.'

'Does the Emperor know of this plan?'

The moment she had been dreading had arrived. Strangely, she was now totally calm and unafraid. 'No.'

'No?' He frowned, then his brow cleared. 'You will tell him?'

'No.' She deliberately dropped the royal plural. 'I am in command from now on.'

He stared at her with grudging admiration, but only for an instant. 'Madam, you realize that I shall be putting myself in tremendous personal jeopardy if I proceed to Agra with the Emperor's private army without his express approval?'

'Of course. You will not, however, be proceeding to Agra, but on the greatest adventure of your life.'

His eyes widened as he grasped her meaning.

She pressed home her point. 'I have watched you closely, General Mahabat. You are the one man in all the Empire who is capable of being the commander of the imperial armies under *my* direction as their commander-in-chief.' She deliberately dropped the royal plural.

He understood. With a sunlit heart, she knew he would accept. A cloud threw a shadow over the sun. Could she trust him? Knowing the answer, she decided to throw in the greatest prize of all. 'The Emperor will soon be dead,' she stated softly. She returned to the royal plural for emphasis. 'We shall then declare our son-in-law, Prince Shahriyar, Emperor. As most people know, he will merely be a figurehead. It is we who shall rule the Empire. You will not only be commander of our armies, we shall also appoint you Prime Minister. You will help us rule the Empire, General Mahabat.' She gazed at him with such intensity that she knew he was aware of it. 'And once my own rule is established,' she deliberately dropped the royal plural again, 'I shall depose my son-in-law and appoint a new Emperor, who will share my rule . . . and my bed.'

'I will gladly lead the army to the relief of Agra,' he asserted forcefully. 'If you would please execute a *firman* to that effect immediately, I shall issue the necessary orders and leave without delay.'

It was obvious that he knew the urgency of the situation and was eager to thwart Shah Jahan's plans. But why had he not responded to her most intimate suggestion? Had he been afraid to presume, or had she once again been abandoned?

Knowing what his reactions would be to her plan, Nur Jehan had not looked forward to her interview with Asaf Khan, who had accompanied the imperial Court to Srinagar, but as Prime Minister, he had to know. She could keep information away from the Emperor, who had reached a stage when he never questioned her decisions, did not even want to be bothered about affairs of State so long as he could enjoy the panoply of his position. Nowadays, he would rather talk, hold forth really, than work, and even his improving health in Srinagar had not altered this. She guessed that the alcohol and opium had permanently destroyed some part of his brain that had once produced initiative, diligence and the consciousness of responsibility. He was a human vegetable marrow now, bedecked with the trappings of a Moghul Emperor. She herself still respected him for his office, cared for him as a human being, but she was not of a breed that could love without admiration and respect for the man.

Now General Mahabat was another matter. He had even begun to represent a challenge to her.

Unlike her husband, Asaf Khan had the reins of administration firmly in his grasp. He knew everything and there could be no secrets from him. Having dismissed General Mahabat with the promise that her *firman* would be delivered to him before noon, she had commanded the eunuchs who had been present nearby, just out of earshot, strutting about the gardens in their finery like peacocks, to summon Asaf Khan.

He arrived in less than an hour, during which time she had dictated the *firman* to a secretary and walked around inspecting her rose beds. She received Asaf Khan in the same pavilion, but extended him the courtesy of a black marble seat opposite her own.

'Beautiful day!' Asaf Khan commented, taking in the scene. He looked as youthful and dashing as ever in a gold tunic and white satin pantaloons. His lean face was more tanned, however, the skin contrasting sharply with the vivid blue eyes, but matching their devil-may-care expression. 'The Emperor was right. This is the ideal place for him to regain his health, for one beautiful day follows the other.' He inhaled deeply. 'The air is like wine, only flavoured with the bouquet of your rose garden.'

Allah forbid that the Emperor should recover his health, she thought fiercely, facing her real desire for the first time. Had her interview with the dashing General Mahabat influenced this? 'We are both creators of beauty,' she reminded him. She wanted to put him in the right mood. 'A family failing.' She wished that, like him, she could grow older without ageing. 'After all, it was you who created the Pratap Garden over there, building it in terraces down the hillside to complement natural beauty instead of replacing it.' She paused. 'Our husband was chagrined that a mere commoner should have presumed to create such an extravagant ornament.' She chuckled at the recollection. 'But we rather think his annoyance came more from jealousy that you had built something more beautiful than any of the Moghul Emperors had done.'

She had hoped to draw Asaf Khan on to her side. He smiled carelessly, but had a knowing glint in his eyes. He fingered his thin moustache. 'Your Imperial Majesty, we have known each other since you were born. Why do you not dispense with these pleasantries and tell me what you want from me?' Years ago, he would have called her 'little sister'. Now the height of her own rank and station separated them. She stamped out the question that sprouted, need the height have made a difference?

He frequently put her off stride by his honesty and directness. She wielded her peacock feather fan involuntarily, then stopped, telling herself that she should not indulge in such betrayals of reaction. She pointed the fan at him with a return of the sisterly coquettishness she had used with him years ago. 'You are so perceptive,' she declared. 'Nothing escapes you.' She hesitated, decided on bluntness. 'Yes, there is something very important for which we need your unquestioning loyalty and support.'

He arched an elegant eyebrow. 'Unquestioning is a tall order.' He smiled. 'But please try me.'

She told him of her analysis of the situation and of her plan, concluding with the orders she had just given General Mahabat, omitting only her future ambitions.

Asaf Khan had listened intently, betraying no emotion, making no comment. He now gazed at the still waters of the pool beneath them, silver coated with bright sunlight, dark within. An unwonted sadness lay on his being. He sighed. 'So the die is finally cast,' he murmured, as if to himself. 'The Moghul Empire has its new mould.' He shrugged. 'It was inevitable.' He shook the weight off his spirit, raised solemn eyes to her. 'I assume that these are not the Emperor's orders.' It was a statement, not a question.

'You assume correctly.'

'And that you will not tell him until the day General Mahabat leaves for Agra.'

How well he knew her. For a moment, she found it frightening. 'Correct.'

'Does this mean that you will be abandoning Kandhar?'

'For the present, but not entirely. Prince Shahriyar will still be there in considerable strength and can help raise the siege, though his combined strength with the garrison will not be sufficient to drive Shah Abbas back to the rat hole from which he emerged.'

Amusement flickered briefly across Asaf Khan's face. 'An imperial rat and a rat-hole Empire. Why not?'

She noted that he had not questioned her local strategy. Why not? Was it because he deemed it the right course of action, or was it that his sympathy lay with Shah Jahan and he dared not reveal it?

With the uncanny gift he always possessed he read her thoughts. 'I want you to know that I neither support nor condone Shah Jahan's conduct. It violates my code.' He leaned forward for emphasis. 'But then, it is his life to live by his own code, to suffer the consequences and reap the rewards.'

A thrill of joy went through her. They had never discussed this openly before, but he supported her view. She had told him of the despatch she had sent Shah Jahan, relieving him of his command and his northern possessions, but had never revealed that they were far in excess of what the Emperor had authorized. Asaf Khan would, of course, never question the Emperor about it.

'I supported neither Prince Jehangir nor Prince Husrau when they disputed the succession.' Asaf Khan's voice had risen slightly, its tone had grown more decisive. 'It was the code that made me – and, I might add, our father – take that stand. The Moghul tradition of succession is so clear that no one, not even the ruling Emperor, may betray it, without cause.'

In the instant, her hopes were dashed. This was no loving brother, but a hated betrayer, abandoning her.

'The eldest son always succeeds, provided he is competent to rule. When the successor dies, his own eldest son succeeds. If such eldest son is not of age, the dead ruler's next eldest brother acts as Prince Regent.'

'If that is your code, why did you not support Prince Jehangir openly and fully at the time?' she flashed.

He smiled faintly. 'Ah, a good question.' His voice had grown gentle. 'There is another, more important code, that of morality. One does not share the lion's spoils until the lion is ready to deliver them. It is a matter of the elementary good manners that exist among beasts, and comprise the beautiful fabric of human society that we offer God.'

What a self-righteous prig, she thought savagely. But she could not afford to antagonize him. All she needed was his support in her present moves. Later, with Agra in her grasp, she would have the strength to proceed on her own. 'How do you think the Emperor should direct the succession then?'

'Even to discuss it while he is alive seems to be a breach of good manners, but I shall commit that breach in the interests of the future. Since Prince Husrau is dead, Prince Parviz is the successor, until Prince Husrau's eldest son can take over.'

'And if Prince Parviz dies or is incompetent?' She already knew the answer.

'Then it has to be Shah Jahan.'

Prince Parviz was due in Srinagar that very week. He would arrive with gold and costly gifts for her and her husband, to gain their favour. He would not dare discuss his rights to the succession with the Emperor. She would make appropriate noises to give him hope that all was well and send him packing back to the virtual exile of the distant east, laden with return presents, honours and hollow assurances. There he would remain until the succession was finally determined.

'You are excused, Prime Minister,' Nur Jehan stated abruptly.

Asaf Khan rose to his feet. Age had not diminished his grace. He bowed, departed in silence.

No old allies. Nur Jehan abandoned again. A determined laugh escaped her. The cobra would shield her until she was ready to act on her own.

Later that afternoon, a secret messenger from Shah Jahan arrived in the Srinagar palace with a despatch for the Emperor. Though it was the siesta hour, the despatch was brought to her reception chamber. The messenger was Lord Aziz, whom she knew to be a trusted friend of Shah Jahan.

A fire had been lit in her chamber against the approaching chill of evening. Nur Jehan took the scroll over to the fireplace to read it.

The despatch had been written from Mandu immediately after Shah Jahan had received the notice of his dismissal in disgrace. He now reiterated his loyalty to the Emperor: 'It is the beginning and end of my life. My stand is not against my Emperor, but against the disloyalty of others, against injustice and a planned subversion of the decrees of destiny. I shall gladly take command of the Kandhar expedition . . .' Without specifying them as conditions, he pleaded for those he had already requested, which now related only to the prestige that being granted the *suba* of Punjab would give him and to the funds needed to carry the Emperor's commands to success.

Without hesitation, Nur Jehan tore the despatch into shreds, dropped them into the fire. With smouldering eyes, she watched the pieces catch the flames, curl up, blacken, crumble.

Having proffered her the message, her Chief Eunuch had remained standing respectfully at the entrance to the chamber, awaiting her instructions. 'Does anyone know of the arrival of the messenger?' she inquired over her shoulder.

'No, Your Imperial Majesty. It being the siesta hour, all except the sentries are resting.'

'Have the messenger, Lord Aziz, and his escort seized and imprisoned until we and we alone rescind this command.'

Chapter 35

It was February 1623. The two Moghul armies faced each other across a green plain near Delhi. The battleground being of Shah Jahan's choosing, he had placed his men beneath low eminences at the eastern end of the plain, so the enemy would have the morning sun in their eyes. At the urging of the Rajput generals, he had earlier appointed the Muslim General Dorab overall commander of the army, with another Muslim, General Shaista, to command one of his three divisions; the other two, being Rajput, were commanded by General Vickram and Raja Bhim. This move had stopped the slow flow of minor Muslim sultans and their men from Shah Jahan's ranks, but he had meanwhile lost the support of the people who had been looted. Sick at heart, he had seen a sacking of the region around Agra on a scale never witnessed since Babur's invasion.

No longer an instrument of destiny, Shah Jahan felt he had become a victim of fate these past weeks. He could either pulverize Agra and take it, or allow the plunder to continue with its own awesome toll. Meanwhile, the imperial army under General Mahabat had been approaching from the north and his own support in the south was being eroded.

Seated on Samt II in the greying darkness, Shah Jahan welcomed today's battle. Here was finality at last. By Almighty Allah's grace, he would win. His family was safe in Mandu. Mumtaz Mahal had suggested this herself. He rather suspected that she wanted to distance both of them physically from the evil that was befalling the people of the Agra region, though she remained one with him in all his actions, good or bad. Her absence often reminded him of the oath he had given her under such delightful conditions. Had that been in another, carefree lifetime? Had it happened to two other people? What utter chaos lay between. All created by one person, Nur Jehan, with her power lust.

General Mahabat had wasted no time in getting to Agra from Srinagar and launching his forces to the attack. He was of princely birth and known to be a daring, aggressive commander, full of ambition and totally ruthless. A dangerous foe, worthy of the speed of Shah Jahan's own lightning strikes.

Shah Jahan had selected a small green hillock for his battle headquarters. The solitary *neem* tree on it, splaying lush branches, was like a banner which all his commanders could identify. General Dorab, a giant Muslim with fierce moustaches and shaven head, mounted on a great Scindhi bay, was at his right, the craggy-faced General Wahid on an unusually tall grey Arab at his left. It was still not light enough for them to see the enemy drawn up at the far end of the plain, which was veiled by a light mist, but Shah Jahan's own troops were disposed in classic battle order, with General Vickram's division in the centre, Raja Bhim's on the right flank and General Shaista's on the left.

For a moment, in the uncertain light, it seemed to Shah Jahan that the scene was an exercise on a vast sand table in military school. The musketeers of each division were drawn up in front, spreading endlessly to the right and left of him. Behind the riflemen, massed columns of cavalry regiments, pennants on upright lances drooping in the stillness, were packed between the lines of infantrymen. When he turned his head he could distinguish the snouts of his cannon. He had decided against using chariots or elephants today.

The sun must have peeped from behind the hillock, for the air lightened and the faint crowing of cocks told of life going on elsewhere despite death lurking on the battlefield. The familiar sounds of readiness for battle stuttered through cool air heavy with the tension of those awaiting the advance, a shouted command, quiet conversation, a ribald joke of bravado followed by artificial laughter. A horse whinnied, another snorted, clearing its nostrils, a barrow creaked, its cannon balls rattling. The odour of horse-sweat on leather mingled with a sharp camphor scent which General Dorab had used. Why not? If one had to go before the Almighty, one might as well smell clean. All the Muslims on that plain had already answered the *muezzin*'s call to *subh* (morning prayer), kneeling at their posts to face Mecca. If the battle lasted long, there would be no *zuhr*, *asr*, *maghrib* or *isha* today. For some, never.

He cast the dismal thoughts from his mind, tightened up on the pre-battle fears that were churning around his guts and closed the door to conjecture of the outcome, except for one vital link. He half-turned to General Dorab, whose grey had begun restlessly pawing the ground. 'Can we be sure that General Abdullah will transfer to our side at the right time?'

562

General Abdullah, commander of one of General Mahabat's divisions, had secretly promised to cross over. This was vital to even the odds, because Shah Jahan's forces were outnumbered. General Mahabat had reportedly left Srinagar with two divisions, each of ten thousand men, but had been joined along the way by two divisions from the Kandhar expeditionary force and another division loyal to the Emperor. Together, excluding General Itbar's Agra garrison, the enemy totalled fifty thousand men while Shah Jahan himself could only field three divisions, following the attrition of his forces.

'Anything is possible, my lord,' General Dorab responded. 'But General Abdullah is an old comrade at arms with whom I have shared many a campaign tent.' Typical of the true soldier that he referred to a tent rather than to battles. 'I have been in constant, close touch with him through the years. He is disgusted with the way the Empress has eliminated His Imperial Majesty from the scene and seized power. He was in Srinagar with his division when General Mahabat was commissioned by the Empress to undertake this expedition. He learned about it the same day, received orders for the move and was warned that preparations for it were to proceed with the utmost secrecy because the Emperor was unaware of it. He sent a fast messenger to me, and my own response reached him along his route to Agra. I am as certain of him as I can be of myself.' He grinned wryly. 'But there are times when I cannot even be certain of myself.'

The blare of distant trumpets drifted across the plain. The enemy had begun to advance. The air had lightened, the mist was being driven westward towards the enemy by a steady breeze that had sprung up. A good omen, Shah Jahan thought.

His own trumpets blared around him. His ears began to sing. He could make out an extended line of tiny figures in the distance. The enemy approached, Muslim against Muslim, Rajput against Rajput, each Indian race against the other. A chill gloom seized him. With a tremendous effort, he flung it away. He was Shah Jahan, a Moghul, the man of destiny.

Suddenly, like a volcano erupting, the sense of his destiny returned, flung exhilaration and confidence through him. His battle spirit revived, bursting through the hideous confines of conscience and dejection of the past weeks.

Commands rang out from his lines. Matches flared. Spurts of flame were followed by the thunderous roar of his cannon. The earth shook. His ears became plugged. He could not hear the whistling of the cannon balls lofting their way to the advancing enemy. Smoke drifted from the cannon, slowly obscuring them, curling the acrid stench of burnt gunpowder into his nostrils. In the distance, some of the tiny figures vanished. His artillery fire was accurate. And no wonder, the distances had been carefully measured days earlier. He exulted.

As the plain lightened, he watched the battle unfold its classic pattern. His musketeers advanced on foot in double line to meet the enemy. Artillery fire from across the plain fell short of them, but the next barrage took its toll. Men fell in their tracks. The screams of the wounded arose. He had steeled himself not to react with pity for his men, but with hatred for those who caused their death and maiming. An insensate desire to plunge into the battle seized him. It communicated itself to his charger. Samt II impatiently tossed his neck, lowered his head, pulled against the bit.

The roar of artillery fire resounded again. All around him was incredible noise, smoke, the reek of gunpowder. Only when the opposing ranks were within range of the musket fire did the cannon lift their barrage, the roar fading into an ear-splitting silence broken by the splatter of fire from kneeling front ranks and standing rear ranks of musketeers.

'Prepare to advance! Ad . . . vance!' The commands broke through the singing in his ears.

His centre line of cavalry moved forward with a drumming of hooves. Tired pennants began to flutter bravely.

'Extend into line. Ex . . . tend.' The column wheeled out into an extended line, a brave display of trotting horses.

'Level lances.'

The line of cavalry became a serried rank, like a pike-ditch horizontally reaching as far as the eye could see.

'Prepare to charge. Chaa . . . arge!'

Canter, gallop. The thunder of hooves reached him seconds after he saw the line streak into smooth speed.

His cavalry cut through the enemy musketeers. Horses neighed, squealed, fell, limbs helplessly pawing empty air. The shouts of men, spewing hatred, screams of agony became an infernal medley.

His cavalry wheeled, re-formed. With a fierce drumming of approaching hooves the enemy cavalry charged through his musketeers. His infantrymen advanced. Soon the single battle in the centre of the plain became a series of engagements, swaying back and forth.

For three hours, the fierce battle continued. Shah Jahan sat an impatient horse and General Dorab muttered, cursed and gave directions that could not be conveyed. Then the sun was directly overhead, glaring down at them, watching the vast tide of the enemy slowly pushing Shah Jahan's men back.

'Time for the flank attacks,' Shah Jahan directed General Dorab.

The general shook his head. 'I'm afraid our flanks are fully engaged, my lord.'

A moment of despair.

'What is General Abdullah doing?' His only hope.

At that moment, the mass of the enemy on the right flank parted like a vast fallow field before a gigantic plough. Great masses of them turned around, bewildered.

'General Abdullah has kept his word!' General Dorab roared. His laugh soared to the heavens.

The tide of battle had turned, but fighting raged on for another hour. Then slowly, inexplicably, Shah Jahan's men began to retreat. 'What has happened?' General Dorab shouted his bewilderment.

Shah Jahan knew the truth with a sinking heart. 'Mahabat has recognized General Abdullah's defection and led in his reserves.'

Slowly, ever so slowly, fighting every inch of the way, General Vickram's division was being driven back by General Mahabat's merciless attack down the centre of his line.

'There he is!' General Wahid pointed to the leading edge of the enemy. The throng had cleared for a few seconds. Shah Jahan saw a powerful figure on a great chestnut indomitably cutting and chopping his way. That was the man he wanted. He tensed, ready to dig his heels into his horse's flanks. General Wahid placed a restraining hand on his arm. 'Not yet, my lord,' he warned. 'No personal engagements as yet. See, General Vickram is rallying his men.'

True enough, the tall Rajput on a great bay had galloped back, circled and was now leading a group of his men in counter-attack.

'What a warrior!' General Dorab muttered. 'A true Rajput.'

Indeed, it seemed as if General Vickram could win the battle by his ferocity alone. Followed by his Rajput warriors, he slowly pushed the enemy back. He seemed to be wherever the battle needed him. For another hour Shah Jahan watched him with breathless admiration. 'He's done it! He's done it! The enemy is retreating!' General Dorab was almost babbling in glee.

And sure enough, the enemy had turned in full retreat.

Then it happened. Shah Jahan distinctly heard the splat of a single musket. In an instant, he knew he was meant to hear it above the murky clamour and din of battle. General Vickram's head was shaken back. His hands groped blindly upwards. His body slowly collapsed sideways. His horse threw him and bolted.

'Dear Allah!' General Dorab groaned. 'A stray shot hit his head.'

In an instant, the enemy took new heart, while General Vickram's men paused in confusion. The tide of battle turned again. Relief had come from the flanks. Raja Bhim and General Shaista had ridden to the rescue.

But soon, Shah Jahan had to watch, helpless, as his troops were driven back across the plain, still fighting valiantly.

It was hopeless.

'Have my bodyguard follow me!' Shah Jahan commanded General Wahid.

He trotted Samt II down the slope. His bodyguard of one thousand cavalrymen cantered up.

The battle had eased. The enemy was regrouping.

Raja Bhim and General Shaista galloped back to him, hot, sweaty, blood-streaked. The Raja had a red gash showing through the right shoulder of his black tunic. 'My lord prince,' he gasped. 'Forgive me, but the battle is lost. To attempt an attack on the enemy now would be an act of folly. You must flee and rally loyalists to our cause again.'

'Men have died for me,' Shah Jahan ground out. Trembling, he pointed a shaking finger at the grisly apparition of wounded men staggering back through the near darkness, bleeding from terrible wounds, one of them holding up protruding pink entrails with his hand, some without arms, others hopping on single legs, men gasping for breath, screaming with pain. 'What have I got to live for?' He gathered up his reins.

Raja Bhim squared burly shoulders. 'For those very wounded. For those who died on that plain.' He slumped in the saddle. 'For General Vickram.'

Shah Jahan stared wildly at the scene. Hell must look like this. But nothing could resemble the hell within his head.

Moved by some force other than himself, like a wheel turning without oil or volition, Shah Jahan slowly reined his horse around. Today, he had not fired a shot or wielded a sword. Nor had he ever before returned from a battlefield in defeat.

He rode through the night, accompanied by his remaining generals, making for Ajmer, where Mumtaz Mahal had moved from Mandu. He was numbed by the defeat, but utterly dejected at General Vickram's fate. He paused at dawn for a couple of hours to take a head count and rest his battle-weary men, many of them severely wounded, wearing makeshift bloodstained bandages. Less than ten thousand remained of his proud thirty thousand army corps. The rest had either failed to join him or had deserted, some perhaps to the victorious enemy, or were lying dead or wounded on the battlefield. Knowing General Mahabat, he was certain that the wounded would be massacred.

When they reached Ajmer the following morning, news of the defeat had obviously not reached the city. Since Shah Jahan had taken control of Ajmer, he had no difficulty gaining entrance this time, but it only required the sight of his small force, which made camp on the *maidan* outside, for the inmates to know the outcome of the battle. Defeated armies bear an unmistakable stench.

He was shown into a private reception chamber of the

palace by the same flabby eunuch who had once escorted him to Princess Jemaliya's chambers and the quarantine suite.

Mumtaz Mahal awaited him. One look at his face and she flew across the room to him. To his amazement, for the first time ever, instead of clinging to him, she took him into her arms. His child-bride had grown up. He clung to her, trembling, his head buried on her shoulder, able to release the emotions which pride and the need to maintain a cheerful, even poise before his men had held back.

'We lost.' His voice was muffled.

'I know.' She sounded very calm. 'I have known it since evening the day before yesterday.'

He was stunned. Yet he understood and her quiet strength restored some of his own.

She placed a gentle palm on his head. Only when he felt that soothing touch did he realize how fevered his brain had been, how torn and racked by the 'if onlys' of despair. 'We must accept this defeat as part of your destiny,' she said. Her voice carried the calm certainty of a high priestess and for once he was content to let her take the lead. 'You have never known defeat, my husband. If victory had been yours today, the imperial crown would have been on this noble head,' her grip tightened, 'immediately, with no hardship, while your father, a sick, dying man, was still alive. Knowing you, I say that it would have been more difficult for you to bear that prize than the setback you have now suffered. And history too would have judged you. I had to endure years of misery before you married me. I proved my love then and it was all to the good that I did not win my prize with ease. So too with you, my beloved husband. Rejoice in this defeat, because it is the will of Almighty Allah to make you more worthy to receive the imperial crown.'

'But the shame, the whole future . . .'

569

She reached for his head with both hands, drew it back, gazed intensely up into his eyes. 'The future is not tomorrow. Each tomorrow leads to the future.'

'I have only ten thousand men.'

'That is nine thousand eight hundred more than the Emperor Babur once had. He proved his worth and established an Empire. Now it is your turn.'

'I have come so far. How can I go back?'

'You are where you are. You do not go back. Are you less than Babur then?'

He squared his shoulders, straightened up. 'Never!' he grated.

'Are you less than Akbar the Great?'

'Never.' He had bled enough. Now he would rise and fight again. 'I shall assess what I have and base my strategy on it. I shall overcome my enemies and wear the imperial crown.'

'That is my beloved Shah Jahan speaking at last.'

'We cannot remain here. General Mahabat will descend upon Ajmer swiftly. We must leave for Mandu immediately. You and the children will be safe there.'

'And where will you be?'

'Wherever it is necessary to escape my father's wrath until I can fight for the throne again.'

'You will have to go diverse ways before that happens, my husband.' A prophetic note had entered her voice. 'You will be pursued like a common criminal. Your men will desert you, your friends and allies will hold you to scorn. The birds of the air have nests, foxes have their holes, but you will have nowhere to rest your head.'

Rage sparked against her, but the love and tenderness in her expression dimmed it. 'I still have money, treasure, remember, plenty of it. I can hire mercenaries to our cause.'

She reached out gentle fingers to touch his face. 'Will your money last as long as the Emperor's life, my precious darling? I fear that Almighty Allah intends grinding you into dust before using that dust to re-create the man into an Emperor.'

He was shocked. 'You believe that?'

'I have always known it.'

'You never told me.' He was tempted to turn on her.

'Would you have believed me?' She was eyeing him levelly.

He stared at her, then dropped his gaze. 'No! I was too arrogant.'

'You had to discover yourself.'

His eyes remained downcast, like his spirit. '*If* what you say is true, I have to get you and the children to a place of safety.'

'Our only refuge is you.'

'What do you mean?' He lifted his eyes to her again, ready to pounce.

'Wherever you go, we will go. That is the only security we have. We shall share your hardships. If we are a burden at times, you will have the reward of our presence in your hours of need. I love you. I belong to you. I shall be by your side as long as I live.'

He wondered at the shudder that escaped her, but could not help crying out. 'I love you. I did not marry you to bring you hardship. I shall have to go my own way at times.'

'Never! You gave me your oath on it.'

He stared at her in disbelief. She was firm, immovable in her determination.

He had never loved her more.

The Emperor Jehangir was not pleased as he held his *durbar* in Agra, with Nur Jehan on her throne behind him. For once, he had had cause to doubt his beloved's judgment and the thought still rankled in his mind.

When she had informed him in Srinagar that General Mahabat was leaving for Agra to bring Shah Jahan to heel, he had been furious that civil war was being invited without his consent. He could easily have countermanded Nur Jehan's orders, but that would have involved the kind of confrontation for which he was neither physically nor mentally ready. Instead of criticizing her, therefore, he had pretended that he did indeed endorse her actions. But he informed her that in order to carry them to a logical conclusion, the imperial Court would be moving back to Agra the following day.

Not only was he shocked that Nur Jehan should have taken such drastic action on her own, but he did not think it proper that a military expedition against one of his sons should be led by anyone other than himself or at least another son. Besides, he had been left with no other protection than his personal bodyguard, while General Mahabat would soon have command over a huge force. If the man prevailed against the rebel forces, it would give him enormous prestige and power. The Emperor mistrusted General Mahabat's motives.

Finally, the Emperor was jealous that Nur Jehan had selected another man, a young, dashing figure at that, for such a dominant role in the Empire's affairs. It made him take stock of himself for the first time: no longer young or dashing, his figure gone, his health at its lowest ebb, his virility ended. He saw General Mahabat as a rival in every sense of the word.

He had reached Agra with his entourage three days ago, only to find that General Mahabat had pressed on towards Delhi, accompanied by General Itbar and his men, to give battle to Shah Jahan there. He had sent word immediately to General Mahabat through a fast messenger to wait until he arrived to take command of the expedition, but word had come back that he was too late. The opposing forces were already drawn up for a battle. It must have taken place yesterday, the Emperor had deduced.

News of the victory had been carried through the night and had reached him that morning, along with the head of General Vickram, which General Mahabat had sent him as a trophy. What a barbaric act! The Emperor shuddered at it. General Vickram had been a fine soldier, who had served Shah Jahan since the first Deccan campaign and been rapidly promoted. The Rajputs had believed that he was blessed by their Creator God Brahman and was indestructible. Chopping a dead Rajput hero's head off and not giving him a decent cremation was an act of desecration which they would not forgive. It would have its repercussions.

'What is the point of being a victorious general if you are also politically incompetent?' he had irritably demanded of Nur Jehan.

Now here he was in full *durbar* and General Mahabat had been announced, requesting audience. Of course he had been obliged to invite the victor to his presence but it annoyed him to observe the stir which the general's arrival had created amongst the nobles and officials gathered below his elevated pavilion. A man who the other day had been just another general was commanding more interest than their ruler. All these courtiers had the hearts of sycophants beneath their splendid attire. Oh, he was so very, very tired, holding up his own magnificent jewelled tunic and turban only with a tremendous effort of will. His body was sore, his head ached, he had difficulty breathing, but he did not show it. What did these commoners know about the nobility required of a monarch?

He glanced back at Nur Jehan. Had her interest been quickened at the prospect of seeing the dashing young victor? By Allah, if that were so, it would not be a defeated enemy's head, but a victor's balls that would be forfeit.

* * *

When he became Rana of Mewar, he had promoted Selvam, his personal aide, to the rank of colonel. The promotion was not merely a reward for past services, both very personal and official, but also signified the end of their sexual encounters, since Rana Chara preferred younger men or boys. Older men were like mature goats, tough mutton! In Selvam's case, the promotion also signified his liking for the man and his confidence in him. Nothing more, for Rana Chara never trusted anyone.

He was seated alone at his mahogany desk in his private chamber, studying the reports of his tax gatherers that afternoon, when Colonel Selvam burst in, almost unceremoniously. Since Selvam knew that he retired to this sparsely furnished upstairs room overlooking the courtyard only when he wanted to be alone, his intrusion had better be for a good cause. 'Yes, what is it?' he demanded brusquely.

Selvam knelt to him hurriedly, rose to his feet. He was plainly agitated. 'Forgive my disturbing you, my lord, but the news warrants it. Shah Jahan was defeated by General Mahabat in a great battle outside Delhi five days ago. He is on the run with about ten thousand men, marching through Mewar towards Mandu.'

Rana Chara restrained the impulse to show his amazement. He knew of General Mahabat's advance, but had never dreamed that Shah Jahan would be defeated. His brain cool, he examined the possibilities and excitement fountained within him. 'Did you say he is in Mewar now with only ten thousand men?'

'Yes, lord,' Selvam responded, adding hopefully, 'They will all be battle-weary and disorganized.'

'Precisely.' The fountain became a surge. His moment had arrived at last. Cause and effect had delivered his mortal enemy into his hands.

* * *

General Mahabat's virile presence irritated the Emperor more than ever. Even the obeisance the general made seemed to be tinged with condescension. It had deeply hurt Jehangir to learn of Shah Jahan's rebellion, for this had been the son he admired most, who had shown him the greatest loyalty. Why were his children so untrustworthy? General Mahabat's victory over even a rebellious son belittled imperial stature.

'We must congratulate you on a remarkable and timely victory,' the Emperor proclaimed.

'I am honoured to have been selected for the role, Your Imperial Majesty,' General Mahabat responded. His green eyes shot a glance in Nur Jehan's direction.

It infuriated the Emperor. There was some undercurrent here. 'We would of course have preferred you to give General Vickram a decent Rajput cremation.' Noting the angry flash of those eyes, he decided to put this upstart in his place. 'But your knowledge of our style will come with experience.' He could sense Nur Jehan becoming restive.

'I regret that I may have caused Your Imperial Majesty displeasure,' General Mahabat countered curtly. 'I have laboured valiantly on behalf of the Empire.'

'Oh, you certainly have and we are most delighted.' An answering of condescension was called for. 'We shall of course give due deliberation to suitable honours and rewards. Meanwhile,' he paused to make certain of everyone's attention before he loosed his thunderbolt, 'we deem it only proper that the final victory over a rebellious son should be achieved by us personally. Since our health does not permit it, we shall send for our eldest surviving son, who is by law and tradition our heir, to return to Agra and lead the imperial army in pursuit of Shah Jahan.'

He definitely heard the hiss of Nur Jehan's indrawn breath, but General Mahabat's only response was a mocking smile.

* * *

The more he thought about it the more Rana Chara was certain that destiny had delivered Shah Jahan into his hands. Defeated in battle, with no more than ten thousand dejected, weary men to support him, Shah Jahan's only escape route was through Rajasthan to Mandu and the Deccan, where he could regroup his supporters in a region traditionally hostile to the Moghul Emperors. 'Ask our army commanders to attend me immediately,' he ordered Colonel Selvam. 'We can eliminate Shah Jahan in Rajasthan.' It was as simple as that.

'Yes, Your Majesty.' A broad smile crossed Selvam's face. He saluted, turned on his heel to leave.

Something nagged Rana Chara. 'Wait!' he commanded.

Colonel Selvam paused in his stride, turned around.

'If we remove Shah Jahan from the scene, the Emperor will be the stronger.' He was speaking aloud, but to himself. 'With General Mahabat leading the imperial armies, the Moghuls would have a replacement for Shah Jahan who would not be a source of civil war.' He frowned as a sudden thought struck him, placed a finger between his teeth in contemplation. 'On the contrary, once General Mahabat assumes greater command, his own ambitions will inevitably lead him to try and seize power. Hm . . . m.' He stared out at the afternoon sunlight glinting on the flagstones of the courtyard. 'No. Let the two lions destroy each other. That will weaken the whole imperial pride of lions. We shall do nothing for the present.'

He was beginning to enjoy his new role, shorn of any ambition to become the Maha Raja, the Great Whore.

Nur Jehan had already barely been able to control her fury at the Emperor's decision, which had taken her completely by surprise. She had grown so used to making such decisions herself and to his concurring with whatever she did that she had been close to ignoring his existence as

Emperor. He was merely the crumbling platform of the imperial throne – which she alone occupied – and her energy had been concentrated on ensuring that she did not need any platform when he died.

She had remained silent and uncommunicative during the *durbar*, but before it ended her native cunning told her that she should tread warily. Something was bothering her husband and she had best not step out of line. If rebellion was on his mind, he could have her imprisoned, and it had also become obvious to her that even Asaf Khan would entirely approve such a move.

Where did all this leave her? If she was not careful, Prince Parviz, who loathed her and who would never allow her to manipulate him, would inherit the throne. She would become another Salima Begum, head of a *harem* instead of an Empire. The thought terrified her. Some instinct for believing in the Hindu doctrine of *kharma*, in its sense of retribution, warned her. History must not repeat itself in her case.

When she returned to the *harem* from the *durbar* that evening, she expressed her rage by smashing the goblet of fruit juice which Mano had brought her. The violent act released all her pent-up anger. By the time the Emperor came to her bedchamber that night, she was her cool self again.

He seemed somewhat different when he entered the room. 'Ah, you grow more beautiful each day, star of my soul,' he declared, pausing at the entrance door.

'And you grow more magnificent by the hour, light of my life.' What an accursed lie she thought savagely, noting his paunchy body beneath the blue silken robe, the legs grown spindly and the sagging skin. Even his once commanding expression had become obtuse. 'And you *were* magnificent today. Such wisdom. Such decisiveness. Such imperial majesty.'

'I was good, wasn't I?' He sounded relieved, his need for her approval obvious. If he had not thwarted her designs, she would have found it pathetic.

'You always are. You may pretend because you love me that you have delivered the Empire to me in exchange for a glass of wine and a few morsels of food, but no one, least of all I, can have any doubt as to who is in command.'

'Good, good. I now command you to bed and ministrations.'

'First, please tell me what bothers you, lord of my life.'

'What, what?' He had developed the habit of repeating his words whenever he was agitated.

'I know you better than you know yourself. That is how Almighty Allah intended it, so I can better serve you. It is He who tells me that you have something on your mind.'

'Nothing, nothing.' He was taken aback, hesitated. 'Except that I was not going to put up with the arrogance of that dog Mahabat.'

'You are jealous because *I* appointed him, are you not, my lord?'

'Hr . . . rmph.' Her directness had really put him off stride. 'Well . . . well, I suppose you could say that.'

'My lord, you are the Emperor. There is no one on this earth who can even stand in your shadow. You are a human god, second only to Almighty Allah. Why should you descend to the level of ordinary mortals, especially when you have the total love, loyalty and fidelity of your wife? You are my day and my night, my sun, moon and stars. You are my whole life.'

'People are human beings,' he responded bitterly. 'When the flesh of my flesh can betray me repeatedly, what can I expect from anyone else?'

'I am not flesh of your flesh, nor blood of your blood, nor bone of your bone. For that very reason, I could never betray you.'

'Oh my beloved, do you really mean that?'

'Of course. I am your mother too. A son may betray a father, but would a mother ever take the milk away from her son?'

The time was right. She produced the whip from behind her. His eyes widened. Only then did he notice that she was in her black riding attire. 'Take your robe off and come here, Jehangir,' she commanded him. 'You have been a naughty boy. You have to be punished.'

It had been so long since she had done this. As on that first night, she wondered how he would respond, trembling inwardly.

Long moments passed while he gazed at the whip, fascinated.

He slowly began taking off his robe.

Chapter 36

By some miracle, not of love but of tenacity and determination, combined with the fact that he had obviously not touched any liquor that evening, she had been able to get the Emperor to rise and come. He now lay back on the mattress, his eyes closed, exhausted but grateful. 'It has been so long,' he whispered. 'You are a miracle worker.'

She reached out and took him in her arms. 'The miracle is our love,' she rejoined softly. 'We have only each other. We must protect each other.'

'Of course,' he agreed sleepily.

'Will you let me help you as before?' She was approaching her objective fearfully.

'I need your help, always.' He hesitated, debating in a return to his befuddled state. 'I know my commands were somewhat harsh this evening. In order to help you save face, I shall appoint General Mahabat senior army commander to Prince Parviz in the expedition against Shah Jahan.' He suddenly seemed very weary. 'But only on condition that you direct the campaign by personally giving General Mahabat his instructions.'

A thrill shot through her. This was precisely what she had hoped to ask of him. She would send for General Mahabat tomorrow. Surely there were many ways of skinning a cat. Tonight she had done so with a whip and an ejaculation.

It was strange having one of her own race other than family in her reception chamber. In fact, Sir Thomas Roe had been the only outsider who had been there alone and he was a foreigner, an Englishman. She missed him.

Nur Jehan had deliberately selected the early afternoon for the audience to which she had summoned General Mahabat because the Emperor and most of the palace household, other than the eunuchs and the female Uzbeg guards, would then be resting. She had awaited his arrival with an unfamiliar eagerness. He arrived punctually at 2 P.M., but she deliberately kept him waiting a few minutes before she made her way to her side of the chamber, behind the green velvet curtains.

Since she had a private entrance from her bedroom through the inner chamber, she was able to take her seat on her divan without his knowledge. He was seated on the chair that Sir Thomas Roe had favoured. Dressed as usual in his well-fitting cavalry uniform, he seemed very much at ease, despite the unfamiliar surroundings, gazing out at the courtyard which was so grey under an unseasonal pall of cloud that the chirping and whistling of the birds in their cages sounded puzzled. He had the remarkable capacity of remaining relaxed while sitting erect like a soldier and exuding power as a man. For the first time in her life, faint as a moth's orgasm, Nur Jehan felt a stirring of her womanhood. What was happening to her? Was it being totally alone in a private chamber with a man who exuded raw sexuality that was causing this? She had best put such thoughts out of her mind.

Exercising her tremendous willpower, she simply threw the notion aside. 'Good day to you, General Mahabat.' She deliberately kept all warmth from her golden voice.

General Mahabat casually turned his head in the direction of the slit. He rose to his feet and bowed. 'Good day to you too, Your Imperial Majesty.'

'Please be seated.'

She waited until he had resumed his seat. 'You may find the environment of this meeting, with a curtain separating us, rather strange, considering that we met face to face in the palace garden at Srinagar and even in *durbar* yesterday.'

'Hardly face to face, Madam.' He laughed good-humouredly. 'Veil to face would be more accurate, don't you think?'

She warmed to him. 'Well put, general. Only here, we have to observe another set of rules, those of the *harem*. You can be assured that our discussion is neither heard nor observed, nor will we be interrupted. So you may speak as freely as you wish. We always had the regular conference of what people chose to call the Nur Jehan Cabinet in this chamber. And we ourself have had many a discussion here alone with Sir Thomas Roe, the ambassador from England.'

'So I understand, Madam. Did I rightly hear you say we are not observed and will not be interrupted?'

'Yes.' Now why had he asked that? Did he have some secret matter to discuss? 'Let us first give you the proof of that. We wish to extend our regret for any pain of mind you experienced from your audience with the Emperor yesterday. We feel responsible because we selected you for the role you played in confronting the rebel Shah Jahan and defeating him. You acted with remarkable speed, courage and gallantry. You deserved more than the promise of honours and reward.'

'You are most gracious.' He fixed his gaze through the slit in the curtain. She knew that he was certain their eyes had met. 'Why? What can you want of me, especially now that someone of higher rank has replaced me?'

'We have taken steps to ensure that the omission has been rectified. You will be the overall army commander, only nominally under Prince Parviz, in the military operations against Shah Jahan.'

'To whom do I report, Madam?' He sounded almost brusque.

'All operations will be under our personal control.'

'Yours, Madam? How will that be achieved with the distance separating us?'

'You will make field and command decisions. We shall dictate policy.'

Head cocked to one side, he thought this out, then smiled, teeth showing very white beneath the reddish cavalry moustache. 'Do you have any policy decisions to give me now?'

'Yes. Your troops are presently located at Ajmer. What is their strength?'

'Four divisions, totalling forty thousand men.'

'What losses did you take in the battle?'

'Over four thousand killed and twice as many wounded.'

'Are your divisions up to strength then?'

She could see that he appreciated the question. 'Yes, because our numbers have been increased by detachments that deserted Shah Jahan's cause.'

'You shall make immediate preparations to pursue Shah Jahan. When we have concluded this discussion, we shall send you to the Royal Treasurer, with whom you shall make arrangements for payment to your troops and the supply of your army. You can be in touch with us, here in this chamber, any time through our Chief Eunuch. Is there anything else you need?'

'Yes.' He stood up abruptly.

'What?'

'You.'

A gasp escaped her, a hand flew to her mouth. Taken completely aback, she was about to erupt in outrage when he began moving towards her. The swing of his solid loins excited her. The green eyes were boring into her through the slit in the curtain.

This is the cobra and I for once am the transfixed bird.

She felt her womanhood really stir this time, stood up involuntarily to flee. He had parted the curtains by then and stopped, looking at her. His face had turned cruel. 'You need me, Nur Jehan,' he said quietly, his lustful gaze reaching through to her soul. 'You need me as the Empress and you need me even more as a woman, for as a woman you are totally unfulfilled. If you wish to satisfy your needs as a woman, the Empress cannot afford to reject me. I am going to take you now, whether you like it or not. You can scream, call for the guards, but I shall rape you before I am imprisoned and executed.'

'You would risk all that just to take me? Why?'

'Because I need you as a woman more than as an Empress. Never in my life have I been so excited by any woman. Your sheer presence fills me with lust.' He bared his teeth. Gone was the suave man of the world before the jungle animal. 'And the price will be worth it. Death in exchange for a few moments' bliss.'

'You would not dare.' The words escaped her, but she did not mean them. Death in exchange for a few moments' bliss, he had said. Oh dear Allah, how wonderful. Her brain was swimming, her head whirling and the invisible connection to him held her in thrall.

'I dare everything for the vibrance of you, the melody of your voice. For the feel of my cock in your flesh, thrusting, thrusting. I dare to dare because if you reject me, the Empress will have no one to help fulfil her ambitions. She will have nothing.' He paused to let his words sink in. 'So I shall rape you, or blackmail you into submitting, but I know you will yield to me instead, because of your own lust.'

The truth of this statement hit her, stark and clear. If she delivered him to the guards, she would be left with nothing. To one who was allowing a husband to blackmail her, why should it matter . . .

'The woman too would be left with nothing.' He said it very, very quietly, but there was no doubt about his dominance.

A sob escaped her, but it was not from sorrow. She did not know its cause, nor did she care. In a few strides he was on her. Grasping her roughly, he shoved her on to the divan. His strength was incredible. Dimly she recognized that she had never experienced it with any man. Sher Afgan had been brutal without strength.

General Mahabat leaned forward, tore off her veil, pulled up her *kurtha*. Reaching beneath it, he tore down her pantaloons. He gazed a moment at her white limbs and the dark pubis.

'Oh Allah!' he gasped. He undid his belt, dropped his breeches.

She lay back totally lost, gazing at his huge, erect organ in fascination. It was so long. He grasped her ankles, tore her legs apart, knelt between them. He placed his organ on her labia, moved it around with one hand. She could feel her slippery wetness. And the incredible thrills.

He centred, pushed, fell forward. She raised her limbs,

her knees almost touching her breasts. Oh, the wild ecstasy of having a hard, long penis inside her, pushing aside the virginity of the years. Suddenly it reached a spot within her that sent wild throbs shooting from it. A place never before touched. Almighty God.

He did not make love to her, he humped her. Every stroke swift and sure. He whipped her, a joyous punishment. He went on and on steadily, his face set and stern, taking her, possessing her, his breath harsh.

Then unexpectedly, she turned the corner. And came. For the first time in her life without artifice. No deliberate clutchings and spurting. No moans. Only wild cries of ecstasy she could not hold back. She just came and came. She could not stop.

She seemed to come forever before she started jerking to a close, relaxed, exhausted.

But he would not stop. He went on whipping her limp body until she revived, came once more.

This time he groaned. And ejaculated inside her like a great spouting pump.

The odour of his emission remained in her nostrils all day. Her entire pelvic region felt weak, but in her heart there was fierce exhilaration. She pleaded a severe colic and stayed away from the evening *durbar*.

Strolling by herself in the palace garden that evening, Nur Jehan sorted out her feelings. She was not in love with General Mahabat. She was no impressionable young maiden to swoon before a man who satisfied her sexually. In spite of his seeming self-sufficiency when he domineered his way to sexual conquest, General Mahabat had needed her. Otherwise he would not have taken such hideous risks to couple with her.

She had found what she in turn needed to fulfil her ambition. When General Mahabat established himself as the strong man of the Empire, he would want to be the ruler with her at his side. That was not what she had worked so hard and made such tremendous sacrifices for all these years. She would manipulate him, use him and kill him.

A brown praying mantis was perched on one of the garden seats. Almighty Allah had sent her a sign, for this was the insect that copulated with the male then ate him up.

For all her calm, she could not prevent the recollection of a strong body and a long penis from intruding. Or the ceaseless, delicious thrill within the whole of her. And that spot the penis had reached, her sexual soul.

When she saw the Emperor's naked body on her mattress that night, the protruding stomach, the spindly legs, the sagging flesh, the wrinkled skin, the limp member, she was so revolted she fled to her privy and vomited.

How fortunate it was that she had made the excuse of a colic that afternoon. It explained everything.

Chapter 37

From the Diary of Shah Jahan

My grandfather, the great Emperor Akbar, had no great education, but he took pains to learn about war, politics, government and religion from the great ones. Perhaps the military genius he admired most was the Emperor Sikander of Macedonia. My grandfather instilled into me many of Sikander's policies.

Two of these are most important to me today, as I contemplate my future.

I must have a goal, an ultimate object that I am striving for and I must drive relentlessly towards that goal. My goal is to be the Emperor. My military strategy should therefore always be planned with that object in view. It is only in Agra that I can finally reach that goal. A war is not won until the victorious infantryman stands in the enemy citadel. This is why I drove for Agra . . . and was defeated. Some day, I will have to thrust back. I shall have faith, faith, faith.

We have sped southwards through Rajasthan towards Mandu. The presence of Raja Bhim made the Rajputs of the area assist us, but I am specially grateful to my brother Rana Chara for not taking advantage of our pitiable condition to attack us and avenge all that he and his kingdom suffered at our hands ten years ago. Our ultimate destination will be Buran. None of the imperial armies of recent times, other than that which I once led, have been successful in Buran.

Mumtaz Mahal has missed her monthly period. I believe she conceived on that wonderful night in Ajmer when life was so full of hope. She is now the one person in the world on whose total approval of my decisions I can depend. To my generals my 'infallible' judgment was once proved wrong and there is no easy way back into their confidence.

We crossed the River Narbada today, an arduous operation for an army at best. Some of my men mutinied. I put down the mutiny, but in such cases, a commander can take only one course of action to prevent a recurrence. I had all the mutineers, nearly two thousand of them, put to the sword.

It is a black night for me. Not even the fair countenance of my beloved can bring light to my gloom. I cannot even begin to describe how I feel. So it is not 'Good Night' but 'Hellish Night'. Oh Allah, where am I going? What am I headed for? What can I do?

I feel no better this morning. I have distributed most of my treasure to the remainder of my men. As the Christians might say, thirty pieces of silver!

What will I do to support this army in the months ahead? Almighty Allah will provide. I can only look to the present.

Oh God of the Prophet, the most unkind cut of all.

Immediately after he received his share of the treasure today, a letter written by General Rahim, one of my senior commanders, to General Mahabat was intercepted and brought to me. General Rahim has offered to defect provided that his support of me is pardoned and his rights and property are secure.

Muslim Judas. Is he responsible for Mumtaz's miscarriage?

I feel lost. It is all too much. I would kill myself were it not for Mumtaz Mahal.

General Rahim was brought before me just an hour ago. He admitted his guilt, did not seem the least penitent, only requested that he be suitably punished. I have removed him and his son, who is also in my army, from their commands and ordered imprisonment for both father and son and their families.

Our first ray of hope today. We captured Asir without firing a shot. The commandant capitulated when we encircled the fort. I gave him, his family and inevitably his valuables, safe conduct back to Agra.

A minor victory. But it has given confidence to my men, restored hope and therefore morale, and allows a period for rest and the replenishment of our ammunition, supplies and treasury.

After much reflection, I sent my brother a despatch today. I stated, among other things, that my rebellion was not against our father but against the injustices being perpetrated in his name. Injustices which he would never have condoned. I regretted that the only course open to me was military action . . .

'The unity of the Empire and the Moghul dynasty are as dear to me as to you,' I said. 'I have pledged before God that I will protect them,' and I begged him to intercede on my behalf.

It was such an abject letter. Such abject surrender. Though I have deliberately sent it on the heels of my minor triumph, I am so ashamed.

Yet if by this means I can safeguard my Mumtaz Mahal and the children . . . I am so tired.

The reply to my plea did not come from Prince Parviz but from General Mahabat. He demanded the release of General Rahim and his son as evidence of my good faith.

I invited General Rahim to my private apartment in the Asir palace. In the presence of Mumtaz Mahal, I actually fell on my knees and implored General Rahim to negotiate on my behalf for an honourable settlement.

How low I have fallen. Below the knees, below the earth, to the uttermost depths of the Hell of Shame. And I once spoke so bravely of self-esteem.

Meanwhile I am courting General Malik Ambar and Sultan Adil, once my adversaries. But they are only playing with me.

When a man reaches the utmost depths, he cannot sink any further unless he is a fool. Upon General Ambar's final refusal to make common cause with me, I decided to move east, rather than south where I can expect no support.

It is now 11th September 1623. I crossed the river Tapti yesterday with fifteen thousand loyal troops. We have been on the run for six months and eighteen days. The imperial army is still north of the River Narbada. I am making for Orissa and the east where the imperialists have few friends.

A reckless move, but perhaps it is the long, long road back. I must only negotiate with my enemies from strength, not weakness. Mumtaz is pregnant again.

Oh joy! Sultan Qutb of Golkonda has helped me. He has given me a loan of nearly two million rupees, great quantities of food, supplies and equipment and a command to all his officers to permit me and my army safe passage east through his territories.

I have paid up all arrears of salary to my officers and men with my own remaining funds and bought all that I need for the long journey east.

May Almighty Allah bless Sultan Qutb. More than money and material, the sultan has given me hope renewed.

I have conquered Orissa, once again without firing a single shot!

I made love to Mumtaz Mahal last night, for the first time in weeks. Her stomach is getting a little rounded. How dear.

Success upon success. Advancing farther east today, I met an imperial army under Ibrahim, Governor of Bengal, at

Burdwan, where Nur Jehan's late husband Sher Afgan was *faudjar* at the time of his death. After a fierce battle, I defeated the imperialists. Governor Ibrahim was killed in hand-to-hand combat with my General Abdullah.

Within two months, two rich provinces, Orissa and Bengal have fallen to me.

Appointing General Dorab as Governor of Bengal, I move west again intending to capture the remaining eastern state, Bihar, until recently the domain of my brother, Prince Parviz.

This seems like poetic justice. Prince Parviz was at my tail. I am about to seize his head!

When one is in the ascendant, one should push on up. The time has arrived to circle back and make for Agra. I have sent General Abdullah to take Allahabad, and General Darya, one of my new commanders, to subjugate Qudh. I await the outcome at Jaun.

Appalling news once more today. General Abdullah battered the Allahabad fort for seven days without being able to take it. Suddenly, General Mahabat and Prince Parviz appeared, seemingly from nowhere, at the head of a massive army, and General Abdullah has withdrawn with casualties. Our thrust has been blunted, but Raja Bhim is eager to take on the enemy. Buoyed by my recent successes and the belief that my luck has turned, I have decided to do so.

We fought our battle near Jaun. We lost. Raja Bhim was killed. Like General Vickram, he was a valiant soldier and a true, loyal friend.

Once again, we fought all day. I am still bleeding from a bad cut on my left shoulder. This time we were overwhelmed by the sheer weight of General Mahabat's numbers. The final count started when General Mahabat personally led a crack division of Afghan troops into the fray. With imperial might behind him, the man is invincible.

I wanted to fight on and die on the battlefield, but General Abdullah led me away by force. We galloped to safety in the darkness through a corridor of the dead bodies of my men.

We shall head for the impregnable fort of Rohtas in Bihar

tomorrow morning with the tattered, bleeding remnants of my army.

Why?

My beloved Mumtaz Mahal gave birth to yet another boy today, here in Rohtas. We have named him Murad, Soul Wish. Perhaps his horoscope will end my terrible period of misfortune.

The only light in my life is Mumtaz Mahal. What would I do without her? We are one in body, mind and spirit.

Dreadful news again today. General Dorab, whom I appointed Governor of Bengal, has abrogated our agreement and will cede to the Emperor. I feel so hopeless that I cannot even blame him. This is, however, a mortal blow. I no longer have the security of the east. My best hope remains back in Buran.

Leaving two of our sons, Prince Dara and Prince Aurang, in Rohtas, we shall leave immediately for Buran. I am dismayed by Prince Aurang's reaction to my decision. He is only six years old, but his response was that of an adult. He stated very respectfully that since we were taking his brother, Prince Shuja, and the baby with us, his mother and I are betraying and rejecting him.

Is there no solace anywhere?

As we approached Buran, my spirits were raised. General Malik Ambar came to meet me and we have executed a pact to cooperate in peace and war. However, he gave me no support whatever in my siege of Buran and I fear that he wants the imperial army to lose, but not me to win. He is playing a waiting game. When the lions have worn themselves out fighting each other, the black gorilla will pounce.

A messenger has brought me news that General Mahabat and Prince Parviz with another massive force have appeared on the northern horizon. What kind of a miracle worker is this General Mahabat?

I am finished. Bone weary in body, totally devastated in mind and exhausted in spirit.

I have never, never given in before, but this time convictions of honour and good sense must prevail. I cannot expose those loyal to me to the mortal dangers of a lost cause.

I have sent a despatch to the Emperor through my brother Prince Parviz, seeking forgiveness for my acts and permission, in the name of Almighty Allah, to don the dress of a dervish and embark on a journey of self-purification through service and non-attachment.

All I want now is to spend the rest of my days with Mumtaz Mahal. She alone is my world.

I believe my timing is right. Prince Parviz will support my plea at long last because our father is dying and, with Nur Jehan plotting to place Prince Shahriyar on the imperial throne, the legal heir should not allow himself to get bogged down chasing me in the Deccan. He should be in Agra, at the centre of things. As for our father, a dying man is more likely than one in good health to extend compassion to an erring son.

How the mighty one has fallen, Shah Jahan.

Peace at last.

After months of suspense, I have received a despatch from my father. He has forgiven me. I can live wherever I wish in the south on condition that I surrender the fortresses at Rohtas and Asir and send my two sons, Prince Dara and Prince Aurang, to the Agra court as hostages.

In the midst of my relief, I remember Prince Aurang's earlier words of protest.

Am I now making both these sons the hostages of fortune, *my* fortune? Will my acceptance of this condition come back some day to haunt me?

I have no choice. I thrust aside my anxiety and accept the Emperor's terms.

Chapter 38

When Rana Chara received Nur Jehan's invitation to visit the Agra palace, he knew that a fresh crisis must be brewing.

The conqueror of Mewar, Shah Jahan, had bitten the dust. Rana Chara derived enormous satisfaction from his part in bringing about this end, more satisfaction than from the downfall of his arch-rival or the expectation of achieving additional power from it. He had been clever in his handling of Nur Jehan, General Malik Ambar and the flexible neutrality of Mewar. And he loved to be clever.

Gone was Prince Chara with the ambition to become a Great Whore. His place had been taken by Rana Chara, whose deep fulfilment sprang from playing the Great Master Mind, working from behind the scenes as a director of the stage play, Life. By taking control over his destiny, and incidentally that of others, he had achieved personal Enlightenment, a Buddhahood of his life's direction. Without stooping to the crudeness of military battles he had become the superior of every politician in the Moghul Empire.

He had made it a point to visit Nur Jehan at least once every six months during the nearly three years of Shah Jahan's rebellion, so he had first-hand information as to what was going on in the capital, including General Mahabat's rise to power. Although the seeming cause was the general's outstanding brilliance as a military strategist, Rana Chara was convinced that the original cause went beyond matters military. Nur Jehan had her favourites, always worked through men she trusted. In a strange way, he himself was one of those favourites. He rather suspected that in General Mahabat's case some added personal emotion was involved.

When he was ushered into Nur Jehan's reception chamber that warm, summer Friday afternoon, he was surprised to find two little boys present. They rose and greeted him with the respectful obeisance due to an elder and a Rana, and he concluded that these well tutored children were Shah Jahan's sons, now hostages in the imperial palace. They were both too old to be housed in the palace *harem*, so what were they doing here this afternoon?

Having sat down, he swiftly studied the two boys. Prince Dara was very like a young Asaf Khan, with a triangular-shaped face, the bones delicate, the skin fair, the hair contrastingly dark with almost reddish tints. Something almost feminine in the large, brown doe-like eyes told of great sensitivity.

Prince Aurang was so like his father that it was incredible. Rana Chara placed imaginary Mongolian moustaches beneath the long nose, the nostrils flaring upwards and the face with its already heavy, handsome bones, wide cheeks, strong jaw, and the whole was Shah Jahan. He removed the moustaches and the expression in the eyes, haughty, brooding, and the set of the face were those he remembered of the boy who had judged the elephant battle twenty years ago and whom he had hated from that moment.

Prince Aurang, on the other hand, offered other possibilities. Some sixth sense told Rana Chara that beneath the polite, seemingly unconcerned exterior lurked the Prince Chara of his own youth, angry, sullen, bitter. It was like discovering a double and it seemed to him that Prince Aurang had recognized this too in some indefinable way. He certainly was cool towards his brother, Prince Dara.

Now here was an interesting situation. Considering the

way Moghul princes clawed their way to the succession, if ever Shah Jahan . . .

His reflections were interrupted by the warm, golden voice of Nur Jehan. He rose with the two princes and gave her salutation.

'We see that Prince Dara and Prince Aurang have already introduced themselves to you, Rana,' Nur Jehan observed when they had resumed their seats. 'They have such nice manners despite having spent the last two years mostly in military camps around the countryside, don't you think?'

Prince Chara's eyes flickered towards Prince Aurang. The boy's eyes widened slightly, the nostrils dilated briefly, but he gave no other indication of the anger that had flashed within him at Nur Jehan's condescending tone.

'With due respect,' Rana Chara responded, 'people with nice manners are a breed apart. They are not the product of environment but of creation.' He knew without looking that he had scored a point with Prince Aurang.

'Ever the philosopher, Rana Chara.'

'Your Imperial Majesty brings out the best in me.'

He heard her hands clap once. 'Ever the charmer too.' She paused. 'That is one of the reasons why we arranged for the two princes to be present today. We wanted them to meet you. They have no parents since their father has rejected them . . .'

'That is not true!' Prince Dara interrupted fiercely, without any concession to deportment. 'Our father was compelled to send us away.'

'For his own safety,' Prince Aurang sneered.

'And we have just remarked on your good manners, Princes!' Nur Jehan flashed. 'Now repeat after me: We shall never again interrupt the Empress when she speaks.'

The boys looked at each other, then repeated the words, Prince Dara mumbling, Prince Aurang defiant and loud.

'Thank you. As we were saying when we were so rudely

595

interrupted, the two princes have been rejected by their parents.' So it was 'parents' not just 'father' this time, to dig the knife deeper in the boys' wounds for that interruption. Rana Chara enjoyed the subtle expression of Nur Jehan's streak of cruelty. 'While we can teach them languages, mathematics, history, politics and, of course, *deportment*, with the Emperor busy and ailing, there is no one to whom they can turn for personal guidance. Though you are so far away in Mewar, we can think of no better person than you, Rana Chara, especially as you do not have to take care of children of your own.' She must have known that he had no special fondness for *little* boys! 'You would be someone they could look up to, talk to at times. This could be achieved during your visits to us here in Agra. And if you would be so kind as to have them attend you in the Chitor palace from time to time, they could also absorb some Rajput culture, which is part of their heritage. What do you say, Rana?'

What *could* he say when the Empress was offering to deliver to him two human beings whom he could shape as the causes that would have far-reaching effects on the destinies of others in high places and certainly on the destiny of the Empire? He would be the granite circumcision knife that shaped the ends of two Muslim boys! That was amusing.

Nur Jehan waited impatiently while Rana Chara conversed with the two princes. He was easy with them, did not condescend or try to win their favour. She could not wait for the princes to leave, however, because what she needed to discuss with Rana Chara involved one of the most momentous decisions of her life.

When she missed her period, Nur Jehan's first reaction was panic. Only General Mahabat could be the father. He had humped her – it was the only way in which she could describe his performances to herself and it gave her secret delight to think of them as such – each time he came to Agra from his chase of Shah Jahan and reported to her in the palace. Those Friday afternoons had become special to her, but she had taken pains not to be careless of discovery.

After her initial panic, she calmly thought of what she would do if she were indeed pregnant. Firstly, she could easily make the Emperor imagine that the baby was his. Even if she failed to get him erect, she could always make him so drunk that he would believe her if she told him when he was sober the following morning that he had been a magnificent stud. The problem of functioning effectively as the factual head of the Empire remained, but she would learn to cope with that. Dear Allah, she had always believed that she had gone barren after giving birth to Ladili. Women were taught to believe that if they did not produce children the fault was in their wombs, not their husband's seed. Her pregnancy made it obvious that it was her husband, the Emperor, who was sterile.

Having brought her fears under control, she had informed the Emperor that he had made her pregnant. To her surprise, he was elated. It would prove to the world that he was still very much a lusty, virile man even though he was so sick. He had bragged about it during his *durbar* the very next day.

Nur Jehan was horrified when the months went by and, instead of a growing stomach, she had occasional spells of bleeding, moments of irritability and bouts of depression. She finally came to the conclusion that she was experiencing the menopause. Damn Allah, the menopause!

At forty-eight, looking as if she was in her early thirties, she had passed into another phase of her life. She was old! How would she charm the Emperor with her sensuous beauty when her skin became wrinkled and her breasts began to sag? How would she keep the lusty General

Mahabat her devoted lover and slave? Her husband would die soon, but General Mahabat?

Having pretended to the Emperor that she had had a miscarriage, she had the answer to the second question when General Mahabat came to Agra after the Emperor's peace agreement with Shah Jahan. He told her very respectfully that he had met a high-caste girl of twenty from South India while in the Deccan and had taken her for his mistress. He was getting on in years, a widower without children, and needed a more permanent relationship.

For the first time in three years he did not hump her.

Nur Jehan's world had shattered. She had never loved General Mahabat but he had rejected her for a much younger woman. She politely wished General Mahabat happiness, but her hatred of him knew no bounds. It found its first outlet in secret scorn. This man who had seemed so strong and self-sufficient *needed* a woman in his life. Next came the blazing determination to wreak vengeance on the wretch who had betrayed her.

Which was why she had sent for Rana Chara.

She was glad when the princes departed. Prince Aurang, who had been taciturn throughout, gave Rana Chara a backward glance at the door that was significant.

'Did you enjoy your luncheon?' she inquired of the Rana.

'Enormously.'

'We sent you a young pheasant especially for your pleasure.'

'Ah, so *you* were responsible, Madam. We do thank you indeed. There is nothing in any of the religions that preach unselfishness that can match the sympathetic unctuousness of a well-roasted young pheasant lying on its back on a cushion of dark gravy in a gold platter, its well-browned legs raised upwards in a plea to be consumed.'

She laughed in spite of herself, then grew serious. 'We have a matter of even greater importance than the religious virtues of a dead pheasant on which we would like your advice, Rana.' As always, she came quickly to the point.

His smile was almost indulgent. 'The Empress of multi-millions of Muslim people and she seeks the advice of a Rajput!'

She knew he was referring to her dead father, to Asaf Khan, to Shah Jahan and more recently to General Mahabat, on all of whom she had depended. She curbed her first reaction of anger. 'Not to mention an Englishman,' she reminded him.

'Ah yes, the Englishman. A very special breed of fish, named Roe. Which reminds us, have you not also summoned the Persian Parsee architect, Ustad Isa, to attend you from distant Shiraz and design a monument to your dead father? We understand he has arrived in Court and has already commenced work.'

'Indeed. Ustad Isa is a genius. His preliminary sketches are of exquisite form and symmetry.' She paused. 'But it is the architecture of the entire Empire that we are concerned about today.'

Rana Chara stretched slim legs, ran a thumb-nail beneath his black moustache. 'The Empire is at peace . . . er . . . thanks to General Mahabat.'

She saw beneath his seemingly casual observation. He was so astute, he somehow knew that it was General Mahabat who concerned her and was giving her the lead. 'It is precisely General Mahabat that we wish to discuss. His very usefulness to the Empire, which has brought us peace at last, makes him a source of war. Speaking frankly, success goes to people's heads. General Mahabat rendered us valuable service, now he is exacting his price.'

'And what may that be?'

'He has openly spoken of seizing the imperial crown and has been robbing the imperial treasury scandalously.' This lie was just the beginning of her revenge.

Amusement twitched the sides of Rana Chara's face. 'A small enough price to pay for his services,' he countered lightly. 'But if he really has designs on the throne, that would be another matter.'

'He has sounded out certain senior commanders with just that end in view.'

'Ah now, that is a logical conclusion to robbing the imperial treasury. After all, why not get his hands on everything?' He flicked an imaginary speck of dust from his knee. 'Is anything the general has planned imminent?'

'Not that we are aware of, but remember we are dealing with the god of lightning.'

'A twin of that other purveyor of lightning whom he has eliminated . . . er . . . temporarily from the imperial firmament.' He cocked his head to one side. 'You cannot summarily dismiss General Mahabat without dire consequences. Assassination is of course possible, but that is an untidy solution.' He clicked his fingers, stared through the slit in the green velvet curtain. 'We have it. Promote him, Your Imperial Majesty.'

'He is already at the top of the ladder.'

'A vacancy exists in Bengal where Shah Jahan's appointee, General Dorab, is merely a defector with temporary tenure. Promote General Mahabat to the rank of Sultan and send him into the same exile as the Emperor once sent Raja Man and . . . er . . . your late husband.'

A cynical smile had touched Rana Chara's lips. Did this man who sometimes displayed the genius of a devil incarnate guess at her real relationship with General Mahabat? Did he know that his advice would deprive her of the opportunity to destroy the general totally? She imagined General Mahabat humping his twenty-year-old South Indian girl. Bleak certainty told her that the humping was his reaction to her alone. He would probably be very tender with his mistress, as strong men, such as the Emperor

Akbar, could be. Dear Allah, why are you punishing me in this way? Do you have that old bitch Salima Begum in Paradise, laughing at me?

'The one problem that could arise is if General Mahabat pretends to accept the honour but decides to do something about his banishment,' Prince Chara continued. 'We strongly suggest that the Emperor and you leave for Srinagar again, on the grounds of His Majesty's ill-health, immediately upon issuing General Mahabat's *firman* of appointment. Do not under any circumstances issue the second *firman*, demanding his explanation for misappropriation of imperial funds, until he has started for Bengal, when you will be safe from any retaliation and he can be discredited without being able to answer in person.'

'Good!' she exclaimed. Merely promoting General Mahabat would have been some sort of reward for his services. Discrediting him immediately afterwards with lies would be the sort of cruel and inhuman punishment he deserved. 'Would it be safe to leave Agra at this time? If we do leave, will you ensure peace in Rajasthan?'

'There are no contenders for the imperial throne in Rajasthan.'

How well he understood her motives. 'And the Deccan?'

He frowned. 'Have you not heard the news, Your Imperial Majesty?'

'What news, Rana?'

'Prince Parviz, whom you will want to keep there at this time,' he grinned conspiratorially, 'can now ensure peace in the Deccan. We had word by special courier this morning that General Malik Ambar is dead.'

She had faithfully carried out Rana Chara's advice, but with one exception, prompted by her feminine desire to witness her betrayer's humiliation. It had caused her to summon General Mahabat to her presence and confront him with her allegations, appropriately on Friday afternoon, the day before the imperial Court left Agra for Srinagar. His only reaction had been a smile of contempt, but she should have known that a man of General Mahabat's calibre would later react aggressively.

Her one concern about the move to Srinagar was that she and Prince Shahriyar would not be in the capital when her husband died. But with Prince Parviz in the Deccan, her absence from Agra should not create any problems of succession, because she would arrange for the Emperor to name Prince Shahriyar his successor from his death bed. The Prince had developed a disease which was causing his hair, moustache and even his eyebrows and lashes to fall. This was all to the good: it would keep him from the public eye while she ruled through him.

Now, with the Court encamped on the east bank of the River Jhelum, General Mahabat had, in one of his lightning moves, suddenly appeared on the scene with a force of five thousand Rajputs. He had sent a delegation to the Emperor requesting that he be 'permitted to give an accounting to His Imperial Majesty in person'.

When Nur Jehan received the message late that morning, she was relieved that General Mahabat's despatch was couched in respectful language and his intentions seemed peaceful, because Asaf Khan had already crossed the river with the main body of the imperial army and the Emperor's tents were only lightly guarded. Even as she dictated the Emperor's reply to General Mahabat, she could not help but wonder whether she was being imprudent, but pride and bitter hatred for the General got the better of her. Her response was brief and peremptory. Under no circumstances was General Mahabat to attend the imperial Court until the Emperor summoned him.

Her husband was lying in bed, so weak that his signature on the document was barely legible.

Summer had already arrived in the region. The plain on which the royal party had set up camp was hot, dry and dusty. Nur Jehan was resting on her divan in the royal *harem* that same afternoon when she heard the commotion.

Her chief attendant, Mano, came rushing in, made hasty obeisance. 'Madam, Your Imperial M-Majesty, we must flee!' She was stuttering in fear.

Nur Jehan immediately guessed what had happened. She swung to her feet. 'Why?' she inquired curtly. 'Stand up and speak up.'

Mano came erect, her large eyes round with terror. 'General M-Mahabat rode to the Emperor's quarters accompanied by about two hundred Rajputs on foot, carrying spears and shields. They thought the Emperor was in his bathroom and started tearing down the boards around it, when the Emperor appeared from his bedroom. General Mahabat requested the Emperor Jehangir to mount the royal elephant and accompany him out of the camp.'

Fear such as she had never known before churned in Nur Jehan's stomach. Her head felt light, dizzy, her mind whirling inside it.

'Why didn't the imperial guard stop them?'

'It was all made to seem so routine that they did not dare to interfere. General Mahabat even escorted the Emperor to the royal elephant and helped him on to the *howdah* at the entrance to the royal enclosure before they left.'

Hope released the clamps tightening on either side of Nur Jehan's head. 'Did you say they left?'

'Yes, Your Imperial Majesty.'

'Good.' She thought with feverish speed. 'Pack us a light bag.' She reflected a moment. 'Tell Prince Shahriyar and Princess Ladili to join us immediately. Prince Shahriyar must disguise himself as a eunuch. Get the grooms to bring us an ordinary wagon. Hurry now. We have not a moment to lose. We must get across the bridge to the safety of the

603

main body of the army. Who knows how that fiend persuaded His Imperial Majesty to his will, but he managed to do it in a peaceable manner. Now, as soon as the Emperor is lodged in his own camp, he will come after us.'

'General Mahabat's Rajputs hold the bridge, Madam.' Mano was gibbering with fear, wiping the snot from her nose with the back of her hand.

Nur Jehan stepped forward and slapped the young woman hard across the face. 'Compose yourself!' she commanded tersely.

Mano was shocked into silence. She became quiet immediately. The violent act and the description of the situation filled Nur Jehan with great calm. 'The Rajputs will have orders to prevent the imperial army from crossing back to the rescue. They will not prevent a wagon containing a man disguised as a eunuch and three women in *purdah* from going in the opposite direction.'

Nur Jehan thought, with icy satisfaction, *purdah* to the rescue again!

Despite some anxious moments at the entrance to the bridge of boats, the wagon crossed without incident. Asaf Khan was in his tent when she reached the camp. He made obeisance to her, straightened up quickly. He was sweating from the heat, she noticed. 'Thanks be to Allah you are safe,' he said. 'But I understand the Emperor is a prisoner.'

'Yes.' Now that she was safe with the imperial army again, her fury was beginning to mount, against Asaf Khan too, though unreasonably. 'Since we were left without adequate defence on the other side of the river, the Emperor was easily captured by that spawn of a sow's entrails, may his soul rot in hell.'

'We shall try and get his body to rot on earth first.' Asaf Khan flashed his daredevil smile briefly, then grew serious.

'As for leaving the Emperor unguarded, we merely followed the order of march he gave us, which we have no authority to alter.'

'The Emperor's advisors are expected to recommend changes when prudent.' She knew she was being unjust, but needed someone on whom she could vent her rage, for suddenly the planning of years, based on sacrifices and betrayals, had crumbled. Within a few minutes, her entire world had come apart, the upheaval from an earthquake named Mahabat. God, how she loathed him.

Asaf Khan shrugged. 'I was totally unaware that General Mahabat had reason to follow the Emperor.' He obviously just discovered the reason for General Mahabat's 'visit', which she had been careful not to divulge to anyone other than the general himself. 'We have a grave situation now, whoever was responsible for it, and we must meet it.'

'What do you propose?'

'My every instinct tells me to launch an attack across the river and rescue the Emperor. General Mahabat would not dare to injure him because as a hostage the Emperor is his most precious weapon. But my brain says, parley with General Mahabat first. A river crossing is one of the most difficult of military operations. Let us find out what the general really wants and see whether it cannot be granted, or some compromise effected.'

'Bargain with a traitor?' She spat the words out in scorn, but her brain told her that she should not permit parleying because it would expose her own part in the affair. 'That is an act of cowardice.'

He would normally have been stung to a sharp response, or have responded to such a barb with his good-humoured wit, but his grave countenance told her that the responsibility for the Empire rested heavily with him. 'You are in command, Your Imperial Majesty,' he replied icily. 'What are your orders?'

'General Mahabat has only five thousand men to our twenty thousand. Attack across the river tomorrow morning and rescue the Emperor.'

Asaf Khan brought his horse pounding up the hill from which she had observed most of the fighting, which had gone on since dawn. The imperial army had first tried a direct thrust across the bridge but had been beaten back. A three-pronged assault across the river had also failed. Reports coming to her at the command post confirmed the evidence of her eyes. Several thousand of her men had died in the operations. It seemed to her that the river was tinged red with the blood of the dead men and horses being swept down it, while the bridge was strewn with corpses. By noon, Nur Jehan was beginning to realize the truth of Asaf Khan's assertion that an attack across a river was a most difficult operation.

Now the Rajputs were counter-attacking across the bridge.

Both Asaf Khan and his grey Arab stallion were streaked with dust and sweat. The stallion's flanks were heaving. Asaf Khan had a bloody cut across his chest.

One look at her brother's face and she knew the worst. 'We have lost, haven't we?' she demanded even before he reined in his mount.

'Yes.' He was panting. 'Our only hope is to withdraw with our remaining men and make a run for the great fort at Attock.'

'No.'

'In the name of Allah, why not? We must keep you safe at all costs.'

She had already decided what she was going to do in the event of defeat. 'You go on to Attock and try to marshal forces loyal to us who can destroy this monster, but my place is by my husband.'

He eyed her incredulously. His horse snorted, its flanks still heaving. 'That is most noble and devoted of you, but not in the best interests of the Empire,' he grated.

'While he is alive, the Emperor *is* the Empire,' she declared. She was making a pronouncement for the people and for history, but only she knew that her actions were based solely on self-interest.

She had coldly reasoned that her one source of power was her husband. While she was with him, she might be able to use his influence to manipulate General Mahabat's troops. And who knew, she might even be able to influence General Mahabat himself.

Alone, she was nothing.

PART V

Promises

Chapter 39

Every evening at this hour, Shah Jahan climbed the roof of the Nazik palace *harem* with Mumtaz Mahal, though it continued to throw back the heat. Standing by the parapet wall in the shade of canopies, he scanned the north for the return of the second secret messenger he had sent to Shah Abbas of Persia. The first messenger, Lord Zahid, had taken months longer than he should, because the Shah had kept him waiting for an audience.

'I only hope that Shah Abbas does not keep Amir Prince Khwaja waiting as long as he did Lord Zahid nor send him, too, back with the scant comfort of a homily on filial piety!' Shah Jahan remarked to Mumtaz Mahal. He had said this to her daily for four months. Today would mark the twenty-third time for March 1627. But that was one of the joys of being in love with one's wife and certain of her love. Every concern bore repetition as if it were for the first time.

'The Amir is more aggressive and erudite than Lord Zahid.' Mumtaz Mahal uttered the comforting words also for the twenty-third time that month. She glanced northward, pointed. 'Look, let us hope that is the Amir and not simply a sandstorm!'

At first it was like a wisp of beige cloud, far across the vast barren earth, wilted scrub and dark skeletal arms of gnarled trees that formed the arid desert, just where the horizon would have been had it not succumbed to shimmering heatwaves. The wisp grew larger and larger beneath the glare of the still fierce evening sun, a huge revolving disc without edges halfway across the burnished western sky. Black specks appeared at its centre, moving rapidly, smudged at first then gradually resolving into horsemen. So it was not a sandstorm but a group of men, when even fleeing armies tried to avoid moving until the worst of the afternoon heat was over, the sun's rage tempered by its approaching bedtime.

Shah Jahan's pulse had quickened as he followed her pointing finger. 'I assured the Shah that I was indeed moved by filial piety,' he muttered. 'My father is the victim of scheming, unscrupulous people. He must be rescued.' He wiped the sweat pouring down his face with a white linen square. 'The Shah is our only hope, now that General Malik Ambar is dead.'

'General Ambar was our *false* hope,' Mumtaz Mahal retorted bitterly. 'He used us to give himself hope. Everybody supports the victor until he bites the dust. The Hindu ranas and the Muslim sultans betrayed you as soon as you experienced your first reverses. But you will rise again when the time is right. It is in your stars. Even surrender has not been able to keep you low. You hung down your head and played the penitent, sincerely, but it was not you. Within a few weeks you were up and trying again. I am so proud of you.' Her voice had grown vibrant, her eyes glowed.

He melted as always before her love, then grinned mischievously. 'I suppose I selected Nazik for my retreat from the world because it is in the heart of the Deccan, beyond the formal frontier of the Empire, so we would be safe.'

'You selected Nazik because deep inside you was the conviction that you could gather your forces again here and move to Agra. You are an arch plotter. You would align yourself with the devil to fulfil your destiny.'

'I have,' he teased, 'with a she-devil.'

'Whom you lay on her back every night, except when she has her bleeding,' she countered. 'A she-devil who has fertilized your seed eleven times already to spawn little devils.' He knew her mouth had twisted piteously. 'Six of whom were taken to Paradise before . . . before . . .'

He laid a hand on the slender white fingers that trembled on the hot red sandstone of the parapet wall. 'Hush, my darling beloved. It is enough that we have each other.'

'Yes, indeed. I thank Almighty Allah for you, five times a day and every hour in between.' She hesitated. 'But I fear the hand of death. It has hovered over us since we were married, whether at home or on the battlefield.' She had one of her abrupt changes of mood, laughed wistfully. 'I shall give you countless children before I die.'

'I shall die before you.'

'Do you love me?'

'Of course I do.'

'Truly, truly?'

'Truly, truly.' His heart contracted with love.

'Then you will let me die first, so I don't have to live on this earth and suffer . . . as Salima Begum did.'

Her strange illogical logic had never left her. He shook his head in wonder. 'You are Almighty Allah's most priceless treasure to me. Let us pray that when we go it will be together.'

She was about to say something, but changed her mind. She nodded towards the approaching group of horsemen. 'See, they are almost here.'

The drumming of hooves reached his ears. He became conscious of the hot, dry smell of the burnt desert, raw inside his nose, as if the wind of their approach had wafted it. He recognized the leading figure, a lean-faced man with a white beard beneath his burnous. 'Amir Khwaja, back already!' he exclaimed. 'The news must be good. I must go and meet him.' He turned.

She laid a detaining hand on his arm. 'Would it not be more fitting for you to await the Amir in the palace, lord?'

* * *

613

Amir Khwaja looked like an *imam*. Dressed in long black tunic and white *jodhpurs*, he was a very thin, tall, scholarly man with a high forehead and fine, ascetic features accentuated by the white moustache and beard. His eyes were so sharp and black the lids seemed to be edged with *kohl*. He entered the reception chamber of the palace slowly and with dignity. Since the palace was no more than the mansion of a small ruler, it was furnished in Deccanese style with solid, dark teakwood furniture and brightly coloured cotton rugs on the red flagstone floor.

Shah Jahan scanned the Amir's face as he bowed, right hand to heart, mouth and head. It was impassive.

'Pray be seated, Prince,' Shah Jahan bade him, indicating a low sofa-divan. 'You have ridden long and hard,' he added, taking his own seat on a high settle across the room. 'I particularly appreciate your having travelled the last miles in the evening, without waiting for the cool of night.' He was tempted to add that the Amir's news must be important for him to have done so, but the rules of decorum forbade it. His heart was beating a shade faster with the suspense. His whole future hinged on Shah Abbas's reply.

'It was the least I could do for a most worthy prince.' This was not the battlefield so he too was prevented by the rules of decorum from being direct.

'Some refreshments perhaps?'

'I have already been given some melon juice. I had it in the foyer, while waiting for you to come down. It was delicious. Just right for this appalling climate.' He mopped his brow with a large white linen square. 'The service here is as good as your own hospitality, Prince, but not the climate.'

They chatted pleasantly about the Amir's journey and his observations on Tehran, while Shah Jahan curbed his growing impatience. Finally the Amir worked his way into the Tehran palace and his meeting with Shah Abbas. 'I am afraid the news is not good,' he stated. Shah Jahan's heart sank. 'I had three meetings with the Shah and did my best to persuade him that he should send an army to help you liberate the Emperor. There were times when he seemed disposed to grant my request, but I believe his Council was against it. His final word was that he cannot intervene because of fraternal feelings for "my brother Jehangir", as he called the Emperor whose territory he invaded not so long ago, without a direct appeal from the Emperor himself.'

It was hopeless. Shah Jahan found it hard not to let his shoulders slump and rush out of the chamber to reach the depths of his depression alone, but he smiled at the Amir through the pall of gloom. 'You tried,' he stated. 'I am most grateful and I shall remember when my time comes. Mine was the hope but it was you who endured the ardours of the long journey to Tehran and back. Your disappointment must be greater than mine, for your mission has ended while mine continues and my hope will never falter.' Not true, when his heart was as bleak as his prospects, but he owed the lie to this loyal man.

'Thank you, Prince, for your customary generosity.' The Amir brightened. 'But I do have some good news from Agra.'

Shah Jahan's interest quickened. 'What might that be?'

'General Mahabat is being promoted into virtual exile as governor of distant Bengal.'

'What?' He could not believe his ears.

'You heard me. Those in high places say that the Empress fears his growing power and influence especially at a time when your father is dying and that the general has obviously overreached himself.'

'Allah be praised.' He thought feverishly. 'In that event, the military pressure on us will be reduced. I hate to admit this, but my men have been getting restive again and my

615

forces, which were small enough, have begun to dwindle.' He tried to make his laugh light instead of bitter. 'It is one of the hazards of depending on mercenaries who look to some hope at least of loot to augment their salaries.'

'I know only too well, Prince.'

'That is why I thank Almighty Allah daily for loyal friends such as yourself who support me with no expectation of reward.'

'I believe in your independence, so vital in a ruler, and your integrity, therefore I support your cause.'

'Thank you from the bottom of my heart.'

'Not at all, Prince. It is my duty before God.' The Amir paused. 'Two other interesting developments have taken place, though they both relate to depressing subjects. The Emperor and his entire entourage, including the Empress and your father-in-law, Asaf Khan, are moving to Srinagar. It's sad to think that this is to enable your father to die in the place he loves, the vale of Kashmir.'

Shah Jahan received the news with mixed feelings, the most dominant of which was a white flash of knowledge that Agra, the capital, had been left virtually defenceless. And yet, Agra had always proved invincible. Then a thought struck him with the force of a battering ram. 'That will leave Prince Parviz a clear run for the capital!' he exclaimed.

'Not so.' Amir Khwaja shook his grey head sadly. 'When I passed through Mandu on my way here, I learned that your brother, Prince Parviz, had died the previous day.'

'My brother? Dead?' He shook his head to rid himself of the shock. 'How did he die?' Could Nur Jehan have had him murdered too?

The Amir looked grave, almost stern. 'I regret to say that alcohol, dissipation and a dissolute life finally caught up with him. He is said to have died of a sudden heart attack. I wish I could offer you my sympathies.'

Four brothers, two of them gone! How sad. It left only Prince Shahriyar and himself. Prince Shahriyar? This time, the knowledge burst forth in a great flash of wonderment.

His two older brothers were dead. He was the legal heir to the imperial throne.

Except for Nur Jehan's machinations.

By Almighty Allah, he would seize what was his.

Amir Khwaja seemed to have sensed his thoughts. 'I advise you to move with caution, Prince. Let events unfold before you act. Having been expelled, General Mahabat is not likely to lie back with his legs up and allow those in power to stroke his stomach. He will act. Meanwhile, start consolidating your position and prepare for your day, which is drawing close. Wisdom, not impetuosity, will give you victory.' Once again he seemed to have anticipated Shah Jahan's reasoning. 'There are those in the Court, including your father-in-law, who will at least try to thwart the base aims of the Empress.'

Before they left Agra, after his discussion with the Empress, Prince Chara had learned that Prince Dara and Prince Aurang were to be left behind in the palace when the royal party headed for Srinagar. He immediately requested permission to take the two princes with him to Chitor. 'After all, they both have Rajput blood,' he said to Nur Jehan. 'They should learn something of the manners, customs and traditions of that heritage.' The look in his eyes conveyed his meaning to her. 'As you yourself once suggested.'

'Supposing Shah Jahan tries to snatch them since Mewar is close . . .' She changed her mind. 'He would not dare. Certainly, take them with you, Rana.' Her voice had become underlaid with irony. She knew him well enough. 'You are most gracious.'

For a few weeks, Rana Chara had allowed the two princes

the opportunity of enjoying themselves without pressure of any sort. When he received news of General Mahabat's pursuit of the royal party, ostensibly to explain away the allegations against him, he made shrewd forecasts as to subsequent events.

Today he had learnt of the death of Prince Parviz. The time had come to commence Prince Aurang's education. While all these fools, the Emperor, Nur Jehan, General Mahabat and Shah Jahan, strutted the stage of today, he, Rana Chara, the wisest man in the world, the Enlightened One, was setting the stage for the fools who would be strutting it some day in the future.

It was Nur Jehan who had caused the Emperor to execute the personal directive to Asaf Khan to surrender when General Mahabat surrounded the Attock fort. The journey there had been strange. General Mahabat had accepted her own voluntary surrender and her plea to be permitted to join her husband with an amused glint in his eyes. He knew her well enough, saw through her sham and undoubtedly had respect for her brains. If he desired her, he never revealed it on the journey to Attock. It would have been impossible anyway, not least because she confined herself to the royal *harem*, giving an appearance of total docility and virtue.

Some day she would bring down this man who had spurned her, but once again, as it had been before she became Empress, it had to be with guile.

General Mahabat had diverted north-west in order to take Attock. He now proceeded south-east, intending to cross the river at Rohtas before heading north-east for Srinagar.

Meanwhile, the Emperor, under her direction, seemed content that they were on their way to Srinagar. If he felt any resentment at the changes that had taken place, he did not show it or cast blame on anyone. He had been a figurehead for years, content with asserting himself occasionally, as if he needed only that sop to feel assured of his power. Nur Jehan now managed to make him accept General Mahabat not as his warden, but as a loyal guardian angel.

As the days went by, it became increasingly obvious to Nur Jehan that the Emperor's mind had become unhinged from the realities of life. He had exchanged his Empire not merely for a glass of wine and a few morsels of food, but also for an actor's role in life and with death ahead in his beloved Srinagar. His occasional flashes of lucidity had become increasingly rare.

There had been method to Nur Jehan's madness when she commanded Asaf Khan's surrender to General Mahabat. Since the general seemed disposed to allow her husband's secretariat to carry on with the business of governing the Empire, of which he, being first and last a soldier, had scant knowledge, it meant that Asaf Khan must spend a great deal of time with the Emperor on their slow journey towards Srinagar. This gave her access to her brother.

So, as they headed towards the distant snow-capped Himalayan peaks, she had done everything in her power to lull General Mahabat into a false sense of security. She even sent him messages through Asaf Khan, asking his advice on various matters of state, while ensuring that her husband complied with the general's every request. At the same time, under her direction, Asaf Khan was discreetly sounding out General Mahabat's junior officers.

'You were right, Your Imperial Majesty,' Asaf Khan reported to her one day, when they were alone in her *harem* tent. 'Many of his officers are puzzled as to why General Mahabat has not assumed supreme power, executed you and the Emperor and departed for Agra. They see his actions as a farce, the entire situation as a comedy. All of which leads me to believe that one of the wisest decisions you made was to demand my surrender to General Mahabat.'

'You see its wisdom now?' She was elated by the old note of admiration in his voice. She had been through the blackest period of her life. She had plumbed the depths, but she had never given in. Now she could tell, merely from the tone of her brother's voice, that the way up had begun to clear again.

'Certainly. If I had allowed myself to be besieged in Attock, I could have been starved into submission within a few months, with no hope of succour. By surrendering to the enemy, we are in his camp and can assemble forces that may not necessarily be loyal to the Emperor, but are certainly afraid of him. The invincible Rajputs especially are far away from home in a situation of uncertainty. General Mahabat is a superb military commander, brilliant, the god of lightning strikes, but being politically a novice, he does not know how to handle the situation he has created. Soldiers and their commanders do not react well to indecisive leadership.'

'General Mahabat also made the mistake of allowing our own forces to augment his five thousand Rajputs, believing that more is better, which is curiously at odds with the basis of his original success against us, that fewer would be best!' She pondered a while. 'Do you think the time is right?'

He flashed that daredevil smile. 'As right as it will ever be.'

'Very well then.' Her voice was decisive, but she felt almost dreamy with anticipation. 'We shall arrive at Rohtas tomorrow. Inform General Mahabat that the Emperor desires to review all his troops at dawn, before we leave.'

Asaf Khan looked puzzled. 'What would that accomplish?'

She smiled her secret smile. 'You shall see.'

Chapter 40

The Emperor was seated in his *jarokha* in the tent that served as an audience chamber whenever he travelled, with Asaf Khan standing as usual at his right. He had been advised by his beloved Nur Jehan to exclude everyone else from this interview. He felt unusually fit and strong, after a night when his sleep had been uninterrupted by his attacks of asthma, and this sense of well-being brought back the memory of the last time he had seen such an elaborate encampment, now spreading over many square miles on the plain fronting the river at Rohtas. It had been twenty years ago, before he defeated Prince Husrau in battle on the Barowahl plain. How splendid he had been, in spite of having had a severe cold on that occasion.

The dawn was cool and grey outside; the gem-studded throne emitted the delightful scents of the ambergris in its hollowed arms. He was dressed in a long gold tunic sparkling with diamonds and rubies that hid his paunch. He wore the imperial crown, with the plume of hern-tops, the great ruby dangling on one side, the huge diamond on the other. He was glittering again on the outside and this morning felt the sparkle inside him as well. When he reviewed his troops, riding his tall white charger, they would see him as the messenger of God, fresh from his morning prayer.

General Mahabat was shown into the tent and announced. He stood at the entrance and saluted. In his cavalry uniform, red tunic, baggy white trousers tucked into black riding boots, long curving sword sheathed at his side, he looked smart and soldier-like, but he was obviously impressed by his Emperor's renewed majesty.

'Good morning, General Mahabat.' The Emperor adopted his most imperious voice, as Nur Jehan had advised. She was such a jewel, so wise, so brave, so loving. What woman would have sacrificed herself as Nur Jehan had done by volunteering virtual imprisonment so she could be beside the man she loved? 'We trust our troops have commenced assembling in readiness for our review?' He was pleased to be thinking so clearly this morning.

'Good morning, Your Imperial Majesty. Your troops are ready, eagerly looking forward to offering silent submission to their commander-in-chief.'

'Excellent, excellent.' The Emperor's mind had begun to wander, but he pulled it back again with a sudden effort.

He rambled on, as had been suggested by Nur Jehan, asking questions regarding strengths, dispositions, an artillery salute, to keep General Mahabat off guard. Something told him that he should hate this man, but he could not help liking him. Those strange eyes, the colour of a cobra's hood, the square and chiselled features – he particularly admired the cleft chin – spoke of strength and resolution, combined with a respectful attitude. What had the general done that was wrong? Something, something. The Emperor could not remember what. It was enough that Nur Jehan had told him of it. But was this not the man who had humbled Shah Jahan, the rebel, the pariah dog, the pig's entrails who had dared to lift lustful eyes at his chaste Nur Jehan? By Allah, he had forgiven Shah Jahan his rebellion, because that was politically desirable, but he would have the bastard's balls some day for his impious act.

He finally came to the point. 'Tell me, General Mahabat, do the feuds that have been a regular feature of the imperial army in the past still exist? We mean regiment against regiment, Rajput against Sikh, Pathan against Gurkha?'

'I am afraid so, Sire.'

The Emperor deliberately passed a hand over his forehead, as if suddenly tired. He was enjoying playing the role assigned to him. 'There have been occasions when fighting has broken out between such factions even in the imperial presence. Are you aware of that?'

'Yes, Sire.' The general seemed puzzled by the drift of the conversation.

'Today's review will be the last formal one of its kind until we reach Srinagar and leave it for Agra once more.' He had no intention of leaving Srinagar if he could help it. 'We desire it to be a harmonious event. The regiments that are likely to clash with each other should be kept apart. What do you think?'

General Mahabat pondered this deeply a few moments. Then his eyes gleamed. 'A splendid idea, Sire. You have the wisdom of Allah.'

The Emperor's pulses quickened. He had done it. This was no usurper but a loyal commanding general. Why had Nur Jehan? . . . no, no, his beloved wife was always right. 'Which are the regiments most likely to quarrel over matters such as precedence and protocol?'

The general smiled, briefly touched his reddish moustache self-consciously. 'The Rajputs, the Sikhs and the Pathans, Sire.'

'It was always so. Religion and race play a great role in matters of precedence. Do you think you could separate these regiments on the review ground? Keep each of the two groups a mile or so apart from the other? We would enjoy the extra length of the ride on a beautiful morning such as this promises to be. Will it be difficult? Create problems?'

General Mahabat brightened. 'Your wish is my command, Sire. It will neither be difficult nor create problems. It might solve them. The Rajputs are the fiercest on matters of honour and precedence and all of them happen to be under my direct orders. I shall place them at the south end of the review.'

'Thank you, General. We appreciate your loyalty and cooperation.'

'It is no more than my pleasure and my sacred duty, Your Imperial Majesty.' He paused. 'May I now have your gracious permission to withdraw and carry out your commands?'

'Certainly, General Mahabat.'

The general saluted, backed out of the tent, departed, a tall, strong figure of a man.

Nur Jehan glided into the *jarokha* from the adjoining room, where she had listened unobserved. 'It is working,' she declared quietly. She turned towards Asaf Khan. 'Are the loyal troops ready, Prime Minister?'

He smiled. 'As ready as they will ever be, Your Imperial Majesty.'

'We want that traitorous dog brought before us in chains. We shall first have his balls smashed and his penis cut off.' The Emperor was startled by the crude language and the unwonted viciousness in Nur Jehan's normally warm voice. And yet, why not? His beloved had suffered so much at the hands of General Mahabat.

What had General Mahabat done? What had the light of his life suffered? He did not remember. The fog was closing inside his brain again.

He was so very, very tired.

Nur Jehan surveyed with fierce anticipation the long line of imperial troops, their serried ranks stretching over a mile northwards in the direction of the distant pine gorges of the hill country.

The Emperor had begun to feel increasingly unwell immediately after the audience he had given General Mahabat, so he had decided to undertake the review of his troops from the golden *howdah* on the back of the royal elephant, a giant tusker, rather than tire himself further by riding one of his chargers. Nur Jehan regarded this as a heaven-sent opportunity to accompany the Emperor and personally witness the downfall of General Mahabat.

The army was drawn up in review order on the west bank of the river, a huge, flat plain stretching for miles with never a tree or bush on its grass surface. The regiments had their backs to the broad, swift-flowing river. With the red sandstone ramparts of Rohtas rising sharply on the opposite bank, the river served as one of the defences of the fort.

The elephant brigade occupied the centre of the parade, straddling the broad highway leading to the drawbridge that served the west entrance of the fort. The huge grey beasts were caparisoned in red or white linen saddlecloths bordered with cloth of gold and studded with circular brass knobs and squares of mica fretwork. The *howdahs* on their backs carried uniformed men armed with muskets. Mahouts in red and white livery stood by the elephants' trunks. The cavalry regiments were massed on either side of the elephants, their banners and the standards of their commanders limp in the still morning air. Grey, bay, chestnut and black horses were grouped separately, but all the cavalrymen wore the standard imperial uniform of red and white with black boots. Men of the artillery standing beside the ugly snouts of the cannon came next. The front row of thirty guns soon to fire the imperial salute before the Emperor commenced his inspection were placed far enough from the elephants so they would not panic. Barrows containing cannon balls and mules to haul the cannon were gathered behind the great guns. The infantry divisions stretched to the north. This was part of Nur Jehan's plan, the artillery and swift-moving cavalry being closest to the gap of another mile southwards that separated the loyalist imperial troops from General Mahabat's elite corps. The silence of thousands of men and animals was incredible, broken only by the jingle of elephant bells.

The sun had just cleared the fort's rampart walls, which were thronged with onlookers. Before noon, the mettle of General Mahabat's elite corps would be tested, its ranks reduced to nothing. There was only ice in Nur Jehan's heart at the prospect, for her plan was that as soon as her husband finished his review of the entire line, he would give the signal to the artillery commanders to wheel left and take off south, followed by the imperial cavalry. When they came within range of General Mahabat's men, the big guns would commence a savage bombardment. This would be the signal for the imperial cavalry to charge General Mahabat's corps and slaughter it. Her orders were explicit: General Mahabat alone was to be taken alive.

The Emperor's inspection on the slow-ambling elephant took three hours. They finally returned to the central review stand facing the drawbridge. It was still an hour before noon, but the heat of the sun was causing them both to sweat. Nur Jehan ran a tongue over lips gone dry. Her pulses quickened with anticipation.

The drumming of hooves reached her ears. A single horseman was galloping madly towards them from the south, his whip alternating in a regular beat on either flank of his great Arab mount in his effort to make it move faster.

What could have happened?

The horseman slowed to a canter when he saw the royal elephant surrounded by the mounted aides in full dress uniform. Even before he reined in, Asaf Khan on a great

Scindhi bay had broken through the group to reach him. The rider delivered his message without dismounting.

Had General Mahabat moved to attack first? Nur Jehan's skin turned cold beneath its film of sweat. She feared the man.

Asaf Khan spurred his horse back to the royal elephant. He directed his gaze at her rather than the Emperor, who was obviously too worn out and listless to pay any attention.

'General Mahabat has vanished,' Asaf Khan stated grimly.

'Vanished? Where?' she demanded. 'Five thousand men do not evaporate into thin air.'

'He probably suspected or had knowledge of what we had planned and kept on moving south. He obviously insisted on being at the south end of the line, in order to give himself free passage.'

Her enemy had escaped. Damn him. Damn him to hell. Nur Jehan could barely control her fury. 'Send our cavalry after him immediately.'

'Too late,' Asaf Khan advised, his face grim. 'Remember, he had at least a four-hour start and he and his men move like lightning. Our cannon can never catch up with him and if our cavalry did succeed in reaching him without artillery support, he would turn round and rend them.'

Once again a beige wisp had appeared in the horizonless distance. By unspoken consent, Mumtaz Mahal and he had continued their practice of standing on the rooftop of the Nazik palace *harem* every evening. This time it was because Shah Jahan's instincts and reasoning told him that messengers would come to him from the north with word of the political situation. Yet a part of him kept clamouring to burst forth into battle again, to wrest his destiny by force.

'Look, a sandstorm.' He pointed in the direction of the

wisp, hoping it was men and not searing sand. 'We had best get inside and have all the doors and windows battened down.'

'It is not a sandstorm,' Mumtaz responded with calm certainty. 'It is men.' They watched across the shimmering air of the scorched brown soil, scrub and blackened trees. The wisp became a cloud, the cloud was pierced by specks that materialized into figures on horseback. The faint drumming of hooves was like the thunder of a monsoon approaching from the distance. 'There must be thousands of them.'

'Almighty Allah, it is an army!' Shah Jahan thought: Oh God, not another disaster, please. The stench of two rotting corpses of rabid dogs that had been shot by the musketeers became acrid in his nostrils. 'I must get the troops to man the walls.' He reached for the ever handy bellrope hanging from a canopy.

Before he could even touch it, the alarm bells jangled across the blazing hot air. The great gates began squeaking and screeching, then creaked shut. 'The sentries have spotted them.'

Ears singing, he watched musketeers and bowmen pouring out to the lower parapets, while artillerymen ran to the embrasures to man the cannon, their mates following with splashing pails of water which they poured on the stacked cannon balls to permit easy handling. Light steam rising told of the heat that had been absorbed by the metal.

Shah Jahan shaded his eyes from the sun to his west. The cloud had increased to enormous proportions now, spreading east, west and north above the vast columns of men approaching at a canter. The desert now reverberated with the thunder of their horses' hooves.

They were led by a single man. Shah Jahan tried vainly to distinguish the colour of the man's horse.

Mumtaz Mahal placed cool fingers on his arm. 'This too we shall survive,' she declared.

He placed a moist palm on her fingers, but absently. His every attention focused on the approaching column, his mind was suddenly working fast and cool. His men had perfected the drill for repelling an invader. They would hold out at all costs.

'Load! . . . Load! . . . Load!' The commands rang through the air. Artillerymen carrying damp cloths reached for the barrows. Cannon balls rattled, clanged into the gun barrels.

The column was almost within range of the guns. 'You had best go down,' he bade Mumtaz Mahal.

'No!' she said. It was not a protest, but a declaration.

He was about to turn and remonstrate when the leader of the column raised his hand, signalling his men to slow down.

Mumtaz Mahal followed Shah Jahan's intent gaze. A surge of relief rose within him. 'At least they do not have artillery,' he muttered. 'Their leader wants to keep them beyond range of our guns. I expect they will fan out though and surround the fort.'

The vast column slowly came to a halt. The upright lances of the cavalrymen sprouted behind their leader in dense, spiked array. To Shah Jahan's surprise, the leader slowly walked his horse forward alone, while his men remained motionless behind him. Who could it be?

'Hold your fire, commanders!' he shouted down to the parapets below.

'Hold your fire . . . ! Hold your fire . . . ! Hold your fire . . . !' His command was echoed along the rampart walls.

Within minutes Shah Jahan had his answer. There was no mistaking the strong erect figure on horseback. 'By the beard of the Prophet, it is General Mahabat!' he exclaimed.

We are lost, he thought, but did not speak the words aloud. His stomach had turned to jelly.

'Good!' Mumtaz Mahal exclaimed fiercely. 'Now we can test our mettle against him.'

'I thought he had gone to Bengal,' Shah Jahan said helplessly. 'What is he doing here?'

'Nur Jehan must have forgiven his sins, so she could resurrect him to destroy you,' Mumtaz Mahal rejoined calmly. 'This time you shall send him to hell, my husband.'

'He is obviously coming in alone to parley with me and demand my surrender, but I shall *never* submit or yield,' he gritted. His jaw clenched. 'He will have to tear down the fort block by block first.' He watched the approaching rider. 'I shall go down to the reception chamber and receive him in state.'

It was the first time he had met General Mahabat face to face. The man was so tall that though Shah Jahan had seated him on the lower divan while he himself took the dark teakwood settle, their heads were almost at a level. He exuded power and alertness, in spite of his obviously long and tiring ride through the near desert, which had left his uniform, riding boots and even his face tanned almost black by the sun, all covered with dust. It was, however, the large, strange-coloured eyes that impressed Shah Jahan most, dark emerald green with brown flecks.

Real fear from General Mahabat's arrival had combined with the heat and closeness of the evening, notwithstanding the swaying *punkah* overhead, to give Shah Jahan a headache. He did not want to be kept in suspense any longer, came to the point. 'What is the purpose of your visit, General?' he demanded brusquely, immediately they were seated.

The general's face relaxed in appreciation of such directness. 'I have come here with eight thousand men to place my sword at your disposal, Prince,' he replied.

The simple words, quietly spoken, re-echoed in Shah Jahan's head with the clangour of joy bells. He was so amazed he could hardly bring himself to speak. In a few seconds the tide had turned in his favour. The greatest general in the imperial army had defected to him. Why? He must either be dreaming or touched by the sun.

Anticipating his question, General Mahabat explained how it had happened in clear, concise sentences.

Shah Jahan listened without interruption until the general had finished speaking. 'What made you suspect that a trap had been set for you when the Emperor commanded you to separate your troops from the main body during the review?' he finally inquired.

'It was obvious, was it not? Especially against the background of my knowledge of the Empress's designs and plots. The whole thing made no sense. I pretended to agree wholeheartedly with its rationale when the reasoning behind it was flawed. I left the Emperor's encampment, issued a general review order to the corps commanders, stating that my own corps would take up position a mile south of the drawbridge. I must admit that I selected this position in order to have a clear passage to safety in the event of any trickery. When I left the encampment about half an hour later, the imperial troops had taken up positions for the review. This meant that they had already received orders, which seemed odd. Then I found that the artillery regiments were being placed immediately south of the drawbridge with only cavalry to their own south. My men and I were being segregated, obviously to be made the victims of an artillery barrage before the imperial cavalry charged us and finished the slaughter. So I issued orders to my commanders in the hearing of those whom I considered to be the enemy to take up the expected review positions and, once they did so, I simply had them wheel and gallop away.'

'Did the imperial army pursue you?'

'My rear guard patrols reported a large force, but there was no way in which they could catch up with us. Skirting Lahore we came directly south, through Bikaner and Ajmer. I avoided Agra too. Once in Rajasthan I had no great concern, because my men are mostly Rajput. We were never once attacked along the way.'

Shah Jahan smiled. 'Your reputation preceded you.' General Mahabat had had the opportunity of a lifetime, but had let it go. He was a leader of men first and last, proud, cool, fiercely independent, never a ruler. His story merely confirmed Shah Jahan's belief that it took far more than tactics and strategy to win a crown. 'We both have speed, audacity and aggressiveness,' he asserted. 'Together we can conquer the Empire.'

The cobra eyes shone; the reddish moustache bristled. 'Give me and my men a day and night of rest,' the general stated eagerly. 'And we shall be ready to march with you to Agra. We can seize it before the Emperor returns from Srinagar.'

'How is my father?'

'In extremely poor health. I doubt that he will live long enough ever to see Agra again.'

Shah Jahan sighed. He felt sorry for his father. In some ways he would miss the man to whom he had begun to draw close until that monstrous Nur Jehan began her evil machinations. 'And my father-in-law, Prime Minister Asaf Khan?'

'A brilliant, fearless man, dedicated to doing what is right. I have enormous respect for him. Being the person he is, he had no option but to fall in with his sister's plan, because with him it is not a matter of *who* is right, but *what* is right for the Empire and the Emperor. I am convinced that, when the time comes, he will support the traditional heir to the imperial throne.' His cheeks twitched sideways.

'You.' He paused. 'Which is another reason why I am here today.'

Shah Jahan pondered the situation a while, conscious of General Mahabat's unwavering gaze. 'You and your men will have longer than a day and a night for rest,' he finally stated. 'We have just one more chance to achieve our object. If we fail, it will never be ours again. I have sources close to the imperial Court who feed me regularly with information.' He laughed. 'As a matter of fact, I will probably, as usual,' he smiled wryly, 'receive news of your departure from Rohtas a week or two hence, because you move so fast. As good generals, let us gather all possible political and military intelligence and then strike,' his eyes twinkled, 'this time with the speed of two shafts of lightning, instead of one.'

He felt light-hearted for the first time in three years. His headache had vanished.

It was the happiest evening they had spent together in a long while. Mumtaz Mahal grudgingly allowed Shah Jahan to do his duty and attend a welcoming dinner for General Mahabat. Shouts and peals of laughter from the dining hall faintly penetrated the *harem*. She thought they would never end. She wanted her husband to return.

Although the *harem* opened out on to its own private courtyard, which was cooled by a splashing fountain, being cloistered, in summer it was the hottest part of the palace, when women and eunuchs simply stewed in their rooms, while on winter nights it was bleak with the desert chill. This was definitely a summer night.

Seated on a low stool in her small reception chamber fronting the courtyard, with Sati braiding her hair into its long plait for the night, Mumtaz Mahal simply ignored the heat. Moths fluttered against the brass hanging lamps. A tinge of burnt oil punctured the scent of camphor incense from smoking braziers. This was far removed from the luxury of the Agra palace, but nothing mattered tonight, not even the stifling air outside.

She looked at her image in the tiny mirror she wore over her thumbnail. 'H'm, not bad,' she observed. She moved her thumb forward to take in the image of Sati behind her, deftly twisting her dark brown hair strands. 'Tell me, Sati, am I more beautiful than Nur Jehan?'

'Why do you want to be compared with that spawn of Satan?' Sati inquired. She had no time for the woman whom she held responsible for the fate that had befallen them all, especially her little one. 'Do you want to displace her in the Emperor's favour?' Sati too was feeling more light-hearted this evening.

'And do you really want to be as horrid as usual to me?'

'Any other little girl would feel lucky to have someone as horrid to them as I am to you.'

'You are right, Sati.' She laughed, swung to her feet, twirled around in a dance. 'Not bad for a woman who has conceived eleven children and intends getting pregnant tonight, eh?'

'Not bad for an ageing woman.'

'Oh, you are horrid.'

'You said that before.'

'You were horrid before . . . and before . . .' She was about to stamp her foot again just to tease Sati when a sudden thought jolted her. She stared out at the red-gold of the flare-lit courtyard, became aware of the squeaks of rats from the dark shadows beyond. 'I wonder how many children I shall have.'

'At the rate you are going, I would say at least a hundred,' Sati answered her drily.

'I don't know, Sati. I don't know.' In one of her sudden swings of mood, she had grown serious. She walked to the window, stared unseeingly outside. 'Children, especially male children, can be so difficult. Look what has happened to the Emperor Jehangir. Prince Husrau rebelled against him and he blinded his son and heir. Prince Parviz became a drunkard like his father, died while still young. And when the Emperor was Prince Jehangir, he rebelled against his own father, the Emperor Akbar. History repeating itself. Most tragically, it happens to once-mighty Emperors only when they are old and ailing.'

'You should not concern yourself with such things, little paddy-bird. There is no solution.'

Mumtaz Mahal swung round fiercely. 'There *is* a solution,' she insisted. 'Follow law and tradition. Let the eldest son of the Emperor be the heir so long as he is competent. I know that my father believes this too with all the passion of his being.'

'That is why he did not support Shah Jahan in his rebellion?'

'Yes. And I respect him for it. He would give his life for that principle, because to him, the Emperor is the symbol of the Empire and the Empire can only endure on principles.'

'Then our beloved Shah Jahan should be the next Emperor by right.'

'Of course. And I shall instil it into him, extract his most sacred oath – and you know how he feels about oaths! – that when the time comes to name his heir, it shall be Prince Dara, our eldest boy, and no one else. I remember telling him, when I was carrying Prince Aurang, that I would kill the baby in my womb if I thought he would attempt to usurp that right.' She flushed at the recollection of the ferocity of her feelings.

'You feel even more passionately about it than your father,' Sati observed wonderingly. 'You and I have talked about everything under the heavens, but never this.' She shrugged plump shoulders. 'Rebellion, especially of sons against fathers, is a fact of life, the will of Allah.'

'No, Sati, remember the Emperor Osman, who killed his male children except the heir? Do you know why he did that? It was not to avoid the will of Allah, but the curse of the Moghuls, the Moghul legacy.'

A light wind had cooled the courtyard of the Chitor palace. The summer sky blazed with countless stars. Having become used to the two boy princes in an objective sort of way, Rana Chara had started walking with them after dinner in the flare-lit courtyard. The dark bulk of the palace was broken by glowing golden squares of light from the windows. Up there were the rooms that had once belonged to his father. He occupied them now. A chink . . . chink . . . chink from the darkness beyond the Indian cypress trees reminded him of the cobra he had used to kill his father. Or was it the poison that had done the trick? Unaccountably, he shivered.

Prince Dara picked up a stone from the flagstone walkway, threw it into the dark silver sheen of the pool. The plop! sounded distinctly above the splash of the waters from the fountain. Rana Chara paused to watch the tiny ripples widening towards the pool's edge. Prince Aurang paused with him.

'Do you know the latest news?' Rana Chara inquired.

'What news?' Prince Dara turned to face him.

'*The* news,' Prince Aurang asserted. 'My brother does not know, but *I* do.'

'All right then, what is the news, Prince Know-all?' Prince Dara challenged.

Prince Aurang's fists clenched. Rana Chara already knew that the boy had the quick temper that goes with fierce pride and extreme sensitivity. He himself had been like that once. Yes, once, a long, lo . . . ong time ago. The scar on his face itched at the recollection, but it only left him wistful.

'The news is that General Mahabat got angry with our grandfather the Emperor and that foul bitch, Nur Jehan, and took off for the south with his Rajput corps. He passed through Rajasthan two weeks ago and is headed for Nazik, where our father has holed out.' He ejected the last words contemptuously.

Rana Chara had made it a point never to curb the boy princes' expressions of rage. On the contrary, he rather helped Prince Aurang to cultivate his sense of rebellion.

'Our parents are neither rats nor rabbits to hole out,' Prince Dara flashed. He thought swiftly. 'If General Mahabat joins our father, he will help our father become the next Emperor, which is his right, because he is now the eldest son and the heir.'

'Ho! ho! ho!' Prince Aurang stood with his legs apart, arms akimbo, dark eyes blazing. 'Do you really think that someone can become Emperor merely through a birthright?'

'Certainly.' There was quiet assurance in Prince Dara's tone. For a moment, Rana Chara glimpsed Asaf Khan here. 'When our father becomes Emperor, *I* shall be the heir.' With a quick jerk of his left hand, he pointed towards his chest.

Rana Chara remembered irrelevantly that Prince Dara was left-handed. He had taken good care to coach Prince Aurang secretly and subtly in the rights of accession, rather than succession. The results were already evident in the hostility between the two brothers, which had existed even before he got to know them and witness their bouts of aggressiveness towards each other.

'Our parents abandoned us,' Prince Aurang declared, his piping voice shrill. 'So they have no heirs, no rights, no traditions. If the man who fathered us,' this was a nice distinction Rana Chara had covertly supplied him with, 'ever becomes Emperor, when he dies,' the boy's pause was deadly as a cobra's sway, 'or is driven from the throne, he will be succeeded by the most brave, daring and powerful general.'

'It's ho! ho! ho! to you too,' Prince Dara shouted fiercely. He returned to Rana Chara. 'The Empire will then belong to me, will it not, Your Majesty?'

The feud had already commenced. Rana Chara chortled inside himself. How fortunate that he had no wife to play favourites or children to challenge him. 'To the victor belongs the spoils,' he asserted.

Prince Aurang eyed him levelly. 'You are so wise,' he declared. 'You should be the Emperor today and I should succeed you.'

Rana Chara chuckled. 'It is when I became wise that I ceased wanting to be the Emperor.'

Chapter 41

October 1627
Nur Jehan was frantic. Within a few months, the Emperor Jehangir, a living, breathing ruler, had become a vegetable. He had suffered a massive heart attack in her suite in the Srinagar palace that evening.

The Court physicians had just told her that he would never recover.

This was a contingency Nur Jehan had not anticipated. Fully believing that the Emperor had at least a few more months to live, she had overlooked the possibility of a sudden heart attack and had agreed that Prince Shahriyar and Princess Ladili could leave for Lahore. That had been four weeks ago and the couple had departed immediately because Prince Shahriyar found that warmer climates were better for his disease, which had been diagnosed as a form of leprosy.

Nur Jehan had definitely not wanted Prince Shahriyar to go to the even warmer climate of Agra because that would take him too far away from the Emperor. She wanted her son-in-law close enough to Srinagar for her to summon him the moment her husband's condition took a permanent turn for the worse, so that the Emperor could place the imperial turban on his head and hand him the royal sword in its bejewelled gold scabbard.

She had managed to assist the Emperor to the uphol-stered divan in her reception chamber before he finally collapsed. Having commanded everyone else to leave the suite after the physicians had departed, she stood alone beside the divan looking down at her husband.

This hulk, clad in a jewelled robe, lying back on the gold cushions had been the young prince of her romantic dreams. She recalled the youthful, vigorous body, full of vibrant dynamism, that had first attracted her attention when she saw him at the private dinner party given by Asaf Khan. She sighed. It seemed a hundred years ago, when both of them had been different people. She had been helpless to do anything about her future then, but by slow degrees and superhuman efforts she had taken her destiny into her own hands. Now she was a near-goddess. No one dared cross her.

Her husband mumbled incoherently, his head jerking from side to side. She bent down to distinguish what he was saying.

'Oh, poor blind eye.' The words were so distorted she could hardly decipher them. 'Go away! . . . Get out! . . .' His face began working, the Mongolian moustache quiver-ing in obvious terror. She knew with a chill that he was seeing Prince Husrau's blinded eye.

'You too . . . I did not kill you . . . Get away . . . Get away from me . . .' His whole body was agitated, jerking in violent spasms.

Her mind spun back through the years to the secret they had shared. He had conspired through Sher Afgan to have Hakim Ali poison the Emperor Akbar.

Ghosts of the past were finally haunting the Emperor in the last hours of his life. Was it all the guilt he had known through the years, ghosts finally released from their hideous confines, emerging to torture him, taking their toll at last? Or had the ghosts of the dead, who had waited in the wings until he had acted out his life, finally emerged on stage to terrify him with their dread vengeance?

There was nothing she could do to help him. His death was an eventuality she had faced up to and now she was ready for it emotionally. She would miss the fact of him in her life, but not the bloated body and flatulent mind. Within a few hours, she would be completely on her own. She had best take care of her interests. She took one final look at his anguished countenance. His face was wreathed with terror. Two tear drops were poised beneath the closed eyelids.

She went to the writing desk at the far end of the room, sat down at it. The whirr and crackle of a moth against one of the hanging lamps seemed harsh in the stillness of the room.

She stared bleakly at the bright-coloured silken tapestry on the wall before her. In soft greens and pinks, it depicted a Moghul garden. She could almost smell its roses from the attar-of-roses scent she herself was wearing. For a moment she was tempted to write out a *firman* appointing Prince Shahriyar his successor, back-dating it, placing the Emperor's palm on it and forging his signature. She abandoned the thought. It would be too risky. If the deception were ever discovered, it would be the end of everything she had planned and worked for, including the result she had hoped to achieve from the forgery.

Instead, she seized a scroll, opened it. Picking up a quill pen, she dipped it in the black ink and wrote out a *firman*, marked secret, to Prince Shahriyar, authorizing him, in the name of the Emperor, to take over the imperial treasury both in Lahore and Agra immediately and then report to Srinagar. The *firman* would leave by fast messenger at dawn.

It was an essential requirement of government that the successor of an Emperor be named immediately the Emperor died, so that there was not the slightest gap in government. The Emperor Akbar had even placed the imperial turban on his son's head a few days before he died. She could either await her husband's death, hoping that he would remain alive until Prince Shahriyar returned to Srinagar in time for his father to declare him the new Emperor, or . . . Grimly, cold-bloodedly, she considered the other possibility. In that event, she would summon Prime Minister Asaf Khan immediately and command him to name the absent Prince Shahriyar the Emperor forthwith.

The latter alternative was more attractive.

She rose from her desk, returned to the divan. The Emperor was still unconscious, but his face was contorted, his whole body involuntarily quivering and jerking as if fighting off attackers.

She gazed at him. In her mind, she shed the wrinkled skin, the sagging flesh, the present torment, reclothed the unmistakably strong frame and the bones of his face with the flesh, blood and pride of youth. When the image of the man she had really loved was imprinted forever in her mind, she slowly reached out for one of the gold cushions.

She owed what she was about to do to the romantic young prince of her dreams.

* * *

The secret messenger had arrived at the Nazik palace from Srinagar at nightfall. Summer had dried Shah Jahan's skin so much that it had caused an itchy rash on both sides of his face and painful cracks on his lips. Yet none of this mattered to him any longer. It was the inaction that had been bothering him increasingly of late. Two months had passed since General Mahabat had arrived and pledged allegiance to him. During this time, the general had frequently urged him to launch his drive, but somehow he had not believed that the timing was right.

Shah Jahan had thought carefully about the implications of the news during dinner with General Mahabat. Now they were seated alone in the reception room, sipping hot, black coffee that was causing them both to sweat even more. The aroma was, however, pleasing, the honey in the thick black liquid was giving him tiny new surges of energy.

'I had word from Srinagar earlier tonight,' Shah Jahan informed the general, who had just raised his steaming coffee goblet to his lips. 'Prince Shahriyar had just left for Lahore where the climate is supposed to be better for his . . . um . . . condition.'

General Mahabat carefully replaced his goblet on the table beside him, stared at Shah Jahan. Lifted eyebrows conveyed the inquiry. 'That places the heir presumptive some distance away from the succession, does it not?'

'Certainly. Meanwhile, as you know, our own forces have been increasing in size, and we have been receiving a stream of men, funds and pledges of support from nobles, ranas and sultans, who are very concerned about the state of the imperial Court.'

'They are also finally aware that Nur Jehan does not rule on behalf of the Emperor, but in her own right,' the general responded quietly.

Shah Jahan knew that General Mahabat had fallen in love with a Hindu girl, who was now living with him. He guessed there was some connection between this girl and the general's breach with Nur Jehan, but it was none of his business. General Mahabat was his most valuable asset on any battlefield today. 'Strangely enough, there has also been some disquiet in the minds of many over the mausoleum which Nur Jehan is causing to be built in memory of her father,' Shah Jahan added. 'Anyone can build a public monument with their own funds, as Asaf Khan did with the Nishat Bagh gardens on Lake Shalimar.' He smiled. 'That may have annoyed the Emperor, but the people did not care. You would be surprised at the number of those who are outraged that this mausoleum to Ghiyas Beg in Agra which my friend Ustad Isa of Shiraz was brought over to design, is being built with public funds and not from Nur Jehan's vast personal treasury.'

General Mahabat eyed him hopefully. 'Surely the timing is now right for us to proceed to Agra. With due respect, my advice is that the farther away Prince Shahriyar gets from the Emperor, the nearer you should be to Agra.'

'You are right, General. We must certainly leave before the monsoon breaks. How soon can you be ready?'

The general rose to his feet, saluted. 'Our vanguard can leave at dawn tomorrow.'

Shah Jahan relaxed on his settle, grinned. 'I thought that is what you would say.' He laughed aloud. 'I have known all along that you are tired of summer in the desert and have been straining to get where it will be cooler!'

The gold cushion was almost on the Emperor's face when his body jerked in a tremendous convulsion. Nur Jehan whipped the cushion aside. The large almond-shaped eyes were open, staring at her in consternation, while the open mouth clamoured for air.

He *knows*.

Her heart nearly stopped beating. During that second,

he was so alive, so conscious that she half-expected him to leap off the divan and smite her down.

An expression of intense grief such as she had never before witnessed crossed his eyes. His face crumpled. A great gasp escaped him. The horrible faecal breath smote her nostrils. His body stretched once, then relaxed. He had simply let go. The dead eyes remained staring at her.

Had he died of a heart attack, or a broken heart? She would never know.

She flung the cushion aside, sprawled on his body. Without thought, this always controlled woman started keening.

One never recognizes what lies in the secret recesses of one's heart. Nur Jehan was amazed that she should have given way to the primitive instinct of the Muslim woman by keening when her husband died. On reflection, however, she was pleased that it had happened because it would show to all Muslims that beneath the trappings of State, the proud, haughty Empress was still a woman in her love for her man. Nur Jehan spent the next hour issuing instructions for her dead husband's formal lying-in-state in the great assembly hall of the palace, when hundreds of thousands of his grieving subjects would file past his bier. While the embalmers were busy preparing and perfuming the body, she ordered a magnificent ebony casket with gold fittings, lined with cloth of gold to be built for the final rites.

Try as she might, she could not get rid of the image of her dead husband's last look, those accusing eyes underlaid with stunned disillusionment. It would haunt her dreams for the rest of her life.

But now she had to face the world of reality. For years she had endured the gross creature that her husband had become, in order to wield *his* power. Now, absolute power was finally hers.

She was glad when Asaf Khan was announced, seeking audience. News travels fast in a palace and she had expected him earlier. She received him in the ante-room because the embalmers were preparing the body in the reception chamber. The sickly sweet smell of their unguents lay heavy everywhere. Female attendants and eunuchs tiptoed through the room from time to time, carrying their auras of mourning. On such occasions, she reflected, underlings vie with each other in demonstrating grief, ranging from the openly tearful, highlighted by an occasional sob, to the strong, silent type who showed deep sorrow restrained.

Asaf Khan strode in, his shoes click-clacking on the marble floor. He made obeisance, his expression unusually grave. She silently indicated a low, heavy, gold-upholstered chair of French make, one of the two that Sir Thomas Roe had given her as a present. She had transported them to Srinagar after the English ambassador departed, as being more suited to the cooler climate. Which brand of grief should she display to her brother? The keening over, she thought the strong, silent image best, particularly because she alone was now wielding the Emperor's power.

She took her seat on the higher of the two chairs. 'The suffering of the Emperor is finally over,' she declared. 'He is even now in Paradise.' She thought that a perfect opening statement.

'The Emperor's gain is our dire loss, Your Imperial Majesty, and I offer you my deepest sympathies,' Asaf Khan responded sombrely. 'As Edward Terry, Ambassador Roe's chaplain, once said, the disposition of the Emperor can be compared to extremes, from the barbarously cruel to the exceedingly fair and gentle. History will see him as such.' He reflected a few moments, shook his head. 'How did the end come?'

She told him the facts, a tear in her voice where appropriate, only omitting her move towards using the cushion. He listened in silence.

'You are brave to organize the lying-in-state when you are prostrated with grief, but then you always had remarkable courage,' he declared when she had finished. 'I shall of course inform all relatives, the Court in Agra, the neighbouring rulers, the ranas, sultans and senior nobles immediately and also make arrangements for the State funeral. Do you have any special wishes?'

She placed her elbows on the arms of the chair, leaned forward, steadied her breathing despite the beating of her heart. 'Yes, Prime Minister. As you know, we cannot have a gap between Emperors. The Emperor is dead, long live the Emperor. In affairs of State, the living must bury the dead. It is our desire, as the Empress, that in accordance with the late Emperor's commands, Prince Shahriyar be named immediately as the successor.'

Asaf Khan's jaw tightened imperceptibly, the daredevil blue eyes frosted. 'Did the late Emperor leave a written will, or issue such a command before reliable witnesses?'

She held back her temper. 'No, we alone are the witness.'

'Your Imperial Majesty alone?'

'Yes.' She lifted her head imperiously. 'It is enough.'

'Not really,' he rejoined, mildly now. 'I am already aware that the late Emperor left no public instructions as to the succession. Even if he had, anyone other than the legal heir would have had to receive the imperial turban and the royal sword personally from the Emperor for such a deviation from law and tradition to be effective.' He grew solemn. 'You are of course aware of these requirements.'

Anger and frustration caused her to respond without thought. 'In that case, it is our edict, here and now as the Empress, that you acclaim Prince Shahriyar the Emperor immediately.'

His smile became wintry. He rubbed his chin with his thumb. 'Unfortunately, and I regret to say it, here and now you lack the authority to issue such an edict. Your powers as the Empress derived from a live Emperor. In the absence of any appointment by him as Regent, prior to his death, you are legally incompetent to issue edicts.'

Rage such as she had never experienced before swept through her. Knowing that she was on the edge of a precipice, however, she held it back. 'Very well then, our edict was issued prior to the Emperor's death,' she declared airily.

'Prior to the Emperor's death only he had the power to make such an edict.'

He was very sure of himself, almost playing with her. The angry snarl of a cat in the courtyard outside was followed by the squeak of a mouse. Nur Jehan shivered. Her eyes went to the mantelpiece. A long matchlock rifle, similar to the one she had used in the Agra palace to kill Tafari, reposed there. She resisted the urge to seize it and shoot her brother. 'We know why you are rejecting our legitimate commands.' Her voice had a dangerous edge to it.

'Why, Your Imperial Majesty?'

'You want your son-in-law, Shah Jahan, named Emperor, so that your daughter can be Empress.' The very thought of it made her brain raw. 'She shall never be Empress. As for your son-in-law, he is a parricide. He and Prince Husrau drove our husband to an early death.' Her voice rose almost to a screech. 'You want to rule the Empire through your family.' She stood up, her finger pointing accusingly, and he rose with her.

He placed his hands behind his back, fingers locked together. Even in her anger, she could not but note his enormous dignity, though clad only in the white tunic and *jodhpurs* he had worn for the occasion, with no jewellery or

647

ornaments. 'You are right to believe that I want Shah Jahan to become Emperor,' he rejoined soberly. 'But not because he is my son-in-law or since it would make my daughter Empress. I have only one concern, the welfare of the Empire. That does not mean the princes and nobles, but millions of common people, leading ordinary lives full of the joys and sorrows that can be caused by their ruler. It means the land, the scent of the blossoms, the stench of manure, the hills and plains, mountains and valleys, rivers and lakes of this mighty Moghul kingdom. It means the insects, the birds and the beasts. Finally, it means our religions and culture, which will enrich our lives and influence the whole world forever. No man is perfect. Shah Jahan is the only one of those eligible who can guide us as close as possible to the attainment of our ideals. I beg you even now to reconsider your decision. Let us jointly name *him*, not the son of a palace slave, as the successor, in the interests of national security.'

'Never.' Her finger pointed imperiously again, this time at the door. 'Begone. You are no longer Prime Minister of the Moghul Empire.'

'Summarily sacked?'

Why was he laughing? 'Summarily sacked,' she confirmed.

He drew himself to his full height. 'As I have just stated, you no longer have the powers of the Empress, so you cannot dismiss me. Only the Emperor can do that.'

'But he is dead.' This interview had turned into a nightmare.

'The Emperor is dead, long live the Emperor,' he quoted her. 'A council of princes and nobles met before I came here. Having agreed that there is only one available heir at present, we have named him Emperor.'

She recoiled, then a laugh escaped her. 'The Emperor Shah Jahan! We shall see how long he will last.'

'No, Your Imperial Majesty. We have already placed the imperial turban on the head of Prince Dawar, who was readily available in the palace. He is the other of the two eligible heirs by law and tradition, being the eldest son of the late Prince Husrau.'

Her incredulity knew no bounds. This was a move she had never anticipated. For a full minute, she could not bring herself to speak, merely stared her hatred at him. 'We shall overthrow Prince Dawar by force,' she finally said with deadly quiet. 'And then . . . and then . . .' she could hardly breathe . . . 'you shall hang, be pulled down from the rope before you die, disembowelled . . .' She was sputtering, incoherent.

'Spare yourself the vicarious thrills of a sadistic mind,' he interrupted her coldly. 'You are in no position to hang a flea outside this palace even if you had an invisible rope.' His blue eyes held a cold hostility. 'As from now, having rejected my plea for unity, being bent upon taking control over the Empire, thus creating civil war, you are confined to your quarters in the *harem*. You are under arrest.'

The long march to Mewar had been accomplished in record time. Far from opposition, Shah Jahan and General Mahabat received the support reserved for a victorious army all along the way.

Shah Jahan had intended by-passing Chitor. But to his utter surprise, he received a visit from Rana Chara while he was encamped for the night a few miles from the Mewar capital.

It was a typical evening for an army on the move. Cooking pots containing stews hung on tripods above crackling fires; bread was baking in field ovens above glowing embers, whole lambs were being turned on spits. Their odours mingled with the clamouring of men's voices, filled the camp, were wafted into Shah Jahan's tent by a sudden breeze. General Wahid presented Rana Chara and left. They took their seats on the settles at each side of the table. Trumpets suddenly blared outside, announcing five o'clock.

Rana Chara had changed. Shah Jahan recognized it the moment the man entered his tent. It was not a question of growing older, with the black hair now streaked with silver, some wrinkles on the skin once tight-drawn over the hatchet face, but of a changed personality. Gone was the old restlessness, the seething discontent, the undoubted bitterness. Great calm had replaced them. And yet the deepset black eyes held something he could not place, except that it was more an absence, more the look of a void than a presence. If Rana Chara was surprised at the plain dealwood table and settles, the rolled up mattress, that were the only furnishings of the tent, he did not show it.

The months during which Shah Jahan had ravaged the Mewar countryside seemed far away. The land too had been restored. Change, change, change, always change.

'You have done us great honour by calling on us,' Shah Jahan opened the conversation. 'If you would exchange the bountiful board of your palace for a soldier's fare, we would be even more honoured to have you join us at dinner.'

'On the contrary, it is a greater honour to be invited to share a soldier's simple meal than an Emperor's banquet.' Rana Chara lightly scratched the scar running down his face with an extended little finger. 'We regret that we have been denied the pleasure of having you stay as our guests in the palace.' An amused glint flickered through the dark eyes. 'You seem to be making it a practice.' He was referring to the last time Shah Jahan had been in Chitor to accept the surrender of Mewar; then too he had camped in his tent for the night. For a moment, Shah Jahan was uncomfortable. He could not escape the feeling that the Rana was playing with him.

'But on this occasion, we do understand.' Again that amused glint. 'What you have at stake is more important than the lamb steaks from our kitchens.'

Shah Jahan laughed. It was rather a strained joke, but he needed the laughter in dealing with this man. 'I wonder whether that is really so,' he responded. 'A good roast lamb is more enjoyable at times than sending firework rockets into the heavens.'

Rana Chara's smile was wry. 'Your words come from the lips of one who is tonight's firework rocket, making for the imperial stars. And as to that, we have much news for you, Prince. Your father is dead.' He made the announcement bluntly, man to man, as if it were the demise of some unknown peasant.

Shah Jahan felt as if he had been punched in the stomach. 'My father . . . dead?' Fathers somehow seem so invincible. He remembered thinking that of his grandfather too.

The news began to sink in, but not all its implications. Rana Chara exposed them to him. 'He died suddenly in Srinagar, of a massive heart attack. Prime Minister Asaf Khan, in consultation with the Council of Princes and Nobles, proclaimed your cousin, Prince Dawar, Emperor. He also placed the Empress under arrest.'

'What?' This time it was Shah Jahan's head that felt battered. No, no, no! He would never accept that. He would seize the throne by force. What a traitor Asaf Khan had proved to be, naming Prince Dawar Emperor.

Rana Chara's voice broke into his furious thoughts. 'The Empress had already sent word to Prince Shahriyar, who was in Lahore, to seize the imperial treasury there. Though shorn of her powers, she instructed him to raise an army of mercenaries and give battle to Asaf Khan on his way to Agra with the Emperor Dawar and the imperial army. The foolish prince did as she commanded and hastily assembled a great force of mercenaries. The two armies met in battle just north of Lahore. Prince Shahriyar's rag-tag bunch was no match for the well-trained imperial army, ably led by Asaf Khan. The rebels were routed and Prince Shahriyar was taken prisoner. Asaf Khan then removed him permanently from the ranks of contenders for the imperial crown.' He relapsed into a deliberate silence.

'Did Asaf Khan have Prince Shahriyar executed?'

'No. Asaf Khan has too great a sense of justice for anything so crude. He had Prince Shahriyar blinded, as your father once blinded Prince Husrau for rebellion against the crown.'

'Blinded?' Shah Jahan was aghast. And yet, why not? One could not wield supreme power without supreme ruthlessness and cruelty. His reading of history told him that. All the great conquerors, Alexander the Great, Julius Caesar, the Great Padshahs of Persia, Babur, had ensured law and order through cruel and inhuman but fitting punishments. He thought of what even the Emperor Akbar had once advised him: the best way to ensure a safe throne is to eliminate competition. No, he could not blame Asaf Khan.

'Yes,' Rana Chara affirmed the news with indifference. 'Do not let it shock you. Like your eldest brother, Prince Shahriyar was always a blind fool. The loss of his sight is merely a physical extension of the disability. Our own advice to Prime Minister Asaf Khan shall be that he treats Prince Dawar's appointment as a temporary measure to meet constitutional requirements. You are the legal successor to the imperial throne. When you do ascend it, or before, if possible, you should have your competition, including Prince . . . er . . . the Emperor Dawar, eliminated. The others would logically be Prince Shahriyar, who should equally logically prefer a swift death to his lingering blindness, and your two cousins, the sons of your father's brother, Prince Daniyal.'

Much to his own surprise, Shah Jahan was not shocked by what he would have regarded as dreadful suggestions five years earlier. His only disquiet was the strange flicker of satisfaction that went through Rana Chara's eyes at his silent acquiescence.

'We are also pleased to report that your sons, Prince Dara and Prince Aurang, were in good health two days ago when we sent them back to Agra. As may have been reported to you, they were our guests in Chitor for a few months. We did not want to be responsible for the future of hostage princes.'

Why had Rana Chara really sent his two sons back to Agra when he must have known that their father was on his way through Mewar? Was he honouring his word to the late Emperor that the two hostage princes would be kept separate from their father? And had Rana Chara sent them back to Agra before or after he received all the news he had just imparted?

It did not matter. Rana Chara would live and die the ruler of Mewar. He was not an important part of the imperial scene.

'When you become Emperor, what will you do with Her Imperial Majesty, Nur Jehan?' Rana Chara flung the question into his musing.

Shah Jahan instantly recalled the stories he had heard of Rana Chara's regular visits to the Agra palace. His suspicions aroused, he feigned indifference, smacked at a buzzing fly that had settled on the table, missed it. 'I have not given that any thought. What would you suggest?'

'You could always have her executed, but that would be a rather childish tit-for-tat, unworthy even of your present, still dubious, position. Besides,' a malicious twinkle crossed the dark, deep-set eyes, 'the sweetest revenge is that which can be witnessed and savoured. Rulers who condemn their enemies to death miss all the fun of relegating them instead to a life of obscurity. As for the rationale,' the eyes twinkled again, 'punishment should be remedial, retributive and deterrent. Execution remedies nothing for the victim. Now torture, on the other hand . . .'

Shah Jahan was fascinated. 'Go on,' he urged. 'What about retribution and deterrence?'

Rana Chara chuckled. 'People imagine that being deprived of life, especially when trampled by elephants, is retribution. It is a swift reward for a lifetime of crime. An accused person should be sentenced to a lifetime of suffering instead. Thus alone can all men, particularly potential wrongdoers who have notoriously short memories, continue to witness the living consequence of a lifetime of crime.'

'Excellent.' Shah Jahan had never suspected that this Rajput king, whom he only knew as a warrior without peer, had such depth. 'I am glad that my two sons have had the benefit of acquaintance with you. May I send them to Chitor from time to time in the future, to benefit from your tutelage?'

A strange expression crossed Rana Chara's face. Was it triumph? Why would he know triumph at being given some charge over two boy princes? Could it be the expectation of rewards when he, Shah Jahan, was Emperor? A firmer foothold in the royal palace? That must be it. Shah Jahan thrust aside the disquiet that had briefly stirred in him.

'We would be honoured.' That annoying fly had returned. Rana Chara smacked it four-square. He flicked the tiny corpse away with a jewelled forefinger. 'Now back to your first question,' he asserted. 'We would recommend that you banish Nur Jehan to a city away from the centre, Lahore perhaps, from where she can have the mausoleum being built in Agra for her father completed while contemplating the errors of her past. You would be hailed as a merciful Emperor, while you secretly exult in her ignominy. People have a remarkable capacity for extolling a single act of seeming public virtue, regardless of private motives. If a Muslim prophet were served up in a pork stew, they would believe that he had sacrificed himself to purify the pig's flesh and would confer sainthood on him . . . er . . . and even on the pig.'

Shah Jahan's laugh rang out. 'That certainly explains the divinity an act of seeming compassion would confer on me, but what about the scheming Nur Jehan? Would she not cultivate my enemies?'

The black bushy eyebrows lifted superciliously. 'In the *harem* of a provincial capital? No, Prince. All she could cultivate in the Lahore palace would be prominent Muslim ladies and her rose garden.'

The eventful news of the evening was capped by the delegation from Asaf Khan that rode into the camp while Shah Jahan was at dinner with Rana Chara, General Mahabat, General Wahid and his army commanders.

The most important part of the scroll presented to him made his head swim.

'You are hereby urged to proceed directly to Agra, where the temporary appointment of Prince Dawar will be abrogated and the imperial turban placed on your head.'

In a daze he read the message aloud to all those present.

Rana Chara had the last word. 'You must be blessed by the Christian God,' he declared. 'Under the Christian calendar, today is the first day of January in the year 1628.'

Chapter 42

February 1631

He was in the European room of the Agra palace that morning when Asaf Khan brought him news of the crisis in the Deccan. It seemed incongruous to Shah Jahan that the region which had been his refuge during the years of virtual exile should have turned against him now that he'd been Emperor for three years.

He had maintained this room exactly as his grandfather had furnished it fifty years ago. Having moved directly into the imperial palace in Agra on being named Emperor, Shah Jahan had proceeded to embellish it, replacing the sandstone with marble, which he loved. Fascinated with jewels, he had even commissioned a peacock throne to replace that of the Emperor Akbar. It was surrounded by twelve emerald pillars holding up a canopy topped by a tree set with rubies, glittering diamonds, emeralds and lustrous pearls, on either side of which were two peacocks, bedecked with the same jewels. This one room, however, he had insisted on leaving unchanged, as a tribute to his grandfather. It must surely be even the same silver sunlight pouring in through the open windows, the same wind rustling through the cypress branches in the courtyard below. It certainly was the same Persian carpet, soft beneath his feet, the same gilt French sofa on which he now sat, with Asaf Khan on the matching chair opposite him.

Receiving the news from Asaf Khan, he understood again the repeated crises his beloved grandfather had faced and overcome, many in that very room. The example was an inspiration to him.

'I deeply regret having to bring you the news today, on the third anniversary of your coronation.' Asaf Khan smiled wryly. 'But that is one of the prices we have to pay. As in the saying which the Thebans of old handed down to us, the price of honour is death.'

'You are right, Prime Minister. It took only three months after our coronation for Prince Jauhar Singh of Orcas to create problems. He hates Moghul rule, but is now serving us well as the imperial commander in the Deccan. Then came the Afghan Prince Lodi, who has not submitted even after losing so many battles to us. Now you say he has reared up again. He is like a snake with many heads. We have always wondered whether he is not inspired and aided by Nur Jehan. She is wealthy enough in her own right. Three years of almost ceaseless losses, his defeat last month, and he still persists. His movements around the country have been rather similar to our own when we were pursued by our father's armies.' It was his turn to smile wryly. 'And of course we had problems from Shah Abbas of Persia in Kandhar.' He tapped the coffee table insistently. 'In spite of it all, we have been consolidating and expanding our territories. We shall bring the whole of India under our direct suzerainty during our lifetime, something no other Moghul Emperor has ever done.'

'Well, Sire, Shah Abbas of Persia is dead. It will be years before his son, Shah Safvi, dares to move against us.' A mischievous expression crossed Asaf Khan's face. A fore-finger scratched one side of his reddish moustaches, now flecked with silver. 'Abroad, that is,' he added. 'For his ambassador has been making serious expansionist moves within Your Imperial Majesty's Court.'

Shah Jahan failed to see any humour in the situation. He was honest enough to realize that the passing years had made him increasingly arrogant, even full of self-import-ance. For instance, he had taken the Emperor Akbar's entire imperial train with him and occupied the royal tents when he led the campaign against Lodi and Jauhar. It was not fitting that an Emperor should occupy an ordinary tent, like a common soldier. But deep inside him, something told him this was wrong. The commander-in-chief of the imperial armies should have the same attitude towards his men as the prince in exile, but this was only a despairing cry from the past. With each campaign, that cry diminished in intensity until it was finally extinguished by the conviction that an emperor was not a person, but a demi-god. Today, he himself was Shah Jahan only in name. He was an institution without either the rights or the needs of self-determination of a human being.

The Persian ambassador had repeatedly insisted on his position as representative of the head of a parallel sovereign empire. He had persistently refused to bow low enough in audience to satisfy Shah Jahan, who had no option but to accept whatever obeisance the infidel made to him. Exasperated, Shah Jahan had finally hit upon the expedient of having an overhead wicket installed in the path of those approaching the imperial *jarokha*, above its entrance door. He had thought this a rather clever move, because the ambassador would have to bow low to enter beneath it. At the *durbar* this very morning, to his utter consternation, the ambassador had paused at the wicket, then calmly turned around, bent down and come through the entrance, presenting a broad posterior to the monarch.

'You ambassadorial wretch!' Shah Jahan had roared in an uncontrollable fit of rage. 'Did you imagine you were entering a stable of asses such as yourself?'

'Indeed I did, Your Imperial Majesty,' the ambassador had retorted urbanely. 'Being faced with such a door, who could believe otherwise than that he was entering a stable of asses? I but presented that part of my anatomy which Your Imperial Majesty invited.'

The recollection of the incident filled Shah Jahan with renewed fury. 'We shall administer an imperial kick on that infidel's rear some day,' he vowed. 'He has made us the laughing stock of the world.'

'You are too revered by all men, not only by virtue of your position but also because of your unique attainments for anyone to dare laugh at you, Sire,' Asaf Khan soothed. 'The civilized world will laugh at the ambassador and his master for being barbarians who travel arse first.'

Shah Jahan clapped his hands. 'Ah! That's good.' Asaf Khan's words had made him feel better. 'A pig's arse where the manhood should be!' He laughed uproariously, then sobered instantly, as was his wont. 'You say that Prince Lodi, having suffered last month's defeat, is now defying us in Buran?' He crossed his legs, leaning forward on the sofa in anticipation of Asaf Khan's reply.

'Yes, Sire.'

'Once *our* stronghold.' It was from Buran that he had achieved some of his greatest triumphs. It was in Buran that his brother, Prince Husrau, had died, probably at the hands of assassins. He could not suppress a sigh. 'We shall leave for Buran without delay. How long will it take for us to have twenty thousand men ready to move?'

Asaf Khan's cheeks twitched. 'Twenty days.'

'Good.' The excitement of the coming campaign had begun to stir Shah Jahan's blood. It was wonderful to lead men into battle from the power of the Emperor's position, to be proceeding with mighty armies to crush instead of defending with the proverbial seven men and an elephant. 'Send word immediately to General Mahabat to join us at Ajmer with ten thousand men. He will, as always, enjoy the campaign trail instead of sitting in Ajmer, as governor of the State. Inform General Wahid of our decision on your way out.' He paused, remembered something totally unconnected with the coming campaign. 'Now that the architect, Ustad Isa, has completed his design for the pearl mosque, he must not return to Shiraz. We have other plans for him which we shall need to discuss on our return from the Deccan.' He had not been able to spend any time with the young, white-haired architect with the haunted eyes. When the Deccan was finally subjugated, he would devote himself more to philosophical communion, as his grandfather had done.

Things had certainly changed, Shah Jahan reflected with fierce satisfaction, as Asaf Khan rose, made obeisance and departed. Even crises which had once seemed like the buffetings of fate were now merely challenges. He was a fortunate demi-god, especially because of Mumtaz Mahal, who would, as usual, insist on accompanying him even though, this time, she was pregnant with their fourteenth child. Thirteen children, five of them still alive, healthy and vital, from the same woman in nearly twenty years of marriage, the testament of two people's exclusive love for each other.

Yes indeed, he was blessed of Almighty Allah.

The imperial army departed from Agra twenty days later, proceeded west to Ajmer, where Shah Jahan was joined by General Mahabat with ten thousand cavalrymen, then headed directly south and reached Buran at the end of April. Prince Lodi refused to surrender, so Shah Jahan's army sprawled for many square miles on the flat lands around the city, which put up a stout defence for over five weeks.

Shah Jahan occupied the royal tents within the movable imperial stockade created by his grandfather, with Mumtaz Mahal in the *harem* adjoining. Since she was heavy with child, the delivery being expected any day now, Wazir Khan, her physician of many years, attended her daily. Shah Jahan could not get her obvious discomfort out of his mind. The summer heat was dreadful enough for him and his men, what must it be like for a pregnant woman?

Mumtaz Mahal's birth pains commenced one evening while he was in conference with General Mahabat after dinner. To Shah Jahan's surprise, General Wahid, who had maintained contact with the *harem* regarding Mumtaz Mahal's progress, requested leave to enter his pavilion. Had Mumtaz delivered the baby already?

Shah Jahan rose to his feet, met the craggy-faced general at the entrance. 'You have news?' he inquired anxiously.

General Wahid's normally dour face was wreathed in a smile. 'Certainly, Your Imperial Majesty. You are the father of a lusty baby girl weighing seven pounds. My heartfelt congratulations.'

'Praise be to Allah.' He glanced instinctively at the clock hanging on the tent wall. 'Ask our secretary to note the time, 10.29 P.M., for the royal astrologers to prepare the girl's horoscope. It is the 8th day of June, is it not?'

'Yes, Sire.'

General Mahabat came up to him, saluted. 'My congratulations too, Your Imperial Majesty. I pray Almighty Allah's blessings on the mother and child.'

The mother! General Wahid had made no mention of the mother. Unaccountably, Shah Jahan's heart started beating faster. 'How is the Empress?' He kept his voice steady only with great effort.

General Wahid seemed surprised. 'I assume she is doing well, Sire. No mention was made of her.'

'Tell the Chief Eunuch to find out for certain and report directly to me.' Shah Jahan could not keep the curtness from his voice. 'You will not be required for this session, General, so get some rest.'

'I certainly will. Pray forgive me the omission.' General Wahid saluted, backed out of the pavilion and vanished into the darkness beyond the red-gold flare-light.

By custom, a man was not permitted to be with a woman during her times of bleeding, whether it was from her monthly period or from childbirth. This was meant more to protect the woman than the man, as was the rule that she should not be entered sexually for thirty days after the birth of a baby. Fists clenched, Shah Jahan started to pace the tent restlessly. 'The important thing, our wife's condition . . . and nobody cares to tell us,' he gritted. 'When will . . .' He stopped short, not wishing to be critical of General Wahid. 'We mean, surely those eunuchs should know better. Their brains must have gone with their balls.' He had found himself becoming a little more loose with his language in recent years, but it helped ease some of the enormous tensions he so frequently experienced. And it did not matter any longer. He was the Emperor. He set his own standards.

'Surely if the news had been bad, it would have been brought to you,' General Mahabat volunteered. 'If you will pardon me the liberty, let me ask one of your attendants to bring us specific news of the Empress.'

'Good, but these accursed eunuchs . . .' He pounded his thigh with a fist.

By the time General Mahabat returned, Shah Jahan had calmed down. 'Let us continue with our planning, General. We regret having permitted a domestic crisis to intrude upon the business of the Empire.' He took his seat on the imperial throne fronted by a white marble-topped table that matched the lit crystal oil-lamps hanging from the roof of the tent, but an inner restlessness had seized him. It was almost at this very spot, fifteen years ago, that Prince Husrau had died in an army tent after he had drawn close to his brother for the first time. Tonight, amid the splendour of Persian carpets, gilt furniture, crystal glass and marble accessories, the heavy odour of incense smoking in braziers, the only common factors were the pungent smell of burnt oil and the feeling of being close to another human being. Mumtaz Mahal was the light of his life. Oh Merciful Allah, keep her safe!

Two hours later, their tactics for the next assaults on the city complete, ready for the following day's general staff's planning session, General Mahabat saluted and departed. 'Let us hope that no news is good news,' were his last words, for no message had come from the *harem*.

The trumpets blared forth the midnight call, a lonely sound in the crowded silence of the warm desert night. Shah Jahan started pacing the tent again, alone this time. It struck him forcibly that at times of crisis even an Emperor was isolated. Whether it is our subjects, or those who love us personally, no one can really experience or share our anxiety or grief, he reflected. Not even the closest communion with a loved one can mean a complete sharing. As of this moment. I love Mumtaz Mahal so completely. But I do not know what she is enduring. And if I were by her side, I would still not be able to live her pain, nor she my misery.

He reached for the little golden bell on the white marble table. Its tinkle was pleasant, but it jarred on his ears. The chief attendant, Kasim, clad in purple and gold livery, entered the tent and made obeisance. 'Why have we not had a response from the *harem*?' Shah Jahan roared even before the man rose from his prostration. 'What are we? Some forgotten child of no consequence?'

The silver-haired Kasim's wrinkled cheeks quivered with fear. 'We are awaiting word from the chief eunuch, Sire. We have sent repeated messages to him with no result.'

'Tell the Chief Eunuch that if we do not hear from him immediately, we shall have his balls.' The words were barely out of his mouth when he realized their stupidity. An involuntary laugh escaped him. 'Go now and inform the chief eunuch that the Emperor demands an immediate report. Remain outside the *harem* enclosure until he gives it to you.'

He resumed his pacing. Minutes passed. The soft tread of his shoes on the carpet became louder in his ears. The silence it penetrated was deafening, the warm, close air within the tent began to overpower him.

Crump, crump, crump, crump.

His own footsteps had become those of an elephant. He had an insane desire to quicken them to galloping speed so he could crash through to news of his beloved.

Crump, crump, cr . . .

It was too much. Gasping for breath from a surge of anxiety, he stumbled outside the tent. The air was cooler here, but still balmy. The new moon had long set. Countless brilliant stars lit the sky. The jewels of the night. His passion for jewels was so great that he had sometimes been more fascinated by the jewelled garments of dancing girls than by their sensuous movements. Ah, jewels! The sparkle of the only jewel of the night, of his entire life, might be extinguished already. Panic seized him.

I am the Emperor. I have the power to bring death to anyone. But not life. Have I created a new life only to have it destroy my co-creator?

A rustle of garments brought him back to sanity. He swung round. Kasim appeared through the light of the hissing flares, smiled as he made obeisance. 'All is well, O Emperor,' he announced, still on his knees. 'The Empress was in danger of losing her life, but has just recovered. Hakim Doctor Wazir Khan advises that she is very, very tired from her hours of labour and certain complications after the birth. She has fallen into a healing sleep. The Hakim begs that she be permitted to rest undisturbed.'

Shah Jahan lifted his eyes to the heavens in deep thankfulness. He had known that something was wrong with his beloved. They were a single strand of the lyre of existence, making the music of one beneath the Great Creator's plucking fingers. They might not share every experience, but even when apart they each knew when the light, soaring thrills of joy escaped the other, or when the deep haunting strains of tragedy were struck.

Now, like his beloved Mumtaz Mahal, he could sleep in peace.

There is no greater exposer of others than a downfall, Nur Jehan reflected as she gazed out of her bedroom window that night at the sky brilliant with countless stars. She had been the glittering firmament once. Now she was nothing. She even lived in a *house* in Lahore, not in the palace.

During the three years of her exile, she had learned to cope with her bitterness, but there were occasions in the deep of the night when she would lie on her divan bed, unable to sleep, restless, smothered by the silken sheets and cushions, remembering, remembering. Like tonight. Then she would get out of bed and pace her room, a tigress caged by her own despair.

Losing power was like the death of a much needed relative. Family and friends immediately crowded her residence, filling its emptiness and the hours that would otherwise be lonely. Soon came the burial. As the sods of earth were tamped down on the coffin, the flood of sympathizers ebbed. Then suddenly one day the mourner was alone, more alone than she had ever been in her life. And it would have been better if she had been left totally and completely isolated from the first moment of the bereavement.

It had taken weeks in her case for the stream of syco-phants to run dry, but it had done so steadily, accelerating as nobles, courtiers and friends increasingly smelled the stench of death. Only vultures remained, eunuchs who wished to capitalize on handling her wealth, the indigent who fawned on her for charity but who earlier would not have been permitted to come within a mile of her, except at the Emperor's *durbars*.

Her one true friend had been Rana Chara. He had journeyed to Lahore once each year to visit her and he was the only man outside the palace that she talked to in person. He was a changed individual, at peace with himself and the new purpose of his life, which was to ensure that the cycles of cause and effect had their most logical force, especially in devastating those he hated. A strange attitude, but one she wished she could cultivate. He was a guest at the palace tonight. The two of them had one thing in common, hatred of Shah Jahan. Rana Chara did not share her jealous hatred of Mumtaz Mahal who now occupied her place. The thought of that little bitch of a niece residing in her rooms, using her eunuchs and attendants, exercising her former authority, infuriated her so much at times that she thought her head would burst and she would go crazy. As for her brother, Asaf Khan, she could only pray for the vengeance of Allah on the head of that supercilious, conniving bastard. She even prayed for their dead father to invoke hell-fire and damnation on him.

A hyena howled from a nearby hillside. Neighbourhood dogs began barking in response. One of them echoed that dismal howl. Unusually, an elephant's trumpet blared from the nearby palace stables.

She recalled Rana Chara's words of yesteryear. 'It is even more difficult to await the outcome of revenge than the fruits of endeavour. They both involve wisdom and cunning, courage and unswerving purpose. You are already facing your position in life, the fall from the divine grace you bestowed on yourself. Learn to accept it, as I did the uselessness of my ambition to become the Great Whore, then everything will fall into place. You disengage, regroup, consolidate and proceed in a new direction. It is like converting one's sword to a ploughshare, one's spear to a pruning hook!'

Two years had gone by before she had eventually been able to accept her position as final and irrevocable. Events moved fast in the outside world. Men did not pause for a former Empress, least of all the men of ambition – Prince Jauhar, Prince Lodi – who refused to bow to the new Emperor. Rana Chara was right. Her day was over. Only vengeance remained. She prayed that she would live long enough to witness Shah Jahan's downfall. She believed Rana Chara's assessment of the source from which that downfall would come, aided by his deft manipulation.

But it was not enough.

Driven desperate by bitterness, she gazed through the glow of the night at the darkness within all light, the original darkness of the deep. 'Oh Great Shaitan, take the woman Mumtaz Mahal away from this world to thee. Let the void in Shah Jahan's life be as formless as Thy original deep.'

More exhausted from the strain of worrying about Mumtaz Mahal than he had ever been before or after a battle, Shah Jahan's sleep had been deep. He would see his love in the morning. Yet like the soldier drugged with exhaustion on the front, but still alert deep down inside, he responded immediately to the alarm.

'Sire! Sire! Please awaken.'

He was alert on the instant, came erect, swung his legs out of the divan bed. 'What is it?' Mumtaz sprang to his consciousness.

Kasim was on his knees, tears streaming down his wrinkled cheeks. 'The Empress came out of her sleep, but has suffered a relapse. She begs you to come to her.'

His brain spinning, he was barely conscious of being

helped to dress. He splashed water on his face, wiped it with the linen cloth and dashed out of the tent.

Hakim Wazir Khan met him at the entrance to Mumtaz Mahal's tent, made scant obeisance. 'Your Imperial Majesty, I regret to inform you that the Empress has taken a sudden turn for the worse. I suspected this would happen when she told me earlier tonight that she had heard the baby cry in her womb. Her whole body is infected. The other physicians and I have done our best.' A sob escaped him. 'She is dying.'

'No . . . o . . . o.' The cry that escaped Shah Jahan was that of a wounded beast. 'She shall not die.' All deportment forgotten, he was screaming now. 'We are the Emperor. We decree that she shall not die.'

Vain words. An Emperor can only decree death, not life.

Out of the depths of his despair, the well-springs of love fountained. Mumtaz Mahal would need all his strength and dignity. He squared his shoulders and walked into the tent. In the light of a single, shaded lantern placed on a table beside the divan bed, as in a nightmare, he saw the group of physicians and a veiled white-robed woman in *chador* sink into obeisance. He gravely acknowledged their salutation, avoided looking at the still figure on the divan though his heart clamoured for it.

'You may all leave,' he commanded. 'Only Sati need remain. We thank you for your help. You shall be suitably rewarded.' A devil inside him shrieked, You are all responsible, why do you not save her? He jerked his head back at Wazir Khan. 'Please be within call, Hakim.'

He calmly waited until the tent was empty. Should he ask to see the baby? It was not important. She was probably being breast-fed by a wet nurse even at this moment, sucking away at the sustenance of her own life after bringing death to her mother. Finally, only Sati remained, standing respectfully at the far corner of the room, a veiled figure in a *chador* echoing the deep vibrance of tragedy.

He looked towards the divan bed, where his beloved lay still beneath the bed clothes. A sense of unreality gripped him. This could not be happening. It must be a dream.

'My beloved husband, I kneel to you in my heart . . .' The words were whispered in a voice so weak it tore at his brain. Absurdly, it spun him back to the time she had been so sick with their first baby. The happy time.

'Oh heart of mine!' He rushed to the divan bed, knelt beside it, fearfully touched the dark hair, breathed the sick-smelling sweat on her head. Her face was pale and drawn, her breathing shallow. Black hollows beneath the closed eyes accentuated gaunt cheeks. 'Heart of mine!' he repeated, his own heart near breaking.

'Why, my love?' Her eyelids trembled, fluttered, opened. He gazed in horror at the glazing brown eyes of a dying doe.

The tremendous effort she had made to respond to him carried through. 'I am going, Shah Jahan.' He had to bend forward to hear the words. 'But I . . . shall never . . . leave you.' A long pause, deeper breathing. She swallowed to speak again. 'Promise me two things.'

'Anything, anything,' he declared hoarsely.

'Prince Dara . . . our . . . our eldest is to be your heir.' She swallowed again, her face twisting with pain. 'If any other of . . . our sons fights for the crown . . .' She raised her head, fire sparked for an instant in her eyes. 'Kill him . . .' Her eyelids drooped shut, her head flopped back. Even that slight effort had been exhausting. 'Your oath . . .' she murmured.

'My oath on it.' The royal plurals were forgotten. The Emperor was on his knees to the higher king, love, but with a parched, aching throat, a stifled chest and a raw brain.

'Good . . . good.' She seemed to fade back to semi-consciousness.

'The other thing you wanted,' he prompted, the words ending in a sob. 'Mumtaz . . .'

'What, my love?' Her eyes suddenly opened again. 'Yes, the second thing.' She smiled, a hint of the old elf in her expression. 'Place my ashes somewhere really beautiful, so all men will know how much I loved you.' The words came out crystal clear, as if she were not sick at all.

His whole being clamoured to say, You shall not die . . . Please, please don't leave me . . . I cannot live without you. But the dread truth slowly spread inside him, chill as a tomb.

'I swear I shall build you the finest memorial in the history of man,' he promised, the words gentle but firm. 'It shall endure forever. And all who see it will say with awe, *this* is Mumtaz Mahal. She and her love inspired the eternal love of a man, who happened also to be Emperor.'

'Good. I like that.' She smiled and closed her eyes. 'Both promises.'

As the hours passed, Mumtaz Mahal drifted in and out of consciousness and spasms of pain. He knelt beside her in torment, wanting every precious moment with her. Whenever she was lucid, they murmured the dear, sweet words of lovers. He would stroke her hair tenderly, place his cheek lightly against hers, kiss her hands. He longed with his whole being for her to caress his face, to feel her cool fingers on his fevered brow. He knew she did not have the strength. What would he do without the one human being who cared for him as a person? To whom alone he could show his love?

He wanted to blubber, to weep continuously with a puckered face, devoid of tears, like a child. His last weeping had been at his grandfather's deathbed. He had given the dying man his oath that he would never weep again. His oath, his sacred oath! What good was any of it? He would not weep now, but only because his grief went deeper than the wellsprings of tears.

And all the while, Sati, the other mother, stood out of earshot at the far end of the tent, a silent symbol of his own grief.

He was barely conscious of the lightening of the earth. Mumtaz Mahal's eyes opened in one swift moment. They were clear again. The elfin smile appeared, crinkled her eyes. Hope touched his spirit. She was going to live. As if a shutter had been moved, her eyes became fixed, staring, blank.

She was dead.

Some hidden power of love had enabled her to give him that one last moment of grace.

He requested Sati to leave the tent, closing the flap behind her.

For a day and a night, he sat alone with the dead body of Mumtaz Mahal. He talked to her at times, reliving the past, sharing the future, until some wave of tenderness moved him to touch her face and jerk his hand away at its coldness.

He knew his mind was unhinged, but he did not care. Better madness with Mumtaz Mahal than sanity alone.

Twenty-four hours after she died, the madness left him. He kissed her chill, hard lips without even the hope of a single breath. He rose to his feet and stumbled out of his tent into the grey dawn.

He walked with lagging steps to his own tent, followed by General Wahid. 'We are not to be disturbed by anyone,' he commanded the General. 'Not for anything at all. Arrange for the body of the Empress to be prepared and placed in a gold casket with a white satin lining. It shall

671

accompany us wherever we go until it reaches the last resting place which we shall create for it.'

He stumbled into the gloom of his own tent.

For seven days and nights, he remained alone in there, without food, sipping an occasional fruit juice for sustenance. The only sound that emerged from the tent was his almost continuous moaning.

On the eighth morning, the Emperor emerged from the tent, blinking at the warm, silver sunlight.

General Wahid, who had been standing by during the entire period, came forward, saluted and paused in shocked disbelief. This was not the Emperor, nor even a man, but a creature with a bent back and staring eyes, looking smaller in stature. His raven black hair had turned completely white.

'We wish to renounce the imperial throne.' Shah Jahan barely whispered the words.

General Wahid eyed him sternly. 'Sire, you and your revered lady who has just passed away have endured too much for you to toss the imperial crown away as if it were some worthless bauble. Too many men have died for their faith in you and what you can do for the Empire. The fate of millions more is in your hands. A hundred years ago, I presumed to jolt you back to your duty when temptation faced you. I presume to do so again today. The Empress is even now in Paradise. Would you diminish her enjoyment of the eternal bliss she has earned by entering a hell of your own making?'

PART VI

The Eighth Wonder

Chapter 43

General Wahid's words jolted the Emperor Jahan with the force of a lightning bolt. They brought him back to a world of reality as the general had done in Lahore all those years ago, when a young prince had lost touch with reality before the spell of the dancer, Nadia. He had sworn to himself then that he would never be less than any other man, yet here he was again, less than this brave, loyal warrior.

As he met the general's unwavering gaze, he suddenly found himself staring at the Emperor Akbar. If he had to be diminished, who better than this man to be diminished by. He straightened his shoulders. Through the miasma of his whirling brain, he knew with white certainty what his dead Mumtaz Mahal and countless others, living and dead, expected of him.

I shall let it be known throughout the world, he thought, and in the annals of history, that a man died with his wife on the ninth day of June in the Christian year 1631, leaving behind an Emperor.

The Emperor decreed an indefinite period of mourning for the entire Empire, forbidding all popular music and public amusement, all use of cosmetics, perfume, jewellery and brightly coloured clothes; he himself would wear nothing but white during the period. Offenders would be brought before the Magistrates. If found guilty of disrespect to the dead Empress, they would be executed.

If a dead man has to play the role of Emperor for the people, let the people share his torment.

The tragic miracle which turned his hair white overnight

was a gift from Mumtaz Mahal, pointing the direction in which some solace might lie. The hair of Ustad Isa, the architect from Shiraz, had also turned white the day his own wife died. Ustad Isa and he, linked by the common bond of their tragedies, could create the memorial he had promised Mumtaz Mahal, the building of which would bring some lightening of his torment. New purpose could be the antidote to his soul-shattering grief.

But in order to ensure that the monument would not merely be a wonder of the world, but would *be* Mumtaz Mahal herself, revealing the depths of her character and her swiftly changing moods, the Emperor decided to pay renowned architects from all parts of the world to come to Agra and submit their schematic designs so that he could choose the best of them. He had messages sent to Bandara in Ceylon, Veroneo of Venice, Ahmed in Lahore, requesting them to arrive in Agra by January the next year, to prepare designs.

Until then, he unleashed attacks of savage fury on the Deccanese rebels, personally leading his men into battle, inviting death.

One month after Mumtaz Mahal died, the Emperor took Buran, but Prince Lodi escaped and was reported on his way to Daul, Ahmad or Bija.

They say that death goes in threes, the Emperor reflected, when Sati, Mumtaz Mahal's 'other mother' died. The purpose of her life ended, she succumbed to a slight infection. The previous day his most loyal subject, friend and constant companion, General Wahid, had also died, of wounds sustained during the final assault on Buran. What a sadly historic place Buran had become.

In January 1632 the Emperor returned to Agra completely victorious, the entire Deccan under total subjection to a Moghul Emperor for the first time in history.

He had Mumtaz Mahal's coffin placed in a special crypt in the Agra palace while he examined the preliminary design concepts of the four architects. Veroneo's was too ornate and European and did not capture the spirit of Mumtaz Mahal. Ahmed's design proved to be parochial Indian, whereas the grieving Shah Jahan sought something universal. Bandara's concept was a masterpiece of tranquillity; the huge bell-shaped dagoba of Sinhala Buddhist architecture, with its grand pinnacle and spire thrusting, like Mumtaz Mahal's soul, towards heaven, was classic in concept. Yet this image too was foreign to the genius of Moghul India.

Ustad Isa, however, produced the perfect blend of Moghul and Indian. Yet it was at the same time universal, the concept chaste but with a quiet magnificence and the elusive elfin quality that characterized Mumtaz Mahal. It seemed to represent the lost love of all bereaved men, not a monument but a memorial to every unfulfilled longing. Three weeks later excavation for the building commenced.

During the first four years of his reign, the Emperor had commissioned so many major works that he already had in Agra the finest engineers, carvers and stonemasons of the world, including the stonecutter Amir Ali from Balkh. Now, he sent for others to join in his endeavour.

Ismail Effendi of Turkey, designer of hemispheres and builder of domes.

Qasim Khan of Lahore, the famous worker with precious metals, who would cast the solid gold finials to crown Ismail Effendi's domes.

Chiranji Lal from Delhi, the lapidary who would be his chief mosaicist.

Mukarrimat Khan, whom Ustad Isa recommended from his native Shiraz, and the veteran Abdul Karim, whom his father used a great deal, would oversee finances and supervise day-to-day construction.

Amanat Khan, the master calligrapher, also from Shiraz, would adorn the façade and the burial chamber with Arabic lettering, assisted by Mohamed Khan of Baghdad and Roshan Khan of Syria and the Arab Zeman Khan.

Inlayers from South India, a specialist in building turrets, another who carved marble floors.

Red sandstone from local quarries; marble from the hills of Makran; jade and crystal from China; turquoise from Tibet; lapis lazuli from Afghanistan; crysolite from Egypt; rare shells, corals, mother-of-pearl from the Indian Ocean; topaz, onyx, garnets, sapphires, blood-stones, forty-three different types of gems from all over Asia.

He would bring the talent and wealth of an entire world to lay at the feet of Mumtaz Mahal.

He would create another Moghul legacy, this one dedicated to true love, which, in honour of his lost love, he would call 'Crown of the Palace' or Taj Mahal.

Abdul Karim estimated that twenty thousand workers with their families would be needed to build the Taj. In addition to the capital from his Treasury, Shah Jahan endowed the revenues of thirty villages to sustain the city, complete with dwellings, warehouses, bazaars and entertainment centres, that would accommodate these people.

He was on his annual visit to Nur Jehan in Lahore, the fourth since she had changed from a resident in the Srinagar palace, ruling an Empire, to a lonely widow living in a large house near the Lahore palace, filling her days with sweet works and bitter regrets.

Rana Chara made it a point to see Nur Jehan regularly not from any feelings of loyalty or compassion, but because he believed that she would somehow be one of the causes of the effects he hoped to bring about on Shah Jahan. The Emperor had been foolish to heed his advice and not have Nur Jehan put to death. If he, Rana Chara, had become

Emperor, he would either have had Nur Jehan executed or made her his Prime Minister!

Nur Jehan had used her ingenuity and wealth to convert the two-storey house she occupied into a miniature palace. The dining room in which they sat tonight, after his superb dinner, was furnished in European style, with a large oval table in the centre, twelve straight-backed chairs and chiffoniers against the walls, all of dark Indian mahogany. The chairs were upholstered in white satin brocade, matching the white marble floors covered by a large dark red Venetian carpet. Sparkling crystal lamps were reflected in gilt mirrors adorning the walls. Ivory and gold ornaments on the chiffoniers glittered with the emeralds and rubies that encrusted them, which lapis lazuli statuettes helped to subdue. Through the open windows, the courtyard was a fairyland of pools and fountains beneath red and green lamps hanging from the dark branches of trees that bordered it.

She must have caught his renewed appreciation of her creations. 'I have come to believe that the essence of art can never be exposed by spending money on vulgar ostentation,' she quietly commented. They had come to drop the royal plurals in private conversation with each other. Also, since she was head of this household, she made her own rules of social conduct, within the requirements of *purdah*, so she would sit with him while he dined, but would not share the meal, because eating would require her to remove her veil. 'I have always found joy in creating works of art.'

'Like your attar-of-roses perfume and this unique meal,' he responded. 'Each time you come up with something even more extraordinary. Tonight, you have taken me on a rare adventure of the oceans, the air and the earth, from oysters to quail and locusts, from plovers' eggs to lamb.'

'I find time nowadays for some of the things I really enjoy. Your advice to me through the years was right and has had its effect. I have exchanged the delights of the trappings of power for the power of God's trappings. I find much pleasure in little things which I now pause to savour.'

Rana Chara tapped the mahogany table gently in applause. 'There is a balance in all things,' he declared. 'The human brain has certain capacities for enjoyment. When we let go our pursuit of material things and ambition, a void is created in that part of the brain, which has to be filled. Other things can then flood in and we can fill that void through expanding joy from little things, like the touch of cold marble to bare feet on a warm day, the scent of a single jasmine or the cooing of a solitary dove. It is the difference between the diffused delight of seeing a whole bed of flowers, and the concentrated ecstasy from a single red rose with a dew drop on it. True epicurean delight lies in the depths of the exquisite, not in the breadth of the splendid. So too with power.' He smiled cynically. 'One single bowel movement is more satisfying than giving an entire Empire indigestion.'

Her mellow laugh rippled out freely from behind her *yashmak*. It pleased him. Pity I am a homosexual, he thought. You and I could have shared many an emotional delight. 'It was fortunate for both of us that the Emperor was alive at the height of your power.' He grinned. 'If we had got together, you and I, we might have been cursed with an Empire on our hands.'

He caught her wistfulness. This time, her laugh was somewhat forced. 'You are laughing from the dictates of good manners,' he interjected. 'Not because your life's course has earned it. When you can laugh at your bitter experiences, you will have achieved the next level of your liberation.'

'Misery frequently goes well with the way we Muslim women do our hair,' she rejoined, more light-heartedly. 'Which is why we hide it under the veil!' She paused. 'But you are right. If I had joined forces with you, we could have achieved supreme power.'

'And been consumed by it. People imagine that power is something that only flows outwards from one's grasp. Very much to the contrary, for here too we have the balance of life. Each experience of power seeps a like amount inwards, to seize us in its own grip, so to the exact extent that we make others the victims of our power, we in turn become its prisoner. It is essential for our well-being to accept circumstances, to let go the things for which we crave. We should not strive for entities but for a deliberate acceptance of life, without effort, fulfilling our duties but not fighting for rights we can never possess. Then we will be happy all the time. Think of yourself as being in the eye of a hurricane, with the wind and noise, dust and confusion, alarm and terror swirling all round you, while you are at peace. Then you can enjoy the grandeur of those seemingly adverse circumstances. Like pain, which is physical, mental or emotional. If you have a backache, it is unbearable at first, but when a few hours have gone by, you find yourself barely conscious of it. Or a grievous loss, which you suddenly find you have lived through. All pain is a message to the brain. It is possible for us to accept the message, to say, yes I have received the cry for help from an organ, the mind, or the heart, I am conscious of it, but I can do nothing about it, so it now exists outside the inner me which remains happy every conscious second.' He realized that one of the reasons why he enjoyed her company was because she listened to his philosophy with interest, not because he was the Rana addressing one of his subjects. She comprehended his statements immediately.

The hoot of an owl poised above the croak of frogs outside, followed by the chink . . . chink of a cobra. 'My protector!' she exclaimed. 'Perhaps it is a reminder to me that it is you who now protects me with the hood of your wisdom.'

He was touched. 'If it has been of service to you, Madam, then whatever wisdom I have will not have been in vain. And yet, we must always remember not to relinquish *everything* we desire, like vengeance, for instance. The art of vengeance is to watch the individual wreak it on himself.' He ran a deliberate thumbnail beneath his moustache, remembering similar advice he had given Shah Jahan about her nearly five years earlier. 'Take Shah Jahan, for instance. The tragedy of his life was not the death of his wife, but the effect of that loss. For he is now heading towards the end of his power. His desire to build a memorial of surpassing beauty has become so overwhelming that it has acquired a life of its own. The original cause has been taken over by its consequent purpose, which is now in the process of destroying lives.'

'How so?'

'With any human being an aim becomes an ambition, an ambition a compulsion, a compulsion an obsession, which can only destroy that human being. Imagine the vast numbers of men and the quantities of material needed to build what Shah Jahan calls the Taj Mahal. I mean, twenty thousand men alone to be fed, clothed, housed and paid wages for endless years. A huge army, on top of all the imperial forces he must maintain.'

'All of it will cost far more than his personal treasury and the Empire's revenues can sustain.'

She had caught on instantly, he noted. And why not? She had years of experience with an Emperor's budgets, most of them under the guidance of one of the most astute financiers ever, her father, Ghiyas Beg.

'The only way Shah Jahan is going to be able to meet all this expenditure is by taxing the people,' she continued. 'He will have to bleed them. And he is the man who once

682

protested against the taxes I imposed in the Deccan! After the people are bled, he will need increases in his standing armies, to hold down the revolts of the poor, bloodless wretches, so he will have to bleed others yet, all of it the continuing vicious cycle of a debtor who keeps borrowing to service his debt!'

'Meanwhile, his preoccupation with his dream, so characteristic of the Moghuls, will cause him to remain in Agra, watching that dream come to life, seeking out others to quell the people's inevitable rebellions against overwhelming taxes.' He eyed her levelly. 'Which is why I am grooming the one candidate who will ensure the effects you and I desire for these causes. It will take time, but it will happen. The day he calls on his sons to lead his armies so that he can remain in Agra to watch his monument grow, you and I will hear the fanfare of trumpets heralding his doom. Not even his precious daughter, Princess Jahanara, who has emerged from the obscurity of the *harem* to rule it for him, will be able to save him.'

'I had heard that the little nothing has become queen of the *harem* by default since the death of Mumtaz Mahal has not driven Shah Jahan to the pleasures of other women's bedding.'

'He has become wedded to Mumtaz Mahal's memorial.'

Chapter 44

Asaf Khan's face was unwontedly grim when he gave Shah Jahan the news at his *durbar* in the audience hall of the Agra palace that evening. Eight years into his reign and Asaf Khan, who had grown older gracefully, was still his Prime Minister.

In embellishing the palace, Shah Jahan had covered the red sandstone parapet of the balcony that housed the pavilion built by the Emperor Akbar with pink marble and it was on the peacock throne of his own creation that he sat cross-legged.

Shah Jahan was in no mood today to consider any news bad. 'Peace reigns throughout our territories, Prime Minister,' he declared. 'We subdued the Deccan, the Punjab and the north-west, with armies we personally led. Our forces under General Qasim drove the Portuguese out of Bengal, bringing four thousand prisoners across the continent to be paraded before us here in Agra.' He smiled at the recollection, for the Portuguese had refused to help him when he was so desperately in need while in exile in Bengal. 'Serve the bastards right.' He nodded to acknowledge the sycophantic titters that arose from the gaudily dressed courtiers and nobles standing in order of rank in the huge hall below him. He fleetingly remembered a prince who was once the epitome of refined speech, but that prince had died in a tent in Buran. 'Our Empire is well under control. Why then do you look disturbed? Give us your report and we shall prove to you that you are worried by shadows.' He lifted his eyebrows inquiringly.

'Your Imperial Majesty, may we discuss my news in private?'

Shah Jahan gestured grandly towards those assembled below him. 'Any news concerning the Empire affects these, our loyal subjects. Even if our planning has to be done behind closed doors, we shall share the events of our realms with *all* our subjects. You may therefore speak freely.'

'Very well then, Sire.' Asaf Khan did not hide his displeasure well. 'Raja Jhujhan of Orchha, whose territory is, as you know, but one hundred miles from Agra, has been growing so steadily in wealth and power that he built himself two magnificent palaces in Orchha and Datia. He has once again refused to pay the imperial taxes, claiming that his people have already been bled to death. Meanwhile, the Deccan too is simmering once again for the same reason.'

Asaf Khan had repeatedly warned him in recent years of the harsh effects of his taxation policy, but he had chosen to ignore the advice. 'What is your solution, Prime Minister?' Shah Jahan demanded impatiently.

'We can send punitive expeditions to bring rebellious rajas, ranas and sultans to heel, but that will be removing the symptoms, without curing the disease.' Asaf Khan's response, though quiet, was delivered in clear tones. 'The disease is a people brought to their knees by the burden of taxation. Millions are starving. Others have left their ancestral land holdings and become nomads, because they can no longer afford to pay our tithes and taxes. Whole villages have been evacuated, leaving vast regions desolate. In days gone by, when there was drought, famine or pestilence, the Emperor opened up his private treasury to provide the people with grain, but we have remained aloof because we ourselves are the instruments of their misery. Nor do we suffer any more from merely sporadic disasters.' A bitter note entered his voice. 'It will take as many years to restore the prosperity of these regions as it did in Rajasthan after we devastated the kingdoms, or in Agra following the looting and plunder of General Vickram's and Raja Bhim's Rajputs.'

This bold reminder of the atrocities he himself had commanded roused Shah Jahan's wrath. His former father-in-law was attempting to berate him, the Emperor, in public? But he had invited plain speech. Besides, the Prime Minister had always been palpably honest. He might dismiss Asaf Khan some day, but not yet. 'We are taxing the people fairly to build them a monument of which they can all be proud,' he asserted, holding back his anger.

'When the Taj Mahal has been completed, the burden of taxation will end.'

Asaf Khan hesitated, ran a forefinger thoughtfully beneath his moustache, now fully silver. The blue eyes flashed when he made up his mind. 'With due respect, Your Imperial Majesty, the Taj Mahal is a memorial to your late Empress, who was also my daughter. She would never have desired it to be built on the foundations of human misery.'

'Have a care, Prime Minister,' Shah Jahan growled, his voice low. He remembered his promise to the dying Mumtaz Mahal, but his obsession set aside its intent. That promise had been the key to the door of his life. His love for Mumtaz Mahal was as undying as his need for her, a need that had not diminished through the years, but had merely grown more bearable to live with because of his marriage to the Taj Mahal, which had even kept him celibate all these years. How dare Asaf Khan speak to him of Mumtaz Mahal's desires? He was about to issue a harsh rejoinder when Asaf Khan turned his head slightly. Something about the cheek bones flashed a reminder of his beloved through his brain, searing it in an agony of recall. 'Our Imperial Diwan, whose name inappropriately is Wazir, which means Prime Minister,' he smiled at his oft-repeated joke, 'assures us that, having purchased most of the material needed for the actual building, we will soon need less revenues for the work until the time comes to decorate the interiors. We shall therefore reduce our taxes in the affected areas. Does that satisfy you?' He cocked an eyebrow at Asaf Khan, waved a graceful, heavily bejew-elled finger at the murmur of applause from below. 'We look after our subjects.'

The Prime Minister continued to seem troubled. 'It is something, Sire, but only you in your infinite wisdom can decide whether it is enough.'

'Almighty Allah has granted us infinite wisdom, which is why he placed us on this throne.' Shah Jahan glanced around him at the glittering emeralds and rubies that formed his pavilion, then down at the jewels encrusting his robe so heavily that he had had to be supported by his aides from his robing room to the throne. He was indeed the Chosen of Allah. An insidious thought from the days of his exile intruded to mock him: you are an imperial peacock on your peacock throne! He flung the thought away angrily. He was no peacock strutting around the palace garden, but an Emperor given to ruling with strength. 'As for what you call the symptoms of the disease, Prime Minister, we would have you know that we are the imperial physician of last resort, blessed by God with sons who are now of age. Prince Aurang is sixteen years old. It is time he proved himself. Let it be recorded that, in the Christian year 1635, he led his first military expedition, an imperial army, to Orchha to drive Raja Jhujhan from his palaces.' Rana Chara had first suspected this.

'Sire.' Asaf Khan's voice held respectful protest. 'I beg you to remember that history repeats itself. Surely it is your eldest son, Prince Dara, who should lead this expedition.'

'No. Prince Dara remains at our side, assisting us with the government of the Empire.' He would not confess to anyone the reasons for this decision. Prince Dara, whose marriage to Princess Nadira he had arranged that year to keep him settled in Agra, was so like his mother in appearance that it inspired him to have the young man's constant presence while he watched his beloved Taj Mahal slowly rise. Also, from the experience of his own youth, he believed uncompromisingly that the eldest son and heir should always be beside the Emperor, against the eventuality of the Emperor's unexpected death. This was the line of succession he had promised Mumtaz Mahal on her death bed. This was what he himself wanted with all his heart.

'But, Your Imperial Majesty,' Asaf Khan began.

The Emperor held up his hand for silence. Vaguely a recollection of the resemblance between himself, Prince Aurang, the Emperor Jehangir and the Emperor Akbar disturbed him, but he quickly assured himself that this was only in looks, not in temperaments or ambition. 'We would lead the army to Orchha ourself,' he asserted, 'for the thrill of battle calls.' He paused deliberately. 'Sadly, a sterner duty demands our constant presence in Agra, the creation of God that *is* India, that nothing and nobody shall stop, the Taj Mahal, which shall endure forever as the Moghul legacy.'

Rana Chara had received news of Prince Aurang's campaign from the Emperor without amazement. Prince Aurang was a true Moghul, cast in the great Moghul mould. Rana Chara's influence on him had been subtly and cunningly exercised through the years, because that was the only way in which the proud, headstrong Moghul prince could be manipulated. It had, however, made him the only person whom the young prince trusted.

As he sat in the European room with Shah Jahan, Rana Chara's mind went back many years to another such morning in this same palace, when the Emperor Akbar had talked to him. That was when he had been plotting to have the boy Prince Jahan kidnapped and killed.

'Your recommendation that our son lead the expedition against Raja Jhujhan was admirable.' Shah Jahan opened the main conversation without preamble. 'As you know, Prince Aurang cut his way through impenetrable forests,' a slight exaggeration with which Rana Chara could find no fault, 'and took the Orchha palace, located on a monkey-infested peninsula, within a few months. Raja Jhujhan fled south and we spared ourself from our duties here in Agra to join the prince. Although we do not have the time to spare for a campaign, we moved with him against the Deccan, and our very presence with such a powerful military force caused the rulers of Bija and Golkonda to sign treaties of allegiance.' He pushed forward the leg he favoured, straightened his head from its slight sideways tilt, scratched his white hair. 'We owed a great debt of gratitude to the former ruler of Golkonda, who assisted us most nobly when we were in exile, so we gave his son easier terms.'

It would not have been so easy for you if General Malik Ambar were alive, Rana Chara thought. 'We understand you left Prince Aurang behind in command of the Deccan when you returned, Sire.'

'Yes, he was needed there, while our presence here is even more vital.' Shah Jahan smiled deprecatingly. 'Our architect, Ustad Isa, will not move hand or foot without us.'

'That is perfectly understandable,' Rana Chara responded smoothly. 'For the Taj Mahal is *your* creation. We would like to make another suggestion, Sire.'

'Certainly. Your wisdom is of the utmost importance in our deliberations. And after all, we two have been brothers since the Mewar campaign ended.'

And you left my land devastated, with me and my fellow Rajputs enduring eternal shame, Rana Chara thought fiercely, but without heat. 'Being in command of an entire region that has been traditionally hostile to Moghul rule, Prince Aurang faces an extraordinarily difficult and complex assignment. It is now eighteen months since you despatched him to Orchha and look what he has achieved already with your help and guidance. Would it not be wise to appoint Prince Aurang Viceroy of the Deccan?'

'What?' The question emerged like a musket shot.

The scar down Rana Chara's cheek itched. He fingered it unconsciously. 'You heard us, Sire.' He eyed Shah Jahan levelly. 'It would be a fitting reward for the prince's services, while giving him the power to govern without turning constantly to Agra for decisions.' He added his shrewdest thrust. 'It would also enable you to spend your time in Agra without having to travel frequently to the Deccan.'

Shah Jahan blinked once before comprehension dawned on his face. The strong nostrils distended with pleasure. He raised a hand sparkling with jewelled rings in acknowledgement. 'A splendid idea, Rana,' he stated warmly. 'We are most obliged to you for your fraternal concern. We shall issue the imperial *firman* this very morning.'

Rana Chara contrived to have the last word. 'Your decision will give all India much pleasure, Sire. Your peoples share your interests in the well-being of the kingdoms and the magnificent monument you are building is for us all.' Knowing what Shah Jahan considered the Taj Mahal to be, he deliberately added, 'The Moghul legacy.'

The report from Kandhar had placed Shah Jahan in a quandary. 'Just when we have established peace in the Deccan and our son, Prince Aurang, has restored good government there as Viceroy, the product of a sow's tits from Persia has to turn the north-west into a sty,' he flamed.

He was in private conference with Asaf Khan in the French room of the Agra palace that morning.

The Prime Minister shrugged slim shoulders beneath a finely tailored gold tunic. 'That is part of your imperial honour, Sire,' he responded, good-humouredly. 'If you will recall, it was the Emperor Akbar, may the Lord rest his soul in Paradise, who said that if a ruler has no wars on his hands, he should create them, to keep his armies active and give his mercenaries opportunities for loot!' His expression turned grave on the instant, in the quick change of mood Shah Jahan knew to be characteristic of him. 'Which reminds me that I have received disturbing reports from the Deccan as well. Your Imperial Majesty's Viceroy has commenced desecrating every place of Hindu worship in his territory, allegedly on a plan evolved by his chief *imam* Nazrullah.'

It was a relief for Shah Jahan to direct his attention from the threat at hand even for a few moments. 'What has he done?' he inquired, without concern.

'The Muslim *izan* has been called from the places where the Hindu temple deities are enshrined. Prayers are being said in your name as the Emperor in the temples, followed by the sacrifice of cows in the holies of holies.'

Shah Jahan recalled Asaf Khan's former protests over the pitiful condition of the over-taxed people of that region. 'Are you complaining that the cows that were sacrificed were not given to feed the poor, starving, over-taxed Hindus?' he inquired maliciously.

The Prime Minister's vivid blue eyes flashed. 'Sire, with all due respect, I submit that these acts of sacrilege cannot be laughed away. Almighty Allah has exalted you to the position of ruler over *all* the Indian people to safeguard the rights of *all* religions and races.'

So I finally got you, Shah Jahan thought with private glee. That will teach you not to preach to me. 'What other horrors has our sacrilegious son perpetrated?' he inquired.

Asaf Khan hesitated. He knew that his report had made no impression. 'Hindu priests and temple caretakers have been deprived of their houses and *jagirs*. They have been commanded not to live within specified distances of their former temples. The images of Hindu gods and goddesses have been smashed and flung into the nearest lake or river. In one temple, the venerated image of the Hindu god Shiva was blackened with coal then smashed to bits with hammers.'

'Very proper!' Shah Jahan commented. 'From the days of Babur, we have destroyed graven images.' He injected a pious note into his voice. 'They contradict the tenets of our religion and are a blasphemy against Almighty Allah.' He was enjoying his Prime Minister's discomfiture. Fleetingly he remembered a boy who once rode each morning on the *maidan* of the Agra palace with a man he admired and hoped would one day be his father-in-law. 'We have also learned that Prince Aurang has discovered a new source of revenues with which to keep his armies happy. Hindu temples have amassed vast quantities of gold and silver over the centuries. When he was alive, our grandfather possessed more gold and silver than all the other Emperors of the world put together, but we understand that Prince Aurang has uncovered more than our grandfather ever owned.'

Asaf Khan's face grew stern. 'Most of your revered ancestors looted places of worship,' he stated sombrely. 'But not your illustrious grandfather, who was a model of tolerance.'

A flash of irritation caused Shah Jahan's temper to explode. 'Stop preaching at us, Prime Minister,' he roared, thumping his thigh with a fist. 'That is not one of your duties.'

'On the contrary, Your Imperial Majesty, as you are well aware, my one concern has always been the Empire and it is my sacred duty to bring to my Emperor's notice anything that affects the peace and well-being of even his humblest subject.' His look was fearless as ever.

'Oh, your infernal addiction to principles!' Shah Jahan sneered.

'Yes, Sire,' Asaf Khan confessed, the admission taking the trot out of Shah Jahan's mount. 'Even if you, in your infinite wisdom, consider the source of my addiction to be the infernal regions.'

'All right then, you have made your report and we shall give it due consideration.' He was not amused by Asaf Khan's attitude, but he needed the man for more important things than reporting the rape of a sacred cow. 'Now, to return to the more pressing matter at hand. Shah Abbas II of Persia has attacked Kandhar again.'

'I am not surprised, Your Imperial Majesty. He probably thought the time was opportune because you were preoccupied with the Deccan. He could not know that you would bring the Deccan campaign to such a speedy and successful conclusion.'

'Oh, you concede then that we and our son Prince Aurang can do *some* things right.' He could not help the jeer, but quickly returned to the subject that had been nagging him. 'We shall send an imperial army of fifty thousand to relieve Kandhar. Order the generals to attend a staff conference in the war room at six tonight.'

'Will Your Imperial Majesty be leading the army?' A hopeful note had entered Asaf Khan's voice.

'Of course not.' Shah Jahan slashed his hand away for emphasis. 'General Mahabat shall lead it.'

'I regret to inform you that General Mahabat is seriously ill.'

'What?' Shah Jahan was dismayed. 'What is wrong with the imperial governor of Ajmer? He has always kept excellent health. This is a passing ailment, perhaps?' He glanced hopefully at the Prime Minister.

'I am afraid not, Sire. General Mahabat suffered a stroke three nights ago, possibly from over-exertion while lying with his young mistress. He is not expected to recover, or to live very long.'

'By the beard of the Prophet, we always suspected that he went at it too hard.' Shah Jahan directed a level glance at Asaf Khan. 'Even with Nur Jehan, though the fornication was never discovered. Oh well, life must go on. Whom do you recommend as leader of the Kandhar expedition?'

'You, Sire.'

'Us? Us? No, no, no. We cannot leave Agra.'

'Your Imperial Majesty, many years ago when Shah Abbas's father threatened Kandhar, your father led a huge army into the north-west. He quickly brought the Persian Emperor to his knees, merely by a show of force. I strongly urge you to do likewise. You can end the Persian invasion by showing the flag, and your personal presence will strike even more terror into the hearts of our enemies than that of your revered father, for you are the greatest military commander of this century.'

The words were so sincerely spoken that they reached the deepest recesses of Shah Jahan's heart. Asaf Khan was never given to idle praise or flattery. His Prime Minister was indeed a treasure, the only man left from the old regiment of his loyal followers, now that General Mahabat was stricken.

'If you desire to complete the Taj Mahal in peace, you must be prepared to go to war, Sire.' Asaf Khan's words added to Shah Jahan's certainty. 'You may never find a more opportune time to strengthen your north-western frontiers. If Shah Abbas II takes Kandhar, Kabul will be lost and the entirety of Afghanistan and the Punjab will be open to him. Having conquered the whole Deccan and brought peace to it, something that none of your illustrious ancestors achieved, you cannot let Kandhar go by default. Since Prince Aurang is Viceroy of the Deccan and Prince Shuja is doing a good job keeping Bengal under control, I submit that only you can lead this expedition, Sire.'

The reluctance to leave his beloved Taj Mahal intruded. 'But our monument requires our personal attention,' he protested, aware that he was vacillating and annoyed at himself for it. 'The body can look after itself only if the heart is sound.'

'By Allah's mercy the Taj Mahal is at a stage of construction which demands your imperial presence less than the frontiers of the Empire,' Asaf Khan urged. 'The building is slowly but surely rising, the staking out of the gardens has been completed. For the next few years, only the completion of the superstructure, the excavation of the gardens and the layout of the irrigation system need to be done. Ustad Isa can surely ensure that all goes well in your absence.'

Asaf Khan had forced him to return to reality. 'You are right, Prime Minister,' Shah Jahan declared. 'We shall personally lead the greatest army the north-west has ever known into Kandhar!'

'And Prince Dara will act as Regent here in Agra during your absence?'

Shah Jahan knew instantly that Asaf Khan was trying to prevent the role of Regent being conferred on Prince Aurang, who had his own ambitions. 'No, Prime Minister, we have another nominee for that post.' He felt a childish desire to play with this self-possessed man.

Asaf Khan's face showed his concern. 'And who may that be, Sire?'

'You.'

'Me?'

Shah Jahan savoured the Prime Minister's shock, noted the way his eyes then lit up with just a hint of pleasure. Asaf Khan never displayed emotion or grief, not even when his daughter died. He nodded at the Prime Minister. 'An excellent choice, don't you think?'

'Admirable, Sire!'

Asaf Khan's quick grin had been his reward. 'Prince Dara shall accompany us on this campaign,' he added. Somehow the words had a historic ring.

Chapter 45

Shah Jahan knew that he took his daughter, Princess Jahanara, very much for granted. Now in the year 1644, having been his best friend for thirteen years since her mother died, at twenty-seven years of age she was at death's door.

Through the years, Shah Jahan had come to depend increasingly on her friendship. She looked more like his side of the family than her mother's. He had sometimes wished that the solid, handsome features, long nose with dilated nostrils, dark slanty eyes and stocky build had been born instead a replica of the elfin Mumtaz Mahal.

On the death of her mother, however, the Princess Jahanara, though barely fifteen at the time, had on her own initiative stepped into the vacuum created in the imperial *harem* and immediately assumed control, with typical Moghul authoritativeness. Since then, she had made his well-being the one goal of her life, even refusing his plans that she get married, because that would diminish what was now her life's work.

She had given Shah Jahan all the female companionship needed, making it easier for him to abstain from the readily available sexual delights of the *harem*, while continuing studiously to fulfil his duty to visit the ladies daily, chat to them and look after their material needs.

'How did it happen?' he demanded furiously of the Chief Eunuch, who had fallen to his knees when the Emperor burst into the familiar reception chamber that had once belonged to Nur Jehan, then Mumtaz Mahal and was now Princess Jahanara's domain.

The man, a black Nubian, rose to his feet, trembling, his shiny, dark face agonized. 'The p-princess was wearing a d-dress of f-fine muslin tonight, Your Imperial Majesty. She thought to p-please you with it at d-dinner. She surveyed herself in the m-mirror, then swung round in a d-dancing motion and a candle on the d-dressing table set her dress on f-fire.'

His breath caught. Oh dear Allah! He remembered the childlike way in which Mumtaz Mahal would pirouette for him when she wore a dress that specially suited her. The ache for his Mumtaz returned. It had not diminished with the years. 'Why was the fire not put out immediately?' he demanded, anger replacing horror.

'The flames burst all over her in a trice, Sire.' The Chief Eunuch had acquired more control over himself now. 'Two maids threw themselves on her to stifle the blaze. They succeeded in doing so, but died in the process.'

Oh, how pitiful. He could not be angry any longer.

'And the princess?'

'Is in grave condition, despite the best efforts of the Court physicians.'

'Is she in severe pain?' His breath caught with the realization of how precious his daughter was to him. She was all he had. How dearly he loved her!

'She is unconscious, under sedation, Sire.'

'Thanks be to Allah for that. We must see her immediately.'

'Sire, the l-laws of the Koran,' the Chief Eunuch began in timorous protest. 'They are laid d-down by the *imams* . . .'

'Damn the *imams* and the sacred Koran. Lead us to our daughter.'

Extracts from the Diary of Shah Jahan

Though my beloved daughter's entire body has been so terribly burned, by Allah's grace her face has been spared.

But for what? To be a corpse with a living face? I have never realized until now how much I love and need her.

What is it about fate that forces me repeatedly to my knees beside the death beds of those I love? First the Emperor Akbar, next my Mumtaz Mahal, now my devoted daughter. The wellsprings of grief are beneath us, I have discovered. They flood the same for grandfather, wife, or daughter.

I have taken up residence in the *harem*, leaving it only to attend my daily *durbar* and for my visits to the construction site. In the *harem*, I am constantly on my knees, praying to Almighty Allah for Jahanara's deliverance from death. I rise from my knees only to eat and sleep.

General Mahabat is dead. Oh dear Allah, help me. Do not take my daughter from me too. I cannot stand another calamity. In this, I am no Emperor, merely a human supplicant, like the millions of other human beings under my rule. I shall not demean myself or Thee by making promises, or offering vows. I only pray for Thy mercy. Take this bitter cup from my lips.

I have sent for my sons, Prince Shuja in Bengal and Prince Aurang in the Deccan, to join their eldest brother Prince Dara and me in Agra, so we can unite in prayer at their sister's bedside. Being one family under God, we must be together at such times of torment and perhaps our joint prayers will reach the Almighty sooner than the single cry of a fearful heart.

Noting the stubborn set of Prince Aurang's features, Shah Jahan was reminded of himself in youth. Since living in the *harem*, he had begun using Princess Jahanara's reception chamber for private audiences. The blue pool at the entrance with its sparkling silver fountain, the huge Persian carpet, the gold-upholstered divans, the whistling of love-birds in the sunlit courtyard outside and especially the attar-of-roses scent from the smoking incense braziers were frequent reminders of Nur Jehan and the days when he was a member of her Cabinet. This morning, noting Prince Aurang's obvious disagreement with his wishes, Shah Jahan also remembered his own rebellion against Nur Jehan.

'The people of the Deccan should not be compelled to pay taxes for the implementation of imperial policies that will not bring them direct benefits, Sire,' Prince Aurang stated flatly.

The familiar words tumbled Shah Jahan's memory back many years to the morning when he himself had protested against Nur Jehan's decision to tax the Deccan, but he would not be diverted from his course today. 'The Empire is a single entity, Prince,' he stated, mildly because recollection of the past made him somewhat sympathetic towards Prince Aurang's feelings. 'The Deccan benefits from the prosperity of the other principalities, so it must contribute to the whole.' He turned towards his eldest son. 'What do you say, Prince Dara?' Aware of the latent hostility between the two brothers, he could always depend on one of them to support any of his policies with which the other did not immediately agree. It amused him to play one brother off against the other, but he also had a very practical purpose in fomenting their jealousy. It would prevent their uniting to seize his throne.

'Your divine wisdom always gives you divine inspiration, Your Imperial Majesty!' Prince Dara exclaimed.

Prince Aurang's eyes flashed. He leaned forward in his settle. 'Even God extends his mercy towards suffering people,' he declared. 'My people . . .' The word 'my' had escaped without thought. He became conscious of it instantly, noted the lift of Shah Jahan's eyebrows and deflected its impact. '. . . The people whom you have entrusted to my care, Sire, should not be taxed any more. They have very little left to give.'

'Their taxes help defray the cost of our revered mother's tomb,' Prince Dara asserted hotly. Shah Jahan noted the quick glance in his direction for approval. 'The Taj Mahal will belong to all the people of India, so the Deccan must

699

contribute towards it.' He was mouthing Shah Jahan's words.

Shah Jahan realized that Prince Dara had shrewdly cornered his brother, who would not dare to criticize the building of the Taj Mahal, knowing how dear it was to his Emperor's heart. He decided to watch the verbal tug-of-war for a while, without intruding his authority.

'When people are dead of starvation and disease they will never appreciate monuments, not even their own tombstones,' Prince Aurang retorted bitterly.

This was too much. 'You are overstepping the bounds of respect for our policies, Prince Aurang.' Shah Jahan could barely suppress the anger that suddenly flooded him. 'We and we alone decide on the fiscal policies of the Empire. We encourage free speech from you, but beware of insolence. It can have grave consequences even for one of the Emperor's sons.' He abruptly changed the subject. 'Your sister's condition shows slight improvement this morning.'

'Praise be to Almighty Allah!' Prince Dara exclaimed fervently.

'In that case, may I have your leave to return to Bundel in the Deccan without delay?' Prince Aurang demanded.

Shah Jahan still kept his temper in check. 'We have all been united here as a family because of your sister's tragic accident,' he stated. 'She is not yet out of danger. Why do you seek to run away at the first glimmer of hope?'

'Do I have your permission to speak out, Sire?'

'You certainly do, Prince, so long as whatever you have to say is reasonable and couched in respectful terms.'

'Then I respectfully submit to you that a greater call of duty exists for Prince Shuja and me. He is Governor of Bengal and, by your grace, I am Viceroy of the Deccan. The best way in which we can serve you is by returning to our duties without delay.'

'You hold your appointments by virtue of your family

connections, so your first duty should be to your family.' Shah Jahan's voice was quiet but he deliberately gave it a dangerous edge.

'I would like to think that Prince Shuja and I have earned our appointments.' Prince Aurang was twenty-six and quite fearless.

'What is more important to you than your sister's life?'

'My father's well-being, Sire, and the lives of the millions of people I govern on his behalf.'

'You are getting close to presumption.'

'I submit that it is not I but the truth that seems presumptuous.'

'You are concerned about the effect of our taxes on the people you govern?'

'Yes, Sire.'

Shah Jahan finally exploded. 'Then why have you robbed their temples and levied your own taxes to enrich your private treasury?' he roared. 'Do you think that we are unaware of all your activities, because we are so far away? You sit there preaching about the lot of your people. Who are they? The Hindus, whose temples you have desecrated? Why do you not give them relief from the wealth you have accumulated from them? What kind of hypocrite are you?'

Prince Aurang relapsed into a tightlipped silence.

'Answer us!' Shah Jahan roared again. 'You are a person with loyalty to no one, not to your family, not to those of your subjects who cannot be of use to you, only to yourself.'

Prince Aurang flushed. 'I submit that I have been loyal to you, Sire, and have risked my life many times for it.'

'Never for us. Whatever you have done has been to further your own ambitions.'

'Are we not all men of ambition, Sire?' Prince Aurang flared, obviously stung.

'Success has gone to your head,' Shah Jahan stated,

forcing himself to a deadly calm. 'It is time we restored you to sanity.' He paused, to regain control of his voice. 'You wish to return to Bundel?'

'Yes, Sire.' There was a defiant lift to Prince Aurang's head.

'You shall leave immediately.' His smile was deadly. 'But in your personal capacity. You are no longer our Viceroy.'

Prince Aurang had arrived at the Chitor palace unannounced – a measure of his trust in Rana Chara – on his way back to the Deccan. The Rajput made a point of dining alone with the young man that night, in order to discover the reason for the unexpected visit.

The attendants cleared the dining table and left them alone, with the gold salvers containing *pan* on the Indian mahogany table and the porcelain coffee cups emitting their delicious aroma.

'Well, Viceroy, now that we are through with the formalities of good manners and good cheer, tell us what brings you here as our most welcome guest.'

Prince Aurang sprang unexpectedly to his feet. 'I am no longer Viceroy of the Deccan.' He gestured helplessly with both hands. 'One moment I am the Viceroy, the next I have been summarily sacked.' He pushed back his chair, began pacing the room like a captured tiger.

Rana Chara hid his elation beneath a sympathetic exterior. The conflicts had surfaced. 'Tell me all about it,' he quietly requested.

Continuing his restless pacing, Prince Aurang gave him the details of the final discussion with his father, pausing whenever he wanted to emphasize a point. 'The Emperor is mad,' he ended. 'When my mother died, he ceased to be a rational human being.' He halted facing Rana Chara, gripped the back of a chair so tightly his knuckles showed white.

'The Emperor has had time to recover from his bereavement,' Rana Chara advised. 'After all, it's been over thirteen years now, and he has even led a few successful military campaigns since then.'

'The whole Empire is in a shambles,' Prince Aurang burst out. He pounded the back of the chair with a clenched fist. 'The shame of it! The utter shame of having to go back in disgrace to the kingdom I conquered and ruled.' He jerked his fist repeatedly at his chest. 'I . . . I . . . I . . . while he was a mere figurehead.'

'The entire Deccan knows that,' Rana Chara soothed, cunningly adding, 'It is the prerogative of Emperors to be capricious. We are all whores servicing them!'

'I am nobody's whore,' Prince Aurang grated. 'I shall raise an army as soon as I get back to Bundel and march on Agra. Will you join me?'

'You will not march anywhere.'

'Who is going to stop me?'

'Not who . . . what.'

'What, then?'

'Your own military good sense.' Rana Chara gestured towards Prince Aurang's chair. 'Sit down, Prince. Behave like a rational human being and I shall tell you why.'

The prince hesitated, ready for defiance, then abruptly sat. 'It had better be good,' he muttered.

'Good sense is always good,' Rana Chara rejoined blandly. 'Take a sip of your coffee and relax.'

Prince Aurang grinned suddenly, reached for his coffee cup, took a sip. 'M'mm, not bad,' he said. A malicious glint entered the slanty eyes. 'You Hindus make almost as good coffee as we Moghuls who introduced it to you.'

'We are not a Hindu.' Rana Chara raised a cynical eyebrow, ran a forefinger beneath his silver grey moustache. 'We started drinking coffee after we learned that the Christian Pope had banned it as the "infidel's drink"!'

'You are an infidel?'

'Yes. It came from our agnosticism, which also tells us that it would make good sense for you to fight the Emperor only from strength, not from weakness. You, who want to be a future Emperor, should not be moved by petulance. If you attack Agra now, you will lose and end up in the same miserable situation in which your father put himself as a rebel twenty years ago. The military might of the Emperor is awesome. Brew your coffee before drinking it!'

'I am not afraid.'

'That is what every petulant schoolboy says. Bravado is no substitute for wisdom. Being filled with shame, you are allowing it to cloud your judgment. Remember this for all time. No one can shame you. Insults, humiliation may be offered you, or heaped upon you. There is no shame if your spirit remains proud, so all men can see that you are unconquered.'

Prince Aurang slipped slowly down in his chair. Shoulders hunched, he stared into space. 'You say my time will come?'

'Without a doubt.'

'How do you know?'

'We acquire some wisdom with age. Do you know the story of the old bull and the young bull?'

'No.'

'Let us tell you. The old bull and the young bull were both quietly grazing on a mountain slope when the young bull suddenly saw a herd of cows in the valley below. "Do you see them?" he inquired excitedly of the old bull. "Yes," was the calm reply. "Let's rush down and mount one of them," the young bull suggested, all worked up. The old bull shook his head. "No, let's sneak down and mount the lot."'

'Wonderful!' Prince Aurang rapped the table in a quick change of mood. 'That's good advice from an old bull!'

'We would also remind the young Moghul of our old Indian saying, Softly, softly, catchee monkey.'

'You are so wise. You should be the Emperor.'

'You said that to us once before, when you were yet a boy and we have the same reply to give you.'

'Then age has not given you new wisdom.' Prince Aurang was laughing now.

'There is no such thing as new wisdom. Whatever is wise exists to be picked up. It is eternal.'

'How will I know when the time is right for me?'

Rana Chara thought of all the plans he had made over the last forty years, many of which he had set aside. He could not restrain a sigh. For what, he did not know, except that each aborted plan had taught him so very much and yet there was so much more to learn. Aloud he said, 'We shall tell you when the time is right.'

Never for a moment did Rana Chara doubt that he would be the one to direct Prince Aurang to the imperial throne. Death would not take him away until he had fulfilled his own destiny. This he knew.

Chapter 46

When she began to have persistent spells of constipation, accompanied by stomach pains, Nur Jehan's physician had prescribed the usual strong laxatives, which relieved the immediate symptoms without abating their recurrence. Then came terrible stomach cramps and pain in the lower abdomen, with bleeding in her stools. Her weight began dropping rapidly and she had spells of nausea and dizziness.

Some instinct told her that she did not have long to live. The knowledge did not frighten her. On the contrary, she had nothing and no one left to live for, except the drag of day-to-day life itself. She only hoped that she would go before becoming bedridden or a walking vegetable. As a Muslim, she could not take her own life and risk a denial of Paradise, whether it existed or not.

As she grew weaker by the day, she felt that the only person who might care about her passing was Rana Chara. So she sent a special invitation to him to visit her in Lahore, without mentioning the cause.

When he neared Lahore, Rana Chara heard rumours that the former Empress was bedridden. He guessed that something was wrong and sped on with a small escort, ahead of his entourage, moved by some inexplicable sense of urgency and a desire to meet Nur Jehan before she died.

He missed her presence at dinner on the night of his arrival, but her Chief Eunuch informed him that she would receive him in her reception chamber the following morning.

Some whim, perhaps some desire for self-torture, had caused Nur Jehan to turn the reception chamber into a small-scale replica of the one in the Agra palace from which she had ruled an Empire. The pool at the entrance had a fountain gushing forth silver water. The Persian carpet was fronted by a gold-upholstered divan at the far end of the room with matching settles around it. The brass braziers emitted the customary attar-of-roses perfume and love-birds trilled and whistled from the courtyard outside. Only the green velvet curtains with the slit of a peep-hole were absent.

Each time he visited this room, as now, Rana Chara remembered Sir Thomas Roe, the English ambassador, with affection.

Nur Jehan was alone in the chamber, lying on the divan,

propped up by gold cushions. Moved by some impulse, Rana Chara made obeisance to her.

Though he could not see the face beneath the *yashmak*, he knew that she smiled her acknowledgment.

A weak hand was feebly raised. Gnarled fingers – fingers, he suddenly realized, that he was seeing for the first time ever – beckoned to him once, then flopped back, as if devoid of life, on the cream silken sheet covering the inert form.

Not all his amorality prevented a gush of pity from surging through Rana Chara. He moved forward, knelt beside the divan, bent his head close so he could hear her speak.

'Ever the . . . all . . . gallant Rajput,' she whispered. 'Pity our hand . . . has to be old and withered . . . the first time you set eyes on it. Our . . . fingers were once . . . full and beautiful. But no matter.' Her voice grew stronger. 'Change is inevitable and it will be the last time you see this hand.'

For once, Rana Chara was at a loss for words. The former embodiment of physical power and beauty, this woman who had enslaved an Emperor, had been stricken so low by change! He could not help recalling that Gautama Buddha, who had once been a prince of Nepal and heir to the throne, had renounced all of it and the world to seek Enlightenment when, as a young man, he encountered disease, poverty, old age and death for the first time. He, Rana Chara, was the Enlightened One of triumph over the effects of causes on others, but he now faced certain questions he simply could not answer. What had happened to Nur Jehan, what lay ahead for her? Why his present unaccountable grief for another human being?

'You must not grieve for us, Rana.' Notwithstanding her weak condition, Nur Jehan had picked up his feelings with the uncanny instinct she had always possessed. The trill of the love-birds took on an angry note. A harsh flutter of feathers told of fighting in the cage. 'Our time was at hand, but we delayed it until your arrival.' Her breathing became laboured. The chest rose and fell rapidly, rasping sounds emerging from it. 'You must not diminish our faith in your strength by showing the weakness of compassion now. Our only regret is that we shall not live to see the downfall of our arch enemy, Shah Jahan.' Her speech was clearer now.

'You can have the satisfaction of knowing that he is heading for that downfall,' he responded hoarsely.

'Prince Aurang will cause it? He is in disgrace now.'

'His disgrace will cause it.' He could have added that both Emperor Jehangir and Shah Jahan had risen to supreme power from disgrace, perhaps through it.

He gathered all his resources of calm with a superhuman effort. 'Please also be assured that what we are displaying is not the weakness of compassion, Your Imperial Majesty, but the strength of love.' He smiled gently at her, the power of all creation suddenly vibrant within him. 'You knew we would come.'

'Yes. There are things we must tell you.' In halting speech she revealed her affair with General Mahabat to him, then went on to tell him of her near-attempt to suffocate her husband with a cushion.

He listened in amazement. 'You needed to confess this to someone?' he marvelled. He recollected the story of the Greek hero. Even Achilles had his heel.

'Yes.' The effort to speak had been too much for Nur Jehan. She sagged back on the cushions, but her confession had enhanced her in his eyes.

Rana Chara's head lifted as tremors ran through Nur Jehan's body. He stared at her wide-eyed, speechless. This was different from witnessing death on the battlefield.

Suddenly, the quivering figure beneath the cream silken sheet went into convulsions. 'No! No! No!' she cried aloud, the voice strong with undisguised terror. 'I did not kill you, star of my soul.' She went on jerking, her hands rising above the sheet as if to ward off an attack. 'The cushion?' She screamed out the question. 'I only took it in my hands to restore your youth. But you were gone before . . . before . . .' She began gasping for air she simply could not reach. 'I swear to you on the sacred Koran . . .'

Gibbered words followed, unintelligible to Rana Chara, the hands flailing, the body twisting this way and that, the face snapping violently from side to side.

Rana Chara gazed at the tormented creature in appalled silence. Nur Jehan was finally facing the ghosts of her past.

Suddenly her body straightened, the shoulders pulled back. The chin under the *yashmak* lifted. 'We are not afraid of you, Jehangir,' she stated calmly and lucidly. 'We are not afraid of the Devil himself, nor even of Allah.'

Her body tautened for a moment. The breath rattled in her chest and throat. She stiffened, sighed and relaxed.

Nur Jehan was dead.

From the Diary of Shah Jahan

Nur Jehan is dead. I shall not honour her with an epitaph of either praise or contempt.

Praise be to Allah, my daughter lives.

We are entering the final phase of completion of the Taj Mahal. Its embellishments have been far, far more costly than the entire structure, the total cost much greater than I ever expected. The people must pay even more for their historic monument.

Having relieved the Prince Presumptuous, our third son, Aurang, of his power and responsibility in the Christian year 1644, we have observed that he has lived a blameless life in Bundel with his wives and children during the course of a whole year. He is a devout Muslim. His belief in the invincibility that God has given him, reminds us of our own boyhood years, but he, in his military campaigns, goes even further than we did. He not only lives in a tent when in the field, partaking of the same daily fare as his men, but he

709

never wears armour nor carries a shield into battle, his trust being in God. And when the time comes for prayer he has been known to lay out his mat, kneeling on it to his Creator, with the battle raging around him.

Since trouble has broken out again in the troublesome Gujarat, I am sending him to that province as governor.

It has taken Prince Aurang less than a year to bring Gujarat under control. I therefore intend dispatching him to far distant Badakh, the territories of my ancestor Timur, in northern Afghanistan, where Prince Murad, my youngest son, has, contrary to my commands, left a successful summer campaign to return to the fleshpots of Lahore. I have punished Murad by relieving him of all his appointments and forbidding him to show his face in Agra. Prince Aurang will take over the imperial army of fifty thousand men.

This campaign will be a severe drain on the imperial treasury, but I am determined to take Badakh, which even the Emperor Babur failed to conquer.

Prince Aurang has led his army back to Kabul, with tremendous losses of men, animals and materials along the way. The two-year campaign has cost the imperial treasury a fortune, with no success.

This is the first campaign failure of the Emperor Shah Jahan. Perhaps I should have led it personally. The knowledge depresses me. The capture of the Deccan rebel, Lodi, brings me no satisfaction despite seeing his head displayed on a pike.

My failure in Badakh has had its inevitable consequences. This year, 1649, Shah Abbas II besieged and retook Kandhar. This city is more than a gateway to Kabul and India, more than a junction of vital trade routes. It is part of the Moghul heart. This despicable Persian, while professing eternal friendship to me, has robbed that part of the Moghul heart.

I have appointed Prince Aurang to lead an army, which I am assembling, to recapture Kandhar. It will take about one year more to cast the cannon and assemble the weapons and men necessary for this tremendous enterprise.

* * *

Strange news, even disturbing, from England, the country of my former adversary, Ambassador Sir Thomas Roe. Some common people, led by a man named Karim-el, having seized their King Charles, tried and executed him this year, 1649. The country is now governed by this Karim-el, not as the king, but as Lord Protector, which is what he calls himself. Such events must be hidden from our people, who might otherwise get ideas.

My dream of the last nineteen years has been fulfilled. Let me describe briefly what Ustad Isa and I have created.

The main highway leading from Agra leads to a common where the grounds of the Taj Mahal commence. You can see the massive exterior gates of the compound half a mile away. On either side of the road are two octagonal buildings. The left one is the Tomb of the Serving Ladies, the mosque is on the right.

Within the exterior gates is the financial centre of the new city of Mumtaz. It is served by a long arcade, which leads to the central courtyard, enclosed by galleries of residences. At either end is a tomb. In the first the remains of Mumtaz Mahal's 'mother', Sati, who will guard her ward in death as in life, have been placed, in the other, those of my first wife.

The main gates of the Taj Mahal are a huge guarded portal opening to the south of the courtyard. An impregnable gateway is essential to save the priceless gold and jewels of the monument from robbers, but it also serves as an imposing herald of what lies beyond. Symbolically, this is the entrance to Paradise. Standing one hundred feet high, the three-storey gateway has a gigantic arch at its threshold. The massive door of the lowest storey is made of eight metals and is studded with knobs. Beyond it, a multitude of rooms with hallways create a labyrinth for those with base intentions.

On the southern façade, framing the central portals, are verses in Arabic from the Koran. These increase in size gradually from bottom to top, to give the illusion of being all the same size. This device has also been used on the main doorway of the Taj Mahal.

When viewed from these portals, the Taj Mahal seems small and far distant. As you approach it, the building begins to grow and grow with the great central dome expanding

711

until the whole appears colossal when you finally reach its base.

The dome represents the bell-shaped tents of my Tatar ancestors. Its finial is two hundred and twenty feet from the ground. Each time I see the dome, however, I am reminded of the plenitude of my Mumtaz Mahal's generous breasts, perpetually filled with milk for the fourteen children she bore me within twenty years.

From the entrance, you receive a first glimpse of the garden, a carpet of green, enclosed by a large wall, extending to the base of the Taj Mahal. This garden is divided into squares and has a stone pavilion at each corner. At its centre is a fountain.

In Persian the word for 'garden' in their regions of sandy wastes, where water, grass and trees are blessings, is the same as the word for 'paradise'. Since four is the sacred number of Islam I have caused my paradise to be laid out on a quadrate plan; the two marble canals, lined with fruit trees to symbolize life and cypress for death, cross in its centre, dividing it into four squares. In the middle of these squares is a great marble pool, positioned to reflect the Taj Mahal perfectly in its clear waters. Goldfish in the waters, peacocks on the lawns, nightingales in the branches give life to what would otherwise be a mere mausoleum.

Guards in white robes patrol the grounds. They are armed only with peashooters to drive away birds of prey. Man shall not hurt nor destroy in this holy sanctuary.

I shall sometimes cause my throne to be placed in front of the fountain, so I can gaze at its bubbling waters and commune with the spirit of my dead love.

At the northern end of the garden, in the centre of an enormous rectangular platform, the Taj Mahal rises in that strange combination of simple majesty and grace that was Mumtaz Mahal. On either side of it, the buildings of red sandstone are twin three-domed mosques. The mosque to the east does not face Mecca so it shall never be used for prayer, but is a symbol of the emptiness that is Hell, architecturally counter-balancing Paradise, the western mosque.

Four marble towers, topped by minarets tapering to a height of one hundred and thirty-eight feet, guard the Taj

Mahal. Angels will descend regularly from heaven to act as their sentries.

Enter through the massive portal of the Taj Mahal into its marble room, stranger, and gaze upon the tomb of Mumtaz Mahal.

Is this a tear drop that has smudged my manuscript? Impossible!

I swore an oath, many thousand years ago, when I was a man, not just an emperor, that I would never weep again.

Three months after the grand opening of the Taj Mahal, Shah Jahan was beginning to feel restless. He had created one of the wonders of the world, but now the work was completed and it was as if he had nothing left to do. The drive had gone out of him. As the amazement of the visitors who thronged the first viewing slowly became commonplace, he experienced a curious emptiness.

He broached the subject with Ustad Isa when the two of them were alone together in the European room of the Agra palace one morning, after a routine discussion of construction defects and deficiencies.

'We feel that we have been propelled back nineteen years to the time our Empress died,' he stated. 'It is as if, with the completion of the Taj Mahal, a prop has been removed and the platform of our life has sunk back into an abyss.'

The architect nodded his understanding. The years had not wrought many changes in his appearance except that there were wrinkles now on the sharp features; his skin had become tanned from exposure to the sun on the construction site and his trim moustache and pointed beard were liberally sprinkled with silver. 'I know exactly how you feel, Sire, though I could never probe your mystery. When my wife, Laila, died, I made my work the purpose of my life, but it was not enough.' The dark pools of his eyes revealed their haunted depths. 'Assisting you with the creation of your Taj Mahal brought purpose again to my life. Now that purpose is ended and I too am back where I started.'

Shah Jahan nodded gravely. 'It seems as if we have a common problem once more. What shall we do?'

'I wish I had an answer. For my part, I suppose I shall drift on and be as I was before.'

'Gazing in the direction of your homeland at sunset every day?'

'You remembered, Sire?'

'How could we forget? We were but a boy then, untouched by most of life's grimmer tragedies, but how does one compare tragedy? To the boy of twelve, the death of his grandfather had been world-shattering. It seems there is an equation in life.'

'A balance, Sire. We know the same dimensions of joy and sorrow whatever our age. To a baby, physical hunger is a cause for crying aloud, as tragic an occasion as soul hunger is to an adult. It is the law of cause and effect, which creates a kind of universal equality.'

'It is the will of Allah.' Shah Jahan always curtailed projections of non-Islamic philosophy when he was troubled, being superstitious about inviting God's wrath. In this he was even more superstitious than his grandfather, but then his emotional situation was nothing like as secure as that of the Emperor Akbar had been. 'We shall be leading imperial reinforcements into Kabul after Prince Aurang leaves for Kandhar next month. You shall accompany us on your way back to Shiraz?' The question was a command, but he mentally held his breath for the architect's reply.

'It would be a great privilege, Sire,' the architect responded. His expression became animated. 'A fitting finale to these nineteen years which will be the inspiration for my work during the remainder of my life.'

The words hit Shah Jahan between the eyes, piercing

through to open a blind spot that had lain beneath. Ustad Isa had just said that the past nineteen years would inspire his work for the remainder of his life. What was to prevent him from recreating the Taj Mahal elsewhere, perhaps even producing a more exquisite model? Never! The Taj Mahal was his, Shah Jahan's creation. An architect could produce a concept, but the development of that concept into a life-form required another artist, the man who conjures a theme and converts it into a melody, the kind of melody which reaches people, touches their hearts; then takes all the risks, makes the most supreme sacrifices to create that work. The Taj Mahal was the product of his own genius, the expression of all the love of his ancestors for beautiful buildings and gardens, the sensitivities that were uniquely his own, products of the suffering he had endured, which alone could reach out and touch the sorrows of all humanity.

He would never permit this architect to duplicate the Taj Mahal or create something even more beautiful.

Ustad Isa was an enemy who could capture his citadel.

How could he defend it?

Every Moghul instinct suggested that he put the architect to death. But that would belittle him in the eyes of the world and history. The eyes! Inspiration flared. Cold-bloodedly, dispassionately, he decided what he would do.

'I hope I have not offended you, Sire.' The architect's quick perception caught his change of mood.

Shah Jahan smiled with his mouth, not his eyes. 'No, no! On the contrary, we have just been inspired by a new idea.' He paused, staring through the grilled windows and the silver morning sunlight at the endless blue heavens. 'We too are mortal and shall not live forever,' he stated calmly. 'The Taj Mahal is the epitome of white marble. We shall have you commence immediately a design for an exact replica of it in black marble across the river, which shall be our own final resting place.'

'What a sacred idea,' Ustad Isa began; then his face clouded. 'You said, I should start design work immediately, Sire?'

'Yes.'

'I had hoped to visit other members of my family in Shiraz. I have been away for nineteen years.'

Shah Jahan deliberately lifted his eyebrows, gave the architect a piercing glance. 'You would place that above your duty to your Emperor?' Ustad Isa's Emperor was Shah Abbas, but framed this way the question brooked no negation. 'And also above your mission to honour your dead wife?'

For once the architect had no answer.

Shah Jahan hit home. 'It is settled then. In order that you may lose no time in completing the design of the black Taj Mahal and then go back for a short visit to your family, you shall not accompany us to Kabul, but shall have the schematics ready for us by the time we return.'

He would keep this master architect a virtual prisoner in Agra forever. If he himself died first, he knew what he would do to ensure that the Taj Mahal remained unique.

Chapter 47

Rana Chara had learned the procedures for protecting Shah Jahan against poisoning by the simple expedient of asking the Emperor, on the grounds that he wished to institute the same methods in his own palace in Chitor. If his intention had been to poison Shah Jahan, it would have been impossible. Tasters in the royal kitchens tasted every one of the ingredients, even the spices, used for preparing the Emperor's food, while others tasted the prepared foods before they left the kitchens and others yet stood by the dining room to check everything Shah Jahan chose to eat.

But it was not Rana Chara's purpose to poison the Emperor. That would have been too quick and clumsy. Where once he had merely wanted to kill Shah Jahan, the bitter fruit he had been forced to eat through the years now compelled him to manipulate the man by the same slow degrees. Besides, there was more intellectual pleasure in such a process.

He reasoned that the completion of the Taj Mahal must have brought about the end of Shah Jahan's obsession. The man must now be in the vacuum of the very goal he had set himself, above drink, sex and women, above ruling the Empire, above extending his dominions, all of which he had placed outside himself, as merely objective goals, in the years since Mumtaz Mahal died. Shah Jahan would now reach for something to fill the void created by, as Rana Chara concluded with quiet cynicism, the death of his second wife, the Taj Mahal. Under construction, it had a life. Completed, it was dead.

He had openly carried the gold flask into the dining chamber as a gift for the Emperor. Being a trusted and honoured guest, none of the officials had made any demur when he was conducted into the dining chamber and took his seat cross-legged on the low pink-silk divan immediately to the right of Shah Jahan's.

This dining chamber was one of the smaller ones used for private meals, and Rana Chara had been elated to learn that Shah Jahan would be dining with him alone once again. It was not entirely unusual for rulers to dine alone with someone with whom they desired private conversation or a philosophical discussion. Like his father, Shah Jahan had come to appreciate Rana Chara's unique ideas, but particularly now, when the Emperor was exploring every possible resource to discover the meaning of his seemingly meaningless life.

The divans, with marble bases and gilt legs, were just high enough to enable diners to reach for the food, in golden trays on the low tables of filigreed ivory before them. Rich silken tapestries in matching colours enlivened the walls. The entire chamber glowed warm and pink beneath two great crystal oil-lamps. Ornaments were not needed in a room where the golden serving dishes, bowls and platters provided decoration enough, but the scent of camphor incense came from jewelled gold braziers suspended from the ceiling.

The twenty-course meal had been sumptuous, but was no match for the exquisite delights of Nur Jehan's composition and too heavily spiced with basil, oregano, coriander and sweet anise for Rana Chara's more austere tastes. He noticed that Shah Jahan had started drinking wine. Good. The Emperor was reaching for substitutes.

Rana Chara had placed the gold flask openly on the table before him. He waited until the attendants started clearing the food, expertly burped his acknowledgement of a fine meal, a custom that he still considered vulgar, before leading into the subject he had in mind. 'Your Imperial Majesty is leaving shortly for Kabul, we understand?'

Shah Jahan nodded. 'The army which Prince Aurang will lead against Shah Abbas II in Kandhar has finally been assembled. It leaves next month and we shall let Prince Aurang go north-west to relieve Kandhar and proceed directly to Kabul.'

'Ah! The beloved home of the Emperor Babur. Kabul, the mystical city.'

Shah Jahan stared sentimentally into space. 'Indeed.' He sighed. 'Perhaps we shall find peace there, some purpose to life on a spiritual plane.'

'Your Imperial Majesty, we respectfully submit that you have been searching in the wrong areas of life.' Rana Chara deliberately half-turned to secure Shah Jahan's gaze. 'The purpose of life lies within each moment, wherever we may be, whatever we may be doing.'

'How so?' Curiosity had sparkled in the dark, slanty eyes; the white-topped head, tilted slightly to one side, became alert.

'Whatever our beliefs, our lives consist of countless seconds and fractions of seconds. After all, it takes only a fraction of a second sometimes for a living creature to die or be unalterably changed. Each fraction of a moment is a life,' he paused deliberately, made his gaze hypnotic, dropped his voice, 'or a death.'

Shah Jahan's head swivelled back, tilted more to the other side as he contemplated that idea, while Rana Chara awaited his response with an expectancy foreign to him. 'You are right,' Shah Jahan finally conceded. 'One moment, Mumtaz Mahal was alive, the next she was dead.'

'And Shah Jahan, the man, died with her,' Rana Chara declared softly.

A tremor went through the Emperor. 'How did you know?' he whispered into space.

'Some God-given secret, meant for Your Imperial Majesty, was whispered into our heart.'

'Give us of it.' Shah Jahan continued staring into space.

Rana Chara knew that the Emperor's mind had tumbled back in time. 'We have the phenomenon of a dead man then and a live Emperor, but the Emperor, being a man, needed to fill the void in his life, not created by his loved one's death but by his humanity. So he built a monument. Brick, tile and mortar, marble, sparkling water and gleaming gold could never fill the void. How can material things replace the spirit? It was the creating of beauty that became the Emperor's life, for in this, he was a man. Now it is over.

719

He prepares to create another thing of beauty, this time in black marble, that will be a joy forever, but he is not the same Emperor of nineteen years ago, and the monument is not for his lost love but for himself. So it is not enough. Besides, being mortal, he might die before the work is finished.'

This time Shah Jahan shuddered. 'Death has no terror for us,' he stated hoarsely. 'It will reunite us with Mumtaz Mahal in Paradise. The time in between . . .' He paused, leaving the sentence unfinished. 'How can a place in history ever fill the void made by a living being?'

A thrill of triumph ran through Rana Chara. The attendants had cleared the room, leaving only the gold cups lightly steaming with black coffee and the gold flasks of honey. His timing had been impeccable. He now had to accomplish the deed before the poison taster, standing to the rear of the Emperor, left the room. 'Which brings us back to my original thesis,' he volunteered, 'that each fraction of a moment is a life which we *can* indeed fill. That is how the Creator, whether you call Him Allah or Brahma, Ahura Mazda or God, has ordained creation. If we follow that code, we will not know the emptiness which hungering for a permanency that can never exist brings.'

'Eat, drink and be merry for tomorrow we die?'

'Not so, Sire, for that is a creed of permanence. Think, feel, say and do in each moment what will bring you happiness.' He looked away. 'Your father attempted to fill many of the lives of each second with the eat, drink and be merry outlets of wine and opium. That was not living the reality of each moment, but creating a fantasy for moments strung meaninglessly together.' He could not resist a flash of admiration at his own cleverness with words. 'The Creator has afforded us many joys for each moment. We often make the mistake of wanting joys that we think are permanent. This springs from the biological urge to be eternal, as with perpetuating ourselves through progeny.' He bared white teeth in a dare-all smile. 'We have had no such problems in our own life.'

Shah Jahan glanced curiously at him. 'You do not miss having children?'

'Do you, Sire? Especially you, as Emperor, watching his sons wrangling over his crown before he even becomes a corpse?'

'You do not care who succeeds you as Rana of Mewar?'

'Certainly not. What satisfaction can it give us today to know that a son may make a good Rana or a bad Rana after we are gone and have no control over the kingdom? That way, we suggest, lies horror! A Greek philosopher once told the young Sikander, To be an Emperor you must trust no one and learn to be completely alone. Our own view is that this advice must even extend to our attitudes towards our children.'

The slanty eyes narrowed. 'You are right,' Shah Jahan remarked. 'Our four sons are all manoeuvring to succeed us.'

Not to *succeed* you, Rana Chara thought maliciously. Prince Aurang at least plans to *displace* you. Shah Jahan placed an elbow on his bent knee, chin on his palm. 'Tell us, Rana, do you give the same advice to everyone?' he inquired.

Rana Chara smiled. 'Everyone does not seek our advice, Sire, and if they did, we would be selective as to who should receive it. To answer your real question, however, we believe that there is no such thing as absolute reality. Each entity has its own separate reality, right down to the components of our bodies. Any advice we may seem to give is really the wisdom of the receiver, mirrored in our words.'

'You do not believe that there is such a thing as absolute truth?'

'Absolutely not, Sire.'

'What about the religions of the world?'

'They are each and every one of them an expression of the reality of its individual founder. Moses said, *I* have found the one God. Prince Gautama said, *I* am the Buddha. Jesus said, *I* am the Christ. Your own Mahomet said, *I* am the Prophet. I, I, I . . . . How can there be an eternal verity based upon the *I* syndrome?'

'What else can prophets say?'

'They can talk about their philosophy, religion, whatever, objectively, without trying to establish their credentials as if they were ambassadors or crippled beggars. And what are they all trying to achieve? The salvation of people according to their own images, as if those created by the Almighty, or by Nature, are insufficient. Patronizing bastards, all of them, I would say, patronizing even the Almighty in their attempts to improve what the Almighty has created. And before these prophets prove that they are mortal, by dying like anyone else, they issue *jagirs* of the faith to their priests, who live off the revenues, fulfilling the duties of their respective offices.'

'Do you not believe that man is capable of sin?'

'Sin was created by man, not by God or Nature. Priests and the religious set up the obstacles, so that they can be the ones to help people overcome these shadows of their own creation.'

'Surely religions provide for the soul?'

'Ah, the soul, Sire. That marvellous entity which enables men to believe that there is no end to them in their present form. They will know peace only if they acknowledge that death is the transition to another form. Even if you believe in Paradise, it is not necessary for you to imagine that you, the Emperor Shah Jahan, will be the entity to enjoy its bliss.'

Shah Jahan's black brows furrowed. He had been listening intently, obviously endowed with his grandfather's faculty to absorb the truths of philosophies other than his own. Finally, he smiled. 'The *imams* would consider your words blasphemy.' A sad look crossed the handsome features. 'Even our late wife would be horrified if she could hear you.'

'Unfortunately, blasphemy only occurs when words are spoken. It is the truth that blasphemes, but how does one burn the truth at the stake?'

'True, but our *imams* would surely want to inflict the direst punishment on you as the purveyor of the truth.' A malicious glint entered his eyes. 'In the same way that pimps and panderers are punished! You would be considered beyond salvation.'

'What is salvation? A mirage of the religious desert pointed out to us by those who have never traversed it. How can there be conditional salvation? You live thus and so and the kingdom of heaven is your legacy. What about all the poor living creatures who existed before the prophets spoke of heaven or Enlightenment? As far as we are personally concerned, we would accept a philosophy of heaven after death if it were free of conditions in this life. That being so, we return full circle to the thesis, make a heaven of every fraction of a second. Your heaven, based on your individual reality. Let the past enhance rather than cloud your present.'

'Remarkable!' Shah Jahan exclaimed. 'You have given us much food for thought.'

It was time to seize the beard of the Moghul lion. 'We understand, Sire, that with the completion of the Taj Mahal, you have very recently turned for some solace to the joys of the *harem*?'

Shah Jahan hesitated. He looked around and dropped his

voice. 'Such joys have not been complete,' he confided, then sighed heavily. 'We are old and out of use.'

Rana Chara seized the moment with alacrity. 'We rather guessed that to be the case.' He injected a pious note into his voice. 'The Creator has imparted some of His divine wisdom to us for your benefit.' He reached for the flask, held it to the light. Had the sparkle from the gold been evil? 'You have aphrodisiacs in the *harem*, we know, Sire, but they seem to have failed. Here is a divine preparation that will restore your power without harming you. It has been in our family for hundreds of years. As you are aware, evidence of virility is a requirement of Indian as well as Moghul rulers. We even have a Raja who has to ride stark naked through his capital in public in an open carriage once a year, his bared organ proudly erect, after which his subjects weigh him in the three precious metals which are then donated to his private treasury. Since our custom pre-dates yours by several centuries, far more cunning is contained within this flask.' He paused to allow his words to sink in. 'Let us have your poison taster sample the contents.' He smiled his amusement. 'The only effects he will suffer are his wife's protests.'

He noted the gleam in Shah Jahan's eyes. It is but a short cry from one obsession to another, he reflected.

'If it will have the effect you promise, there would be no harm in our trying it.' Shah Jahan sounded eager.

'It will be the resurrection of your erection, Sire. And in order to make assurance doubly sure, we have brought with us on this visit a *nautch* dancer from South India to complement the contents of the flask. What they cannot achieve, she in her divine experience can. She is the daughter of a famous belly dancer who moved from Lahore to Madras to marry a South Indian actor.' He became deliberately casual. 'She adopted her mother's name when she took to the profession, in the South Indian medium of course. Her name is Nadia.'

He knew why Shah Jahan's eyes had widened with shock. It had taken many years of inquiry and a stroke of luck before the antecedents of the famous *nautch* dancer had been revealed to him.

By the time she came to his bed-chamber in the *harem*, the aphrodisiac had begun to work. Shah Jahan's organ, flaccid for so long, was erect to bursting point. His brain had no control over it, only the glands running along his prostate and below his testes, which were thrilling with the fiery blood pumped into his penis.

The music that was intended to soothe him had changed to a familiar beat. What was it? His fuddled mind could not find the answer, but its throb was that of his desire. He reclined on the gold cushions of his divan bed and gazed expectantly towards the entrance door. The entire room was pink, he realized. It had been so long since he had occupied it that he had forgotten, but the pink glow from the hanging lamps jogged his memory.

The music stopped abruptly. Moments of silence followed. A single drum started a slow *tap . . . thari-kitha . . . thari-kitha . . . thari-kitha*. A reedy pipe took up the beat, dissolved into the haunting traditional belly dance melody.

Where was he?

Stringed instruments joined in. Slow tinkling cymbals announced Nadia's arrival. He listened, breathless. The sudden jangle of brass ornaments made him gasp.

Still breathless, he awaited Nadia's entrance. A tiny voice whispered: You are the Emperor. You can have any woman in the world. Why have you become a mere youth tonight?

When he could not bear the suspense any longer and would have let his anticipation go, she appeared at the door, tiny bells beating their seductive tattoo. A tall sinuous figure, with a tiny waist, flaring hips, full thighs and generous breasts, wearing the diaphanous seven veils.

His mind raced back. A hip swung seductively and it came to a stop. Nadia, the belly dancer. The figure, the dress, even the eyes above the veils, were those of Nadia from a thousand years ago. This was no *nautch* dancer, the young Nadia, but her mother, the belly dancer.

How had this happened? Who knew about the past? General Wahid was dead. His Mumtaz Mahal, to whom he had confessed his near fall in Lahore, was dead. So was Sati, the woman with whom Mumtaz Mahal had prayed and saved him.

Tonight, there was no one to save him.

But he did not want to be saved. He was a lusty young man again.

She glided into the room, her feet beating a muffled thud on the pink marble floor, anklets jingling. The skin of her arms and the face above the veil was ivory, contrasting sharply with long hair gleaming jet black, tight drawn from a noble forehead and held in place by a glittering tiara of diamonds.

'A divine gift of Allah!' he muttered to himself. And ejaculated.

Shame turned his cheeks warm and crimson.

To his amazement, his erection did not subside. The swollen member hurt while Nadia danced. When her dance ended, she gave her hands, her mouth and her body to him. He lost count after his fourth orgasm. His organ remained erect all the time, without yielding, even when he finally fell asleep.

Chapter 48

From the Diary of Shah Jahan

The aphrodisiac which Rana Chara gave me had some amazing effects. In my eagerness, I took more of the liquid than he advised and could not get my erection down for three days. Meanwhile, I even had the wet dreams of my boyhood at night and these, combined with my sexual play with Nadia, whom I did not seem able to resist, so debilitated me that on the fourth day I collapsed in bed. After years of being damned, the flood-gates of my sex organ had opened only to swamp me with the products of my own repression.

Rana Chara departed for Chitor only when he was assured that I had recovered. Since then, my sexual appetite has returned and I have learned to regulate my use of the aphrodisiac.

I accompanied Prince Aurang and his imperial army up to the River Indus, where we parted company, he proceeding north and west to Kandhar while I headed directly north for Kabul. I had expected to find peace in Kabul, city of my Moghul heart, and joy with my young Nadia, who is as naturally insatiable as my aphrodisiac makes me artificially, but Almighty Allah willed otherwise.

For the first time in my life, disaster has struck my health.

It started with retention of my urine. I just cannot make water readily, though I have the need and the desire. A frightening situation, which my physicians have eased somewhat with decoctions.

Then came the itching of my skin, thirst, a craving for sweets and, of all things, the need to urinate frequently.

My physicians have diagnosed the two conditions, distinct and separate from each other. They have placed me on a strictly vegetarian diet, with no wine or aphrodisiacs, plenty of exercise and abstinence from sex.

Just when I rediscovered my sexual youth, I have to act

as an old man. Nadia created so many problems for me with her demands for my sexual attentions that, on the advice of my daughter, I have sent her back to Madras, with a goodly pension.

Summer has ended and Prince Aurang has failed to take Kandhar. I have commanded him to withdraw the imperial army to Agra. His failure is disgraceful. He will return to the Deccan, but I shall reappoint him Viceroy, because I do not wish to heap humiliation on him and drive him to revolt as I once did. With my health deteriorating, I find myself increasingly in the position of my father, the Emperor Jehangir. I see in Prince Aurang, of all my sons, the young Shah Jahan.

I do not wish to become his victim.

My eldest son, Prince Dara, took over the Kandhar campaign in the hopes of succeeding where the brilliant Prince Aurang failed. One year later and he has had no success either. The alternatives are to take over myself or to withdraw. I am too worn out in health to lead a major campaign and too old to face the prospect of defeat. Besides, I am immersed in the planning of the second Taj Mahal in Agra. I fear that Kandhar will never more be a Moghul possession.

I now know how my father felt in his final years. Like him, I shall spend what remains of my life wielding the balance of power between ambitious sons, an imperial juggler on the peacock throne.

I am so tired at times.

The discussion which Rana Chara intended having with Prince Aurang that evening was so far-reaching that he had decided that it should take place in the Chitor palace gardens.

They were completely alone when they paused by the fountain. This was to be a historic meeting. Rana Chara sensed an inner excitement in the prince, that of a war charger who knows a battle is about to commence. The large almond-shaped eyes did not have their usual contemplative expression, but were restless. The black Mongolian moustaches dipping down into the well-kept beard that flowed from trim sideburns quivered occasionally. Rana Chara found himself responding to the momentous occasion, his blood vibrating like the screech of bats in the darkling branches overhead and the splashing fountain. Summer had ended, so the silver-grey air moved by a steady breeze was cool as water. Pale golden rectangles of light had already appeared in the palace windows. Such peace!

Sensing Prince Aurang's restlessness, the Rana decided to approach the subject he had in mind obliquely. 'We are in the year 1657 by the Christian calendar,' he remarked as he stooped to pick up a large brown leaf and throw it into the pool. He watched it float. 'As the leaf is at the command of the water, you, Prince Aurang, have been caught up in the insane drivel of time and the appalling gibberish of imperial circumstances. You are now thirty-nine years old, the father of five sons. What is your appraisal of the current state of the Empire? Your father has relinquished day-to-day powers to your brother Prince Dara, the legal heir, whom he has raised to the unprecedented rank of sixty thousand *zat/sawar* before recalling him to Agra. Prince Shuja, in Bengal, has already declared himself the Emperor.'

'That bastard has even had a new coin struck in his name,' Prince Aurang cut in furiously, 'which he has changed to Abdul Fauz Nasiruddin Mohamed, Timur III, Sikander II, Shah Shuja Bahadar Ghazi. He is having the *khutba* (Friday's mid-day sermon) read in these names. The man's mad.'

'A megalomaniac who sees himself as the reincarnation of Sikander the Great and Tamburlaine. His vaulting ambition will overleap itself and fall on the other side.' Rana Chara was quoting Ambassador Thomas Roe with affection. 'Even your youngest brother, Prince Murad, has been putting out feelers for support from the ranas and nobles. You alone have displayed remarkable restraint.'

'Under your tutelage, Rana,' Prince Aurang muttered. 'But it has not been easy. Many is the time I have wanted to erupt.'

'Meanwhile, you have indeed occupied yourself, forging your own alliances, using promises, bribes or threats where appropriate.'

Prince Aurang darted a sharp glance at him. The shrilling of bats increased in a crescendo. 'How do you know?'

'We make it our business to know,' Rana Chara replied airily. 'Not being directly involved has its advantages. Bribery and promises, which are after all another form of bribery, have probably won more campaigns throughout history than the battlefield. The Emperors Ky-roos, Sikander and your own ancestors and, more recently, your father, were past masters. It is part of imperial wisdom, which you have obviously inherited.'

Unexpectedly, Prince Aurang exploded. 'How could I sit still while my father puts me on the shelf!' There was more pent-up hatred in him than even his mentor had imagined. 'Do you know the humiliations I have endured for the last five years? I have been engulfed by a constant stream of reprimands from the Emperor, as if I were some damned servant who shopped at the wrong market-place. My pleas for funds to revive areas of the Deccan smitten by years of crippling taxes, natural disasters and warfare have been rejected with the accusation that I am merely attempting to enrich my personal treasury. Almighty Allah! Can my father no longer comprehend what it is to *feel* for the people one governs? What has happened to our cherished ideals of kingship?'

'We know the whole sorry scene,' Rana Chara soothed him. He did not believe in all the mumbo-jumbo of politics. One merely ruled as needed for survival and prosperity.

But this was not the time for a debate on the non-ethics of government. 'You have also been accused, falsely no doubt, of misappropriating presents that should have been sent to the imperial treasury. You have been conspicuously excluded from the Emperor's generous gifts. During your previous period of eight years as Viceroy of the Deccan, you were invited north four times on your visits to the Emperor's court. During the last five years, you have not received one single invitation.' He thought it wise to remind Prince Aurang of all this as a prelude to what he intended suggesting, even though it was obvious that this caged tiger needed no incentive to break loose.

'Talking of presents, do you know what I have just been accused of? Keeping the Emperor's favourite Deccanese mangoes for my own table, instead of sending the crop to Court.' The statement was half-growl, half-roar. 'Are we governing an Empire or a bazaar?'

'You have achieved marvels of administration these past five years and all you have received is criticism. Your supposed incompetence has been discussed openly in the Court. That is not right.'

'Do you remember that my last two campaigns against Golkonda and Bija were halted on orders from my father when I was poised for victory both times?'

'Yes.'

'Well, I learned only last week that this was caused by the intervention of Prince Shuja with the Emperor. That son of a bitch . . .' He raised a hand at Rana Chara's lifted eyebrows . . . 'Yes, my mother was a bitch who favoured my other brothers, especially Prince Dara, and discriminated against me. From as far back as I can remember, she hated me.' He grinned savagely. 'Feared me too, no doubt, because she knew she had conceived a rebel in her womb.'

'Does that make you too a son of a bitch?' Prince Chara inquired with feigned innocence.

'Oh, I am a son of a bitch all right.' Prince Aurang grinned mirthlessly. 'The difference is that I know I am . . . and exploit it. Prince Shuja poisoned our father's mind against me to prevent my successes bringing me imperial rewards.' He gritted his jaw. 'I shall have my revenge some day.'

'What about your younger brother, Prince Murad?'

Prince Aurang threw back his head and laughed aloud, white teeth gleaming through the black moustaches and beard. 'I have made him believe that all I want out of life is a hermit's cell, but that it is my duty, as a good Muslim, before retiring to it, to set right the succession, which should be Prince Murad's, as the most devout, orthodox Muslim of our family and should never go to our free-thinking eldest brother.'

'Prince Murad believed you?' Rana Chara sounded as incredulous as he felt.

'Certainly.'

'We are not surprised. There is no greater folly than extreme piety. Anyone dedicated to folly has of necessity to be both foolish and a fanatic fool. Such a one, being totally consumed by self-righteousness, must end up a foolish fanatic.' He paused. 'Have you really been able to win Prince Murad to your side?'

'Of course.' Prince Aurang's face clouded. 'My only major problem is that Prince Dara has summoned my secret ally, General Mir, whose army is in the Deccan, back to Agra to support him against Prince Shuja and doubtless also against Prince Murad and me, though I have made no open moves.'

'That would certainly be a blow.' Rana Chara thought rapidly. 'General Mir is the most brilliant of the generals. Are we certain that he is secretly your ally?'

'Absolutely.'

'Then have him arrested . . .'

'What?' Prince Aurang's dropped jaw remained there until comprehension slowly dawned in his eyes, when it gradually closed. He shook his head slowly from side to side. 'You really are a clever bastard, aren't you?' He nodded. 'I can arrest General Mir, with his own consent, on a trumped up charge and take over his army.' His dark eyes shone. 'Brilliant.'

Rana Chara shrugged. 'Elementary! What is simple always seems brilliant. Meanwhile, just in case Murad, the foolish fanatic, decides that you are too good to be true, execute a written agreement with him, whereby in the event that you do not finally retire, he will have Afghanistan, Kashmir, the Punjab and Sind, while you retain the right to the rest of the Empire. Also arrange to share the booty from your first joint victories. In order to lull him into a false sense of security, demand two-thirds for yourself while the balance goes to him. You cannot afford to depend entirely upon your claim to a non-existent holiness. Even the *imam* who severely chastises your lack of morals will expect you to invite him to your sumptuous board immediately afterwards.'

'That will certainly lend me greater credibility, and I can also reassure Prince Murad that when I become a hermit he can have it all.' He bared his teeth in a grin. 'The "when" of it will of course never occur.'

'Meanwhile, allow Prince Dara and Prince Shuja to destroy each other in battle, then strike with Prince Murad as your ally. Prince Dara will learn of your alliance with Prince Murad soon enough and send an army to prevent your two forces from uniting. That is when you will act.'

Prince Aurang's whole face lit up, a tremor went through his body and his wide nostrils distended from a deep breath. 'Praise be to Allah. You think the time will then be right for me to march?'

'Undoubtedly. You are going to be very busy during the

months ahead. In case we do not meet again before you become Emperor, we would like to give you some advice about what to do with your brothers once you become the victor.'

Rana Chara found immense satisfaction in repeating the advice he had given Shah Jahan years earlier, when he was about to become Emperor.

Yesterday the thunder of distant guns from the battle taking place on the sandy plains of Samugarh had reached the Agra palace. This morning an eerie silence prevailed, because Prince Aurang had emerged the victor.

The atmosphere in the European room of the Agra palace should have been tense and grim, yet his visitor was relaxed. Shah Jahan himself felt a strange peace. Here we are, two white-haired men at the tail-end of our lives, he reflected, yet faced with our worst crisis ever.

In spite of being nearly ninety years of age, the debonair Asaf Khan, his slim, erect figure impeccably clad, still had a devil-may-care elegance. Indeed, the heavily wrinkled skin of his face made the blue eyes seem to glitter all the more, as streams do in scarred ravines.

'So Prince Aurang finally stands with his army outside the gates of Agra,' Shah Jahan observed. 'We are glad the months of turmoil and uncertainty have ended, though we are not amused by the outcome. When the imperial army routed Prince Shuja in February this year, we thought that Almighty Allah was on our side. But then Prince Aurang severely defeated the force we had sent under General Singh to prevent the prince's joining forces with Prince Murad and we knew that the tide had turned in his favour. So reminiscent of our own rise to power, eh Prime Minister?'

Asaf Khan nodded slowly. 'Those were stirring times,

Your Imperial Majesty.' His voice had become weaker, husky and cracked with age.

'Indeed. Your loyalty to our cause finally brought us victory.' He could not help a sigh. 'Prince Aurang does not have an Asaf Khan to assist and guide him. A pity.' He sighed again. 'Prince Dara made a grievous mistake when he decided to march out immediately and prove his own worth in the field. Prince Aurang sprang and struck as we once did, like lightning.' He smiled at the recollection.

'Prince Dara is neither a strategist nor a general, Sire,' Asaf Khan asserted cuttingly. 'Your support of him has cost you the Empire.'

His Prime Minister had not changed through the years. Suddenly Shah Jahan was transported back to the days when he really ruled the Empire before Mumtaz Mahal died, before his urine retention, dire thirst, itchy skin, a failing virility which he kept trying to prove, especially with young girls, the time when he was a man in addition to an Emperor. It filled him with euphoria, but the feeling lasted only a few moments. 'You are right, Prime Minister. We understand that our eldest son, being too ashamed to face us, took refuge in his own palace here in the Agra fort at about nine last night, but ignored our sympathetic request to call on us and slipped out at three this morning on elephants with his wife, children, some slave girls and a small escort. We learned of his intention on our sleepless bed and sent mules laden with gold coins to accompany him. We have also dispatched instructions to the governor of Delhi to place our treasury there at Prince Dara's disposal.' He shook his head sadly. He was paying for having tried to keep his promise to Mumtaz Mahal, as to the succession.

'I shall leave immediately after this conference to lead the delegation which you are sending to Prince Aurang, inviting him to visit you in the palace to discuss the succession.'

Asaf Khan's face tightened, causing the wrinkled skin to shine. 'As commanded by you, I shall take your famous sword, *Alamgir*, Seizer of the Universe, as a symbolic present to Prince Aurang. Since Prince Murad was severely wounded in yesterday's battle, Prince Aurang has certainly seized our entire Universe.'

From the Diary of Shah Jahan

Prince Aurang sent word back to me through his son, Prince Mohamed, and Asaf Khan that he would accept my invitation to visit only if I permitted his officers to take over the Agra fort.

Naturally, I rejected this condition. The man must desire to humiliate me. Years ago, I would have been furious. Now, I am just sad.

All these tensions make it impossible for me to find joy in the pleasures of the *harem*. I do not seem to be able to get it up even with the youngest and most beautiful of my slaves.

Prince Aurang has surrounded the fort and laid siege to it. My defenders are resisting loyally and with indomitable courage. My one hope is the secret messenger I have sent to Prince Dara to use my money to raise an army of mercenaries and come to my rescue.

Oh dreadful day! Prince Aurang is a devil incarnate. What he failed to achieve by force of arms he has succeeded in attaining by low cunning. Three days ago, he seized the gate to the River Jumna through which all the water is carried to the fort. We have been without water all this time. I have no option but to surrender.

I have begged Prince Aurang to permit me to retain the title of Emperor for the few remaining years of my life, while he exercises the power. What has happened to me, the once proud Emperor? It is Allah's will.

The European room had become a refuge for him from the harsh, arid realities of imperial life. Here, Shah Jahan could live in a make-believe world for a few hours, dreaming of the past.

There were three white-haired men in the room this morning. In addition to Asaf Khan, Ustad Isa, who had requested an audience, was present. The architect had turned seventy, but his small, slight figure, clad in the white robes of the Parsee, was erect, the face barely lined and the moustache and beard, now as white as his hair, were trim. The deep, dark eyes remained haunted.

'First, your news, Prime Minister,' Shah Jahan bade Asaf Khan when they were seated. 'When will Prince Aurang call on us?'

Asaf Khan shook his head sadly. 'Never, I am afraid, Your Imperial Majesty. He had mounted his elephant early this morning to ride in triumph through the city, to visit you, when some troublemakers informed him that your Tatar slave girls had planned to assassinate him when he approached you.'

Shah Jahan was outraged. 'That is not true,' he burst forth. 'We are incapable of such treachery.' Remembering his past acts of treachery, he relapsed into silence, gazed through the windows at the blinding sunlight and the silhouettes of cypress against a cloudless blue sky.

Asaf Khan ignored the protest. He too must know it was not the truth. 'Prince Aurang decided not to be turned back at a threat from the *purdah* brigade. When he arrived at the entrance gates of the fort, however, Your Imperial Majesty's messenger to Prince Dara was seized and produced before him, with the letter in your own handwriting to Prince Dara, requesting him to rescue you.'

'But that letter was written some days ago.'

'Unfortunately, it was undated. Prince Aurang remained outside the fort and sent for me. I attended him immediately and he commanded me to convey his decision to you.'

Shah Jahan's heart sank. He knew it was all over. 'His

decision? How dare he?' The old reflex lasted but a few moments. His shoulders slumped. 'What is his decision, Prime Minister?'

'He is withdrawing to Delhi, where he will take the title of Emperor of India. He will rule the Empire from Delhi. Since you have clung to the title of Emperor all these years, you shall retain it.' Asaf Khan's eyes glistened with tears. 'You shall be Emperor of the Agra palace, to which you shall be confined, with full imperial powers of life and death over every palace resident.'

'Oh dear Allah!' The expression escaped him without thought. His eyes drifted to a window. A thought struck him. He rose to his feet. The men stood up with him, as was the custom. He hurried to the window. There, to one side, was the Taj Mahal, etched against the sky, its white marble cupola and towers rising above the treetops like exquisite gifts to heaven. He gazed at it, entranced. Suddenly, it was incomplete.

Shah Jahan's heart, mind and spirit told him why. Desperate, in a rush of fevered anxiety, he turned around. 'The black marble Taj Mahal, our own final resting place, the Shah Jahan of the Mumtaz Mahal. Surely, we can at least build that?' He looked eagerly at Asaf Khan. 'What do you think, Prime Minister? Can we not persuade our son to extend this one crumb of mercy towards us?' His eyes darted to Ustad Isa.

'I am so sorry, Your Imperial Majesty.' Asaf Khan's voice seemed to cut in from a distance. 'Prince Aurang has already decided that your revenues, like your activities, must be confined to the needs of the palace. He expressly forbade any construction work on the black marble Taj Mahal as a sheer waste of money.' His voice broke. He cleared his throat. 'You may recall that he always opposed expenditure even on the white Taj Mahal.'

Shah Jahan heard the hiss of escaping breath. He thought

it came from Ustad Isa, but immediately realized that it was his own. 'Oh God, then there is nothing left in life. Not even hope!'

In his despair, his grandfather spoke to him.

Rise and fight again.

What do I have to fight for?

Your dignity and self-respect. Even if your Empire extends only within the palace walls, rule it.

He straightened up, glanced at Asaf Khan. 'We shall no longer need a Prime Minister,' he said. 'You are hereby relieved of your post with all honour.'

Asaf Khan's face crumpled, but the tears would never fall. 'All these years, Your Imperial Majesty. All the striving, the battles, the triumphs, the betrayals, for *this* moment?' He shook his head. 'I still cannot believe it.' He paused. 'I would rather remain here with you, in any capacity, but your command has always been my wish.' General Wahid had once said that.

'What will you do? You are free to serve the new Emperor Aurang.'

'Never, Sire.' Asaf Khan drew himself erect. 'When I have served a Shah Jahan for thirty years, why would I trade my service to a god for a muleteer's yoke?'

Shah Jahan nearly broke down then. 'We thank you,' he whispered hoarsely. 'How will you occupy your days?'

Asaf Khan grinned. 'Since I no longer have the right to remain in my official mansion, I have decided to go to Kashmir, where I shall live the simple life of a hermit on a houseboat, contemplating the Himalayas, my navel and the struggles, beneath the boy's stick, of the worm we call mankind.'

Oh, fortunate man, I envy you, for you have found liberation.

Shah Jahan directed his glance towards Ustad Isa. 'And you, architect, why did you request audience? You have heard the sad truth. What can we possibly do for you now?'

Ustad Isa bowed low. When he raised his head again, his dark, haunted eyes were filled with tears. 'Your Imperial Majesty, I requested audience immediately I heard the news, by accident, of Prince Aurang's refusal to permit the building of the black marble Taj Mahal. I humbly request that I be permitted to return to my native Shiraz.'

'You made that request five years ago and we refused.' Shah Jahan smiled tenderly at this man he had loved from the first day he met him in Kabul. 'Your eyes are forever turning towards Shiraz, but we thought that this occurred only at sunset!' His inquiring glance at Ustad Isa held a hint of mischief. 'It is yet morning.'

The architect's lips tightened. 'Ah Emperor, that is indeed true. But is not the sun setting on your Empire?'

Shah Jahan's heart pounded at the words. The entire period of the past months suddenly seemed unreal to him. 'You will go back to retire within your family circle?' he inquired, idly, to hide an access of grief.

'I can never retire, Your Imperial Majesty. Once an architect, always the artist. I shall practise my profession in Shiraz.' Shah Jahan turned towards the window again. The Taj Mahal shimmered before his gaze, virgin, immaculate.

You would return to Shiraz and build a replica of my life's work? This beautiful dream, to which I gave reality, to be brought to life again in some other land?

'Never!' The thought exploded into the word. He stared at the Taj Mahal, his mind made up, inflexible, enduring as the beauty of his creation. 'The remains of our life are out there, for I died with the Empress Mumtaz Mahal twenty-seven years ago. You shall never build another Taj Mahal.'

'I have no such intention, Sire.'

Shah Jahan swung round. The pain and frustration of the years, the Moghul desire for vengeance, could at least be released on this one individual who had become the symbol of all that he had lost. Ustad Isa had the power to take away from him the only unique thing remaining to him, which would endure when the puppet Emperor of the Agra palace, Shah Jahan, died.

'Ustad Isa, we are the Emperor of the Agra palace, with all our imperial powers, including life and death, over all who dwell in our domain.' A mad laugh escaped him. 'You are one of our subjects, are you not?'

The architect looked puzzled. A subdued gasp from Asaf Khan indicated that he knew the Emperor's mind.

'Ustad Isa, we hereby decree that you shall never leave our borders during our lifetime. And if we die before you do, you shall be blinded.'

Epilogue

Eight years of exile in an imperial domain. During the first year there had been some hope that one of his other sons might rescue him. The first to rise again had been Prince Shuja. Within a few months, he had raised an army in Bengal and began marching towards Agra. Reminded of his own triumphs in Bengal, Shah Jahan had been heartened by the move.

Supported by General Mir, Prince Aurang raced to meet Prince Shuja and narrowly defeated him in battle early the following year. Prince Shuja escaped and was pursued by General Mir. After a campaign lasting fifteen months, Prince Shuja fled with his family to Arakan, east of Bengal. Nothing more was heard of the prince or his family. They were probably murdered by pirates, who infested the region.

Prince Dara had used the immense wealth that he, Shah Jahan, bestowed on him, to raise another army. In March 1659, his forces had been over-run by Prince Aurang's army, near Ajmer. Prince Dara had fled to Ahmadabad, then across the blazing Sind desert, where his favourite wife, Princess Nadira, died of dysentery and exhaustion. Prince Dara himself was betrayed by a local chieftain, named Malik, whom he had once befriended. The Emperor Aurang had Prince Dara and his male children brought to Delhi, and paraded them, clothed in rags, on a doddering female elephant through the streets and bazaars of the city. The once debonair Prince Dara, so like his mother and his grandfather, Asaf Khan, in appearance was then imprisoned with his sons, all still in rags. Prince Dara's popularity was such, however, that the Emperor Aurang had the entire family butchered in prison on 30 August by slaves.

Prince Murad had been in prison since his elder brother seized power. The Emperor Aurang evolved a devilish plan to eliminate him. Prince Murad had once executed his own Finance Minister and, under Muslim law, a dead man's relations can demand justice. The new Emperor prevailed on the Minister's second son to demand that justice. Rejecting the alternative of compensation, in December 1661, the plaintiff witnessed Prince Murad's execution.

All Shah Jahan's sons and his sons' sons, all except Prince Aurang, were gone, eliminated by the new Emperor. Only the Princess Jahanara was left. How could such a fiend as Prince Aurang have been nurtured in the womb of the gentle Mumtaz Mahal?

Each time Shah Jahan recalled his own actions when he himself became the Emperor, eliminating his brothers and their sons to prevent any threat to his sovereignty, he knew that it was from his own seed that the Emperor Aurang had emerged.

It was the Moghul Legacy.

* * *

Rana Chara could not prevent a totally unfamiliar twinge of pity when he saw the fallen Emperor lying on the divan of the European room of the Agra palace. Although he was now eighty-two, the Rana had not aged with the years. His lean, tall frame was still strong and his mind alert. The dark skin had puckered though; the hawk nose was more prominent and the hair and moustache had become white.

The scar running down his cheek itched.

Shah Jahan had been bedridden for months, following his collapse one night when he had taken too much of the aphrodisiac to prove himself to a young concubine. Rana Chara's spies in the palace had sent him regular reports of Shah Jahan's condition. When it had taken a turn for the worse a week before, the Rana had hastened to his side. Today, he had been summoned from his room at dawn. Shah Jahan desired to speak to him.

Seated on a settle beside Shah Jahan's divan, facing the windows, Rana Chara took in the prone figure lying very still on the pink silken cushions, beneath a matching coverlet. The large eyes were closed, the skin over the once-rugged features had sagged and wrinkled. The arching eyebrows, Mongolian moustache and beard were, like the hair above the sharply sloping forehead, white and sparse. Yet there was majesty here, even in the lifeless figure that looked like a great rag doll clothed in a pink silken coverlet.

Was this the once magnificent Emperor, his robe so laden with sparkling emeralds, rubies and pearls that he had to be supported to his glittering peacock throne?

Why was he, Rana Chara, here today? To be in on the kill? To witness the final success of his lifetime of endeavour? To triumph over his enemy at last by letting him know, at his last moment on earth, who had really been the instrument of his destruction?

He recalled that first morning on the rampart wall of this very palace, fronting the *maidan* on which the elephant battle to determine the succession was to take place. He had experienced his first hatred of this man on that day. Had it been sixty-one years ago? Or in another lifetime?

Suddenly he felt a curious disassociation within himself, Rana Chara separating from Prince Chara.

Shah Jahan stirred, slowly lifted his eyelids. At first, he could not focus. Then the dark eyes, glazed with age, gradually slid towards the Rana. He smiled. 'One friend at least from times gone by.' The lips framed the words that his breath could barely produce.

The scar on Rana Chara's face began to burn. 'Yes, Sire,' he responded steadily.

'All is well, we are about to find everything we lost, in Paradise.'

A man goes where he believes he will.

The knowledge jolted Rana Chara. He watched Shah Jahan with heightened interest.

'Our one regret is that we cannot have one last look at our beloved Taj Mahal,' the Emperor continued. 'We have not seen it for weeks. We crave for sight . . .' He began to mumble in his beard.

'Can you not be carried to the window, Your Imperial Majesty?'

The tired, wan face smiled at the title. 'Ever the gallant Rajput, Rana Chara!' Shah Jahan paused, breathing heavily. 'No, the physicians say it would kill us.' The sad eyes twinkled briefly, like a star to be eclipsed by a cloud. 'Dying is all right for the physicians, so long as we do not die!'

Rana Chara comprehended that no one in the palace, not even the Princess Jahanara, would dare to take the responsibility of being the immediate cause of their ruler's death.

He thought it was the beginning of a death rattle, but it was only an insistent knocking on the door. He observed Shah Jahan's slow nod. 'Enter!' Rana Chara commanded.

A slim slight figure, clad in the white robe of the Parsee, carrying a bulky package in a wrapping of white linen, entered and made obeisance.

Rana Chara had met Ustad Isa several times before. The architect bowed low to him, then addressed Shah Jahan. 'I am Ustad Isa, your architect. I request your Imperial Majesty's leave to give you a present.' The words were uttered in clear tones. 'May I have your permission to display it?'

A barely perceptible nod of the head was the only acknowledgment. The architect moved across the room to the window, avoiding the settles and tables with a strangely youthful step. 'I had to await the full rising of the sun before bringing it to your royal presence.' He stood by the window and removed the wrapping. As it fell away, to Rana Chara's astonishment, a large mirror was revealed.

The architect held the mirror to the window, aligned it. 'Look, Your Majesty.' His words were a command.

Shah Jahan responded by reflex. His eyes opened wide, slanted towards the window. For one second, he stared uncomprehending, then his gaze lit up. 'The Taj Mahal!' he exclaimed in wonder. The sides of his eyes crinkling, the mouth twitched in a glad smile. 'Almighty Allah has vouchsafed to us the blessed gift of one final vision. Ustad Isa has given us the gift of sight.' The words were clear, the speech strong. 'Now we can die in peace.' His eyes closed. 'Within sight of our Mumtaz Mahal, who awaits us.'

Rana Chara realized with amazement that the architect had cleverly set up a system of mirrors to enable the dying Emperor to see his creation one more time. This man, who had been condemned to be blinded as soon as Shah Jahan died, had given his judge and executioner the clemency of sight.

'Your Imperial Majesty, here is the final reality of your vision and your creation,' Ustad Isa continued. 'Here shall your body rest in peace beside that of your beloved Mumtaz Mahal. Here is your love that never ended and will now endure forever. Accept it as my final gift of love to you.'

Who was this Ustad Isa? Vaguely Rana Chara remembered a man who had lost his own wife at childbirth and had inclined thereafter to the Buddha's doctrine. *Ahimsa*, forbearance towards all, especially your enemies. *Maitriya*, loving kindness to the entire Universe.

The time was short. Moved by a frantic impulse over which he had no control, Rana Chara reached out and grasped the bony shoulder beneath the pink sheet coverlet. 'Your Imperial Majesty, one final boon for a vassal Rana, I beg you.' The royal plural, embedded in him through the years, was forgotten in the moment's urgency.

'What is it?' the lips formed the words.

'Islamic justice. An eye for an eye. Sight for the man who gave you final sight.'

Shah Jahan's eyelids fluttered. You deny me this and I shall strangle you with my bare hands, Rana Chara thought savagely. What thoughts are churning inside your cruel Moghul brain?

Long moments of suspense.

A teardrop appeared beneath each slanty Mongol eye.

'Yes.'

Relief and joy such as he had never experienced before swept through Rana Chara. He forgot his purpose, the one last moment of triumph over his enemy. Recalled it. Cause and Effect. He had no use for such a petty victory.

'Mumtaz. My beloved Mumtaz, you have come for me.'

The Emperor Shah Jahan died with the words on his lips.

A man goes where he believes he will.

Crash! Rana Chara's head swivelled in its direction as he reached for his sword.

The stunned architect had dropped the mirror. Blinded by tears, he was gazing stupefied at the shattered remains of what had once held the image of the Taj.